TWO IN ONE VOLUME

THE SECRET CLUB AND THE MANAFULS

SECOND EDITION

DORIMALIA WAIAU

AND EASA MOHAMED

The Secret Club and Ejad the Inventor

The Secret Club and Ejad the Inventor and The Secret Club and the Manafuls, Second Edition, Two in One Volume Copyright Registration Library of Congress Number: TX 9-437-497

Cover and interior book designs and formatting by miblart.com
Back cover author image by Monica H. Waiau
Be Manaful Logo ™ 2024
Printed by Dorimalia LLC., in the United States of America, 2024
Dorimalia LLC website: dorimaliawaiau.com

For Our ‘Ohana

BE MANAFUL

ACT I

PROLOGUE

Manaful World
August 1, 2000
ʻŌmaʻomaʻo Hopohopo City
Protectors' Academy
Twenty-two Years Ago

He was a hell of a killer for being the runt of the family. Ejad Honua could become a top assassin easily. Elder Uli, the Protector's Academy owner, instantly knew this. The diminutive Hopohopo, empowered with self-made gadgetry, walloped his bullies on that ominous night. Uli saw the entire take-down.

A foot shorter but miles smarter than most dwarves, teenaged Ejad defended himself with gadgetry. Uli was lucky to be near enough to sense the intense emotions involved. He arrived at once to investigate. Upon teleporting to the Academy, the Elder admired Ejad's small switchblade baton. It was at full extension, dripping maroon droplets.

Elder Uli levitated in the twilight over the empty parking lot, studying the dismembered hands of two Hopohopo teens on the ground below him. His bioluminescent elder's robe glowed in the spectrum of greens from emeralds to aquas, floating around him with a mind of its own. The magical cloth's power uplifted him physically and spiritually. Source's eminence filled his every turn and nod with beauty. But his dark personage lessened its vibrance. He smirked at the fleeing bullies, a blonde and brunette, who sobbed with arms pressed against damp chests. Their severed hands lay haphazardly mismatched, the pale one beside the brown, fingers twitching on the now bloodstained asphalt.

Ejad tapped a button on the metal baton in his hand. The blade folded on itself and disappeared into the weapon's tip. He closed his eyes and bowed his head as if in prayer, completely stoic. He wasn't breathing hard nor shaking. He held his shoulders back almost proudly, strangely giving him a taller presence. Backpack at his feet, he rested his weaponed arm against his leg. Uli considered teleporting the weapon back to his mansion in a blink of the eye. But instinct told him the baton wasn't the most valuable weaponry here. The Elder descended gracefully until the youngster was bathed in the glow of his robes.

"Where'd you get that contraption?" Uli's deep baritone echoed in the lot. His feet came to rest in front of Ejad, whose eyes had widened into orbs of surprise. Uli waved at the dismembered hands at their feet. The body parts and stains vanished into thin air.

Ejad jumped in awe, having only heard of Elder Uli. Never dreamed of meeting him. It's a breathtaking moment akin to meeting the monarchy. There was protocol for this sort of thing.

The teen immediately kneeled on the ground before his Elder. Ejad's plain green sarong rode up his thighs, revealing rippling hamstrings from squatting to tend to his machinery and training at the Academy staff's gym. Ejad didn't reply to Uli about the weapon.

"Speak up!" Uli yelled, impatient by-half already that he had to voice his thoughts. Mind-reading and projecting one's thoughts was the Manaful way. Why won't this student answer? The youngster continued to kneel with nary a projected thought nor a spoken word.

The elder sighed, staring at the teen at his feet. With skills like that, the boy could have been a prized Academy member instead of a tech assistant. Uli squinted to peer into the shaggy, overly-long brown head. Huh, that's not the regulation cut. Come to think of it, the little fighter wasn't wearing the required teal sarong of Academy students nor the forest green of employees. His was a darker hue, deep moss.

Uli realized this boy must be a full-fledged Hopohopo. However clever they may be, they couldn't match a Manaful in anything. He shrugged at the ease of the task. These Hopohopo failed to mentally communicate much less screen their minds. Their thoughts were unshielded, practically screaming aloud on cartoonesque bubbles above their heads.

"*Tell me your name,*" Elder Uli telepathically projected (TP) into Ejad's head.

"*I am Ejad, a lowly tech assistant, Great Elder!*" Ejad thought carefully, sensing Uli's intrusion into his mind.

"I accept my punishment for maiming two of your students. But I am not in the wrong. Reach back into my brain for my rationale. They deserved this and more."

Uli's left brow rose in curiosity. Though Ejad's head was bowed, his thoughts rang with confidence and self-assurance. Such bravado to an elder was something Uli rarely saw in a young dwarf, not to mention a Hopohopo. He suddenly wanted to hear the boy speak aloud.

"Stand up! Use your words!" Uli commanded.

Ejad came to his feet smoothly like a breakdancer, arms and legs loosely relaxed. He didn't speak a word. He lifted his chin, waiting for the elder to kill him or scramble his brain. Ejad emanated stillness and serenity despite having just assaulted two other young dwarves. His eyes were ice.

Uli's normal disregard for *other's* feelings or concerns dissipated. This young one fascinated him. He peered again into Ejad's brain. He saw flashbacks of the injured teens bullying Ejad over the last few months. Each encounter was a snapshot of humiliation for Ejad. The humiliation came from having to restrain himself. Uli zeroed in on the events of this evening, viewing the memory clearly.

The three dwarfs were in an empty Academy classroom. The dirty blond student towered over a stoically serious Ejad. The former squeezed the life out of a furry hamster. He dropped the lifeless pet at Ejad's feet. "I guess little Hammy can't help with your experiments any more!" The blonde bully cackled.

Ejad looked down at the pet. He neither grimaced nor cried. His lack of reaction irked the bullies. The dark haired student opened a Jackson chameleon's cage, grinning. Ejad's breath finally hitched. His eyes narrowed. This jazzed both bullies. Without a care for the pet's ribs, the second bully crushed the chameleon's body like gelatin with his bare hands. The bullies only laughed at the grotesque crunch of its bones. The student dropped the lifeless yet still beautiful rainbow reptile to the floor next to its deceased furrier companion. Ejad swallowed whatever screams were awakening in his throat. His eyes widened into saucers. He had yet to move.

The dirty blonde shouted, "Let's get out of here before he calls the Chief!" He was referring to Ejad's technology supervisor who normally ran the very lab they stood in. Being too poor to land a full Academy course, Ejad Honua had chosen part-time employment and attending free staff-only classes as the path to achieving his dreams.

"Sure thing! Let's bail!" The brunette answered as they exited much quicker than they'd entered. There was no rhyme nor reason why they chose to "visit" Ejad daily. This particular encounter had been by far the worst. Ejad's lack of verbal response nor reporting of their daily insults and slurs had urged them on. How'd they escalate from name-calling and toppling furniture to killing pets, Ejad couldn't guess. He'd get revenge.

A rodent scurried on the fire escape behind Ejad, bringing Elder Uli back to the present. He stared down at the young dwarf, who was at least a foot shorter than the elder. Ejad raised his brow as if to ask, *Got what you needed from my brain?*

Uli nodded at Ejad. His foray into the youngsters mind had shown him the Hopohopo's ingenuity. He had manufactured the multi-purpose switch-blade baton from scratch on his own using springs and clockwork mechanics. He was an inventor. This one was a keeper.

Uli's Song: Uli's New Pet:

"This one's a keeper –can it get any better?
This one's for me I know things are looking up now.
Asked Source for at least one worthy of me somehow.
Waited a millenia for others to shape up– step up
Find me one that's not wimpy and quivery when I say, "Shut up!"
One who doesn't care whether he lives nor dies by my hand.
One who sees past my foibles and occasional need to grandstand
A youngster who is trainable in my wily ways
A faithful acolyte who will not stray.
A true killer –with none of that heart of gold mess
Ejad will even call me out on my BS.
I can't thank Source more for this makana of all makana
Oh, boy! We're gonna plan, we're gonna scheme. I wanna!"

Ejad stood at attention and stared grimly at the Elder as if awaiting orders. This brought out a smile on Uli's sour face. The Elder lifted his chin. "*You're coming with me to the sandalwood forest.*"

Ejad mutely blinked his agreement.

The rest was history.

Chapter 1
Ari's Moody Moods

Earth
Storyteller in Papakōlea, Hawai'i
August 4, 2022

At twelve years old, Ari had the spunk of a girl twice her age. She was often left to her own devices while her parents kept busy. She often hatched plans to amuse herself unbeknownst to whichever adult was keeping an eye on her. She still missed her parents and got into her little moods.

Aunt Ellie read her mind, "You can't have it both ways. Either you want them around a lot or you want space."

"Can't they give lots of kisses and hugs like you do?" Ari mumbled.

"Oh, well, you have to admit: there's only one of me!" Aunt Ellie winked and smooched Ari's cheek to change the mood.

Ari giggled, yet her thoughts lingered on her parents. They did give her the occasional hugs and kisses. Just not as much as she wanted. They never phoned when they were at work, instead trusting her loneliness will be fixed by her Aunt.

"I don't think they love me as much as they should," Ari said.

Aunt Ellie almost laughed, but kept her lips pursed. She shook her head instead. She moved as fluidly as a forty-nine year-old could manage from the settee where she'd been re-hemming her culottes to the couch. She gracefully joined Ari who lounged on it. Dropping a hand on her niece's shoulders, she bent down to peer into Ari's dark brown eyes.

"They love you in their own way," Aunt Ellie insisted.

She continued, "Remember there's food on the table and clothes in your closet."

Ari rolled her eyes, wishing her Aunt understood that provisions aren't enough. It takes affection and patience from a parent for a child to feel appreciated.

As if mind-melded, Aunt Ellie kissed Ari's cheek saying, "We all love you. We are all here for you, although I speak more for myself than your parents. Yet, the trust they instill in you and I to be strong without their continuous presence is precious. Everyone has their own unique way to kāko'o others."

Ari shook her head stubbornly. "You can't call this 'support'."

Aunt Ellie just held her tighter and said, "I can and I am. They definitely love you."

Ari teared up and hugged her Aunt. It lasted exactly six seconds. Then she abruptly leaped up and ran to the front porch, leaving Aunt Ellie blinking at an empty spot on the couch.

"Hey, where are you going?"

Ari shouted over her shoulder, "A walk in Tantalus trails. I'll be okay."

Aunty Ellie frowned, debating whether to follow the pre-teen. She was never one hundred percent sure how safe it was on the hilly trails. It was a block behind her mountain residence in Papakōlea. There were wild boar, feral chicken, and even wilder teens smoking marijuana in their trailside hideouts.

"I'll be fine!" Ari said from the doorway. "It's homestead land where everyone knows everyone. You're such a worrier!"

Aunt Ellie watched the girl rocket off into the afternoon humidity. She scratched her graying head and got up to pace the living room. Keeping Ari by her side all the time was getting increasingly difficult as the girl aged. Recently she'd created an entire story to keep the preteen distracted from her absent parents. It had helped Ari recover from the tumultuous years of the COVID pandemic.

Aunt Ellie stopped in her tracks. The story! Ari needed The Secret Club in her life more than ever. Perhaps the story needed more spice. That'll bring Ari back to herself.

"I can get her to sit still longer that way," she told herself. She paced to recall where she'd left off in the fictional story.

In the magical world of Manaful, accessed through Shimmery Walls, her three young heroes witnessed the unfolding of Elder Uli's plans to take control of the Elder Council and the whole Manaful World. They had seen his eventual demise by the hands of Maka, his grandson. However, the malevolent Spirit Lapu, who had empowered Uli, still controls part of Manaful. Nicole, Pierre, and Malie - the Secret Club - are molecularly traveling via the Shimmery Wall right into the aftermath of one of Lapu's destructive rampages.

One problem was Aunt Ellie's inability to answer all of Ari's questions. The preteen didn't like waiting a whole day for the next part. Her niece was most inquisitive about mind powers. And Lapu. *I'm going to have to stretch my imagination*, she thought.

Aunt Ellie hummed a song of hope to herself and returned to her rehemming and waited for Ari's return. Her mind worked as fast as her fingers as the story evolved. The clock hanging over her decorative fireplace depicted native Hawaiian birds instead of numerals. It ticked towards the ʻōmaʼo thrush that represented two o'clock.

Aunt Ellie's Song of Hope:

"God above helps us when we are lost.
Our sacrifices sometimes have a cost.
We grow through these changes daily.
What would we do without family?
Praise be for those who stick together.
Facing the good and the bad weather.
Trust one another to be there still.
No matter how things go downhill,
Love provides this deep inner hope.
Remember that united we can cope!"

CHAPTER 2
LAPU'S MIND ATTACK

Manaful World
August 4, 2022
Sandalwood Forest, Elder Territory

"What the heck happened here?" Nicole said, filter-free as always. She burst out of the Shimmery Wall and stood astounded by the devastation of trees everywhere. The Manaful ʻŌmaʻomaʻo (green) ʻOhana's forest was as she'd never seen it before—smoking, in ruins. Nicole had an Amazonian build with burnished cocoa-skin and broad shoulders upon which rested the weight of the world. Her eyes searched the smog to find the source of a forlorn thrush song.

Her two friends Pierre and Malie spilled out into the destroyed forest in her wake. They stumbled into each other in shock. Behind them the Shimmery Wall slowly dissipated in mid-air. It shrunk and dissolved into dispersing rainbow mists.

Nicole stomped on the carpet of broken twigs and ashes. "Why is it so barren here? What is that acrid smell?"

Malie whipped around, arms outstretched, reaching for the loving boughs of the splintered yet still fragrant sandalwood trees. Her hands only touched stumps. Last time she was here it had been a smorgasbord of vibrancy and magic. Now, the daytime light was leached from this magical forest. Around them hung a gray smog. She adjusted thick glasses on a button nose and whimpered, "It's the parched remains of a wildfire, Nicole!"

Pierre knelt to touch the cindering ashes. There was a residual luminescent glow to the scattered tree fibers at their feet. The air was electrified. His skin itched. He said, "There's more going on here; remember, nothing is as it seems in Manaful World."

Nicole and Malie both agreed.

The evening breeze whipped Malie's brown tresses around her face. She wished for a hair tie. Reading her cherubic face, Pierre handed her a decorative pink and green cotton band with a floral design.

"Wow, how did you know?" She smiled at Pierre.

He grinned, "I carry them for my mom. She always misplaces her's and blames it on pregnancy hormones."

Malie smiled in thanks, putting her hair into a ponytail.

Puna, Alaka'i, Maka and Ikaika were busy regrowing the sandalwood forest nearby. Elder Puna conjured the Shimmery Wall after chasing away Lapu from Maka's forest just minutes ago.

Soil writhed beneath the quartet as small plants broke through shyly from the ashes. The smoking remains of the trees couldn't hold back the new sprouts. The verdant surroundings revived with Mana, the magic of the Manaful world. Elder Puna looked up from a riven tree he was healing with Elder Alaka'i, telepathically projecting (TP) directions to his grandson. "*Ikaika,*

The Secret Club has arrived. You and Maka go to receive them. We will join you shortly."

Ikaika nodded at once. He grabbed Maka's elbow. The latter frowned as he tapped into his Mana, his new Elder feathers ruffled by Puna's command. It was slightly irritating to still be told what to do like a child.

Reading his mind, Ikaika's interjected in TP, "*You are still a child. Don't mind Gramps. Trust me, he'll be bossing us both around until we're well past our two thousandth year."*

"You're right, Ikaika. I'm still sensitive about being treated like a 'youngster'... just not as confident tapping the Mana as I could be."

Maka had inherited the Elder title at the death of his grandfather Uli only recently. He was still getting used to freely using Mana. Uli oppressed Maka his whole life into bottling up his magic. With Puna, Alaka'i and Ikaika by his side, he was only now getting the hang of it.

"Here we go," Maka TP. He and Ikaika vanished into the wind.

All three humans jumped when the dwarves materialized in front of them. One in elder robes and one in a sarong.

"Holy fudge!" Nicole yelped.

"Ikaika!" Pierre exclaimed.

"Maka!" Malie beamed. "Good to see you again!"

The two Manafuls preened at all the attention. The dwarves were shorter than the human children at almost four feet. That was their maximum height.

Ikaika grinned. "Same here!"

The dwarf raised a hand for the customary fist bumps all around, inciting giggles and happy hops from the kids. Maka only frowned.

"*I sense Lapu's essence still lurking*," Maka Telepathically Group Projected (TGP). "*Be on guard.*"

Pierre nodded, hugging himself. "Yes, the air is sticky."

"Also icky," Malie agreed. She edged closer to the two Manafuls. The wind howled, kicking up detritus and ash.

"There's definitely something weird going on," Nicole said. She stood further away with her arms akimbo. She faced the others, mass of curly hair bobbing frenetically. Unaware of the dark mist coalescing right overhead. Malie looked in her direction just in time to see.

Him.

"Nicole! Watch out!" Malie gasped.

Elder Maka and Ikaika turned. The blob resembled a jellyfish. The Spirit in this form seemed more fluid or gaseous than solid.

Nicole looked straight up. In barely a blink the cloud of sticky, inky droplets fell on top of her like a bucket of oil. Her yell rang throughout the smoking forest.

Malie and Pierre ran at Nicole. She was now tangled in threads of the sticky blob. Her yells were muffled.

"LAPU!" Maka and Ikaika shouted.

Pierre and Malie forgot their own safety. They ran right up to the blob from which Nicole's weakening yells emanated.

Lapu's essence reached out. Black octopus arms grabbed them both. His inky hold pulled them in, His prey. Disembodied voices infiltrated their minds, all laughing, Lapu was on a roll:

"*Hee Hee Hee*!"

In the blink of an eye the Secret Club was lost to sight in the sticky mass. They became one with the roiling sphere that captured them in His clutches. Dark wormy Medusa tendrils slithered into their heads, impervious to skin and bone, straight into their brains.

"*Coochy coochy coo. Useless little babies playing useless little games. Stupid, freaky, abnormal excuses for children blundering around my world. Pah!*" Lapu snickered.

All three kids fell to their knees. They held their heads and cried as Lapu summoned forth every single hurtful memory It could find in their minds, twisting them beyond recognition. Their eyes blurred with tears.

Lapu rasped, "*Your parents hate you. Everyone hates you. You hate yourselves.*"

Elder Maka centered himself. The robes that had once belonged to his grandfather Uli swam around him in the mossy greens and teals of his 'Ohana. Family Mana flowed into his being from Source. "*Back me up, Ikaika!*"

Ikaika set his jaw and nodded. He planted his feet firmly on the ground. Combat pose. He lent his Mana to his friend, Elder Maka. Their power flowed like heat fumes, or a mirage on the Sahara horizon.

Maka raised his hands. The wind flowed around his wrists like bracelets. The Elder blasted Lapu's smoky essence that was entrapping the Secret Club. The preteens' mentality had been reduced to blubbering infants. They were blind and deaf to everything except their own self doubts.

Maka's burst of wind-power pushed the black mist away. It hit a tree and split in two. It gathered back into a blob. Tentacles out, the Spirit surged back like a hungry predator. Nicole, Pierre and Malie reached out, forming a group hug right before Lapu's fetid influence drowned them again.

"*We need more power!*" Ikaika TP.

Maka nodded. He bent his knees and jumped. Robes whipping, he went for it. He directed the wind into successive blasts.

In synchronicity, as Maka's elemental attack knocked the dark clouds back, Ikaika leaped into the fray and conjured a force field around the children and himself. It was thin and weak. Won't hold for long. He trusted Maka to deal with Lapu's essence immediately. Above them, the enormous black mist torpedoed towards Maka.

Whether Maka would have succeeded in fighting off Lapu was never known because Elders Alaka'i and Puna dropped in just in time. In a rainbow burst of Mana mist, the older pair appeared with their full power on display. Red and white robes flared out around them with fluorescent luminance. Their eyes were unblinking in their alignment with Source.

The revered Elders each raised a single finger. A tremendous white light exploded, zapping the voluminous dark forces. Maka, blinded, fell to the ground. He wiped dirt off his palms and blinked. Lapu's essence had dissipated.

Ikaika let go of his force field in relief. He fell to his knees. The rose red sarong of 'Ula'Ula House was covered in soot. He checked on the humans.

Pierre was crying freely. Nicole hugged her knees to rock back and forth, eyes tightly closed. Malie just lay on her face without moving.

Ikaika touched her on the shoulder. She flinched. "*Are you alright? Please sit up.*"

"Leave me alone," Malie mumbled into a pile of decaying leaves.

Ikaika looked around. "*Pierre?*"

"I wish I was dead," Pierre sniffled. He tried to breathe in deep but only cried harder. He mumbled. "I'm just an imposter... I'm not even that good at football."

"No way, you're a legitimate athlete," Ikaika projected at once.

Pierre shook his head. Nicole had fists on either temple, frozen and staring. She was thinking, *Neither dad nor grandfather wanted me. They threw me away while I was inside mom. Threw us away like trash.*

This was serious. Ikaika and Maka raised their eyebrows at the levitating Elders. Though humbled by the latter, the young Manafuls deeply wished for the children's wellness. Knowing exactly how to deal with the situation, Elder Alaka'i stepped in to heal. He was the first and oldest Manaful. Using that deep power of the soul, he vibrated a soft hum. Lilting rhythms blew gently from his mouth. His breath - his Hā - swam through the air, embracing the children in waves of tranquility. Everyone visibly relaxed.

Pierre rubbed his tears away. He did his breathing exercise. Nicole grimly unwrapped her arms from her knees to stand up. Her gaze was riveted to the sky; she refused to look at anyone.

Malie sat on her butt and pouted. "That was awful. Just awful."

Nicole nodded. "I need to douse my brain in a long, warm shower."

Elders Puna and Alaka'i descended gracefully to the forest floor. Ikaika tentatively peeked into the minds of the three humans. There appeared to be no lasting damage. He let out a held breath with a woosh.

"Apologies for the delay in our arrival," Elder Alaka'i group projected. *"We were tending to the pain of this forest."*

Nicole inhaled deeply and looked at the senior Elders. "Lapu said you two are lying to us."

"Lapu is the one who lies," Alaka'i projected.

"As if you've never lied even once in your life," Nicole sneered. Her obsidian eyes flashed.

"We don't," Elder Puna projected.

None of the three humans met his gaze.

Pierre held out a hand. Malie took it. They got to their feet, holding hands. They looked at their sneakers, still disoriented.

"Lapu said—" Pierre began.

"—that the Elders are just using us for a nefarious ulterior motive," Malie finished her friend's sentence. Pushing her glasses to the bridge of her nose she met Elder Puna's eyes.

"He said the Elder Council cannot be trusted," she continued. Malie bit her lower lip, brown eyes begging for the truth.

"It's true Lapu holds the notion that nothing can be trusted," Elder Alka'i projected. *"He regards every truth with suspicion, infects others with his negativity and doubts... He was not "telling" you anything just now. He was simply creating chaos, confusion and grief using your own fears and thoughts."*

Nicole shook her head gravely. "I don't want that to happen ever again!"

"Me neither." Pierre gave Malie a side hug. He thought that perhaps they should go back to the real world where Spirits didn't sneak around attacking kids.

Ikaika's face fell into sadness. He heard the thought as clearly as if Pierre had spoken it. *Please don't leave so soon.*

Nicole came to Malie's other side and held her as well. She and Pierre looked at their smaller bookworm friend. Malie scrunched up her face.

"We'll stay but not here," Malie decided for the Secret Club.

Ikaika lit up. "*My crib?*"

The Secret Club raised their fists into the air and yelled, "Aye!"

"*We shall stay to work on the forest*," Elder Puna TGP.

He was already busy vanishing the ashy remains and growing grass. Elder Alaka'i poured out Mana for new buds. A zephyr rose up from the pair of elders to herd the smog away.

Maka gave Ikaika a chin-up, projecting solely to his buddy: "*I need a few minutes to...*"

Ikaika gave Maka a hug, not surprised when Maka held him tight for a little bit. They released their hold. Ikaika got it.

"*Say no more, Brother. See you!*"

Ikaika completely understood Maka's need to be alone. He was still a little mind-blown by what just went down. He turned to the Secret Club, who understood Maka as well. Nicole and Pierre fistbumped Maka. Malie couldn't hold back a sniffle, jumping towards Maka for a hug. He patted her back while she fondly ran her hands on his luxurious robe. The radiant spectrum of greens glowed against her hands, warmly returning her Aloha.

"You did your best," she whispered in his ear.

Maka half-smiled his gratitude, "Mahalo, Malie. But it's never enough!"

"Give it time," she smiled softly.

He nodded. She stepped back to the others. Maka raised his hands to magick them to the crib. Lapu had crossed limits attacking humans. Not to mention Heirs and Elders too. He would calm his emotions before he joined Ikaika.

The wind hissed through the forest. Maka Molecularly Transported (MT) Ikaika and the Secret Club to the 'Ula'ula mansion. He'd follow them soon.

Maka's Song: In Time:

"When will I be the Elder I need to be?
How long does fruit take to grow on a tree?
What's wrong with the Mana transmuted through me?
Is there something untapped inside, needing to be set free?
In time, in time, in time I'll see.
What does it take to defeat these great forces?
How do I take a step forward without remorse?
Give me some hints, some Kōkua, oh, Source!
Why do I feel so unsupported, completely unendorsed?
In time, in time, in time I'll see.
Perhaps it's not about me but the greater beings around me.
If I stop pressuring myself, I'll be able to see
that Mana, like everything, flows when it's ready
Like the saplings growing from their roots.
Like blossoms rising from their bud.
Like baby manu bursting from their shells.
Their timing seems out of order, pell-mell,
But it's perfect – I'm simply not privy to The Grand Plan.
So, I bow.
I feel it now, I know the truth: Wow!

My growth, my blooming, my bursting, my life will be empowered
In time."

Chapter 3
The History of Manafuls

Earth
Storyteller in Papakōlea
August 4, 2022

Ari loved her daily hour-long stroll through the Tantalus trails. She returned just as Aunty's bird clock sang out its thrush song. Upon Ari's return home, Aunt Ellie got Ari to shower and join her for storytelling. Ari noticed her aunt's lingering concerns about her being out there alone. She hoped to ease them.

"The mountain is an old and sacred one, Aunty," the kolohe niece began, dark eyes mischievous. "People find their own peace amid the poky yet colorful bougainvillea. It's full of natural birdsong. Hungry mangroves gobbling up every space in sight."

"Maybe you shouldn't be alone on the trails with all kinds of predators!" Aunt Ellie's brows furrowed, wishing to hold on tighter to her niece. She wanted her cuddly, sweet homebody Ari back.

"Aunty," Ari laughed, "Most of the people visiting the trails were either your former students or are related to us. Papakōlea's a small community."

Ari patted her Aunty's knee as she made herself comfortable on an opposing couch in the living room. Their cups of chamomile iced tea refreshed the ladies on that particularly humid summer afternoon.

Tranquil meditation music soothed them and floated around like pixie dust bringing calmness. Ari saw Aunty's laptop beside the couch, excitedly awaiting the rest of the fantasy story.

The preteen was a little scared of the Secret Club's most recent visit to Manaful. The sandalwood forest being burned down breaks one's heart. That's a tragedy. Yet, nothing's spookier than Lapu. She anxiously wanted to know more about the Spirit. For example, where did Spirits come from?

Aunt Ellie's face brightened with an inner glow, grateful for her niece's interest. She explained, "Manaful world is a place created to hold all the unused magical power. When it accumulated in Manaful dimension a Hill was formed as its core point. On it grew three magical relics."

"Oh, like those found in museums?" Ari interrupted. "Aunty, Kumu Ala taught us that relics represent significant meanings in many cultures."

Aunty Elle nodded, "Yes. Now, let me cover a bit of the Manaful World's history. All of Manaful's geography originates from Old Hill. He is exactly what he sounds like. An old hill."

"He?"

"Yes, Let's say he is the Manaful equivalent of Earth's concept of Gaia. Know her? 'Soul of the Earth'?"

"I've read of her. That's pushing it."

"Look, I'm aiming at storytelling over here. Hopefully educational too. Give an old kumu a break."

Ari giggled. She was interested in the story. Now that her ideas were showing up in the tale, she felt like it was her story as well.

Aunt Ellie put a cushion on her lap and went back to Manaful, "The rest of Manaful land is simply the periphery of Old Hill like robes around a king. He magicked up three relics to keep him company."

"Boo."

"Why?"

"I want to know about Spirits of the Manaful World."

"The Spirits also come from Old Hill. Please be patient before you know the whole story. For now, just know one thing. When the Spirits touch Mana, they taint it."

"Tainted? What? The Spirits make bad Mana? They're bad beings and Manaful are good? Why'd Source make Spirits bad?" Ari plucked at the yarn balls that popped out of the older quilt. She coiled the loose sunflower yellow string around her fingers as she shot off her questions. *What's going on with those Spirits*? She thought.

Aunty Elle squeezed Ari's yarn-wrapped hand reassuringly. She continued to expound, "Source created the Manaful to counterbalance the existence of Spirits. Manaful purified Mana. But Spirits remain strong because the Hopohopo ban themselves from using Mana. Unused Mana saturated their world. Spirits gleefully fed on this unused power. Spirits aren't inherently bad, but they become dangerous forces once let loose. They grew strong on unused Mana. Among them, Lapu is the strongest one. He wants to take over all of Manaful."

"What's stopping him? I mean."

"A huge amount of Mana is needed to realize Lapu's dream of taking a corporeal form. More Mana than even the Elder's can harness."

"Corporeal form? Like a physical body. What's he doing to harness that much Mana?"

"A lot of things. One of his perpetual battles is with nature – trees, rocks, rivers, animals. Natural ecosystems are always harnessing Mana. The imbalance in the system came because the Manaful population dropped below a certain point."

"I thought there were plenty of Manaful."

"Don't you remember the Hopohopo? Those are dwarfs who refused to submit to Source. They were blocked from Mana by their own actions. They have shorter lifespans than Manafuls. The Hopohopo refuse to tap into the Mana flowing into their world. This leaves plenty of room for Spirits to hijack the flow. Spirits consume the excess Mana and evolve into powerful forces."

Ari shook her head in wonder, "Then real-life beings counteract the power of Spirits! The very existence of the Hopohopo is the reason imbalances persist!"

Aunty Ellie nodded. "Exactly! That is why Spirits destroy natural growth, to reduce nature's inherent power. Spirits need nature's balance to be tipped and there to be more Hopohopo than Manafuls. Spirits believe they can grow strong enough to manifest in physical form. On Manaful and Earth."

"Or so they hope," Ari cringed.

"Lapu is a strong leader of the Spirits. As far as we know, he is the only Spirit currently trying so hard to manifest," Aunty shivered too.

Ari sipped her tea thoughtfully, asking, "Can Hopohopo society be changed? If all of them become Manaful, the Spirit power-balance problem will be fixed. It's just one simple solution."

Surely the Spirits can coexist with the other life forms in Manaful. Weren't the Spirits part of Manaful nature too? A part of Source? She was confused.

Aunt Ellie noted her niece's questions on her laptop. They helped develop the story further. Already new ideas were blooming.

"What exactly did Lapu do to the Secret Club?" Ari asked.

"He brought forth their insecurities and doubts. Those feelings became stronger than their natural state of loving, confident acceptance of the world," Aunty Elle replied solemnly.

"Some people do that too."

Aunt Ellie was surprised. She tickled Ari's arm. "You sure have a lot to say about people for someone so young."

Ari giggled, setting her cup on the saucer, "It's true. Some kids at school are always saying mean things to others. Their hurtful words cut everyone in hearing range." Ari popped up from her seat. She paced. Excess energy bubbled inside. She wanted to wiggle, dance, and sing. Aunty Ellie nodded encouragingly. Ari couldn't contain herself any longer.

Ari's Song: No More:

**"Why is it easier to be naughty than nice?
Some simply jump on you like mice.
Can't let you go or be.
Just let you have your tea.
Something about you makes them feel less.
Maybe it's the way you talk, walk, or dress.
Putting you down makes their day.
Wish they'd see they're enough! Hey,
Bully, talk to your mirror, affirmations
that build you up– confirmations
that tell of the truth inside of you
That you're hurting; this is true
Let me hug you, let's be friends
Step by step, your heart will mend.
They say, 'Hurt people hurt,"
Take my hand, stop spitting dirt.
Your days as a bully are no more
Let love win, come, let's explore!"**

Ari spun around the living room happily singing and sharing her heart. She ended her song with a grand stage bow. She even clapped for herself. Catching her breath, she laughed when Aunty Ellie jumped up to catch her. They shared a swaying hug and giggles.

"That was delightful! You're a Broadway performer in the making! I should sign you up for drama classes!"

Ari bowed over her aunt‘s hands, kissing them affectionately, “I owe any theatrical talents to you, dear Aunty. Mahalo.”

“Awww...dancing and singing was decades ago for me, my love! I’m touched. You remember that?” Aunt Ellie pulled Ari down to the couch.

“Of course, Aunty!” Ari smiled and patted her aunt‘s leg.

“Your song gets to the heart of the matter in Manaful and in real life. All beings need Aloha and to mālama themselves!” Aunt Ellie patted back, but on Ari‘s hand.

She continued on that line of thought, grateful for the segue into the Manafuls. “People who overly favor pessimism end up being bullies. They use other‘s insecurities against them. It’s the same as Lapu’s tactics on the Hopohopo. He creates doubt that poisons the mind slowly over time.”

“Hey, can’t the Secret Club screen their minds from stuff like that?”

Aunt Ellie reined her niece in. “You‘re getting way ahead of yourself, Ari! Although you did give me the idea of mind-screens in the first place.”

She took a sip of chamomile, taking a deep breath. Preparing herself. She picked up the story where they’d left off, reading from her laptop screen.

Chapter 4
@Crib for a Mind-Screen

Manaful World
August 4, 2022
Koa Forest, Elder Territory
Ikaika's Mansion

The Secret Club appeared in Ikaika's 'Ula'ula mansion in the sky. It was completely transparent and devoid of any furniture until and unless an inhabitant imagined them up. All three collapsed to the see-through floor. They landed in a gigantic plush couch that appeared right on time for their butts to land on.

Ikaika magicked up separate seats. A coffee table filled with snacks and chilled boxes of fruit juice appeared. A Turkish rug unfurled at their feet. The air cooled considerably. Everyone sighed comfortably. Below them, the verdant canopy of the Koa forest stretched on for miles under a forget-me-not sky.

"Maybe next time we can step right here from the Shimmery Wall?" Nicole suggested, snatching a raspberry juice. She sucked so hard on the straw that Malie burst out laughing at the slurpy sounds.

Ikaika shook his head. "*Puna made this place impervious to Shimmery Walls for traveling. Only the viewing kind here.*"

"Makes sense. For security." Malie nodded. She grabbed a handful of sugared candy from the pile on the table, stuffing her face.

"I feel better already." Pierre hopped up to stretch, as usual unable to sit still. There was some iced water on the table. He really needed it after all the crying earlier. He chugged it greedily. Then he felt like burning off his excess energy. Maybe exercise would drive away the lingering worries Lapu had seeded in the boy's mind.

A stationary bicycle appeared in a corner. Pierre grinned at the Manafuls. "*Thanks, Ikaika!*"

"*Huh? Excuse me! That was me!*" Maka projected sourly. He'd just MT to the crib.

Maka was a few inches shorter than his friend, and had a pointy face with the ability to wear a darker scowl. Ikaika's heart shaped face lit up to see his buddy, as did Pierre's.

"Oops. Thank you, Maka, I didn't see you arrive. Glad you're here!" Pierre smiled at the young Elder before hopping on the bike and pedaling furiously.

Ikaika was laughing at Pierre, but gave Maka a sidelong look. "*You ok, Brother?*"

"*I'm good,*" Maka grinned.

Ikaika grinned back and projected, "*Are you going to tell Pierre it's the mansion's embedded magic, not ours?*"

Maka laughed, already feeling 'normal' again being with this little team. "*No, let him think we've got all the power.*"

Ikaka smiled and shook his head. "*You're funny!*"

Nicole finished her drink loudly. "I still feel like I need a shower. I don't like how Lapu touched my mind."

Maka and Ikaika exchanged a look.

"Don't you use group telepathy when we ask you to?" Nicole snapped.

"*Sorry. I apologize for what happened to you*," Ikaika TGP humbly.

"I don't want that to happen to me ever again." Nicole threw her empty juice box away. It vanished instead of hitting the floor. She stared at the space her rubbish disappeared from! "What the?"

"*That was mansion magic!*" Ikaika and Maka TGP simultaneously.

Pierre's brows went up. He pointed at his stationary bike, looking at Maka quizzically. "Mansion magic?"

Maka laughed and nodded. Pierre tutted at the lame joke. His bike whistled out Queen and David Bowie's "Under Pressure" which encouraged Pierre to pump even harder.

Malie put her book down and gave Maka a serious look, worried for him. She'd noticed he stayed back in the forest. Priorities. She agreed with Nicole – she never wanted to be possessed by Lapu again.

"Me neither," Malie said, unaware of a growing sugar mustache as she chewed candy. Pierre huffed agreement from the bike. The Secret Club unanimously voted No to Lapu.

"*There are mind screens that will help*," Maka projected.

Nicole perked up and Pierre stopped pedaling. Malie leaned forward. She said, "Oh yes! I remember Puna talking about it on our first visit."

"Correct. Mine was placed by Gramps long ago," Ikaika projected.

"I want one!" Nicole banged the table with a fist. "Give me a mind screen at once!"

Pierre and Malie laughed at her spoiled toddler impression. They earned a very dark scowl. The Secret Club sobered up and nodded at the Manafuls. They all wanted screens.

"I don't know how to do it." Ikaika was apologetic. Maka bristled and blushed. He admitted, *"Me neither."*

Malie scrunched up her face. She screamed out a thought: "*Elder Puna, we need you here at once!*"

When she opened her eyes, she found Puna standing there frowning. The others gaped at him.

"*Wow, Malie!*" Ikaika ogled the tiny girl. "*That was LOUD!*"

"*What happened?*" Puna looked around at the youngsters scattered on various pieces of furniture. His red robes rippled around him.

"We want mind screens," Nicole burst out.

Puna's caramel eyes landed on Malie, projecting to her. "*That was an immense attempt at projection, little one. I've never before seen anyone without Mana send an SOS so powerfully. Well done.*"

Malie was too surprised to react. She hadn't known it would actually work. She was beginning to really like telepathy. She projected back, "*May we please get our minds screened from Lapu, dear Elder?*"

"*Of course,*" Puna TGP. "*Elder Alaka'i was just advising me to do the same.*"

Noting the trio had become fearful and distrustful after Lapu's lies and the pain of his infiltration into their minds, Puna didn't waste time. "*Please sit still, all of you.*"

Pierre, Nicole and Malie quickly arranged themselves, bumping elbows and settling in comfortably squished up on the couch.

Puna extended his hands towards them. "*You might feel funny.*"

"*Don't fight it or it won't work.*" Ikaika advised.

The Elder's robes coruscated light as he channeled Mana. The human children fidgeted nervously, staring at the glowing fibers. Their skins tingled with gooseflesh. They remained as still as they could. Malie's breathing slowed down. Nicole's heartbeat decreased to near bradycardia levels. A coolness penetrated their skulls, causing a light headed, almost sleepy feeling. Their heads drooped.

"*Stay awake!*" Puna TGP forcefully.

Nicole snapped her head up. Malie sighed lethargically. Pierre was the least affected; he scratched his hair as his scalp crawled. Then the feeling was gone as suddenly as it had come. The peppermint coolness withdrew.

Puna used a diver's OK signal. The preteens shook their heads No then Yes, eyes wide open.

"*There. I have placed mind screens on all of you. You have to actively push back against the sort of intrusion you experienced today. You don't need Mana for that. Just the strength of will, enough to activate the mind screen.*"

"*Thank you!*" The Secret Club thought in unison. Overwhelmed with gratitude they forgot they could speak.

Puna turned to his grandson. "*Advise them. Help them become extra vigilant within their minds.*"

The SC relaxed and spread out across the large sitting room. Riding the stationary and gaining a mind screen successfully soothed Pierre's nerves. He was now in full lounging mode. He asked the magic mansion for a waterbed. It gurgled out of thin air right next to him. He dove into it and let the oscillating, rippling waves comfort him.

Malie asked for a velvet loveseat with a couple of books. At the same time, Ikaika summoned his puppies Cookie, Cupcake, and Brownie. Nicole lay down on the silky Turkish rug to play with the three labradors. Abandoned, the plush couch faded away.

Puna was pleased with his grandson's instinct to put the kids at ease right away with refreshments. The wise elder thought it was time the Secret Club learnt more about Hopohopo life. They needed to learn how their generational rejection of Mana affected the Hopohopo communities.

Being the second most powerful Manaful in this world after Elder Alaka'i, Puna's telepathic projections were the softest of touches. The kids absorbed the information he supplied while they were engaged in their respective activities.

"Uli may be dead, but Lapu keeps many of the green elder's plots still alive and well. His work is carried out by Uli's Hopohopo network. We have yet to root them all out."

"I thought Uli owned only the Protector's Academy," Malie said. She rifled through the pages of Nānā i Ke Kumu, a book on her bucket list.

Puna nodded. "*He did. But ever since Maka took over we have noticed several discrepancies in how it is run. We fear it may be a dummy institution. It actually functions as a mercenary business. Most of the control is in Hopohopo hands.*"

"Just read their minds. Can't Manafuls find out any secret in just a few seconds?" Nicole asked.

"I am not the only one who knows how to place mind screens," Puna sighed. "*It seems Uli was an exceedingly busy Elder. There isn't a single Academy administrator without one of his mind-screens.*"

"More like mind-blocks," Maka interjected. *"It feels more than a simple mind-screen. It behaves differently, chaotically. There's a whole lot we don't know about Uli's schemes. Or how he used his Mana."*

The Secret Club didn't know how to respond. They'd only ever seen Uli on a screen. A Shimmery Wall for viewing, to be precise. While they were safe and sound in Ikaika's crib.

"We're thinking of approaching this problem from the back," Ikaika picked up the thread.

Elder Puna regarded the youngsters. "*That is correct. I need all of you to visit the 'Ōma'oma'o Hopohopo territory. See if we can get new leads on exactly who Uli's merchant network comprises outside of the Academy.*"

Maka jumped to his feet and pumped a fist into the air. *"I am ready!"*

Nicole looked up from a handful of puppies. Malie put down her book. Pierre bounced on his face on the waterbed yelping, "What! Right now?"

"Whenever you are ready," Puna projected. He shot a stern gaze at Maka that told the young Elder to avoid forcing the

Secret Club into anything. *"Feel free to enjoy your time here any way you please."*

Puna MT away in a swirl of rainbow Mana mist. Ikaika looked around at everyone. Despite his previous yelping, Pierre fell out of the waterbed excited. "You know what? I do want to see the Hopohopo up close. But I also want to go back to check on mom now. We're having a baby."

"You've told us a thousand times already about this baby," Maka sniffed.

Malie nodded. She snapped the book closed. "Definitely need to get back to Earth."

"Agreed. See you later, puppies," Nicole giggled around a pair of lolling tongues. She deposited the puppies onto the rug. The SC left in a blink to the Koa Forest floor and then to Earth.

Right out of the gymnasium Shimmering Wall, the trio immediately grabbed one another in a tight group hug. They felt tremors running through each other. They were breathing heavily.

"Why does returning to Earth bring a sudden rush of emotions?" Malie asked her pals. She patted Nicole's and Pierre's shoulders.

"I don't know," Pierre groaned, fighting tears. "Maybe stepping out of the portal brings a reality check. No distractions. No magical buddies. No tricked out crib. We're forced to face only facts."

"Which are?" Nicole said through her exhalations.

"We almost died!" Pierre hyperventilated. "We were attacked!"

Nicole didn't like those reminders. She was breathing too fast already. Malie broke away to do owl breathing.

"Whoo! Whoo! One...two...three..." Malie counted. She waved her hand at Pierre to help. The breathing exercise came with flapping your arms in time.

"Whoo! Whoo! One...two...three..." Pierre breathed with her. They urged Nicole to follow.

Nicole finally let out a huge breath. She bent at the waist. When she came back up, her arms were spread open. She went along with her buddies. "Whoo! Whoo! Whoo!"

Malie grabbed Nicole's wrist and timed her pulse. She nodded in approval, "Better. Your heartbeat is slowing down!"

Nicole nodded with a big sigh.

Pierre watched his pals. A tune bubbled up from his chest, from a place he could only call Source.

Pierre's Song: A Heartbeat Away:

"Dark forces tried to bring my mentality to a halt.
Big issues and pain – it was a total fall out.
Those memories that I'd rather forget.
The stupid mistakes that fill me with regret.
Dark forces will bring them all to mind.
Even that hateful incident I cannot rewind.
Little did I know peace was a heartbeat away.
The inner strength is always here to stay.
Holding awareness of my true connection inside
To a large Source and Mana no one can hide.
From the power and solace if one accepts it, indeed,
Set aside the fear and always pay heed
To the love and great warmth found every day

Source defeats Dark Forces –It's just a heartbeat away."

Pierre closed his eyes to savor the moment. The song washed him with happiness. Malie grabbed his hands, kissing both of his cheeks like his French dad does. He laughed at that. Nicole grabbed his arm, squeezing it hard. She was made of tougher stuff, no kissing.

"That was beautiful!" Malie skipped away feeling light hearted.

"It does change the vibe in here," Nicole pointed to her heart, nodding.

"I'm glad, girls. I don't know how to explain what Source is. But I believe every word that comes from there," he said. His eyes smiled though his voice was serious. He felt his cell phone shiver in his back pocket. Oh, he'd put it on vibrate.

Malie swatted a fly from her leg. She spotted fresh dog poop by her sandal. Thank goodness she hadn't skipped into that!

"Yuch! Let's get out of here." She hopped away from the doody.

Pierre was still checking his messages. Gabe texted to check on him. With Shelly's delivery date coming soon, his father kept close tabs on him. Did he or the girls need a ride home? The girls called their moms to tell them Gabe Martin was bringing them home. Of course, Kaleo wanted Gabe's number, adding, "Put him on the phone."

"OMG, Mom!" Nicole complained. But Gabe didn't mind talking with Kaleo.

"My mom's good. She says, 'Mahalo!'" Malie relayed her mom's consent to Pierre, closing out Pili's text messages. She whistled, eager to rest. It's been a long afternoon. The SC arrived at their homes less than an hour later. They were all relieved and grateful for each other and their ‘ohana.

CHAPTER 5
THE SECRET CLUB VISITS A HOPOHOPO TOWN

Manaful World
August 5, 2022
ʻŌmaʻomaʻo Hopohopo Community

"*Remember, the Hopohopo distrusts Manaful and our allies,*" Ikaika told them. "*Stay close to us.*"

It was another day. The Secret Club stepped out of the Shimmery Wall into Maka's sandalwood forest for a fresh round of Manaful adventures. The fragrance of the ʻiliahi hung thickly in the air. They felt giddy inhaling it.

Maka nodded at them and gestured. In a split second their molecules burst apart and zoomed several miles to the south. When they were put back together, Pierre put his hands between his thighs and squeezed. "Woah! That felt funnier than usual."

"My navel is tickly," Nicole agreed. This time she patted herself all over just like Pierre. That called for a rare Malie eye-roll.

"*This is the furthest we've traveled in the Manaful world so far,*" Ikaika explained. "*You'll get used to it.*"

They were standing in a field on the outskirts of a small town. In the distance they could see the high rises of the city proper. A dirt path led through open gateways into this Hopohopo community. A log fence painted green circled the perimeter.

The preteens followed Maka and Ikaika down the path towards the town.

"Why didn't we MT right in there?" Malie asked, ever picking up on subtleties.

"Hopohopo panic when Mana is used in their vicinity," Ikaika explained. "*We have to be careful and try not to worry them.*"

"Which is a useless endeavor, because Hopohopo are worried all the time anyway," Maka interjected.

Nicole snorted but kept mum. She stomped along with Pierre. Malie followed her cautiously. Soon they passed through the gates into the brick paved Main Street. Rickety rickshaws, mopeds and bicycles creaked around the citizens who ran about as busy as locusts on a feeding frenzy. Maka and Ikaika earned several ugly looks. The stares directed at the human children were openly curious.

"There's a town hall meeting happening right now," Maka noted. He scowled up at the pigeons arrayed on electric cables overhead. Beneath them a fresco of pigeon poo painted the paving bricks. Maka quickly stepped away from range.

Ikaika grinned. "*Perfect timing.*"

They wove through the crowd till they found the city square. In the middle of the cobbled courtyard stood what looked like a ridiculously big barn. It was riddled with tinted windows. It had a weathercock on top of the A shaped roof. On either side of the front doors stood two House Green Protectors with their lances at rest. Nicole and Malie recognized them at once. They ran the rest of the way yelling, "Kōkua! Maika'i!"

Kōkua and Maika'i were Academy trained 'Ōma'oma'o Protectors, experienced across multiple fields. They were also Maka's aunts. They'd helped reveal Uli's schemes and pulled Maka out of his grandfather's tyranny. They turned against Uli after he'd tortured them with his Mana.

Maka bowed his head respectfully. The Protectors thumped their breastplates with their fists. "Elder Maka! What brings you here?"

Maka was grim. "*Finding clues to solve a mystery.*"

"We thought you quit being Protectors," Pierre said.

Kōkua and Maika'i fidgeted uneasily.

"We want to," Kōkua said. "But we need coins until we become fully Manaful."

Ikaika nodded sympathetically. "My grandfather's Manaful Center for Aspiring Hopohopo is still welcoming recruits. Free of charge across all territories."

"We have reached out to Elder Puna. We requested special admittance, since we are 'Ōma'oma'o. Thank you." Maika'i smiled gratefully.

"We are also working as part-time healers at the Elders Medical Center. Anything to have a roof over our heads and food on the table," Kōkua updated them.

"The Medical Center is where we learn most about channeling Mana hereabouts," Maika'i said.

Maka blushed, suddenly very aware he was the boss of 'hereabouts'. "I give my word that a similar Manaful center to

Elder Puna's will open right here in green territory as well," he promised intensely.

Kōkua nodded vigorously. "Can't wait to be Manaful and live life without worrying about money."

"What's this meeting about?" Nicole asked, pointing her chin at the hall.

"Oh, just a bunch of merchants complaining about the ban on cutting down House Green woodlands around here," Kōkua sighed. "They hired us for two hours of guard duty while they heckle."

"Please enter." Maika'i swept her hand at the City Hall. "There's no way we're barring our Elder and the 'Ula'ula heir from this place."

Maka bowed his head and marched up to the double doors. They creaked open to admit them. There was a collective frenzy of rustling and whispering. Seated Hopohopo turned to see who was interrupting them mid-meeting. A rotund Hopohopo with a top hat who was behind the stage podium spluttered mid-speech. He lost his train of thought. Adjusting a large monocle, he stared open-mouthed at the little group marching down the aisle towards him.

The town hall was filled with top Hopohopo merchants lined up in seats. Unlike Manaful dwarfs, the Hopohopo came off more like trolls than beings of light and magic. They all wore frowns. And headgear.

"*They sure love hats*," Ikaika TGP.

Nicole snorted. She almost choked swallowing her laughter. It was true. Every kind of headwear and headdress imaginable bobbed over the creaky pew-like bench seats.

The Hopohopo stared with saucer eyes at the ʻŌmaʻomaʻo Elder, the ʻUlaʻula heir, and the three humans. Just like out on the street, the humans got the most attention. There was some muttering.

They reached the front row. An important looking Hopohopo in a fez pointed at a few empty seats by the stage. Apparently a few VIP's had skipped the meet. The five new arrivals sat down, smiling politely. Top Hat, behind the podium, realized they wanted him to finish his speech.

Top Hat cleared his throat. "Ah-yes. As I was saying, the Elder Council is a bunch of crackpot fools with poi for brains. They should lift the ban on logging and poaching at once. And that is all I have to say. Bye."

Maka's nostrils flared. Top Hat scurried down and slid into a third row seat. A Hopohopo in a cone hat strode up to the podium microphone. He said, "Thank you, Merchant Logan, for that eloquent and accurate elaboration on the pathetic creatures that we call our leaders and Elders. Speaking of which... it appears our own dear "Elder" has graced us with his presence. I wonder if he has something to say to us. Aloud."

Maka nodded. Cone Hat said, "It seems the new Elder of our Uli House wordlessly affirms he does have some words. But first, he would listen to what we have to say if he knows what's good for him."

Waves of mocking laughter rippled through the crowd to echo in the moldy rafters. Cone Hat proceeded to invite various merchants to march to the community podium. They gleefully shouted their complaints at Maka, who slowly started to steam at the ears.

Finally, after a particularly vociferous rant by a merchant wearing a baseball cap, Cone Hat returned to the podium. He glared at Maka, waving him up, "Let us now see what our Elder has to say about the troubles faced by our community."

There was grim silence. Maka stood and went up to say his piece. The young Elder dwarf looked at the sea of scowls before him. He was grateful when Ikaika projected calming thoughts. "*You can do this, Maka. Keep them distracted. I'll sift through these hatted heads.*"

Malie put her hands together in prayer. Pierre followed suit.

Nicole mumbled under her breath, "This could get ugly!"

Ikaika silently agreed.

"First of all, I want to make it very clear that the ban on logging and poaching stands in all territories by order of the Elder Council," Maka began. His voice was drowned out by a cacophony of boos. He gave Ikaika and the Secret Club a pained look. They gave him identical *You Can Do It* brow lifts.

The noise did not die down. A thundercloud passed over Maka's face. His patience expired. He blasted a strong TGP across the hall: "*SILENCE!*"

The Hopohopo were shocked at the blatant mind-intrusion. They obeyed without even realizing it. Under the assorted brims, mouths were open like goldfish. Maka threw his shoulders back. His emerald robes slithered to life. There was no point in reducing himself before this uncouth gathering.

"I am your Elder, your leader, and every decision we make is meant to improve all of our lives and our world as well," Maka said. He also mentally projected the words he spoke. His statement rang so hard in these hatted heads that they wouldn't even think of interrupting him anytime soon.

"Already the Hopohopo has spread much destruction throughout these outlying lands. The Elder Council has informed you a thousand times: you do not need to destroy the world to survive. You don't need excessive trade to get by. Your coin system exists only because the Hopohopo reject Mana. There are many institutions in the Territories that teach Hopohopo to become Manaful. Green territory will have its own soon. Why not reach out to us in humility? That is the solution to all of your problems."

As Maka's speech stretched out into several minutes, Ikaika mentally sought out Uli's conspirators. He peered into several dozen minds seated in the building. "*All I can read are superfluous fears, worries, greed... no Uli related conspiracy in sight,*" Ikaika TGP to the Secret Club.

"What about hate?" Malie whispered.

"*Lots of that! But that's a good idea, Malie... I'll follow the strongest threads of hate.*" Ikaika's brow furrowed. He expanded his mind. It was taxing for him to mind-meld on a large scale. Puna trained him well, so he managed to do it one by one relatively quickly. It was a tough crowd in more ways than one. Maka bought him time with words.

Maka progressed into a new topic. The Protector's Academy. Ikaika perked up as he detected strong waves of hate from the Hopohopo in the fez who had shown them their seats. But most of his thoughts were concealed and his memories jumbled as if tampered with.

"*Got one,*" Ikaika TGP. "*He's completely mind-blocked.* "

"Every problem Hopohopo communities face are self-induced," Maka continued to speak volumes as the Hopohopo came out of their previous shock. They muttered among themselves again. "You favor division instead of unity. You encourage suspicion in place of trust. You pursue the coin system only because of greed and the fleeting illusion of power."

Maka's young, inexperienced mind failed to see the total Hopohopo interdependency on coin flow. The generations of power imbalances between haves and havenots were lost to the child-leader who grew up without that inequality. The norm of Manaful World was one where everyone has what they need with utopian equality for all via Mana.

Maka's brash judgment of the Hopohopo kindled an uproar, as he saw them as beings who want and demand self-ruin. The merchants raised their voices as one. They stamped their boots on the floorboards. Some clapped their hands. Others waved their hats over their heads.

Hopohopo Merchant Song:

"What does he have to say for himself?
How can he ever redeem himself?
How can he say that about us?
Why must he come here causing a ruckus?
You know what?
You know what?
Will he cancel the obnoxious lies?
Let's not listen to those Elders' cries
Steal our livelihood.

Oh, they certainly would.
Think we're no-good money grubbers
They're just goody-goody fixer-uppers
Hoping to bring our people together
Where we can soar as one forever and ever
Should we unite with them? Two become one?
Ha, ha, sure, giving up all we believe in is "fun"
Shoving aside generations of loss
and gains all hard won –
Sure, just toss aside beliefs
For mysterious Mana? Good grief!
You know what?
You know what?
We call this all baloney.
This boy's a phony!"

The Hopohopo in the fez stood up to shout, "We're calling out your lies! We don't actively choose poverty and misery!"

There were several "Aye's" and the merchants got to their feet, talking over each other as a push-back against Maka's words.

Maka did not back down. "It *is* true! Everyone of you has the choice to become Manaful. Seize the opportunities! Learn! Stop building these senseless systems that reject Mana at every turn!"

The argument swelled. Jeers rose up till Malie covered her ears. Pierre looked around, fearful at the grimaces and yelling. Nicole fidgeted, wanting to leave at once. She did not like this part of Manaful after all. Although the "normalcy" here was almost indistinguishable from what she was used to back home.

Humans bickered like this regularly on Earth in courtrooms, in malls, in concerts, and more.

"*They are getting too riled up and all emotions are mixing up*," Ikaika lamented. "*It's all hateful ignorance now. These merchants have deep financial investments to protect. Maka, please change the subject.*"

It was too late. Over the thunderous voices Maka told the crowd that the least the ʻŌmaʻomaʻo ʻOhana and its business partners can do is focus on tech innovation and sales. But he was ignored entirely. The attendees rose, forming little discussion groups among themselves. Maka trailed off. He bit his lower lip, meeting Ikaika's gaze.

"*I think it's best to leave now*," Ikaika TP. Maka nodded. He strode away from the podium. The Secret Club and Ikaika joined him as he beelined for the doors. The merchants gave them a wide berth.

"Good riddance to all that," Nicole muttered. They walked out of the heated confines of the Town Hall.

CHAPTER 6
HOPOHOPO TOWN SQUARE

Manaful World
August 5, 2022
ʻŌmaʻomaʻo Hopohopo Community

Maikaʻi and Kōkua stepped back as Elder Maka and Ikaika strode out with the Secret Club on their heels. Maka's annoyance was apparent by the way his robes swung around agitated. His bushy eyebrows were knitted tight.

"That didn't sound too good," Maikaʻi observed.

Maka rubbed his smooth chin. "When are you two going off-duty?"

"It's already been two hours. The meeting seems to be over," Kōkua said, peering into the hall. Attendees were surging towards the exit enmasse.

Maikaʻi hefted her lance upright with both hands. "That's right. We're done here. At your service, Elder."

"Good. We have important business to share with you," Maka said.

"We shall summon you to Elder Puna's to discuss new information about Uli," Ikaika TGP. Maka's aunts nodded solemnly.

Just then, Nicole felt something wiggling into the butt pocket of her jeans. Instinctively, she reached around and grabbed a slim arm. Twisting around fast she slammed the Hopohopo picking her pockets to the ground, hard. The dust cleared. Her 5'3" was enormous compared to the dwarf that was revealed. She quickly released the two foot Hopohopo, raising hands to her face. "Oh! I didn't mean to!"

Pierre went to his knees to help the Hopohopo sit up, saying, "Sorry to disappoint you. We don't carry anything on us, pickpocket."

"Not even lint," the pickpocket agreed bitterly. He held Pierre's hand looking at how big it was. Pierre let him, wrist limp.

"Nothing comes through the Shimmery Wall except the clothes on our backs and my glasses," Malie said knowledgeably. She blinked owlishly down at the now blushing pickpocket.

The Hopohopo got to his feet and glowered at Ikaika and Maka. "I need silver for food," he said curtly. He was entirely unabashed by his attempted theft. Certainly not the usual humble beggar.

"No silver nor gold needed for that," Maka TGP, including the pickpocket.

The street urchin jumped at the voice in his head, unaccustomed to telepathic projections. This was his first time. His eyes widened when an armload of paper bags appeared in front of his face. The survivor swiped the bags in a jiffy. Tucking the gifts close to his side like a rugby player's ball, he poked his grimy hands in to claim the prize. He squealed with pleasure at finding pears, kiwis and apples inside. The food was a beautiful and welcome sight for the hungry youngster.

Overwhelmed, the pickpocket's tough-guy, ruffian face dropped for a second. Grinning, he said, "Fruits galore, oh my! Thank you!"

"See how easy it is when you just ask?" Nicole said, crossing her arms and looking down sternly at the dwarf. Her temper still sizzled at the unwelcomed touch earlier, though a kernel of empathy began to blossom within. Grand-dads would have only aloha for this street urchin. They'd hope Nicole would treat everyone, especially a starved-looking pickpocket, with patience and generosity.

Malie smiled at the foodbags and the raggedy Hopohopo hugging the makana tightly to his chest. Murmuring and grumbling voices approached the SC. She looked around with nervous hiccups in her chest. Their little run in with the pickpocket attracted a lot of attention. Malie shivered under the curious gazes of those in the square, particularly a red faced fruit seller.

The merchants trooping out of the Town Hall surrounded them. Malie became claustrophobic. The merchants couldn't keep their eyes off the humans. The Hopohopo seemed more familiar with Nicole's fiery temper than the calm yet cold facades of the Manafuls.

The Hopohopo in the cone hat strode up. He said to the pickpocket, "Give those back at once. There's no such thing as a free meal."

But the pickpocket just blew a raspberry. He ran off to discover that the reverse was, in fact, truer. Cone Hat shouted after the urchin, "Hey! I'm the Mayor around here! Show some respect! I'll have you arrested on vagabond charges!"

"No you won't!" Maka said, bristling. He was ignored by everyone. The fruit seller was particularly peeved with Maka's food conjuring. Where would his business be, if Hopohopo simply snapped their fingers, "Poof!", and fulfilled their grocery needs?

Cone Hat studied the three humans. "What manner of creatures are you? Giants?"

"Humans from Earth," Pierre supplied.

The gathered Hopohopo murmured among themselves. Some had heard of humans. Others ascertained that humans weren't Manaful and therefore good. The Secret Club was suddenly bathed in dozens of appraising gazes.

Someone shouted, "Do you use Mana?"

"We can't use it," Malie said, her voice small in the face of all this attention. She felt like a mouse in need of a burrow. She stood half hidden behind Pierre's athletic figure.

"What are you doing here with these horrible Manafuls?" Cone Hat jabbed a thumb at Maka and Ikaika, who hid their offense at being sidelined.

"Wow, rude," Nicole burst out. Nobody talked about her buddies that way!

Cone Hat was surprised. "Rude?"

Malie stepped around Pierre, trying to reach Nicole. She hoped the SC could avoid a Hopohopo confrontation. Pierre grabbed her hand and shook his head. He chin-nudged toward Nicole and nodded. Malie raised her brows at him. He nodded again. Malie let out a deep breath, nodded, and stepped back behind him. Ikaika smiled at the silent exchange. Those two were already mind-melded.

Nicole missed her pals' agreement to let her at 'em. No biggie. She didn't need anyone's consent nor approval. Overcoming bullying taught her that no one deserved to be stepped on or mistreated.

She faced Cone Hat straight-on, raising her voice, "You heard me. You lot are rude. No manners. No love or support. You're just busybodies who throw their insecurities around pell-mell. And it's not like you're aware of that either... you're just packed full of bitterness, hate and small-mindedness."

Wow, she was on a roll.

The Hopohopo were shocked for the second time that day. Many reached up and held tight to their hats. Their ears were probably ringing loudly.

Fez Hat protested, "That doesn't sound anything like us!"

"It sounds exactly like you," Maka said, pointing a trembling finger their way.

A chorus went up in the square, "Shut up!"

Maka clenched his hands into fists. He stopped himself from blasting the entire place into smithereens. These Hopohopo were really testing his patience. And to think these belonged to his own House!

Remember your calming energy, Maka, Ikaika reminded his lifelong buddy. *Align with Source. Let me do the rest of the talking.*

"We refuse to be harassed by Manafuls and your allies on our land," Cone Hat was saying.

Maka's chest puffed up from restraining himself with the interjection: *Excuse me? No, this is all MY 'Ohana land.*

Hearing that thought, Ikaika winced and shook his head at his buddy. He smiled, spreading his hands out towards the Hopohopo like a seasoned politician. He kept stepping closer to the crowd. "We apologize for any offense that may have been caused. It is not our intention to criticize or judge you. We are simply here to deal with an issue that poses much danger to our world."

That riveted everyone's attention on the 'Ula'ula heir. A cry went up: "What danger?"

"Lapu gets stronger everyday," Ikaika said in a carrying voice. A collective gasp went up in the town square. A baby started crying. Mothers quickly towed toddlers away from hearing range. Spirits were a taboo topic here.

The Hopohopo weren't the only ones impressed by Ikaika's charisma. Malie came out from behind Pierre, grabbing his shirt sleeve excitedly. She met his eyes, brows up and wiggling excitedly by what was to come: truth and strength of words. Pierre patted her hand and nodded in acknowledgment, feeling that same pride for Ikaika. Nicole rolled her eyes. Those two were twin-thinking again. She turned, putting her hands up to signify her personal space bubble as the wide-eyed Hopohopo drew in closer.

Cone Hat, the Mayor, was the first one to gather his thoughts. He harrumphed. "Uli told us in a memo that humans are more dangerous than Spirits because they bring diseases into our world."

"That was a lie, as was made clear after Uli's fall and Maka's ascension," Ikaika said in even, calm tones. He opened his arms wide, a warm and welcoming gesture that matched the serene expression on his brown face. Like a hula dancer, he used his body in the most smoothly hypnotic way.

"COVID was a real issue back on Earth, but here it was just a trumped up fear mongering campaign," Ikaika continued. "Yet even Earth fixed the issue as quickly as beings without Mana possibly could. Even if viruses crossed between the worlds, Manaful would have found a faster, instant solution. There was never cause for worry. Uli's words hold no water through and through." He lined up his facts with clarity, without being uppity. He wisely knew nobody, especially the Hopohopo, likes being talked down to.

After some muttering among themselves, the Mayor said, "If Uli really was as nefarious as you say he was, that's all the more reason for us to distrust Elders. He can't be the only rotten egg in the crate."

"*Exactly*," Maka projected to Ikaika, surprised he was agreeing with a Hopohopo. "*Grandpa was working with a small, devious circle. We need to get to the bottom of the schemes he left behind.*"

Ikaika shook Maka out of his head. "The Elder Council was aware for a long time of Uli's attempts to sow distrust. We just couldn't catch him in the act for a long time. Rest assured, Uli was an exception. Neither the Elder Council nor Manafuls intend to harm the Hopohopo. We seek only to empower."

"I second that!" Pierre said. "We have known the Manaful for almost a year now and they have been nothing but good to us."

"They only speak of the Hopohopo wanting to help," Nicole added.

Malie perked up, happy for this positive turn of conversation. She agreed with Nicole, "The Elders only wish to improve your quality of life. Your capabilities are huge from providing food supplies to developing occupational training." She giggled to herself, "*I sound like a campaign!*"

Ikaika winked at her, projecting, "*You are campaigning. For us, for the Manafuls! Keep it up!*"

The Hopohopo Mayor sized up the humans. He was surprised by the humans' fearlessness. "What exactly are you doing here? How did you arrive?"

"Through the Shimmery Wall," Nicole answered only the second question, hands on hips.

"The Elders are opening portals to other dimensions!" The Mayor was scandalized.

"There is no risk in opening portals as nothing dangerous can pass through under the watchful eyes of our Elders," Ikaika said.

"But why bring humans here?" The Mayor scratched his head, confused.

Ikaika looked to the sky for a moment. He chose his words carefully, "To learn from them and teach them how our worlds are linked."

"Learn from them? What can a Manaful learn from humans who have no Mana?"

"Many things. Manafuls can learn from humans as well as Hopohopo." Ikaika smiled.

The Mayor took off his hat, suddenly deflated. "Learn from *us*?"

Ikaika nodded. "Manafuls are always open to learning new things. To use what we learn in ways that will benefit all the worlds. That is the way of life we hope to teach you. It is the way favored by Source."

Malie touched her heart as his thoughts were unifying.

"As for us, how we live without Mana is sure to give insight to beings who know only power," Pierre grinned, sweeping bangs out of his eyes. He looked like a poster for a movie about hair.

"Take my word for it, your Hopohopo society seems to be an exact replica of human societies," Nicole said. She laughed to herself recalling her many talks with her mom about human choices, often unexplainable. "We're not that different."

The Hopohopo mulled this. Humans lived without Mana just like them. The currents of distrust and fear in the crowd lessened. One didn't have to be a Manaful to feel it.

"Elder Alaka'i and my grandfather, Elder Puna, believe if they can prove humans can become Manaful on their own, the same would be true for the Hopohopo," Ikaika revealed.

A young dwarf stepped forward to introduce himself to Ikaika. He looked the same age and was hatless. His wavy, dark hair was crew cut except for long tendrils of burgundy highlights on top. Ikaika's eyes brightened with appreciation as the breeze blew the longish black and red bangs into the handsome Hopohopo's light eyes.

"I am Kimo, Mayor Ethan's youngest. I believe you fully," Kimo said resolutely, ignoring the wary glances his father, Mr. Cone-Hat Ethan, was shooting at him. Kimo's gray eyes held only awe for Ikaika's eloquence. He held out a hand that Ikaika took to shake slowly, their eyes meeting. Sparks flew between them but they were quickly distracted. The merchants demanded Ikaika's attention.

Ikaika resumed his steady speech. "We will return to share what we know of Lapu's plans. Right now, we have business elsewhere. Thank you very much for hosting us despite our unannounced arrival."

There were murmurs of "You're welcome."

Malie was trying to avoid the Hopohopos' staring by hiding behind Pierre's broad back. When Kimo said his name, a chill came down her spine. That was her dad's name. Her chest caved in like someone punched her, making her breathless. She suddenly wrapped her arms around Pierre's waist, hugging him from behind. He patted her arms. He telepathically sensed her need for comfort without attracting attention to herself. He knew she'd lost her dad, also named Kimo, when she was seven. She'd been young enough to recall her dad's aloha. His memory strengthened Malie in that moment along with Pierre's presence. She said a silent pule to her dad's spirit, giving Pierre a final squeeze before releasing him. He glanced at her over his shoulder and sent her his thoughts: *You good back there, Halfing?* She laughed and gave him a thumbs up. Smiling at his 'halfling' thought, unfazed that she caught the TP. Malie has been sending telepathic messages periodically to Ikaika and Maluhia over the past year. She was pleased Pierre's telepathy was growing too. His halfling moniker had become a private joke. Ikaika shared that some Hopohopo and Manafuls were born extra small. They grew up with cute petite frames. The term halfling was an insult among Manafuls, a taboo. Hopohopo halflings were made of sterner stuff, embracing the name and becoming stronger inside than their taller peers.

Speaking of which, she noticed a masked halfling in a wheelchair by the city hall. The figure was wrapped in a checkered cloak. She frowned. The figure had been near the Hopohopo town hall when they'd arrived as well, barely noticeable in his stillness. He held what looked like an old battered beatbox. Looking at it, Malie felt her skin tingle. Mana alert. She looked at Maka and Ikaika. They didn't seem to notice the figure. These extra-sensory perceptions alarmed her. Why didn't the others feel it? Maybe they were all too caught up in the moment.

"We came here hoping to clarify the disinformation that abounds in Hopohopo communities," Maka said in a shame-on-you tone of voice. "But I see now that you are not welcoming of our efforts."

"Maka! Tact!" Ikaika TP. Aloud, he said, "We are thrilled to have been part of the meeting. Would you be willing to meet us again for talks?"

Mayor Ethan titled his head, fussing with the hat. His son Kimo was transfixed on Ikaika but he pointed at the Secret Club. "Only if you come with them."

"Deal," Maka said. "Bye."

Before anyone could do so much as raise a hand to wave goodbye, Maka promptly MT them away. They arrived in the woodlands on the outskirts of the town. He'd disregarded their earlier concern of bothering the natives with Mana use. After that mess of a town hall meeting, Maka was over being courteous and tactful.

"Whew! Am I glad to be out of there!" Malie said, immediately coming out of her momentary shell. She was relieved that those strange sensory feelings were gone. The grateful girl ran around the group in circles chasing a cloud of butterflies frenzied at their sudden arrival.

Pierre laughed at her antics. He remembered his limestone rock. There was a soft thump behind him at once. He turned to find the familiar green, smooth limestone boulder in the knee high grass. He hopped onto it easily and beamed at the Manafuls. "Thanks!"

Ikaika grinned and nodded at Pierre's appreciation. He turned to Maka and both dwarfs began conversing telepathically as the kids unwound. Nicole curiously wondered what they were discussing. She was so mentally exhausted by that community visit that she didn't bother asking them to TGP. Sighing, she wandered up to the edge of the woods to get a breather.

An odd, wheezy voice spoke up in her head. "*Well met, human!*"

Nicole jumped. She twisted her head this way and that but saw only butterflies, dragonflies and trees. There was a gentle hoo-hoo right above her.

"*Up here. We've met.*"

She looked up to find a pair of gigantic orange orbs regarding her with the calm wisdom only owls can manage. She was thrilled. "Maluhia!"

The big white bird ruffled his feathers. He looked like a giant fuzzball. Malie ran over to join Nicole, clapping her hands when she saw the owl. Malie wanted to snuggle his fluffiness close. Nicole wanted his mind powers.

Wind chimes of laughter floated into their heads as Maluhia TGP, "*You two can have neither of that, but I'm glad you're here.*"

"What are you up to?" Malie asked.

"*I am directing animals away from a new Hopohopo logging area,*" Maluhia projected, squeezing his powerful talons on the branch he perched on. "*Care to follow me for a look?*"

"Yes!" Nicole and Malie chorused.

Maluhia hopped off the bough. He spread his wings to catch the breeze. The manu swept over their heads and circled directly over Pierre, who sat up and hooted up at the magical bird. His exuberance was contagious, bringing laughter all around. Pierre jumped down from his limestone and ran after the owl. Maluhia circled back to the girls, wings luminous in the breeze.

"Let the tour commence," Maluhia projected. The bird was leisurely in his flight. But the humans still had to run to keep up. Pierre nimbly jumped over the gnarled roots and rocks that littered the ground. A born hurdler, the natural obstacle course was a joy to run through. His heart soared watching the manu glide on the wind currents. Pierre never felt freer than that moment with his pals near and the amazing Maluhia above. Equally excited though not as recklessly free-spirited, Malie and Nicole picked their way more cautiously.

Winging under the canopy, Maluhia came to rest on an old oak that looked like it had been blasted by lightning not long ago. Various animals milled around the blackened trunk. They stopped to wiggle their noses at the new arrivals. It was a gathering of sorts for furry, poky, scaley, and feathery animals of all shapes and sizes. The squawks, howls, and chittering on low hanging branches added flavor to their ears.

Pierre looked around in surprise. "What's happening here?"

"They're animal refugees," Nicole said knowingly. She told them about the logging. Nicole's heart melted remembering the wildlife shows she watched with her Grand-dads. Some of the traveling veterinarians risked their lives to save suffering animals just like these.

"The Hopohopo have so many flaws it's no wonder the Elder Council has no idea how to deal with them," Malie said. "How can they not understand themselves and their inner potential? They're blindness harms these beautiful beings' habitat."

She squatted and held her hand out to a group of squirrels. The creatures scurried up to swarm her lap. She giggled at their bushy tails tickling her all over, sensing a keen intellect and curiosity in them.

A colony of bunnies frolicked among bushes adorned with golden flowers. Nicole wandered among them looking at the various huddled creatures of all species. "Isn't the land a free-for-all for the animals?"

Maluhia rotated his head almost 180 degrees, saucer eyes following their movements among the animals. *"In Manaful, animals are deeply attached to the bit of land they were born and raised on. When their land is destroyed, they become depressed. I have gathered them here to give them the inspiration and courage to move on. They will disperse from here as they gain strength."*

Nicole's heart was instantly touched by the homeless animals' depression. She knew what that felt like. At least, second hand. Her mother Kaleo had been thrown out of her home when Nicole was just a growing fetus in her belly. If not for Granddads John and Court Fine, Kaleo and Nicole could have both died. She almost cried for these lost souls. She sniffled, and lips quivering, looked to the treetops high above for peace.

Maluhia fluttered his wings and projected, "*Owl breathing time?*"

The hilarity of an owl suggesting that broke the melancholy mood. Laughing now, Nicole pointed at Maluhia, "That was funny! No, I don't need the 'Whoo...Whoo 1,2,3's at the moment, thank you very much." She was enjoying the majestic owl's company. Malie and Pierre wandered around, visiting with the other forest foundlings.

"Is this part of the forest safe from logging?" Nicole asked, a row of minuscule birds arranged in rows and twittering on either shoulder. They pecked her hair.

"Sadly, no. This woody swathe belongs to the Hopohopo. But the Elders still visit from time to time to heal devastated areas." Maluhia fell silent. He watched the children give the animals much needed love, scratching their fur and feathers, playing and frolicking. Then he lifted his wings, stretching them out to full width. He flapped them slowly. The air swirled like water around his feathers, glittering with a rainbow sheen.

"Wow!" Malie gazed at the magnificent creature. "Is that Mana?"

"Yes. Mana mist, a natural, condensed state of Source's Mana. It helps the animals."

The colors broke into rainbow droplets that floated down to the grass, where the animals jumped to catch them. The droplets caught in their fur and feathers, getting absorbed. Joyous animal calls abounded. Many of them disappeared into thin air.

They watched in awe. Maluhia's projections took over his calming hoots. "*Animals can drink or absorb the Mana mist. They gain special powers temporarily, mostly to MT.*"

"How different is Mana Mist from Source's Mana?" Malie asked, watching a possum curl up into a ball of fur and rapidly decrease in size until it vanished with a soft *pop*.

"It is the exact same thing but in a different form, Maluhia projected, amber eyes staring at her glassily. "*Don't you know about water? It's always present around you in vapor form. It steams upon heating and condenses to liquid when cooled. Cooled further it turns to ice. It remains the same thing but takes different forms."*

"Of course," Malie slapped her forehead. She had been thinking of Mana as something far too mysterious and indescribable to understand. But it turned out her mom Pili was right. A few years ago, whenever young Malie found something overwhelmingly inexplicable or strange, Pili would say, "There is a science and art to everything. We just have to investigate and find out the answers. Knowledge is power. So never be needlessly scared of the 'unknown', my beautiful Baby Manu."

"Mana mist consists of energetic powers tapped straight from Source." Maluhia continued to educate them. "*Even so, only a select few animals like me are capable of telepathy and teleportation using the mist."*

Maluhia's assistance and abilities would help all of these creatures. Nicole gazed at the animal with new eyes. The owl was like an elder to the animals. Respect!

"Owls, ravens, and parrots are masters at working the Mana mist in the animal kingdom," Maluhia said. "*That is why we are known as Forest Guardians."*

"Can humans get Mana powers with the mist as well? Can we drink it?" That was Malie the scientist.

"No, it works only on beings that fully belong here."

"Aw shucks," Pierre said.

Maluhia allowed them a few more minutes before they all received Ikaika's TGP: *I have opened a Shimmery Wall. Ready to go back?*

The Secret Club looked at each other. They were all tired after their adventures. Maluhia read their minds and rose up into the air. *"Follow me back to your Manaful companions."*

After returning them to the Manafuls, Maluhia wished them a good return. His feathers rustled in the wind as he MT away in a rainbow burst. Maka and Ikaika were sitting on Pierre's green rock. Beside them The Shimmery Wall Portal shone bright in the sunlight, with the frozen gym backyard visible on the other side through the haze. The edges sizzled like soda fizz.

"This was definitely our wildest visit so far," Nicole said.

"Yep. I feel like a nap," Pierre yawned widely.

"There's a lot to digest from our journey today," Malie agreed. "Hello home, mom and comfy bed."

The SC thanked Ikaika and Maka profusely. Ikaika hugged them all as Elder Maka nodded his goodbyes. Malie, Pierre and Nicole stepped into the portal. Bodies tingling as their molecules broke apart, they were transported back to earth.

Chapter 7
SC Mom Talks

Earth
Honolulu, Hawai'i
August 6, 2022
Various home locations of the Secret Club
Malie Manu's home

"How's the gang?" Malie's mom, Pili Manu, asked, peeking through the kitchen window while cooking dinner. A cool evening breeze swept over Malie who was doing yoga on the living room floor.

"We're not a 'gang'," Malie replied. "We call ourselves The SC. The Secret Club."

"What is it you do together?" Pili stirred the mixed vegetables, maintaining a steady and not too nosy tone.

Malie turned to her side on the floor, lifting her right knee to her chest. Stretching eased her mind and body. Solitary exercise was becoming her way of being strong. How Pierre handled team sports was beyond her, much less the necessary roughness of tackling others.

She turned her head towards the kitchen, but couldn't see Pili directly. Malie heard the concern in Pili's voice. Her mom pounded the pots and pans against counters and stoves. They say cooking releases tension. It's undoubtedly true.

"It wouldn't be a Secret Club, if we told our parents every detail of our affairs," Malie lilted cheerfully. She appreciated her mother's love. She'd share generalities about Manaful World. It was truly too spectacular and incredible. Malie knew she had to share *something* with her mother or Pili would feel left out.

Malie spoke clearly and deeply, "We learn more about each other and ourselves with each meeting. There are personal problems that seem difficult to deal with alone like bad memories. Together, we support each other in getting past these insecurities through storytelling."

Pili gasped and dropped the cooking spoon. "Who are you and what have you done with my daughter? Are you Malie Two – pod person visiting from outer space?"

Malie giggled. "It's just me, Mom. I'm growing up!"

Pili returned her focus to boiling a large pot of water for the pasta noodles.

Malie was talking more than before so Pili wasn't complaining. She was both bemused and glad. Nowadays Malie's reading time wasn't her biggest priority of the day. Her sweet bookish kid now had many things to do. Busy, energetic, talkative. Texting, phone calls, giggling. In the face of this curious change, Pili now listened more than talked. Something about her daughter's stories and anecdotes made her feel like some lines were being blurred. As if there were some bits Malie refrained from sharing with her. She couldn't shake off a feeling that something was amiss.

Pili did not voice the suspicions that her daughter was keeping secrets from her for fear of disrupting her daughter's joy. She was stuck in a mental battle - is her daughter all right upstairs? The intense book-reading of the past few years was fine. She still feared an active fantasy storytelling club was detaching Malie from reality further after the prolonged period of isolation.

I should get to know Malie's SC friends better, Pili decided, starting on the pasta sauce.

* * *

Pierre Martin's Home

At home, Pierre was growing increasingly fascinated with Shelly's tummy. She was ready to pop, huge.

Shelly's mother, Tūtū, cleaned the cabbage from their home garden for their dinner coleslaw. It would accompany the barbequed chicken Gabe, her son-in-law, was grilling outside that minute.

"Mom, may I get you some iced water or decaf herbal tea?" Pierre was ever catering to her needs, praying for his sibling in her uterus to come out healthy and bouncing.

"The months have flown by, Mom! I can hardly wait for 'Delivery Time!'" Pierre would be here on Earth not in Manaful for the birthing. He had a mind to even ditch SC meetings, if

Shelly seemed uncomfortable. This morning she told him to stop henning her and go enjoy his summer with his friends.

Pierre's excitement for his baby sibling was escalating his need to reveal his sexual orientation... he wanted to tell now. It felt like "coming clean", a way to deal with just one of the secrets that was quickly piling up in his life.

Shelly enjoyed the automated tapping and bumping of her reclining massage chair. She stared up at her agitated son. Pierre bounced in circles like a boxer waiting for the referee's bell to ring. Sensing his urgency to share, Shelly inquired, "How are your guy friends lately? You bond with SC often. How are your football teammates doing?"

With a relieved sigh, Pierre knew this was his opening. He lowered his shoulders and sat before her on an ottoman. Reaching for her swollen cankles, he grabbed the Dōterra Mālama essential oil they both loved. He soothed her with it, mixing the fragrant liquid with some almond oil and lathering it on her skin with strong fingers. She closed her eyes and smiled.

On this day, they would finally have the talk. Pierre took a deep breath and launched into the little speech he'd prepared. He came out. It was easier than he thought.

"Mom, I think I'm zesty."

"What's that? Gen-Z speak?"

Pierre nodded, lips dry.

Shelly was enthralled. "Does it have anything to do with lemons?"

"Mom. I'm gay."

That was it. His fingers ran circles on the soles of her feet. Beneath the apprehension there was an enormous gratitude for his parents and life, bolstering him.

"I am proud of you my dear boy!' Shelly exclaimed. The chair squeaked as she leaned forward to hug his head to her bosom. Pierre felt her joy for him in her heartbeat.

"How are you so calm, Mom?" He knelt at her side and pressed the massager function off on her recliner. It was making his nose itch.

"My love, your father and I have known this truth for a while. We were simply waiting for you to face your truth yourself."

Pierre started with surprise, his eyes widening. He started trembling as it dawned on him that many at school might have "known" as well, just like his parents. *Am I that obvious?*

"We love you and worry for you as the world isn't a graceful, accepting place," she reached for his shaking hands and leaned forward to rub her nose against his like she did when he fell as a toddler.

To his surprise, Shelly started crying and laughing at the same time. She could not stop until Gabe entered a few minutes later with the barbecued chicken ready to be eaten.

"Our boy's finally come out," Shelly blurted through her giggles. Gabe gently placed the hot pan of chicken on the table and rushed to his wife and son.

Both of his parents hugged him, sharing an overjoyed moment of acceptance. Gabe wondered aloud if Pierre's new friends ought to be included in the family to share the joy. Maybe the SC girls and their mothers could come over for dinner soon?

Shelly shook her head. "We shouldn't rush things. The kids will do things at their own time and pace."

Pierre agreed with energetic nods. He didn't really need to bring any more joy home at the moment. He wanted his mom to rest. And soon, he will bond with his newborn sibling.

* * *

Nicole Moku's Home

Nicole was proud to have dealt with her bully issue, but now felt like a tattler. She was anxious people would call her that, though her fears had proved baseless so far. Now that summer was closing and classes starting soon, she was stressing out again.

She stood in her mom's office to study the legal books. Being among her mom's treasured things calmed Nicole. Her worries had driven her here. The idea of kids at school making fun of her made her stomach turn.

"Kids are cruel sometimes. Why can't people be dry and emotionless like the law?" she asked herself, thinking she was alone.

"Trust me the law is a cruel being too except when we learn to manipulate it," Kaleo Moku, her mother, squeezed her shoulder from behind.

Nicole was never fazed by Kaleo sneaking up on her. She bent her head to press a cheek to her mom's hand.

"What do you mean, Mom?" Nicole turned, twisting her puffy hair into makeshift ringlets. Keeping her fingers busy helped to sidetrack worries.

“You will learn one day that all things, especially the law, are open to interpretation.”

“Oh, you mean someone’s opinion may be different from yours, but it doesn‘t make them good or bad?” Nicole perked up. This was juicy and explained a lot about the Hopohopo and Manafuls.

Her mother watched her for a moment. Nicole knew that examining gaze. Kaleo was determining how much details she can persuade with her lawyer skills out of her daughter.

Nicole realized the bullying after effects were something her mom could clarify for her.

“Hey, Mom, remember when those boys bullied me in the school gym?” Nicole straightened up proudly and released her hair. She opened her hands and reached for her Mom’s fancy courtroom lapel. She guessed her mom had a hearing or presentation that required her to suit up.

Kaleo went with the flow of her daughter’s assistance. She spun and dropped her arms, allowing the blazer to fall onto a chair. Nicole patted the couch where clients sat to discuss their legal issues with her mom.

“Relax, Mom. I’ve got some sharing.”

Kaleo smiled as her daughter plopped not so ladylike onto the couch beside her. She sighed. Her daughter needed to work on the plopping. Kaleo leaned her shoulder into Nicole‘s and they interlaced fingers.

“After reporting the bullying, to my surprise, I’m getting eyebrow raises and some smiles at school,” Nicole said. “No one taunted me for tattling. Not that I know of. But I still worry.”

“Rattle off the positives, love.”

"Alright. My world is getting more colorful with new approaches... possible new connections. Remember Kona? The main bully's younger brother and sixth year student who gave me strength to counter the bullies? Yeah. He bounces up to me everyday to say Hi and Bye. Kinda nice but also annoying."

Nicole had shared about Kona's timely appearance with her mom the very day of the bullying. Nicole initially wanted to stay mum, but he really deserved recognition. Kaleo was both appreciative and surprised by Nicole's annoyance of the youngster. She supposed it may be a matter of her daughter's pride – not everyone likes to be saved.

"New contacts aren't a bad thing," Kaleo reasoned. "Why not just welcome his friendship?"

But Nicole was lost in her own thoughts. She couldn't share how much Kona bugged her as Kaleo liked him. Before school let out for summer, Kona would sometimes catch her at lunch to show her the latest comic he was reading. He always waved at her in the hallways. The brat seemed to idolize Nicole to a fault for reasons she could not understand. It was second nature to check if the puny kid was sneaking about before she went to SC meetings on school grounds. If Kona overheard their talks, their secret would be out and he might want to be part of it.

Nicole didn't think the SC was ready for a fourth member. Especially not a smaller kid like Kona.

Nuh-huh. Nope. Not happening, ever.

Chapter 8
Cat and Ari Snuggies

Earth
Storyteller in Papakōlea, Hawai'i
August 7, 2022

"Eager to resume classes next week?" Aunt Ellie asked over the pages of *The Book of Love and Creation* she was reading on the lanai settee on the porch.

Ari was sitting on the steps petting a stray cat that crossed her Aunt's front yard every day before the sun set. She called him Maui as his meows sound like the Hawaiian demigod's name. They hānai the feline beauty, but had yet to get him to stay put. He was a creature of the night. He could get any species to mālama him. He did make it a habit to visit in the mornings for a can of wet cat food and extra cuddles. Ari was grateful for his sporadic rubs and head-butts. Always felt loving and kind. She returned to the convo about school with her aunt, unexcited like most students to go back.

"No," she sighed, "Being in eighth grade will have its ups and downs, including making new friends."

"Why? What happened to last year's buddies?"

"Aunty, many of them changed schools. Middle School is the deciding time for families: private schooling or redistricting to a "good" school neighborhood. Being the one left behind can be demoralizing. What does that say about our community? Are we second rate?"

"Never! You're always first rate."

"Mahalo. I enjoy my summers with you, Aunty. I am blessed to see you before and after school during the school year. You're my hānai mom. Love you!"

Aunt Ellie lowered the book to her lap and knelt to hug Ari. They swayed back and forth like a sitdown waltz as they did when Ari was a toddler. Except back then Aunt Ellie could actually pick little Ari up. She loved Ari's affectionate moods, felt honored that her niece was comfortable sharing her heart.

Ari was dropped off at her Aunt's for the entirety of her parents' office hours, 6 am to 7 pm daily. That was a lot of time together. Thank God for the big house, yard, neighborhood park and pool, and the Tantalus trails. Otherwise, on these sweltering hot summer days, they'd have cabin fever. Her sister and brother-in-law aren't forgetful of their daughter. Both worked hard seven days a week to thrive amidst Hawai'i's horrendous cost of living. Aunty Ellie was fortunate to be a retired, single, non-parent, who made wise financial investments.

For most of Ari's life, she and her parents, Hoku (Ellie's sister) and Hassan, lived with Ellie in her Papakōlea home. Mothering Ari was joyous for the sisters as Hassan worked his way up the corporate ladder. Hoku had been a stay at home Mom and college student. Ellie took over watching Ari after returning home, a winding-down high school educator. Hoku got some respite and post-secondary studies done then. Ellie babysat Ari full time every summer. Hoku received her Certified Public Accountant credentials and joined the workforce with Hassan. Her return to work coincided with Ellie officially retiring to begin collecting her pension from teaching.

Ari's parents now owned a condo and dropped Ari off to Aunt Ellie's before work and picked her up after dinner. Ari's ambitious career-minded parents rarely had a sit-down meal with their daughter. With Aunt Ellie, Ari would always be safe, happy, nurtured, and loved. What more could a kid ask for?

"Mauuu-eee. Mauuu-eee."

Maui, the cat, woke Aunty Ellie up from her memories. Shaking her head, she sighed.

"I am the blessed one to have you, my dear!" Aunt Ellie said emphatically.

Maui who'd run a few steps down from the hugging pair, reapproached the ladies. The black cat came in for one last scratch on his triangular head before he padded off into the hibiscus trees lining the home. Maui was probably going off to hunt after all the love. Ari looked up at her Aunt's caring eyes. There was a comfortable silence for a moment. They smiled as the cat leapt up onto a trash dumpster and over a fence into a neighbor's yard.

"Aunty, what are the Secret Club doing today?"

Aunt Ellie was resettling herself on her chair by the lanai railing. She was just picking up her book when Ari's out of the blue question caught her off guard. She almost threw her book over the railing and into the yard in her eagerness to continue her story.

Ari giggled as her Aunt tossed the book to the porch floor instead. She dragged a stool near Aunt Ellie and sat. She motioned for her hānai mom to put up her feet for a soft massage. Aunt Ellie obliged, leaned back, and commenced storytelling.

Chapter 9
The Lost Legend

Manaful World
August 7, 2022
Koa Forest, Elder Territory
Ikaika's Manson

Wright Middle's summer program is over with fall quarter beginning next week. The SC felt relatively safe on campus at 12:30 pm. Nicole was the last to arrive after looping around all over the building to shake off any possible stalkers. Namely, Kona.

"Maybe it's a good idea to tell Puna to summon the Shimmery Wall at our homes like last Spring," Nicole said.

Pierre and Malie frowned. "What are you talking about?"

"Never mind," Nicole sighed.

The trio's skin tingled as the soft hum in the air that was the Manafuls' welcome song sought them. They walked casually around the gym to the back. A pack of mongoose scurried into the ferns. The preteens stopped before the familiar mossy wall that began shimmering brighter and brighter until the

Shimmery Wall opened before them like cascading, liquid light. Beyond was a kaleidoscope of swirling colors like a hologram, the verdance of Manaful.

Malie clasped her tiny hands in front of her. "Ooooh, I'll never get tired watching that happen."

They stepped through their school gym's Shimmery Wall. The Secret Club materialized in Koa Forest beneath Ikaika's invisible mansion in the sky.

Ikaika and Elder Maka appeared before the trio as Pierre double checked if his body was still intact. Malie laughed at his silliness and Nicole rolled her eyes.

"What's happening?" Nicole demanded.

Ikaika grinned and pointed up. In an instant they MT up to the dwarf's seemingly empty gym-sized crib, knowing whatever was needed would simply appear. Sure enough, Pierre envisioned bouncing on a trampoline. Before the girls could blink, their tall buddy was climbing on the gymnasium apparatus.

"Seriously?" Malie giggled. "A trampoline?"

Nicole considered a soak in a jacuzzi filled with yogurt ala the retro Madonna video she had recently seen on YouTube. Reading her mind, the Manafuls laughed at her dairyfood day dream. She was set on her crazy thoughts. She was not doubting for a second that her magical hosts could conjure a swimsuit and tub of creamy cold Greek deliciousness. She raised a brow at them questioningly. Ikaika and Elder Maka smiled, nodding simultaneously. Sure enough, Nicole's wild idea materialized in the corner opposite Pierre's trampoline. A clawed Victorian tub brimming with dairy goodness, with rose petals sprinkled on top.

Malie had already found herself a reading nook with a red velvet loveseat and a cache of her favorite author's novels. It was a predictable if sweet sight. She contentedly thanked Ikaika, "I wish I could take these books home."

Nicole laughed, "Malie, most popular novels are blackmarket published or posted online."

Malie gasped in shock. "I can't download those; it's cheating the author of their rights and profits!"

Nicole covered her face and shook her head, muffling her laughter. She was unsurprised by her friend's consideration for authors the world over. She got into the tub wearing the exact swimsuit she'd imagined. The Secret Club got lost in their separate activities for a few minutes. Ikaika and Maka sat still with eyes closed. Probably communicating with Elders Puna and Alaka'i.

When they opened their eyes around ten minutes later, Pierre was tiring out on the trampoline. Nicole remained in the tub, feeling ridiculously pampered and not guilty about it even an iota.

Ikaika began, "Our visit to the 'Ōma'oma'o Hopohopo community got us an important lead." Frowning, he continued, "The Hopohopo in the fez had a mind block. He is a spare parts merchant called Malachi, Mayor Ethan's best friend. Influential in the town's administration, Malachi is in contact with a wide network of traders in every Ōma'oma'o township. Frighteningly, they're even in the main city. We followed those threads of connection to find mind screens and blocks of varying degrees on almost every trader."

Unnerved, Malie moved closer to Pierre. He squeezed her hand.

His mouth fell open, "That would mean an Elder placed them!"

Maka nodded and TGP, *"I'm confident it was Uli, my grandfather. Some of the merchants aren't even aware of the mental manipulations placed on them. They are controlled remotely like robots."*

Even Ikaika shivered at that, saying, "These manipulations are signature Uli mind tools. They muddle the host's memories and thoughts to confuse anyone who attempts to read their minds. Mind blocks are against Council Law, which decrees mind manipulations must never interfere with the host's memories or sense of identity."

Nicole's eyes widened, appreciating that her mind screen was purely benevolent. She tapped her temple, saying, "Ever since Puna placed the screen, I have actually felt calmer and can recall memories better."

"Exactly," Ikaika said. "Screens function to help and protect the host from outside influence. They don't mess with memories. But Uli's screens intentionally conceal his schemes, achieving this by muddling their memories."

"Like editing film reels," Malie said. "Memories of their own lives were re-edited by Uli until they forget who they are!"

"You got it!" Ikaika gave Malie a thumbs up.

"Fortunately, the merchants' exchanges are clear as day," Maka picked up. "*Once we knew what to look for, we quickly identified Uli's screens and ended up with a network of fifteen merchants."*

"What's the merchants' agenda?" Malie was intrigued and her fears allayed. "Also, how are the screens still functioning with Uli dead? What are they hiding?"

Both dwarfs frowned and nodded in agreement. They had a lot to say. Ikaika chose TGP to continue his update of recent discoveries. "*Uli's twisted screens remain despite his death. Probably through Lapu's workings. Uli really wanted his influence on the Ōma'oma'o communities to outlast his life. His entire existence was geared towards oppressing Mana because the last thing he wanted was others to be as powerful as he was.*"

The Secret Club shared a relieved look that Uli was dead.

"*My grandfather used our Protector's Academy to train Hopohopo assassins instead of teaching Manaful defense and combat strategies.*" Maka spit out frustratedly, not at them but at the fact that he couldn't figure out how to fix the Academy.

Ikaika's projections remained cool though, unmarred by intense emotions. "*The assassins, who can at minimum TP, are hired by coin-greedy merchants for various purposes. Mostly the assassins help them maintain their monopoly on the Hopohopo communities. They drive them ever away from Manaful contact and assistance.*"

"*We also suspect that the assassins murder Manafuls and Aspiring Hopohopo who advocate to solve the Hopohopo issue once and for all,*" Maka TGP.

Ikaika shot a sideways glance at his friend. The Secret Club, even Nicole who was still neck deep in yogurt, saw something flicker in Ikaika's eyes. Oblivious, Maka continued, "*Even in Uli's absence this network continues to carry on his work like a cohort of brainwashed zombies. They're groomed into a habitual routine that they likely don't even know why they uphold anymore. This sort of mind control is just sad to witness."*

"Isn't there anything Elders Alaka'i and Puna can do about it?" Nicole asked sleepily, muscles completely relaxed.

"Not without breaking their minds entirely," Ikaika chewed his lower lip.

"Since I inherited Uli's Mana, I'm the only one who can safely deal with the hijacked minds of these Hopohopo merchants," Maka sighed. *"But I don't dare do it as I still have so much to learn."*

Pierre stretched, saying casually, "I don't think this is much of a problem, is it? Since Uli's gone, they're just gonna lose steam over time. Right?"

Nicole's eyes snapped open. She stood up to drip yogurt. "Um, excuse me, but since when is murder 'not much of a problem'?"

Pierre blushed.

Malie came to his rescue with, "What he means is that without Uli's presence the assassins and this merchant network have no compass, no real goals."

Pierre shot his petite friend a grateful look, nodding so hard he looked like one of those bobble-heads on car dashboards.

"We sure hope so," Maka and Ikaika TGP.

"Well, I sure hope you find out what these Hopohopo are up to," Nicole said, oozing out of the tub. The moment her feet touched the floor, the tub, yogurt and her swimsuit vanished. She was the regular Nicole Moku again in her jeans and sloganned tee. She sat on the rug with Malie, as Pierre bounced around the room.

"Thank you for your support," Ikaika smiled at her.

"Guess this calls for more trips to Hopohopo territory," Malie said, leaning back on her arms. The labrador puppies bounded in from another room, climbing into her lap and licking her face. She giggled, scratching behind their ears.

Ikaika smiled, happy his puppy distraction worked. The convo had gotten deep.

Maka sniffed, stumped. He got up and shuffled across the translucent floor to a wall, drinking in the clear sky and passing birds to seek peace. There was still tenseness in his shoulders. "Maluhia, the owl, advised me to be wary of my temper when dealing with the Hopohopo," he grumbled more to himself than his friends behind him.

Ikaika came up to his pal and squeezed his arm reassuringly. He'd considered sharing about Lapu, but decided the kids had had enough. Not to mention, that Spirit had already done a number on the SC. The ʻŌmaʻomaʻo ʻOhana would sort out their businesses in time. No sense in rushing and increasing the pressure on poor Maka.

"Maluhia speaks true. It is wise to heed his advice," Ikaika projected. *"The Hopohopos' suspicions must be handled with tact and wisdom."*

Maka winced at the reminder of his people's distrust of him. He mumbled, "Why won't they just believe that we have their best interests at heart?"

The room was solemn after his comment. Ikaika stood silently with his hand on Maka's shoulder. They breathed in unison.

Ikaika came out of deep thought to TGP, *"There is something Puna and Alaka'i shared with me recently that you'd find interesting."*

"*That's right, the quest!*" Maka turned on his heels, his momentary misery forgotten. His excitement was catching. The girls jumped to their feet wide eyed.

"Quest?" Pierre howled, bouncing around the room.

Ikaika grinned. "*Yes. Let me summon grandfather. He puts it far better than I can.*"

It was done in a split second. Elder Puna's red robes cascaded out of the air to reveal his kindly, brown face and chocolate eyes. The second most powerful Elder in the world chuckled at the youngsters. "*Ah, it seems you took your sweet time calling me.*"

"*We had some updates to share,*" Ikaika said, bowing his head respectfully as an apology.

"*You should have just gone ahead and told them about the Old Hill,*" Puna patted his grandson's head as if he were a baby. "*After all, the idea for the quest came out of your brilliant head.*"

"Old Hill? Oh, tell, please," Malie skipped around the hopping Pierre, making Nicole snigger into her hands at the twin bundles of energy her pals were.

Elder Puna crossed his legs. He did this while standing. The children appraised the final surreal effect of him sitting calmly in midair with robes swaying around him in wine and rosy reds.

His melodic projections drew them in. "*According to our legends, The Old Hill is at the Center of Manaful World and part of the Manaful Creation Song. It isn't easy finding the Center of our world. Elder Alaka'i was the first dwarf to find it, becoming the first Manaful of this world. On his journey to align with Souce, he learned from the relics of Old Hill.*"

The Secret Club was intrigued, Pierre and Malie joining Nicole in a gigantic lounge chair.

Elder Puna glanced at Ikaika. "*Will you continue the legend?*"

"*Gladly, grandfather,*" Ikaika TGP. "*The Relics on Old Hill were a tree, a stone, and a cloud.*"

"Woah," Pierre said while laughing. "Those don't sound like your regular relics."

"*The Old Hill* is *rather irregular, as it forms the core of our magical world,*" Elder Puna agreed.

Ikaika picked up the story. "*Elder Alaka'i said the stone is the only Relic he met only once. As it turns out, stone is also the most valuable. It has Songs etched on it. These Songs could turn Hopohopo into Manafuls. Elder Alaka'i learned only one Song before the stone "lost itself", according to the elder.*"

"What sort of songs?" Nicole asked, momentarily too invested in the story to solve riddles.

Malie giggled. She and Pierre said at the same time, "Like the Welcome Song, Nicole! Duh!"

"Jinx!" Pierre howled.

"Songs aren't really needed for making magic around here," Nicole nodded up at the levitating Elder Puna. "He could be telepathically communicating with any being down in Koa Forest while sharing the legend of the Old Hill. And he's not singing. Think about it."

Malie wanted more of the legend. "You said Elder Alaka'i retrieved the Manaful transformation Song from the stone. Is that what he taught you, how you became Manaful as well?"

Elder Puna nodded. He swept a hand to paint a vision across the transparent walls of Ikaika's mansion. The forget-me-not sky above Koa Forest was replaced by a cyan field that rolled up to form a rather large hill. Two small caves formed its eyes. A grooved ridge that resembled very pursed, rocky lips lay close to its base. Where its nose would be, a single, very pretty tree grew tall, majestically reaching towards a halo of pink clouds.

"Oh wow!" The human children exclaimed. They all ran to the wall to plant their hands on the clear surface. They ogled the fantastic landscape.

"Have we traveled to the Old Hill?" Malie asked, taking off her glasses to rub squinty eyes. She also cleaned the lenses on her cotton lapel. She put the frames on for another eyeful of the turquoise scenery.

"This is simply another unique capability I integrated into this mansion," Elder Puna had a note of smugness in his telepathic projection to his rapt audience.

"*We can call it a vision, I guess*," Ikaika projected.

"More like a hallucination," Malie said, awed.

"Or Virtual Reality," Nicole's mouth hung open.

"Augmented Reality, you mean," Pierre said dreamily.

"One can only find Old Hill with physical locomotion beyond a certain point in the world of Manaful," Ikaika said, unfazed by the immersive vision on his walls. Hands behind his back, he walked around and switched to vocal storytelling.

"Elder Alaka'i found it 4,000 years ago," Ikaika pointed at a small figure walking up the hill in the distance. Elder Puna pinched the air and the scene zoomed into the figure. It was a very young Elder Alaka'i.

Chapter 10
Old Hill and Alaka'i

Manaful World
August 7, 2022
Koa Forest, Elder Territory
Ikaika's Mansion

"This is way better than IMAX!" Pierre announced. He imagined up his waterbed from earlier. It appeared bigger to accommodate the whole Secret Club, Maka and Ikaika. The latter couldn't sit still though and kept pacing. Everyone else jumped on the wobbly bed eagerly. Popcorn and honey almonds appeared in various fists.

Beyond the mansion walls, they watched the young Elder Alaka'i using a staff bigger than himself to help him up the slope of the Old Hill. His feet flattened soft, feathery cyan grass adorned with fluffy flowers. They burst in his wake to be swept away on a breeze that tinkled like bells. There were butterflies trailing Alaka'i along with excitable dragonflies, solemn paper wasps, and furry bees. Every flap of their wings created music.

All the while, a rainbow mist fell like rain on everything. Overhead the pink annulus clouds giggled and rippled. A bit of it broke off and came down to Alaka'i. Its music got louder the closer it got.

"You'll never find it," Cloudlet chuckled. "Why won't you just give up?"

"A Manaful never gives up," Alaka'i said resolutely.

"A Manaful now, eh?"

"Correct. I sang the Song of Mana. It was on the pearly facet on the stone. And the Old Hill blessed me as the first Manaful of this world. Source has come to me."

"I know. I was hanging around to see all that, remember," Cloudlet formed a hand so that it could point a finger up at the sky. Then it zoomed erratically around Alaka'i, who tried to shoo it away with the staff.

"Why do you doubt that I have become Manaful?"

"You haven't made a Manaful out of anyone else yet. Being the one doesn't really earn you the appellation. Just my opinion." Cloudlet was doing annoying bounces all over the slope now.

"I'll get to it," Alaka'i said.

Cloudlet laughed. It burst apart in a shower of music and was gone. The pink clouds above changed into lime green. It continued to giggle from afar, obscuring the sun just enough so that Old Hill never got too hot nor too cold.

Alaka'i finally got to the tree. It was twiddling its twigs and looking worried.

"Surely you must know how to find Stone," Alaka'i demanded by way of greeting.

"Oh, dear, can you check my backside please? I think I'm leaking resin." Tree fretted and swished her lavender head of foliage.

"Why would you be leaking resin?"

"I moved."

Alaka'i stepped back and blinked. It was true. There was a nasty gouge across the side of Old Hill's face where the roots had broken the soil. It looked like Old Hill had developed a dark brown mustache.

"Where are you trying to go?" Alaka'i asked sternly.

"Just..." Tree a-hemmed sheepishly. "Since Stone just rolls off so easily, I thought... perhaps maybe I can go on a stroll as well."

Alaka'i rolled his eyes. He went round to the side of the tree opposite the very mossy, holey "face" and discovered a rip in the bark.

"It's not that bad," Alaka'i called up.

"You're saying I AM leaking!" the tree wailed.

Alaka'i strode back around and pointed his staff at the plant. "It's perfectly fine, bark heals just like skin. Will you just tell me how to find that stone?"

Tree sighed and dropped some berries that ran away on tiny little legs.

"I can't. Stone is very hard headed," Tree bemoaned. "He's very closed in. Doesn't share much with me or cloud. It's impossible to penetrate that granite head. I say the only one who can help you is Old Hill himself."

"He went to sleep."

"He's not going to wake up anytime soon, I guess. He spent a long time teaching you. He needs his rest." The tree suddenly started laughing hysterically. The reason soon presented itself. A family of chipmunks were running over a particularly ticklish groove between her boughs.

Tree's giggle-fit subsided and the chipmunks retreated into a hole.

She said, "Besides, The Song of Mana alone can give rise to the first age of the Manaful world, with you as their Elder."

"Elder?"

"A leader, a teacher, a healer."

"But it's just one Song!"

"It will inspire others within you. Besides, don't forget the Creation Song Old Hill dictated to you himself. You actually know two of the most powerful songs in existence."

Tree suddenly stopped speaking. The ground rumbled. A pair of boulders moved away from the caves closer to the summit. Below them, the ridge thunderously broke apart to reveal a maw of black soil and rocks for teeth.

It seemed Old Hill wanted to butt into the chat.

"Don't you know, you can now sing your own songs, Elder Alaka'i," Old Hill rumbled. "Search within yourself. Go to your people. And sing your songs. They will become Manaful."

Alaka'i fell to his knees in the grass. Tree dropped berries all around him as the hill vibrated gently with speech, and the little fruits hopped up the dwarf's legs. They seemed afraid to run on the trembling ground and clung to his white robes instead, squealing.

Alaka'i spat out a berry hanging on his lower lip before speaking. "Old Hill, the stone promises so much more power...

so much more magic than just one song can give! I feel that this world needs them all!"

"You are correct in that feeling," Old Hill said.

"Oh, why do you always wake him up," Tree muttered grumpily as her leaves fell off to float around in the air currents. "I'll go completely bald if this keeps up."

Old Hill continued his reassurances. "But the time is not now for everything to be known. And there is a price. Each Stone Song costs a Manaful life."

Alaka'i's head snapped up. "What?"

"This world will learn the Song of Creation and the Song of Mana and all of the songs you can invent on your own. Anything extra comes at the cost of your own life."

"What does that mean?" Alaka'i became visibly apprehensive.

Tree piped up with, "It means death has been fated for you."

"Not exactly," Old Hill corrected slowly. "It means the stone will only be found after your death, Elder Alaka'i. By another Manaful, whose death in turn will cause the stone to be found a third time."

"And so on and so forth," Tree said, trying to hold her leaves together with spindly boughs. She added, "End of story. Now go to sleep, Old Hill, if you please."

"One needs the virtues to read Stone. Be patient and righteous, Alaka'i," Old Hill mumbled. "For you and your emissaries, I will always wake up."

With that, the boulders moved back to close Old Hill's eyes—the caves. The ridge closed up at the seams. Old Hill remained still yet ever aware.

"Whew!" Tree said. She creaked as she straightened up.

Alaka'i sighed. "I guess that settles it. Time to return and teach what I have learned."

"*That is all for now,*" Elder Puna TGP to the audience in Ikaika's mansion. He motioned with his hands. The scene zoomed out and faded until they were once again looking upon the canopy of Koa Forest. The show was over.

"*The magic is strong at the center of the world of Manaful,*" the 'Ula'ula House Elder projected. "*It is pure Mana made physical and its mist is heavy in the air like water vapor. The power of Manafuls is nothing compared to the concentration of magic on Old Hill. Even Elder Alaka'i could not reveal all of its mysteries.*"

"*We're wondering what will happen if humans visit the place,*" Ikaika said.

"*Ikaika thinks if the Secret Club finds the Stone this world will learn a third Song while Elder Alaka'i is still alive,*" Maka tilted his head at the humans.

"Us? How can we find something even the Elders cannot?" Malie asked.

"*That's Ikaika's wild idea,*" Maka smiled.

"*That's what we want to find out,*" Ikaika projected at the same time. He and his buddy exchanged looks and laughed. "*Do the natural laws of Manaful apply to humans? Perhaps humans can read multiple Songs on the Stone unlike the one-per-Manaful rule Old Hill has set.*"

"*It is Source that sets all the rules,*" Elder Puna reminded gently. "*Everything else simply obeys.*"

Nicole jumped off the waterbed. "Hey! This is exactly what Lapu was saying! This proves you *do* have ulterior motives!"

Elder Puna hovered to Nicole, putting his hands on her shoulders. "*My dear Nicole. We have ideas and test them. We don't plan schemes to intentionally harm anyone. Least of all the Secret Club.*"

"Remember to fight against the suspicions and doubts that always rise up in our minds," Pierre said. Malie nodded and gave Nicole a reassuring gaze. The taller girl closed her eyes to take deep breaths. *Whoo. Whoo. Whoo.*

"Owl breathing!" Malie giggled, spilling out of the bed to run to Nicole. They held hands and did their whooshing breathing exercise together.

Elder Puna stepped back with his eyes twinkling kindly. "*The screen works when you set your mind on it. Always be on guard.*"

Sure enough, when Nicole opened her eyes they had regained their softness. "I'm sorry I keep paying attention to the doubts Lapu planted."

"*The screen will grow stronger as you work on it yourself,*" Maka projected.

"Is that all there is to the legend?" Pierre wanted to know, rolling around with the waves of the waterbed.

Ikaika nodded. "*For now, yes. We will soon travel the world searching for the Stone. We are convinced that the Songs etched on the Stone will help transform the Hopohopo into Manafuls much faster than we are able to right now.*"

"*Finding it brings a new Manaful Age according to the Legend,*" Maka TGP.

"*Most of the Elder Council refuses to view the Legend as important,*" Elder Puna sighed. "*But Alaka'i and I think Ikaika is onto something and wish to support him on this quest. Perhaps the Old Hill and his Relics treat humans differently from Manafuls."*

"We're all for it," Malie said at once. Nicole looked a tad doubtful but Pierre whooped agreement as he bounced.

"*Perfect*," Ikaika projected.

"*And now we have to get back to investigating these Hopohopo merchants,*" Maka projected.

Pierre was the last off the waterbed. The Secret Club stood before the three dwarfs. Nicole raised her chin and said, "Alright, I'm in as well. For the quest, I mean. All of this is a bit too much, to be honest. I agree exploring the Manaful World is super exciting. Just not today."

"Awesome!" Pierre crowed.

Not long afterwards, Ikaika took them down to Koa Forest, where the Shimmery Wall opened up between two giant koa trunks. The trees reached out telepathically to tickle the minds of the children with aloha.

"See you soon!" The Secret Club waved. They ran into the portal, molecules vibrating apart into music and song. They headed back to the real world. Good ol' Earth.

ACT II

Chapter 11
Ari Drives to Aunty's

Earth
Storyteller in Papakōlea
August 8, 2022

Ari sat in the backseat of her mom's car, pondering eighth grade starting next week. On their drive to Aunt Ellie's, she stared out at the rolling hills outside and remembered Old Hill.

Hoku glanced in the rearview mirror at her daughter. She parted her lips to speak, but only sighed. How could she possibly catch Ari's interest? Nothing came to her. She turned back to the road. No need to worry. They were almost at Ellie's. Hoku's thoughts became consumed with her office schedule, a safer bet.

Ari spoke first, mentally shaking Hoku out of work mode. "Do you know Aunt Ellie's writing a story?"

"She's always writing some silly story," Hoku blurted before she could stop herself.

"They're not silly," Ari said coldly.

"It's a habit she picked up from her Kumu days," Ari's mom continued, turning a corner into the street where her sister Ellie lived.

"I love her stories," Ari continued to stare outside.

Hoku got a call. She was soon speaking breathlessly into her Bluetooth headset as they rolled into Aunt Ellie's driveway. Ari shook her head disappointedly. Her parents were rarely able to be present in the moment with her. They prided themselves in doing exactly that when they attended to work associates. Everything, except their work, was always sidelined.

"That's what 'silly' really looks like," Ari muttered to herself, pointing at the back of Hoku's head.

"What's that?" Her mom asked, flustered as she finished her call. She hit the brakes in front of Aunt Ellie's squat two storey suburban house and smiled back at Ari. Her daughter was already exiting the car. Ari wasn't in the mood to see the smile her mom could have given her when their drive began.

Hoku bit her lower lip, watching her daughter and sister in a tight hug. They seemed so close.

A pang of jealousy made Hoku look away. Come to think of it, when had she last hugged her daughter like that?

Her phone beeped crazily as her work notifications stacked up. She lowered the window to shout a quick 'Bye, Love You! Umwah!' before reversing out of the driveway. Once she was out of eyeshot, Aunt Ellie led Ari up the porch steps by the shoulder.

"Everything OK?" Aunt Ellie asked.

Ari just sighed. "The usual. My dear parents are busy around the clock working hard to earn money apparently because they love me."

Aunt Ellie knew that it was best to maintain a kindly silence at times. One of these days Ari would better understand her parents. She got Ari's backpack and deposited it on the round table by the front door.

"Hope you've been working on the story," Ari said, plopping down on the couch. "That bit about Old Hill was kind of awesome."

"Thank you!"

"What's the quest about?"

"In time, in time," Aunt Ellie disappeared into the kitchen for refreshments. She returned with two glasses of chilled pomegranate juice and watermelon slices, "Before storytelling we always share life updates, remember?"

"There are no updates. Everything's the same as always."

"Tsk."

"Alright. I'm anxious about my online Math class' final. Having numbers-loving accountants for parents is intimidating."

"Take out your notes and online resources, then. We'll go through the lessons. Ask me anything you're too shy to ask in the discussion forum."

Ari grinned and ran to unload her backpack. "I'm so glad my hānai mom worked her whole life at a school."

"Mind you, I'm not helping you solve anything," Aunt Ellie warned. "I'm just guiding you."

They were done with Ari's studies in twenty minutes flat. Ari sat back and whistled. "Wow. That was easy."

"Remember the owl breathing of the Secret Club?"

"Yeah. What about it?"

"They do it when they feel anxious, to clear their heads. You might be having trouble focusing in class due to anxiety. Deep breathing exercises help overcome it and deal with the present better." Aunt Ellie tucked Ari's iPad and heavily doodled notebooks into her school bag.

Ari nodded. She inhaled and exhaled for a few minutes as Aunt Ellie put her bag away again. It was true. Her body relaxed and her head felt lighter than it had been in days.

Whoo, whoo, whoo.

"Better?" Aunt Ellie asked, coming back round to smile at her breathing exercise.

"Definitely," Ari pouted. "Now, how about the story?"

Laughing, her Aunt lowered herself to the couch and gave her niece a side hug. They toasted their glasses of pomegranate: "To the world of Manaful we go, then."

CHAPTER 12
RHODA & UNCLE EJAD

Manaful World
August 8, 2022
"Ōma'oma'o Hopohopo Community

The Hopohopo City was too stifling for Rhoda Ūlialia. She hadn't anticipated this when she moved here to start an apprenticeship program. Her parents put great faith and coin into her career exploration.

This city was as far from the rural farmlands of her 'ohana as possible. Dozens of haphazard high rises stacked together to form a rainbow labyrinthine knot of alleys and streets. Poorly maintained, the buildings were occupied by a chock full of people who preferred motor scooters. She preferred the rural townships beyond Hopohopo City's tall buildings and narrow streets.

Uncle Ejad Honua lived there, in a backway town with thick wooded areas that held abandoned factories. Visiting her uncle was an excuse to get out of her fifth floor apartment flat. Riding the public bus, she held a bag of gifts from her parents. It was their aloha on behalf of Ejad's parents Kalo and Kamana Honua.

Rhoda was the only one who knew her uncle's whereabouts. He'd threatened her into secrecy with, "I'll vanish, if you tell anyone where you meet me." That alone should've hinted at his eccentricity.

She hadn't really known Uncle Ejad growing up. Only ever heard people talk about him, really. That is, until last year right after she was kidnapped by Uli. Upon her recovery and return home, he approached her out of the blue. He introduced himself and told her where he lived. His fedora was low on his brows as he'd hugged his trench coat around him.

In a gravelly voice, he'd said, "Come see me, if you need some quiet time. If you want to tinker with gadgets. I need an assistant."

That convo was one of the longest they'd ever had. He was a dwarf of few words.

This was Rhoda's third visit.

Honestly, her first occupational choice was becoming Manaful with Maika'i and Kōkua rather than taking engineering lessons from Ejad. But Uncle's home was a giant workshop filled with such marvelous contraptions that she couldn't stay away. Truly fascinating to watch the little machines he built.

She alighted at the last town, where the headgear of the Hopohopo merchants got out of hand. Hopohopo city residents had artistic flair. Headgear was part of fashion and one flowed with the trends. In Ejad's town, it was a disaster for the senses.

Rhoda adjusted her fashionable checkered tiny-hat on her red curls, hurrying away from the main courtyard into a more isolated area. Wind blew through the abandoned factories. She ducked into an alley, hugging her blazer closer and checking behind her. Assured she wasn't being followed, Rhoda pressed a button beside a black metal door. It slid open.

She walked in and headed down steps leading into the basement corridor. Her shoes echoed on the perforated metal. She felt safe there with the electric lights in wall sconces that lit up the plush green carpet. Yellow wallpaper brightened it all up. The ceiling air vents kept Ejad's underground workshop fresh. But it was too dusty for her liking. Huge double doors squeaked on their hinges, admitting her into the first section of her uncle's workshop.

"What opportune timing," rang a curt, hoarse voice. That was Ejad – no small talk nor pleasantries. Pointedly, he said, "My assistant appears. Hand me that piece of paper."

Rhoda put her bag of gifts on a wheelchair covered with a checkered blanket. There were several devices on the round table beside it, including what looked like an old-school beatbox.

Ejad had his head stuck inside a ring of iron, etching something on the metal. Goggled eyes peered at her. "It's under the fish bowl."

Rhoda found a sprawling desk with a solitary fighting fish in a tiny bowl. A slightly damp sheet of paper lay under it. She snatched it up and took it to Ejad. He was working hard on what Rhoda thought looked like an enormous wedding ring.

Rhoda tapped the metal with a fingernail. "Are you proposing to a giant, by any chance?"

As usual, Uncle Ejad did not laugh at her jokes. He leaned out to grab the paper. There were symbols scrawled all over it margin to margin. He studied the script closely.

"They're runes," Rhoda said.

Ejad looked up, nodding at her. She felt his approval at her learning. She peered closer at the metal ring and the runes he was etching deep into it. He engraved with some sort of small wand that shone a thread of red light. He pressed a button and the light vanished.

Ejad flipped the tool in his hands to offer it to her. "It's a laser pen. Want to try it?"

Rhoda reached for it, but Ejad snatched the pen back. He showed his teeth. "Not yet. I'm busy. Go fetch that screwdriver."

She snorted but obeyed. Uncle Ejad was eccentric and may come off funny. Unfortunately, her previous two visits proved he was also short tempered.

When she got the screwdriver, he told her to affix something to the gauntlet on the workshop table. It was hard to miss. Fascinated, Rhoda touched the chrome surface of the arm piece, "it's like a perfect glove, but metal."

"Wait till you see what it does."

There was only one piece left to attach. It was a small bit of metal shaped like an anchor that fit nicely into a groove of the same shape. When placed correctly, it hid a battery cell that had the emblems of three Elder Houses stamped on it. Rhoda proceeded to screw the cover on, hiding the cell from view.

"You sure have a lot of projects going on at the same time," Rhoda observed as she worked.

"Pay attention to what you're doing," he ordered. When Rhoda was done, she lifted the gauntlet to show it to Ejad. He switched off his laser again. Checking the runes on the ring, he nodded and took off his goggles to approach her.

Uncle Ejad had olive skin and eyes that were tawny, although she'd never seen real warmth in them. He swept his black hair back and reached to lift the gauntlet out of her hands.

"I'm 100% sure this version will work," Ejad said. He put it on.

Since being rescued from the deceased Uli's pandemic plot, Maikaʻi and Kōkua had taught her basic telepathy. She'd warily tested it recently. She suddenly wanted to read Uncle Ejad's mind as the gauntlet latched around his thick forearms. Filaments of light flared up in the metal as it activated on its own.

"Wow!" Rhoda looked up at her Uncle. His eyes flickered with the metallic light, unmoving on the gauntlet that he flexed experimentally. She reached out with her mind to peek into his.

Can this kill an Elder? he was thinking.

Rhoda gasped aloud. Uncle Ejad's eyes snapped to hers in an instant, and his forehead seemed to split down the middle as he scowled. "How dare you!"

Rhoda stumbled back. "What?"

"Don't act dumb. You just used telepathy on me!"

"No I didn't—"

Ejad raised the gauntlet at her and it sparked menacingly at the fingertips. Rhoda screamed mid-sentence. Although she wasn't harmed, she held her arms up across her face as she backed away.

"Don't lie to me!" Ejad hissed. "When it comes to using Mana around me without my permission, I will cull even my own family. Elder Uli's commands."

"Uli is dead," Rhoda dared to say, though she stammered. She straightened her blazer, shuffling backwards.

Uncle Ejad's eyes widened for a moment. Confusion? But then a shadow washed across them and his face contorted, mouth a rictus of bared teeth. He hissed like a snake, "Then it shall be done by Lapu's order!"

Electricity flared up from Ejad's armored fingertips. His niece realized that he was telling the truth. He *would* hurt her, if he's told to.

Rhoda cried and ran away. She felt her hair rise up in the air as if being pulled back. Ejad directed an electric charge towards her from his gauntlet. Spine tingling, Rhoda escaped out the doors and through the corridors wildly looking for the exit.

He's plotting to murder an Elder! She thought frantically, wishing she knew how to project long distance. *I have to tell someone! The Protectors! Oh, Source, help me!*

* * *

A post-Uli world was a confusing one for the deceased elder's Protectors. Even when he was alive, everyone suspected the guards were just a front. Most of Uli's soldiers were given just a bit of power to manipulate the already fearful and Manaless Hopohopo.

That's why ʻŌmaʻomaʻo Protectors Maikaʻi and Kōkua had a sturdy understanding of telepathy. The Academy trained graduates with several telepathic skills. Manipulating Hopohopo had never sat well with Maikaʻi and Kōkua. Since Uli's death, they sought a more virtuous path of life. Part of that was volunteering at the Medical Center and teaching seekers like Rhoda what they knew of becoming Manaful.

They received Rhoda's call while at the Medical Center. Neither of them could MT Rhoda there, but she would bus there and meet them by lunch time.

True to her word, Rhoda appeared at noon and immediately hugged Maikaʻi tight.

"What's the matter?" Kōkua asked, alarmed. They sat on the shaded benches on the center grounds. Volunteers, staff and patrons moved busily around not noticing the trio.

"I had the most horrible encounter," Rhoda sobbed.

Maikaʻi was suddenly alert. She held the younger dwarf tighter. "Is it Lapu?"

Rhoda shook her head no. She sat back and dried her tears. "My— I ran into an inventor."

"What sort?" Kōkua tilted her head.

"The masked Inventor," Rhoda said carefully.

Maikaʻi sighed. *"I feel much fear in you. You are trying to conceal something from us. May I look into your mind so you won't have to say it?"*

Rhoda nodded at once. She sat still as Maikaʻi massaged her scalp gently. The Protector and Healer still required physical touch to mind-meld.

Kōkua reached and placed her hand on Maikaʻi's shoulder to lend her Mana to the process. Maikaʻi reached into Rhoda's mind and plucked her most recent memory. Her eyes snapped open.

"That is your uncle?" Maika'i asked.

Rhoda nodded. "*Please don't say that aloud. Anywhere. Please.*"

Maika'i and Kōkua exchanged a look.

"This sounds like news for Elder Maka," Maika'i said.

"Or we could reconnaissance his factory first," Kōkua ruminated.

Rhoda grabbed Kōkua's hands. "No, please don't go there! You don't know how his mood swings around!"

"I do, in fact," Kōkua said. "Sounds like a very bad case of bipolar disorder to me. We learned about it recently here."

"His likely illnesses aren't relevant! Safety is! Don't go there!" Rhoda was adamant.

"Be reasonable. We need to investigate him before reporting to Elder Maka," Maika'i told Rhoda. "We need actual evidence. Your three memories don't tell us anything about the person."

Rhoda was relieved that her friends weren't saying Uncle Ejad's name aloud. She relaxed a bit.

"Come home with me," Rhoda said. "My parents always have a lot to say about everything and everyone, including relatives. They'll even serve you dinner."

Maika'i and Kōkua grinned.

CHAPTER 13
ELDER COUNCIL MEETING

Manaful World
August 9, 2022
Koa Forest, Elder Territory
Elders' Council Chambers

Elder Alaka'i pounded his gavel on the koa table to commence the meeting. The room was filled with the rainbow robes of Elders. They were all lively, ignoring his presence.

"That never works," Puna smirked, nudging Alaka'i's foot. "Why do you use that mallet? You're 4200 years old, simply blast a TGP in their heads!"

Glowing opalescent in his dancing, shimmery robe, Alaka'i stood majestically at the head of the table. He gave Puna a shrinking side glance and grudgingly followed his advice.

He TGP the Elder Council: "*The sooner we start, the sooner you can MT home. Let me honor your time. Please settle down and take your seats!*"

That immediately got everyone's attention and the echoes of dragging chairs on the koa floor made Ikaika's ears wince. Maka sat beside Puna at his ʻŌmaʻomaʻo leader's chair, while Ikaika sat behind his grandfather as a guest for the quest proposal. The scent of nutty kukui oils filled their senses as levitating burning nuts simultaneously diffused the air and provided a glow that lit the room.

Elder Alakaʻi nodded at everyone and projected mahalo to each elder with gratitude for their cooperation and attention. Puna rolled his eyes and flapped his hand, signaling 'Let's get this show on the road!'

Maka's eyes widened at Puna's joking irreverence. Ikaika smiled as he was used to his grandfather's behavior towards Alakaʻi.

The Council listened as Elder Maka presented Ikaika's proposal to find the Legend of the Lost Songs.

"Why are you wasting our time on this?" said Elder ʻĀkala in her voluminous fuschia-pink robe. She nibbled on her toasted lox bagel. The elders always had the munchies at these meetings. The food distracted them from the onus of being there. They were like a disgruntled family, having obligingly served for millennia together. Not to mention, they were telepathic beings at heart. Talking aloud was a chore. Food made things better. Thankfully, their host Alakaʻi allowed them to conjure up their own snacks with a snap of their fingers. Their taste buds were so eclectic it kept everyone happy.

Elder Polu raised an eyebrow at Elder ʻĀkala's bagel. "Don't you have enough on your plate with your Hopohopo merchants? Mine are always a handful to manage. They are insistent that their coin system is the answer to every issue. They're blind to the fact that feeling aloha and tapping Mana are more beneficial,"

Elder Polu shared a conspiratorial glance with his peers around the table. His lively dark navy blue robe rippled around him as if he were wrapped in ocean waves.

"The Hopohopo have chosen their fate. I have no more desire to run begging after them anymore," the House Blue Elder concluded.

Every elder could relate to what Elder Polu mentioned. They all had Hopohopo in their tribes, spread over the Territories. Polu received many nods and heavy sighs of agreement. The rainbow of ʻohana saw a spectrum of Mana-acceptance among their Hopohopo. It ranged from fringe believers to outright killers of Manafuls. The concept of songs changing the stubborn dwarves into Manafuls was far-fetched.

Maka raised his shoulders and sincerely held his hands out in a 'What are you gonna do?' expression. The elders closest to him patted his shoulder comfortingly as Maka was laughed at by the others.

Elder Alakaʻi came to the young elder's rescue. He proclaimed, "The Relics are the key to our survival! The stone is real. I've seen it. The songs on it use Mana mist in ancient, powerful ways."

Alakaʻi was riled up. He switched to TGP. He revealed that as the first Manaful, he had learned all of the mind-melding and Healing he knew from a song on the Stone. He chastised the rest of the council for laughing at the very thing that carried all the technical knowledge behind their powers.

Elder Puna agreed that it is high time the Manaful World solved the mystery of the Stone, or at least got a hold of it. Beyond singing the Creation Song for wake-up prayers, nobody took The Old Hill and Its Living Relics stories and songs all that seriously. Besides, most of it was lost to time.

Once attentiveness was restored and the munchies removed, Maka tried again. He spoke of the quest with the SC to hunt for Stone. The Manaless humans may be able to sneak up on the magic resistant geological pain in the butt. This time they heard him out.

The Elder Council took an eyeful of Elder Alakaʻi's glowering face and finally agreed to test this theory. They voted Yes to Ikaika's proposal.

* * *

Elders Alakaʻi and Puna remained in the Chambers after everyone left, putting up a powerful mental Shield for privacy.

"*We have to deal with Lapu.*" Elder Puna began. "*He's getting out of hand.*"

Elder Alakaʻi nodded. "*He's indestructible, but we can weaken him.*"

"*Confronting him is too dangerous.*"

Alakaʻi smiled around his pearly, flowing mustache. "*Not as dangerous as finding the Stone. That would literally cause my death, remember?*"

Puna's chest filled with grief. He placed his hand over his heart. "*Sometimes I pray the Stone won't ever be found.*"

"*It is simply fate, my old friend. The Stone's discovery is linked to me.*"

"*Even if it's the SC who finds it?*"

"Even so. I am willing to take the risk if it means seeding an utopian world of Manaful."

"You are very noble, Brother Alaka'i."

"Mahalo. In any case, we can weaken Lapu in many ways. We can do wonders when we mind-meld and combine Mana on a large scale."

"Yes, he can't be eradicated, but we can weaken him," Puna agreed. *"We will need back up."*

Elders Puna and Alaka'i thought of the entire Elder Council. There were as many Elder Houses as the colors in a rainbow, if not slightly more. While Uli's treachery had been unprecedented, the Elders' philosophies were quite varied. It was difficult to determine which Elders would fully support their wild ideas.

A good place to start was excluding everyone who'd allied with Uli over the long Manaful years.

Elder Alaka'i finally projected a name. *"Elder Lilinoe. She always listens to me, eager to learn and experiment. She hated Uli."*

"I trust her," Puna nodded.

"She is also quite the genius. After all, she invented the Mana Battery Cell that powers some of the best technical innovations of this world. The Hopohopo are grateful for her."

"Not a single-handed accomplishment, though. She couldn't have done it without her sisters Elders Laka and Pele."

"I am comfortable having Elder Laka on our team as well. What say you, old friend?"

"Why not Pele?"

"Not her. Not yet."

Puna steepled his fingers and tapped his chin thoughtfully. He considered the two nominees. *"I am content with four on the team."*

"Five. Including Maka."

"Isn't that too dangerous?" Elder Puna knew he was voicing this single worry too much. He couldn't help it. Maka was only a little over a thousand Manaful years old.

"Yes, but he must learn." Elder Alaka'i stood abruptly. *"That is my decision. The five of us will travel to a place where we will attempt to cage Lapu and drain his essence."*

Puna felt a tremor of apprehension. There had never been a true Manafuls versus Spirits battle, and he wasn't eager to start one. But world peace was at stake.

"Are you talking about the Rift where the Old Hill once stood?" Puna ventured.

Elder Alaka'i nodded solemnly. *"The Elder Council should have fully investigated the Rift over the past few years and discussed how to heal it, restore Old Hill, and balance the Mana of this world."*

"Instead we always bicker," Puna shook his head sadly.

"No point in crying over spilt milk. We start as soon as Elders Lilinoe and Laka agree to the quest. Please make sure Maka is free."

"I shall ask Ikaika and Maluhia to accompany the Secret Club. They will be Team One. I will inform Maika'i and Kōkua to be on call. Lapu will target our closest and dearest once we trigger this confrontation. We must help them if any danger arises."

"Perfect." Elder Alaka'i's and Puna's robes reached out and grabbed each other as if hugging and shaking hands. The white and red luminance of their respective robes resulted in a pinkish glow where their clothes met.

"Looks like everyone's going off on quests," Puna grinned like a youngster. *"I feel decidedly excited."*

Chapter 14
The SC Finds Relic Tree

Manaful World
August 10, 2022
Wintergreen Forest, Elder Freelands
ʻUlaʻula Manaful Center

The Secret Club visited Manaful World a day after the Elder Council meeting. They stepped out of the Shimmery Wall and onto the grounds of the ʻUlaʻula Manaful Center. Only Ikaika awaited them. The children were breathless by what looked like a Christmas tree farm. Though not a cold environment, Malie expected soft snow flakes on her face. The smooth white marble structure contrasted with the pokey pine cone branches.

Entering the building, the children gasped at the twirling patterns of light glimmering from giant fireflies everywhere. Both frightened and amazed, the SC watched Ikaika put his hand out for one. Though physiologically similar to Earth fireflies, these were the size of cell phones. The black belly and orange head of the insect was fuzzy. The tiger pattern hypnotized the kids. Ikaika's firefly was friendly with flirtatious blinking lashes, making Malie giggle. The navy blue of its wings swiftly lifted the insect to the ceiling. Its glow source was on its backside, a radiating light bulb within. Nicole was in love with them! Her hands were cupped for one to jump onto her palms. One did. She gasped and appeared teary eyed for a second. Malie nudged Pierre. They smiled, touching their hearts with their own palms in their twin way. Before they knew it, Nicole's giant firefly lifted off and joined its friends. The SC looked at each other in silent understanding that this was a blessed place.

Ikaika agreed.

"Where's Maka?" The Secret Club wanted to know.

"He is off on a quest with four other elders," Ikaika projected. He'd brought them down the flatstone paths to a swaying cypress thicket on campus grounds that ran along the boundary wall of the center. The ribbon of conifers bulged in happy shades of lime and forest green. Voluptuous and tall. The forest was usually deserted except for a lot of birds. The manu were friendly too, coming to sit on branches right next to the kids whistling their greetings. Some were rainbow parrots and what looked like African Grey parrots. The big manu held their orchestras among the fuzzy boughs and pines.

Ikaika summoned Pierre's limestone boulder on the wild grass that carpeted a generally even terrain. The kids climbed it gleefully. He filled them in on the Elder grapevine.

Nicole was upset on Maka's behalf. She paced beside the boulder with her arms folded over her chest.

She grumbled, "They laughed at his presentation? Where's the respect? Where's the kākoʻo for someone trying to improve everyone's lives? What the?"

Malie and Pierre frowned in unison. They both knew where this was going. Don't let Nicole start on her defense of the underdog–any underdog. That is, even an Elder with thousands of years of ʻohana Mana transmuted into him. Pierre hopped off the limestone, giving Malie a friendly hand down. She smiled in mahalo.

Pierre and Malie each took a side of Nicole, grabbing her hand and each other's, forming a SC circle. Ikaika TGP: "*Hey, I want in!*"

Smiling, Malie opened the circle grabbing one of Ikaika's hands. Touched by their aloha, Nicole grabbed Ikaika's other hand. Laughter sprung from Pierre's throat at the hodgepodge group they made. Malie read his mind, winking at him. Ikaika grinned and closed his eyes to TGP a song.

Team 1's Unity Song:

"Stay with me through thick and thin
As their laughter fills me with chagrin.
Your kākoʻo gives me that drive
To not just hang in there, but to thrive!
Others don't realize when everything's
Said and done, there'll be no lingering
Doubt that we are the ultimate team
We go all out, we go to the extreme
To lift each other up, when one falls

To hold on tight, to make tough calls
Facing the fire, braving it out
In unity, in unity, we will shout:
We are one!"

Once the song died down, they spent a silent moment of appreciation. Then everyone jumped when Ikaika said, "Who's ready to go find Tree, then?"

The kids were excited to be on Team One. They have a quest! Ikaika was unsure of where or how to start looking for Stone. It's only ever been found once since its creation. Asking Tree was an easy shot at it.

The problem was, Tree was nomadic as well. The Relics constantly traveled all over the Manaful world on separate paths.

"Maybe Maluhia knows where she is with his bird's eye view of Manaful," Malie suggested.

Ikaika blinked at her. "*How on Earth do you fit that brian inside such a tiny head?*"

Malie laughed. "*Tiny? Speak for yourself!*"

Ikaika looked into the distance as he sent out a projection like a pulse, an animal call. Maluhia soon appeared.

Whoo-hoo. "*Tree is easy to find. Follow me.*"

The giant owl flapped up into the air currents. Ikaika rose into the air pulling the humans up with him. They all squealed and giggled as they bade goodbye to gravity. Hovering them en-masse, Ikaika flew, pulling the Secret Club after him. He followed Maluhia's tail feathers with his Mana. The wintergreen trees hundred feet high became smaller as they rose into the clouds. They weren't cold nor afraid of dropping to the ground far below. The invisible hovering platform kept them safe, as long as they didn't grab anything. Varicolored manu glided behind them as if to say, "A hui hou!" and glistening dots of light danced amid the tree tops, making Nicole wave. One of them was her firefly. A tear came into her eye; she'd come back.

* * *

Manaful World
Elder Freelands
Redwood Forest, ʻUlaʻula Territory

Maluhia flew for a long time. Ikaika and the SC hovered past several forestscapes with a multitude of tree scents filling the air from sandalwood to oak to pine. Some of the Hopohopo cityscapes saddened the children. Poverty wasn't only on Earth. The shack towns and rubbish piles of a few Hopohopo villages broke their hearts. They hovered over a wide raging river of rapids a rafting team would love. It was treacherous to behold. They were finally staring down at an expansive redwood forest in the Elder Freelands.

"They're huge!" Pierre said.

"Sequoioideae, otherwise known as redwoods, are coniferous trees that hold the record for growing the largest and tallest. They also live for millennia," Malie said as she gripped Nicole's shirt tightly in a fist. She tried not to look down but she couldn't help it. There was nothing but air beneath her sneakers. It made her queasy.

Nicole chortled and pulled her friend close to ease her tiny fear of heights. Nicole felt a platform beneath her, albeit invisible, and knew it was secure. Malie will overcome her fear. "Who needs Google when you have Malie?"

"Why aren't we molecularly traveling there, again?" Pierre asked. He looked down at his feet deep in thought. *Why doesn't this invisible platform have railings? Why not walls like an elevator?*

"We don't know the exact coordinates since Tree has also taken to moving around," Ikaika projected. Ikaika loved long distance hovering. He has lived for hovering since he first learned the magical transportation mode about eight years ago.

Pierre didn't understand how coordinates mattered. He just shrugged and let himself hover over the tops of the redwood trees. He could get used to hovering. They were shielded from the elements, went fast, and the scenery was thrilling.

Maluhia looped around suddenly and dived into the canopy. He left behind some choice hoots that didn't need telepathy to carry the note of 'follow me'.

Ikaika stopped in midair and the three humans slid forward to bump into him. They dangled around the dwarf confusedly.

"What's happening?" Nicole spat out Malie's hair. The three preteens were hanging on each other's shoulders, excited.

"We're going to descend slowly. Please mind your elbows," Ikaika projected solemnly like an airplane pilot. As they lost altitude the redwood branches bent like rubber to allow them through, as if pushed back by a platform. Pierre reached for a branch in fascination. *Did hovering conjure something like the forcefield around their platform, but invisible like Ikaika's mansion walls? Would his fingers contact bark or glassy walls?*

The Secret Club landed on the ground. Nicole looked around. "Where's Pierre?"

"Up here! Help!"

They looked up to find Pierre hanging on for dear life to the branch he'd grabbed mere seconds earlier. "I didn't think I could actually grab it!" Pierre howled.

Nicole and Malie burst out laughing and fell on the grass to roll around holding their bellies. Ikaika sniggered as well, but gently unlatched Pierre from the branch and levitated him safely to the ground with his Mana.

"Let that be a lesson to you for being *too* curious," Malie said, still giggling.

"Hmph." Pierre rubbed his bent nose, his heart still beating hard from imagining landing on it had he fallen, breaking it a second time in his life. *Am I glad to have this nose!* He started laughing as well. "OK, that was stupid. My bad."

Nicole dried her tears of mirth. "Where's Maluhia gone off to?"

Ikaika seemed to smell the air and pointed north. They ran some yards through enormous bushes as branches scratched their forearms and calves. Malie wished she'd gone first, since Nicole kept forgetting to hold the branches once she walked through them. Each whip on Malie's face was punishing. They finally emerged into a small clearing where an extremely gnarled, mossy tree sat in the middle. It sat on its side like an elderly person popping a squat suddenly during an afternoon stroll. The tree's bottom stump and roots stretched out before it. It wasn't as tall as the redwoods, being a bit stooped and leaning. Its leaves were hued by the purples and turquoises of a peacock's feathers. There were pink and beige leaves as well closer to the spiny, pokey brown branches. Its mish mash of spring and autumn colors made the SC speechless, too stunned to speak. The bizarre tree stood out amid the plainer forest canopy surrounding it. It was an odd ball sight, beautiful surely, but out of place.

Maluhia circled the tree and sat on one of the lateral branches that resembled an arm sticking up at the elbows. The Tree shivered to life at once.

"Oooooh, that tickles," Tree creaked. Maluhia flexed his talons and the tree added, "That's right. Manu always hits the spot."

Ikaika hopped forward and discovered TP didn't work on the Tree. So he called up, "Aloha, Relic Tree. I am Ikaika, Heir to Manaful 'Ula'ula House. We seek your sage words."

"Sage words," Tree repeated, bemused. The bark squeaked as it turned to find the speaker. A knotty, lichen encrusted face peered at Ikaika and the SC. It blinked.

"Can you receive our projections?" Malie asked.

"Why, no, my dear little weed," Tree said. The roots lifted laboriously, seemingly walking, as the old girl rearranged herself in the humus. She faced them now. Tree wished to avoid another nasty, leaky wound in the trunk from trying to be way more flexible than wood really was. She wasn't a young spritely gal anymore. It was amazing to witness how the mllenniums had changed the being they'd glimpsed in Elder Puna's vision.

"Thought so," Malie nodded. "I've been sending thoughts at you and you never noticed."

"I'm a Relic. I don't work like a Manaful or animal... I'm not really a tree either, it seems. Old Hill told me. I'm unique."

To everyone's surprise, Tree started shedding resin tears. "That means I'm the only one of my kind in the whole world. My name is just a borrowed noun! Waaah."

An entire family of ants got trapped in Tree's resin tears and were frozen forever before Ikaika thought of something to say. Forest creatures chittered around them with their aloha as they explored their verdant world.

"Elder Alaka'i speaks highly of you saying he will cherish you forever," Ikaika said.

Tree stopped crying. "Elder Alaka'i? Are you his emissaries?"

"We are!" The Secret Club said in unison.

"My word! Apologies for mistaking you for weeds," Tree swayed her boughs. "I must say. It feels nice being remembered and appreciated."

"Elder Alaka'i is noble and loving," Ikaika said loyally.

"Why have you found me?" Tree got down to business. She suddenly seemed wary. As if she suspected something nasty.

Ikaika hesitated. Nicole bought him time at once with, "You can't even read our minds?"

"Right! Go ahead! Rub it in my face, why don't you!" Tree shook so hard a helping of her dark purple leaves fell off. She had neither flowers nor berries anymore.

"It's just strange after being with the Manafuls," Pierre said. He walked over the twitching roots and put his hands on the bark to feel the texture gently. Maluhia did his talon work. Hoo-Hoo. Tree relaxed.

"I bet there's a Song to make you telepathic," Malie said out of the blue.

Tree said, "Mmmm?"

"Elder Alaka'i told us the Song of Creation and Song of Mana made him the most powerful Manaful in the world," Malie continued. "He found it on a stone. A stone that may contain more powerful Songs, even one that will help you get what you want."

Tree's knotty eyes were fixated on the tiny human. She bent down creakily to look closer. "And what is it you think I want?"

Nicole jumped in. "To grow to your full potential."

Pierre said at the same time, "To telepathically connect with the rest of the world!"

Tree harrumphed. "You're telling me! You're babies. I don't know where Rocksie is. Goodbye."

They all waited. But Tree could move only very slowly and went nowhere. She pouted and crossed the branches that resembled arms across her trunk, uncaring if they ripped at the seams.

"Elder Alaka'i said it is fated that all Relics meet each other at least once every thousand years," Ikaika said sternly. "When's the last time you, Stone and Cloud got together?"

"888 years ago," Tree sighed.

"That's when the Rift happened," Ikaika said.

This was news to the SC. "Rift?" they chorused.

"Old Hill broke apart and Lapu materialized," Ikaika explained. "Lapu is the first Spirit to become fully sentient. He identifies as an individual with a right to a physical form of existence. Old Hill permitted him to try."

"I'm guessing he succeeded."

"Lapu ate Old Hill," Tree lamented suddenly. "That bad Spirit ate up my wise Old Hill! Made him crack open and turn into the Rift!"

Tree's Ode to Old Hill:

"When Source said 'Hear thee!'
Old Hill came to be
On his face were Relics three
There's Cloud, Rocksie and Tree
If you haven't noticed, that last one is me
Together we make this world's Mana flow free
But in Old Hill's belly woke a restless Spirit
Named Lapu, whose greed you'll intuit
Shot the arrow that wounded Old Hill's knee
Lapu arose, seeing more than there was to see
The Spirit grew strong through malevolent deeds
Lapu will kill who he must until he succeeds
Despite it all, Old Hill keeps his cool
He knows how it ends, he's nobody's fool.
Old Hill shall outlast Lapu's unrest
He sets us upon the Spirit like a test
For us to grow through, metamorphosis
For Old Hill's completely aligned, no hit or miss!"

Ikaika went to join Pierre on the roots to pat the tree bark. "Elder Alaka'i and my grandfather say the Rift can be healed and Old Hill put together. They're out there fighting Lapu on ground zero as we speak."

"Those two alone can't defeat Lapu at full power at the Rift!" Tree exclaimed.

"They're not alone," Ikaika said resolutely. He breathed deeply thinking of Maka and his grandfather. *He will pull through. They will be alright.*

Chapter 15
Ejad's ʻOhana

Manaful World
August 10, 2022
ʻŌmaʻomaʻo Hopohopo Community

Kōkua and Maikaʻi fortunately learned quite a lot about Ejad Honua's childhood from his sister. They enjoyed dinner last night at Rhoda's. The pair were struck by his sibling's love for him despite his eccentricities. Ejad's family touched the Protectors as they understood The Inventor's need for solitude and creativity. Rhoda was fortunate to have devoted parents. They were kind folk who ran a hair salon. It was a small but successful shop on the first floor of their flat building in the City. Rhoda was the middle child of their five children and the only one with red hair. Everyone else was brunette like Ejad.

The Honuas provided quite a feast of noodles, soup, salads, beech mushrooms with honey marinated carrots, an entire tandoori chicken, and vegetables mixed in jasmine rice. While enjoying chai of three different flavors, Maikaʻi and Kōkua learned that Ejad ran away when he was just ten years old. The pair were recalling Asha Honua's passionate responses.

"Mom and dad were distraught," Asha, Rhoda's mum, had wailed. She'd hit her forehead with the back of her wrist dramatically while still holding her fork. She'd spilled veggies on the laden table. "I missed him," she'd mumbled after settling down, "I called him my Halfling, affectionately. I changed his diapers and wiped his nose! He'd always take machines apart and put them back together even better than before. A little genius. He would raid my closet, trying on my shiny boots and metal belts. He had a fresh sense of fashion beneath his quiet intellect." She'd wiped her teary eyes. "Why am I talking about him like he's dead? That's why I approved of our daughter interning with him. Even sent gifts for him. I hope for a happy reunion one day." She'd sniffled.

Rhoda's maternal grandparents, Kamana and Kalo, were rural Hopohopo farmers who maintained a small farm. Out of their three children, Ejad had been the youngest and smallest both in build and farming skills. His head was always in the clouds. His sister Asha had done more farm labor than he ever had.

Ejad wanted the same thing as his parents—to find a way out of hardship and earn a comfortable life. Kamana and Kalo had a secret they kept from their Hopohopo community, though. They wanted their children to become Manaful. The Hopohopo way was too muddled and burdensome, as they'd learned throughout their life. By the time they had Ejad, they'd decided they would strive to make all their children Manaful. They dreamed of the day all their children found homes in Elder Territory.

"However, Ejad believed in finding ways to become Manaful without associating with the Elders," Asha Honua had supplied. That was why he ran away when his parents contacted Elder Puna's Manaful Center to take him on as an intern.

"Maybe his 'Ōma'oma'o loyalty ran too deep," Maika'i surmised as she and Kōkua mind-melded in the apartment they were sharing in the City. They were replaying last night's dinner together and building a picture of Rhoda's enigmatic uncle. They sat knee to knee on opposite chairs, hands on thighs, eyes closed.

"He definitely did not want to go to 'Ula'ula territory," Kōkua agreed.

"He is now middle aged… forty human years?"

"Just over thirty."

"Rhoda's mum is his older sister. She is Kalo and Kamana's second youngest."

"So if she says he is emotionally 'messed up', we ought to believe her," Kōkua said. *"She'd know best. Ejad was closer to her than the eldest brother, Jamel Honua."*

Maika'i nodded. Ejad had no real past trauma to justify the bipolar explanation to his actions. They were most likely dealing with what the Medical Center identified as either a psychopath or a sociopath. Possibly. Only, Ejad didn't wantonly harm people. He just remained aloof and detached. The Protectors were very fascinated with this Hopohopo.

"We should find out more about him at the Protector's Academy," Kōkua projected, opening her eyes. *"Rhoda's memories show him telling her this much. He worked his way up from Uli's Academy when he reached the City after running away from home."*

Maika'i came out of the mind-meld as well. "Ugh, we're definitely going to bump into familiar faces."

"I never like visiting there," Kōkua agreed. "Something's wrong with quite literally everyone in the administration. No offense to Elder Maka."

Maika'i and Kōkua debated whether to investigate Ejad's factory workshop first or get more information on him at the Academy. Rhoda's mum had also informed them that her eldest brother now lived and worked in Elder Polu's Blue Territory. Asha Honua herself was trying to shift to Elder Puna's. This little family was all over the place.

"Too many nests to poke our noses into," Kōkua tutted.

They resolved the issue by telepathically reaching out to Rhoda, who was baking star shaped cookies at home. She was bemused when the two Protectors stepped into her head asking for a vote from miles away.

"He's my uncle and I want to find out more about him as well," Rhoda projected with some difficulty. Long-distance telepathy was still a challenge for her. She had to stop what she was doing and stay very still. She would have the ability to project like they did soon.

"I vote for you to pay the Academy a visit when you are ready. And I'll go visit Grandma and Grandma for a sleepover after packing these cookies. If you manage to catch my uncle Jamel Honua at Elder Polu's Territory, we'll have enough info by sunset. We'll compare notes tonight and visit Elder Maka tomorrow. Hey, you two, no storming Uncle's workshop!"

"Perfect," the Protectors agreed. *"If we're lucky with the eldest Honua, we'll meet you at your grandparents' farm before bedtime. The Academy can wait."*

* * *

Maikaʻi and Kōkua landed an appointment with Jamel easily. By seven pm, they drove an auto-carriage over to Rhoda's grandparents' farm on the outskirts of a Hopohopo town.

Rhoda received them practically hopping with glee. "They have a *lot* to say," she said delightedly. The Protectors followed her into the modest farmhouse to receive a blast of cooking fumes to the face.

"Is that taro laulau?" Kōkua asked, mouth watering.

It was. Along with kimchi, roasted ʻuala and grilled iʻa. Elder Lilinoe's House Gray branded Hui I ka Wai Hua to wash it all down. The mixed juices included Kōkua's favorite, manako—mango, and Maikaʻi's lifelong love, puluma—plums.

Rhoda grinned as the Protectors agreed to stay for dinner. Grandfather Kalo and grandmother Kamana were very chatty, and it helped that they were so opinionated when speaking about their offspring and themselves.

Ejad Honua's parents, Kamana and Kalo, were raised on the fringe where Hopohopo and Manaful homesteads met. Even here, Mana was rejected more often than not. Ejad's parents always desired the Mana their community disliked. They were in awe of the Manaful's abilities to conjure anything they needed. Basic needs were simply met by those with Mana. Worries about labors and bills were nonexistent for the Manaful nearby.

Unfortunately, generations of Hopohopo on both sides of his parents 'Ohana brainwashed them of the evils of Mana. They were told that those with Mana are slaves to Source. Manaful beings used telepathy to control each other. There's no free will for Manafuls. Thoughts such as these were imprinted into children as soon as they could learn to speak. Telepathic abilities were immediately stomped out of babies, as the inherent Mana sprouted from their beautiful fresh minds naturally.

Ejad chose to believe in only the ill will of Mana. He never sought the proper training once he reached his age of majority. At which time, a Hopohopo could choose the society or House Territory they wished to reside in.

Hopohopo were dwarves, like the Manaful, reaching at best 4 feet in height. Nonetheless, Ejad was a petite two and a half feet, truly a runt amid his towering three and a half foot siblings. Every day of his life, they reminded him of it. Pejoratives such as shorty, shrimp, shortstack, and worse of all 'the nothing' were common insults thrown at him.

Ejad was a genius with numbers and mechanisms from an early age. He isolated himself often, preferring to tinker and build things alone.

The homeschool system of both Hopohopo and Manaful societies were formed to nurture family bonds. One generation teaches the next the 'ohana's trade. Other 'ohana hānai, or adopted, children who have different vocational interests than their birth 'ohana.

Ejad's family were kalo farmers; kalo was the precious plant from which his father got his name. To gain his father's approval, the young scientist built ingenious mechanical irrigation systems when he was barely out of diapers. A true engineering prodigy, he'd swell with pride when his father's crops grew bigger and healthier than any other farmers'. Their land was owned by coin-wealthy Hopohopo investors. Long ago, a generational cycle of coin-power had taken over their Hopohopo society.

But on farms brawns are sometimes more favored than brains. Rhoda piped around a peppered drumstick with, "That's true for all Hopohopo communities. Brainy Hopohopo are often feared."

Kalo refused to send Ejad to a Hopohopo 'Ohana in the factory or engineering trades. His children were all he really possessed, albeit temporarily. He feared never seeing his son again. Though a silent man of the soil and roots, Kalo loved his youngest son. Some parents simply didn't have the emotional or social capacity to show affection and love as others did. While not abusive, this emotional withdrawal from Kalo hurt Ejad in subtle ways – causing him to be emotionally distant to others. This learned stoicism helped him later in life. Ejad was ripe for the maniacal Elder Uli's picking.

All this Elder Maka's aunts Maika'i and Kōkua learned over the hefty dinner that went from laulau to full roast chicken. Rhoda listened with rapt attention over pudding. The whole picture now clicked nicely. Jamel Honua had supplied them with what he knew of Ejad's Academy exploits earlier that evening. The trio hit it off immediately. The Protectors were in awe of Jamel's scientific knowledge, realizing the brothers shared savant characteristics.

The Protectors appreciated learning about both of Rhoda's uncles. After dinner they were treated to a tour of Rhoda's grandparents' house.

Ejad's quarters were up in the attic, behind a padlocked door. The wood's moldy fragrance greeted them as Kalo swung it open. The modest loft was dusty with a pallet for sleeping in the corner. Cobwebs abounded and scurrying mice scrammed into nooks.

"It's exactly as he left it decades ago," Kalo told them. "Feel free to look around. Not you, Rhoda. Come down to clean the dinner table with us."

Maika'i and Kōkua discovered a stash of blueprints for odd machinery among the many desks and shelves strewn about the room. Kalo came back up to tell them about some of the clockwork models his son had built and left here.

With Rhoda out of earshot, the Protectors updated Kalo on Ejad's situation. His youngest is the prime suspect in leading an underground merchant network linked to assassinations and drug trade.

Worried about his son's activities, Kalo told them to feel free to take evidence with them.

In their auto-carriage on the highway, Maika'i said, "We'll store the evidence at our place till Elder Maka gets back." She and Kōkua drove back home that night after thanking and wishing Rhoda and her 'ohana "Goodnight!" The young Aspiring Hopohopo would sleepover at her grandparents'.

The Protectors got back close to midnight; it had been a two hour drive. They were lucky they weren't on the bus or railway tram. Both modes of transport took an hour longer. Kōkua wished she could just MT to places, already.

Chapter 16
Ejad Invents & Kills

Manaful World
August 10, 2022
Sandalwood Forest, Elder Territory
Elder Uli's Abandoned Mansion

He was sitting on a mountain of gold. Literally. Elder Uli's oldest mansion was the bank of 'Ōma'oma'o 'Ohana. The devious Elder had minted a reservoir of coins, using it to monopolize the Hopohopo economy. When Uli hānai Maka, he had hidden this mansion for security purposes. He'd built a new one far away for the same reasons. Only Ejad Honua had access to Uli's bank.

Elder Maka may have inherited the 'Ohana Mana and the majority of the 'āina, or land, upon Uli's death. However, Ejad inherited a large portion of his fiscal wealth and assets. All of which, Uli's blood heir was oblivious.

Ejad now controlled over forty percent of Uli territory, as an invisible beneficiary. Documents showed him as a 'research' section under the Protectors' Academy Administrative Fund. Ha ha.

If the network of puppets Uli had installed held, Elder Maka would never access all of Ejad's hideouts. His Mana Battery Cells kept the force fields up. The telepathic shields were going strong.

His recent hideout, the abandoned Hopohopo town factory, was unusable now. He wouldn't be returning there anytime soon, due to his momentary weakness hiring his niece. He'd thought Rhoda could make a possible sidekick in his endeavors. He'd inadvertently scared her a couple times. She likely sought Manaful Elder help; who'd in turn, glean its location from her.

Rhoda must have already snitched. Periodically, Lapu whispered nasty things about her in the recesses of his mind. For Ejad, this was normal.

In fact, Ejad mistook it for his own inner voice. His exchanges with Lapu were delirious at best and quickly forgotten. Right now he was fully focused on himself, being hard at work and feeling very confident in his autonomy.

His excitement for the current project was palpable, as he breathed the smoke fumes it emitted. The engine hummed loudly, echoing across the vast emptiness of the theater-sized room. Uli had recently used the cavernous space for spying on Earth via multiple Shimmery Walls. Without Uli's Mana, the room ceased to function as it did. Recently made wealthy, Ejad hired minions to clear out the entire mansion of its designer furniture. All of it had been useless, as Ejad practically slept standing up. When his body forced him to lay down, all he needed was a pallet. Luxuries like king sized beds with extravagant thread counts were irrelevant. Inventions were his life. He surrounded himself with machines, pipes, work tables and books.

One cork board showed his sticky notes:

"Why do Elders refuse us full radiowave, magnetic and electric energy access in the Mana Tech sector?"

"Why do Elders ban the use of Mana Battery Cells (MBCs) for home experimentation?"

"Why do Elders insist that MBCs are unsafe and unstable for modern weaponry?"

"Why do Elders deny the use of MBCs for inventing entertainment devices?"

"Smart Slates have been possible for thousands of years, yet the Elder Council still claims the tech is in 'testing' stages."

"I will invent my own Smart Slate with long-distance communication capabilities."

"Is it possible to become Manaful through technology? Let's find out."

The dwarf was busy attaching metal legs to the engine core of his latest project. He donned goggles and a violet scarf to cover the lower half of his face. A thick high collared coat protected him from the cold ventilation. Cool air was a necessity wherever hotly heated metal parts were at work.

Ejad manned his projects from behind his protective cubicle, using robotic assistance controlled by levers. Hydraulic joints, counterweights, and springs all did the heavy lifting for him. Almost as if he were channeling Mana. Almost.

His dashboard screen showed that he was on track. He'd harvested his own Mana Battery Cells over the years and was now integrating them into his engines. The project was all juiced up and working fine. Lit green.

His machines were getting bigger and bigger lately, as were his welding and metalsmithing expertise. Most impressive was his rune work (Scripting), if he did say so himself. With his eidetic memory, he'd simply read a book once and remember it wholly. His 35 years was enough time to consume a lot of books.

From behind his plexiglass cubicle, Ejad's heartbeat picked up and chest swelled. She was coming forth. His lips formed a slight smirk of pleasure, when the sparks died down to reveal a metal skeleton the shape of an arachnid. She still needed a few more parts and then a full chrome chassis. Ejad licked his lips, nodded, and took off the goggles.

As he took a sip of water, his eyes caught the calendar. August 10th. Incidentally, there was the ‘Ōma’oma’o House emblem lying right below it. Maka now wore that emblem on the sash of his elder robes.

Maka whose parents Ejad had murdered with his own two hands.

Well. A finger, to be precise.

One press of a button.

* * *

Manaful World
August 10, 2012
‘Ōma’oma’o Manaful Zone

Uli's Grove, Rose Hale
Ten years ago

"*My grandson, Maka, is with me,*" the elder's projection rang in Ejad's head. "*You'll find no trouble in the mansion.*"

"*Message received, Commander Uli.*" Ejad trusted his master. The Manaful House Green was third most powerful for a reason. Uli accumulated a lot of Mana by taking the easy route. Murder. His master had cleared the mansion of household staff and Protectors. This was a simple in and out assassination.

"*What do you do when you inherit extra Mana when a House member dies?*" Ejad monologued to himself, pushing through the pikake bushes. He never noticed the miniature white buds nor their breathtaking fragrance. Ejad sauntered into the garage free as can be. Instead of cars, there were floating koa logs akin to human bobsleighs. Maka's parents lived in the Manaful Zone, which meant their architecture melded with the nature it stood in. This home was all about flowers and trees.

"*Why, you kill your family members, of course!*" Ejad almost smiled as he answered himself. He made his way on the pebbled patio path. "*If Uli says I'm a genius, then he is too, though decidedly of a different variety. The old coot looks like a tree stump struck by lightning but he sure has presence. He makes me want to become Manaful, sometimes.*"

Ejad shook his head, pushing aside any feelings for his master. He breezed through the doors and up a gently curving rose adorned staircase. The place was all clear. He took what looked like a plastic water gun from his flax coat. He'd nicked it from the Medical Center. It used to be for pre and post surgical euthanasia. Now it euthanized, period.

Uli was true to his word. The estate was empty except for his son and daughter-in-law. Ejad simply took a hovercraft there and walked in. In plain sight.

Ejad felt Uli's watchful presence in his head. He'd felt constantly watched ever since his Academy days. As if more than one being was always breathing down his neck, 24/7.

"They will be in the master bedroom, maybe in the adjoining study," Uli projected from Source knew where. It wasn't Ejad's business and he never wanted it to be. He only wanted the coin.

"Be vigilant and look everywhere." Vigilant? Hah. Uli could be so obnoxious.

"I can handle these two easily."

Uli felt his overconfidence and bristled. "*These are two Manafuls we're dealing with and you are only one Hopohopo, you ginormous idiot.*"

"I have a tool in my favor."

Uli lost it. "*You are the tool in MY favor! Shut up and get the job done. If you fail, I will scramble your brains on the spot.*"

Ejad ignored his boss's cussing, striding past orchids on floating lattices. He circuited through a winding corridor, narrowly avoiding geranium baskets on every available space. He finally came to a large set of sandalwood doors, designed with intricate vines. He swung them open.

He entered a sitting area with a water wall that probably served as a Shimmery Wall Viewer, activated by Mana. It had the House Blue emblem on a corner; the manufacturer stamp.

Victorian couches were accentuated by garden tables laden with more overflowing plants. Maka's parents had eccentric tastes.

Speaking of whom... where are they?

He padded through an archway into presumably a library. There they were. Listening to a radio, their backs to him. Listening to an Elder Council performance report, as per a Hopohopo station.

"*See how they spy on the Hopohopo in their free time,*" he told himself. His inner voice sometimes became gravelly, like rusty metal pieces banging together. This was one of those times. His head rang with the strange fury in his inner voice. "*Manaful are to be culled. Spirit power is better.*"

His fist tightened around the tiny gun. He wore gloves to reduce chances of electrification. That was a pity. The modified medical tool was unwieldy with wires going haywire, but it was the only way to achieve the sort of blast he wanted.

He called it a Baby Ray Gun. BRaG. Funny, eh? It was just one of his hundreds of experiments. Ironic how it was once used to heal Manafuls.

Ejad's soft leather shoes were silent on the mahogany paneling. He was halfway across the room before the Manafuls were alerted to him. Uli's mind screens got weaker the closer he got to them.

His victims turned around at the same time. Victims? No. *More like assignments,* Ejad thought to himself. He raised the BRaG.

"Who are you?" Maka's mother gasped. Her husband raised a hand to defend themselves. Probably to put up a force field, which was the least anyone with Mana could do. But before he did, Ejad calmly pressed the button.

The little gun zinged and there was only the slightest ripple in the air originating from the nozzle. Maka's parents felt a tingling sensation wash over them. In an instant, both of them contorted, heads snapped back, and screamed. Their screams caught in their throats and went no further, turning instead into gurgles.

Ejad twirled the gun on a finger and studied them. The Manafuls collapsed to the ground; their bodies became concave from the inside. Their flesh hung and pooled like jelly.

"*Ah, so it destroys the skeleton first*," Ejad observed. "*Interesting*."

Maka's parents sank to the wooden floor a bubbling mass of flesh, smoking only lightly. What was left of them tangled in their wraparound 'Ohana robes. The little pile of Manaful flesh dried up, turned to clumps of soil, and blended with the mahogany. They took just one minute to disintegrate.

"*Wouldn't have gotten an elder, though*," Ejad studied the ray gun. "*How can I absorb their Mana before killing them? That would be an improved feature to my weapons. I will figure out the storage and utility of harvested Mana as well. Hmmm.*"

Already distracted with these new ideas, Ejad circled around the study. The residual burning stench dissipated as the air vents exuded a gardenia fragrance. The room was filled with medical books. Aww, Uli's family had been healers. How sweet. He plucked a rose from a vase and brought the soft petals to his cheek. *A couple as sweet as the roses strewn all over their Victorian home.*

Ejad noticed a small pile of brochures on a nearby table. One of the titles said: "Are the Hopohopo killing themselves?"

Ejad put the BRaG down and picked up a brochure for a deeper look. In a corner text in tiny print warned it was a WIP—Work In Progress. On top of it the paragraphs were watermarked across every page. This was apparently not yet ready for public dissemination. His eyes narrowed as he read the first few lines: "Our results show that some Hopohopo illnesses are linked to their rejection of Mana. A sad but vicious side effect of refusing the Source's gifts. We must educate them of this risk and liberate them."

Ejad rifled the pages, annoyed. *What is this? All medical issues faced by Hopohopo stem from our rejection of Mana? We have 'genetically reduced' ourselves? What nonsense!*

Fascinated, he pocketed the brochure draft and picked up another. Then another.

"*Well?*" Uli's iron voice piped up. "*I sensed something. Is it done?*"

"*Yes, Commander. They are dead.*" Ejad pocketed a couple more leaflets.

"*Excellent*," Uli said.

Before Ejad could pick up the ray gun, the elder molecularly transported him to his basement workshop. The BRaG had served its purpose. Ejad wasn't frantic to have it back. He had new ideas to work on.

* * *

August 10, 2022
Sandalwood Forest, Elder Territory
Elder Uli's Abandoned Mansion
Back to the present

Ejad shook his head to bring himself out of the memory. He sighed, partly relieved that Uli was gone. But was he in a better place now with Lapu? Has Lapu always been there in the background with Uli? That persistent growling tone? He picked up the 'Ōma'oma'o emblem beneath his calendar, caressing the tiny runes along its edge with gloved fingers. He'd discovered Scripting and rune work, around the time he'd assassinated Uli's 'ohana. It was next level. He began using his runic knowledge years after their deaths. The ray gun did not have rune faculties. It was an old prototype with a messy pre-rune design and wiring. Speaking of which, where'd he put that gun? He must have left it at the town hideout.

Scripting was a rare knowledge amid Manafuls. Ejad's machines were imbued with magical attributes using runes used to write spells for this technique of magic. The runes were typically empowered by Source's Mana, but in his case he used an alternative energy supply. Runic knowledge had always been stashed away in the archives, wastefully. He gave new life to it.

Uli used to tap Ejad's experimental runic machines with Mana in their secret sandalwood workshop. Now Uli's dead.

In Uli's absence Ejad worked around the problem. Mana Battery Cells were the answer. They 'triggered' his Scripted machines, allowing for project testing and improvements at each iteration. The MBCs fueled his automatons. He'd collected every

Cell he could get his hands on, busily storing over a hundred by now. Just waiting to be used.

Runes are a lost language, and Ejad still had a lot to learn about them. He had been lucky Uli shared the power of Manaful runes. His master encouraged him.

Maka's parents, especially his mother, worked with runes too. His father had been a full practicing and teaching Healer. The Scripting leaflets he'd found at their murder scene were another reason he finally invested so much time into its study.

Ironically, Ejad accepted Maka's parents as among the best Manafuls to have lived. They'd been community workers despite Uli ordering them not to "flaunt their magic shamelessly". Uli had brainwashed them to self-restrict their use of magic. When Uli was alive, 'Ōma'oma'o 'Ohana Manafuls were expected to restrain their magic. These calculated blocks disabled their reflexive magic capabilities. After years of Mana oppression, Maka's parents could not react fast enough to Ejad's appearance. Neither of Maka's parents had reached for Source's power in those few seconds his BRaG was aimed at their faces. Ejad had actually smirked before pressing the button. The Manafuls just hugged each other as they died at the hands of a Hopohopo of the same 'Ohana.

He hadn't felt any remorse back then. He'd seen them as just another pair of elite Manafuls, spoilt in their privilege of luxury and power.

"I don't regret it now either," Ejad sneered, chucking the Green emblem away. It clinked on the concrete floor.

Being from a middle-class Hopohopo 'ohana, Ejad didn't know any Manaful "royalty" until he began working as an assistant technician at the Protector's Academy. He worked, saved funds, and studied Mana-Tech part-time. Upon graduation, he became an engineer for Uli's House.

Elder Uli liked Ejad for his stoicism. Every time Uli dispatched him to kill, Ejad did it. Coldly. Perfectly. Uli's Protectors were overpaid babysitters, while his Mercenaries were run of the mill assassins. Ejad's methods were clever and fast. Uli chose him often.

Ejad circled to the other side of his cubicle to admire his spider-like assemblage. Runes skittered and crammed thickly all along its legs. There were various shapes on the engine body too. Not glowing yet, since the Mana Cells were currently inactive.

The Inventor sneezed and waved his arms as a lot of smoke suddenly arose. "*Wait a minute... What is this stuff?*"

Inky, oily droplets condensed around Ejad in the cool air currents. He whipped around as the droplets formed into an oozy dark cloud hovering a few inches off the ground. "*Hello, my new commanding officer*," the blob rasped.

"*Lapu!*" Ejad shivered in fear. The Spirit's voice was familiar to him, resembling Ejad's own inner voice. Come to think of it... that rusty, echoing growl was *exactly* like the Hopohopo's on-and-off inner voice.

How is the Spirit materializing so well? Usually, he was just a looming presence Ejad felt in his head. But low and behold, here was the Spirit's essence. Lapu was perfectly visible, if a bit gaseous.

"*I have achieved a great victory*," Lapu told his minion. "*I've just struck down an elder. Literally seconds ago. Now what of our long-awaited plans to leach elder powers for ourselves upon their death? Can we circumvent the transmutation process? There isn't a time riper than now to put our theories to the test."*

"Struck down?"

"Incapacitated. He's just a sitting duck now. Ready for your taking. Let's take his power and kill him in one blow."

"Which elder is it?"

The oily figure chuckled, sliding around the chamber. "*Important things first. Can your machine harvest elder power?"*

"The prototype can harvest Mana mist. Needs extra glyph-work. I have Scripted many more capabilities into this one."

"Will it work?"

"That remains to be seen."

Lapu's annoyance was visible as the oily thing bristled as a spiky ball.

"You are rash, brash, far too daring; careless of self preservation."

Ejad stared at Lapu's form. Unresponsive.

"Uli at least had survival on top of his list. You're barging into this not even knowing if this thing will work."

Ejad scowled. *"I don't know what you mean. I am always careful. My machines always work one way or the other. I make them work."*

"You are careful only in your studies and engineering, not in your confrontations. Your assignments may have all been successful but you are a careless little dwarf."

Lapu was a genius at hammering in one's weaknesses.

Ejad silently watched the oily blob ooze up the half-completed machine. Lapu probed the engine. The Spirit's taunting niggled at Ejad's worries. Was that true? Was he a poor combatant because he chose to test his weapons on the go? Would that be his downfall?

Lapu dripped off the engine and coiled around back to him. *"There is a team of five elders on my case. They annoy me immensely. Test this contraption on them, starting with the one I weakened."*

"Consider it done."

"I will lead them to you, when you are ready." With that, Lapu's essence dissipated as suddenly as he had arrived.

Ejad returned to the machine and took out his laser pen. The tactile motions centered and distracted him from Lapu's bullying. The Inventor cringed at the tar-like scent lingering around him. Focusing back on his project, he inscribed runes on pieces of the chassis cover spread out on his work table. Mana-tech only worked when perfectly etched with runes and glyphs. Ejad's scripting was exquisite. Thanks to his basic rune studies at the Tech Academy and Uli's intense teachings of the more secretive glyphs. The power of Glyphs was older and hidden. Well... at least from other Hopohopo.

Ejad unrelentingly experimented with Scripting over the decades. Espousing runes and glyphs into a new type of Mana Tech. Armed with this secret knowledge, he knew he was incomparable and unmatched in the Manaful World. He called his innovative machines Mana Mech, a step up from Mana Tech.

It took Ejad, the Inventor, an extended period of thinking, planning, measuring, testing, building, and hammering to create Mana Mech. He's very patient, sacrificing Hopohopo.

Chapter 17
A Show of Power

Manaful World
August 10, 2022
Rubber Forest, Elder Freelands

Ikaika and the SC's encounter with Tree gave the 'Ula'ula heir hope. He projected, "*We shall visit Tree often now that she has warmed up to us.*"

"Mahalo, Tree, for letting us know your travel path," Nicole smiled gratefully. The notorious world traveling Relics bemused her.

They ascended again on Ikaika's invisible platform high above the canopy. The Secret Club waved bye to the swishing Tree as they zoomed under soft fluffy clouds of a sunny evening.

Maluhia was a speck in the sky, flying behind them this time.

"Maybe we can MT to your crib now?" Malie suggested, grabbing Nicole's tee as they left the redwood forest behind.

"I rather like the view," Pierre said.

"Just don't grab any branches again," Nicole laughed.

"Back home? Really? Don't want to hole myself up in the mansion before I hear from Maka and grandfather," projected Ikaika. "*I'm just too antsy.*"

"What are they up to now?" Malie appreciated the distraction of the conversation.

"Casting a spell to weaken Lapu. Spells are possible only when Elders from different 'Ohana combine and channel their Mana for a united, specific purpose.

"Is the Rift a dangerous place?" Pierre inquired, his curiosity about the center of the world piqued. He dreamily looked into the distance where clouds snagged on the summits of blue mountains.

Ikaika nodded. "*Perilous. Before Old Hill was "eaten" as Tree calls it and broken apart, it was a safe haven. The center of Manaful World. Now the Rift is a dark place overrun with confused Spirits led by Lapu.*"

The Secret Club snuggled around each other. Though they had no knowledge of Spirits here, the mention of them was scary.

"Are you communicating with the elders?" Nicole asked.

"No. Long distance projections are blocked in the Rift. We must wait until they enter Elder Territory."

"Ironic how powerless they are in such a Mana full spot," Malie shook her head.

Ikaika suddenly halted again. The SC gasped, grabbing their tummies as their body fluids sloshed nastily. They hovered over the borderland of a forest. But the woods were a blackened, smoking ruin.

Ikaika exploded. "*An entire rubber plantation burnt to a crisp! In 'Ula'ula territory too!*"

They descended so fast their hair stood straight up and their diaphragms tickled. Ikaika's small feet slammed down into the ashes hard, sweeping them away in a ring around the small group.

Woah, never seen Ikaika this mad, Malie thought. She looked up as Maluhia beat his wings to decelerate, hooting softly. Pierre covered his nose with a hand.

"There are several animals with burns and injuries," Maluhia TGP. *"I am rounding them up immediately."*

"*What else do you see?*"

"Animal traps all over the place. And... Some sort of machine, not far from where you are. Go due east and you'll find it."

Ikaika extended his arms and swept around in a circle. Small blasts of wind kicked back the ash and charcoal away. Then he leaped forward and left a clear path behind him for the SC to follow. They went in a straight line till they found what Maluhia was talking about.

It looked like a barrel mounted on four stubby legs. Only, this was chugging like a generator, with smog sucked into one set of vents at the front and oily droplets spilling out from another set at the back.

Ikaika walked around it with a frown. "*I've never seen the likes of this machine. Mana Cells are powering it. No one can purchase Mana Cells without going through Elders Lilinoe, Laka and Pele.*"

"They supplied the Cells powering these killing machines?" Malie asked dubiously.

Ikaika shook his head. "*They'd never sell in ignorance. They always check what projects their Cells are used for.*"

"We should ask those elders to make sure," Pierre said. Nicole nodded in agreement. The easiest way to avoid misunderstandings was to just come right out and say things, ask things. Nicely.

The machine growled away. Ikaika motioned them back, conjuring a cloth to wipe the tears and perspiration from his face. "*The barrel's sucking in Mana mist, tainting it, and transforming it into Lapu's essence. A twisted, lower form of Mana. I can't control it at all like other machines.*"

The Secret Club was dumbstruck. Nicole recalled something Elder Puna had let slip in their first ever visit last year. *Mana can be used with good and bad intentions.*

She'd gone nuts at discovering Uli and the "bad" parts of Manaful World. Now her hackles rose again. This was troubling. So much for magic.

Ikaika closed his eyes and the humans heard his projection calling for his friend Elder Maka and grandfather Elder Puna.

"I can't pick up a reply," Malie said, looking around. "Can you?"

Everyone shook their heads no, including Ikaika. "*They're still occupied. Let's do what we can here and leave in a while.*"

The Secret Club ran to Maluhia who was resting on a stump. He bade the humans to retrieve him animals too weak to move. Then he rose up with Mana mist swirling around his great wings to flap the smoke away with powerful air currents.

Ikaika stood near the machine and directed his Mana to the forest floor. The soil writhed and the destroyed trees started reviving. Though limited by his training, he did his best. His power wasn't strong enough for healing further than a fifteen foot radius.

As the team replenished the woodland, Lapu's essence flowed stealthily around them like grease on a hot pan. So this was one of the annoying heirs he'd heard of. Lapu studied Ikaika closely, his essence itching to harm the dwarf.

Oozing around a nearby tree, Lapu knew exactly what Ikaika telepathically heard when the young dwarf suddenly stopped and screamed. Lapu chuckled.

"Elder Alaka'i is incapacitated!" Ikaika exclaimed. "Maka and Puna just contacted me!"

The Secret Club ran back, unsure if they'd heard right. They could hardly believe Ikaika's news. That's when Lapu decided to mess with the thunderstruck youth. The Spirit slithered towards Ikaika.

The Manaful was too distraught to react in time. Lapu's essence wrapped around him like a swarm of bees. Before the Spirit could reach Ikaika's mind, though, the dwarf shut down. It was a dangerous if neat trick Elder Puna had installed, when his grandson was just a child. Ikaika's mind was now impenetrable.

Ikaika fell to the fresh grass he'd grown, knocked out cold. Mana mist shimmered and glowed around him, a self preserving force field that would protect him until he woke up.

Lapu turned on the Secret Club.

They were ready for him. Nicole, Malie and Pierre clenched their hands into fists. But Lapu penetrated their minds as easily as he did the last time. The SC were struck with terror, sadness and hopelessness. He hit them with a barrage of negative, self-deprecating thoughts.

"*You are all weak! You will achieve nothing in life. You will never amount to anything worthwhile,*" He poisoned them, hissing. "*Freaks, that's what you are! Freaks!*"

No, Pierre suddenly thought. *That's not true.*

He remembered Shelly laughing-crying after he came out. Her big belly wobbling, she'd held him tight in a hug. Then Gabe came in with the chicken and threw it aside to run to them, covering them in his bear hug. Fuzzy warmth rose up in Pierre's chest as he shouted back, "Your poison won't work on me this time, Lapu!"

He relived the beautiful memories with his ʻOhana. His mind cleared instantly. Elder Puna's mind screen was up.

"Find the kākoʻo," Pierre shouted. Being a transplant from continental USA, the Hawaiian word rolled off his tongue funny. Distracted from Lapu by Pierre's accent, Nicole and Malie shook off their weaknesses. Both threw their shoulders back, grasped one another's hands, and sang. Their voices rang out with such strength that it woke Ikaika. His force field expanded to include the humans. The song rose up from deep within each of them, unifying and fearless.

SC Rally Song:

Pierre:

"Loved ones wrap us in Aloha
Lapu's words cannot ever control ya.
Don't believe the untruths he spouts.
Won't let him win, we're going to rout.

Take control of our own minds.
Our strength is one of a kind."

Nicole:

"Lapu cannot use my regrets unless
I let him and surrender to the mess.
He tries hard to break my heart
But we shape our lives, creating art.
Believing in our own unique beauty
Filling our souls with equanimity."

Malie:

"Truth is not hard to dig up.
Lapu thinks we're just pups
To push around, to lead astray.
We are bigger than that, I say.
He doesn't stand a chance.
Our love's like a warrior's lance."

Ikaika:

"Mahalo, my team, my family, my friends
I am grateful to you, this love never ends.
Our unity is what pushes Lapu back.
With our bond, we withstand any attack
On the mind, on the heart, on the body.
Beneath it all, Lapu's Mana is shoddy!"

Ikaika's force field stretched thin from protecting so many, dissipated. Inspired by the children, he gathered Mana from his piko. He conjured a powerful energy blast at Lapu. Ikaika hadn't conjured such a blast in his eight hundred years of life.

Lapu was pushed back. His essence was weakened. He swirled warily, losing power the longer he stayed in either a liquid, gas or solid form. He was almost out of charge, having materialized too much for that one day. It was easier to back off.

He ducked away behind a tree, but the Spirit kept an eye on them. He had underestimated the SC and the heir. But a visit to the Rift will recharge him back up for a stronger assault. He wondered how to best use these young ones.

"I'm impressed by how you took control of your screens, Team One!" Ikaika projected. He was proud of the SC, but remained crestfallen.

"Lapu came here after a horrible attack that felled Elder Alaka'i," he TGP. *"They've just reached House Opalescent grounds, Alaka'i's Villa. No one else was harmed."*

Lapu stopped interfering for the day. When the team MT away, the Spirit let the winds take him away too. Invisible. This was how most Spirits existed. They rode within the winds, waves and woods, unseen. Barely awake. Theirs was an easy existence.

But Lapu was different. He wanted to be seen, to taste a more grounded life. He had a sense of identity. And the power to possess.

Riding the winds, he mentally reached out to his connections. He tugged on his threads of various puppets scattered all over the 'Ōma'oma'o territory. Puppets from both the Hopohopo and Manaful. He'd use them all. Milk them dry to reach his goal. He'd Manifest.

Chapter 18
Ari and Aunt on Maʻi

Earth
Storyteller in Papakōlea
Earth
August 12, 2022

"Aunty Ellie, Lapu is a monster. I pray to never confront a being like that. Though sometimes I feel like there's a monster like him in me."

"What do you mean?"

"I'm an irritable snappy turtle on a good day, but I'm a monster on the worst," Ari frowned. She slouched off the couch to plop onto the rug. The tea table was just inches from her head. She folded her legs beneath it, and knocked her forehead lightly on the glass. Knocked it again.

"Woah, woah! Stop that!" Aunt Ellie squatted beside Ari, wrapping her arm around her niece's head. "Careful, the poʻo is sacred. Mālama it always," her aunt insisted, hugging Ari to her bosom.

Ari began to cry and shiver.

"What's happening, my child? Where's this coming from? Do you want me to stop the story? Is the SC's Manaful journey too traumatizing?" Aunt Ari's voice raised with worry.

Ari shook her head and wrapped her arms around her aunt. She just sobbed and Aunt Ellie held her, moving the tea table back for space. The rug was fluffy with swirly gray and black patterns. Aunt Ellie stretched her legs out, willing to stay there a while.

Ten minutes later, Ari nodded and looked up at her Aunt through puffy, red eyes. Her messy hair bun falling and nose stuffed. Aunt Ellie gave her precious silence, nodding with an encouraging expression. Eyes dampened too, her aunt tried not to frown.

"I'm a monster too. I got my period for the first time. Felt so alone. I wanted to tear up my clothing, my blankets, and scream. I had to stay silent because it was the middle of the night. I couldn't tell Mom about my ma'i. She already disapproves of me. I don't think she wants to help me. I was scared." Ari started to tremble again as the words tumbled out.

"Hey, hey, you're okay. Breathe. We're together. You're not alone." Aunt Ellie hugged Ari, swaying soothingly. Repeating words of reassurance. She was feeling so many things. Anger at her sister. Disappointment in the world. Impatience with herself for not explaining menstruation earlier. Just letting this huge life milestone slip through her fingers unthinkingly. She shut down the negative line up of "should haves". She closed her eyes, taking a deep breath. It's not about her. It's about Ari.

"Ari, talk to me when you're ready. We'll sit here for as long as necessary. Do you have supplies now? Did your mom finally help you? What can I get for you?" Aunt Ellie rolled her eyes at herself for messing up again. Trying to get her brain to shut up, so Ari can talk.

Ari shook her head. Then nodded. Then shook her head. Her eyes scrunched up like she was going to cry again. "Ahhh...I..."

"Yes, okay, Babe!" Aunt Ellie nodded as if understanding what Ari couldn't get out. She guessed that Ari found feminine products. Maybe her mom's stash. Maybe she made her own from old rags out of necessity, hence the term "being on my rags." She shook her head and frowned at herself for going off on such a trivial tangent when Ari was the main concern here.

"I got stuff," Ari whispered. "I found pads. Took a shower. Had to hide my linen and bloody clothes in the hamper."

Aunt Ellie let out a huge sigh that Ari mālama herself best she could. Wishing there was a way to convey that she shouldn't be ashamed. Wishing her sister had been more cognizant of her daughter's maʻi coming. Oh, maybe she was to blame too? Weren't they all sort of co-parenting? Didn't her sister rely on her to have these kinds of healthy body talks with Ari too? The regrets just snowballed in Ellie's head. She closed her eyes and reached for Ari's hands. Looking down at her niece's smaller, softer fingers, Ellie came back to the present. She came back to the realization that it didn't matter. All of the "what ifs" were irrelevant. What's important is to mālama Ari right now and in the future.

Ari stared at her Aunt, "You okay, Auntie? Do you need water or some rest?" Ari released her aunt's hand, checking the latter's forehead.

"You're burning up, Aunty!" Ari looked concerned.

Aunt Ellie grabbed Ari's hand and laughed, responding, "No, I'm fine. It's you I'm worried about. I'm just frazzled by what's happening to you."

"Oh, that's really sweet, but you need to take care of yourself too!" Ari's eyes got bigger and she hummed wisely.

Aunt Ellie couldn't stop smiling now, sort of a deliriousness coming over her. Can this really be happening? Her niece was worried about her after sharing about last night's first ma'i day?

Ari stole a side glance at her aunt as she got up. She ran to the kitchen for ice water and a cool wet cloth. She ran back, looking at her aunt who was now lying on the rug. Aunt Ellie's arms and legs were stretched out like she's making a snow angel. Her eyes were closed and she was smiling at the ceiling dreamily. Ari placed the wet cloth on her aunt's forehead and squeezed her bicep, kneeling beside her head.

"Aunty, drink this!" Ari cupped her aunt's head under her arm and lifted the glass of water.

Aunt Ellie opened her eyes and accepted the water and aid. She was amazed at her niece and humbled too.

Ari, sat back on her knees, staring at her aunt. She sighed, saying, "Aunty, I don't understand what's happening with my ma'i. But I do understand that you have to be careful of your blood pressure, stress levels, and mindfulness."

Aunt Ellie turned over with her head on an elbow to look up at Ari. She was taken aback and proud of her niece's selflessness. She fistbumped Ari's left knee and told her, "I love you and am grateful for your concern. I also apologize for not being there when your ma'i happened."

Ari shook her head and groaned, "Aunty! You can't be perfect! You can't predict every little thing that's going to happen to me! You're not the author of my life!" Her voice was raising a little with impatience. She was talking with her hands and shaking her head left and right. Her eyes had gotten big again, eyebrows hiked way high into her hairline.

Aunt Ellie sat with her hands up in surrender. She smartly stayed silent. She let Ari have her say and vent all her stressors.

Ari's head wanted to explode. She couldn't believe her aunt thought she could solve everything and be there for all things. Really? Really? OMG! She closed her eyes and practiced what she preached minutes ago. Watching her own blood pressure and being mindful of her own thoughts. Owl breathing!

She did the count: "1…2…3…Whoo! Whoo! Whoo!" Eyes still closed, she heard Aunt Ellie's shuffling clothing, likely sitting more comfortably. Then, her voice came in to count as well.

"1…2…3…Whoo! Whoo! Whoo!" Aunt Ellie chorused with Ari.

The counting worked.

Their heart beats settled and their thoughts cleared. Aunt Ellie lay back down. Ari lay down beside her. They stretched their arms out but their fingers met, intertwining. After what seemed like a while, Aunt Ellie said, "I'm here."

Ari was quiet for an even longer while. Her aunt respected that silence. Finally after an interminable moment, Ari said, "Mahalo."

CHAPTER 19
ALAKAʻI FELL

Manaful World
August 12, 2022
Wintergreen Forest, Elder Territory
Elder Alakaʻi's Opalescent Villa

The SC saw the grayish, unconscious Elder Alakaʻi for the first time two days after he fell. They arrived at the Villa infirmary just seconds after exiting the Shimmery Wall. Ikaika led them to the large green healing room. Elders Puna, Lilinoe, Laka and Maka looked around from a floating resting flower pod. In it, Alakaʻi lay prone, his robes dulled and unmoving.

The Elders all levitated at human eye level. A young Manaful girl held Elder Alakaʻi's temples in her hands. Her robes shimmered faintly of all ʻOhana colors. The SC were too distraught to notice her at first.

Malie couldn't hold back her tears. The pod resembled a floating lotus with waving fuschia and white petals. In its soft embrace Elder Alaka'i was lost to the world.

"Don't cry, little one," Elder Puna's mind caressed Malie's mind. "*Allow us to calm this grief.*"

Elders' robes glowed as their Mana healed the SC's and Ikaika's sadness.

Elder Maka TGP, "*He is not dead. There is still hope yet.*"

Ikaika grimaced. "*But I cannot feel Elder Alaka'i's mind in his body!*"

"Earlier, that panicked us too." Elder Puna stroked his long beard and added, "*but Charmaine assures us that his spirit is alive and can be brought back.*"

The Elders levitated near the girl, as their bioluminescent robes reached out to her. She sat prim and ramrod straight on the edge of a cushioned lily pad. The stem curled up around her waist forming armrests. Her seat levitated beside Alaka'i.

More like a throne, now that I think of it, Pierre thought in awe. Before seeing this beauty, he'd been accustomed to being the prettiest one around. He'd been brought down a peg.

Charmaine's eyes were closed, oblivious to their stares. Her dark brown hair was braided elegantly like an intricate laurel. It was held up by three fan-shaped pins. The accessories from the front aligned to make the emblem of House Momi, a pearl wreathed with Mana mist tendrils.

"She's so beautiful," Nicole clasped her heart, grief forgotten. Her eyes had almost turned into heart shaped emoji. Pierre scoffed then saw Malie even more smitten. He studied the pretty Manaful.

She appeared around fifteen human years old, which would make her only a thousand and fifty Manaful years old like Maka. She had a petite frame swathed in silky robes printed with moving geometrical patterns. The cloth itself was not alive like the elders', but the swirling patterns mesmerized the SC.

"This is Elder Alaka'i's daughter, Charmaine," Elder Puna introduced them. *"Heir Charmaine, these are the Secret Club: Pierre, Nicole and Malie."*

"Pleasure," Charmaine TGP, her eyes still closed. She sent a wave of happiness to the SC, making them smile goofily. That was it from Charmaine for now.

"She's communicating with Elder Alaka'i in the Spirit Realm," Elder Maka TGP. *"Charmaine can go there. She's leading her father back to his body."*

"Better not disturb her, then," Pierre suggested. He turned around to glimpse the worst case of Charmaine idolization so far. Ikaika was a goner. No wonder he was so silent.

Elder Maka cleared his throat. He was clearing his throat a lot. Oops. Spoken too soon, Maka's with Ikaika. Maka said, "Charmaine is a master at all crafts. She will fix this. She's the best." He looked shocked he had spoken aloud. He cleared his throat, 'Ahem-Ahem'.

Elders Puna, Lilinoe and Laka kept their grieving faces on.

Pierre shook his head. Everyone except him was blown away by Charmaine, Heir Apparent of House Alaka'i. He gave her another once over when she opened her kalakoa ombré eyes with a small gasp.

Elder Alaka'i also gasped and opened his eyes. Rainbow Mana mist glistened around them. Color returned to his milk-coffee face and his robes fluttered weakly about him like a fussy yet confused nurse.

"Brother!" Elder Puna joyfully projected. He threw himself on the pod. Elder Puna's red robes shone brightly infusing with Elder Alaka'i's. In a pink burst of light, the Elder Prime rose up from the pod in his shining robe. Everyone was glad he was awake, despite his light being noticeably weaker than his previous glory. Puna stood grinning ear to ear.

"*Thank you, dear daughter,*" Elder Alaka'i reached for Charmaine. She floated up like a princess and inclined her head formally, both hands on the ribboned sash around her waist.

"Oh, come here and give me a hug," Elder Alaka'i harrumphed. "*You just literally saved my life.*"

Charmaine shrugged with a regal If-I-Must expression and embraced her father. He showered her with kisses. She brushed the corner of her eye with a lace gloved finger.

"Is she for real?" Pierre projected at Ikaika.

The 'Ula'ula heir unwillingly broke his gaze away from Charmaine. "*What do you mean?*"

"She reminds me of Queen Elizabeth." Pierre put an imaginary crown on his head and held an imaginary scepter. He puckered his lips and fluttered his lashes for good measure.

Ikaika scowled his displeasure at Pierre's teasing about the reverent Child Prime. "*Charmaine was raised like a queen, so it's unsurprising she may come off as such. I wouldn't think it was a problem.*"

"*This particular Manaful takes it way too seriously,*" Pierre concluded, blissfully unaware of the lines he was crossing.

Ikaika's ears turned magenta. He looked back at Charmaine. Pierre watched Ikaika melt.

Elder Alaka'i released his daughter and TGP to everyone, "*My body's response to my mind is still flawed. I will need my Elder team to help with recovery. I fear Lapu may try to strike me while I'm still weak.*"

"He did not follow us after we left the Rift," Elder Puna projected. He mind-melded with Elder Alaka'i, creating an expanded sphere of consciousness with everyone in the chamber. Now they could share each others' thoughts and experiences to get on the same page.

"Lapu assaulted Ikaika and the SC in the rubber woods," Elder Puna summarized. He pulled up images of the machine Ikaika and the SC encountered for closer study.

The SC felt the mind-melding as a fantastic collective swoon. Their knees buckled hard with the strange experience. They sank onto ottoman-like puffball mushrooms to experience their full blown large scale mind-melding situation. Everyone had access to each other's thoughts. They could file through each other's minds at once.

"*Those machines had our House Emblems on them,*" Elders Lilinoe and Laka said. "*The Mana Battery Cells. They're from our factory. Tita Pele supplies the hardware.*"

"These are Pele's hardware?" Puna wanted to make sure.

Elders Lilinoe and Laka shared memories of their work life and visits to their sister's hardware factory. "*They are. But it's all mashed together like a—a—*"

"Frankenstein's monster," Malie supplied.

The horrible machine flared up in their shared mind's eye. Curious, Elder Laka simultaneously pulled up movie clips of Frankenstein's monster from Malie's mind. They watched Ikaika's attempts to break the machine over and over again while the 70's TV version of Frankenstein's monster screamed in the background. Nicole brought up Lapu's attack scene into it. Like B-Roll footage, she and Pierre supplied them singing their rally song with some metal music backing tracks. They were delighted it all rocked nicely, fist-bumping in their minds.

Then the mind-meld was over.

"Hey, what about the Rift? You didn't share those memories with us," Pierre protested. His head buzzed at the experience. Awesome! It was possible to affect mind-melds with stuff he wanted! "*Cooler than at Ikaika's mansion!*"

"*That was fun,*" Nicole agreed solemnly. She rubbed her arms because they still tingled from the mind-meld.

Elder Laka looked dazed. "*Um... with all due respect, perhaps it is easier for us to do our work without human distractions, for today. Just a suggestion.*"

Elders Lilinoe and Puna also cleared their heads with a good shake. Pierre listened to a vast range of music and why he'd chosen metal for the memory replay was anyone's guess. The poor Manafuls had never been so shocked. Ikaika was now blushing all over.

"*We apologize, dear Elders. The humans are still adjusting to Manaful ways and certainly not yet familiar with mind-melding and its code of conduct,*" Ikaika apologized.

"We're just joyous that Elder Alaka'i is OK," Malie said. She shot her fellow SC members a sympathetic look. "Sorry for messing up the mind-meld."

Elder Alaka'i waved a weak hand dismissively as if to say 'nobody ruined anything'. But he only sighed and held Elder Puna's shoulder, Charmaine still by his side. The Secret Club noticed his eyes were having trouble staying open.

It was Charmaine who spoke. Her voice was like a bell. "Thank you, human visitors. I have been working to bring my father back for two days. Only in your presence did my Mana grow strong enough to overcome barriers between the spiritual and physical worlds."

"Why would our presence make your Mana stronger?" Nicole was flabbergasted.

"The strength of your love. The purity of your thoughts. The beauty of your memories. These are just a few of the many reasons. Thank you for arriving here when you did."

Charmaine bent her neck, lips pressed into a line. She was obviously not going to say 'thank you' a third time.

"You're welcome, er, Heir Apparent," Malie said quickly. She elbowed Nicole.

"Huge...HUGE privilege to meet you," Nicole babbled. She elbowed Pierre.

"Glad to be of any help we can give," Pierre said soberly. Charmaine shot him an unexpected smile. She'd heard his Queen Elizabeth thoughts. He finally blushed like the rest of them.

They were all distracted when Elder Alaka'i moaned. He held his head muttering, "The Spirits keep pulling at my mind, trying to trap me in their Realm so that my body will remain a vegetable here."

The Elders hugged him, urging him back to the resting pod. Elder Alaka'i lay down in the heart of the flower and sighed. Charmaine levitated by his head and placed both her hands on his temples. "*Rest, father. Elder Puna and I will watch over your body and mind.*"

Elder Maka broke away to approach Ikaika and the SC. "*This is the safest place in the Manaful World. They will all be fine here. Elder Alaka'i needs time to fully recover. It's best for us to give them space.*"

"*Agreed,*" Ikaika projected.

Before they left, the SC saw Elder Alaka'i sinking back into a trance with Charmaine watching over his mind.

Chapter 20
SC Texts

Earth
August 12, 2022
Malie Manu's Home

The trio were solemn at home. Overwhelmed by the enormity of Alaka'i's predicament, they chose mindfulness and being in the present.

Sensing Malie's deeper than usual worry, Pili decided she wanted an official introduction to the SC members. First she had a hot shower and mālama herself with shea butter with a drop of lemongrass oil. She spritzed on Gypsy Water, one of Malie's favorite scents. Then she went to catch her daughter at opportune timing, putting that goal out there.

Malie assured Pili it'll happen, returning to her silent introspection after agreeing. Pili didn't interfere. Contemplating the Manaful World alone, the preteen kicked back and texted her buddies. The SC were checking if they had any budding telepathic abilities.

SC texts

Beep. Beep. Beep.

SC group text notifications came in.

Malie: What did I just picture?

Pierre: Sheep.

Malie: Yes!

Nicole: I dunno. I didn't see anything.

Pierre: Iykyk. Again, Malie.

Nicole: Umbrella? Pony?

Malie: No. No.

Pierre: Sksksk.

Nicole: Wait.

Malie: Try again!

Nicole: IMHO, this is a no go!

Pierre: Malie! You're picturing the Hopohopo Town Hall!

Malie: Slay!

Nicole: Pierre, you're good at this game.

Pierre: Wow! HMU again!

Malie: I was trying to tell you something specific. A picture of the Town Hall works too. How clearly did you see it, Pierre?

Pierre: As clear as day! There was even a cloaked Hopohopo in a wheelchair who felt out of place by the door.

Malie: That's it! You got it!

Pierre: This is so weird but cool!

Nicole: Hey, maybe you guys really are developing something. This is amazing!

Malie: It's J4f, Nicole, no worries.

Nicole: I want mind powers!

Pierre: Period!

Malie: TBC!

Nicole: THX!

Pierre: TTYL!

Malie: HAK!

Pierre: Ditto!

Nicole: TY!

Chapter 21
SC Moms Mobilize!

Earth
August 13, 2022
Wright Middle School

The next day, Malie introduced Pili to Pierre and Nicole when her mother came to pick her up. The Secret Club was on the curb chatting about classes when Pili Manu rolled up in her chartreuse Toyota Corolla.

"Hey Baby Manu! How's the company?" Pili said, blasting a warm smile at her daughter's two friends. She knew their names. "Pierre? Nicole?"

Both kids nodded and grew shy at meeting a new adult. Pili couldn't ignore how tiny her daughter looked between these two taller kids with stronger builds. Malie seemed at least three years younger.

"It's a privilege meeting you," Nicole broke the ice, "Listening to Malie talk about you, you're a Super Mom."

Pili Manu burst out laughing. "Oh, stop it. I'm just a single mom playing nurse."

"You were on the front lines of the Covid pandemic," Pierre said. His chin jutted out. "You're awesome. No two ways about it."

"I'll take that," Pili couldn't stop grinning. What a pair of nice kids. She resolved to meet their parents. Pierre took her number and promised to tell Shelly to ring her.

"See you!" Malie shouted through the car window. Pili rolled it up as they turned into the main street. She adjusted the air conditioner and shifted gears. Malie threw her school bag behind her and settled into the passenger seat.

"You OK?" Pili ventured. Malie seemed fine but there was a tint of worry in the preteen's aura. In her years of medical experience, Pili knew people open up when they're ready. She wasn't one to dig up answers. Even from her own daughter.

"I'm fine," Malie said, looking at the scenery whooshing past. "Just school stuff. Assignments. Minor worries."

"Remember, I'm all ears whenever you want to talk about anything."

Malie nodded. Pili let Malie be for the rest of the drive home. In the silence a wild hope kindled in her heart. Then a question. Could she befriend the parents of her daughter's new friends? Did she have the courage? OK, just one question.

"Pierre's mom is preggers, right," Pili said. Her daughter confirmed with a nod, lost in a daydream. Malie took off her glasses, fussing with them in her hands. These kids sure had a lot to talk and think about, it seemed.

And here I am, going past thirty with barely a social or familial circle.

Perhaps Pili Manu deserved some new friends too. Adulting was hard enough, let alone mothering and aging towards the elderly strata every passing year. She pule for Shelly's imminent birthing.

You know what, she told herself as she gripped the steering wheel. *I'm going to organize a baby shower. Arrange everything and call Shelly Martin and Kaleo Moku to drop the invite. I'll do it within the next five hours,* Pili promised herself.

But Shelly beat her to it before the sun set that day. In Pili's defense, by then the chicken was thawing in the sink and she'd dug out some frozen patty's from the icebox.

* * *

Pierre Martin's Home

Shelly's world was a hazy existence filled with her medical needs. If she wanted to, she could sit on her butt all day ordering Gabe and Pierre around. Those two were at her service 24/7.

But they were also riding the waves of gestation and imminent baby delivery along with her. In Pierre, it was akin to a near-constant fever.

Today her son was not as joyously bubbly as usual. She glanced briefly at him as she waddled to the massage armchair Gabe had hauled in. "Solely for your enjoyment," Gabe had said.

Shelly groaned and lowered herself into the plush black leather. An enormous sigh escaped her like a prolonged squeak from a rubber ducky. Pierre sat doodling in a notebook in front of the TV sofa.

"Son," she called.

Pierre jumped up at once and was beside her. There was far too much worry on his face for her liking. Before he spoke she said, “I told you to stop worrying about the delivery! Everything is fine!”

Pierre looked hurt. “But I’m not.”

“It’s written all over your face,” she said. She pinched his cheek, which earned her a pearly white grin at once.

“I can’t help but overthink it, mom!”

“What’s your little Secret Club for if you can’t distract yourself?”

She had a point.

Pierre tried to smoothen his face out. Plaster that grin on perpetually. He failed. The image of Elder Alaka‘i bedridden kept flashing in his mind’s eye. Then Alaka‘i would transform into Shelly, and his heartbeat would speed. Mom might be bedridden too soon, if there were any complications. How could he not worry?

“I said stop it,” Shelly tsked. She leaned back heavily. The whole chair creaked. She felt like a rhino on steroids.

“It’s not all about you, Mom!” Pierre protested. He found the button to make the chair vibrate. Anything to shake off this line of questioning.

Shelly said, “Oooooooo yes,” when her swollen form started jiggling gently.

“I’ll just go back to...” Pierre shuffled towards the sofa.

“Tell me,” she said curtly. Pierre ran to the icebox and got some cucumber slices. He went to Shelly and dropped them on her eyes. She smiled.

He almost snuck back. Shelly said, "Something's off. You can't fool me. Tell me at once."

Pierre shuffled back to the massage chair. At least she couldn't see his face now. He'd chosen thick cucumber slices.

"It's school," he began carefully. He shared a locker room incident. A couple of boys on his team had teased him about Nicole and Malie. Pierre insisted both girls were just his friends. Another boy said, "Only gays have girls as *only* friends." Everyone laughed.

Pierre's face burned like a Fourth of July bonfire just rehashing it. Shelly caught him down and hugged him. The cucumber slices slipped off. Gabe would find them later. She talked him through it.

She told him to be strong against teasing. He will face more in the future, so he needs to be solid in his emotional and mental well-being. He had to reduce his insecurities, learn to be proud of who he is, and be firm in his identity.

Pierre told her about meeting Kaleo and the Drs. Fine in the last few months. Plus, Gabe had been chatty with Nicole and Malie on their ride home the other day.

"Am I the only one left to bloat?" Shelly said.

"You're ges-gestating," Pierre tried out the relatively new word. He smiled and patted the heaving globe that was her midriff.

"I want to meet your friends' families," Shelly said. She was going to boldly approach Kaleo and Pili. Two girlfriends were more useful to a pregnant woman than one and a half men.

"But mom-"

"No buts. Give me their numbers. I'm calling them for a baby shower."

Pierre supplied Pili's number. He didn't mind their moms talking to each other. He was concerned about the timing. His mother really was all... ripe.

Shelly asked Pierre to get her phone. The moment he did, she dialed Malie's mom. Pili picked up on the third ring.

* * *

Nicole Moku's Home

Alaka'i almost died. Lapu might one day cross the world. Basketball division finals were coming up.

Nicole was at her wit's end, pulling at her puffy bangs.

She scrunched her face, wishing for ideas for handling Kaleo's questions about her sad mood.

Hiding in her room she texted Pierre. He just shared a real life problem with his mother to hide the truth about Alaka'i.

Nicole told her mom she was still dealing with being bullied.

Kaleo demanded if there have been more incidents. Nicole calmed her down and escaped back to her room without further questioning, barely avoiding an impromptu Fines appointment. She dug out her pastel oils and horsehair brush to sit on the bedside rug and paint. Every loud color she used was therapy.

Malie texted an invite to a baby shower for Pierre's family. "Moooooom! Check your phooone!" Nicole hollered. She forwarded the text to Kaleo.

Chapter 22
Baby Shower Splash

Earth
August 13, 2022
Malie Manu's Home

"This is a beautiful yard," Gabe Martin said as he helped Shelly out from the front seat of their minivan.

She was in her 37th Week. Shelly complained about not seeing her feet. She was beautiful to him, and really hadn't gained much weight at all. He was smart enough not to even mention the words tired, weight, or fat in her presence. Ugh, ugh. Never. When she wasn't looking, he admired how her belly protruded like she'd stuffed a basketball under her shirt. Her whole body became a heavenly statue of maternity and fertility. He loved pregnancy.

Shelly didn't. She hated pregnancy. She'd begged her doctor to induce labor days ago, but she was still a few days shy of her due date. Her Braxton Hicks had been coming for weeks, totally throwing her off balance. The pains though infrequent made her irritable. It could happen at any moment as anything could naturally induce labor: sex, urinating, being dehydrated, and more. Walking was torture on her cankles. Yet, ambulation helped, as well as warm baths and herbal teas. Not to mention, Pierre's peppermint oil foot rubs were heavenly.

What didn't help was Gabe being underfoot 24/7. Humbug, she needed him for the simplest things like getting dressed and even brushing her hair. She got exhausted so fast. Shelly sometimes considered chopping her long, waist-length, thick black locks. Her scalp constantly sweated, perspiration trailing down the locks, making them sticky. They'd been her pride and joy as a hula dancer. Now her hair was a pain in the behind. Speaking of which, even making #2 hurt. Sitting on the toilet as the baby dropped low in her uterus, she felt like she'd tip over while making bowel movements. Then she would holler for Gabe again. How could she need him so much but not want him around too much? She was simply a mess of emotions and thoughts. Her brain was fevered with worries and stress about the delivery. She definitely didn't want a giant epidural needle in her back. It was the stuff of nightmares. She may poop during labor. Her vagina may become torn and mangled. She may need a C-section. She may die. Nope. Shelly Martin did not like pregnancy. She lived for the reward at the end.

Pierre stared at his mom. *Is the baby shower a good idea?*

Mom was looking ready to literally pop. She walked so slowly it was like watching a time lapse video. His dad's forehead was sweating, wrinkled with strain as he helped her along.

Pierre wished for molecular transportation powers to simply deliver his mother to the hospital ASAP.

Deliver.

Delivery.

Delivering. "D" Time. That's the ultimate word now. He pulled out the emergency Hospital Bag for his mom from the car. He gripped it tighter than he'd ever held a football. Cannot put this thing down. Ever. Must have it. Must be ready. "D" time was coming. He didn't need Mana to know this.

The moment Pili's eyes landed on Shelly she knew; Pierre saw her expression go from casual to professional in a snap. Today's the Day, Pili's face said. As a former neonatal registered nurse, she was compelled to act. She ran to Shelly's side and without preamble said, "How far apart?" Meaning, how far apart were the contraction intervals?

Pierre, mouth hanging open, looked from Pili to his mom. What was this secret Mom Speak?

Shelly looked into Pili's wise, confident eyes. Something went pop in her ears. She took a great big breath and shoved Gabe off her.

Here was a tita who Shelly could trust. A huge load lifted from her shoulders and tears sprung up in her eyes. She let out the big inhalation and said, "Twenty minutes!"

Pili grabbed Shelly's hand and nodded up at Gabe. The trim medium-height Caucasian-Hawaiian woman had caring brown eyes and hair the same shade to her shoulders.

"It's Pili. We've spoken a couple of times before. Whenever you drop off the kids." she pointed to herself then raised her other arm in welcome, "Aloha, Shelly, Gabe, and Pierre. Welcome finally to my hale!"

"Gabe, will you help Court at the barbeque for a little bit, while we ladies get better acquainted?" Pili looked pointedly at Shelly's husband.

Shelly turned to Gabe and nodded, sending him reassuring thoughts with her eyes. *We'll be fine, Dear. Need to walk this out.* Shelly held her belly which she'd been carrying low for a few days.

Gabe looked lost. He wanted to follow them, knowing the contractions were decreasing in intervals. He bit his lower lip, fisting and loosening his hands.

Pierre watched him warily. He hugged the precious "go to" bag for his mom. He poked his dad's arm, "Breathe, Dad!" After a few seconds, Gabe turned to his son, his breath "Whooshing" out.

"Backyard's that way," Pierre pointed with the bag. Gabe blinked. Right.

"Let's go barbecue, Son!" Gabe made a fake grin. He wasn't fooling Pierre, but the latter just went with it. He made a fistbump motion, which made Gabe really smile this time. He fistbumped Pierre back. They turned together, though Gabe threw a backward glance towards the garden path. He didn't see his wife, but something told him she'd be fine with a nurse.

Malie had watched the entire entrance and exchange, flabbergasted by her mom's confidence and aloha. She knew Pili had interpersonal skills, but she hadn't expected her mom to kidnap Shelly so quickly. Perhaps because Pierre's mom looked ready to pop and her mom's medical instincts told her to mālama NOW. Yeah, that's it. Malie grinned. Her mom rocked! She followed Pierre and his dad to the grill.

Nicole Moku's entire assemblage was in the backyard parked at the picnic bench. They'd arrived early and got to work at once. The Moku's loved Pili's excellent backyard grill. The heat was already on.

Doctors John and Court Fine were a handsome pair in their board shorts and t-shirts. One would never guess they were in their early sixties. They kept fit surfing and bodyboarding whenever they could get out of the office. Thankfully, the tanned mixed-race couple owned their own therapy practice, making their own hours.

They'd adopted their son, Nicholas, upon completing medical school together. They'd timed it to their thirtieth birthdays, both being born in the same year. They hadn't anticipated the late nights of sleepiness it took to mālama a newborn. When the agency called to say their baby was here, the Drs. Fine said, "We'll be there!" without hesitation. They'd picked up their baby at the hospital thirty years ago and never looked back.

Court, who was balding a little on top, was manning the barbecue chicken station. He was trim like a runner, yet had a pot belly. A small 'baby bump'. Just a small sign that those COVID years affected him as well as his clients. Everybody binged a little in their own ways: on food, on sex, on alcohol, on anything. His was red wine and cranberry juice. Oohhh, that was his daily poison. Just a glass a day. Okay, maybe a biiiigg glass. A guy's gotta let loose somehow, right?

John Fine was still quite fine. He was part-African American and part-Japanese. He was a model during undergrad, which helped pay the bills and was how he met Court. He'd been at a photoshoot at the beach. He'd just completed that booking and said his Mahalo's to the crew. Instead of going home to clean off the make-up, he'd simply dived into the water and swam out as far as he could. John had needed that people-free time just feeling the waves, the tide, the sun on his back. No more call sheets. No being camera ready. Just him and the cold liquid surroundings. He hadn't been paying attention where he was going when, "Bonk!"

He wasn't knocked out, but heck it hurt!

"You okay?" someone shouted from a surfboard to his left. "Oh, crap! What can I do? Come!"

John, a muscular and toned six feet two model, was no light weight. Thankfully, the salt water's buoyancy helped Court lift him partially onto the surfboard. John hung on for his life. His sight was going in and out. His breathing was irregular.

"You might have a concussion! Hold on in the front, and I'll pull the rest of your body on to the board long ways," Court husked.

A long-time lifeguard during his teen years, Court confidently checked John's vitals. Thoroughly. Then he jumped into waves behind John on the longboard, paddling them shorewards. It was all done very professionally.

John had stayed cool. He wasn't completely oblivious to the tanned, slender yet whipcord strong surfer manhandling him. He was also aware that his heart was pumping so much blood so fast he forgot the pain in his head by the time they made it to the beach.

"And that's how we met," Court narrated to their audience of SC families as he flipped the hot dogs and chicken. He grabbed John's hands for a loving squeeze, their eyes locked and twinkling with silent giggles. Their souls never aged.

John hadn't had a concussion. Just a bump. Funny enough, he was grateful for that bump on his head. He'd met the love of his life. They'd met at the beach again for John's surfing lessons; Court's a good teacher. Coincidentally, they both were Pre-Med/Psych double majors. Different universities, Mānoa and Chaminade. It was pretty much fate. Even thirty years later, John, who went to set the salad bar across the patio, stared back at Court with warm fuzzies inside.

The touching How-We-Met story finished and food prepped, the SC hurried to the kitchen to sample the crisp burgers. The adults had conjured it all up nice and quick. Kaleo carried the plate indoors and her foster brother, Nick, carried the soda.

Nick Fine winked at Malie, Pierre and Nicole. The kids were rehashing his parents' love story as they tucked in. He grabbed a burger as well, watching his dad watch his other dad dreamily. Holy-moly, they never quit. That's love for you. As a gay man like his parents, Nick understood the value of a solid, strong relationship. He'd never had one, but he knew it existed somewhere, sometime for him. His dads were a living testament.

Though he wasn't tall at five and a half feet, his pure Japanese heritage gave him a lovely porcelain complexion and a ballet dancer's tight frame. He had a long, slender body, often seeming to look taller than he really was. Soon, his niece, Nicole, would be taller than him.

Speaking of whom.

Nicole, Malie and Pierre huddled together at the kitchen counter on red rattan covered high stools.

Malie's feet never reached the stool legs. Her mom would make fun of her about that. She wished she'd gotten her mom's tall genes. Her dad, Kimo, was an attractive, compact guy.

Pierre was flustered. His mom was gonna pop any minute now. They were praying it would be a safe and healthy labor.

Nicole was anxious on arrival as her ENTIRE family decided to join. She couldn't get over it. Did they ALL have to come! She wasn't embarrassed by them; she was more afraid of what they'd say about her! Those baby stories nobody wants people to know about? Yes, those. She blushed imagining them.

An hour later, it happened. The families had been sitting around a grand table in Pili Manu's pastel decorated home. One minute they were talking about the upcoming Labor Day Sales. The next minute they heard a "Shwoooosh!" followed by an entirely blasè, "Oh, shoot!" from Shelly.

The hale fell silent.

Shelly added, "Guys. There goes my water."

Sounds exploded to life. Everyone clamored, heading in one direction. The point of convergence was Shelly. She was standing now, her knees rapidly going numb. They all reinforced her in time.

Kaleo got a large beach towel ready to wrap around Shelly like a sarong. Nick and his dads ran to the garage, making sure Gabe's car was not blocked. Nicole and Malie ran to the kitchen for tupperware to pack food for the Waiting Room Picnic during delivery. Pierre had The Hospital Bag practically growing on him, ready to go. He charged around people in quick-stepped quarterback moves, and was at his mom's side in seconds. Gabe was kneeling on her other side, unsure what to do about her soiled clothes, slippers, and legs. He wielded a napkin. Shelly did her breathing as her contractions were at the 5 - 1 - 1 stage already.

"We have an hour," Pili barked. Everyone heard. Everyone got it. That was the labor countdown. Pili's manner became brisk and practiced. She suddenly commanded the whole group.

Shelly focused on breathing and counting. She felt a surge of strength through the pain as she took note of the blurry shapes orbiting her. *This is my second time. Plenty of people to help. I got this. I got this.*

Chapter 23
Aliyah Is Born

Earth
August 13, 2022
Stanton Hospital
Midnight

Teddy bears dancing on rainbows were scenes Pierre would remember forever as the digital clock signaled another minute passed. A minute in which his mom could live or die. His sister could come then leave this Earth. He wasn't sure why the maudlin thoughts haunted him. Surely he could clear them away. Maybe pule. Maybe his buddies would get their behinds here ASAP. When a guy needed his pals, he could text or call. He had neither capabilities. Left his phone at home. Hey, he remembered The Hospital Bag.

Ten points for me, he thought. Points were adding up in his head. That's how he can remain positive. *One point for not crying in fear. One point for not falling asleep with exhaustion. One point for not pacing the waiting room floor. What other points do I deserve? Hee hum, this game is not working to take away my anxiety.*

Breathe. He should breathe. He closed his eyes, pulling the air into his lungs. Then, he heard it.

"*Come through the Shimmery Wall!*
Miss you, Pals!"
Come through the Shimmery Wall!
Can't you hear my call?"

It was Ikaika.

Is he watching me at this very moment? Pierre thought, waving up at the Teddy bears before him. Button eyes gleamed in the fluorescent hospital lighting.

How does Ikaika see me? From the back? From the top? It was a fascinating thought that struck Pierre as hilarious. He was grinning now at the Teddy bears. He got up and looked at the ceiling, the four walls, and the floor. For a moment he saw the waiting room as if through the eyes of a fly on the wall. He reached up to the ceiling and the Pierre he saw in his mind's eye did the same.

Was he going crazy?

Shimmery Walls aren't like CCTV cameras. Pierre shook the thoughts from his head and laughed at himself. That was what Malie and her mom saw, as they rushed in. He looked delirious, smiling and pointing to the ceiling.

"Pierre! Are you alright?" Malie grabbed his hand to pull him to one of the cushioned loungers.

Pili followed with a rolling cooler the size of a small table, packed with goodies. Malie's mom lifted the lid. "Do you need some party food?"

Pierre's stomach rumbled at the sight of chicken, corn, sticky white jasmine rice, potato salad, fruit mix, pies, and more lined up neatly in labeled tupperware. He raised his brow at Malie, thinking *Really? Labels? Who in the world had time to do that?*

As if reading his mind, Malie nudged his ribs with her elbow and grabbed a container. She pointed to the blue painter's tape with the words "fruit mix," and said, "Yes, I'm the food label maker! It helps my stress levels to organize foods, toys, books, etc."

Pierre nodded. He already knew that. He grabbed a container too and smiled around a forkful of watermelon slices. He didn't judge Malie. Organizing was a good habit to have. He wanted to be like that. Don't ask him what his bedroom looked like. Malie would have a fit seeing it. The first thing she'd do, after a humongous sigh, is make piles of things. Categorizing the books, socks (clean and dirty separately), food snacks, bags, and anything she got her hands on. He'd let her at them all. Sometimes it was wiser to let Malie let loose like that. Whatever settles her mind and shaky hands worked for Pierre. She loved him for it.

Pili nodded to the kids and made a hand signal to Malie. Her daughter nodded. Pierre raised a brow, but didn't bother asking. Food. He had food, so the world was sane again. That is, until he heard from his parents in the delivery room. His thoughts went back to worrying: *Ooh... hope they're...*

No he wasn't going back to those sad vibes again. Uh-uh. Patience was the best virtue. And food.

The potato salad in the cooler called to him. He lifted the plastic cover, drooling over the variety of chunky starches from 'uala to baby red potatoes to good 'ole Idaho spuds. All chopped up nicely with carrot shavings, minced boiled eggs, sliced black olives, and a dab of mayo. Ohhh, heaven in a tupperware rectangle. He knew he was double-dipping with his fork, but he didn't care. He made a face as if saying, *Hey, first come first serve. Do you see anyone else here?*

Malie playfully chided him for his audacity – other people want salad! He was good enough to look guilty for half a second, before letting out a laugh with his mouth full. She passed him a napkin to avoid food falling out. He thanked her with a wink and nod, thinking, *Nothing like good food with a buddy.*

Malie giggled and hummed along with the happy symphonic music on low volume coming from the Bluetooth speakers above the Teddy bear mural. The woodwinds soothed her. Pierre swayed too, though his eyes were focused on the next food box –macaroni and four-cheese casserole. Malie had a ladle and recyclable paper products on her: bowls, plates, and cups. She pushed the ladle in front of Pierre with a serious expression. Better late than never, she did her job of rescuing the food from Pierre's double-dipping hunger. The world was saved.

Nicole and her entire family ran into the Maternity Waiting Room. It could be considered a large room with a dozen cozy chairs, a maternity magazines rack, an iced five gallon water cooler, and a small table with a single serve coffee maker and complimentary K-cups in a stand-up cabinet all organized by flavor and caffeine content. The K-cups made Malie dance happily. She loved coffee. *What great service this waiting room provided.*

Uncle Nick, the Grand-dads, Kaleo, and Nicole bundled on chairs near the door. They each had varied degrees of worry and concern on their faces. Kaleo noticed Pierre and Malie were unsupervised. She was the first to speak.

"Where's Pili? Is your grandmother coming?" she asked the boy pointedly. Her mind was frazzled being in this room. Between worrying for Shelly's labor, wondering if the kids should be alone, and fighting back the flashbacks triggered by the word 'baby', Kaleo was falling apart.

Nicole glanced at her mom funny, sensing something was up. She looked at her buddies on the pale pink cushioned lounge. There was just enough space for her on the other side of Pierre. Stuck between checking on her mom and her pals, Nicole bit her lip and bounced on her feet. Right then left. Her Grand-dads noticed her fidgeting and indecision. In a silent couple-convo with their eyes, the spouses nodded and separated across the waiting room. Court stepped towards Nicole, while John slid up next to Kaleo. Court put his arm around Nicole, turning her towards her buddies. Then he grabbed a tupperware of barbecued chicken, Nicole's fave, and insisted she sit beside Pierre. He grabbed a ladle and some paper products for Nicole, placing them on the empty reading table on her other side. She smiled up at him and nodded her thanks. He squeezed her shoulder putting his hand up for a high-five. She slapped his palm eagerly. He waved his hand for the other two kids. They laughed and high-fived him as well. Having done his duty, distracting his granddaughter, Court turned to check on his husband and daughter.

John had grabbed Kaleo's hand as soon as he'd reached the lovely, slender Hawaiian young lady. Well, thirty wasn't young, but she was half his age and he'd practically raised her as his own.

"Dad, you have that look!" Nick said, pinching John's thigh as he joined Nick and Kaleo on the opposite lounge chair.

John winked at Kaleo, "Oh, what look would that be?" Kaleo laughed knowing where this was going. Nick often teased his parents for being living, breathing, cuddly cats. They loved to lean into people for rubs and hugs, tenderly giving them back. They purred often and nudged their loved ones for TLC.

"You have that, 'She needs a hug' or 'Let me at her for some rubs and love' expression," Nick laughed and pinched his dad again.

"Hey, stop that! If I'm the fuzzy kitten giving and taking rubs, you're the grumpy red crab on the sand! Put away those pincers!" John grabbed Nick's fingers.

This made Kaleo laugh as she was just as familiar with said pincers. Nick simply wasn't a soothing, hugging kind of guy. He was as snappy and sharp in intellect as his fingers were in pinching.

It had started when they were little, as the Fines raised Kaleo and Nick as water people. While one dad went surfing, the other built sandcastles with the kids. Catching crabs was little Nick's thing. When Nick caught one, he'd admired its pincers endlessly before setting it free. He'd say, "Look how sharp they are! They are true survivors! Wow, I want to be a speedy, snappy guy like them!" Kaleo would always laugh, loving him for his oddness and his appreciation of the creatures.

The crab memory made Kaleo smile. She'd always be grateful to her family, having learned young that love is deeper than blood-ties. Her frown returned, pondering her father. Ironically, it was this same Maternity room they'd been waiting in twelve years ago. Well, not with the Teddy Bears and cushy pink lounges, and definitely not the K-cups. Ha-ha. The days of her pregnancy had been an emotional rollercoaster. She'd had no female figure in her life. Her Dads and brother were beautiful, warm, kind people. But she'd needed a mother. Kaleo had read books and attended support groups at the Community College. Those ladies were gentle and patient. Even her gyno had been helpful, answering endless questions.

At seventeen and a half, Kaleo had been on the honor roll and on the Debate Team. How'd she end up pregnant?

It was just one dumb night.

She'd gone out to celebrate the Debate Team winning State Championships. Her bestie, Phoebe, got a hold of fake IDs for them. They went to a nightclub. Dancing in the strobe lights and lasers over deafening music, Kaleo's almond eyes landed on The Man.

Marcus had been handsomer than any high school boy. He was an Army Ranger with muscles for days and half a foot taller than her 5'8", which brought her to her knees. Tall, strong, African-American guys blew her mind! Marcus was all that a guy should be.

It was just one night.

Kaleo hadn't gotten his number, nor his last name. Stupid. Truly. She'd also been underrage, which was likely why he didn't offer those details. Had he suspected she'd used a fake ID? Maybe or maybe not. Had it been her first and only time having sex? Yes. Was it consensual? Yes. Though as a minor, consent is moot. Marcus was looking at statutory rape and court marshaling had he been caught. That probably explained why she'd woken up alone in that motel room the next morning. She's lucky to be alive. It could've been worse.

The ping of her phone brought Kaleo back to the present. She sighed and looked at her brother and Dads. Her daughter and her friends. Could she really feel remorse, when life had turned out so wonderfully?

"Hold up! Hold up! Don't let her deliver without me!" said a crotchety, older woman as she wobbled into the waiting room with her cane. It went 'Clack-Clack' against the Dettol mopped tiles.

"Tūtū! You made it." Pierre ran to her side.

"Of course I made it! What! Did you think I'd die of old age on the way? Putting me in a coffin before my time! Where is my daughter?"

Pierre swallowed a giggle. Grandma under pressure was a force to be reckoned with. He said, "Dad left a message, but we weren't sure if you'd hear over your CPAP machine, mask and hose blocking sounds."

Pierre guided his grandma to an open spot. He offered her some food and refreshments. "There's a lot of 'ono food here, Tūtū, are you hungry?" He'd finished the potato salad, much to Nicole's disfavor, but there was a lot of tupperware to be explored.

"No, no, I'm not hungry! I want to see my daughter!" Tūtū was getting a little distraught. Pierre's eyes welled up and he bit his lip. His fingers began to shake, so he hid them behind his back. Malie, who sat behind him, looked at his hands. He looked over his shoulder, meeting her reassuring eyes. His were widened and shell-shocked. She intertwined their fingers, holding on tight trying to send him the message, *It's going to be alright. We'll help. We'll get Tūtū settled. This is not all on you!* His eyes closed for a split second, tightening then loosening his grip on her slender digits. Then, he took a deep three-second breath in and "Whooed!" She smiled back, knowing he was owl-breathing. He smiled back and turned back to his grandmother, still holding Malie's hands behind his back.

Granddad Court watched the pre-teens' comforting less-than a minute long exchange. It warmed him greatly. He instinctively met his husband's eyes. The older couple smiled, likely sharing the thought, *Our granddaughter's blessed to have such caring friends.* The two therapists nodded in agreement.

Nicole of all people was the one to settle Pierre's grandmother. She reintroduced herself and asked about the organic plant deliveries that day. Tūtū loved her garden, keeping it up and running as best a seventy-five year old widow could. Tūtū never tired of sharing about it. Nicole smiled and even added her own ideas about plants that she'd learned from Malie and her Grand-dads' love for nature shows.

Kaleo smiled at her daughter's decisive subject change. Nick winked at his sister thinking the same thing: *That's our girl!*

Pili was the next surprise visitor to the Maternity Waiting Room. Malie waved at her mom and pointed at Pierre, who'd been the primary enjoyer of her mom's tupperware picnic. At that moment, his grandmother was in deep conversation with Nicole, attacking their own food boxes.

This time, his was corn on the cob. The butter had melted long ago, but Pierre loved the salty goodness of each kernel. His appetite was colossal. Pili laughed, thanking Pierre for digging in. It would've been a waste of energy hauling it up here otherwise.

Pili explained that she'd been conferring with her old boss and co-workers in the Neonatal Ward about Pierre's mom. Though they spoke hypothetically for patient confidentiality purposes, Pili had learned that a woman of Shelly's description was still in the Delivery Suite. She was safe and sound, actually yelling at Gabe for his miscounting of breaths. That got Tūtū laughing, which infected the rest of the group. Pili smiled too.

Pierre's family welcomed a baby girl a few minutes before midnight. They named her Aliyah Ivy Martin. The doctors allowed them a look before sending everyone back to the waiting room.

Tūtū and Pierre sat outside in the family area. Hugging each other, they pule in gratitude for his sister's and mother's health and well-being.

Pierre wished his Grandfather was still alive to meet Aliyah. Just a glimpse of the precious bundle had sparked a huge relief in his soul. Tūtū assured him that her husband is with them in spirit. She saw him standing right there in Stanton Hospital with them.

CHAPTER 24
NICOLE'S IMMINENT THERAPY

Earth
August 14, 2022
The Fine's Home

Nicole and her family (grandfathers, mom, and uncle) returned home after getting to see Aliyah cocooned in her fuzzy blankets. After farewells and hugs to Pierre and Malie, Nicole and her mom followed her grand-dad's car to their place.

They gathered in the sitting room to celebrate and recap the birth.

Her grand-dads sneakily inquired about Nicole's mental health per Kaleo's request. Nicole seemed happy enough and the night had proven she had two good friends in her life. But they wanted to make sure.

Nicole painted a picture of emotional stability, proceeding to distract them all by showing how much she has learnt from Kaleo's legal textbooks. The Grand-dads weren't fooled by her surface layer of hunkydory. Yet the day and night had been long, so they chose their battles. She said her Goodnites followed by rounds of kisses before heading to sleep. She lingered in the doorway of the guest bedroom adjacent to the sitting room. Her room was too far away. She knew they'd begin the real talk now.

John sat on the couch beside Kaleo again, waiting for Court to return from the kitchen. Court found cranberry juice in the pantry.

"Kaleo, be a doll and open the wine cellar for me, please? "

Kaleo laughed and got him his favorite burgundy, teasing him about his splash together method of mixing juice and wine.

"A splash of this and a splash of that make for delicious refreshment!" Court bopped happily at the kitchen counter.

Nick laughed from the couch, shaking his head at his dad's singing. It was for healing.

Nick sang his Dads' most frequent therapy hymn: '"Even if you can't carry a note! Sing from your heart, unashamedly emote!" Court gave him cheers, joining them as John let out a sleepy yawn. Kaleo laughed as she released the tension from her neck. Her head sank back into the satin quilted pillows.

They decompressed with their drinks under the whirling ceiling fan and watching the sashaying dance of the palm fronds on their porch. The moonlight glistened off the crystal windchimes, their gentle clattering soft xylophone mallet beats in the air.

The Fines smiled at their daughter and sister, Kaleo. This 'ohana had provided a nourishing, safe harbor for her since she and Nick had been preschoolers. The two had been both outcasts in a sad ethnically fragile community. Nick was a Japanese-American four year old with interracial, gay adopted parents. Kaleo was an impoverished native Hawaiian child. Kaleo's widowed, single-father was too busy surviving to pay attention to his daughter. Preschool Nick would bring Kaleo home like a lost puppy. Her father had actually thanked the doctors repeatedly, as they'd saved him after-school funding. The Fines adored the small brown child with her messy pony tails and church-donated mix-matched clothing. They'd hānai little Kaleo immediately. Their son and Kaleo had been inseparable for more than a dozen years when Kaleo became pregnant and homeless at 17 years old. It had been a no-brainer taking her into their home. She'd been stubborn about it. Though she was balancing community college courses and being hāpai, Kaleo insisted on doing household chores daily in exchange for room and board. They'd gone along to save her pride. Now that Kaleo and Nick were "grown ups," John felt proud for having a hand in raising such wonderful individuals. His heart felt warm and fuzzy looking over at his son and daughter. John worried for his son, Nick. Sometimes love takes a while to catch up to a person.

Nick closed his eyes, soaking up the lavender breeze from his dad's favorite diffuser. Their chicken coop outside rattled and a few peeps and squeaks floated through the patio window. Nick smiled to himself recalling the luminescent ʻehu and oranges of Marv the Rooster from the Naʻiwi's next door. Marv was likely paying a visit to his girls. Boy, how can a manu get lucky and not him? He didn't need a pen full of lovers, Heaven help him. Just one faithful one, please.

Practicing law likely didn't help the "man search." Especially as the Assistant Honolulu District Attorney. He got the bad guys. But who wanted to date the "Good Guy?" Only in the movies do the heroes win the fair lady, or guy, in his case. It's the rebels without a cause, who got the hotties, so to speak. Here he was, sounding like his niece with her colloquialisms. The hard part about finding a partner was his elected position. The ones he was really attracted to sometimes came with some 'unacceptable', by some idiotic standard, background. He hated it, but that was his life. He was appreciative of his loving dads, and especially of his Tita, Kaleo, and niece and namesake, Nicole. Yes, that was enough.

* * *

"Hmmm...poor Uncle Nick.

Nicole sat on the tatami mats she'd pulled out from the guest room closet. The adults whispered and stared off into nothing while drinking their decaf coffees and wine. Side note: Malie would laugh over the decaf. Like, what's the sense of having coffee without the kick? For flavor? Suck on a coffee candy. Save the water, coffee grounds, and electricity! Anyway, Uncle Nick looked really forlorn out there. Her neck cranked from peeking around the corner. She'd gone from twisting her body at the doorway to sinking down on the mat from behind Grand-dad's old clothes. Moth balls. Ugh. Those white plastic insect repellents rolled out from behind the retro outfits. A mixture of detergent and carpet cleaner permeated the air as she kicked the rolling irritants away.

Saving Uncle Nick. She often saw his face in those hidden moments when he thought no one was watching. Well, they weren't hidden at all. She saw how sad he was. A lot. Nicole was resolved now to intern at his office. Uncle needed love. She'd help him find it.

Chapter 25
Pili's Questions

Earth
August 14, 2022
Malie Manu's Home

Upon returning home at 1 am that early morning, Pili and Malie went right to bed. It had been a long, emotional day and night. They woke up still exhausted but the party clean up called to them. Everyone had run to kākoʻo Pierre's ʻohana, leaving a big after-party mess. It was worth it: Aliyah's healthy and Shelly's fully supported and loved.

Pili watched Malie scrub the tupperware from the Waiting Room Picnic. She smiled remembering how much Pierre could gobble down. That young man's appetite was fierce. Malie had a small smile on her face. The sun shone through the kitchen window creating a bluish glow to her dark brown hair, luminescent like a crow's wings. There was a bubble of soap on her turtle-rimmed eyeglasses. The preteen contentedly hummed to herself some elevator music from the Waiting Room. The high and low "la, la, la's" made Pili laugh. That captured Malie's attention.

"How's the living room mom? Do you need help breaking down the extended table, folding the leaves down?" Malie continued to sing melodic sweet sounds.

"I've got it. I have another load of laundry to put in and vacuuming to do." Pili watched Malie wipe the dishes dry.

"After you finish that, can you fold these dish towels and cloth napkins on the dining room table?" Pili asked. Malie gave a thumbs up. Pili smiled, putting the basket down by the table for Malie. She turned towards the washer and dryer outside, then stopped herself. The music Malie hummed made her recall Stanton Hospital for some reason. Particularly memories of watching the kids.

Something had been bugging her about Malie and her friends. Meeting their families made Pili happy but didn't chase away this... this niggling, wiggling, feeling that something was *off*. These kids were extraordinarily close and seemed to talk in a silent language.

"Hey, Malie, will you put that down and come here for a second?" Pili kept her voice light and not too inquisitive. She sat at the dining table and patted the seat next to her.

Malie nodded, put the dish towel down, and joined her mom. She sensed where this was going. All morning her mom would suddenly stop what she was doing to stare at her. She didn't wonder about the staring, having a hunch it was about the Secret Club. Last night was the longest she'd seen them all together. Malie sat sideways to face her mother, her hands folded, her demeanor open and calm.

Pili studied Malie, simply surprised by her countenance and presence. *Who is this child? Is this MY child?* She thought. "Who are you? Are you Pod Person Malie again?" Pili joked, as she often does now, about Pod Malie.

"You say that a lot, Mom," Malie giggled, taking everything in stride. "Am I that different?"

Pili nodded her head vigorously. "Yes! You used to hide behind your books and not talk to people, even if it affects your grades in class. You had social anxiety issues longer than my arm!" Pili was stretching the truth a little, but her daughter got the point.

Malie laughed at that, knowing her mom didn't want the old Malie back. She just didn't understand who THIS Malie was. "Hee, hee, you've got me thinking in third person now like a hip hop rapper in an interview."

Malie wiggled her eyebrows and lowered her voice, grabbing a utensil from the rack at the center of the table as a pretend mic. She mimicked a rapper: "Mr. Foxy loves these interviews. Keep asking me about my new album!"

Pili broke out laughing! "You are incredible! Mr. Foxy! Ha. Ha. We all think in third person in our head. When we do it outloud, then it's humorously pretentious like that!"

Malie laughed too, "Yes, those performer's and influencer's interviews are a bit uppity to see on YouTube, but entertaining for sure!"

Pili pointed at Malie, "You see, that's what I'm talking about. Your sense of humor and gregariousness is off the charts." Pili smiled with her hands up in the air like she couldn't explain what was happening.

Malie nodded but didn't feel the need to explain herself nor her personality. She had wrapped up her research on adolescent sexual reproductive health way before she got her ma'i. Now she was just waiting out for the storm of puberty to pass.

Pili watched her daughter in wonder. The calm, comfortable-in-her-own-skin young lady was not Baby Manu. Was she? Maybe the New Malie? Certainly not Adult Malie yet.

Malie smiled at her mom, nodding in understanding as if she could read her mom's mind. Maybe she could? Maybe her sensing her mother's confusion about her behavioral changes was part of her mental growth? Understanding that she can't control how her mom feels. She is only in charge of her own feelings. Malie was maturing.

Pili had a hunch Malie had nothing else to share about her personality. Pili switched gears, asking, "So, about Pierre and Nicole. How is it you all get along so well? You're very different. Different lifestyles, ethnicities, and family types."

Malie raised her brows and was quiet for a minute. Then she suddenly broke out in laughter and responded, "Mom, we're not different at all!" Their similarities outweighed their differences. She raised her delicate palm up and ticked off the SC's similarities with her fingers.

Malie explained, "All of our mother's were teen Moms struggling with poverty while pregnant with us. We all suffered socially and mentally during the COVID shutdown. We're all part-Hawaiian and struggle with that identity. Most importantly, we all support each other's interests, preferences, and difficulties." Malie put her hand down and nodded. Her voice was steady and confident. Yet, her eyes teared up a little as if thinking of her friends touched her deeply.

Pili leaned forward to hug her daughter. Malie hugged back and patted her mom's back, strangely reassuring the elder Manu, "I'm okay, Mom. The Secret Club is wonderful. You don't need to worry about them or their affect on my personality!"

Pili released Malie and squeezed her slender shoulder. Her daughter was much smaller than her, taking after her father, Kimo. He was a gorgeous, slim, dark-skinned man. Petite but svelte and stylish. Her daughter took after him in body structure, fashion sense, and aloha. Malie was filled with a lot of love. Pili instinctively knew her daughter was the heart of their Club.

CHAPTER 26
IKAIKA'S LONELY DAY

Manaful World
August 14, 2022
Koa Forest, Elder Territory
Ikaika's Mansion

Being just over eight hundred Manaful years, Ikaika looked the same age as a fourteen year old human would. But everything from his thoughts to his mannerisms spoke of a Manaful past his thousandth birthday. An upbringing such as his isn't ordinary even by Manaful standards.

Having lost his parents years ago, Ikaika came into adult-thinking much earlier than his contemporaries. For years, his lessons were made of universal concepts of healing, psychology, and Elder Ethics. Puna raised him and spoke to him, as an adult. In Earth years, he'd barely been out of second grade when Puna began his leadership training. They'd counsel, dropping in to visit every Elder in Manaful from Elder Pele at her volcanoes to Elder Polu within the abysses of the ocean.

Ikaika was both a "grown up" and a child in Manaful ways. That day, his childish side shone through. The SC didn't mind skipping a visit to him. Yet, Ikaika was bored out of his mind without them. Sure, he could magically conjure any game, book, movie, series, or electronic device imaginable. Or molecularly travel all over the world. Can one imagine how wild a human child would go with that kind of Mana at their fingertips? Nonetheless, none of that material entertainment or distractions mattered to Ikaika. When a being needs company, nothing else matters. He hovered around his crib feeling like he hadn't seen the SC since *forever*. Alone in his mansion in the sky, Ikaika sang for his human buddies.

Ikaika's Song: Missing Pals:

"What is it like to miss one's pals?
Tears you up–love those guys and gals!
The pleasure of their company, incomparable
We were blessed, we were inseparable
Talking about anything in the world
Singing and laughing, life's a whirl
Wind of joy but sometimes there's misunderstandings
Which is expected when our minds are meandering
From this topic to that or this issue or that
I feel like it's been forever since we just sat
And breathed together, appreciated what matters
Each other's presence and love rather
Than what's missing or one's weaknesses
In the end we are each other's witnesses

Of growth and truth like rays of light
Knowing that with patience we might
Bond again. Hug again. Be together again."

Ikaika sighed, eyes closed to relive his memories with the humans. Pierre's fears of rejection by his teammates and their increasing misdeeds toward him. Ikaika sometimes watched the football players via the Shimmery Wall, disliking how the teammates mistreated Pierre. Their bigotry was subtle and vicious in its slow chipping away at Pierre's confidence. Ikaika took a deep breath feeling upset on Pierre's behalf. He unclenched his fists as he prayed to Source for levelness of mind and spirit.

Malie's laughter rang in his mind, bringing a fuzzy warmth to his heart. *Mahalo, Source.* His bookish pal was ironically the strongest of them all. Malie's the backbone of the SC with her fierce kākoʻo of her pals and aloha for all that they are. Ikaika smiled, remembering her kindness to the many animals under Puna's care. Ikaika couldn't think of a bigger hearted being than Malie.

Now, Nicole was still a mystery after all this time. Ikaika scrunched his lips together. He frowned and closed one eye as he squatted on his Turkish rug to wake up his puppies. The lapping of their tongues and soft fluffy ears tickled his cheeks. Holding them was getting harder as they grew bigger every day. An armful for sure.

The puppies loved it here. Fresh grass grew where they ran. Rubber squirrels and bunnies squeaked about to get caught and shaken as they played. From time to time frisbees hovered around Ikaika and he would throw them to much excited yapping.

Nicole loved his pups, playing with them every chance she got. Every visit here, she'd make time to roll on the rug with the labradors. Cookie loved to jump on her belly. Brownie insisted on climbing her shoulders and resting his furry head on top of hers. His paws would balance on her ears. If he could, he'd telepathically say, *"I'm the king of Nicole Mountain!"* She let them do this to her – such a softie. Yet, when speaking with her, she was a tough cookie. Sassy. Snappy. Smart. Ikaika took a big breath again, scratching under Cupcake's chin like he loves.

"Miss them! Auwe!"

Before Nicole, Pierre and Malie appeared in his life he was always invested in his training. Those days were endless with the taskmaster kumu Gramps is. When he'd first learned to hover, he kept tripping on the invisible platform.

"Is it moving, Gramps?" 420 year old Ikaika (first grade like) asked Puna who was levitating beside him.

"No, the hovering platform stays still. It moves when you tell it to." Puna patiently explained.

"Oh, like human skateboards? I step on and roll off to my destination?" Ikaika got excited and started to hop. "Those boards are really neat! The wheels are soo tiny, yet they hold the human's weight all balanced like!"

Gramps smiled but shook his head, "No, Ikaika, those boards move on wheels and without human will, if there's an incline or fierce wind."

"Oh, yes, I've seen accidents like that in the Shimmery Wall! Okay, so the hovering platform is not skateboard like. Umm, then what is it like?" Ikaika lifted his leg and attempted to step into thin air.

"Ohhhh!" He shouted. "Going to fall!"

He did. But not on the ground. He was on his butt – levitating.

"Gramps! I'm levitating like you! You didn't say I could do that!"

Puna shook his head and let out an exasperated breath. This was taking longer than he thought it would. His bioluminescent maroon and ʻehu robe lifted and danced with humor. It wooshed around the elder's legs, almost touching Ikaika's head as Puna knelt in midair beside his grandson.

"I levitated you. You're on your own hovering platform now. Get up, young one!"

Ikaika mumbled in his mind, *Well, if you told me I could levitate, then I wouldn't have been nervous of stepping on thin air and falling on my butt. Which I did anyway! Except in midair!*

Heard that! Puna projected into Ikaika's head, and continued to TP, *Now you're on it. Stand up and tell the platform where you want to go.*

I don't understand! Little Ikaika whined, still sitting on his butt in midair.

Puna looked up to the sky as if asking Source for help. He took a deep breath, reciting a prayer. Then he looked at his now pouting grandson. He lent Ikaika a hand and helped the two-foot Manaful to his feet. He dusted off imaginary specks of dust from Ikaika's chubby knees and slowly projected, *You are still learning. Be patient with yourself and me. Be persistent with the Mana.*

Ikaika nodded, sucking his upper lip under his teeth. He took a huge breath, puffing his tiny chest out with determination.

Puna smiled encouragingly, *Now, Ikaika, tell the platform how fast you want it to go. How high. Imagine how big you want the platform to be – as big as your bedroom? As small as your jacuzzi? You are in control of the platform. Don't forget that!*

Ikaika released his lip as a tiny smile formed and got bigger across his face like a gradual sunrise. Brightened and excited, the little Manaful peered up at his grandpa and clapped his hands, *I'm in control!*

"Control" had been the magic word.

After that day, Ikaika hovered everywhere. He took himself on mini-tours around towns, within forests, and above seas. Manafuls were used to seeing Puna's heir whizzing by, 'cause this one liked to go fast!

"Roof! Roof!" Cupcake's barking and pawing at Ikaika's arm woke him up from his memory reels. Ikaika smiled, thinking of his younger self. He laughed. Ikaika shook his head admitting to himself that he'd been a slow learner at times stretching Puna's patience.

Aside from his grandpa, Ikaika didn't have other Manafuls or a group of buddies to hang out with. The only friend he had growing up was Maka. Sadly, that dwarf would disappear for long periods of time when Uli had one of his fits.

During those days and nights, Maka had been imprisoned and abused in his own house. Those had been frightening times. Ikaika had missed him dearly.

Puna says, *Never wish ill will on others or be glad for one's death.*

But Uli pushed that rule to the limit.

Ikaika remembered one night years ago asking Puna to telepathically 'check in' on Maka. Ikaika had tried continuously but was always blocked. He would hover over the Sandalwood Mansion daily wishing to get in there and make sure his buddy was alright. On one evening three years ago he'd hovered too close. It had almost been perilous.

Ikaika's Shimmery Wall Viewer showed his dark memories like a movie projected on a theater screen. The Sandalwood Mansion glowed in the evening light. Fireflies glittered amid the browning puakenikeni petals on the mossy forest floor. Rustling branches waved at him when a racoon mom scampered through, creating a pathway for her trailing young.

Ikaika's hovering platform wooshed to a stop from his normal speedster pace, violet sarong swinging against his leg. He looked up at Maka's window. It had been dark but he saw Maka's face through the curtains. He must've been standing on his desk. Maka waved.

Ikaika TP, "*Brother, are you okay in there?*"

Maka shook his head. His hand came up. His hand formed a puppet mouth talking with his four fingers together being the top lip and his thumb being the bottom. Then he covered his puppet's mouth with his other hand.

Ikaika couldn't believe what he was seeing. Hand motions? What's going on? Ikaika's TP was worrisome, "*What's happened to you? Why can't you TP?*"

Maka shook his head again. Ikaika heard sniffles and muffled wheezing, whimpering. Was Maka crying? What the heck?

"*Are you hurt? Can I do anything? Can I help you?*" Ikaika's TPs were becoming frantic. He TP Puna, "*Gramps, I'm at Maka's, something's happening to him. Know it. He's in trouble up there! Gotta get him out!*"

Puna had been silent for a moment. Ikaika heard him breathing, but not a word for what seemed like a lifetime.

"Grandpa? Well? Can you check on him?" Ikaika's projections became anxious.

Soothing waves preceded Puna's voice. *"He's physically safe, Ikaika, that's all we can ascertain. Otherwise, we have to respect Uli's methods of parenting."*

"What about mentally? Doesn't that count for something? Uli can't keep him locked up there indefinitely, can he?" Ikaika twisted his sarong with his hands and kept bumping his shoulder on a boulder. He turned and leaned his forehead on the cool limestone. Groaning, he grumbled to Puna who, as usual, waited out Ikaika's moods.

"Why do I feel so powerless?" Ikaika cried against the boulder.

"We all do sometimes," Puna TP, *"Lift up your worries to Source. Do your reciting of prayers always. Maka will be over at 'Ula'ula hale in a few days or so, like he often is. We'll help him then, like we often do."*

"I know. I know," Ikaika understood. This was how things were.

Puna signed off, but not before warning Ikaika to stay away from the force field surrounding the mansion. They were energized akin to electric fences that kept animals from leaving or entering yards on Earth. Ikaika wondered if that made Maka a caged dog. Of course, like most youngsters, the word "don't" was a red flag compelling them to "do" the exact opposite.

Ikaika waved at Maka who waved back. Despite Puna's warnings, Ikaika slowly approached the window. The force field crackled and turned red as he neared it.

He shouted, since TP was not an option, "Maka! Did you check the control rooms? Can you turn the force field off?" Ikaika knew Uli lacked the patience for self-created mental force fields, preferring to use Mana-cell generated ones.

Maka shook his head again, pantomiming a door and key, then throwing away the key.

Ikaika ran out of steam and was about to leave.

Zap! Ikaika ducked as a lazer shot pinged past his left leg, leaving burn tracks on his outer thigh straight through his sarong. Ikaika nimbly ducked behind some palm fronds.

"Ack! Oh, Shhhhessh!" Ikaika screamed.

"Ikaika!" Maka finally spoke.

"Maka! I'm good. I'm okay! Are you okay in there?"

But Maka was suddenly gone. There was no more noise. Not a peep. Ikaika wanted to shout at Source. *Why is this happening?* He lifted his sarong, lightly touching the burn mark. He winced. Getting on his hovering platform, he looked back at Maka's empty window forlornly. Prayed his brother was safe. Went home.

Days later, Maka visited and appeared fine physically. Mentally he was a little out of sorts. As the week went by, he loosened up, enjoying himself. Nourished again with Puna's and Ikaika's love and respect. Joy, too. That helped Maka the most.

Swoosh! Wooshh! Ikaika flushed the toilet, looking at his present day self in the mirror, washing his hands. The bathroom disappeared when he walked out.

Ikaika was grateful to be older. Thankfully those days of witnessing Maka's imprisonment were long behind them. He sighed. That's how it had been for Maka. It had been a vicious cycle. *Sorry, Puna, but I'm glad Uli's dead!*

Maka was literally forced to kill his Gramps.

Now Maka is an elder, always on elder business. Ikaika was still a mere Heir. If it were not for Puna's insistence, Ikaika would be unaware of what elder business meant.

As it were... Ikaika suddenly perked up and turned to the walls. He spread out his hands. Beyond the walls, the starry sky of Manaful and the velvet darkness of the Koa Forest canopy swirled away. The landscape was replaced by notes and reports of the Elder Council.

Who exactly supported the Elder Council to be so Closed Doors? Ikaika questioned himself as he looked through the official documents. *Why all this secrecy? Elder Alaka'i and grandfather certainly don't support it.*

The 'documents' of Manaful world didn't exist as paper unless it needed to be. What Ikaika saw on the walls was the content prepared for Hopohopo education, stored in the Manaful 'Hive Mind'. The Manaful Hive Mind was not exclusive to elders, as it is a part of Source. It is a mental space shared by all Manafuls, and its existence is why telepathy is possible in the first place.

In short, the collective Hive Mind was equivalent to the Internet's 'Public Domain'.

Ikaika found records of an ancient council meeting that had voted to 'filter' its meeting minutes from the public. This is it, Ikaika told himself. This is when it happened.

He was not surprised when he found Uli at the bottom of it. Keeping Hopohopo ignorant and without advancement had been to his extreme benefit. The majority of the council had taken Uli's side and passed the motion. Thereafter, the Elder

Council always put out a sterile record of its meetings on the Hive and kept juicy details for itself.

Ikaika frowned and harnessed his Mana to shift to his own memories. He found Puna telling him years ago about the Elder Council choosing to limit the technology available to Hopohopo. Advanced Mana Tech would give the Hopohopo more power. The Council had feared advanced Mana Tech would be used for a rebellion against Manafuls. The treatment of them like a second-class society was clear in the hidden records.

They made the decision to limit Mana-Tech only after the motion for secrecy was favored. The Hopohopo only knew what the council wanted them to know. The whole system currently in place was the result of Uli's various meddling in Council Decisions. He monetized this fear and oppression.

There is a moral question to this that I feel is difficult to answer. I really wish the humans were here, Ikaika thought, looking up. The original view returned so he could see the stars. *Or maybe just see them.*

Wait a minute. He was Manaful. Ikaika burst out laughing, rolling around in midair. Right side up, he brushed tears from his cheeks and went to the Shimmery Wall for viewing on a blank wall, still levitating. Instead of his own memories, he tuned it to his Earth Loved Ones.

There they were. Ikaika's Shimmery Wall was powerful enough to allow sounds of laughter and the smell of grilled buns to pass between the worlds. The dwarf took lungful after lungful of that yummy barbeque goodness, grinning. His eyes glittered to replay the hospital scene. That was yesterday. He swiped the air to move to today.

The human children were with their families. They were getting together a lot. Mostly at Pierre's. Shelly seemed to have bounced right back up.

Ikaika smiled to see Malie, Pierre and Nicole at peace with no worries. Now that they'd found each other and grown closer, would the Manaful World become useless to them? *Will they stop wanting to visit?*

Ikaika felt a tingle in the air. Powerful Mana was concentrating here. As if a whole barrel of it was enroute to visit Ikaika. Sure enough, Elder Puna appeared a nano-second later. Rather more than a barrel. His arrival sent a golden pulse through the transparent walls.

Sorry for the rude intrusion, grandson. But there's much work to be done.

Work?

Yes. You are part of the efforts to improve this world. By default. Remember?

Ikaika sighed. Right. He may not be an elder but he was Puna's Heir Apparent. That was a job title. He had always helped his grandfather with healing and nature-tending work. Ikaika happily thought he would be doing that for the rest of his life. Those didn't feel like 'work' because he loved the beauty, sounds and smells of nature. Times were changing. Lapu sprang new conflicts often, using the Inventor to create a thousand and one ways to bamboozle the Elder Council.

Ikaika shrugged. *What's new?*

Puna obliged with, *"Ejad has done a lot without a soul being aware - dozens of machines are being uncovered in isolated patches of nature."*

Once the Mana mist in the area was depleted, Hopohopo poachers and loggers would arrive and decimate the whole place. In the meantime many of the machines would somehow disappear.

Mind-melding, Ikaika saw that the Elder Council was moving the barrels to the mountaintops. The cold would slow them. No one could deactivate the machines.

"We have no idea how much Mana mist has been harvested already," Puna fretted.

Ikaika gasped and pointed at the Koa Forest below. A huge patch of trees lost color as they watched. The patch grew like a quick cancer.

Elder Puna held down Ikaika's shoulder to keep him from MT down there. *"Be patient. These Mana barrels are strange and new. I'd prefer you kept out of this."*

"How did they place it on our property?" Ikaika was livid. But he stayed put and allowed his grandfather time to collect his wits.

Inhaling and exhaling deeply, loudly, Elder Puna MT down to the Koa Forest alone. He found a Mana harvesting barrel at once.

Elder Puna cooled the air around the machine. Snowflakes appeared in the air and the metal turned white with ice. Puna was able to thicken the ice till the machine was encased in a block.

But the runes lit up red. The ice it contacted melted into rainbow mists that it sucked up. It released an oily essence that threaded through the ice as if looking for a way out. Puna lowered the temperature further to thicken the containment.

"Freezing slows it down, but not significantly," Puna TP to Ikaika, who was watching from above. *"Don't come down. I will freeze it and move the entire block."*

Puna levitated and let loose. Where the machine stood a glacier grew to enormous proportions. Before hovering the machine to another location, he regrew the dead koa patches. He really loved this Koa Forest he'd gifted Ikaika.

CHAPTER 27
SPYING PALAPALAI

Earth
August 15, 2022
Wright Middle School

Wright Middle School stood on a hill all by itself, lording over the suburbs below since 1932. Half the school grounds had been reconstructed a decade ago and the other half remained old. The entire gym constituted the old half. The CCTV cameras always looked odd against the withering, cracked walls and corrugated rooftop.

Behind the back wall of the old gym, accessed through a narrow passage between stairwells, grew a thicket of mangrove, hala and ʻākala shrubs. They were seemingly defended along the edge by a heavy growth of feathery ferns that were called, according to Malie's new phone app, palapalai. Families of mongoose, rats, cats and birds used this pocket of green as a safe space away from traffic and people.

There was scurrying within the ferns that Malie was sure were mongoose. *Could the plural be mongeese, I wonder?* she giggled to herself. She'd been startled by their scurrying often when the Secret Club first started to meet here. Now she listened to twigs breaking and foliage rustling with a soft smile. Malie liked waiting here alone for the others. She was listening to a particularly feisty robin song when footsteps came round the corner: sneakers that skipped instead of stomping. Pierre.

"Hey, did you hear they're going to build a new gym?" Pierre said the moment he saw her. He took off his cap and rubbed his head of hair. It had gotten shaggy, growing over his ears.

Malie was surprised about the gym getting knocked down. She didn't usually keep track of sports-related school activities. Including the gym. "Really? When?"

"Probably next year. They say it's gonna be hugely extravagant like a professional athletics center!" Pierre was excited. It didn't take much to excite Pierre ever since Aliyah came along. His energy was lively and fun, always tickling her heart.

Malie touched the spongy moss on the wall. It held a special piece of her life, connected to her recent growth and friendships. She looked around the pocket of nature and breathed in the smells of dirt. The animals would be pushed out and plantlife uprooted. "That means they'll knock this down."

"Yep. And we get a fully locked and loaded gym that will boost our school to new heights!" Pierre did a shimmy and mimicked a slam dunk.

"You got that right out of Coach's mouth didn't you?" Malie said.

"Got what out of who's mouth?" Nicole said in a carrying whisper as she ran around the corner and slammed herself against the wall. She peeked round the corner as if to make sure she wasn't being followed. Malie's brows raised at Pierre who simply smiled knowingly. He'd seen little Kona following Nicole around campus.

"Gym's being rebuilt," Pierre launched into his scoop again.

Absentmindedly, Nicole gave him a high-five for the news and nodded appreciatively. The school did need new facilities. Instead of picking up her friend's excited conversation, she checked her phone for the time.

"Listen, our parents are gonna text any minute so we better step out and back into this dimension real quick," Nicole said.

Malie gave Pierre a funny look projecting her thoughts *out and back real quick?* Pierre frowned and shook his head at Malie, silently answering, "*What's the rush?* Malie shrugged.

Nicole missed their exchange, still looking at her phone. She noticed the silence, looking up at Pierre. "How's Aliyah and Mom?"

Pierre beamed. Loved talking about his baby tita. "They're doing great! Malie's mum keeps checking up on us. Dad's taken a short leave. Uncle Trevor might drop by soon. He's an actor like dad and he's meeting with some TV producers here about a long-term gig. Dad's over the moon and proud of his buddy."

Nicole and Malie often heard Pierre mention his godfather Trevor Mālama. Nicole suddenly felt a clenching in her piko, something sparked about his uncle. A memory. Aha! Yes!

"Pierre, did you say once that your Uncle Trevor was a famous, handsome gay model turned actor?" Nicole now ignored her phone and was bouncing like Pierre. A bee was in her bonnet now. Malie laughed at her friends' joyfulness, though she wasn't sure where Nicole was going with this. She looked at Pierre questioningly, silently asked, *What's happening? Why are you so happy?* He made a funny face and laughed, *Don't know but she seems happy, so that makes me happy!* That thought made Malie laugh too. She turned back to Nicole excitedly.

Nicole noticed the half-second mental exchange, but was used to their twin-mind speak. She rolled her eyes and asked Pierre, "Well, my Uncle Nick, remember him from the baby shower and the Maternity Waiting Room?"

Pierre and Malie nodded their heads and said, "Yeah!" at the same time. Then, "Jinx!" again, at the same time.

Nicole shook her head at them. "You twins never quit! Anyway, he's been really sad lately and I think it's because he keeps bringing home loser guys!"

Pierre and Malie were shocked by her description of her uncle's personal preferences.

Malie frowned and pointed to Pierre, silently saying, *Uhh, you take this one!*

Pierre frowned back and gave a big sigh, but gave her a fake mad look with his eyebrows scrunched up, answering, *Ohhh! Okaayy, but only because it may be about my gay uncle!*

Malie winked at him and gave him a thumbs up for encouragement.

Pierre turned to Nicole, "Riiight, you've mentioned him. Said you grew up with positive, gay role-models: your grand-dads and your uncle Nick. That I should meet with them more often." Pierre was shuffling his feet now with hands behind his back. He was still unsure how to converse with gay adult men. Even his Uncle Trevor.

Nicole got closer and patted his arm. She frowned, thinking to herself, *Should I continue the convo about our uncles?* Her piko told her to go for it, that these men might be made for each other. You never knew.

She said, "I'd like to play matchmaker for our Uncles. Will you do some reconnaissance work for me? Check if he's single. Send me his IG handle or pics?" *There, I got it out. See, I'm brave.*

Malie giggled at the matchmaking. Pierre looked at the girls questioningly. Unsure what he was getting into.

He went for it, "Uhh, I'll do what I can."

Malie clapped her hands.

Nicole gave him a thumbs up and a "Mahalo, this will be great!"

The otherworldly traveling tune started in their heads. They knew it was Ikaika by the bouncing, jolly vibe all the way through.

Ikaika's Song: Please Come Back:

"The crows call for your lovely visage
Come on, I'll even throw in a massage
Things get funner when you three are here
Is funner even a word? Look my rhyming's in gear
Making up words for my buddies on Earth
Give me some room on stage - I've got girth!
Love that you're all happy over there
It seems like forever - look, I've grown my hair!
No, really, join me just for a second or two
Give a guy a hug, please, no more "Toodeloos!"

I await your kindness and lovely faces
Your open hearts and warm embraces.
I know each minute disappears like in a sieve.
Oh, Mahalo to Source for any time you can give.
Please come back, miss you, my dears
Please come back, to waylay my fears."

"Aw, he sure sounds like he has a lot to say," Nicole noted as Pierre and Malie bumped shoulders with hers excitedly. A soft breeze played with their hair and the knee-high grass at their feet.

"I just want to check on Elder Alaka'i," Malie said. Pierre nodded, pursing his lips seriously.

The Shimmery Wall opened. They stepped through, not noticing that apart from the schoolyard mongooses there was one human secretly watching them from the ferns: a very nosey sixth grader.

CHAPTER 28
PUIE FOR ALAKAʻI

Manaful World
August 15, 2022
House Opalescent Territory
Elder Alakaʻi's Villa

The SC arrived via the Shimmery Wall directly into Elder Alakaʻi's conservatory. There were no walls, only an invisible force field that strangely still welcomed the makani. Natural light and plant life abounded as the room stretched seamlessly into a forest beyond.

The kids were both excited to see Alakaʻi and more of his Villa. Pierre wanted to cry upon entering the heavenly place. His late grandpa had been an organic farmer, and this was his grandpa's dreamworld. He took a deep breath and looked at Malie, knowing she'd feel like him. She gave him a heart gesture, thinking, *I know. I love it too!*

Nicole wasn't as into the landscaping, preferring to see how form met function. She was approached by a floating table-sized sunflower with a tray of refreshments nestled on the fluorescent orange head. Not at all shocked, as this was Manaful World, Nicole grabbed a wooden mug without hesitation. Yummmy. Iced guava juice. The cookies appeared to have chocolate chips with walnuts. Oh, her favorite. *Did they get that from my head?* She thought. *Probably.* She ate that too. The sunflower table waited for her to say, "Thank you. That's all," before gliding at waist level towards Malie and Pierre. Malie's "Oh, so pretty!" got a laugh from Pierre who took his share before politely sending the flower away.

They'd seen floating kukui nut lights before, but they never witnessed a floating burning coconut oil torch. The wooden torches were soldier-like in efficiency and stationed a few feet apart on the perimeter of the room. The smell was unforgettably decadent like sunbathing on a gorgeous beach rubbing coconut oil all over. "Woah, love that smell!" Nicole whispered. Pierre and Malie nodded in agreement.

They turned to Ikaika's voice.

"Elder Alaka'i keeps falling in and out of trances," Ikaika projected to the SC.

He was awake but stared blankly at the world through slitted eyes. Elder Puna projected understanding among the SC. The Spirits had severed Alaka'i's mind from his body. That meant the elder's mind was no longer anchored to his brain. Malie held her heart as the pained to hear of the Elder's predicament. Pierre squeezed her shoulders. He looked for somewhere for them to sit and take it all in. A brown and gold shaded kamani tree bench popped out of nowhere. Malie and Pierre sat gently and leaned in for the update.

"It is something we all take for granted," Puna fretted. *"We've never thought of this before. What can we do if the brain stops being our mind's physical anchor?"*

"Elder Alaka'i is unable to tether himself to the waking world," Malie said tearily, her hands pressed together in prayer. "Even while he is awake, like a person in a coma!" A soft handkerchief appeared in her hand. She said, "Mahalo" to Alaka'i's magic hale.

Pierre asked the hale for a cold, icey glass of orange juice, having returned his cup to the sunflower. His OJ appeared in a snap. He sent a silent thanks to the powers that be.

Puna nodded. "*Charmaine has to constantly pull his mind back into his brain, holding it there. When she goes away or rests, Alaka'i drifts away.*"

Elder Alaka'i's resting pod bobbed near human eye level, with Puna and Ikaika hovering beside it. The children lost all thought. They were amazed by the ginger bud as big as a king sized bed. Its glowing fuchsia petals looked cushiony soft. There were no medical apparatus connected to it.

Nicole realized their medicine was of the magical variety.

Ikaika nodded.

The senior elder's robes hung like damp sheets below him, still glowing, but with a waned light.

"*My brother is no different than a log in this state. His mind roams in the Spirit Realm.*" Puna's pained tone echoed in their minds, breaking their hearts.

The SC held hands and sent silent prayers to the Elder Prime.

Puna's calm facade cracked. Stricken and grieved, he covered his face with his hands. The Elder's red robe hugged him tight.

An ochre felt comforter appeared around his neck like a puffy scarf. Ikaika gasped, recognizing his baby blanket. Touched that his grandfather called it to him for peace. Nostalgic memories pervaded their cores. Puna sank to the floor and remained with his head bent, face in cupped hands. The comforter as if alive spread out around his shoulders and arms. His thoughts were open and clear to all present. He was praying and sharing his prayer with them telepathically. The depth of aloha in his thoughts captivated everyone.

Ikaika and the SC joined their thoughts to Puna's. They all prayed for Elder Alaka'i's full recovery.

"*He really wants the quest to be completed,*" Elder Puna TGP sadly. "*If I were to be selfish, I'd tell you to avoid finding the Stone for a while longer. But as it is... Ikaika, go travel the world.*"

Team One bowed and honored his wishes. As they were transported away, the SC felt the weight of the elders' pain and their kuleana.

Chapter 29
SC Hails Relic Cloud

Manaful World
August 15, 2022
Violet Mountains, Elder Territory

Ikaika MT with the SC. When their molecules were put together, the SC found themselves standing on a peninsula. The children appreciated the beauty of the water all around except for the base of a mighty mountain range.

"*The Violet Mountains,*" Ikaika said. "*That's Elder Lilinoe's Territory, and beyond that would be Laka's. Their sister Pele's Territory are the lava lands ever farther beyond.*"

"Is there a map of the Manaful world?" Malie said. It was all so beautiful, she needed to see it in hardcopy. A map would help. She smiled at Pierre, thinking, *Aliyah would love it here with all of nature before us!*

Pierre nodded and thought, *Hawai'i still has lovely places like this beneath it all!*

She nodded, *Yes, definitely!*

Ikaika caught their quick mental convo and smiled. He TGP. "*There can be maps, Malie.*

'Ae, Hawai'i has many beautiful places to harmonize with nature as we do here!"

Malie loved Ikaika's thoughts and was happy he heard her convo with Pierre. She felt her telepathic abilities strengthening. She was proud of Pierre's growth too, hoping Nicole releases her self-induced mind blocks soon.

Ikaika shared a thought with Malie: *She will. In her own time.* He pulled Malie's map request out of thin air and handed it to her. Dark brown parchment with an elaborately painted map. Her mouth dropped open. "Wow. Like an original artist's creation. No printer needed."

"How'd you imagine up the entire Manaful world to put on a map?" Nicole demanded to know as Malie perused the sheet. Mana continued to be a confusing topic, much less the use of telepathy.

"*I didn't have to,*" Ikaika projected. "*It's already on the Manaful Hive Mind, the repository for all the shared knowledge of Manafuls.*"

Hive Mind? Making Manaful sound like bees, Nicole chuckled to herself.

"*It's like your Internet, the 'Public Domain',*" Ikaika TGP, reading her mind with a sideways head tilt. "*All the knowledge of Manaful is there. A pocket all to ourselves within the everlasting pool of knowledge and creative power, Source. Once Manaful, we can summon any information into and from the Hive via Source and materialize it using Mana.*"

Nicole was impressed, wiggling excitedly, "No devices needed. No IPN. No sim card. No wifi hub! Simply think of something and 'Pizzazz!' it appears in the flesh."

"Speaking of materializing," Pierre said, scratching his belly. "How about some ice cream, Ikaika old buddy."

The rest of the Secret Club agreed with whoops and fists to the air. Blobs of Almond Praline, Cookies and Cream, and Classic Choc budded out from thin air. The hefty waffle cones floated upright, balancing the tasty work of art. The preteens caught them greedily.

As they slurped their flavors on Pierre's limestone (yes, it appeared), Ikaika looked to the skies and watched a speck grow larger. It was Maluhia. The giant owl rode the air currents down to them.

"Whoo-whoo. Cloud is exactly where Tree guessed she would be. Messing around with mountain tops." Maluhia's TGP was a low bass as majestic as his wingspan.

"Did you talk to her, Maluhia?" Malie said around a chocolate mouthful. She folded the map with one hand and stuffed it into her pants pocket.

"Yes, but not for long. She speaks in rhyme nowadays and it gets a tad tedious," the lovely owl blinked, one eye at a time. He perched on a bough.

"Tell us about Cloud," Pierre said. All his fingers were sticky with praline but he still had lots left to go in his cone.

Maluhia told them stories of the wondrous things that happen over land and water that the ancient Mana Cloud passes over.

"Old Tree is sure turning out to be the dustiest of the bunch," Nicole said, finishing her cone and licking her fingers clean. The SC managed their first big laugh since Lapu broke Alaka'i.

"*Time to MT,*" Ikaika projected. "*We're going mountain hopping.*" He snapped his fingers for effect. The kids smiled at his flair.

They all appeared on a table mountaintop where the air was cold and the wind billowed wildly. A small herd of grazing goats, surprised at their arrival, jumped off the edge.

"They'll die!" Malie shouted, running to the lip of the fall. The entire family of goats looked up at her. They were standing on the seemingly vertical edge of the cliff. Perfectly safe. Her heart almost pitter-pattered out of chest.

Scared as well, Nicole and Pierre ran up and kneeled to look down. They couldn't help but giggle at the stern yet cute faces arrayed below them. One of them baa'd up at the SC as the wind gusted.

"*Mountain goats can chill on walls, almost perpendicular to the ground,*" Ikaika projected. "*They're fine. Come, look over there.*"

The Secret Club rose up to return to where Ikaika levitated, pointing at the snow tipped mountains close by. Pierre swept hair out of his eyes and whistled in wonder. Those snow-capped tips reminded him of family road trips as a child to Big Bear, California. *Those were the best days! Did your family have those?* He thought, looking at Malie.

She squeezed his arm, *Yes. My dad took me to see the snow at Lake Waiau on Mauna Kea before he died. Love snow too!*

Pierre nodded and made a prayer gesture with his hands, bowing in memory of her father.

She made a heart signal back.

Nicole, accustomed to their twin signaling, smiled sadly. She had a hunch it was a sad topic and was a little relieved to be left out.

Ikaika, who'd picked up all three SC's thoughts solemnly bowed as well.

A gigantic canopy of cloud lay over a pointy mountain, pulsing all the shades of blues up to lavender. Pink lightning lit it up on the inside, although what they heard on the wind were not thunder but tipsy bass strings with violin accompaniment. Cloud was having a jam session up there.

Nicole tapped her chin. "Is Cloud in a mood? I can only imagine what her cheerful musical feelings look like."

"What could a thundering Cloud possibly be feeling?" Pierre said sarcastically. "Of course she's in a mood!"

"Cloud's not thundering, and she's not in a mood. She's singing a song. I wanna dance; it's divine!" Malie said confidently with a side to side shimmy. She laughed with Ikaika. "Well? Didn't you say 'mountain hopping'? Let's hop."

Ikaika laughed and went with the flow, "*Here we go.*"

They MT again. This time they were directly under the cloud on the snowy mountain peak.

"COOOOOLD!" Pierre howled. Nicole and Malie ran into his arms and they formed a warm human ball. Over the blizzard they heard snatches of a haunting orchestra, the Cloud's Song.

Ikaika moved his arms around quickly. He looked like a bird flapping its wings. The snowstorm struck a clear bubble around the dwarf and SC, shying away to leave them untouched. Snowflakes drifted in the sudden stillness around the group, bouncing off their protective shield. The SC breathed silently while listening to the Cloud's music. The melody brightened their Spirits like overhead music speakers at a carnival. Aqua and pink light flickered on the snowdrifts around them as the musical lightning bolts zigzagged across the sky.

Ikaika imagined warm clothes for them. At home, the Secret Club hardly had the need for winter coats and boots, with thermal underclothing. The cozy textures of their winter attire were luxurious. Despite Ikaika's forcefield, the air inside their bubble remained chilly, so the new wardrobe was a great idea. The SC broke out of their huddle and compared their outfits.

"How do we make ourselves known in this racket?" Nicole finally asked. Her breath misted in front of her face. She cupped her mouth and yelled, "No offense, Cloud!"

The music went on. Ikaika telepathically projected greetings that simply bounced off the Cloud, just like it had been with Tree. He suspected he had to wait it out. Sometimes it was best to allow magical beings to do their thing.

But Malie pointed up, clapping her gloved hands excitedly, and said, "Cloud noticed. I see her coming."

It was hard to see at first but soon they all saw a smaller cloud detach from the canopy and drift down to them. It had a golden glow.

"She's just hovering there," Pierre had his hand over his brows to see better. "As if waiting for something. Oh, wait, she's sending a part of herself to us!"

Ikaika waved at Cloudlet. Taking a page out of Nicole's book, he cupped his mouth and yelled up, "Greetings, Relic Cloud! We're Elder Alaka'i's emissaries!"

Malie thought he was humorous, as Cloud could likely read their minds as most ancient beings could.

Cloudlet turned black. Malie nudged Ikaika and TGP, *"Remember what Maluhia said? She's going through a phase. A rhyming phase."*

"Oh! I remember now," Ikaika pulled his ear. *"Let's try hailing it in song. Right."*

Ikaika's Song: Hail the Cloud:

"How do we hail a cloud?
All we can do is shout.
'Cause her music is way too loud!
Oh, can't she see us standing about?
Hey, maybe we'll fly up like birds!
Hail, hail the glorious being!
She shades and protects, I've heard,
Our Manaful world is seeing
Rough problems that greatly effects
Everyone, so bring us your nurturing rain.
Bring new life to the whole domain.
Hail, hail the glorious cloud!"

Cloudlet blushed hot pink and so did the Cloud over the mountain. The whole thing descended, acquiring a golden glow. There was a soft harpsichord in the wintry air.

The voice that rang down from Cloud was clear and crisp. Each note was accentuated by a ping or pang from some mysterious instrument presumably hidden inside the living cloud's wispy yet opaque form.

"Emissaries of Alaka'i! That song sounded like an animal dying. Though... I can't blame you for your lack of trying. You traveled all the way here to find me; pray, were my hereabouts relayed by old Tree?" Cloud jingled.

"No. Spoken to an owl lately?" Ikaika waggled his eyebrows.

"Manu are such gossipers," Cloud tutted.

"Maluhia said you are building ice castles on the mountaintops," Malie piped up. She stepped forward and held up a gloved hand.

Cloudlet, glowing gold again, edged close to her. A little zap of electricity touched Malie's finger. It tickled. She giggled and Cloudlet bobbed around her like a friendly puppy.

She continued, "Is that what an ancient relic ought to be doing when the world is in danger from an evil Spirit, Cloud?"

Cloudlet fled from Malie and rushed up to join with the big Cloud, which kept dipping towards them. She began to rain as she lost altitude. She giggled in a dreamy sort of way.

"Ooops," Cloud said. "Excuse me. Just have to let it all out, vent out the steam."

"More like a stream," Nicole said. Pierre and Malie looked up at the golden cloud in awe along with her. It was nothing like normal rain.

Swirling colors streamed out of Cloud's underbelly until it looked like a rainbow made liquid. Droplets broke off the pool and circled down to the snow dusted granite below rather than fall at the mercy of gravity like a regular water drop. Each drop glowed every color imaginable and weren't affected by the force field Ikaika had put up to protect them from the wind.

The drops flew around the Secret Club and Ikaika. They began to catch on the coat linings and their hair. They flowed like water but also seemed to have a mind of its own, snaking all over the children's clothes to find skin. Once they did, they sank into the kids' pores.

"Woah! It tingles!" Malie exclaimed. She levitated a few inches off the ground. She bent down to make sure, but toppled forward instead. Malie squealed as she went into fetal position to hug her knees, bobbing aimlessly over the snow. She looked like an amateur astronaut aboard the International Space Station. She yelped, "Look! I'm floating!"

"Hey! What's happening?" Nicole said, slapping hands on her bob of hair. Her scalp itched. Green vines crept out from between her fingers rapidly, almost as fine as hair but with tiny leaves. Pierre watched in fascination as Nicole's plant-head bloomed orange flowers.

Cloud's Mana rain slithered over the snow, turning them into intricate ice patterns and raising miniature ice-castles. Here and there patches of tulips broke out and blossomed, their petals made of thin colored crystals. Pierre stepped back from a patch at his feet, which was way smaller than it should be. In fact, the ground seemed further away from him than he remembered.

"There's a lot of magic in the air!" Ikaika laughed. The dwarf stood entirely unaffected by said magic. He craned his neck back to look up to a great height. "Pierre, I'm sorry to say you're quite a noodle."

Pierre looked down at himself and then up. He was very tall and very thin, which meant his head was now in Cloud. No wonder the crystal tulips, which were now tap dancing around his shoes in tune to Cloud's soft, never-ending music, looked so small.

"The music is way louder up here," Pierre said from his satellite position. He blinked as random objects popped in and out of existence around his ears like weird snowflakes.

"What a thrill!" Cloud sang. "I can play with humans!"

"It's rather rude to play with emissaries of Alaka'i, don't you think?" Ikaika said, levitating up to Pierre's chest level. Several bolts of lightning flickered down like feelers around the dwarf. It seemed Ikaika absorbed these bolts like the humans had absorbed the Mana mist. The dwarf's brown skin shone from within, turning it gold.

"Wow!" Nicole said. The flowers on her vine-head swelled to produce clusters of berries. Pierre instinctively reached down—all the way down—to pluck some of them off.

"Stop that!" Nicole slapped at Pierre's spaghetti fingers. His wormy digits avoided her easily and went back up into the sky to Pierre's mouth. She suddenly noticed her feet were growing roots right through the boots.

"You're so tasty!" Pierre called down, curiosity satisfied. Nicole was distracted pulling her feet out of the ground. She stomped around with her head full of vines dragging behind her. She bumped hard into the ball of Malie passing by and sent the latter bouncing up towards Ikaika. Her glasses went flying.

"Tell Elder Alaka'i I am not returning to the Rift," Cloud told Ikaika. "It's not my mandate to fix a Spirit rampage, if you get my drift."

"We're not here to ask you to deal with the Spirits," Ikaika said, catching the passing Malie by a fluffy coat hem.

Malie nodded, flushed. Now anchored by the Manafuls firm grip, she said, "We're only here to find Stone."

"That's just it, you better believe it," Cloud tutted again. "Stone's bad news and Tree's lost in the blues. Alaka'i wants to prematurely bring us together, but it will just cause bad weather."

"No, we just want the Stone," Ikaika said.

Cloud lifted up and down. The musical and harmless lightning increased till it seemed like they were in a laser show. Cloud was laughing.

"Finding Stone means learning a Song," Cloud said. "That always changes the world, a new era according to what is foretold."

"There's something else," Pierre shouted inside Cloud's belly. He blew away wisps of cloud and looked down at the rest of the SC and Ikaika. "Elder Alaka'i."

Ikaika nodded. "Elder Alaka'i's mind has been attacked and detached by Lapu. The Spirit is trying to keep the elder's mind hostage in his realm. Do you happen to know a solution?"

Cloud swirled around them still sending out ticklish lightning bolts. She turned pearly white, Mana mist sprinkling at the edges. The swirling was slowly changing her shape from a canopy to a long serpentine form.

"She looks like a Chinese dragon!" Malie said, floating beside Ikaika. She was spot on.

Cloud was an elegant dragon of the air. She swam in coils around them, revealing an opalescent face with a long snout. Music rang out from her misty cylindrical body. It was a mournful note.

“Oh, poor Alaka‘i,” Cloud said. “That is a devious trick indeed. What Lapu has done is infect the body, somehow. You should be able to find a malignant growth in Alaka‘i’s brain that is fighting against his mind, pushing it into the Spirit Realm.”

“Sounds like a tumor,” Malie said. She was regaining her attachment to the ground, slowly growing heavier. Nicole’s hair was losing its greenery and Pierre gradually shrunk.

“But how can Lapu create a tumor in Alaka‘i’s brain?” Ikaika was stunned.

“Tainted Mana is a terrible thing in the wrong hands,” Cloud said, gently lowering Ikaika and Malie to the ground on her drafts. Snow flurried into the air as she draped herself on the mountaintop. “It is the forces involved in death and decay, basically. Life submits to it, life grows out of it. It is a natural part of the universe. Not bad when left for itself.”

“Some call it Dark Mana or Dead Mana. Others call it Tainted Mana,” Ikaika said, sharing what he knew as well.

“Spirits can use it like elders use the pure creative Mana of Source,” Cloud said. “Originally, they were supposed to feed on Mana Mist only while they were inside Old Hill. The Tainted Mana they ‘excreted’ was used by Old Hill to enrich the underground realms.”

“The Spirits were inside him?” Nicole asked.

“Yes. The Spirits worked in his belly. They weren’t prisoners there. All of us are just working as a magical ecosystem, bound to that spot we were all created in. But one day this Spirit called Lapu dissociated from us. He went off by himself and discovered that instead of working for Old Hill, he could accumulate tainted

Mana to make his own 'essence'. A substance he could call his own, which can evolve into a physical form."

"So you're saying even Tainted Mana has a use?" Nicole tapped her chin.

"There's a Territory called the Undersoil Caverns where this sort of Mana is thick in shadows where no light has ever fallen," Ikaika said.

"Tainted Mana lends power to gemstones as they grow deep underground over millennia," Cloud lilted.

Ikaika nodded. "Powered up precious stones make energy cores for factories, heavy duty engines. Since stones artificially saturated with Mana mist do not produce as much power, Tainted Mana is a prized resource for factories and the big machinery the Hopohopo loves. There's a lot of Tainted Mana in Manaful underground Territories."

"Wait, why are Mana Battery Cells needed then?" Pierre asked.

"Cheaper and safer," Ikaika said. "Juiced up gemstones are just too powerful. Some even explode if light touches them or if they are handled wrong. Even Manaful can die from explosions, so we play it safe. Only Mana Cells for the wary Manaful."

Cloud's beautiful, sleek dragon form grew flowing patches of fur and pearly scales. But the illusion blurred whenever she moved or shifted.

"Lapu is obviously powerful enough now at the Rift to not only invade Alaka'i's mind but place a block in his brain," she said. "You must scan the body thoroughly."

"Thank you!" Ikaika was excited with this information. He sent a TP to his grandfather at once.

"If Lapu is able to infect an Elder's body, times have become dire," Cloud said, rising up into the air, the illusory dragon form shimmering a rainbow of colors as it caught rays of the sun. "We have to stop him. Quickly."

The SC and Ikaika felt their stomachs contract in anxiousness. Cloud had been singsongy. Her forgetting to rhyme in the face of Alaka'i's predicament spelled more urgency than they'd thought.

They heard Puna TGP from far away. "*Cloud speaks true. We looked inside Alaka'i's brain and there is tainted essence there! How is this possible? Meet me at home, quick! And bring Cloud with you!*"

Chapter 30
Factory Shoot-Out

Manaful World
August 15, 2022
'Ōma'oma'o Hopohopo Towns
Inventor's Workshop in an Abandoned Factory

'Ōma'oma'o House had been a large 'Ohana at first. Rather a lot of its Manaful members were murdered over the past thousand years. The remaining few rarely socialized. Why would they? They couldn't even MT without suffering a nervous breakdown.

Maika'i and Kōkua were close to Uli in the family hierarchy. They grew up in his shadow just like Maka. Unlike Maka, the two of them had been sent off to Hopohopo City. When they reached Rhoda's age they enrolled at Uli's Protector's Academy. Uli hoped to make two secret assassins out of them. They were sickened by his constant attempts to groom, gaslight and even sexually molest them. It was their final refusal to kill that annihilated all favor for them in Uli's eyes.

The sisters tread softly on leather shoes as they approached the abandoned factory overgrown with vines and weeds. They found the button to open the garage door as seen in Rhoda's memories.

Inside were steps leading down to a basement passageway. Surprisingly, it was carpeted and wallpapered. It certainly brightened up this part of the factory, but it made for a lot of dust.

They were halfway down the passageway when Kōkua sneezed. She swallowed another one and ended up with momentary tinnitus. The sound echoed in the building and bounced up the passageway like a poltergeist.

Maika'i raised a hand to warn her companion to stop. Echoes of the sneeze died down. Maika'i felt out the space with her Mana. "*I sense someone here*," she projected.

"*I don't feel it*," Kōkua frowned. She knew her skills weren't enough to doubt Maika'i. She was regretting that sneeze when a crash boomed through the building. Both sisters jumped and gripped their lances. Sharing reassuring glances, they cautiously pushed forward.

"*Yep. There's a rat in the burrow*," Kōkua projected, licking dry lips. "*Rhoda was right. Maybe we shouldn't have come here alone.*"

"*No point turning back now. We've made it this far*," Maika'i crept around a corner resolutely. There was another door at the end. Beside it was a barrel-like machine sitting in a pile of scrap.

Kōkua pointed, eyes wide. "*It's one of those things! The machines even Elders can't touch.*"

"*Wasn't here during any of Rhoda's visits,*" Maikaʻi said, jogging her memories. "*That's a recent arrival. How is a Hopohopo moving things around so fast, so well?*"

"*Same way he's doing everything else,*" Kōkua projected. "*Lapu.*"

The very name made them sweat in their clothes. Both wore form fitting dark green jackets, pants and hoods. The material did not rustle or limit movements. It was the ninja outfit Uli doled out to his henchmen, but the sisters had cut out the Emblem on the hood.

They approached the machine. It was not activated. Probably a faulty one he had discarded? Would the elders be interested in it? Kōkua ran her gloved hands over the metal. "*It's a homemade version of an industrial Mana mist factory capacitor.*"

"*I thought they looked familiar! Sharp, tita! This design dates to the Great Hopohopo Revolution. But the functions of this tech are totally different.*"

"*You know what that means? He has access to the Hive. How can a non-telepathic being do that? It's always more questions with this guy!*"

Maikaʻi sent out a mind pulse again. This time she sensed a core just beyond the door. A mind that was very difficult to telepathically focus on. The soul flickered, slipped and slid away from detection till it felt like Maikaʻi was trying to pin down an eel.

"*Totally weird. Which means it's him,*" she decided. She hefted her lance. The weapon had runes too, being Mana Tech. They were laughably simple compared to what was being revealed on Ejad's machines. Academy lances were inscribed with three runes giving them durability, temperature settings and target-seeking capabilities. The most advanced lances had a couple of extra runes to make them explode on impact or shoot electrical bolts.

Neither of them held advanced lances. Plus, they weren't even allowed the weapons anymore since they quit being full-time Protectors and their licenses were revoked. The weapons' return to the Academy was long overdue.

"*Blast the door with Mana?*" Kōkua suggested. She loved blasting things with the force of air. That was her speciality. Her only talent that one-upped Maika'i's skill set.

"*Wait.*" Maika'i was holding Mana in her core, ready to use. "*I'm not sure if he is aware of us or not,*" Maika'i was starting to get very worried. "*He feels wrong. He is neither Manaful nor Hopohopo. He's a- a-*"

"*Creature,*" a voice rasped in their ears. "*My very own dwarfish creature. Any more words I can supply you with, meatbags?*"

Kōkua and Maika'i gasped aloud. They turned as one, lances out, backs to the door they had been about to open. What they saw froze their hearts.

Lapu had materialized behind them. He slimed down the ceiling and wallpaper, the oily essence lifting up to snake through the air in threads. He criss-crossed the passageway weaving a giant web. He grew towards them with a gristly stench. Light bulbs flickered as he passed underneath.

Maika'i and Kōkua put up a force field, a semi-sphere, half of what it could have been. Lapu cackled and shot at them. The collision forcefully threw Kōkua and Maika'i back. They slammed into the door and fell through. It was unlocked!

Maka's aunts turned their fall into rolls and were soon standing inside the workshop. Stacked into a labyrinthine maze, dozens of machines surrounded them blinking red, yellow, green lights. The fluorescent lights above began to strobe when Lapu's essence bubbled through the closing double doors. Instead of attacking them, the essence circled around the room.

"What is he doing?" Kōkua managed through her terror. She got her answer immediately. The cloud came to rest around a figure in the shadow of an incinerator. A figure that was wrapped in a checkered cloak, lower face hidden in a scarf, and goggles glinting whenever the overhead lights flickered on. Lapu settled around Ejad's body, the Inventor's very own cloud of miasma.

"Hands up and knees to the ground!" Maika'i barked with authority. She pointed her lance at the criminal. "The Elder Council has ordered your arrest. Submit at once!"

Ejad wordlessly rose up into the air. Maika'i wondered if he was even a real dwarf. He looked like an overly dressed mannequin. Lapu lay all over him like strings on a puppet. Lapu's essence hissed at the sisters.

"*I'm alerting Maka and Puna at once,*" Kōkua projected. She was panicking. She had her lance extended in front of her, fidgeting.

"*Well. That pretty much seals your fate. Die.*" Lapu's voice slipped into their ears like an unwelcome tongue. Kōkua's eyes widened in fear and bravado.

"Go rot, Undersoil, foul Spirit!" Kōkua screamed. She jumped forward and swiped with her lance. Lapu's essence pulled Ejad out of the way. As if in a dream, the Hopohopo raised an arm. A glowing gauntlet encased it.

The good thing with basic runology was that individual runes can be triggered easily with Mana. Kōkua channeled and the three runes on her lance lit up. In one fluid motion she flexed her weapon arm back. She swung it forward and launched the weapon.

Lapu pulled Ejad out of the way again. The lance turned in mid-air and sought him out, following in a lime green blur. For a second, Maika'i thought the Spirit would hold Ejad up like a meat shield to stop the lance. But he coiled around the Inventor and solidified into a blob. Tentacles whipped out to knock the lance away.

"Look out!" Maika'i screamed. She used Mana to hop an unnatural distance, catching her sister out of the way. The lance hit a machine and exploded. Wires crackling, the machine burst into flames. The sisters rolled to a stop beside a pile of broken shelves. They got on their knees, panting. Maika'i had a forehead cut that blinded her with blood.

"Dammit, my lance!" Kōkua spat. Before Maika'i could stop her, the livid, terror-stricken, yet brave-to-a-fault Kōkua ran toward Lapu and Ejad. She harnessed her full capacity for Mana. The air in the room was sucked to her, ballooning around her four feet height and funneling to her fists. She screamed as she let the blast go.

Maika'i wiped the blood from her eyes and stood up in time to get her heart broken. Lapu jumped in a surge and landed Ejad safely to the side. Kōkua's blast hit the old incinerator. It crumpled to the floor. The crash resounded as Ejad raised his hand again. He was holding a small metal ball. A set of runes glowed on it. Maika'i watched him casually lob it at Kōkua.

Her energy spent on the elemental attack, all Kōkua could conjure was a weak forcefield. The ball hit it and exploded. Purple flashed intensely, with a heat haze following it. Kōkua flew back and slammed high up into a wall. Maika'i covered her eyes to avoid getting blinded.

When she lowered her arms Kōkua's limp body fell into a pile of scrap metal. Maika'i summoned her full capacity for Mana as well. She spent it on a projection.

"MAKA! PUNA! HELP US!" Maika'i ran to her sister. She didn't know where Lapu and Ejad were. Her priority was now making sure her sister was alive. She grabbed Kōkua's body and hoisted it onto her shoulder. Her lance clattered to the floor.

"ELDER PUNA HELP US! HELP US PLEASE!" Maika'i projected as she sprinted towards the door with her precious cargo. She almost lost her balance to use Mana while her body was in mid-action. She was dizzy. But she ran.

The double doors banged open. Her shoes slapped on the carpet. There was a buzz behind her. Maika'i knew it was another attack and instinctively leapt forward with her rapidly dwindling energy reserve. She heard the explosion behind her. The force turned her leap into a projectile. She fell and rolled, scrambling to grab Kōkua's body which landed like a sack of flour. Maika'i looked up in time to see the possessed Ejad standing in the doorway by the discarded harvesting barrel.

"*They're going to kill us,*" she projected hopelessly, seeking Puna's or Maka's minds. Her vision was going dark. She hugged her sister, face streaked with dust, blood, and tears. "*Maka! Puna! Anyone!*"

Ejad raised his gauntlet hand. This time there was no bomb. This time his metal encased arm burst into sparking electric fire.

"No! Please," Maika'i shouted.

A storm of blue bolts shot at the Aspiring Hopohopo from Ejad's metal fingertips. Maika'i closed her eyes tight. Her whole body caught fire. She screamed, neck corded. Then she felt the familiar tug in her navel. Her body tingled. For a split second everything went deadly silent. Elder Puna's Mana suffused soul touched her mind to calm it. His ephemeral presence was like the chime of a bell. Puna molecularly transported the wounded sisters from a distance.

Sound rushed back. Weight returned. Maika'i opened her eyes to find Elder Maka looking down at her. They seemed to be in Maka's Sandalwood Forest mansion. But how could she be sure in her half delirious state? Even her eyeballs were burnt.

"Elder Puna MT you here," Maka gasped, falling to his knees beside them. He heard the projections the same time as Puna, but had been slower to react.

Skin smoking, all Maika'i could say was, "Thank you! Thank you! Source blesses us," before she fell on top of her sister, out cold.

CHAPTER 31
KŌKUA'S BARELY BREATHING

Manaful World
August 15, 2022
Sandalwood Forest, Elder Territory
Elder Maka's Mansion

Kōkua was barely breathing. Her blonde hair spread like an open Japanese fan on the hospital bed in Maka's Mansion. It was the same chamber where Uli had held his Covid hoax victims. The beds were still there, but all of them were empty except for Kōkua's.

Maka sat beside his fallen aunt, head down and weeping. "*This is all my fault*," he sniffled. "*I should have reacted faster. I couldn't MT you in time. Puna had to do it. I am so sorry.*"

Elder Puna had worked his magic remotely from Alaka'i's Villa. He promised Maka he would call soon. The two elders would pay a visit to the factory first.

Kōkua's force field had been weak, but thankfully it saved her life. Ejad's spherical projectile had lifted her off her feet upon exploding. The force field kept her from blowing up on the spot, losing body parts, or having a cardiac arrest. Yet, it hadn't softened her fall. Nor had the force field prevented third-degree burns.

For the millionth time in his life, Maka cursed his Uli for not training him properly. He didn't even know Manaful healing techniques. He was grateful for the company he had.

"*You're not to blame for the influence your grandfather cast over you while raising you*," Maika'i projected resolutely. She had healed her own minor injuries wonderfully upon waking. "Now if you want to be helpful, please lend me your Mana. She needs it."

Maika'i analyzed the injuries as professionally as she could manage, yet her heart broke for her athletic-obsessed, girly-girl tita. Kōkua's entire upper body from head to waist were covered with third-degree burns. Source's Mana would repair her broken, bruised body, especially the nerve endings fried by the metal ball's plasma pulse.

If Maika'i got her hands on that murderer, she'd wring his neck or worse. She breathed deep to erase those negative thoughts. The medical healing from Mana required a clear, loving presence. She raised her brows at Maka.

His Mana flowed into Maika'i, whose body posture grew strong and firm. She half closed her eyes and looked at Kōkua's body. The familiar head rush came. She could see inside the body. Kōkua's skull was fractured, along with some ribs, a femur, the clavicle, and both tibia. Her pelvis had also suffered damage on the left side. Maika'i was relieved to see no internal bleeding or organ damage.

She put her hands close to Kōkua's face and watched the third-degree burns knit up. New skin grew fast from the edges of the wounds. Normally this would take around half an hour, but Maka's Mana was strong.

Kōkua groaned as most of her face was restored and the wounds down her throat closed up. Her eyelashes fluttered. Maika'i eased her back into a sleep. She wouldn't allow Kōkua to wake up to the horrible pain her body must be in. Maika'i quickly went to work on the bone fractures.

After a few minutes, she looked round at Maka with a frown. "Something is wrong. Her skin cells are misbehaving."

Maka felt his heart leap up into his throat. Fortunately, just sitting by Maika'i as she did her work was a crash course. Maka imitated her and was soon analyzing Kōkua's body as if looking at an MRI. Images rushed across his vision. He saw cells dividing at an accelerated rate, then growing ridiculously big before rupturing. White blood cells attacked them left and right. Kōkua's skin cells were self-destructing!

"What is it?" He gasped in horror.

"I don't know! His weapon did something to her cells!" Maika'i's voice caught in her throat. She kept healing her sister even as silent tears sneaked down her cheeks. "And- And I can't seem to fix it!"

"The effect is not in the bones?" Maka scanned Kōkua's skeletal damages. It looked like the fissures were fusing back up. It seemed fine.

Maika'i confirmed his observation. "Healing the bone is working. Everything is going well except for the skin cells. The moment I stop healing they get out of control. Visible on the skin surface as red patches, as a sort of inflammation."

As she worked, Maka's chest hurt as if his heart would jump out; he groaned in emotional agony. Maika'i glanced at her Elder. Perhaps he needed healing too?

Hearing her thoughts, he shook his head. He leaned over Kōkua from the other side of the bed, noting how young Kōkua still was. Barely thirty in human years. He breathed in deep. A sudden need to contribute and be a stronger leader swept his spirit. He closed his eyes and laid his hands upon Kōkua's limp arm, while Maika'i tried to smoothen out the fresh breakout of redness on Kōkua's face and down her neck.

Kōkua sighed in her unconsciousness. The burns on her torso had healed. But the same blotchy patches kept appearing. Maika'i shook her head, continuing her healing. Finally, she said, "I fear something is out of hand. We need Elder Puna."

Maka was silent for a moment as he projected long-distance. He said, "The Elders are relentlessly searching for Ejad. In fact, he is requesting you take Kōkua to the Medical Center so I can MT to him right now."

"The Elders?" Maika'i scoffed. "Come on. You mean only Elders Alaka'i and Puna. None of the others are helping with *anything*!"

"They are," Maka said softly. "The Elder Council will improve. I am giving you my word."

A rather large promise coming from the youngest elder, Maika'i thought. She knew Maka heard her. Didn't care. Her whole being was still trembling but she continued to heal.

"You are very good at what you do," Maka noted between his grief. "I can see you becoming Manaful in no time."

"It's the perfect alignment with Source that is hardest to achieve," Maika'i said as perspiration beaded on her forehead. As an Aspiring Hopohopo, summoning Mana from within herself still produced stressful effects. She'd sweat, tremble or lose consciousness, if she did too much at once. Over time these body stressors would go as the Mana imbued her flesh and mind completely.

"Incidentally, that's about the only achievement you need to become Manaful overnight," Maka smiled, wiping his eyes.

"Any tips?"

"Fight your inner demons and face difficult truths every day. That's a constant effort. Fulfilling your responsibility to yourself makes Source love you. One rarely needs to run to Source. Source simply comes to us when we are ready."

Maika'i paused and looked up at the young Elder, her nephew, with a new light in her eyes. She felt pride at his growth. He was sounding more like an Elder every passing day.

"Your mom and dad would be proud of you," Maika'i said firmly. "She was the middle child, between me and Kōkua. She always took the lead in everything. Became Manaful at four hundred years old. Went on to do so much research. It scared the whole Council."

"Mom scared the council?" Maka passed his hands over Kōkua's blemishes, healing them as fast as they kept appearing. He could get the hang of this.

Maika'i nodded and wiped her forehead with a free hand. "Her mind was fast. Too fast. She wrote things way ahead of her time. Your dad was the only one who always believed in her ideas. Uli made them both out to be crackpots and isolated them. Trapped them indoors just like he did to you. We don't know how he reduced their Mana. Everyone assumes he did. Despite your mother being an amazing Manaful in her youth, she barely used it by the time she had you."

"It's the old Uli and Lapu trick," Maka said darkly. "They were always in the house. You could feel Lapu's sticky itchiness creeping around our properties, the sandalwood forest, and even on the fringes of our minds. He lay over grandfather like a rancid cloak. When Lapu fully possessed grandpa, their unified presence knocked out any alignment with Source."

Maika'i shivered. "I know. Lapu/Uli tried to kill us. The day Uli tried to rip me and Kōkua apart we felt Lapu's presence. Uli was possessed. Kōkua was doubly sure of it. Just horrible."

"Tita… do you know if Lapu ever possessed you?" Maka asked.

Maika'i was shocked at the question. Then she grew worried. "I wouldn't know. It's said even Manafuls may not know, sometimes. And I'm barely there. Why do you ask?"

Maka stepped back. Kōkua's body was healed. But as they watched, the stubborn red patches reappeared. Maika'i at once attacked the malignant cells and healed, kept on healing.

"That is my biggest fear," Maka said. "Lapu can possess Manafuls, but he is not strong enough to do it often nor for long. Grandfather knew when Lapu first came round to our mansion, unseen. Uli spoke to him. Invited the Spirit to possess him. That's how this happened."

"Who told you that?"

"That's not important right now," Maka said, making sure his Elder Mind Shield was up. He didn't mind sharing, but there were Council laws and rules to consider. Till he could change them. He continued, "What's important is this: no one has any idea how to track Lapu's possession rampage. We may be on-guard. We may mind-meld to keep everything transparent and honest, but that is all. There's nothing to be done if Lapu possesses us, uses us, and then simply—"

"Deletes the memory," Maika'i completed his sentence with a hopeless expression. "But how is he able to do that?"

"His essence can exist in the Spirit Realm," Maka whispered. "The world beyond where unseen beings roam."

Below them, Kōkua groaned again. Maka had cleaned and dressed her in a split second on their arrival. She wore a hospital gown that was loose for comfort in her resting state. Her blue eyes cracked open.

"Kōkua!" Maika'i bent down to check her sister's pupils. She held up three fingers. "Can you see me? Hear me? How many fingers am I holding up?"

Kōkua reached up and grabbed Maika'i's hand. "Far too many," she said hoarsely. Then she coughed. A bit of blood came out and Maka rushed to produce a tissue to wipe it off.

"That always happens after heavy internal healing," Kōkua said, trying to sit up. Maka pushed her back down. She stubbornly got on her elbows.

"Yes," Maika'i had to agree. The blood was watery and pink, inside a gob of excess fluids. Just residue. Nothing to be worried about. After Maika'i was done studying it, the tissue vanished.

Kōkua seemed flushed. "Where is he? Did we get him?" She meant Ejad. The last thing she remembered was being attacked in the factory hideout.

For a moment neither Maka nor Maika'i knew what she was talking about. They noticed too many blotches appearing all over Kōkua's body.

"Do you feel pain?" Maika'i blurted out.

Kōkua shook her head. "Just a headache."

"We need to go to the Medical Center," Elder Maka decided. Now that they had the situation under control, they needed more study on what was happening to Kōkua. Maika'i agreed with him.

Kōkua was about to protest but whimpered. She fell back on the pillow, fingers scrabbling at her body as if she had fire ants crawling all over her. "You know what! Ack! I do feel—"

Kōkua retched. Maika'i stroked her head to ease her breathing. But chunks of Kōkua's hair came off in her hands.

Maka didn't waste one more second. He MT to the 'Ōma'oma'o Medical Center with his aunts. His elder robes poised like a parrot's wings over his sisters, the trio hovered right up to the Help Desk. There was a moment where all activity stopped to marvel at the Elder's sudden appearance. But it resumed rather quickly when Maka TGP, "*We need Intensive Care at once!*"

Chapter 32
Ejad's Workshop & Clues

Manaful World
August 15, 2022
'Ōma'oma'o Hopohopo Towns
Abandoned Factory

An hour later, dust poofed out in a sphere as two Elders MT into Ejad's abandoned factory. Puna and Maka levitated in the entry passage of the Inventor's former domain. This was the same town Maka had visited with Ikaika and the SC. He'd never seen these factories before.

They were built during the Great Hopohopo Revolution. Dwarf opposition rose up and rejected Manaful systems of population management. The Hopohopo made their own systems and built factories instead to help them into an industrialisation age. Uli had supplied them with all the technical information he collected from spying on Earth.

This factory manufactured clockworks and machinery parts, judging by the dusty framed pictures along the walls. It must have been abandoned for a thousand years now. This was the only known hideout for the renegade inventor Ejad. The Elder Council was still bent on hunting him down.

Elder Puna scanned the grounds with a telepathic pulse. He saw the whole layout in his mind's eye. It was truly abandoned except for some rats. They were safe. Just in case, he placed a force field around them that was visible only when it pushed against the thickly swirling dust motes.

Elder Puna switched the lights on. Maka immediately spotted a detonation point in the corridor by a set of doors. The yellow wallpaper was blackened and the green carpet was melted like wax. The burning stench still polluted the air. This was where Kōkua had almost died. The abandoned harvesting machine Maika'i reported stood nearby, charred by the second blast.

"*I am glad Kōkua is medically stable now at the center,*" Puna projected as they hovered up the yellow passage and through the doors into a bigger space. The workshop. It had a conveyor belt and work tables laden with gadgetry. In a corner was the blast zone where Kōkua had fallen. Metal parts were twisted, melted from the heat.

"*Her cells had become cancerous,*" Maka replied. "*Professional Mana Therapy will fix them in three days. She will stay at the center till the treatment is over.*"

"*And Maika'i?*"

"*Nothing more than a few scratches. She healed herself. She grows stronger in Mana every day.*"

Puna nodded. He felt waves of worry and sadness come off Maka as they looked around the secret space. Objects sprang up and zoomed around as the pair used their Mana for telekinesis.

This is only one of Ejad's many workshop hideouts. Puna thought. He was determined to uncover them all. He looked around when the energy coming off Maka turned red hot. Why the sudden anger?

Maka was holding a small gun with "BRaG" printed on the side. He was breathing hard as he recalled the last place he'd seen it. In Uli's office. He mind-melded with Puna and relayed the memory.

"Uli must have given the gun back to its inventor," Puna said.

Maka blew out a breath and crushed the BRaG into powder with his bare hands. "*He invents only misery.*"

"*He is being mind-controlled by Lapu.*"

"*Possessed,*" Maka said. "*In which case, we are allowed to put him down!*"

"*Don't rush.*"

Maka took calming breaths. "*I will stop this guy,*" he promised. "*I'll stop him before more people are hurt or killed.*"

"*Please stop talking about this as if it were solely your problem,*" Puna was ruffled. His robes fluttered like a wet bird drying itself with the shakes.

"*The responsibility lands on my shoulders fair and square. Uli's underground crime system is still going strong. I have to stop this.*"

Elder Puna wanted to share his experience with his compatriot. "*Why not appoint teams?*"

"*Teams?*" Maka scowled.

"*We all have clusters of teams. They do different things and we meet up to mind-meld every now and then. We share everything there is to know about projects, prayers, stories. Easiest way to manage giant swathes of Territory.*"

Maka didn't really know many Manafuls since he mostly grew up indoors. How does one make teams without people? Oh wait, he could get help from his immediate family. Maika'i and Kōkua's work had revealed Ejad in the first place. Those two were his first candidates for sure.

"*They're not gonna do it alone anymore*," he decided. He would put together teams to manage his House.

"*Good. Center yourself and let's pick this place apart*," Puna projected.

Elders Puna and Maka shifted objects with gestures. Things came closer or moved away as needed as the Elders sorted through Ejad's towers of trinkets. Maka studied the books and notes strewn everywhere, pages ruffling over clinks of metal. Elder Puna lifted machines thrice his size to roll them over. Sometimes he'd take them apart, noting the various emblems inside.

"*He knows runology very well*," Puna said. "*Once activated, our telekinetic abilities don't affect these machines. They become impervious to our Mana.*"

"*Runology? How do you 'activate' runes?*"

"*With a powerful Mana energy core. He's using gemstones to power the runes.*"

"*What about all these Mana Battery Cells?*"

"*That's mostly for machine parts. Electricity. He's added runes on top and given them unique magical power. He's also using gemstones. It's a direct source of tainted mana.*"

"*No wonder we haven't been able to figure him out!*"

Maka moved his arm in an arc and a row of shelves opened to purge their contents. They swirled about: wrenches, diagrams, aluminum and copper parts. Puna did the same and soon the air was filled with all the junk Ejad had left behind. The bulkiest stuff rattled a few inches off the ground.

"There," Maka pointed at the only object their powers had not affected. A big wooden box at the very back. They approached it warily.

Elder Puna pointed at the padlock on the chest. Maka didn't even notice how precious the box actually was until Puna said, "It's laced with diamonds."

Puna made more light bulbs on the ceiling flare to life. The fragments of diamond embedded along the wood and padlock were minuscule but still flashed in the tungsten glow.

"It's a giant box of gemstones, isn't it," Maka sighed, resigned to the absolute worst.

Puna nodded grimly. "Handle it wrong and we go boom."

"Just great!" Maka sulked. "We can't even MT or levitate this thing."

"That's what hovering's for. Buck up and grab that handle."

The box was heavy. Maka huffed as he followed Puna, who held his end of the chest steadily with a powerfully biceped arm. The Manafuls hovered up and set the chest down between them in mid-air. Puna grinned. "The air cushion always works. Time for a leisurely flight."

But what Maka read in Puna's mind (as he projected updates long-distance to Charmaine and Elder Lilinoe) was, "*This Hopohopo has tapped into Mana without aligning with Source. Ejad has become the polar opposite of Manaful. Something worse than a regular, powerless Hopohopo.*"

"*I see there is an abandoned harvesting machine there,*" Charmaine's projection came like a bell. "*It is deactivated. You should be able to MT it here. We need to reverse engineer what this mad Hopohopo has done.*"

Elder Puna nodded. He transported the harvesting machine by the doors with Mana. He was worried about Charmaine's underestimation of the Inventor.

This "mad" Hopohopo had managed to technologically defeat two trained Protectors. This was unprecedented. Puna needed his buddy Alaka'i badly to discuss current events.

CHAPTER 33
AUNTY ON COMPASSION

Storyteller in Papakōlea, Hawai'i
August 15, 2022

Ari scoffed at Alaka'i's "weakness".

Aunty Ellie disapproved.

"No one is immune to everything, Human or Manaful."

She told Ari that falling victim to an attack does not make one weak or any less respectable. Nicole got bullied, but she still came out on top. She took the advice of her friends and stuck to protocol. She did not beat up her bullies.

Alaka'i has achieved a lot in 4200 years, and there were so many times he has won. This setback simply means that the Manafuls have to step up their game to combat the increasingly powerful destructive forces. What was normal for hundreds of years is now changing... Perhaps the time for new leaders is upon Manaful World? That may be the Will of Source. Whatever happens, Ari must know and respect Alaka'i as a strong, capable leader who tried his best.

Ari agreed with a face.

She said, “I like Elder Puna more.”
She was also interested in Charmaine.

CHAPTER 34
IKAIKA OPENS SWV

Manaful World
August 15, 2022
Koa Forest, Elder Territory
Ikaika's Mansion

The SC met in school and crossed over to Manaful. They were quite used to bouncing back and forth between worlds. Their singing molecules whizzed through the Shimmery Wall.

Ikaika was sitting on Pierre's limestone rock, making a musical box with vines and flowers. It's the sort you'd find in the Manaful Zone bazaar. He'd invited Maka to drop by for this SC visit. But his friend TP, "*We found an entire chest full of bombastic leads. Elder Council duties call. Sorry, Buddy.*" So Ikaika MT there alone to open the gateway for his human friends to cross over. Technically, every time they visited their form was destroyed on Earth. Their molecules were transported pell-mell through quantum foam to reconstruct in this parallel dimension.

If Ikaika wasn't there to receive them, they might not have been reconstructed at all.

His Shimmery Wall Portal fizzled and expanded on a bushy, squat tree. Soon Malie, Nicole and Pierre stepped out of it and stood in front of him beneath the cool shade of Koa trees.

Ikaika handed the music box to Malie.

"What's up?" Pierre, Nicole and Malie chorused.

"*Team Two has located Ejad's hideouts*," Ikaika TGP.

"*Gramps is investigating the locations they've mapped out*," Ikaika continued the SC update. "*Right now Maka is with Elder Polu. Next stop is the Three Sisters' Territory*."

"Who are the three sisters?" Malie wondered. She handled the soft green body of the box tenderly, poking a knobby knot of vines. The leafy lid opened to reveal a tree-fountain in a miniature force field. The baby bonsai tree's roots embraced a stone (secured to the box by a stem). Mana mist poured from its leaves into the globule of water that held it all together. The Mana mist sparkles swirled inside when you shook it like a magical, living snow globe. The box's music was the chirping of birds, lulling streams supported by babbling brooks, with the occasional crow for what Nicole assumed were the rap parts. The girls sighed and caressed the soft, living box. They liked the sounds Ikaika carried in his head, grateful he put them out. Loved that he shared the beauty with them.

"*Elders Pele, Lilinoe and Laka,*" Ikaika TGP.

"The Violet Mountains!" Pierre smiled remembering their mountain hopping adventure. He took the box for a look, shook it for a good laugh, and handed it back to Malie.

Ikaika nodded. "*Ready when you are. We'll MT to my crib for SWV.*"

"We're supposed to watch Elder quests on a screen again?" Pierre complained. He got off the boulder.

"Not a screen, a Shimmery Wall Viewer," Malie said. She wiped her glasses on her blazer with a free hand and put them back on, squinting.

"*Bullseye*," Ikaika winked at Malie. He took the music box and folded it up into a pocketable bud. The humans started in fascination.

"Why can't we MT to the Violet Mountains?" Nicole joined the whining, pointedly nodding at the bud in Ikaika's hand. Pierre stood next to her, his chin jutting out.

"*It's the Mana saturation levels*," Ikaika TGP.

"Cloud's rain was also saturated. But we were fine," Malie observed. She tried to keep a neutral tone.

Ikaika grinned. He handed the music bud to Malie, who stuffed it into a pocket. "*We all saw what happened. I had to save you from bouncing off into the stratosphere, Malie. Humans are chaotically affected when Mana mist over saturates their bodies. You will be totally at the mercy of unpredictable Mana effects.*"

On top of that there's the tainted Mana, Ikaika thought to himself. *Who knows about the effects of tainted Mana on humans?* Ikaika shuddered. He didn't want to think about it.

Ikaika MT them indoors, where furniture popped up all around. Malie admired her favorite art works. Nicole giggled from the rug as the puppies bounced all over her. Pierre grabbed floating trinkets Ikaika had plucked from his finicky mind.

"*I'll tune into Gramps*," Ikaika TGP. He opened a giant Shimmery Wall. The House 'Ula'ula emblem flashed briefly, letting them know this was Puna's mind link.

The SC stopped in their tracks.

Nicole whistled.

Pierre and Malie said, "Whaaat!"

Ikaika's jaw dropped open.

On the screen, they saw the Elders battling a machine with six legs. It looked like the machine was winning. The SC fell on the rugs to watch.

Chapter 35
Project Number Three

Manaful World
August 15, 2022
Lote Forest, Elder Territory
Inventor's Hideout
Three hours ago

The runecraft was meticulous. They were perfectly Scripted into the metal monster Lapu and his little Hopohopo genius had created over the past few weeks. This was a full blown Mana Mech. Made with Mana Tech. By Uli's little pet.

"*Tee hee hee.*"

Lapu had never desired corporeal form more than now. He wanted to feel the rune inscriptions on this metal body. He could try.

A point in front of the machine thickened in midair. Silver and gold globules of Mana mist formed and swirled in the air. Instead of shimmering into the rainbow mist of Elder magic, these darkened into an oily, sticky vapor. It was Lapu essence, tainted Mana.

The substance coalesced into a vaguely humanoid shape. Skeletal, it reached for the Mana Mech and swiped at the surface. The fingers broke off. All of them. They turned to goo and dripped from the metal. The gunk poofed into smoke before it hit the ground. The emaciated form wobbled and collapsed into smog.

"*Gah!*"

He was not pleased with himself.

Ejad shared Lapu's fury of failure in body and mind. After all, the Spirit was using Ejad's own emotions against him. And wearing them too whenever the Spirit pleased, the gall! Lapu didn't have much emotion of his own. That was on account of the Spirit not having a physical body with hormones pumping through him all the time. So Lapu was a serial borrower of everything.

Ejad was just about to test-run his Mana Mech Project Three when the annoying Spirit dropped in. But what to do. The Spirit had power over him until such a day he could turn the table and burn him for good measure. And stamp on the ashes.

Sigh. Ejad was all suited up. He'd spent decades designing this sleek metallic outfit. It was Project One, a Mech Suit. The alloy still made his skin itch though, so he needed insulation underneath. But on the whole, it worked.

Modified Mana Battery Cells - which he had taken to calling MBC's - powered the suit. The runes worked because each MBC now had a sliver of amethyst in them. Technically, his suit was the first Mana Mech to exist in Manaful World.

Problem was it was about as mind-blowing as regular clothes before Project Three.

Project Three ended up a tad too big.

The thing before him kind of overshadowed everything else he'd done by sheer weight. He hadn't given the monstrosity a name yet. Maybe Scuttles? Scuttles could be a nice name.

Ejad was shaken out of christening his finished project when Lapu snuck into his head and interrupted. The Spirit stole into minds like he did buildings. Uninvited.

Lapu blasted a command: "*Your next project is to Script a Mana Mech that will help manifest Us!*"

Ejad held back a flinch and touched his upper lip. His fingers came away red. The Spirit's intrusions were taking a bigger toll on his body day by day.

Mentally he was fine and dandy. He was hundred percent sure of it. He had never had a mental issue in his life. He wasn't going to stand for a Spirit trying to sabotage his honest hobby and life's work: engineering of all kinds.

"*Go manifest by yourself, you foul seed of Rot,*" Ejad pushed back. His skull exploded into pain. He gritted his teeth. He fought to keep his thoughts from blanking out in pain. "*My next project concerns what* I *want.* You *can go rot*, rot, rot."

"*How DARE you speak to Us thus!*"

Blood gushed from Ejad's nose. His eyes watered. A barely audible whimper escaped. He covered his nose with a hand. His fingers trembled ever slightly as maroon drops splattered them.

Lapu rasped, "*You even lost the gem stash I gifted you.*"

Tears began to leak. Ejad growled and hunched up. His chest shuddered as he internalized the pain like he always did.

"*You're a useless, stupid, puny little Hopohopo. Even your parents hated you the moment you were born.*"

The Spirit's essence curled around Ejad, waiting to solidify as soon as he was able. Through the pain Ejad felt like being rude. Pointedly, he thought, "*Blah blah blah.*" That earned the dwarf more hurt. Right in the nerve endings.

Ow.

Uncovering his face he spat blood at Lapu. The red tinged spittle splattered across the floor instead. Lapu snickered.

Ejad hurled his thoughts at the Spirit. "*See? You'll be glad you started out formless. Once you get a body, I'll be the first to spit on you.*"

His nerves were on fire. He lifted a rag from a nearby table with trembling hands and wiped his face. Shaking, the rag came away stained maroon and pink.

"*Stupid Hopohopo. Dumb halfling. I OWN your thoughts. I'm the real Inventor. You're just a disposable mask. My insane puppet.*"

Ejad groaned, eyelids fluttering. Memories rose up like visions. Terrible memories. Uli kept him locked up. Uli visited him often. To do things to him. To make him do things to others. Terrible things. For "training". Ejad bit his lip so hard a fresh river of blood flowed on his chin.

"*Look at you,*" Lapu laughed, poking his tendrils at Ejad, taunting him, a bully that can't be touched or maimed with a switchblade. "*Miserable, pathetic creature. Your ugly face is smeared with all the proof of weakness. Tears. Blood. Pain. Such a weakling. Such a dumb Hopohopo. Ha ha ha.*"

Ejad shook his head and stumbled to the machine. He grabbed a leg, hugging it. Cold, dead metal. His fingernails almost broke on it. But his head cleared. With a few shuddering breaths, Ejad regained control. He threw the rag away.

"*You should be buying time to recover, Lapu,*" Ejad thought. "*Talk about pathetic. One face-off with two lousy Aspiring Hopohopo and you're tired out. You break up into wisps in the air.*"

Ejad walked through the dark mist flapping hands in front of his pointy nose. He wore a 'Pooey' face as if Lapu smelled bad. He went to the table and picked up a set of gray gloves.

Lapu bristled visibly. But Ejad's memories and emotions settled. The Spirit was withdrawing from his head. Ejad hid his vindictiveness the best he could, pulling on the gloves. The tensile material went 'Snap' on his wrists. "*You're, like, a literal fart, Lapu.*"

The Spirit was confused for a moment. Who was poisoning whom, exactly? He tended to get muddled, but in short-lived bursts. Ejad pounced on every opportunity.

"*Use your time well and recover, Lapu. You're only expending yourself needlessly to torture me. You don't even have to direct the Elders to this workshop. They're on a manhunt. They'll find us. You can relax.*"

Lapu shifted around and joined him by the machine, calmer. Externalized. Pillar of smoke. Which was a good thing. Because that meant he was less of a headache for Ejad.

Over the long years the Spirit had accepted the fact that physical brains were hands down the best machine for intelligence. Ejad knew this. Spirits weren't very sharp, to put it simply. They didn't have gray matter.

Lapu seethed in silence.

"*Tsk, you're not relaxed enough, Lapu,*" Ejad said, fully recovering from the earlier pain. Lapu dispersed gloomily into the air. He recognized when to back off. Seemingly.

Ejad fought to keep from hugging himself. He stood tall. Rubbed his elbows instead, feeling the suit's rune warmth through the gloves.

Number Three towered over him. Rhoda had only seen its skeleton and a leg. Its central generator was now hidden by a chrome chassis, which extended to form the housing for his cockpit. Clever joints along the cockpit held the six legs together. Runes crawled up all six legs, etched in squiggly lines. A different set of patterns were etched on the body: big fat glyphs.

If this works I'll feed a starving Hopohopo free of charge, Ejad told himself. *Do you hear me, Source? Are You creeping around me like Lapu as well? Do You have anything to say, huh?*

No answer.

Source never used words. Not to his knowledge. If Source worked in other ways, Ejad was not aware of it. Mana didn't count, in his book. He opened a panel on the squatting machine and pressed a red button. Number Three could have blown up for all he knew.

It didn't.

With a whirr, the round body juddered to life. It rose and balanced nicely on the six legs. This was just the mechanics working on Mana Battery Cell juice. The runes did not light up. Not yet. That needed amethyst power.

Ejad stepped onto a round metal platform on the ground. He tapped it with his pointy boots. Runes lit up in an annulus around him. The platform rose up till he was level with the cockpit. This was Project Two. His second invention which integrated runes and gemstone fragments. He called it the HoverBoard.

HoB.

On HoB's bottom was a cluster of white opal fragments, shock-proofed with treated sea-sponge, and insulated with gas nitrogen. It was all packed tightly into a metal sphere that fit snugly in its two inch thickness. It was a ticking bomb. But also powered the levitating platform. Meh. You can't rule the world playing it safe all the time. Ejad jumped off it into the open door of the cockpit.

Through the plexiglass walls he lorded over this dusty workshop. This one was in the Lote Forest, which bordered the Lava Lands of Elder Pele and the Lavender Fields of Laka. The sisters had grown lax in their security. They considered all three Territories as one and only kept an eye on the outer borders. Lilinoe stood guard to the north and Pele to the south. Laka of the middle Territory was a silly goose who puttered in her fields all day, comfortable assuming her sisters kept both her borders free from danger.

Long ago, Uli had built this place for Laka as a "gift". For reasons Ejad could not yet fathom, Laka seemingly then forgot about it. Uli Cloaked the place, which meant it turned invisible. Later, with help from the teenage Ejad, he outfitted it with more concealment configurations. Elder Laka was entirely oblivious.

Soooo sad sis Laka. Danger came knocking long ago, found a back door unlocked, and it was yours, Ejad amused himself in Uli's voice as he poked buttons on the control panel before him. It was a bulky thing. He was annoyed at the clunky buttons. If only he could get the Mana Slate prototype working. If his theory was right, he could turn these physical buttons into virtual ones on a smooth surface. Like those strange human devices he spotted through Uli's Shimmery Walls tuned to Earth.

"*Oh, snap out of it,*" Lapu said snidely in his ear. He wasn't overly enthusiastic over Ejad's side projects. He always messed up Ejad's daydreams.

Ejad grabbed a lever and slammed it up. That opened the MBC generated current to the gemstone circuit. He actually felt the Mana and electricity charge up the stone deep in the core. It reached the trigger point with a bass 'Whooomp!'. Every hair on his body stood on end. He gasped.

The Mana Mech growled. Macabre noises rent the air. The eerie gnashing, screeching sounds had nothing to do with the machinery itself. He had just activated the thing, not moved it. These were phantom noises.

"*Isn't this considered 'Scary' by Hopohopo standards?*" Lapu asked. Ejad ignored him, casting around in his mind for a cause for the racket.

Oh, no. It's the glyphs! These nightmare sounds came straight from the ancient glyphs he'd incorporated. Screams from the Spirit Realm. Maybe he had overpowered Project Three? It was certainly not a common side effect.

The Mech heated up fast. Ejad was glad he'd insulated the cabin or his skin would blister. Perspiring heavily, he slammed the door closed. It was still unbearably hot.

Meanwhile, Lapu mimicked laughs in his ears. Having no body, he had no idea what mirth was. But he had been observing dwarves for centuries now and could imitate. Lapu lived to lie till he made it. He performed a few of the best Hopohopo laughs in his collection of Voices.

"*Oh, shut up,*" Ejad thought irritably.

Lapu stopped. "*Why? Is that not how evil laughs sound like, hafling?*"

"*It is not.*"

"*How must a villain laugh, then? Pray, perform for your Master, puny monkey creature.*"

Ejad bashed his gloved fist on the control panel. The coolant activated. Inside the cockpit the temperature fell, but not enough. He wanted nothing more than to shut this thing down already but he still had to check if Project Three locomoted.

"All right!" Ejad said through gritted teeth, juggling joysticks. The Mana Mech heaved forward. Two legs, each weighing almost a ton, slammed into the cement. Cracks zigged across the floor. The remaining pair of legs followed, churning the foundation into sand. Machine parts added their din to the other worldly screams emanating from the glyph-Scripts. He shouted the rest of his sentence: "You formless, brainless, Old Hill's Fart: listen up!"

"*Do go on.*"

"Behold!"

"*Still waiting.*"

"THIS is an evil laugh!"

Ejad took a deep breath. A laugh bigger than the Mana Mech exploded from his belly that expunged all the air from his lungs over the course of an entire minute. All the rage, all the grief, all the dreams. At the same time he flicked the final switch. Plasma filaments burst out from the Mech. It looked like one of those Plasma Globes you could get on Amazon for twenty dollars, only, the filaments connected the Mech to every physical thing within a mile instead of a glass dome. Since they were currently in a mansion sized warehouse building, the filaments connected with the walls, furniture, pillars, roof and floor to eat everything up and spit out dust. The destruction left Mana mist behind. Vents around the Mech's body siphoned the mist in rainbow streams, gobbling up the condensed Mana.

Ejad plopped into the leather seat to watch the mass destruction. Plus harvesting. He was mesmerized by the rainbow dust swirling like a galaxy in the midst of the plasma storm. It got better as more light entered through the eaten away, swiss-cheese holes of the building. Made for a beautiful light show. He felt the thrill of power.

If only it wasn't so *hot.*

When the roof fell, it vaporized in a dome around the Mech instead of crushing it. It roared and charged out into the forest. Lote trees unraveled in ribbons, bleeding Mana mist as the life was zapped out of them. The animals ran but were caught in the plasma filaments as well. They were ripped to shreds. Project Three sucked leftover Mana mist, their essence, into its belly. Ejad ran out of breath. His Evil Laugh died out.

The Inventor's head felt strangely empty for a second. Lightheaded. Then:

"*You're such a naaasty little Hopohopo*," Lapu said matter of factly.

He promptly hijacked the Inventor's brain. Feverish, chaotic, amnesiac. Puppet.

"*Such a haaafling little Hopohopo.*"

The Spirit's essence, which had snuck into the locked cabin, seeped into Ejad's pores, into his flesh, into his bones. The Mech Suit didn't help; Lapu could possess that as well. Ejad helplessly contorted as if all his bones were broken.

"*Such a stuuupid little Hopohopo.*"

Ejad's joints snapped back together. He stared right ahead. The stifling heat was no longer registered by his mind, but the Inventor continued to perspire. He pulled the tinted goggles on his skull cap down to hide dead eyes. Lapu enjoyed peeking out through the windows that were dwarf eyes all over this world, when he was doing possession rounds.

Lapu also liked trying out new things.

Like clothes.

This outfit suited the Spirit fine. Goggles, gray bodysuit covered by various chrome attachments that formed Ejad's rune powered Mech Suit. Pointy alloy boots with gold tips. They had the tiniest MBC's on their heels. Very cute.

"*Tee hee hee.*"

CHAPTER 36
ALOHA ALAKA'I

Manaful World
August 15, 2022
Lote Forest, Elder Territory
One hour ago

Elder Puna hovered in a cumulus high over the Manaful World. His robes billowed in the chill currents of high altitude. Around him Mana mist buffeted in frozen flakes that flurried along the wispy cloud vapors like squirrels doing parkour in oaks. Even frozen, the condensed Mana behaved like a curious, crystalline animal, always feeling out its surroundings.

Elder Puna had a forcefield to protect him from the elements. Mana mist crystals swarmed on its surface, crinkling like aluminum foil. Some managed to squirm right in. Puna didn't mind. Mana mist flakes that intruded melted and orbited him in globules that rang like bells. Puna held a long, thin finger out so that a pair could twirl around it without quite touching his coffee skin. He liked moments of peace just by himself, immersed in nature, intimately aligned to Source. His aura was visible up here in the clouds. It was soft magenta.

Source's eternal Song reverberated in his core. Puna closed his eyes. He floated as if lost to the world. His face was serene with braided salt and pepper hair rippling past keen ears that expected a visitor any time now.

The location Puna had chosen was the updraft that lay over the mountain range where Ikaika and the SC had found Cloud. It was the mountainous border cradling Elder Laka's Lavender Fields. Cloud had traveled to Alaka'i's Territory to rain her powerful Mana mist there, hoping its saturation in the Territory would help the Elder Prime heal. Lilinoe's northern mountains were back to normal - no more crystal sandcastles, dancing tulips or ethereal music. Just the howls and whistles of wandering winds.

Puna was beside Alaka'i's pod when he got Lilinoe's SOS. After handover to Charmaine - chaperoned by Elder Hina - he MT to the Violet Mountains at once.

Maka was dealing with Ejad's chest of gemstones. Puna didn't want to draw the youngster into too many things at once. Besides, once he opened the Elder Link, Maka was free to appear by his side anytime as an Elder, an equal.

There was a burst of Mana next to Puna as a Manaful appeared. It was Elder Lilinoe. She projected, "*Mahalo for coming at once.*"

Elder Puna opened his eyes.

Elder Lilinoe's dark gray robes shuddered around her strong form like shadows at nautical dusk, cinereous shades throbbing with Mana light. Iron gray hair framed her worried, plump face like storm clouds.

"*What is the urgency?*" Puna inquired.

"*A monster!*" Lilinoe exclaimed. "*A monster is rampaging across our lands gobbling up Mana mist.*"

Elder Puna stared. Elders naturally mind-meld when they meet, and already hazy recollections of Lilinoe's past few minutes unfurled in his mind's eye. He didn't recognise what she had seen. Just a ball of burning filaments. As purple as Laka's fields.

"*Come. See for yourself,*" Elder Lilinoe projected. She descended through the clouds. Puna lost altitude with her. Levitating and hovering were not quite flying; among the Manaful only Elders ever saw a bird's eye view of the world. The pair of Elders broke through the canopy of clouds. They surfed the wind currents, leaving a trail of Mana mist down the slope in their wake. They skimmed over a shrubby terrain and then came to the fields of Elder Laka where her Lote Forest began.

They had to get closer to the ground before Puna saw the cause for worry. His mouth fell open. "*What is that?*"

"*A machine like the Mana mist harvesting barrels. Only worse! A thousand times worse!*"

From up here the thing looked the size of a garden barrow, round with a dome of blinding filaments around it. It moved at the speed of an elephant stampede. It left a path of destruction with a radius of at least a mile. It stomped through Laka's Lote Forest in a tight spiral, making a circle of dust grow to consume her plantations. Already half the forest was in ruins. Even the clouds above swirled down towards the machine, thundering.

"*I did think the updraft was rather strong today,*" Puna thought, more to himself.

"*The suction gets stronger every passing hour! This is powerful Mana Tech at work. It's the Inventor.*"

Lilinoe and Puna's mind-meld allowed their disturbed emotions to soothe each other without interfering with the task before them. Their robes seemed to hold hands.

Elder Laka appeared. Her robes were paler grays than her sisters', muted watercolors to Lilinoe's dark acrylics. Her platinum hair hearkened fogs and pale clouds. Her elven face made her current emotion extremely clear. She was livid.

"*That thing almost killed me!*" Laka began. Her hair crackled around her exactly like the plasma bolts around Ejad's machine below. Laka's hair often overshadowed her robes.

"*Calmness, sister,*" Elder Lilinoe's robes lovingly reached for her sister. Laka allowed herself to be pulled closer. She mind-melded with the older pair and allowed soothing waves into her soul.

Calmer, Laka pointed a trembling finger at the machine. "*Those filaments break molecular bonds! It is blasphemy!*"

"*You fought it!*" Puna looked around at Lilinoe's younger sister, impressed.

Laka was not in the mood to bask in glory. "*Puna! The point is I failed to stop it!*"

"*Failures trigger new learning,*" Elder Puna TGP. "*What did you learn, Laka?*"

Their mind-meld grew stronger. Puna and Lilinoe gained Laka's insight into the fight. Laka had managed to go through the filament dome right up to the machine.

"*We can't affect the machine with Mana*," Elder Laka revealed. "*It takes molecules apart so that things break down to their very basic components. That releases Mana mist. The machine consumes the mist.*"

"*Storage is below a central engine, alongside a converter,*" Elder Lilinoe observed. "*It's spitting out Tainted Mana.*"

Laka nodded. She made their invisible hovering platform go faster, to get to the edge of the plasma sphere that was destroying her lands. Puna and Lilinoe, acting on cautiousness, slowed her down. Laka already looked tired, and her aura was extremely weakened. They didn't want her to drain herself.

"*It's the runes again*," Elder Puna shook his head. "*That is a legitimate system of magic separate from Mana, do you know. Letters and words carry power. When they are in rune or glyph form, they become power itself.*"

"*But they are always activated with Mana! Our Mana! Source's Mana!*" Laka protested. She was peeved they were having an academic discussion at this hour.

Lilinoe agreed. "*Our Mana Battery Cells use a little bit of harvested Mana mist to generate electricity, the energy source that freedom fighters of the Great Hopohopo Revolution wished for. They don't power runes.*"

Laka frowned. She added, "*We did design Cells that could activate runes.*"

"*Oh yes, Tita! For the Protector's Academy, upon Uli's requests. We did not pursue research integrating Mana Tech with runology but Uli's House always did.*"

They reached the periphery of the plasma dome and stopped over the treetops. Elder Puna raised a hand to warn the sisters from propelling forward. The filaments that fizzled in the air were now sucked up towards the funneling clouds.

"*It's eating all my clouds*," Laka's projection vibrated with indignation. "*And lotes!*"

"*It is a great loss. Lote trees are the single most important resource for both the Hopohopo and Manaful Territories*," Puna agreed. Neither he nor Lilinoe contained the younger Elders' emotional turmoil now. Sometimes it is best to live the moment. This moment called for an emotionally triggered adrenalin rush.

The Elders all took a deep breath and opened their souls to Source. They aligned. Their robes lit up till the glow was a sphere around them, stopping at their individual force fields. Their eyes glowed with Source's sparks.

A cloud of Mana mist erupted and vortexed to reveal Elder Alaka'i. His eyes were also sparking. "*You three are not going into battle with that thing alone!*"

"*Alaka'i! There's three of us. Please go back to your pod at once!*" Puna commanded angrily.

"*Absolutely Not!*"

"*Dear, Alaka'i*," Elders Lilinoe and Laka TGP. "*You are unwell. A battle like this will take a toll on you. Please return to your daughter.*"

Charmaine's voice rang in their heads. "*Mahalo! I have been trying to get through to this stubborn old—*"

"*Charmaine!*" Elder Alaka'i butted in. His opalescent robes were decidedly less lively than those of his companions. But he still pretended he was alright with a proud posture as he hovered before them.

"*Whatever happens, do not MT to this location,*" Elder Alaka'i commanded his daughter. His projection carried tones of sternness. Behind it was the full power of love, the ultimate goal to keep her safe no matter what.

"*Father!*"

"*No!*"

"*You—*"

"*Absolutely Not!*"

Charmaine retreated with a petulant echoing '*Ugh!*'. If she hadn't left, her father would have kicked her out of the private Elder Link, a privilege she got only rarely as it was. Elder Alaka'i glared at Puna, Lilinoe and Laka.

"*The machine breaks objects down and steals their Mana,*" Laka attended to the job at hand. "*Living things give a bigger harvest. But the filaments work slower on Source's Mana and organic matter, especially us.*"

"*Key word: Slower. It does eventually eat away the forcefield,*" Lilinoe noted.

"*What happens after that?*" Alaka'i TGP. He took control of the hovering. He created a single bubble of protection for the Elder team. They were ready to dive in.

"*I didn't wait to find out,*" Laka replied.

Alaka'i eased them into the storm of filaments. They sped towards the originating point. The Mech. Dust swirled in spirals as its vacuuming power kept on increasing.

Puna swept a gust of wind to clear the smoke. The Elders saw runes lit up along the behemoth's leg mechanisms. The forcefield fizzled as plasma filaments attacked it relentlessly.

"*It's a Mana Tech hexapod automaton.*" Alaka'i traced the air in a circle with his palms, patterns appearing before him as Mana mist condensed to align with his intentions. He sent it flying towards Ejad's gizmo. The mist took any form and state he desired from a distance.

Puna, Lilinoe, and Laka joined their minds and powers to the House Opalescent Elder. None of them were able to make Mana mist an extension of their bodies like Alaka'i can. They lent their Mana to the Elder Prime.

Mana mist in Alaka'i's telepathic and telekinetic control swept forward to form a bird-like form, with wings that enveloped the hexapod. Alaka'i crystallized it inwards with force enough to pierce even a block of rose granite.

The Mana crystals shattered against the rune-tattooed metal. The pieces went back to mist state. Filaments jumping off from the hexapod attacked it. The mist dispersed, got caught in the air tunnels, and Ejad's Project Number Three sucked it all up. If this were a cartoon she would have gone 'Burp' in smug satisfaction after the meal.

"*That should have immobilized it completely!*" Alaka'i TGP. "*He is using glyphs! Only runology with glyphs can attract Source's Mana with this force!*"

"*He is using gempower for the glyphs.*" Lilinoe was worried.

Laka clasped her hands, suddenly deflated. "*Even if we do affect the machine with Mana, that will only cause a magical explosion.*"

"*An explosion that will kill us all,*" Puna agreed. He looked at Alaka'i, who was stubbornly taking control of the swirling Mana mist, working it into attacks that just kept dissipating.

"*My force fields will hold!*" Alaka'i was adamant. Said forcefield spluttered like a live electric wire, sparking as it broke down. Alaka'i heaved out a fresh bubble of protection from his core.

Puna decided to add his own specialty to the battle. "*Alaka'i, welcome my heat.*"

Puna's robes erupted into tongues of fire. He herded the flames into super concentrated energy capsules and shot them toward the machine. Mana mist reinforced the orange projectiles in super solid state. The projectiles slammed into the hexapod and exploded in megatons.

The Elders were pushed back with the shockwave. They slid backwards on the gusts. Lilinoe and Laka seized the winds and added their layers to Alaka'i's force field, which stabilized.

The bubble of Elders circled Number Three, reaching into the machinery telepathically to target Ejad. But they met a block. Ejad's mind locked them out securely.

There was only one thing the Elders heard. Over and over again. Like an echo in the hallways of a prison for the criminally insane. And that was:

"*Tee Hee Hee.*"

The Elders throbbed with light. "*Lapu!*"

They stopped throwing their Mana attacks. They instead focused on maintaining their shared force field. They circled and watched as dark goo spilled out of the hexapod. Lapu's essence extended like tentacles over Number Three. They grew of Ejad's body, who sat at the controls as if in a trance. The essence was so strong he had filled the cockpit with a gelatinous substance before the pressure broke the cockpit windows. The stuff spewed out and thickened as he extended into tentacles. Threads of him snaked all over the hexapod.

Lapu's temporary form was anchored to a machine, tainted Mana source, and a dwarf host. An amalgamation, a hodgepodge mixture of parts. This wasn't entirely to his taste yet but he was delighted at how things were going. The Elders picked up on his smugness.

"*Behold the Mana Mech! It will eat you up!*" Lapu TP to the Elders. His voice was every noise that made people grit their teeth.

Number Three lumbered around to follow the Elders' protective bubble. Filaments sparked against the force field. Powdery trails of Mana were already coming off it and getting sucked into the machine.

Puna TGP, "*Let us open the Elder Link and blast this Spirit.*"

The Elder Link was the mind connection the Council members shared. It could be closed and opened at will for privacy. They'd closed it upon the discovery of Ejad's chest of gemstones. Now, Alaka'i nodded to agree with public telepathic broadcasting. His eyes flashed as he opened the Elder Link.

All Elders of the Council paused in their respectful activities across the Manaful World. They received the telepathic broadcast right into their mind's eye. It was like watching breaking news, with four House Emblems specifying points of origin. The pearl and Mana mist helix of House Opalescent captured their interest at once.

Four mind-melded Elders are battling a 'Mana Mech' made by Wanted Inventor Number One, Ejad.

The Elder Council at once connected to the Hive. Manafuls of all Territories got the news in a split second. Many rushed to conjure Shimmery Wall Viewers, tuning to the open Elder Link so they could see better.

"*Now let's contain the whole mile wide radius,*" Alaka'i TGP. He swept them all back rapidly out of the sphere of damage. Number Three lumbered after them, filaments reaching, screaming.

"*Laka, I am very sorry for what I'm about to do to your land,*" Alaka'i TGP. Then he broke the dead Earth around the machine and lifted the whole thing up from the bedrock. The rest of the Elders quickly lent their Mana to the task before Alaka'i crumbled with the weight.

CHAPTER 37
CUT: SC VIEWING

Manaful World
August 15, 2022
Ikaika's Mansion in the Koa Forest sky

The Shimmery Wall showed them a bird's eye view of Laka's destroyed Lote Forest.

"Whaat is that six-legged machine doing!" Nicole shouted, standing up.

"It's eating up the fields and creatures like those Mana Battery Cell barrels we saw before Lapu attacked us that second time," Pierre responded. He and Malie sat closer together, arms linked with the puppies licking their faces. The labradors sensed the children's distress.

"Ikaika? Why won't more Elders MT there to help?" Malie worried for Alaka'i who was supposedly bedridden.

Ikaika TGP. "*We must have faith that my grandfather and godfather know what they're doing.* "

Nicole stared at Ikaika, concerned as he paced before them, hands tightly fisted.

Malie sent him much Aloha and almost jumped up to hug him. His face was contorted and his breathing had picked up, almost hyperventilating.

Ikaika suddenly stopped moving, loosened his fists, and took a deep breath. He closed his eyes to align with Source.

Malie closed her eyes too, bringing her prayer hands to her chin.

Earth shattering sounds like a quake boomed from the viewing portal. The edges of the screen suddenly strobed different colors. The image itself seemed to gain depth. The smell of burning lote trees reached their noses over the sharpening volume.

"*They opened the Elder Link!*" Ikaika TGP excitedly. This time his heartbeat sped up anticipating Elder Kōkua instead of fear for his loved ones.

"How does that work?" Nicole asked, looking away from the Shimmery Wall. Her face was taut with worry for the quartet of Elders battling Ejad's terrible invention. Alaka'i lifting the island of rock was testament to his power. But the Inventor's machine was still on top of it, impervious to damage.

Ikaika had to think how to best explain Nicole's question. "*Remember when all the Elders showed up when Uli and Maka confronted each other?*"

Malie nodded, "Yes! They created a mental connection to kāko'o Maka, a rainbow of Mana mist."

Ikaika nodded at her sharp recall. "*The minds of the Elders are Linked telepathically, all being perfectly aligned with Source. Their collective consciousness constantly 'uploads' information to the Hive as mental bits. Bits of their thoughts form packets of information that can be accessed via Mana, Shimmery Walls, or Mana Tech. Those things are called Link Mediums."*

Malie produced the map of Manaful. Ever since she'd folded it and put it in her pocket, it'd been there. It didn't matter which clothes she was wearing. The moment she stepped through the Shimmery Wall Portal into Manaful World she had the map on her. It was never there upon return to Earth. She waved the parchment at Ikaika. "Is this a LM? We just call it paper."

"The parchment is," Ikaika smiled. "Counts as a product of Mana Tech. Your map will always show where you are, and will update itself like your mobile's GPS. Eventually, I will teach you how to drop pins."

It was true. Malie had noticed the drawings changed as they moved around Manaful. It didn't show her the whole world. Just her surroundings in a certain radius, labeled with a bold type.

"*I used my Mana to conjure a Mana Tech,*" Ikaika clarified. "*Manafuls don't usually need a LM. With us it's all in the mind and soul. I won't need parchment to show a map to a Manaful.*"

"Can you try it on me?" Malie lowered the map to her lap. It seemed like a lame LM compared to the authentic Manaful experience.

"*No. I don't want to give you a migraine. It could hurt because you are not Manaful humans yet. Pule we will find a way to make that happen.*"

"You were telling us about the Elder Link," Pierre reminded Ikaika. He was watching the Shimmery Wall Viewer avidly.

"*Yes. When the Elder Link is 'open', the Link Medium experience gets better. More detailed. Check your map now Malie.*"

Malie frowned and picked up the folded parchment. It looked and felt recycled. It crinkled in her hands as she opened it. Her eyes and mouth made immediate O's.

The map was a three dimensional terrain now. It was like viewing Google maps in 3D. As she ogled, the view zoomed in on ground zero. Small simulations of the Lote Forest and the battle flickered to life like holograms over the surface.

"*Everything is tuned in now*," Ikaika TGP.

Pierre pointed at the Shimmery Wall and at the map. "Same viewing!"

"*Straight from the Hive.*"

Chapter 38
Cut Back: Battle

Manaful World
August 15, 2022
Lote Forest, Elder Territory

Elder Alaka'i raised a hand and blasted Mana towards Ejad, a spell to immobilize.

The automaton lit up, a giant maw-like vent opening to suck in the Mana with a head splitting 'Whirrr'. Elder Alaka'i gasped, unable to stop channeling as he was dragged towards the machine's vents, sucked in with force by his stream of Mana mist. He swayed violently.

His eyes rolled up to only show the whites. He managed a TP: "*Puna! Hold my mind! Lapu is pulling it away!*"

Elder Puna at once raised both hands besides Alaka'i's head and kept his superior's mind grounded in the present. He was not as good as Charmaine at this but he managed. Alaka'i tilted his head back and forth a few times before opening his eyes. He looked forward resolutely.

Number Three roared. It scuttled on the island of rock levitating higher and higher up into the sky. If it fell off the edge, could it right itself? Or would it wave its legs in the air on its back like an overturned beetle?

The Elders rose up with the mile wide island, warily. This was the least they could do to stop it rampaging all over the forest. The machine belched at them, having run out of things to feed on except the rock it stood on.

If it ate the island it would fall.

Elder Alaka'i grinned. He disintegrated the island. The machine fell, fizzling its filaments out at empty space like hungry tongues. Alaka'i sent the rocks smashing into it, the whole pile falling at speed towards the ground.

"*Nothing's stronger than gravity*," Alaka'i panted. As they watched, the machine hit the crater with a deafening 'Whoomp'! The rocks fell on top of it as if covering a coffin.

"*There, it is done. He is dead. The machine is destroyed*," Alaka'i turned to his colleagues. He looked faint, though his eyes still sparked.

"*The Elder Council is calling a meeting*," Lilinoe TGP.

"*Those infernal Elders!*" Puna exploded. "They called a meeting instead of MT here to help?"

Laka nodded. "*May we go mind-meld with them?*"

Alaka'i waved a heavily veined hand at the sisters. "*Go. Feed them what they want. We will join you shortly. We must dispose of the thing we just felled.*"

Elders Lilinoe and Laka bowed their heads respectfully, palms pressed on their waist sashes. They were honored to have fought this battle with the Elder Prime. They wished to keep this team going and defeat Lapu at every turn. The sisters vanished.

Puna descended with his friend towards the pile of rocks. They had crumbled to resemble a heap of sand. Smoke curled up from rubble as if it was hot.

The air buzzed. Maka appeared with a burst of sandalwood scent, levitating. Fraught, he shot over to the senior Elders. He'd been with Charmaine. She'd advised him to come here instead of the council meeting.

"*Are both of you alright?*" Maka asked.

"*Maka! Force field!*" Puna TP.

"*Oh. Yes.*" Maka conjured a force field that shimmered green as it appeared. Elders were supposed to always wear a force field while on duty yet Maka kept forgetting. This was just one of the many reasons Puna worried for the boy. Puna massaged his temple.

Alaka'i released his field and leaned into Puna's shoulder. Puna lay a hand on his friend's spine. Mana flowed into the eldest Manaful's body, nourishing him.

"*Stop that,*" Alaka'i TP. "*You need your strength as well.*"

Puna stopped it.

The three Elders cleared the smog. They stopped a few inches over Ejad's grave. Three metal legs jutted out of the ground, clearly ripped off the main hull. The runes were no longer glowing. The impact had broken the Mana Mech. It was a triumphant moment.

Maka mind-melded with his fellow Elders. He'd missed an epic battle. He had been too busy mind-melding with Charmaine. Maka suddenly frowned.

"*Elder Alaka'i, there was no explosion,*" Maka TGP.

Elders Puna and Alaka'i understood at the same time. No explosion meant—

The mound plumed outward with a roar. Maka blanketed the team from the force. He seized boulders and rocks to reduce them into mineral rich soil, and dispersed them through what remained of Laka's forest on gales of wind. When he landed them among the trees, they saw the machine heave out of the crater.

Lapu's essence bubbled thickly over the chrome chassis Ejad had lovingly prepared over the past few months. The machine creaked and could not balance on its three remaining legs. Lapu's essence formed thick octopus tentacles that helped the hexapod stand. The substance was now rubbery enough to have provided a survival cushion on impact. But the Mech was broken, extremely wobbly on half the total leg count.

The cockpit was busted open like a flower. Ejad sat exposed in his seat. The essence poured out of his body, a miasma. He tapped a button.

Number Three wheezed and coughed. Creaking nastily, a pair of guns extended from the body. Each had glyph Script scrawled all over it. The guns heated up till the metal turned hot fluorescent.

"*Watch out!*" Maka TGP. He MT Elders Puna and Alaka'i in time to avoid twin neon beams that shot for miles in a second. Lote trees imploded out of existence in its path.

"*What in the name of Source!*" Puna gasped.

Number Three wobbled around to take aim again. The guns steamed, heating up. Ejad held the firing joystick, swamped in the thick tendrils of Lapu essence.

Maka MT the trio all over the place, describing a polygon around Number Three. The thing kept trying to lock and load but was far too clumsy to defeat the Manafuls in speed.

Lapu may be totally detached from reality on account of having no physical presence in the world. He was aware this had now become a losing battle. Number Three was busted. Ejad's body was running out of life energy. He didn't want to kill the Hopohopo. Lastly, his manifested essence weakened the more time passed. He had to do something drastic. He allowed Ejad some control. He would know what to do.

Ejad at once flicked a lever. The Mech went into autopilot. "*We can now exit the machine*," he monotoned in the prison of his mind.

"*Weeeee!*"

Lapu's gunky, rubbery essence hopped up as one. He slipped off the Mech, rising into the air. The Mech teetered on three legs, drunkenly stepping sideways till it hit a wall of trees. The machinery sparked and juddered but the filament-storm had died out.

Lapu carried Ejad down to the ground, draped around the Inventor like liquid shadows of midnight. The Mech aimed, and shot another bolt at the three Elders.

Alaka'i MT them to the Mech's back. He raised a storm of Mana mist and sent an attack at Lapu. Lapu dodged, scuttled, hopped, and flared open like a giant squid hungry for dinner. Elder Alaka'i reinforced his force field. Lapu wrapped around it, trapping them in total darkness.

Puna set fire to the essence. But that's when Ejad's form loomed through the syrupy darkness and touched the force field with his gauntlets. There was a bust of sparks.

Next thing Maka knew, Ejad was right in front of them. His suit glowed as he floated like the puppet he was in the middle of the mass of solid essence. The gauntlets sparked plasma.

Maka leaped forward and threw his attacks at Ejad, who hit himself on the chest. A burst of energy pulsed out, knocking away Maka's attack. In the same instant, Lapu tendrils shot at Alaka'i. He grabbed the Elder by the head and threw him away. Alaka'i MT in mid-air to return to where he was beside Puna.

"*Tee Hee Hee.*"

That's when Maka knew the trick. Behind Lapu's viscous form, the Mech took aim. Lapu shot up into the sky. The guns whistled. White hot beams shot at the three Elders.

Maka pushed himself back into Puna to MT them both reflexively. The beam washed the spot they were in with blinding neon light. It may have traveled close to the speed of light but Manaful reflexes, guided by Source, helped Maka.

Maka materialized far from the Mech with Puna. He was sure Elder Alaka'i MT himself away in time. He was so sure.

But as he and Puna watched the Mech lumbering around to face them, they saw it.

His robes.

Clumps of soil spilled from pearl-white robes drifting haphazardly on the drafts behind the monstrosity. The House Opalescent elder clothes were as empty as a plastic bag caught in the wind.

Lapu's essence carried Ejad back to the Mech. They were ready to attack again. Metal glinted in the sun and the ground rumbled with the Mech's steps.

Puna used a ton of energy to send a blast of TGP across the whole world, through the Elder Link: *Charmaine Alakaʻi is Elder Prime! Lend your ʻOhana strengths to Charmaine at once! Transmute!*

The Mech was faster with Lapu essence helping it along. It aimed and shot a beam. Maka grabbed Puna and leaped away.

"*Use your Earth element for a force field or energy blast,*" Puna projected. "*I'll work up a heat blast.*"

Maka nodded. As the Mech clumsily regained aim, he took a deep breath. Centered himself. He was aligned to Source. All the soil in the vicinity vibrated to attention, at his command.

The force field burst out from his core. It expanded at the speed of a bullet with a blood curdling *woosh.* Soil rose up like a magnificent, powdery balloon. Puna sent gales of wind with it and set it on fire for good measure. The force field was an Earthen dome of explosive energy. Trees were obliterated in its path. The very Earth churned up like a wave before it. It hit the Mech, flattening it like a pancake. The automaton exploded, but it was dwarfed and swept away by Maka's force field like twigs in a tsunami.

Boulders and trees smashed to smithereens in the ever expanding circle. In the sky, clouds were blasted away in an expanding annulus. Puna placed a hand on Maka's tensed up trapezius, squeezing hard. "*No more, Maka! That is more than enough!*"

Maka stopped and fell back into Puna's arms, panting. The abrupt disintegration of his force field released a shockwave that flattened the last patch of standing lote trees in Laka's forest. The pain of destruction and death permeated the air, making both Elders tremble.

Dust, powdered glass and Mana mist sparkled and settled on the soil around them in the setting rays of the sun. Elders Puna and Maka looked around the smoking, barren land. On the horizon they saw a dark contrail of ink: Lapu's essence fleeing with his precious cargo. They'd failed to end either Lapu or Ejad.

Puna and Maka's searching eyes found the drifting elder robes and stayed on them. Filaments of lights pulsed like heartbeats through the textile, the intervals growing longer and longer as the sun westered. Their visions blurred at the same time. It was true. Alaka'i was no more.

Across the Manaful world, voices were raised in wails. The Hive was abuzz with prayers. The Elder Link was still open, but not a single member of the Council TGP a word. They were all in the Council Chambers, with three seats empty beneath the burning kukui nuts. They lowered their heads for a moment of silence as the world cried. Grief had to run its course. Not to mention... a transmutation was pending.

Maka and Puna hugged each other, a terrible weight descending on their souls. They lent their Mana to Charmaine's transmutation process. In the purpling dusk, all Puna could think was: *Oh, my dear, dear friend. My dear, dear Alaka'i.*

CHAPTER 39
ARI LOST THE THREAD

Storyteller in Papakōlea, Hawai'i
August 15, 2022

Ari threw a tantrum about the deaths and disappearances, despite saying she found Alaka'i boring. She wondered if Kōkua was healed properly. She wanted to know who the traitor Elder is this time.

Aunty Ellie distracted her by recalling Puna's telepathic call across the world. Ari was piqued. "What about Charmaine? You've mentioned her before."

"Ah, yes. After the fray - as Ikaika comforted Elders Puna and Maka - Elder Alaka'i's pearlescent robes were snatched out of the fingers of Lapu's wind and flew home. The magical robe lit up and was sparkling as all of the Manaful Elder Nā 'Ohana, Source, and all of nature channeled Mana for her transmutation spell. All of the magical forces helped the petite girl over whom the robes finally came to rest. The Manaful cloth flared out and draped itself across her slim shoulders. Hers was a 15 year old body huddled on the camellia seat beside her bed. She did not move because she had her elbows on her knees and her face in her hands. Eyes closed. She is one of those rare Manafuls who doesn't need a Shimmery Wall to see things happening far away. She'd seen her father's demise clearer than anyone else alive. She'd been floating over the Lote Forest in spirit, watching, horrified. Then she had let her spirit flow back into her body in the room, on the flower seat. She wept softly, with absolute control, even in the privacy of her Alaka'i homestead. That is Charmaine."

"Please tell me more about her! Only her!"

"Let me get on with the story, will you!" Aunty Ellie laughed. "Just listen and have patience. You'll get to know her."

* * *

Hoku left work early today to have a 'discussion' with her sister. Ellie had texted Hoku that they must better handle the ma'i situation. Eventually, they would have a convo about adult sexuality with Ari.

Using her set of keys, she let herself in. Her footsteps echoed on the tiles of the front foyer. "I'm here!" Passed the wobbly tripod tabletop in the doorway, dropping her keys there as she had for years. The tinkling of keys as they landed in Ari's ceramic pulelehua ashtray was a happy sound. Hoku smiled, relaxing. It had been a rough day. Working with numbers could be a drain at times. The breezy 'ulu trees outside swooshed in the evening sunlight. Chirps of Paradise Park parrot escapees rattled the century-old mango tree next door. The park is now closed but was once a bird sanctuary in a neighboring Valley. There's a rumor that the minimum-wage park attendants knew they'd be canned during the Covid pandemic, so they "accidentally" set hundreds of parrots free. Oops! Squawk! That explains the plethora of giant green and rainbow birds in Papakōlea.

Ari got up from her spot at the kitchen table, enjoying iced green tea and sliced oranges and apples. Aunty Ellie had just left her niece at a cliffhanger moment explaining just a bit about Charmaine.

"Mom, you're an hour and a half early! Woah, what's happening at the bank?"

Hoku, who rarely hugged her daughter, bent down behind Ari's chair to squeeze her shoulders. She nuzzled daughter's hair as she did years ago. Hoku met Ellie's eyes across the table. Surprised for a second, then happy, Ari raised her arms up to head hug her mom. Hoku laughed as her "work hairdo" became frazzled and frizzy. But she smiled and breathed her daughter's lemon essential oil homemade body butter. Ari had a thing for mixing various carrier oils like almond or coconut oil with her favorite scents: lemon, lavender, peppermint, and sandalwood. Not together. Ha ha.

Ellie smiled at her sister and niece. Hoped they could make it an afternoon habit to meet here earlier than usual. To read together or simply bond. She could be a mediator of sorts for them.

"Mom, Aunty was just describing a queen-like teenager Manaful, sooo beautiful!"

"Is that right? Did I tell you I finished Book One during my lunch breaks this week?" Hoku was proud of herself. She had seen the disappointment in Ari's eyes whenever she'd said, "No,

I haven't gotten to the story yet, Dear." Ari had once mentioned being upset about her calling Ellie's writing, "Silly books." Hoku was proud of her daughter for being unafraid to speak her mind. To call her on things she expressed badly or fouled up on.

"Ellie, your Book One is beautiful, though I found some typos. Who's your editor?" Hoku walked around the kitchen table and pinched her sister's forearm teasingly.

"Oh my gosh, I made the mistake of making changes post-editing. Any mistakes are my fault!" Ellie slapped her own head and groaned.

"I'm sorry about that," Hoku shook her head and reached for the cream cheese in the fridge. She'd make herself some spinach dip. She unwrapped and removed the foil from the dairy and microwaved it.

"Aunty, I hope you fired that guy!"

"I did. I found a really wonderful woman who works for a software company." Ellie's voice tipped up as she winked at her family. With a small happy dance, she took her seat again.

Hoku caught a whiff of the fresh spinach. Loved it. Its greens were the richest of hunter and the leafy texture disappeared in the melted cheese. She'd dip fresh tortilla chips from a Mexican restaurant she loved into the delicious mixture.

"Hey, Mom, did you take off early to read with us or to talk with Aunty about me?" Ari was an astute young lady.

"Oh, I can't put anything past you, huh?" Hoku laughed, taking a seat with her bowl of chips and dip.

Ellie poured her sister a glass of iced green tea. She smiled and shook her head. They weren't sly or subtle.

"Darling, why don't you check on Maui? Maybe our resident stray cat could use some rubs, fresh water, or kibble?" Ellie suggested.

"Huuhhhhh, okaayy!" Ari pretended to be annoyed, but she couldn't hide her smile. She was happy to see her mom and Aunty bonding. She prayed her mom made it a habit to hang out with them more.

Hoku watched her daughter exit the front porch with the bucket of cat food rattling, while shouting, "Maui! Maui! Kitty? Are you here?"

Ellie sat quietly as the bird clock tweeted the six o'clock hour. She knew Hoku had a lot to get off her chest. She heard the crackling of chips, as her sister enjoyed a crunchy bite or two. The salty fried tortilla was a crispy treat.

"I know I should've prepared Ari better for her menstruation. I dropped the ball." Hoku's lingering sad tone brought a frown to Ellie's face.

Ellie grasped her sister's hand over the chip bowl. Squeezing it, she consoled Hoku, "It was a "we" responsibility. We'll do better for the next milestone. There'll be many. Trust me. We must learn and move on. I got you! You got me! Your husband's going to be okay!"

At that last part, both sisters laughed. When she spoke to Hassan about Ari's menstruation and the "sex talk," he'd just about fainted. Ari's dad was not ready. She was still his little girl. He'd grow out of it. He'd step up. His male perspective is valuable.

Ellie laughed, "Okay, maybe Hassan will need some time," she took a sip of tea, "but he's got a lot to share too. Tell him he matters. It's not just a 'woman thing' or a 'woman's convo."

Hoku smiled and dusted off her fingers. She should've grabbed a paper towel from the counter. Ellie handed her wet wipe from a crystal dish on the table. Hoku nodded in thanks. These came in handy. Since Covid, you'd find them in many homes to sanitize one's fingers as much as necessary.

"How's it been since her last monthly cycle?" Ellie asked about Ari's ma'i adapting and comfort at home. Ari had mentioned not feeling comfortable with tampons yet. The insertion of the absorbing tube felt strange. Ellie completely understood and hadn't mentioned it to her sister. Ari was embarrassed after that talk, making her promise to stay mum. She did, until now.

Hoku sighed and shared, "Well, I asked her about her cramps, how bad they are. Checked if she needed special teas or foods. If she wanted to get pain meds, you know, are they bad?" Hoku was pacing now in the kitchen, having taken her dishes to the sink.

Ellie turned around at the kitchen table, still sitting. Watching her sister. Letting her sister talk it out. Let it out.

Hoku stopped pacing and leaned against the oven. "Ummmm.. when we were kids, Mom got us heating pads and ice packs." She reached into the freezer for an ice pack. Needing to touch something. She waved at her sister. Ellie smiled and nodded.

Hoku continued, "Mom purchased us a variety of sanitary pads and feminine products for us to try. I did the same." She puffed with pride.

Ellie put her hand up for a high-five. Hoku patted her hand, saying "Ari was appreciative. I told her not to hide her dirty laundry. Not to be ashamed of soiling them."

Ellie finally said, "Yes, I remember the first night she got her ma'i. She was scared and felt bad about the sheets and pajamas."

Hoku teared up a little, her pretty hazel eyes glistening. She sniffed and wiped the tears away with her forearms. "Oh, mahalo. Mahalo nui loa for being there for her." Hoku frowned and looked down at her hands gripping the sink now.

Ellie got up immediately to hug her sister. They'd all been caught off guard by Ari's menstruation. Hoku didn't have to beat herself up. The sisters hugged tight. They were going to be okay.

Ari peeked into the house from the front porch. She saw her mom and aunt hugging. Ohhh, mushy time. Well, that was better than not talking at all. Ari smiled and returned to massage Maui's furry black neck. They were going to be fine.

CHAPTER 40
CHARMAINE TRANSMUTES

Manaful World
August 15, 2022
House Opalescent Territory
Elder Alaka'i's Villa

"*Father!*"

Why had she been in the Spirit Realm when Alaka'i died? Why didn't she see the battle on a Shimmery Wall like everyone else? It was just a matter of seconds. She missed her father by seconds. Why???

"*Father!*"

Why didn't she MT to the Lote Forest immediately? She should have saved her father, destroyed Lapu, and banished Ejad in one fell blow. What's the point in having all of this Mana, if she couldn't take down one Hopohopo? Why didn't she get any warning?

"FATHER!" Charmaine screamed.

Her scream came from her piko. What was Source's bigger plan for her 'ohana?

She felt her chest shudder as her emotions, soul, and mind aligned. The muscles in her neck were strained with the scream.

Charmaine's eyes snapped open. Her nails tore the white petal edges of her camellia seat, the flower's texture spongy in her sweating hands. Then, she ripped the flower seat to pieces.

Elder Hina, Charmaine's chaperone for the evening, hovered close by. She snapped her finger and the camellia seat became brand new. The kindly House White Elder put a hand on her niece's shoulder, sending healing energy. Hina saw a glow pulsing around the child, a halo of colors across the spectrum. Alaka'i's Hā was visiting in Spirit form. He was there. The Transmutation process will begin when the Mana mist and Elder Prime's robe arrive.

Charmaine covered her face while welcoming Hina's kāko'o. They spent some time like this, in silence. The makani outside picked up a rhythmic pahu beat. It was Source's countdown.

The open Elder Link made their heads ring with the ongoing telepathic broadcast. Grief caused her to tune out the mourning voices. Even so, Charmaine felt the energy from around the world as they cried for Alaka'i.

Voices of nature chanted to her, especially the drumming wind, the makani pahu:

He is dead.

Ba ba bum.

He is dead.

Ta-ta-ta.

Alaka'i is dead.

Boooooooom!

A duality of loss and love warred in Charmaine's head. The kuleana of the change to come would make an average Manaful's knees buckle. She was made of sturdier stuff. Charmaine had been raised for this moment. Born for it.

They were in Charmaine's private chambers on the summit overlooking the ocean. The gossamer curtains on her open window arches blew into the room on the sea breeze. Her tear laced eyes watched dust motes dancing in the flares of kukui floating close to the ceiling. Windchimes, dreamcatchers and furins she and her father made together hung all over her room. They added their melancholy melodies to the makani.

Tear drops rose from her slender fingers into the air. They vibrated and orbited her with a tinny sound. They accompanied the symphonic raptures of the wind, the sea, and the Manaful beings chanting through the Elder Link.

"The Transmutation," she whispered.

Her Spirit conducted the condensed magic, the Mana Mist, as it came rushing to her.

It streamed in through the window arches, swirling around Charmaine. Alaka'i's Hā entered Charmaine's body gently. Source's light pulsed in the room.

Elder Hina stepped back and away, hands on her sash, head bowed. Her pearly robe dimmed and blended till she was just a blot against the walls. She was lending her Mana to the process. Charmaine received Mana from all of the Elders across their world. She opened a Shimmery Wall Viewer for the Elders to witness her Transmutation in real-time.

Source's halo widened around Charmaine, glistening, sparkling, effervescent. Flapping loudly on the wind, the House

Opalescent robe jetted in through one of the many windows on the Mana mist stream. Having no light fibers with the absence of a wearer, it seemed almost transparent, ghostly. Phantom-like, it circled the room and found the Manaful it was looking for. Alaka'i's Hā within her recognized the robes and let her know of the arrival.

Her fingers glowed with readiness and acceptance. Charmaine uncovered her face. The first thing she saw was the veins on her palms. They'd turned into threads of light. She heard the blood pumping through her own body. She took a hold of her emotions. Smoothened the pain on her face back to the collected regality of queens. Her father's Hā filled her from head to toe. Her piko flowered to prepare her for a new life as an Elder.

Charmaine reached out to the lightless robe. The Clothe reached out to touch her finger. Where her finger tip met the robe shone rays of the rainbow. Threads of light coursed through the Clothe, which twirled excitedly, flashing its light showily. Nature's music chorused with that touch. The flutes of the manu, the pāhu of the wind, the crashing of the waves all welcomed their new Elder Prime.

Charmaine giggled through her sadness. The textile's familiarity strengthened her transition. She'd grown up with the robe. It was her comfort and joy. It had been her cradle on days Alaka'i did not want to leave her at home. The Clothe hugged her lovingly then as it did now. Her father took young Charmaine on any number of adventures, often secured by his lively robe. An extraordinary Clothe like no other, the robe recognized her father's Hā within her and nuzzled her hair and face. Clothe missed Alaka'i too.

Being close to Puna growing up, Ikaika knew what that felt like. Puna's Clothe had mothered Ikaika as its own, at once entertaining and protecting the generations of Elders. Maka didn't get it. Uli's Cothe was as confused as its new owner. Maka's stubborn face came to her mind. She smiled. She got off the camellia seat, levitating expectantly to get Robed. The music around her rose into a crescendo of instruments. Movements of light and sound whipped around the room.

Clothe was oblivious to the cacophony of energy, safe within Charmaine's force field. It embraced her gently. Silky ribbons slid up her arms. The robe draped her shoulders. The wide sash, already possessing her ʻohana emblem, tied itself around her slim waist. It fell to her delicate feet in gentle waves like flowing water. Attuning to her tastes, the Clothe tailored itself on her in a style far from Alakaʻi's. The Clothe now held a feminine flair both genteel and regal. She sang as she was Robed, the ʻohana powers suffusing her whole being and shining out from her as rainbow light.

Charmaine's Transmutation Song:

"Pahu pounding of each tree with Father's Hā
creating harmony
With the ocean's flow in my koko as the light
transforms within me
Glistening mists give me voice as Father's energy seethes
all around
The patterns of voices carry from the land, and from Source
are sounds

Waving through me with Mana to help me do what I must
As I step up to guide, to lead, and to be worthy of their trust
My robe supports me and helps me through
All of the choices and orders made anew
Help me, Source, to be the Elder Prime Father had been
The one who gave our people hope, so very driven
My tears fall in gratitude and sadness for all that's
transpired.
The misdeeds of a Hopohopo and a Spirit,
certainly conspired
To change our World forever with mysterious alloy
I will stop them! I pledge my life, my pain, and my joy
Oh Source that is within in me, Aloha wau iā 'oe!"

On Charmaine the robe assumed the tea ceremony kimono style of Kyoto she loved. Mana mist crystals embroidered geometrical shapes through it, always moving and transforming like a kaleidoscope. Triangles of light twirled around in splendid celebration with darker circular threads, providing an interlocked balance of shapes. Her loose brown hair twisted into multiple braids in the coronation style. The silken braids were swept away and up from her face, secured with a fan emblem. Charmaine caressed Source's robe makana, sending a silent mahalo to the thousands of silk-worms used for the Mana Tech textile, their Mana transfused into each fiber. She was thrilled at the coruscating light that fed warmth to her body, mind and soul. She smiled up at Hina. The older Manaful nodded appreciatively, blowing a kiss of aloha to her new leader.

"You will make a fine new Elder Prime of House Opalescent." Hina looked upon her new leader with pride and sadness for the years lost.

* * *

Fifteen years ago, Elder Hina was the first person to hold Charmaine in her arms upon birth. She was the one to hold her heartbroken sister in her arms, when Alaka'i took sole custody of their daughter minutes after she was born.

Charmaine's conception had not been a romance nor a marriage. It had been a mutual agreement. A contract.

Lilinoe had been a beautiful Manaful, with a genius intellect that simply blew Alaka'i's mind. She had been a young, single Elder Lilinoe who had been only 30 years old by human years. She'd just transmuted into her Elder lineage after her father's passing. She'd been in awe of her Elder Prime, Alaka'i, who was fifteen human years her senior. Lilinoe had willingly and excitedly gone along with the Heir plans. It had been an honor. Yet, she hadn't anticipated falling in love with her first baby. Releasing legal custody had been difficult. She'd even signed her title as "mother" to the heir away. It was legally forboden to tell Charmaine she was her birth mother. She had no visitation rights. She was a hānai aunt like all of the lady Elders. Except her heart, mind, spirit, and body sometimes had to be reminded of this. This was why her Elder sisters mālama and chaperoned her eldest daughter more often than she. It was hard for Lilinoe to not see Charmaine as her own.

Hina empathized with her sister's sorrow. She prayed for Lilinoe every day. Her sister would be proud of her daughter's Transmutation. Lilinoe intentionally didn't MT here for the big event, though Charmaine would've consented. Too bad. Her niece was a glory to behold.

"Crack!" The crack of an old fashioned nut cracker brought Hina back to the present. She laughed at the incongruity of the Elder Prime in her flowing robe eating walnuts out of its shell. The crunchy snack brought a smile to Charmaine's face even as she dusted the crumbs off. The walnut shells simply vanished before landing on the floor. Mansion magic.

"Thank you, Elder Hina. May I have privacy?" Charmaine didn't need to ask, yet her father had taught her well. Speaking of whom, she wanted to commune with him. She felt him here. Still.

She nodded to Hina, magicked her snack away, and closed her eyes. Her father's spirit was always accessible for her in the Spirit Realm. It was both a blessing and a curse.

She closed her eyes, transporting herself out of her body and into the Higher Dimension.

Charmaine's light body floated in this ever shifting haven of geometrical shapes outside of her body and mind. She weaved her ghostly fingers with her father's creating prisms of rainbows where the 'skin' met. It was bittersweet and comforting seeing him here. Father and daughter in spirit forms communicated in their telepathic way like in Manaful. She could see his features in her mind's eye still. They were translucent beings, opaque yet vibrant in this Realm.

"Explain to me, Father, why can't I see the future while here in the Spirit Realm?"

"It isn't possible to see the future, my child, as even at this moment, it's changing." Alaka'i's spirit revealed. *"There are many possibilities and eventualities for the future, my child."*

"Bah! Philosophy gives me a headache, so to speak," she laughed, pointing in the direction of her head. She didn't have a body there.

"I wish I molecularly traveled to Manaful, instead of watching you die while in this form!" She pointed to her glowing surface again. Her remorse was great as an ulcer settling in her abdomen. *"I am glad I can say "Goodbye" to you here, Father! The battle happened so very quickly, then the Transmutation steamrolled upon me before I could think."*

"It's not "Goodbye," my love," Alaka'i said.

"I feel as if it is. Many of them piled up at once. A goodbye to my youth. A goodbye to the only way of life I knew. A goodbye to our world as Lapu and Ejad amass an uprising soon. A goodbye to the physical form of you."

Alaka'i's spirit nudged her. *"One day you will see that in Source there is no "Goodbye," but instead there is 'A hui hou'. That is, until we meet again. We are all made of energy and love in Source. There is no death but a transition back to your original formless essence.'"*

"I don't see that yet, Father."

"You will." He said.

CHAPTER 41
THE HEIR TOPIC

Manaful World
March 1, 2006
Verdant Valley, Manaful Zone
Lilinoe's Factory
Sixteen years before

Everyone knew that the Elder Prime pledged his body, mind, and soul to Source. As the first Manaful, Alaka'i prioritized his entire life to leadership. Fatherhood was never on his radar or plans. It was Puna who suggested that an heir would reinforce Alaka'i's 'ohana. They'd been touring Elder Lilinoe's Mana Cell Factory, when the idea of conceiving an heir with Lilinoe came up again. The Shimmering Wall Viewer showed the Mana Cells in varied stages of development. Alaka'i was astounded by the steps and procedures

"*Look at those pumps and firing pistons!*" Alaka'i TP to Puna walking beside him. He was at a loss describing what he saw. He laughed at his ineptness. His opalescent robe jiggled excitedly at seeing another Elder's robe. Sure Puna was here, but the newness was fun.

Lilinoe was near.

"How can Lilinoe have so many gifts of the mind, yet be happy about silly things?" continued, Alaka'i, pointing to the air vents.

Puna raised his brow, *"Silly?"* He TP and mind-melded with his pal. *"Ah, yes, you find the humidifying scents humorous? How she changes it daily."*

Alaka'i smiled, tilting his face to the rafters far above in the cavernish factory. Oranges today. He laughed and enjoyed the citrus scent coming through the vents.

"Right, I've heard Lilinoe surprises her employees with different fragrances daily. It keeps them all hopping and guessing what the Scent of the Day is." Alaka'i noted. The joyful, lightness of the gesture made Alaka'i warm and fuzzy. He admired how Lilinoe could be light of heart yet possess a brain tougher than any brawny fighter.

Such a glorious Manaful gene pool.

Alaka'i cleared his throat.

"Those Elder matchmakers are annoying," he sighed, *"They're at it again about Lilinoe and me."* Alaka'i cringed and fake grimaced at Puna.

Puna turned towards the line of employees headed to the cafeteria. Their happy chattering reminded him of pigeons at a park. The grays and browns of their facility uniforms helped his imagination. Not to mention they all wore smooth, silky black hair caps for protection.

Turning back to Alaka'i, Puna TP, *"I know. The Elder Council matchmakers think you'd be a perfect couple."*

Alakaʻi frowned for real this time, grinding his molars. He was unaware of the keening sounds. Everyone else was.

Puna nudged his friend with his foot. *"You're doing it again! Stop grinding! Your day-time bruxism will chomp away your molars!"*

Alakaʻi bit his lower lip instead, giving him a much younger appearance. Puna laughed.

To add to the younger vibe, Alakaʻi whined, *"I'm content with my Elder Prime kuleana and reciting pule. I don't want a relationship!"*

Puna stopped where they stood, which happened to be outside Lilinoe's New Inventions Department. Puna felt her presence there, working away at molecular and chemical puzzles large and small. Puna pointed to Lilinoe's door, looked Alakaʻi straight in the eye, and cut to the chase. *"Do you think Lilinoe would be a strong egg donor?"*

"Ah! Woah! What?" Alakaʻi almost fell five flights. He didn't sense Puna stopping and was looking over the railing. His robe saved him, as usual. He sometimes had his head in the clouds, literally. This time, he wasn't levitating.

"I've been bugging you for millenia about an heir," Puna nodded as Alakaʻi shook his head. Puna chin-pointed to Lilinoe's Door, positing, *"Over the years, you've never gotten your head out of the books long enough to notice someone."*

Alakaʻi's eyes were bamboocha marble sized now. His breathing was getting so fast, his robe was giving him back rubs to calm him down. It even changed temperature, cooling Alakaʻi's body a fraction.

Puna grabbed his friend's shoulders, *"Breathe. Geez, this isn't a new topic! Just speaking hypothetically!"* Puna popped into his buddy's head to check on his mental state. Suddenly, Puna's eyes grew wider too. *Jackpot!* He thought as he released Alaka'i. *I've hit the jackpot with Lilinoe!* Puna gleaned much passion. A gigantic grin began to grow on his lean face.

Alaka'i closed his eyes, knowing Puna caught his fleeting interest. Okay, he'll be honest: sort of a crush on Lilinoe. Alaka'i covered his face with embarassment. Now Puna knows, he'll never hear the end of it. The silly childhood folklore rhyme rang in Alaka'i's head for some obscene reason:

"Alaka'i and Lilinoe, sitting in the Tree.
K-I-S-S-I-N-G.
First comes love.
Then, comes marriage.
Then, comes a baby
In a baby carriage!"

Puna laughed at the song in Alaka'i's head, his robe jumping up and down in mirth as well. Alaka'i's robe wiped his sweat from his forehead. This was getting too close for comfort.

Puna stopped laughing and answered, *"You don't need kissing, love, nor marriage to have a baby, an heir! But if you like her, then that's half the battle won! Just be nice."*

Alaka'i paced. Thankfully, their robes had a cloaking element. Alaka'i turned his on pronto so Lilinoe's CCTV and her wandering employees didn't think their Elder Prime had fallen off his rocker. Puna followed suit.

The two were in the "space" of the fifth floor corridor but invisible by any eye.

Even an Elder Manaful's vision, especially an Elder Lady Manaful's vision. Source forbid, Lilinoe would not see the state Alaka'i was in. He'd turn into a plum with hilahila, matching Puna's robe.

The stealth layer of their robes blocked out sound as well, though it didn't matter since they were telepathically projecting and mind-melding. Still, their footsteps would've been heard in ordinary circumstances.

"We cannot talk about me and Lilinoe as a couple, Puna! I like her. She's amazing and a genius, but I don't want-want her like that! I just want her genes packed into an egg." Alaka'i bemoaned and groaned.

Puna nodded, as they could still see each other, being mind linked. He watched Alaka'i make an imaginary trail in the marble flooring with off white shoes. He let Alaka'i fume, his tension and stress sure to expire soon. Alaka'i spent too much time in pule and in alignment to get off track by any topic. Puna looked at his imaginary watch, counting time. He'd give Alaka'i five seconds to get back to "normal." 1, 2, 3, 4 and...

"5."

"What were you saying about not needing kissing?" Alaka'i's brows were furrowed now in contemplation rather than irritation.

"Ah-ha! You are interested in the Heir Topic! I've been plugging away at you forever! Finally! Like the SC says, "OMG!" Puna made mind-blown expressions with his face and hands above his head. He actually skipped.

Alaka'i fell all over himself laughing. His robe had to keep him in check again in an exasperated fashion. He wasn't too good on his feet today. You know that saying, "Swept off their feet?" That was Alaka'i today. The idea of "mating" or "making a baby" with Lilinoe simply did that to him.

Puna heard those thoughts and was now practically bouncing on his toes like a ballet dancer. *"You're swept away, huh? Oh, this is goooood!"* He winked at Alaka'i.

Alaka'i impatiently waved his hand at his pal. *"Come on, get it off your chest. What's the grand Heir Topic plan?"*

Puna grinned and pointed at Lilinoe's door. *"We're going to go in there and propose an egg donation and gestational carrier, aka, surrogate duties from Lilinoe!"*

Puna's chest popped up with proud glee. I've done it! I›ve finally found the right Manaful and the right timing for my buddy, my pal, my brother! His thoughts were so boastful and loud Alaka'i was unsure whether to hug him or hit him.

Instead, Alaka'i fainted.

He got over the shock of Puna's idea. He admitted Lilinoe was the Manaful he'd been waiting for to mother his heir. Puna was The Negotiator. He set everything up legally: custody, inheritance, and surrogate payments. Medically, Puna had mālama Lilinoe's health needs as if she were a princess, birthing the next queen. For, she really was.

Alaka'i was way too busy being Prime Elder. Truly, he just showed up and provided the baby batter. Between the hānai brother elders it was all known as the Heir Topic. Except it wasn't just a topic. It was a dream in full locomotion.

CHAPTER 42
THEY MOURN TOGETHER

Manaful World
August 15, 2022
Koa Forest, Elder Territory
Elder Puna's Mansion

The Shimmery Wall Viewer went black as did the bereaved minds of all present in Ikaika's crib. The SC, Elders Puna and Maka, and Ikaika tried their best to stay tuned to what was to come. Soon, they'd witness the new Elder Prime Charmaine's Transmutation. The human children tried to be peppy about this prospect. Having seen Elder Maka's incredibly all-consuming change, this one was going to be a doozy. Yet, their hearts were breaking for the Manafuls.

Said Manafuls' hearts were torn to pieces by the failure. The loss. The death. Each of them had their own burdens. Puna TGP an oli, a chant of the soul.

Puna's Song: Be at Peace:

"Making up for lost time is what I do
Often when it's too late, I realize I threw
Those hours and days away, wasted time
Realizing life has no rhythm or rhyme
I have remorse for the things I did
The problems I caused or hurts I hid
The feelings I left by the wayside
Thinking there's time; it's not our last ride
Our hearts and minds stood together
For millennia, through all weather
I helped you lead as best I could
For all beings large and small should
Remember the biggest thing you sought
That alignment with Source forever be taught
I promise to be positive and have a new lease
On life! Not having a heavy heart. To be at peace."

The group withdrew to their own spaces for a few minutes. Malie, Nicole and Pierre had a group hug before they sat back to adjust to the situation. Malie took out Ikaika's musical flower bud, which unfurled to reveal the tree globe. Sounds of living beings at peace soothed them in the magical mansion in the sky.

Elder Puna left the room for a minute to find peace. Separateness from others was necessary at times. He thought up a garden terrace and the mansion magically churned its core to create it instantly. Puna stepped out onto the landing overlooking Koa Forest a hundred feet below. The evening breeze wafted through his salt and pepper hair sending coolness down his spine. Prickling his arms like a lover's kisses. His robe immediately tucked closer to his strong frame for a toasty hug. The ti leaves swayed and bowed to him as leaned over the cemented terrace walls for lungfuls of fresh high altitude air. Preferring the invisible glass boundaries of the inner mansion, he blinked and the terrace transformed. It became a see-through box protruding from the abode. Birds swan dived through the clouds at eye level. Their playful spirits lifted his spirit for a second. Then, the grief returned. With the children, he'd hid his screaming pain beneath a facade of stoicism. He had not shown his grandson, his young peer, nor the SC what he was truly feeling. That would be a dishonor to his late brother. He was the strong one of their partnership. Well, what was left of their partnership. How does one say goodbye to a soul you've known next to forever? The crushing truth is: you don't. In Source's way, there is no goodbye. Alaka'i was still here and would always be. His body was simply an aspect of him. A single part of the sweet, loving whole that makes up a being. Puna took a deep, healing breath and smiled for the first time since MT back home.

Ikaika and Maka left the lounge through a doorway that opened in the wall, permitting the SC on the rug private time to hug each other. The invisible hallway walls sealed behind them, shutting all others out. They all but ran to the swimming pool. This was Ikaika's 'therapy room'. If Nicole knew she could magick a whole Olympic sized pool up here, she'd go nuts.

The Manafuls dived in fully clothed.

Maka's robe flinched in mid air at the prospect of water. It didn't enjoy getting wet. Maka ignored its tugging pleas to throw it off. The robe stayed on. He needed its presence, its comfort. Even wet, the bioluminescent fibers were enchanting.

Splash!

The 'Ōma'oma'o robes gave up the struggle. In water it glowed brilliantly like iridescent seaweed floating around his arms and legs, but tucked primly around his middle. He dove beneath the surface and ate up the bubbles forming with each leg movement. The churning liquid was cold yet he refused to magically heat up the temperature. He wanted the iciness outside his form to match the frozen bits of his heart. He'd failed. If he was a cowardly dwarf, he'd wish to swallow up all of the water in the pool. Simply and literally drown his sorrows away.

Maka gulped water morosely. Bubbles jetted out of his ears. He can't even drown to death easily. He wallowed in his failures.

Alaka'i always said Elders tended to fail before they triumphed. Look at his grandpa. Oh, boy, was that failing. ALL failures, with a singular triumph in the shape and size of a cactus thorn: the halfling Inventor. If Maka were to magick up the Manaful Dictionary for the Criminally Illiterate, the word 'Fail' would have a picture of gramps under it. Was he like his grandpa now? As if guessing his morbid thoughts, his robe lifted him from his attempts by the scruff of the neck.

I should've derobed, the depressing thought came and went. Water erupted. Soon he was floating above the water, his robe serving as a flotation device. The enlarged textile resembled the baby floatees on Earth, poofy air-tight plastic tubes for an infant's limbs. The lifesaving robe both irritated and warmed his Spirits. He couldn't help but smirk at the sight he must be. Well, drowning had been his idea.

Ikaika jumped into the pool for Maka. Water steamed up around him as his robes comfortably kept dry with its very own heat bubble, the 'Ula'ula speciality. He sensed the downturn of his brother's emotions. He'd seen through the Shimmery Wall Viewer how it all went down. The force field failures. The battery cell failures. The failures in general.

Maka had pretty much tripped at the top of a staircase and never stopped landing on his face and butt ever since. Ikaika wanted to lend a hand. Like Maka he did his best through the Hive Mind, transmitting his Mana and entire soul to save his godfather. He'd failed too in that. Maka wasn't alone in his grimness. Except it had been Ikaika's job since he could walk to mālama Maka. If it meant following him into the pool and being a lifeguard, so be it. Except he didn't need to guard or save an Elder. Ikaika laughed at the sight of Maka sulking on his makeshift robe raft.

"Oh my gosh, if you could see yourself!" Ikaika telepathically projected completely in stitches. The only thing that saved Maka from looking ridiculous was the robe's magnificent green color spectrum. The aquas bled into the teals then bled into the shades of hunter green.

"Shut up!" Maka TP as he paddled himself to the built in stairs. *This is what has become of me. A water balloon.* He thought, tisking.

"Hey, you're a pretty balloon!" Ikaika TP, still giggling. Maka's robe deflated as if sighing in disappointment. It was entertaining to see the fuss it put up. Ikaika MT out of the pool in a jiffy.

Why'd Maka actually walk out, he couldn't guess. Well, he could guess. Maka wasn't all together right now. Who could blame him, really? Watching the battle transpire in virtual reality was surreal enough. Maka had been there in person. He couldn't imagine the torment in Maka's soul now. He sent mind-melding aloha to his brother. They were returning dry, of course, to the lounge.

Though he wasn't feeling the love for Ejad, Ikaika certainly admired Hopohopo's brain power. That guy was next level Einstein caliber genius.

"*What the hell?*" Maka TP to him, giving him the stinkiest, most evilest side eye one could imagine.

"*Oops! Devil's Advocate?*" Ikaika cringed realizing Maka had heard his grudging hero worship of Ejad.

"*Worship?*" Maka stopped in his path suddenly. Ikaika bumped into him like a Three Stooges sitcom. Oh-oh, he'd heard that too? Ikaika was digging his grave deeper

"*Shutting up! I'm shutting up!*" Ikaika tried to be serious, but his eyes were laughing at himself. Foot coming out of mouth.

Maka nodded.

The two Elders and Ikaika joined the SC at the same time from different directions. Ikaika wondered where his grandpa went. He raised his brow at Puna. His grandfather shook his head, lifting his hand to change the channel of the 20 x 20 foot SWV. It was time for The Transmutation.

The SC hadn't noticed their three Manaful hosts missing. It had truly been just a handful of minutes. They'd been distracted by the usual heavenly amenities of the crib. Food for days, pets, luxurious bathrooms, limitless best-selling novels (for you know who), and a VR screen that could pop up any series imaginable. If every streaming network on Earth got married, that's what Ikaika's VR-SWV would be like. Except a thousand times better!

"What's your favorite pie, Nicole? I'm hungry for pecan ala mode! Want some too?" Pierre bounced on his king-size waterbed. His stomach grumbled for some caramelized nuts and brown sugar glazed pecans with frozen vanilla yogurt.

"Pie, huh? Not feeling that. Give me plain ole' chocolate covered peanuts!" Nicole was wrestling with Cupcake, its fur tickling her underarms. Wily pup trying sneaking beneath her arms to chomp on her hair.

"Do you guys only think of food here? Come on, where's the bibliophilia?" She was on her rosy velvet couch. It's pillows were body-pillow sized and made of memory foam. She always asked the mansion for the same set of pillows. They contoured her small frame like warm hands rescuing a lost kitten.

Her SC companions laughed at her pillow-hugging and nodded vigorously. "Yes!" They shouted about the food.

Before their Manaful hosts could return, the SC were all set with floating foldable personal dining tables. The treats made Ikaika smile. Maka wasn't in a smiley mood. Nicole avoided his eyes. Pierre met Ikaika's gaze questioningly, asking Ikaika mentally, "*What can we do to help Maka? What can we say?*"

Ikaika appreciated Pierre's tactful mental question. Better to throw the question out via his mind than blurt it out, disturbing the silence. The boy's telepathic abilities were being rooted right now. Pierre knew Maka could read his mind, but had a feeling Maka wouldn't bother at this point. Malie, ever present to Pierre's thinking, put her book down and approached him.

"I can't speak for Maka, but it'll take time for all of us to heal," Ikaika TGP.

"Yes, we must align with Source. Always." Puna agreed.

"But what does that mean, literally. How does that apply to humans? We're not Manafuls!" Nicole complained, plain confused by this Source business.

Puna sent out threads of glowing light from his fingertips. All ten of them circled Nicole, lighting her up. His TGP and light were as soft as the caress of petals. "*Questioning and answering would be an endeavor counted in millenniums by the time all is told to our satisfaction. May I show you a vantage point to begin striving to answer your own questions?*"

Nicole nodded. The filaments encased her and went inside. She widened her eyes at the others and blinked. Her body was lit from within. For a second they saw the silhouette of her skeleton, flesh wrapped around it like glowing light. The light vortexed into a compact sphere exactly where Nicole's center of balance would be. It moved with her.

Puna's eyes glowed like caramel laced with neon lights. "*What you glimpse is your core, Nicole Moku. Your eyes may not always be fixed on it but it's always there. Everyone has one. Stand on it and come ever closer to fulfillment, as you do even now, everyday.*"

"*Be at peace in your body, mind, and soul, Nicole,*" Maka added solemnly, nodding.

"Amen!" Pierre and Malie said at the same time. They hugged each other and opened their arms for Nicole. "Bring it in!" Pierre smiled at her. Malie wiggled her fingers.

The threads of light emerged from Nicole and retreated back under Puna's fingernails into his body. The nerves in his hands were lit up for a blink before it faded to normal.

"Ahhh! You guys!" Nicole joined the group hug, bundled up in Pierre's arms. They wrapped Malie between them as she was so halfling.

The sad but strengthened group watched Elder Prime's Transmutation in real-time via the transportive SWV.

Each had their own reactions.

Malie burst into tears of awe in Pierre's arms. She repeated between blubbery lipped happy whimpers, "She's so beautiful!"

"It's all so beautiful!" Nicole said, lashes wet.

Pierre simply held Malie tight and nodded against her hair. Silence was golden and he knew it to his bones. He patted Nicole's very still arm, as she'd been in a daze the entire moment.

Nicole didn't have a word to say. Her mind left her body for the time being. That's it. She was simply BEING. No thoughts. No pain. Nothing. Just breath. That was enough for Nicole.

Ikaika held Maka's trembling hands. Maka's own Transmutation had not been that long ago. He'd gone through it riddled with flesh wounds after a terrible fight. Ikaika sent calming, soothing ocean sounds into Maka's mind. He knew water was what Maka loved. Maka accepted his brother's waves of aloha, doing his best to just be, as Nicole was. He used the in and out susurrations of the water currents to ease his memories of the pain killing Uli wrought on him. Praise Source for Water. Water heals House Green in particular.

Ikaika watched his grandfather levitating nearby. Puna sat up straight in a cross-legged yoga form. Ikaika knew his Elder relative wasn't really present. His physical shape and body was present, but his spirit and mind was in Charmaine's presence. He was astral traveling, where his mind, his consciousness, his spiritual being left his body. It traveled to another place, time, or dimension. It took great, supreme alignment with Source to do it. Ikaika prayed everyday for that kind of Mana. Then again, maybe not. He was pleased that Puna was there now, making peace with his brother's transmutation. Source be with us!

CHAPTER 43
SC FACETIME

Earth
August 15, 2022
Secret Club's three homes

The SC transported via the Shimmery Wall one by one. It was a strangely different molecular leap, singly and alone. Yet, after what they'd witnessed that day, each wanted their moms. Just to be held tight. Held close.

The moms didn't mind, though each promised to themselves to figure out what was happening. An SC mom meeting was definitely in the near future.

SC Mobile Meeting via FaceTime

Malie: I call to order The Secret Club

Pierre: Wow, I've missed you doing that!

Malie: Muah! Muah! Kisses to you both as it was a heck of a day.

Nicole: You can say, "hell" Malie, it was that kind of day.

Pierre: It certainly was crazy: the battle, the tech, the magic, the death, the transmutation, the...

Nicole: We got it, Pierre. We got it. It was a lot.

Malie: I want to cry and scream. I want to leap through the phone and hug you all again.

Nicole: Omg, you are sappy!

Pierre: I'm all arms. Come right through the phone!

Malie: Hee, hee, wouldn't that be wonderful. MT on Earth?

Pierre: Yes, yes, totally. There were countless times when my mom was preggers that I wished to MT her to the hospital.

Malie: Awww...you are a sweetie. Yes, at the baby shower I was wishing the same thing.

Malie and Pierre (same time): Twin-mind!

Nicole: I'm rolling my eyes. See my eyes stuck at the top of my head?

Malie: Leave them up there. We're on a roll.

Pierre: Always, Halfing. Always.

Nicole: Hey, don't call her that! No bullying!

Malie: He doesn't mean it in a bad way. I embrace my petite beauty. Besides, did you see Ejad? If I had half of that halfling's power...

Pierre: Ha. Ha. "half" of "halfling". I get it. You're hilarious.

Nicole: Rolling my eyes again. Seriously, is it betraying our Aloha for the Manafuls and Puna's ʻohana and even Alakaʻi's memory to admire Ejad? Are we backstabbing? Should we be cheering or even admiring the "bad guy?"

Malie and Pierre: Breathe, Nicole. Breathe.

Malie: I can see your face burning up. Your volume is going up. Your whole aura is heated up!

Pierre: Owl-breaths. Together. Everyone.

Malie, Pierre, and Nicole: 1...2...3... Whoo! Whoo! Whoo! 1...2...3...Whoo! Whoo! Whoo!

Malie: You okay, Nicole?

Pierre: Should I text your mom? Uncle Nick? Grand-dads? 9-1-1 Emergency?

Malie: Hey, don't get her excited again!

Pierre: Oh, yeah, sorry. No adults. We're good. You're good, right?

Malie: Nicole?

Nicole: Whoo! Whoo! Yes, I'm good.

Malie: We won't talk about Ejad.

Pierre: No. We won't talk about him.

Nicole: I think we should ask Ikaika next time. He'd know how we feel.

Malie: Yeah, I'm sooo confused.

Pierre: You're not the only one. Yet, I also feel blessed.

Nicole and Malie: Yes! We are!

Pierre: Hey, now you're twins. Ha. Ha.

Malie: For the rest of my life, I'll never forget Elder Prime Charmaine's Transmutation.

Pierre: For sure. Guaranteed. Me too.

Nicole: I thought Elder Maka's was mind-blowing. This one stopped by mind. Really. Halted.

Pierre: What? Stopped? You stopped breathing? Oh, like took your breath away? Beautiful?

Malie: No. I think she meant spiritually. Right?

Pierre: Ahhhhh! Ohhhhhh! Yeahhhh! Like Buddha, Jesus, Muhammad, and every Supreme being that ever walked the Earth had visited you in PERSON! You stop being you. You just Were.

Malie and Nicole: Pierre!!

Malie: Holy moly, Pierre. That was inspiring.

Nicole: Ditto!

Pierre: Oh, um, thanks?

Malie: You're blushing.

Nicole: Don't be embarrassed. That was the deepest thing you've ever said since we met.

Malie: Agreed. Hands down.

Pierre: Awww, my heart. Ladies, you touch my heart.

Malie: Do you remember those last words of the Transformation chant? It was super duper beautiful.

Pierre: Ummm...was it Hawaiian?

Nicole: Aloha wau iā ʻoe.

Pierre and Malie: Nicole! How'd you remember that?

Nicole: My heart. The words sunk into my heart.

Malie: That's lovely. You're making me cry.

Pierre: Aloha wau iā ʻoe.

Malie: I'm Googling it right now!

Nicole: I love you. It means I love you.

Pierre: Ohhhh, my heart is melting here.

Nicole: I mean it too, guys. I love you.

Pierre and Malie: Oh! We love you too.

Nicole: Twin-mind.

They went silent for a while. Simply looked at one another. Appreciated each other. They logged off a minute later. Each consumed in their own thoughts. But not lost. Loved.

CHAPTER 44
HONI PU'UHONUA

Earth
September 6, 2022
WMS Hawaiian Culture Class

Pierre met a Hawaiian-Maldivian boy in his culture class their parents put them in. Everything in the class was interesting and new, except for the boy. Well… he was also interesting. Just not as new to Pierre as music instruments, craftsmaking, Hawaiian chanting, and hula dancing. They'd seen each other before. His name was Honi, which means "kiss" in Hawaiian as he'd teasingly told Pierre with a wink upon meeting him.

Honi's face was a familiar face in Wright Middle. They had different classes. Now they'd run into each other here. Pierre vaguely recalled seeing Honi at football practices once or twice too. Now they were in Wright Middle School's Hawaiian Papa or cultural learning class taught by guest teachers from the Hawaiian community. It was a course elective both of their parents insisted they sign up for to sustain their native roots.

Pierre was initially reluctant about it, being a Californian transplant. Pierre was now 110% all for it. He loved seeing all the instruments lined up, hearing the beautiful music, and now the happy expression on Honi's face. Pierre was captivated.

On their first day, Pierre held an hourglass shaped gourd called an ipu by the cinched middle. He imagined the once growing fruit with hair, seeds, and leaves on a tough trellis. His grandfather would've loved nurturing such a gorgeous vessel. His teacher, Kumu Kahea, described the ipu as having ceremonial day-to-day water-bearing and musical purposes. The students weren't to drop the lovely mahogany gourds.

Why, hello there, little music thingy, he thought. It was decidedly a whole new experience to gripping a rugby ball so hard your knuckles hurt. The boy next to Pierre smiled at his handling of the Hawaiian traditional instrument as if it were alien technology. Pierre smiled too. They had been smiling at each other for ten minutes now. They stared after introductions and gazed after establishing why their parents made them register for the elective.

Apparently this was supposed to guide young Hawaiians get in touch with their local roots. The moment they saw each other, Pierre and Honi smiled ear to ear.

"Weren't you on the team?" Pierre asked, placing the boy correctly in his memories.

"Nah, quit."

"Knew it."

Smiles.

"It was just a week."

"Coach called you a quitter."

"Thanks for remembering me!"

"I don't think you're a quitter."

Smiles.

"Coach says a lot of things."

"He doesn't lie. I did quit, after all. "

Smiles.

And so on.

Class was awesome.

On that first day, Pierre and Honi discovered they'd be dancing hula, carving a poi pounding board and stone, and learning to chant in Hawaiian. Over the weeks the boys enjoyed the cultural experiences as their special friendship bloomed.

Pierre still felt lost about Manaful World changes. He didn't share those with Honi, but it compounded the distress he already felt at football practice. He's been sensing a change in the way the other players treat him. He yapped about that.

Honi said it's not his imagination. The team is toxic. That is why he quit. He nudged Pierre's shoulder and said they have better things to do than eat mud.

Chapter 45
Bullies & Phobes

Earth
Sept 19, 2022
DMW Football Locker Room

Pierre has had a good week.

Except.

His team buddies dropped homophobic words seemingly randomly into the light conversations. They said it casually, flowing out of their nasty mouths during training, locker time, bench time. Had they always done it and was he only now noticing it? Has he become sensitive to certain words? Why'd they make that snide comment about real boys not having girls as friends? After his talk with Honi, he was seeing it everywhere!

Whatever the case, his nerves were starting to act up around his teammates. Nobody had bullied him outright... yet. It was the atmosphere that got curiously cramped. He felt like a fly over whom someone was slowly lowering a jar to trap it inside.

He shook off the image of him as a fly in a jar. He had better images to think about. Honi's face floated up in his mind's eye and he smiled at once. That's more like it.

He started staying back in Hawaiian culture class to talk with Honi. His classmate became a new confidante as naturally as fish breathed underwater. Many niche feelings he'd kept bottled up came spilling out. He voiced opinions. Pierre felt good about it.

Honi encouraged Pierre to be strong and grateful for the positives in his life. He should appreciate his great football record, loving family and other close friends like Nicole and Malie. Honi likes listening to Pierre talk about the girls. Though they've all never met, he hears the aloha in Pierre's voice as mentions them. Honi enjoyed making new connections.

CHAPTER 46
WMS GROUNDS

Earth
Sept. 20, 2022
Wright Middle School

Pierre ruminated on his teammates' underhanded bullying as he gave silent company to Malie in the Library. She's absorbed in a giant book. When Nicole texted that she is free, they joined Nicole at the gym.

They walked making small talk. Except for Pierre. The girls noticed but gave him peace. Their sneakers made loose gravel underfoot crunch loudly

"*What's up?*" Malie projected her thoughts to him. Her bag bumped into Pierre's as they walked side by side.

"*Something's up, that's what's up. People are talking about me. In a bad way.*" Pierre thought.

"*Maybe it's not in a bad way,*" Malie ruminated.

Nicole sensed their silent exchange. She looked at her buddies, nose tingling.

Pierre took a deep breath as Malie took his hand. He turned to include Nicole, saying that his team knew he's gay. Nicole stopped in her tracks. This happens when her emotions ball up to cannon out at full force.

Nicole demanded if there had been bullying. Gay bashing is a real thing. Speaking up was best. Pierre shook his head No. This felt different. It's weird.

He held Nicole's shoulders to keep her from hopping around in indignation. She cooled considerably when their eyes met. "No bashing happened, Nicole. Calm down."

Malie squinted to remember something. She had overheard the cheerleaders arguing over whether Pierre was gay or not. The guys fuelled the fire. That's where the gossip originated, from his own team.

Malie voiced her theory and anecdotal evidence.

Nicole agreed. "Ignore the word-dropping in the middle of normal conversations. They are baiting," she said. "Don't respond, keep it cool."

Pierre chewed his lips and worried still. He didn't feel like visiting Manaful today... he wanted to go home to Shelly and Aliyah. He also needed a big Gabe hug.

Nicole and Malie understood. They watched him leave. They don't believe anyone can rob Pierre of his light, because despite the disheartening realization that his team guessed his sexuality, Nicole and Malie's friend still looks bright and happy on general principle.

Chapter 47
MW Postponed and Kona

Earth
Sept 21, 2022
Wright Middle School Gym

Malie and Nicole were ambushed by a squeakily polite Kona on their way to duck behind the gym through the stairwells. He pestered them with some questions about why they go behind the gym wall.

Kona came right out and said, "I watched you walk into the Shimmery Wall!"

Malie stopped Nicole from grabbing the little snoop by the collar. She pulled the kid in by the arm to sandwich him between them.

"Listen," Malie said in a Special Agent voice. "Walk with us. First of all, it's a secret. Second of all—"

"You're the Secret Club," Kona said, rolling his eyes. "I know."

"Holy shiz," said Nicole. She gave herself a very loud and painful facepalm.

Smack!

Malie agreed the situation demanded it. Kona just giggled. They walked around campus and talked till Nicole's temper wore off. She maintained her refusal to make Kona SC.

The girls didn't make it to Manaful that day.

ACT III

Chapter 48
Nicole Bullying Wrap

Earth
Oct 1, 2022
Secret Club's three homes
SC Mobile Meeting via FaceTime

Malie: I call this Secret Club's FaceTime meeting to Order!

Nicole: It's good to see you, Pierre, I was worried about you.

Malie: You've never ducked out of Manaful visits before.

Pierre: It's the football team. I don't feel like I belong anymore.

Nicole: What are they doing?

Malie: Is there something I can do? Do you need us to come over?

Pierre: It's not like that. Not threatening or scary, yet.

Malie and Nicole: Yet?

Pierre: Nothing. Nothing. Just feeling some anxiety. Feeling it about going to practice.

Malie: You sure?

Nicole: Want me to talk to your Coach? You have anti-discrimination rights!

Pierre: No. No. Ummm. Silver lining. I met a boy in Hawaiian class. Honi. You'll love him.

Nicole: A boy? Ohhhh...

Malie: He must be a sweetheart!

Nicole: Well, you've got a mixture of news, and so do we! We've got a Kona-problem!

Pierre: (Laughing his head off)

Pierre: So how's your mom, Nicole?

Nicole: Ken and his gang were suspended for the bullying incident.

Pierre: Did your Uncle Nick's pals from the Juvie Department to help out?

Nicole: No, it wasn't needed. We did mediation and the bullies got community service.

Malie: That sounds generous. Didn't your mom want them expelled?

Nicole: Our school counselor, Tawny Kealoha, calmed everyone down at the Principal's Conference Room that day.

Pierre: I'm happy she did that. For healing's sake.

Malie: That's beautiful, Buddy! I like that – for healing. You need to say that to yourself too!

Pierre: I know. I will.

Pierre: Umm...Thank you, girls. Gotta check on my sis'. Night!

Malie: Call this Facetime meeting to close!

Nicole: Night!

FaceTime ended.

CHAPTER 49
SC MEETS HONI

Earth
Oct. 24, 2022
Pierre Martin's Home

The girls came over to meet Honi for the first time. They've heard of Honi, but they'd never talked with him before.

Honi was an inch taller than Pierre at five and a half feet in height and about fifty pounds heavier. He was the epitome of lovable teddy bear types with his warm, genuine smile and affectionate nature.

Watching him hold Aliyah like a professional nanny, the girls were speechless. They hadn't imagined a big guy to be a gentle-speaking, baby-whisperer. Pierre simply grinned at the girls with a thumbs-up.

Pierre was bursting from the seams and doing a happy-dance that his besties from both sides were meeting.

Nicole and Malie stood on the opposite side of Aliyah's crib from Pierre and Honi. The SC watched Honi expertly change Aliyah's poopy diaper in minutes. They all cringed at the smell, except for Honi.

Pierre stared at Honi in awe. Honi's gentle wheedling to the infant never ceased as he dabbed the sides of her diaper tabs on its front coverage on her miniature hips. He knew Aliyah needed reassurance while being wiped down and bodily adjusted. Still in his baby-whisperer tone Honi said, "I've got four little sisters. Sounds like a screaming hen-house, but I did all their diapers and raised them like my own. Learned to change 'em before I turned five."

As his elder brothers moved to Maldives, their mother's homeland, Honi had been their leader, Prince, and caregiver in early grammar school. He was the eldest of the brood left in Papakōlea, basically managing four younger siblings.

"Sing something," Nicole demanded of Honi as they all escorted the baby to its swaddle of blankets on the couch. Nicole was ticking off everything she liked about this new kid. Honi obliged at once. He sang an abrupt limerick about the rain to Aliyah:

Honi's Song:

"Vaareya bōtto.
Kudhin kulhey nātto.
Thandhoshu oi kātto.
Kaalhu elhi mulhōttō."

The Secret Club didn't know what any of that meant, but was doubly impressed. The Dhivehi words were mystical to their ears. Honi's voice was honey against the pitter-patter of rain on the window panes. Under the auspices of a gaggle of loving preteens, Aliyah cooed and went to sleep before they returned her to Shelly smelling of fresh powder.

CHAPTER 50
EJAD/LAPU, ONE MIND

Manaful World
Oct. 15, 2022
Violet Mountains
Ejad's Underground Bunker System

The Mech Suit saved his life the day of the Mech standoff with the Elders. Ejad Honua had never been this grateful to anything, and that the object of his affection was a glyph-Scripted alloy suit made him grin at himself. Project Number One's HoverBoard (HoB) integrated heels helped him escape into the mountains. Lapu, with his essence, could fly as well, but the Spirit had quickly dispersed as they searched for the cavern entrance. Ejad used a pair of aerosol propellers on his suit after Lapu "left" to go faster.

He flew on HoB heels in the center of an electric force field. The cloaking script was faulty on this one. He faded in and out of vision like a dying bulb. Startled rock lizards darted into the rustling festuca grass at his flickering approach.

This was Lilinoe's Territory. He couldn't stay here long. He and Uli built a cave system that had a hidden entrance here. The tunnels also gave him exits into multiple Elder Territories. The underground system was Ejad's favorite hideout.

Too bad he was going to have to block this particular entrance after he was through. He would miss natural wind and light. Ejad hovered into a rocky crevasse and found what he was looking for. The entrance to his personal underground tunnel system was there. He heaved down a lever that was carved into the rock to be found only by the carver.

After he was through, he tripped a switch wired into the cave walls. Doors camouflaged to look like boulders sealed the cave opening. Thick shrubs hid cracks nicely. Ejad took off his goggles to watch the mechanism in action. The doorway light falling on his scratched up, bleeding face dwindled into a slice. It winked out in his dusky eyes. Ejad was enveloped in layers of darkness.

That was two months ago.

He had lived here ever since the battle. The tunnels led into hundreds of cozy caves. Over the course of twenty years he furnished some chambers free from Uli's meddling. Mostly. Uli let him run this cloaked place, what he called his "Ana Keona," or God's gracious cavernous gift. This specific chamber was Ejad's true home. The floor was polished rock with carpeting here and there, all the plumbing was in place, and he had an entire larder full of canned and packaged rations.

It was here Uli gave him lodgings after the Academy. Forbidden to leave the Ana, Ejad roamed the tunneling flowstones by the glow of bioluminescent fungus to visit caves, chambers, and passages. Columns of limestone and calcite cast deep shadows here and there. Ejad used night vision goggles whenever a luminous fungi generation died out. Otherwise he'd as well have gone blind.

Down here in the system Lapu was everywhere. Outside of the Rift Border, the Spirit did not technically have to move in space and time to travel anywhere, although his essence did. This meant Lapu had the ability to telepathically 'tune' into any location he desired and then Manifest there using tainted Mana. If available. The Ana had a system to suck out all Mana.

These walls stopped the Spirit from manifesting with his essence.

But Ejad was right. The Spirit was there, lurking in the shadows. Watching. Lapu was listening to Ejad's thoughts, tweaking, and whispering. "Invisible".

More accurately, "Unseen". He had not manifested ever since Alaka'i died. A lot of his essence was reverted back to Mana mist in Laka's Territory alone, by now. Ejad's harvesting barrels were confiscated. Lapu's plan to accumulate excess tainted essence in the Manaful air had failed miserably.

Wonder when Lapu will be able to Manifest next, Ejad thought as he enjoyed the feel of frayed throws on cozy armchairs. His bed was queen sized and there was a fluffy rug on the rock floor beside it.

Ejad walked over the rug in circles, furry softness beneath his soles. It was braided and scoured to achieve the fluff. The glow of bonnet mushrooms growing on book-shelf ledges along the walls lit the room. Ejad lifted down a beatbox and carried it to the bed to sit studying it.

Setting it on the bed, he pressed a button. A projector flipped out and a wash of light bathed one of the walls, across a hanging taro leaf-print cement plate. On the screen he watched Mana mist bloom to wiggle and squirm, skittering like a hornets wasp. He fiddled dials. This beatbox was not used to play music. It was an old runnecraft (Mana Tech with integrated runology) he perfected during Uli's last days. It could record environmental and spatial information Ejad's body picked up. When he hooked the accompanying doohickey on his ear the runecraft tuned into his brainwaves. Red button was for record and green for replay. Now he pressed the green button. Images rolled out on the square of light on the wall. He had to twiddle the disks to go through the days. Currently, his memory devices stored 200 days of information. He watched and deleted days from the recording device as he memorized. Most of the scenes were of the Hopohopo Town Halls he frequented with the wheelchair disguise that came with the device. He dialed through time and used the fast forward and rewind buttons often. He was lost in the enjoyment of using his Mana Tech.

He had a communication system here to send memos to Uli's Hopohopo Network. After his analysis and scheming, Ejad sent the memos to the Governors. The Governors would then use Lapu's mind-blocked puppets. As a reward, Ejad would send off cartloads of coins their way. All was possible with the comms wiring. He had an old handle phone Earthlings would call the Alexander Graham Bell style. With it, he whispered to Governors all over the Territory and beyond. Ejad's most recent order was to hide all HoB integrated hovercrafts that were used to move the harvesting barrels. He'd promised the Hopohopo an army of Mana Mech. Soon, he'd need helpers. The Governors would supply him with the assistants he needed.

* * *

Lapu observed Ejad as he counted down the days of the calendar. The Spirit bided his time. Recover. Re-energize. A visit to the Rift was called for. Lapu's work here was mostly done. He engineered the inventor's mind over time making it easier and easier to possess each time. Now, he wouldn't even notice. They were slowly becoming Lapu/Ejad, synchronizing cores. Because even Lapu had a core. He was just unseeable to the naked eye.

The Spirit/Hopohopo needed neither telepathic nor verbal communication. They were slowly becoming one mind; that is, Lapu's mind. Ejad instinctively attuned himself to what Lapu wanted. His body reacted less and less. Soon his limbs were fluid and his body limber as he lived in his secreted underground empire. The scheming was Manaful in a dark way as mental and spiritual manipulation was at hand here. Charmaine sensed him but hadn't yet captured him with her telepathic sphere.

As Ejad sat in his dimly lit chambers to reminisce over his turbulent life, Lapu "left". For real. Going into the Rift was not the same as observing the World. To him, he felt how we'd feel jumping into the sea. The air was a denser medium here. Ejad's mind - and all other minds he had threaded together to himself - got muffled. He was with himself in the Rift Border. Lapu was a hazy humanoid ghost; he flitted towards the Rift to reach the world's core.

CHAPTER 51
MAKA MUST MOBILIZE

Manaful World
Oct. 16, 2022
Manaful Zone

Elder Maka and Maikaʻi were strolling in the Zone to feel the beings around them. There was nothing like planting your feet down on these lands. The vibrational energies of Manaful World soaked up through their soles and attuned them with nature.

The Manaful Zone was where most Manafuls lived. The Elder Territories were all in service to the world in general, not in particular. Everything was a natural ecosystem in the Elder Territories, servicing the needs of beings all over the world. Here, the humanoid beings of this dimension could afford to be selfish. They built families. Homes.

Gardens.

The Manaful Zone was a garden community. Every home was a grove, a hale. A grove consisted of several kauhales that grew together like thousand flowers fragmenting on a single sepal. The inhabitants use their Mana to nurture their grove and community in general. Several thousand groves made up communities, which all added up to the Zone. Since House Green was technically all the same ʻohana under Source, it was all one big House.

The Guardian of this community, a tree that bore trumpet flowers, TGP general vibes to the residents. When it picked up Maka entering their sphere, all it had done was project his location while showering platitudes. Manafuls came out of their treehouses and groves to ogle him and his stolid healthcare sector companion.

They loved him here. Maka felt like a celebrity as he walked down stone pathways bordered with dewy turf. A giant snail looked up at him dolefully, distracted from grazing on the front lawn of a spinachy grove. It sat in a pool of slime under the weight of a brilliantly patterned shell. Manaful and Offspring kids obviously used it as a canvas. Said kids forgot their slimy crayons to scream their heads off at the sight of their Elder. One of them fainted.

"Aloha. Aloha. Much aloha," Maka projected all around. The child elder smiled and waved at several adult Manafuls hovering past. They adorned their hovering platforms and force fields with leaves and berries, going by like an invisible car that had moss and plants growing out of it. The drivers nodded their respect and love. Many Manafuls hovered around like floating seeds. They projected kāko'o. Maka tried to keep a strut out of his step.

As the primary Elder of all things growing from plants to vegetables, a leader of crops and harvesting, Maka was higher in the hierarchy than Elder Laka, whose 'ohana also oversaw the growth of plants. Hers were primarily small flowers.

Maka and Maika'i mind-melded over a hearty breakfast that morning at his old home and digested information over their walk. Aligning their frames of reference and mind sets. The pair voluntarily chose to mute all forms of conversation, vocal or otherwise. They breathed the fragrance of the maile and sandalwood intertwined with the Earth and air, mist and water. All House Green Territories boasted majestic forests of sandalwood trees. Here the boughs were interlaced with organic, living treehouse groves.

There was a lot Maika'i wanted to talk about. But she also knew there was no point. She just had to be patient and let time run its course. What she held in was sheer joy. Her core brimmed. This morning she woke up with the space between her eyes feeling like a powerful radar. All the colors in the world were brighter. Her heart was big and strong.

She was going to become Offspring. Soon.

Like Maka she tried not to strut. Also fought from hopping, skipping and dancing. She knew this weird little phantom itch in the middle eye was the alignment starting to slide into place. She knew it because Kōkua felt it the moment she recovered. At the Health Center's outpatient consultation Kōkua had told the Senior Healer in one long breath: "My head feels like a stick of dynamite with the fuse lit. There's something fizzing towards my eyes, right here, and I really, really like it. Should I be worried?"

She had been told by the clinic that it was a symptom of imminent evolution. Her brain was reconstituting its molecules into something bigger and better. Even her bones tickled and it often made her giggle randomly.

They'd celebrated wildly. Now they will celebrate again, back home when Kōkua got back from her real estate prospecting. Maika'i wouldn't dream of dancing in public here on the lanes of Manaful communities. A huge smile made her face glow in the speckled sunlight filtering in from the canopy overhead.

When Aspiring Hopohopo successfully aligned with Source's Way (Academy students used to call it The 'SWay' in whispers), they evolved in mind and body into Offspring. They physically adapted to increase their capacity to receive Source's Mana. The Medical Center Link clarified to Kōkua and Maika'i that upcoming side effects included losing the opacity of their skin.

There were several Offspring hovering about. They rarely walked, being too excited to use their newfound powers. Maika'i didn't have to use her Healer abilities to see the insides of their bodies. The skins of Offspring were transparent, all the same. Of course, this is why some Offspring feel extremely naked and wrap themselves up in cloaks and body makeup. But the Zone encouraged body acceptance and the former Protector saw several teens showing off their spleens to each other.

A giant butterfly dipped on the breeze and slammed into a flower the size of a building. Pollen exploded like a plume of pixie dust. They rained along with wing dust on Elder Maka and Healer Maika'i. Here the mega flora species designed by House Opalescent were used as Mana mist reservoirs. Their stems and petals were turgid with magic.

Such a heavenly sanctuary.

The scent of a rose grove played with Maka's olfactory memories, bringing to surface echoes of a mothers pampering and a fathers stolid love. Hazy memories. Memories that held so much joy, yet with undercurrents of loss. Maka was so young when his parents were killed.

Chapter 52
Maka and Uli

August 10, 2012
'Ōma'oma'o Manaful Zone
Rose Cottage
Ten years before

At three hundred and five years old, or five human years, Maka looked old. Maka peered into his lilac and ginger scented mirror, his forehead wrinkled. When he thought of his grandfather, a perpetual frown resided on his face. He made a raspberry with his lips to lighten up and mess up his hair a little. He ran his chubby fingers through his dark, curly locks wishing to grow it past his ears. Elder Uli, his grandfather, had rigid standards for grooming. Maka cringed, looking at his manicured fingers. Weren't little Manafuls his age supposed to have grubby hands? Dirt under their nails from looking for pretend dinosaur bones in the backyard? He gargled some mouthwash and spit. A fluffy purple hand towel floated to him at ready. He said, "Mahalo" to the house. The petal window frame opened and closed like a winking eye, and the floor wobbled beneath his bare feet. He was used to his very much alive house's responses. Maka stayed ever steady like a captain on his swaying ship.

The cottage loved him. Maka wiped the water from his chin. He couldn't cry about his parents' murder in Elder Uli's presence. His breath stopped, then he shuddered. His fists held the washcloth tightly. Little threads ripped from its seams. The one and only time he'd cried after his parents' deaths, it got ugly. He'd been exiled. He closed his eyes and handed the rag to the petal wall, which reached for it. He'd had to leave the cottage then. It wilted without him.

Thankfully, Rose cottage was healthy now and it brought him solace with its warm, comforting spirit. His house breathed and healed. It pranced around the acres of his homestead like a young ballerina. His cottage rooted, uprooted, and rerooted itself as if waltzing around the ʻāina. The Manaful Zone's enlivening magic enraptured the souls of its inhabitants. That is, unless they had no soul like Maka's grandfather. Maka's new life with Rose Cottage was companionable. The giant soft petals of the walls billowed inward like violet sails in the wind. His room was in the middle of the rose bud, nestling and cradling their dear child, Maka. He pulled out a picture from the toilet paper storage cabinet. His mother's voice lived on in his head, singing her self-made 'Maka Melodies'. He whispered it to himself, voice catching in his throat.

Maka Melodies by Mom:

"Baby boy in your flower cradle, come here for a hug

Dad and Mom love you, our heartstrings you tug
United, splendid one no matter where we go
Mana lives inside you, just let it flow.
A fountainhead of love resides in my heart
Quenching your thirsty spirit, so brave and smart
Maka is our Sun, our Moon, our Stars
Believe in yourself, don't forget who you are.
Guard your heart and mind from darkness
With a strong faith, you can always harness
Your Mana's inside, made especially for you
So, remember our love, and always stay true."

He loved his pictures of his parents; he had to hide them around his room and bathroom. In this one, his parents smiled up at him from inside the old estate's library. It was the very room he'd found the gun.

"Where's mom and dad?" Shocked, Maka had asked the empty room, looking upon the dust that had been his parents' remains. He and Uli had returned from a merchant meeting. Maka had found the weapon. Uli immediately confiscated it, but not before Maka had examined it. The Baby Ray Gun had pulverized his parents. This he'd instinctively known. Maka had held it in his hands for moments. He'd felt the residual energy pulsing; the Mana Tech intrigued and scared him.

That night, young Maka's mind temporarily separated from his body, choosing to protect him from pain. His mind compartmentalized and saved his sanity. Maka levelly gave the gun to his grandfather, walked to the bathroom, washed up, and got into bed. He was an automaton. That's how Maka survived the night of his parents' murder and the abrupt move to Rose Cottage.

His flowery new home never allowed that robotic Maka to remain. He couldn't live without its garden scents and its soothing massages from "hands" that formed out from the petal walls. The musical lullabies emitted from Rose Cottage's pores all around him. Floating on pumice stone in his bedroom, Maka smiled whimsically at the children playing in a park outside the petal window.

"Maka, want me to come get you? Wanna join us at Koa Forest?" Ikaika TP.

"Yes, give me five to use the lua, then come and get me." Maka projected back. He went back to his bathroom to talk to his mirror and restash his parents' picture. He looked at his serious face. *You're gonna have fun. You're gonna let loose. You're gonna learn as much as you can about Mana!*

His pep talk over, he Telepathically Projected Ikaika, *"Okay, I'm ready. Come to my bedroom!"*

"I love this place. Always has a warm, fragrant May Day vibe!" Ikaika said seconds later as he and Elder Puna MT in Maka's room.

Elder Puna simply laughed. He nodded to Maka and raised a brow. *"Ready?"*

"Appreciate your time Elder Puna!" Maka always thanked Ikaika's guardian, often wishing he could hānai him. Though his grandfather didn't take care of him, Elder Uli would rather lose a limb than ask anything of Elder Puna. Ikaika's grandfather understood the legal boundaries when helping Maka learn

and grow. They were off to Koa Forest and Ikaika's hale. Each moment there was a makana.

Fortunately for Maka, his grandfather paid little to no attention to him. What he ate. Where he went. Who he stayed with. Didn't care. That is, unless he was in a foul mood. Let's say one of his "projects" failed or one of his "incompetent Hopohopo" employees failed. Then, Maka was Elder Uli's punching bag. Except he never literally touched Maka. Manafuls, especially powerful elders, had other means of punishment. Mental ones. Like force fields, solitary confinement and brainwashing. Maka was imprisoned in Sandalwood Forest during those times. Maka frowned at the thought. Ikaika pinched his arm before their molecules shifted to transport mode. Maka didn't flinch. He laughed at Ikaika's playfulness. The sad Manaful was going to Ikaika's home to be happy for a while. If home is where your heart is, then it was his home too.

Chapter 53
Team Kōkua & Maika'i

Manaful World
October 15, 2022
Elder Maka's Mansion
Sandalwood Forest

The SC entered Manaful via Pierre's house to avoid Kona. They checked on Kōkua's healing and Maka's mental wellbeing.

Maika'i and Kōkua had been to the Academy where they turned in their weapon licenses and uniform. Official docs were signed. They were released. They used the visit to have a last tour while chatting with people they ran into. Both of Maka's aunts had picked their former colleagues' brains boldly.

Malie, Pierre and Nicole were delighted to hear that Rhoda's 'ohana allowed Maika'i to hānai her to cross train as a healer and protector.

"What does that involve, Rhoda?" Malie asked. She sashayed to imaginary jazz tunes in her head. The petite one coudn't contain her happiness for her friend.

"There will be mental as well as spiritual training, as Hopohopo are brainwashed from birth to alienate Source's Mana," Rhoda shook her head, praying for her distant and close relatives, including her Uncle Ejad. She was convinced he was possessed by Lapu and hadn't meant to almost kill her new family, Maika'i and Kōkua.

"Maika'i, does the medical training come hand in hand with the mental kinds?" Nicole's brows were raised as she twitched her hands. The subject of mental manipulation still unnerved her. *These ladies were on the "good side" though, right?*

"Medical healing leans closer to the spiritual side, Nicole," Maika'i answered, "yet, I have to connect with the person mentally for permission, prior to healing them."

Nicole went still and felt a strong pull in her heart. These ladies were true-blue. They were helping others and not stealing an individual's personal Mana. She nodded and grinned. Pierre and Malie shared a look. *Our pal's coming around!* Was their shared thought. Nicole caught their silent twintalk and smiled at them. She put out her fist and nodded. They all shared fist bumps and giggles.

Rhoda had a lot to say about Ejad's plans. And the merchant network. "It's actually a Governor's network," she began. The prospect of leaders from each Elder Territory involved in Ejad's schemes were grim. They had a ways to go in their investigations. She wouldn't share her inner hopes for uncle. Despite all the 'evils' the Governor's Network did beneath Ejad/Lapu's leadership, Rhoda believed he was redeemable.

Chapter 54
Pierre Notices Phobes

Earth
November 13, 2022
DMW Field

Pierre Managed to stay on the team. He is the picture of a young jock.

His family distractions (baby sister!) were apparent at school. His many kumu still congratulated him about it. They asked after Shelly and Aliyah.

Pierre's positivity was infectious. Those immediately around him blanketed him from what was beyond: gossip. It kindled the second he befriended Honi.

His team buddies and the cheerleaders drew away from him. Pierre was slower than Ikaika on the uptake. The dwarf noticed many details when he watched through the Shimmery Wall Viewer. For now, Pierre was blissfully unaware. His new baby sister, SC and Honi kept him going 100%.

It was slowly dawning on Nicole that she may be becoming popular. Her basketball skills kept steadily improving. She kept at it to burn off excess energy, really. Not to really win or anything.

Hell, she'd been so bad at it she almost got beat up just a few months ago. Now look at her. Tall girl ruling the courts.

Everyone thinks she's the Pierre of basketball. That was the general vibe that she picked up. She felt like they were expecting too much. Often their gazes made her feel hotter than she should under the orbs of the gymnasium lights.

Speaking of orbs.

A pair brimming with adoration bounced up to her. Kona has basically become her Bag Buddy - he carried her stuff and followed her around WMS whenever possible. Can a person be both irreplaceable and irritating? While Kona did his best to be useful, Nicole did her best to ignore him. The two were a regular comedy skit, bumping into each other (intentionally?) everywhere. Malie couldn't hold back a giggle upon seeing the tall, broad shouldered Nicole and the petite, slender Kona nearly trip over each other. Pierre often hid a smile behind his hands. Nicole gave them pretend evil side-eyes. What is there to do with Kona?

CHAPTER 55
MALIE'S COMPENDIUM

Earth
November 13, 2022
Wright Middle School Library

Malie was documenting things that happen in Manaful disguised as the fiction the Secret Club is "writing". Their mothers, particularly Pili, have been inquiring as to where these "stories" the SC spun in their communications were, exactly. "In our heads" didn't hold up to time. They still needed a valid reason and evidence to show that they were doing something other than sneaking through Shimmery Walls.

Malie was compiling a compendium of Hawaiian mythology. This is what she has been busy with ever since Puna and Ikaika called them to Manaful World first. They reminded her so much of *Menehune.* She'd dug out a book on it with help from Ms. Heluhelu, and also had Google open on the phone in her lap.

Menehune were the stuff of Hawaiian myth and ancient ways. The Polynesian beings were said to be dwarfs who lived in mountains. They were amazing builders. Raising stones without lifting them, these two to three feet beings built heiau - temples. Malie had heard Pili mention the fish pond in Niumalu, Kaua'i. It was supposedly built by the Menehune in one night. Oh yes, that was another thing about the dwarfs. They enjoyed working at night.

The compact book rustled as she turned a page. The paper was yellowing at the edges. These stains were the mark of millions of fingers perusing it over the decades, ever since the paperback came out. There was a musty smell that puffed up from the saddle stitches at the center with every page turn. There were a lot of 'ōlelo in it that she didn't know. She made a mental note to fully use every opportunity to expand her vocab of the Hawaiian language.

Malie was the only one doing all this work. She kept her notes and logs in journals, wrote "short stories" in notebooks, and found a nice app to store her mythology research material (pics, links, notes).

Apart from classes, hale and SC time, all of Malie's attention was on the library. The library's attention was on her in the form of kindly but curious Ms. Heluhelu.

Chapter 56
Uncle Trevor is Flying

Earth
November 13, 2022
Pierre Martin's Home

Pierre was ecstatic over his baby sister, Aliyah, at home. All the time. Even poopy diaper times.

He was only knocked out of his happy reverie when his father mentioned his godfather might visit for the Christmas Holidays next month. Pierre didn't really know the man... Trevor Mālama.

To be honest, Pierre was intimidated to meet such a legendary, almost mythological, figure. Gabe insisted Trevor was cool, not to worry. Pierre nodded and wondered. Was he cool enough for his godfather?

Chapter 57
The Law's Fine

Earth
November 13, 2022
Nicole Moku's Home

Nicole was generally feeling OK as home life described an uptick. She was getting into law textbooks. Really tucking in.

Kaleo was inwardly proud but outwardly horrified that Nicole wanted to go there so young.

They had tea with Uncle Nick Fine, who was stopping by on his drive back home. It was a fun battle of topics between the three. It started and ended with the topic of future generations.

Which meant Nicole's future.

They bore down on the topic. Nicole's internship was just waiting for her to take a hold of it. They thought she was a whizz but she knew she was just a kid. Plus, aiming to measure up to her ʻohana in brainpower was a slow-burn existence of ever hopping to measure up to them. Way over her head.

"Whenever you're ready, Nic!" Kaleo chirped. The adults seemed confident enough in Nicole's brainpower.

Uncle Nick was studying a cookie. Nicole furrowed her smooth brows, looking at him wrapped up in an aura she could only describe as a 'bachelor bubble'. On the spur of the moment, she whipped out her phone.

"Got something to show you," Nicole began.

She produced a pic of Trevor and stuck it in her uncle's face. She watched Nick's model-pouty lips go dry; he sucked in his upper lip and bit the lower. He took a giant - very slow and cautious - breath. He made a tiny noise, 'hmm'. Nick nodded. "Seems like a nice guy," was all Uncle Nick said, as Kaleo walked past carrying a plate shooting a side eye his way.

Nicole was prying her phone from Nick's tight grip with the smuggest smirk Kaleo had ever seen. She'd have a talk with the little matchmaker later. To help her.

Hey, a sister could hope to get her brother's boulders rolling! Kaleo chuckled to herself as she left her kid to do her mischief.

CHAPTER 58
MOM BAKE-OFF

Earth
December 18, 2022
Nicole Moku's Home

The SC Moms gathered for a bake off– just the ladies and kids (minus Aliyah at home with Dad Gabe). Baking with friends is something the Moms all missed since preCOVID.

Pierre, Nicole, and Malie were in Nicole's room dancing and singing Karaoke to retro-Holiday music from Uncle Nick's playlist – what's Christmas without George Michael's "Last Christmas" and Mariah Carey's "All I Want for Christmas."

The peanut butter cookies were freshly forked with sugar and placed in the oven. Kaleo set the timer and Pili refilled their hydro flasks with iced water.

"What is going on with Nicole's matchmaking?" Kaleo asked the SC mothers.

"Ahh, yes, Trevor and Nick, right?" Shelly laughed, wiping tears from her eyes.

"Oh, Nic was at my house for the baby shower turned delivery day!" PIli nodded, smiling as she remembered how cool he was under pressure. Helping out as much as possible.

"Yes, he's been my dear bro for as long as I can remember. Maybe since I was five?" Kaleo sighed happily. Loved her bro, Nick. Been through thick and thin together.

"Trevor will be a good match for him," Shelly touched her chin, brows furrowed and focused. "People make fun of actors being just ditzy pretty faces. However, Trevor's been managing his career for decades with wisdom beyond his years. Was a child model and actor, even before we met him in college."

"That's impressive," Pili smiled mischievously, "Match-making is fun! Let's help the kids on their "put the uncles together" endeavor."

"Ah-ha! Yes, we could make sure Nick and Trevor 'just happen' to sit together or be given kitchen clean-up together!" Kaleo put in, laughing.

"Oh, this will be a fun holiday season," Shelly belly laughed too.

"To Holiday Romance, ladies!" Pili raised her hydro flask like a pretend wine glass.

The SC moms cheered so loudly the kids inside wondered if their moms had really hit the rum cabinet.

CHAPTER 59
ARI GIVES THANKS

Storyteller in Papakōlea, Hawai'i
December 16, 2022

It's the last day of school before Winter Break for Ari and the SC. Ari appreciated her Aunt's presence and recovery. She wondered about the SC's Christmas plans. Her questions were piling up. Ari couldn't wait for more of the story. During her bed rest Aunt Ellie made a pdf file of the so-called *Book Two:The Secret Club* 'Part One'. She shared the link with Hoku, who downloaded it for herself and Ari. Hoku promised herself she'd read snaps of it during her lunch breaks. It had become a personal goal to catch up on her sister's second novel, knowing its importance to Ari.

Ari read the pdf so often she practically knew the Manafuls' story by heart. She liked discussing it with Aunt Ellie over the bird-song filled hours of the day. It gave her a lot to think about in her free time.

She and her Aunt made plans to pick up their Douglas Fir tree to decorate together that weekend. Not to mention fairy lights. Aunty always decorated their front lanai with rainbow lights. They'll pull out their family's boxes of Christmas Decorations from their respective bedroom closets.

CHAPTER 60
SC JINGLE BELLS, HONI'S SWELL

Earth
December 16, 2022
Malie Manu's Home

School's out on Winter Break and the SC visited Malie's home to help her decorate her tree. They baked and frosted gingerbread cookies. Malie loved baking with the vanilla in the air and fruit flavors on her tongue.

The SC invited Honi, who was a baker too – having helped raise his younger sisters. He was talented in the kitchen as his little siblings all had a sweet tooth. The girls really liked Honi, particularly appreciating that he didn't fawn over Pierre. They'd quickly determined he didn't swing that way.

In fact, Nicole, the brazen, blunt one, plainly asked Honi if he was straight, gay, or something else on the spectrum. Honi laughed and went with it, admitting that he liked only girls, for now. He was always open to the possibilities and didn't judge people.

"After all, we all keep growing from stage to stage," Honi concluded.

Nicole loved that.

Malie, a hugger who was getting braver every day, opened her arms, saying, "Bring it in!" Honi, an affectionate and demonstrative teddy bear, gently hugged the petite Malie.

Pierre smiled proudly at his buddies. Their acceptance of his sexuality and of his new buddy squeezed his heart, giving him fuzzy feels.

CHAPTER 61
ALIYAH ENJOYS COO-CHICOO'S

Earth
December 25, 2022
Pierre Martin's Home

The SC and their three families, including the Fines grandparents and Uncle Nick, got together for Christmas. They went for potluck style where every family brings one or two dishes, preferably an entree and a dessert from each ʻohana.

The clan fawned over baby Aliyah, who was extra giggly since it's her first Christmas. Lots of singing, food, walks in the garden, and family fun. Lovely occasion with different personalities who'd been wishing earnestly to feel freer socially since COVID.

Trevor Mālama, Gabe's best buddy from California and Pierre's Godfather was there as well. He's visiting for a few weeks. He has a "talk" with Pierre alone in Tūtū's garden that afternoon.

The breeze swept through Tūtū's banana trees, the long wavy leaves like ceiling fans overhead. Uncle Trevor was a sight to behold at six foot four, tattooed, broad shouldered, and longhaired for a long-term surfer role. Pierre felt chills in his stomach and across his whole body. *This was not gonna go well.* The preteen wasn't comfortable explaining his feelings for things much less boys. Uncle Trevor gracefully sat on a bench near the hen house. It was empty at the moment. His grandmother had spread grains and table leftovers on the other side of the garden. The gardenia filled his lungs making Pierre smile remembering the potpourri his grandfather would make once the petals dried.

"How have you been, Pierre?" Uncle Trevor asked in a mellow, unassuming voice. He smiled and fistbumped Pierre.

"Football season is over and I'm trying an outside gym with my friend Honi." Pierre giggled a little, mentioning his friend.

"Oh, do you feel good about that place? Everyone Is treating you well?"

"Uhhh, well, I can't say. It's still early." Pierre frowned, recalling some snide looks he'd gotten. The whispering in the gym locker room.

"Sonny, let's cut to the chase," Uncle said.

Pierre laughed at the nickname from his late toddler days. Uncle never had kids, so he'd tell Pierre, "You'll forever be like a son! My Sonny!" The memory warmed Pierre to his uncle. He leaned his shoulder sideways, laughing and sighing. Life had been simpler at three years old.

Uncle Trevor wrapped his arm around Pierre, giving him a hug and plainly said, "Gabe told me you came out."

Pierre sat up straighter then jumped up.

"I'm not ashamed!" Pierre announced proudly.

His uncle stayed on the bench, bent forward with his elbows on his knees and hands folded. He met Pierre's eyes and nodded.

"I'm glad. You're perfect and loved just the way you are."

Pierre's lips shivered a little. He turned towards the hen house, counting the eggs he would gather for Tūtū. He heard Uncle's shoes rustling leaves behind him then felt strong hands squeezing his shoulders reassuringly.

"You're good. It'll be fine. I'm always here for you, Sonny."

Pierre couldn't turn around, but he nodded. Tears welled in his eyes, falling down his cheeks and onto his red "We are Mauna Kea" t-shirt.

Uncle Trevor released him. The sound of his footsteps on the cobblestones almost disappeared, then he heard his Uncle shout, "Love you, Pierre!"

Pierre turned around and waved. He put up his thumb, index finger, and pinkie finger in the ASL sign for 'I love you'. Uncle Trevor gave him a screenworthy smile and signaled 'I love you," back. Pierre teared up again, but this time with joy.

Chapter 62
SC Quest Stop: Tree

Manaful World
January 31, 2023
The Relic Tree's Home

For a change, the SC entered the Shimmery Wall from Malie's home. They were still avoiding Kona.

They visited the Relic Tree with Ikaika and the ever-sullen Maka. The Tree was grumpy, though she did provide a few new clues. The Tree somberly said a pule for the late Elder Alaka'i. That brought them all to mournful tears. They'd forgotten the former Elder Prime had known the Relic personally.

The Relic Tree added levity to the situation, teasing them about their lack of luck finding his "Brother Rocksie." She surprised them with a song akin to Relic Cloud's tune. There were some hints on Rocksie's geological mineral makeup, even describing the glittery qualities and ability to control rocks around him by "talking" to them.

Cloud's Song: Finding Rocksie:

"Rocksie's bouncy as he's meant to be
Unlike the leaves that fall off from me
He doesn't blow with the wind to and fro
That Stone has an agenda, don't you know?
To escape capture or ownership by anyone
To be free from those who try to control his fun
They use his songs to empower themselves
He has the Mana to move rocks like elves
Makes them do what he wishes them to
Talks to them, jumps on them like a buckaroo
No matter the size of stone, dirt, or pebble
Rocksie can turn things into rubble
Reshape himself big or small so he's difficult to catch
His crystalline, golden mineral's completely unmatched
Try the Rift Border, for he's always concerned
For that's where Old Hill, our love, was burned
Rocksie has plans, in his hard head, for sure
We must wait him out, sit back, and endure
Bon chance! Ganbatte kudasai!
When you find him, remember, he's our guy!"

The SC left the Relic Tree intrigued and touched. They enjoyed the rest of their trip with Maluhia in the clearing. Ikaika was enlightened by the Tree's song. The Manaful sat on Pierre's rock in deep thought.

Chapter 63
SC Valentine's Day

Earth
February 14, 2023
Wright Middle School

Of the Secret Club, only Pierre received Valentine's gifts. The Student Council held candy and flower gram sales a month in advance. Students order these gifts for their loved one. The grams were delivered on Valentine's Day morning during homeroom class.

"Who sent those?" Rodney, another football player, asked Pierre in class.

"I'm not sure," Pierre was embarrassed to receive them. "They say, "Secret Admirer."

When the hall monitors presented him with his gifts, he wanted to stick his head in a hole. Instead he chose an easier solution: He threw them away.

"There are rumors going around that your admirers are boys," Rodney snickered. "Maybe you shouldn't be so open about your tastes, Buddy!"

Pierre flinched. His tastes?

"You're not my, 'Buddy,' when you say things like that, Rodney!" Pierre's voice rose. The hairs on his arms stood up. His heart beat accelerated.

"Watch it, hot shot. We've seen you schmoozing around with your *boyfriend*."

"Shut it, Rodney!"

Mr. King's brow rose and he made his way to Pierre and Rodney's table grouping. Thankfully, their third partner was absent today. Pierre didn't want a bigger crowd than necessary, if he had to tell Rodney off.

"Is everything alright here, boys?" The teacher had a sixth sense about his students' well-being. He knew the growing tension between PIerre and Rodney was not good.

"Thank you, we're fine. Rodney had rude things to say about my Valentine's gifts," Pierre continued, "I told him to cut it out." Pierre answered Mr. King but kept eye contact with Rodney. They were having a battle of eyeball chicken. The weakest of the two dropped his gaze first.

"Oh, really, Rodney? What did you say?" Mr. King's voice was low and steady. He'd been trained in de-escalation. There'd be no fights on his watch.

"No, no, I didn't mean anything by it," Rodney backtracked and looked down at his loose shoelaces. He broke eye contact, surrendering to Pierre. For now, he'd keep mum about the gayness Pierre emitted. The team cannot have that.

Mr. King studied the boys. He nodded, looking Pierre straight in the eye.

"You good, Pierre?" Mr. King made a fistbump, making Pierre smile. He answered, bumping his teacher's fist with his own.

"I'm fine." Pierre answered. Yet, he wasn't. He still got upset by the Cheerleaders' stuffing "love notes" into his locker throughout the quarter.

Pierre, you are the love of my life, so be my wife! One note read.

Pierre, you bring me joy. Come be my boyfriend: boy meets boy! A second one said,

He knew they were pulling his leg. Their duplicitous letters simply upset him. He knew they weren't really interested in him anymore as a guy or person. As the rumors of his orientation thickened, the cheerleaders and football players stopped sitting next to him in the cafeteria. No one talked to him in the weight training room either. Nobody asked for tutoring like they used to.

Malie comforted Pierre. She was grateful he had a really happy homelife and friends like the SC and Honi.

"Pierre, give me a high-fave," Malie said that day outside of the library. She stretched her hand way above her head, pretending he was a giant. He laughed at her silliness, returning her high-five. She had the softest hands, reminding him to mālama his blisters from football.

Malie knew this was closet homophobia rearing its ugly head. She saw it escalating, beginning here anonymously. Cards in his locker with hateful slurs written on them upset Pierre. He stayed strong with his friends' support.

CHAPTER 64
ARI'S BIRTHDAY

Storyteller in Papakōlea, Hawaiʻi
February 15, 2023

It's Ari's 12th birthday!
Aunty sang happy birthday in Hawaiian.

Special Hauʻoli Lā Hānau for Ari:

"Hauʻoli lā hānau.
Hauʻoli lā hānau.
Hauʻoli lā hānau.
Happy birthday!
I wish you good health
And many happy moments in life!"

Aunty Elle almost forgoes telling a SC story, though Ari immediately waived that idea. She played the birthday girl card. Haha.

Over iced fruit cake and cherry soda, Aunty updated Ari about the SC without giving away too many details. That's what the book is for! Aunty alluded to a Relic Cloud visit which really pepped up Ari. That Relic is Ari's favorite as it transformed the preteens making Ari fall off her chair laughing last time.

After the celebratory dessert, Ari was eager for some storytelling, but Aunty Ellie said they need to have "a womanly talk." Ari sighed. She and her mom had that talk already.

"Auntyyyy, mom and I had that talk last month. The birds and the bees and the three C's." Ari laughed remembering her mom's embarrassment. She'd been more anxious than Ari during that talk.

"Ahh, the three C's?" Ellie giggled, recalling that one. It was a new one the sisters made up during a phone call. They were a better team now, texting often and meeting once a week for story time with Ari. Ari had been a little disgruntled that her mom couldn't get off an hour early every day. Once a week was actually a miracle in Hoku's book. Ellie agreed, knowing how demanding Hoku's accounting career was.

"So, if you already had the adult sexuality talk, we can get to storytelling faster!"

"Yes, let's do that now!" Ari jumped onto the couch and patted the spot next to her.

"Hold your horses, young lady! Come back to the kitchen and help me put things away. The candles, the napkins, the utensils, and other party things go in the bin on the back porch." Aunty Ellie listed. Her hands on her hips with a pretend impatient look. Her face cracked into a smile.

"I got you, Aunty!" Ari skipped to the kitchen to do as she was told.

"So tell me about the three C's," Aunty Ellie nudged Ari's bicep.

"Aunty, you and mom likely made it up. I Googled it and it wasn't anywhere to be found."

"Ha. Ha. Caught in the act. Yes, we did. I'd still like to hear it from you," Aunty was now serious. Her brows went up in that teacher's "I mean business" look.

"The three C's are:

1. I'm to be **Careful** who I talk to, trust, and be alone with.

2. I'm **Cognizant** (I had to practice that word; it's a big one) when my body changes and to ask for help when I'm in pain or don't understand.

3. I'm **Confident** in my ability to make smart choices and problem-solve."

"Wow, that was a really strong re-telling. You'd practically memorized the C's verbatim," Aunty Ellie was genuinely impressed.

"I memorized it. It's important to me. You and mom really care about me. I feel like crying sometimes, but I remember the 3 C's and pray. I pray for guidance and the ability to follow them."

This got Aunty Ellie choked up. She couldn't help but reach for Ari, who met her in the middle of her efforts. They sway-hugged. Ari pushed away first and ran back to the couch.

"Let's get this story started!" Ari sang in the melody of a hit party song from the 2000s

Aunty Ellie followed her, laughing. Who doesn't like the singer Pink?

They did get the story started.

Chapter 65
New Elder Council Chair

Manaful World
February 20, 2023
Elder Council Chambers @ House Opal

Charmaine Momi looked as if she had been Elder Prime for centuries now. In truth this is her first council meeting after the Transmutation. She has wept in the privacy of her bedroom for her father. Out here, her face was golden brown topaz. Not a scratch in sight.

The same can't be said for Elder Puna. He looked like a shattered vase glued back together. Everybody silently lent their grief-healing to him as the meeting progressed.

To start, they officialized Charmaine as Chair of the Elder Council. Each Elder sent a thread of light from their fingers to hers in their respective house colors. The threads spiraled around her thumb and solidified into a band. It was the Elder Link controls. Charmaine declined her chin to acknowledge the responsibility they placed on her. Stars cartwheeled in her opalescent garments.

Charmine handled the pending issues beautifully. She attended to the follow up on the destruction caused over the last year due to Ejad Honua's antics. She proposed a committee to track him down. Appointed a multi-Ohana force of Protectors to be trained further into a machine-combatting army. Plus, she sent pleas for help in countering and safely disarming all of the Ejad's Mana harvesting machines collected from across the world. The priority was tracking and immobilizing Ejad himself.

All Elders at the table marveled at Charmaine's perseverance and wisdom. Pule for her focus and patience. They prayed for light and growth to shower on her.

Charmaine said that Ejad is first and foremost an issue arising from ʻŌmaʻomaʻo territory.

Right. This is my problem, basically, Maka thought, fidgeting. Charmaine did not blink, staring his way with those kalakoa eyes, a glowing ombré of greens, browns, and blues. His Elder Prime demanded he fix the issue. Glumly recalling that time his grandfather skewered him head to toe in sandalwood spears, Maka thought, I can't believe I died for a minute just to get ***this*** job.

He agreed to attend to the matter. He will attend the upcoming Green Hopohopo Governors' meeting. Puna smiled and promised to help Maka. He patted Maka's hand and the second youngest Elder in the room nodded in gratitude.

CHAPTER 66
HOPOHOPO CITY VISIT

Manaful World
February 21, 2023
Hopohopo City

Giggles and laughter were the first thing Malie, Pierre and Nicole heard when they MT with Ikaika to Hopohopo City. Ikaika had chosen an empty playground area shielded by hibiscus shrubs. Rhoda waited for them on a bench, a brown bag on her lap catching crumbs from her dwindling hamburger. She popped the last morsel into her mouth and scrunched up the bag to throw into the rubbish bin.

"She's excited to spend some time with you," Ikaika projected as the Aspiring Hopohopo stood up to run to them. Rhoda waved at the humans excitedly when she closed in, pretty in slim-fit black trousers and green blouse shirt knotted at the navel.

"Oh my Source, you are so big!" Rhoda squealed. Malie giggled and went in for the hugs first. Pierre followed and Nicole, eyes twinkling was last. Nicole's hug caught Rhoda off her feet and sent her little pyramid hat sailing. Rhoda had tears of laughter by the time Nicole put her down.

"Oh, I wonder what it will be like on Earth," Rhoda said, hands clasped under her chin. Her eyes are anime-wide and lashes aflutter.

"Almost exactly the same," Nicole said, pointing at the congested street around the park. Rhoda took her hand and the pair walked off to find a bench, quite chatty. Pierre and Malie shot each other bemused looks as they followed with Ikaika. Rhoda gave them company as they waited half an hour for Maka to finish the Governors' district meeting he was attending. The Governor's Hall was across from the park. Governor's watch over House Hopohopo Communities (Towns and Cities), which meant all Mayors attend these biannual meetings.

Ikaika TGP, *"Maka hopes to determine the situation in the Governor's Hall. He promised Charmaine at her officialization as Chair of Council."*

Ikaika accompanied him there to support him before and after the meeting. Maka's moods were improving lately and he trusted his buddy would do well alone. The Governors wanted no more than one Manaful in the hall for the meeting anyway, so Ikaika had to stay out. He'd MT Rhoda to him, who helped him find a secluded spot to open a Shimmery Wall for the SC. Now they all sat on benches behind trimmed hedges watching the street and the Hall beyond.

The air was full of honking, swearing and screaming. Apart from pigeons, no living things were about. Ikaika TGP, *"Most animals would rather go to the Rift Border to die than live in a Hopohopo city."*

Rebellion posters thickly decorated street walls: "We Demand Secession from the Manafuls Way!" "No to Manaful Elders!" "Freedom for Hopohopo!"

Angry Hopohopo milled around the Governor's Hall calling for a Hopohopo Law to replace the Elder Law. They carried placards and signboards, with aluminum foil hats on every one of them. "I'm so sorry for all this," Rhoda kept saying.

"It's not your fault," Pierre laughed.

"I'm still technically a Hopohopo," Rhoda extended her arms to look at her skin. "I'm not gonna be Offspring for a long while. Do you know Kōkua is translucent by now? Ooooh!"

Ikaika picked scenes from Rhoda's life to share with the rest. They were smiling over life updates when the Governor's meeting ended. They knew because Maka Molecularly Transported right into the middle of the protest. Screams went up. Elder robes startled, Maka hurried into the park.

The crowd found his tracks. "There's a Manaful! Get him!" The crowd ran after Maka, who trampled a flower bed upon spotting Ikaika waving at him from the bench. Rhoda put both hands on her cheeks and jumped into Nicole's lap. The mob followed Maka all the way, brandishing their protest boards. Ikaika quickly stood up to meet his friend and face the Hopohopo crowd.

"Deep breath!" Ikaika projected at Maka, who stopped in his tracks and nodded, eyes wide. He took a few lungfuls of breaths as the SC surrounded him to support.

"They're crazy!" Maka TGP.

"No bad thoughts. Align and sing with me, buddy!"

"You're going to sing?" Nicole asked, pointing at the mob.

Ikaika and Maka nodded simultaneously. They met eye to eye and nodded to face the incoming Hopohopo crowd. Ikaika was a born diplomat and Maka followed him. They levitated, mind-melding, and released their voices with the power of Source behind it.

Maka and Ikaika's Hope for Hopohopo Song:

"We are not that different: Hopohopo and Manaful
If we just understand each other, feeling grateful
Life would be much less grievous
Let us guide you, you're so mischievous
You're kolohe as ever my friends to be
Running around, hurting your families
Come to the light, Source's essence so bright
Why hate others and put up such a fight?
Be malie and centered in all that you do
Find serenity, a peacefulness you never knew
Close your eyes to imagine the beauty untapped
Release your fears and pain inside that's trapped
Lift up your mind, your soul, your spirit
There's nothing better than this: let me tell it
Once again, we are no different all of us
Put away the anger, the weapons, and the fuss
There's hope for Hopohopo."

Their Mana did the job, soothing the crowd into a woozy, somnolent bunch. They didn't seem to remember how to get angry, for a moment. Many of them sat on the grass and scratched their hats.

"Rhoda, I am going to MT you home," Maka said. The Aspiring Hopohopo nodded, eyes still wide and scared. Maka sent soothing energy her way and watched her face relax before he transported her to the flat apartment she shared with Maika'i and Kōkua.

Kimo emerged from the crowd, burgundy hair disheveled. He ran to Ikaika.

"Take me out of here!"

Kimo had come here with Mayor Ethan, who was still in the Hall. The mayor's son did not like the vibe around here anymore. He suspected his father was getting possessed. He didn't feel safe here. Ikaika TP's Puna.

Puna TP back, "*Save that boy!*"

Gramps didn't have to tell him twice.

Ikaika took Kimo home.

CHAPTER 67
CHARMAINE'S PIKO POWER

Manaful World
February 22, 2023
Rift Border, Elder Freelands

An Elder was in turmoil. Charmaine's piko felt a pang on an 'Ohana thread of consciousness. It was an Alert. She was traversing the Spirit World, and immediately summoned a visual. A rose bloomed before her and burst into flames. 'Ula'ula house. She was a pulsing light form in the Spirit Realm, having left her physical body behind. She'd de-robed from the material world. Tall and warrior-like, her light form lacked any distinguishable features. It was her spirit, core energy. Her living piko in action.

The Spiritual realm itself was never settled, perpetually shifting and morphing. It was sublime to Charmaine being surrounded by the shapes and imagery. Geometry was prime. The ground was polygonal with sprouting trees that died minutes later. Triangular cacti drunkenly stacked on top of each other. Bouncing spirals leapt into the sky leaving behind pyramid mountains. Spirit cores congregated there like twinkling stars as far as the eye can see. Some Spirit cores meant well, while others didn't. Charmaine was aware and kept safe. She'd come here often since she was a child to explore and observe. Back then, she'd had all the time in the world to roam around. That was no longer the case. Source just notified her that a loved one was near danger from Lapu.

The Alert displayed the 'Ula'ula emblem's brazen and beautiful rose. She peered at the Elder Puna link on the shimmering object before her. Touching the 'Ula'ula emblem, Charmaine caught her breath as the burning rose grew in size, petals multiplying. The emblem unfurled to reveal the shimmering core. A gelatin pool of liquid revealed an elder in trouble. Her spirit form darkened for a split second upon seeing Puna in the Rift Border.

"What the!"

A tremor ran through Charmaine-Piko. This was how her father had died. She'd received her father's pearl emblem Alert and booked to his location in seconds via her astral form. She'd watched her father die while in spirit form. She'll forever regret not returning to her body to MT to his side, to help him. If she jumped into the shimmery object's gelatin pool, entering the heart of the rose, she'd appear next to Puna. Except, she'd be in spirit form again. It would be as she'd been when her dad died. That's probably what Puna wanted, to meet with her in the Spirit Realm. He'd leave his body behind, unsafe, in the Rift. She did not want any part of him there on the border alone. Period.

She will not repeat her mistakes. She would physically return to her body.

Charmaine-Piko crossed her arms, shrinking into a rose bud. The buds were the remains of her Spirit Core. She'd left behind millions of these buds on the "ground" of the Spirit Realm. It didn't matter if her Cores were destroyed or eaten by other Spirits. Every time Charmaine crossed over, a new bud bloomed. Every time she left, she left one behind. She gently released her spirit, returning to her body in nature's time. Her slim torso filled up with Hā.

Charmaine's chest heaved with air as she awakened in her sleeping pod. She basked in the warmth of her floating kukui fairy lights. Her bed was a lotus bloom that was, according to Maka, as big as the average hale in a Manaful Zone grove. The petals fluttered as they detected her rising up to yawn. The lotus fragrance mingled with the nutty kukui surrounding her with the comforting familiarity of home. Returning was always a slow, groggy process in which she became overly emotional. The bed bloomed with happy wake-up tunes. The mattress of pollen-like fiber she slept on extended multiple little hands to pat her all over. Their massage brought a half smile. The fingers arranged her hair and pampered her face like personal attendants. Satin blankets sought out her cold spots, wrapping her in a warm hug. Sunflower trays busily bustled up with refreshments, wet towels, and water globules. She laughed at their servitude, waving them away to quickly jump off the bed. Her Elder Robes, attuned to her 24/7, swooshed from the hanger to her body in a flurry. Her robes magicked her pajamas away, as a bottle of perfume bobbed up to spritz. Ready in seconds, she blew a wisp of hair from her eye and MT to the Rift Border.

She appeared in an arid patch of rocks and bones, crunching a skull underfoot as she materialized. She MT a few miles closer into a trench. She sighed, recalling her father bringing her here once before. They'd never directly teleported right into the Rift. He'd demonstrated the dangers here, such as how teleportation went wonky as the air density increased. Grateful for her dad's warning, she MT forward towards the border in short spurts. Charmaine MT several more times before she found Puna.

The Red Elder levitated in midair at the edge of the Rift. Deeply contemplative, he stared at streams of magma swimming dragon-like in the air. Desecrating all the land near and far. Relieved to her Piko, Charmaine dropped her tense shoulders and released a big breath. She hovered closer to the elder who was like another father to her. She levitated next to his knee and was about to touch him. "*What is he doing?*"

Puna TP, eyes still closed, *"Studying the Rift Border as you study the Spirit Realm, Child Prime."*

"I am no longer Child Prime. I am Elder Prime. mind-melds with me?"

Charmaine always asked because her Mana's capacity overwhelmed others, even Elders. She couldn't help it. If she ever talked to superman trying to paint an eggshell, she'd be understood by someone. So far, no one else possessed as much Mana as she.

Elder Puna hesitated, gulped, and nodded. Charmaine's tightly coiled brain waves sprung out to devour his mind. Her energy waves consumed him vibrationally and magnetically, waves of light surrounded them. Puna almost swooned.

"Oh. The Rift Border is expanding," Charmaine TP. Her melding withdrew, making Puna gasp at the loss. Heartbeat returning to normal, he nodded at her words. He pointed toward the land that expanded endlessly outward, even past the border. She frowned at the sight. Upon entering the Rift, they couldn't MT in there. Charmaine shivered pondering the long walk.

"There's more. Watch this! The protective layer around the Rift border is a shockwave in slow motion," Puna projected. He swept a hand on the edge of the border. As he touched the layer, a ripple of air occurred as his skin met a force field. The layer was a soft cellophane-like membrane surrounding the Rift.

"Father said the Rift's the shockwave of Old Hill's demise. When Old Hill's foundation exploded upon eruption, he opened his mouth wide. The shockwave destroyed everything up to here. The explosion of sound took on a life of its own, becoming a magical shockwave. It traveled, expanded, dispersed into the world. Over the centuries, the Rift borderlands were formed."

"The shockwave won't stop there, Charmaine. The whole Rift is expanding past the borderlands. Do you understand what that means?"

Charmaine regarded the hazy red interloper. Flat, dusty, dead. Of course, she knew the implications. She wouldn't think about it. *"Let's go."*

"Lapu is headed here."

"How do you know?"

Puna pivoted and pointed in the opposite direction. Charmaine wheeled around. A stinky blob approached them. He was a tar-like figure transforming the bones and grass into dust as he slimed over them.

"Does he know we are here?" Charmaine asked. She was bemused by this apparition beelining for them. His diminutive size surprised her. "*This Being killed my Father? He's your great nemesis?"*

"*Yes. He did. He's curious about us.*"

"*Tainted essence is strong here. Lapu has become so concentrated and heavy It has to walk.*"

Puna nodded. Both Manafuls pushed out force fields from their piko. Ready for a fight, they took defensive postures. Charmaine morbidly TP, "*How strong is Lapu here on the border?*" Lapu certainly wasn't ominous, diminutive and featureless instead. The Elders became in sync like twins in the womb. They could hear each other's breaths and feel each other's stubborn will. Both united in thought and emotion. Puna lifted his two fists, bringing them alight with fire. Charmaine's face was glacial as she remained cool.

They met the renegade Spirit at the edge of the border.

CHAPTER 68
RIFT BORDER FIASCO

Manaful World
February 22, 2023
Rift Border, Elder Freelands

Lapu slouched up a few feet away from the two Elders. The Elders' brows furrowed in unison at the imp-like figure. He appeared to be sulking like a child, though this one was without a face.

"Lying in wait for me, sneaky sneaks?" Lapu bristled and spat.

"No," Puna smirked. "We just happened to be here; going for a stroll over this lovely terrain."

Charmaine rolled her eyes at their droll convo. She whipped her hands around, blasting the Spirit. Lapu yelped, just escaping another burst. Her third blast popped Lapu like an overblown bubble gum. His core became invisible, yet he projected annoyingly, "You're crazy! I didn't do ANYTHING bad just now! Ugh!"

"Begone, foul Spirit," Eyes now white, Charmaine commanded him to leave.

"Excuuuse me!" Lapu protested. "Will you get out of my way? I have places to be!" The disembodied voice sank towards the ground. Wherever he slithered, he created tainted Mana. He absorbed the tainted essence from the mud, the bones, and everything he touched. Charmaine raised her hands threateningly and the blob scurried away. Puna stretched his neck and got some shots in too. A barrage of fire made Lapu squeal and dance. Sparks flew as Charmaine blasted with her index finger. Lapu temporarily disintegrated.

"Will you give me a break!" Lapu snapped. He was now a blob on a rock. Charmaine annihilated him, rock and all. Puna and Charmaine hovered after him, destroying him as fast as he could remanifest. They tired Lapu out.

"All right, all right! I'm here. No motion." He feigned weakness. In reality, tainted essence slowly accumulated around the Spirit core, enriching him. He now stood very still like a rumpled blanket. "What do you want?"

"Stop meddling with our world of Manaful," Voices raised and hearts beating fast, Puna and Charmaine said simultaneously.

"I can't help it! I'm part of it!"

"No you're not," Charmaine put her hands on her hips. "You belong to Old Hill. If you exit the Rift ever again I will Lock you in the Spirit Realm," Charmaine swore, her lips going dry. *This is exhausting.*

"Not possible!" Lapu said smugly.

Puna shook his head impatiently; this was like lecturing his grandson. "Go and remain in your rightful place in the world, free Spirit. We don't know why you woke up."

Puna tried to level with him. “We can assure you the purpose is not to go to war with us. Call off your minions. Stop possessing our people.”

Lapu shifted. The blurry gob shrugged. “Okay.”

Charmaine narrowed her eyes. “Really? You mean it?”

The blob nodded cautiously.

Charmaine exchanged a look with Puna. Lapu chose that instant to unravel into threads. Now with a bigger surface area, he wrapped around the forcefields. He sent powerful projections through their bubbles. Charmaine winced.

The Elders mind-blocked his brainwashing attempts. Their force fields held. Charmaine smirked as the threads of Lapu essence were scrabbling along its edges like a rabid fox trying to get into a henhouse.

“I WILL ABSORB ALL YOUR Mana!” Lapu screamed. “DIE! DIE WRETCHED MANAFULS!”

“This is pointless, Lapu,” Puna projected, tutting. Without rune and glyph power, he was really quite weak. Just persistent. Like a pest.

Charmaine nodded. She had a slight migraine. The Spirit was ineffectual against an Elder‘s mind, much less her mind. She lifted her hands in the air impatiently, “Ay Caramba!” Lapu was going nuts trying to “eat” the forcefield.

Puna gave her an “I got this” wink. He sent out blue fire. Lapu screeched and burned away. This time, he drifted behind a rocky outcrop to brood and gather substance. Gaining tainted Mana was most important.

“Why can’t I trace Lapu with Mana?” Charmaine asked, her head tilted in thought as she searched the borderlands. She couldn’t see Lapu, yet she sensed his presence nearby.

"He's too foul for us to pick up," Puna folded his hand together in prayer. "There's one way to detect and link to Lapu's core."

Her brows went up and jaw dropped in shock, "Really? How?"

"By not aligning with Source," Puna nodded solemnly to her surprise. "We'd stop being Manaful. Hopohopo have generationally chosen the polar opposite of us, choosing misalignment from Source." Puna frowned.

"The Hopohopo are extremely aware of Lapu." The older Elder said it so forlornly she could've hugged him. "They believe in all he stands for, making them wide open for possession."

Charmaine looked up at the dreary sky. The coolness of the night seeped into the force field. Lapu was creeping between the lands and the smog-like clouds. She knelt to the floor of her bubble to pray to Source, exclaiming, "I never want to be away from Source's light!"

Puna nodded. "Be careful what you wish for. It's better this way. Let the Spirit be unseen, let him lurk. We will find other ways to end this."

"Let us leave, dear Puna."

Lapu watched them, grimacing at their ferocity. He couldn't hear their TP either, that was frustrating. He hid quietly, sulkily, behind a boulder. The Elders slowly MT away, mile by mile. He would wait to make sure all was clear. He wobbled, growing. As he waited, tainted essence grew around his core. He couldn't help it. The stuff came to him like iron filaments to a magnet now.

This was good.

Very good indeed.

CHAPTER 69
LAPU WRAP

Manaful World
May 3, 2023
Rift, Manaful World

A daredevil butterfly risked its life flitting in the precarious acres of the wide Rift border. Fuschia sparkles trailed its marvelously intricate wings as it zigzagged somewhat dizzily in the wind. This was a helipad area of land where no beings wished to live. Fetid air choked out anything brave. Animals journey there for their deaths ever since Old Hill died. This particular elderly pulelehua had lived a long life in insect standards. It went there to sleep forever and to never be reawakened. First it determinedly did reconnaissance of this magical place for its friends back home. The Rift Border was a good place to die in. The wind readily carried those ready for this stage. Pinky surfed a wonky breeze down to investigate an obsidian rock. The rock's substance was unfamiliar and alluring. Pinky closed the distance. It hadn't seen such an abnormal thing since the humans from Earth.

Pinky poked the thing with its cute antennas and fuzzy feet. The boulder smelled horrible, was soft, and trembled. Lapu gave no clue to his ominous nature. Pinky was about to leave.

The "rock" jumped up and chomped the butterfly in one oily bite. Lapu chewed thoughtfully with rubbery lips. Glittery pink wings dribbled mixed with oil drops onto his chin. He bubbled and burped for more.

"*Pwah!*"

Lapu shuffled along enroute to his hale. Here and only here he could chew living things to absorb Mana. He had eaten a deer for breakfast. Too bad no dwarfs lived around here anymore. Lapu planned to eat Manafuls one day. He'd absorb all their Mana. That would be so cool.

"*Oooooh, imagine an Elder!*"

But that glorious day was far beyond, putting Lapu in a bad mood. He slouched along like a child's soiled ghost costume. Wherever he went, the grass died. The gravel of the largely barren meadows of the Border rustled at his passing. He came upon a haze of red on dry, dead ground. That was inside the Rift.

The womb of the Spirits and Relics.

He crossed the border. There were no butterflies here. In the Rift, nothing dared live. The grass, the trees, the stones all died there. The Rift was dank nothingness. Clouds of tainted essence whirled around, lit red and purple from within; the light shows were Spirit cores trying to manifest. Lapu sniggered as the essence clouds came to him easily, feeding him, making him grow. He made the others jealous.

Lapu felt Rot, immersing Itself into his density. Rot was the collective mind of all Spirits born at the center of the world.

It was the Spirit equivalent to the Hive Mind of the Manafuls. The Rot's energy grew stronger making Lapu happy. That meant more Spirits were awakening. "*Very good!*"

The first manifested Spirit of Manaful World crouched down, absorbing detritus and creating lanes in his wake towards the open guts of Old Hill. He grew bigger as he went. The Rift expanded via the tainted essence condensed within it, unlike the Outside. Spirits howled to the winds to be manifested. They demanded it upon seeing Lapu, their prototype. Their leader TGP: "*In time, dear fellows. In time.*"

Lapu was here for recreation, for recharging. Nothing would stop his return to the Manafuls. He'd die eating those dreadful little dwarves. Steal their Mana. He knew the Hopohopo communities would dearly miss his ever coveted layers of gloom. They could wait for his return. Lapu distracted the other Spirits with his smoother, more practiced voice. That soothed Rot.

"*Sooooo huuuuungry.*"

Lapu's Song: Hangry:

"Haven't had a decent bite in forever
Famished, I'd eat anything even liver
Right now I can chew an elephant into pulp
Take me to a convenience store for a big gulp.
ARRRGH!
It makes me so hangry, so, so hangry
Wish I could be in some Manaful's pantry
I could eat their food, then themselves too
Working for centuries shouldn't prove futile

My journey has taken me for miles and miles
I'm afraid I might run out of fuel out there
Run out of energy, out of steam, out of air
I must reach my goal, my aim and my dream
To Manifest, and have my own Teams
Instead of being stuck here in this latrine!
Even Spirits need help, know what I mean?
ARRRGH!

Makes me so hangry, contemplating the nasty
Things I could consume, but I mustn't be hasty
I will leave after improving my foibles
I'm sort of weakened, losing my marbles
In the Rot, getting strong, my Spirit will stand tall
Next time I go for it, I'm not gonna fall
I have my dream of conquering the Manaful
I'm gonna win, just let me sit and mull
The Rot renews me: just you wait and see,
Tee hee hee hee heeeee!"

He reached the Rift pit. Liquid death bubbled and gobbled all in its volcanic crater. Lapu swan dived, even achieving a happy little twirl in the air. The sea of despair and loss enveloped his energy. Noxious fumes overwhelmed lost souls. Within his miserable existence, Lapu still possessed hedonistic desires. His favorite Hopohopo's undercurrent of fashionista waves had impacted the Spirit. Though he lacked sensory anchors, he sighed in satisfaction of this spa day of sorts. The lushness of this steaming cesspool, gurgling with sheer toxicity, mālama his "skin". Sooo...

...fetid.

Fantastic.

Lapu soaked comfortably.

He fantasized about being able to eat.

"*Sooooon.*"

CHAPTER 70
PIERRE IDENTITY WRAP

Earth
May 3, 2023
Wright Middle School

Pierre wanted to show his true self, his identity. He'd quit the football team today, meeting one on one with Coach Jackson.

Being a Physical Education teacher at Wright Middle, the football coach had his fingers on the pulse of athletics. Pierre went into Coach Jackson's office during Study Hall time. Coach was indoors proctoring make-up Health tests on the laptops. All but one of Coach's Study Hall students had just left. Pierre had ten minutes until Teacher Administration time began and Study Hall ended. By the serious look on Pierre's face, Coach knew their meeting would be a doozy.

Gabe Martin had called the coach a few days ago. Pierre's dad had been concerned about some gossip and maliciousness in the locker room against his son. After that call, he'd sought those bullies out. Though it was no longer football season, Coach saw his players at off-season conditioning. He'd pulled aside the boys one to one. Some had denied it, while other players outright said they didn't want Pierre near them. They'd admitted to namecalling: queer, pansy, faggot, and worse. He'd told those boys their playing days for him were over. The team had lost two players. It was pono. The Coach had felt great hilahila and kaumaha. He'd watched the eighth grade boys grow over their three years at Wright Middle. He'd shaped them into a championship winning team. Yet, he'd gone wrong somehow. He did not believe in intimidation, fear, and belittlement of others for ANY reason. He didn't condone bullying. He'd failed to instill this in his boys. He'd failed them and himself.

Looking at Pierre standing bravely in his classroom doorway, Coach recalled the pain of Gabe Martin's call. When he'd hung up that night, he'd turned to his wife with tears in his eyes.

"I failed my team, Babe!" Coach Ha'aheo Jackson reached for his wife's hand. She'd been stirring their entree in the crock pot. She'd seen his facial expressions as he paced in the living room on his mobile.

"What do you mean, Dear? How can I help?" Tina Jackson asked, staying calm as she sensed his disappointment. She didn't want him to self-flagellate himself more.

"That was Gabe Martin. He says he's had it up to here," Ha'aheo lifted his hand, still holding his mobile, over his head. "The Martins won't stand the bullying of their son. Pierre's mental health is more important than any championship team."

Tina nodded, supporting her husband wholeheartedly.

Coach Ha'aheo Jackson continued, "I have to talk to those boys. I may lose some players." He frowned and shook his head.

More in disappointment for their negativity than their future team prospects.The couple hugged each other, feeling kāko'o for Pierre.

The laptop cart door slammed closed, bringing Coach Jackson back to the present. "Hey, Shawnie! Be gentle with the old cart!" Coach Ha'aheo pointed at the eighth grader who'd just finished her computer test. Procedurally, the haumāna put away their own laptops, plugged them in, and went home. Shawnie grinned and said, "Sorry, it was a happy slam. I aced that test. Feel it!" The thin blonde girl giggled, dancing in place. Coach Ha'aheo laughed as did Pierre who'd waited to speak with Coach. "I'm glad, Shawnie! Have a good one," Coach smiled and they all exchanged fistbumps. Pierre winked at Shawnie, knowing her from Marine Science. She tried to wink back at her handsome classmate. She'd always had a little crush on him. Her wink came out wrong. Instead, she awkwardly blinked repeatedly. Then, she laughed at herself. Her sweetness warmed Pierre.

Watching the exchange, Coach Ha'aheo smiled too. Pierre was always a congenial person. He pointed to a chair for Pierre and sat down himself. His star football player took a deep breath and got to the point.

"Coach, I'm quitting." he said.

"Your father gave me a heads-up. I feel partially at fault for the things those boys did," Coach Ha'aheo Jackson owned up to his kuleana as a role-model. They said a few more words in gratitude then stood up. Coach offered his hand to shake. Pierre choked up a little and gave Coach a hug.

"You're a great coach!" Pierre remembered a phrase Tūtū used when leaving loving friends behind. He smiled and said from his heart, "Me ke aloha pumehana!"

Coach gasped and touched his heart, a tear glistening in his eye. He couldn't respond; his chest felt heavy. He simply nodded.

* * *

Nicole met Pierre, Malie, and Honi in the cafeteria. Nicole was still riding high on her team's basketball championship win. She'd been named MVP. They picked at the chili and nachos at their lunch table. Children's voices rang around them, some cheerful about events, some groaning about homework.

"I never thought I could play basketball!" Nicole's tortilla chip crumbled out of mouth as she spoke with her mouth full. The melted cheddar dripped from her fingers. Malie handed her a napkin, laughing at Nicole's enthusiasm.

"Trust me, basketball's no joke. My brothers are taller than me. They could slam dunk like nobody's business, but not me! Too short." Honi lifted his hands at different levels denoting himself at chest level and his brothers way above his head.

Pierre smiled at Honi supportively, responding, "You're perfect just the way you are! Your hula in Hawaiian Culture class is really graceful."

Honi made an "awww" face and made a heart sign for Pierre.

Malie nudged Honi and said, "I want to visit your hale and learn to dance from you and your mom."

She had starstruck eyes, in awe of Honi's mom. Shifa Honua was a dance teacher of Maldivian descent. After living here for a decade, she'd expanded her repertoire to hula. She'd joined a halau in her thirties and matriculated through 'ūniki with her Kumu Hula. That was the Hawaiian tradition of hula teacher training. As a practicing Muslim, Shifa respectfully declined the 'ailolo ceremony in which the graduating hula haumāna eats different parts of a pua'a or pig to metaphorically and spiritually obtain parts of its Mana. Still two decades later, Shifa was affiliated and practicing with her Kumu Hula. Honi's mom participates annually in the Merrie Monarch Hula Competition in Hilo, Hawai'i held in honor of King David Kalākaua. Shifa's whole being as she danced in Honi's videos stole Malie's breath. She'd planned to meet Honi's mom soon. It was in her Hawaiian Compendium App under: Priority action/in-person research.

Nicole told Malie, "If you become a haumāna at Honi's hale, I'd like to join you. My Hawaiian grandfather may have kicked me and mom out, but he can't steal my heritage."

Pierre's and Malie's eyebrows went up in synchronicity as they met each other's eyes.

"Did she just say that?" Malie projected to him.

"Yes, she's gained courage to talk plainly of her abandonment issues," PIerre TP back.

Malie scrunched her face up and took a deep breath. She waved her hands in front of her eyes, feeling the tears. Pierre reached across the cafeteria table and squeezed her hand.

"It's alright to feel pride and Aloha for Nicole's growth! Let 'em flow. Cry, Tita!" He projected to her.

Malie caught her breath at the nickname. He called her sister! Oh, this was an emotional day! Honi put his hand on Pierre's and Malie's. Nicole knew they'd been twin-talking in their minds. She hoped they were okay. She put her hand on their lima, squeezing Honi‘s chubby fingers.

Pierre looked at his hānai siblings and felt a song bubbling up. A song about love and being brave no matter what. He stood up and shouted to the cafe, "I'm gay! And so what?"

Pierre's Pride Song:

"Feeling the love from all of you,
knowing you kāko'o me through and through.
Being me no matter what people say
Unafraid to be honest and making a
Fool of myself in front of others to make a point
Don't tell me how to be or get your nose out of joint
I've been there and done that –still hurts–owee
Be honest. Be brave: you can be you, don't be sorry
About not fitting in or being perfect
I tried it and trust me, you can't reject
The real you without hurting yourself real deep
Inside where your secrets come out, you cannot keep
Pushing away your love and your happiness
Surround yourself with Aloha and 'Ohana, and confess
To yourself in the mirror, talk loving to him, her, or them.
Come out of shadows, don't feel like you're unhemmed
There's only one you.
Oh, look how you grew!
Group hug, everyone! Bring it in!
As an 'ohana, we'll always win!"

Honi, Pierre, Nicole and Malie hugged, patting each other's back. They hopped around in place like an athletic team having won a championship game. People around them clapped and laughed at their joy. The bell rang.

Vice Principal Pang nodded, watching over the kids. Proud for Pierre's bravery, wondering if he'd join the Drama Club. He had a great voice and presence. She'd text his name to the Theatre teacher. Kids threw away their plates and texted while they walked out of the cafeteria. The kitchen staff wiped down tables, grumbling about lazy kids who forget to dump their plates or drop food on the floor.

The Secret Club plus Honi dispersed to their classes unaware of the quiet, bespeckled Kona hiding behind the stacked tables. He'd enjoyed Pierre's song and longed to be in their warm group hug. He frowned at always being sidelined. He'd find a way to join their club. "*You all just wait!*" He was determined.

CHAPTER 71
SC UNWINDS @ CRIB

Manaful World
June 1, 2023
Koa Forest, Elder Territory
Ikaika's Mansion

The SC was determined to learn more about Lapu this Summer. They knew he was the key to capturing Ejad, the Inventor. They entered Manaful immediately upon reaching this consensus on Nicole's bed. They met Ikaika on the other side in Koa Forest below his mega-awesome crib.

Though it's been more than a year, the SC were still overwhelmed by the Mana of the place – it was totally lit. Want to take a swim in an Olympic size pool? Done. Want to drive a racecar in your own VR film? Done. Want to eat the yummiest chocolate chip cookies ever baked? Done. It was a dream place.

Ikaika's three puppies came running to greet the SC. Nicole still laughed at their names: Brownie, Cookie, and Cupcake, after Ikaika's favorite goodies. Though they weren't quite puppies anymore. They were lovable and fun to roll around the floor with. Nicole was leery of their licking and slippery, slimy saliva. Gross!

They were headed out soon to meet Maluhia and Elder Maka to learn about nature. The SC wanted to know as much as possible to help their Manaful family. Truly, they were like an ʻohana now.

Chapter 72
Charmaine Abdicates

Manaful World
June 1, 2023
Council House
House Opalescent Territory

Privately, Charmaine, Puna and Hina discussed the future of their world.

"It helps me more to pop in and out of the Spirit Realm than sit around in meetings," Charmaine shared with her seniors. *"I will learn more there!"*

"There may be a few things to be learned through material involvement as well. The title of Chair helps you grow," Hina advised.

Puna's eyes crinkled at Charmaine. *"As one with singular power among us, Charmaine knows best which path to take for herself. She is still reaching her full potential. If we cage her with responsibilities too fast, her piko may suffer."*

As Chair, Charmaine will always be held back from visiting the Spirit Realm. Her full presence was important and demanded.

If she were to run meetings, she had to be present, fully awake at the table.

Besides, the Council Chair had more ethics to consider than the average member. Judging by the way things were going, Charmaine thought some rules had to be bent. That's if the council wanted quick solutions to the threats their world faced. One rule was that no member of the council, especially the Chair, can Mind Lock a Hopohopo. It was allowed for MZ Manafuls to prevent Hopohopo attacks and infiltrations into their Territory. Otherwise it was a giant No.

"I WILL Mind Lock Ejad," Charmaine decided.

Hina's sad eyes lowered to folded hands in her lap.

Puna took a deep breath, his robes reaching to pat Charmaine on the arm. "*We believe you know your way.*"

Hina chewed her lips but eventually nodded.

Elders began to MT to the Opalescent chambers. It was time for the meeting to begin. The trio waited till all the floating pod chairs were filled. The central table was made of sculpted quartz. Charmaine took a deep breath and picked up the gavel. She looked at it for a moment, lips parted, then threw it away to vanish into thin air. She leaned forward, robes rustling in the silence, and smiled. She had the council's rapt attention. How would they react to her decision?

Only one way to find out. She revealed her plans to abdicate. The Elders all sat ramrod straight in their seats, eyes popping. None interrupted till well after she was done speaking.

The Elders erupted only once she concluded, "I will Mind Lock this Inventor."

Charmaine was set on finding and immobilizing Ejad and Lapu with her bare hands if need be. Aunty Hina would do the pleasantries in Council Chambers. Charmaine had other, more independent plans. She sat back and stared calmly around at all the Elders shouting at her.

Chapter 73
Ground Zero Revisit

Manaful World
June 1, 2023
Lote Forest, Elder Territory

Maluhia asked Ikaika to meet him at Lote Forest where Alaka'i had fallen. The group MT-ed from Ikaika's crib in the sky. They were headed to the scene of the crime, where Ejad's deserted, burnt out explosion remained. It felt haunted. Malie shivered. Pierre put his arm around her. She looked up and smiled. The information to come may not be what they want to hear...

"*The soil is dead*," Maluhia projected plainly.

Maluhia called it Dead Mana. All the tainted essence Lapu/Ejad produced with the Mech settled into the soil. Laka could not leach the fine mist out with her core. The Elder Council didn't want to unite their powers to interfere there. Let nature do its course, they said.

"*Nothing will grow here for some time. Cloud has been visiting to drizzle often*," Maluhia hooted, begrudgingly ruffling feathers in fondness at the memory of that puff of vapor.

The Forest Guardian did not seem to mind Cloud much nowadays. He said that with Cloud's help the hauntedness will heal half as fast. Already natural growth is happening as grass. They grew slower in the barren soil of what had been Elder Laka's beloved Lote Forest. Maluhia said Laka's core needed to calm down as well for her land to grow faster.

Maka lent his energies to heal the land.

("And that is the end of part two, Ari.")

CHAPTER 74
AUNT ELLIE'S SNEAK PEEK

Storyteller in Papakōlea, Hawai'i
June 1, 2023

"OMG! No, Aunty Ellie, please don't end it here! Mom! Tell her to continue for you. She's so happy you're here. She'll do it!" Ari was on her tippy-toes with her hands in the air. She looked like a ballerina ready to leap. Her mom and aunt laughed from the couch, putting the laptop down next to their tea and cookies on the side table.

Hoku was pleased to be there. It wasn't her first time sitting in. It has been almost half a year since she'd started her once a week adventures here. It was a thrill to see her daughter really happy about reading. She prayed that the reading bug never went away.

"I adore Kona. He's really sweet for Nicole and she keeps bossing him around. I can see Malie and him bonding a little down the road. Please, let's continue?" Ari had by now sunken to her knees pleading.

Aunty Ellie pulled her up onto the couch between her and her mother. Hoku patted her daughter‘s hand once she sat down.

“If you let me explain, Babe, I assure you we’ll return ‘apōpō. I‘m a little tired and sore now.”

She put her hand to her belly, scrunching her nose and eyes together in a pained expression.

Ari‘s face immediately became sympathetic, and she intertwined her fingers with her aunt‘s hand still resting on her stomach.

Hoku grabbed her sister‘s arm.

“Hey, we can stop. Do you need something?”

“Oh, Aunty, we shouldn‘t talk for hours like this, if you‘ve got cramps! Tell me sooner, and we‘ll stop so you can nap!”

Aunty Ellie smiled at her sister and hugged her niece, “Who‘s the adult here? But mahalo, you‘re right that I must tell you how I feel. Keep you in the loop like you do for me when your body‘s sore. We share our inner ups and downs, right?”

Ari pulled on a loose red thread hanging on her basketball shorts. Biting her lip, she nodded. It was still weird having her mom and aunt talking about her ma‘i in front of her. Maybe they could go to the kitchen *without her.*

“We share. Right, Ari? Remember the 3 C‘s?”

Ari let out a deflated breath, a balloon running out air.

“Of course, Aunty. I’m Careful, Cognizant, and Confident! I still feel weird sometimes about menstruation.”

“Trust me, many do, even at my age! Ask your mom,” Aunty Ellie looked at Hoku.

Hoku responded with a wink and nod to her sister. "She's right, Babe. Body issues and questions never go away! They will be with us forever."

Hoku made a fistbump for Ari who giggled then fistbumped her aunt.

Aunty Ellie tucked Ari's loose 'ehu tendril behind her ear and said, "I like your honesty on such a sensitive subject. I know you don't talk to your dad about it, but your mom and I are always here."

Ari blushed and hid her face behind her hands. Hoku patted her daughter's back.

Aunty Ellie pulled Ari's hands down and bent to meet her eyes, smiling into them.

Her voice was extra tender with her niece, "We're beautiful wāhine, unafraid and with no hilahila about our body's changes and needs. We love and mālama ourselves."

Ari teared up a bit, her pupils glistening in sweet pools.

Aunty Ellie caught her teardrops with her thumbs, as Ari smiled shyly, responding, "Remember not long ago you helped me when I was overwhelmed by the spotting on my linen and favorite clothes? When my whole body felt like I'd been run over by a truck? When I didn't understand how to use the feminine products? I love you, Aunty!"

Aunt Ellie noticed her sister looking excluded. She said, "Group hug! Bring it in, Sister. Niece!"

They all were a bit teary yet happy.

Aunty Ellie's stomach still hurts a little. She sighed, "So, we'll share one more scene. Afterwards, let's rest a bit."

Ari instantly perked up exclaiming, "Oh, Aunty, what about that sixth grader? He's really cute and feisty. Does he find out more about the SC?"

Aunty Ellie laughed, then cringed as her cramps were still rough at times. She could do this. End their reading with a small glimpse of what's to come. Her sister nodded encouragingly. Yes! Resolved, Aunty Ellie sat up straighter. "Ready for a sneak peek of the new SC?"

Ari just about leaped out of the chair. Bopping her head like a rocker, "Yes! Tell!"

Aunt Ellie smiled and closed her eyes for a second. She did the owl-breathing.

"About Kona ..."

Epilogue

Earth
June 3, 2023
Wright Middle School

School is on Christmas Break. It's time for our characters to mill around WMS grounds exploring and socializing till classes resume. But of course, family time at their homes were prized most of all.

The SC assumed ("You said ass," Ari giggled) they were safe to use the Gym Shimmery Wall. ("Or maybe not!")

Malie and Pierre found Nicole already at the usual spot, fighting with Kona over a packet of jelly beans.

"Get off of me!"

"Give those back, you little sneak!"

Kona hopped away, hugging the candy to his shirt. It looked like a hand me down. The sleeves hung on his small frame like a deflated parachute. His voice was high pitched and timid. But also spontaneous and stubborn. Kona was a lot of things.

He demanded: "Promise me!"

"No!"

"Nickyyyyyyy!"

"DON'T CALL ME NICKY!" Nicole lost it. She ripped out a bit of her hair. She blew it at Kona menacingly. Kona blew the wisp away.

Kona has been demanding to join the Secret Club for weeks now. Since discovering what he was up to, the SC were getting better at foiling his plans to jump their meetings. Today, Kona is demanding either the jellybeans he'd knicked from the side pocket of Nicole's school bag or the Shimmery Wall for him to go through.

"Please! Be nice!" Malie said timidly.

Nicole snorted. She gave Kona the jellybeans and told him to get lost. Malie had a soft spot for Kona. He was a nerd and a geek, which she assumed must mean he is some sort of genius in disguise. Besides, she'd like to taste those jellybeans. In short, she's fine with taking Kona across. She looked at Pierre, brows raised and wiggling.

Pierre was dubious. "Shouldn't Elder Puna be the one to decide who visits Manaful?"

"You tell 'em, Pierre!" Nicole said.

Their discussion was interrupted when the scintillating Mana substance poured down the gym wall like water, and the Shimmery Wall opened up. The original moss wall looked like a holograph falling away into a vista of a glorious landscape.

"IT'S GIVING!" Kona yelled. He was jumping so hard his glasses joggled on his button nose, beady eyes popping as he pointed in awe.

"You can SMELL the greener grass on the other side! Wow!"

"I know! I love it every time as well," Pierre nodded, grinning at the tiny ball of energy beside him. For a blink of the mind's eye he saw Kona crouching in the ferns behind them, watching them enter the Shimmery Wall. He almost turned around but stopped himself. The ninja was out in the open this time, right beside him. He remembered that Kona had watched them for weeks. Hanging on to Nicole hoping to be included.

The kid really, really wanted to be in the Secret Club. Remembering how his teammates had silently pushed him aside last year, Pierre patted Kona on the arm. That was an extension of the twang of sympathy in his core.

"No offense. But you don't have to be an SC member to be our friend," Pierre said without a smile. He was impatient to go off to Manaful World minus Kona, despite his quickly thawing soft spot. Deep inside he thought, *If I can't bring Honi, Kona can stay out too.*

Malie shook her head and squeezed Pierre's hand.

She persisted, "This means Elder Puna and Ikaika are fine with him. Why else would they open it for us when he's right here? He's meant to join us."

Kona offered to high five Malie but she thought that's pushing it. So he did a geeky victory dance instead. He'd put paper clips along his backpack straps and they clinked merrily with his movements.

"But he's still not an official Secret Club member!" Nicole fumed.

"We didn't vote! I'm not letting him through!"

"I WILL go!" Kona stamped his sneakers.

"Over my dead body!" Nicole yelled, stomping hers.

Kona blew a raspberry. He said, "You can't stop me now ha ha ha!"

"You little—" Nicole began.

Kona dived into the Shimmery Wall. His body unraveled into smaller and smaller bits which were sucked into the substance and beyond. It was the first time the SC saw what they must look like from behind when they MT through a Shimmery Wall. It was glorious. Kona had seen it a couple of times. The cloud of his molecules turned around in slow motion and flipped them the bird before they coalesced into the hazy form of the sixth grader on Manaful soil. The brat looked around in awe, looked at his body, over his shoulder, and then ran off. They saw Ikaika's rippling form run where Kona had appeared as if wondering whether to chase the newcomer or wait for the trio.

It was strange seeing Ikaika's form through the surface for the first time. He looked tiny from here, ghostly in the swirling colors. Like a doll in a fiery sarong held under rippling water.

Nicole yelled, "AFTER HIM!"

The Secret Club snapped out of it. Pierre and Malie ran after Nicole and Kona into the Shimmery Wall. The portal bubbled at the edges like Coke with Mentos, ringing with breathy bell-like tunes. It closed up behind the humans, flowing away into the hearts of moss, stone and wind.

Soon, it was just the regular wall.

To Be Continued...

GLOSSARY 1 Manaful World

Aspiring Hopohopo - A Hopohopo training to become a Manaful via intense, life-changing study in Mana magic via a connectivity to Source.

Cloaking - Invisibility via rune scripting used by Ejad or via Source Mana by Elders

Dead, Dark or Tainted Mana - Mana Mist changed by Lapu in Old Hill and continued by Lapu's soldier Spirits to enrich the underworld or Rot. It's used similarly to Mana from Source, as magical fuel.

Ejad Honua- Primary Antagonist (an heir of Uli and possessed by Lapu). Ejad Honua is THE Inventor of the novel's title and quite simply an all-consuming Hopohopo for this series. Magical in his own genius and Tainted Mana ways. You will love him too!

Elders - the royalty of each family or 'ohana. Each 'ohana only wears one color. The Elders hold the greatest magical power in their family and in the Manaful World.

Elder Council - Manaful World is led by royal Elders. All Elders have a seat in the Council, a governing body. Some Elders are more magical and powerful than others. Upon their death, an Elder's Magic is passed down to the living relative (male, female, or agender) designated as the Heirs. The Heir takes their seat in the Council. The Original Elder Prime or Council Leader is Elder Alaka'i.

Elder Robes - Elders wear a magical, bioluminescent, living robe of their family's color. They don their robes with a belt over their undergarments and clothing. Only Elders have the power to wear these magical robes. The robes are sentient and can travel independent of their Elder.

Elder Link - Telepathic multisensory real-time broadcasting on a private or public mental communications line between Elders across Manaful World.

Forest Guardians - Owls (like Maluhia), Ravens, Parrots, and some trees (like Koa) are examples of Guardians who have symbiotic connectivity to Source. They are high in Mana/ Mana Mist capabilities. Similar to Old Hill, the Relics, and the Elders, the Guardians are extremely aligned to Source and allies of Manafuls.

Forcefield - A Mana-produced magical bubble that needs a substance to work. The 'field' used varies in density, size, and danger. Usually it is made when Mana condenses into Mana Mist, which warps into a repulsive energy field that deflects all other material. The force fields can be made with other things like trees, rock, fire, electricity, water and even light (photonic energy) if one was powerful enough.

Glyphs - Hieroglyphic graphic symbols carved by ancient Egyptians and borrowed in this text by Ejad. These carvings possess historic Manaful powers and energy fueled by Source.

Healing - Manaful powers of energetic medicine where the Elder or Manaful healer runs their hands above a being and regenerates or recreates cells back to normal or improved functioning.

Hive Mind - Akin to the Internet's Public Domain. Data gathered over thousands of years of accumulated shared experiences by every living Manaful. It's always accessible to them. Like the Web, information from the Hive can be filtered or misinterpreted.

House - A Manaful 'ohana in charge of a specific domain and led by an Elder.

Hovering - Levitating with a traveling element and always standing straight up. Imagine standing in an unwalled, invisible box. One steps onto a flat, invisible craft that lifts quickly or slowly, the expert Manaful-user controls the velocity. The craft takes the rider to and fro. Once on the craft, the being cannot fall off. They can jump off if the Manaful deems a specific perimeter. Riders are safe from weather. They can also reach out and touch things. It is the most scenic way to travel in Manaful World though much slower than the instantaneous MT.

Lapu - Primary Antagonist. A Spirit force created inside Old Hill and older than the Manafuls. He's accumulated and consumed Mana essence, turning it into Tainted Mana or evil magic. His biggest goal, aside from taking over the world, is to have a body. Meanwhile, he possesses dwarves and other beings, using them like puppets to steal control from the Elder Council by any means necessary, encouraging even murder and genocide.

Levitating - Floating above the ground in a controlled manner with Mana used by very powerful Manafuls. Could be standing, sitting, or laying down. Always in one place.

Link Medium (LM) - The minds of the Elders are Linked telepathically, all being perfectly aligned with Source. Their collective consciousness constantly 'uploads' information to the Hive as mental bits. Link Mediums are items that give access to the information being broadcast through the Elder Link. Manafuls may conjure them in physical or virtual form at the snap of their fingers.

Mana/Magic - Mana is the magic of the Manaful World that permeates everything but is unseen. It is felt and picked up by the soul. The body can channel this empowering creative force to do magic. In a real world sense, it is "Learned" knowledge that accumulates over time. In the fantasy world, one becomes more Manaful by increasing their knowledge and capacity to successfully share that knowledge through love. In Manaful, the source of Mana is Source, the One creator of the Manaful World. A being achieves the most with Mana by 'Aligning with

Source' with love, which is when one is completely in line with the universal laws revealed to Elders through their connection to the divine.

Manaful - Magical dwarf (4 feet is the tallest) beings of humanoid biology from a separate dimensional world from Earth. They are advanced in technology and magic, speaking telepathically or orally in all human languages. They may travel by foot, but it's more natural to them to travel by transporting themselves molecularly or to hover. They wear only one clothing color, their family color.

Mana Battery Cells (MBC) - Akin to human portable batteries of various sizes and capacities, except fueled by contained Source energy and magic, Mana.

Mana Tech - Any computerized, mechanized, engineered, or robotic programing system large infrastructure sized or small handheld in sized, all powered by Mana.

Mana Mech - Specialized mechanical inventions by Ejad, similar to Tech, except fueled by Tainted Mana as well as the ancient powers of runes and glyphs.

Mana Mist - Like water vapor, Mana remains largely invisible but in virgin nature can condense to form a substance called Mana Mist, like dew drops. It is seen, and can be a source of nourishment for the animals, Hopohopo, and humans within Manaful World when consuming water and plants/fruits. It is indirect Source-Mana for humans and Hopohopo, but they can come a step closer to a Manaful's capacity to tap straight from Source. A select few animals, mostly birds, have the ability to consume it and become magical beings that can use it almost like how Elders use Mana. Understandably, those that use Mana Mist are considerably weaker in magical power than the Manaful, who use unseen Mana straight from source.

Mega Flora - Gigantic plant life, possibly two stories or bigger, designed by House Opalescent. They are used as Mana mist reservoirs, exuding the magical essence like a plume of pixie dust. They rain their special dust on beings in the Manaful Zone. The mega flora stems and petals are turgid with magic.

Mind-meld - to mentally connect and remain connected with another Manaful. Only done Manaful to Manaful. While mentally connected, Manafuls can share past and present thoughts and memories. Only very powerful Elders and Spirits can use mind-melding to combine their powers to build things or to heal others.

Mind Lock - to mentally lock another being using the mind-meld and only done by Elders or Spirits upon other beings of less Mana capabilities. Essentially creating a mental box within the victim's brain to control them. Everything the locked being does, thinks, and perceives is from the controller's perspective or for the controller's purposes.

Molecular Travel (MT) - Magically changing your body into molecules to travel through time and to different places. Manafuls can MT themselves and humans anywhere in Manaful. Manafuls can MT humans to and from Earth and Manaful. Forced molecular travel without permission is kidnapping and punishable.

Old Hill - Aunty Ellie described it as originally a hill in which "The rest of Manaful land is simply the periphery like robes around a king." It's the Center of Manaful World as it forms its magical core. It was once a living, breathing hill. It used to house Spirits occupied with Mana essence. Old Hill, even in Rift-form, is an all-powerful being second only to Source.

Offspring - Former Aspiring Hopohopo who have metamorphosed into Manafuls though not fully so, as they weren't born so. Their skin pigmentation decreases till it becomes transparent. Their Mana magic varies according to their training. When they complete aligning with Source, their skins regain opacity. This temporary effect is a physical and spiritual process of evolution where the entire Hopohopo is reconstituted into a Manaful.

Possession - A Spiritual taking over of the entire body and mind, though the soul can be protected by the being, for malignant purposes.

Protectors - Manaful bodyguards, security agents, and in some cases mercenaries and assassins, originally created by Elder

Uli but passed on to Elder Maka and via silent partnership, Ejad Honua.

Puppets - Spiritually possessed Manafuls and Hopohopo who are mind locked to do the bidding of Ejad or Lapu.

Relics - Cloud, Stone, and Tree are the ancient (older than all Manafuls) creations and "children" of Old Hill. They possess Mana and travel around the world freely, often hiding from dwarves. They still love and miss their "father" Old Hill.

Runology - The study of ancient alphabetic inscriptions and symbology used and empowered by Ejad for its indirect Source energy.

Rift - A crater in the center of Manaful World which is all that's left of Old Hill's post volcanic explosion caused by Lapu. The Tainted Mana there is especially potent and dangerous to all beings, especially Elders.

Rot - The Hive Mind for Spirits in the Rift, a collective repository of their energy there.

Source - God figure for the Manafuls. It (no gender) exists in all things, living and not living. It created all Manaful World and all of its beings, even Old Hill and Lapu. Elders have direct communication with it. Elders encourage all Manafuls to access this communication too. Elders say, "Align with Mana" to mean talk to God. Mana or magical powers come from Source. By aligning with Mana, a Manaful taps Source's love, protection, and magical powers for positive purposes.

Scripting - Ancient, powerful and sometimes dangerous method of inscribing or carving something with magical powers for good or evil purposes. All letters have an inherent power; Scripting uses the rune and glyph lettering of early Manaful World.

Spirits - Beings of good and bad powers originally from Source though some are trained and led astray via Tainted Mana by Lapu.

Spirit Realm - A Spiritual dimension where Manafuls, Hopohopo, and Spirits transition to upon death. Only a handful of the most powerful Elders can visit this Realm while still alive, including Alaka'i, Puna, and Charmaine.

Telekinesis - Ability to move and manipulate physical objects with the mind. Not easy to do. Some physical laws are not easily overcome by Mana. Every applied force has an equal resistive/opposite force, tension and torque and also atomic forces apply while manipulating physical objects. Meaning: a physically unprepared Manaful cannot telekinetically lift a weight exceeding its own without suffering some bodily damage. Telekinesis also expends a lot of energy and is taxing to do on a large scale. But it is used minimally within reason by all Manafuls in their daily lives (eg: to retrieve the TV remote). Phonons (vibrational energy) and electromagnetic energy is used for blasting or moving things. When tapped in the nuclear forces, telekinesis can allow for objects to be taken apart and put together into new things as well, but that sort of magic is of the highest level.

Telepathy - The gamut of mental powers in which one communicates nonverbally and including any of the following: Mind reading, thought projection, astral projection (out of body visiting), telepathic group projection, mind-melding and more.

Telepathically Project - To telepathically send out or mentally project your thoughts privately to one person only.

Telepathically Group Project (TGP) - To telepathically communicate with a group sending mental messages, like group texting. The projected thoughts go to only specific and select individuals from your brain to their brains.

Transmutation - The changing, transferring, and moving of magic, energy, and spiritual powers from one Manaful to another. It can be lent to another Manaful in spurts or large amounts. It can be passed down entirely (all an Elder's powers) from one Manaful to their Heir upon death. Whether Mana can be transmuted upon death to non-family members has never been tested.

GIOSSARY 2 'Ōlelo Nouveau

All Hawaiian language definitions come from Ulukau's Hawaiian Electric Library: Nā Puke Wehewehe 'Ōlelo Hawai'i at www.wehewehe.org

'Ae - Yes

'Āina - land, earth (soil not the planet Earth, that's Honua)

'Ahinahina - gray or white/gray; name of Elder Lilinoe's (female) family/house

'Ākala - pink; name of Elder 'Ākala's (female) family/house

Alaka'i- Main Protagonist. Means to lead, leader; name of oldest elder, founder of Manaful people; highest ranking Manaful family

'Alani - orange; name of an Elder's (female) family/house

Ana - Cave or cavern

Ana Keona - God's gracious cavernous gift (Ejad's favorite home underground in Elder Lilinoe's territory)

'Aumakua - Family or personal god(s); deified ancestors

Auwe - an exclamation of wonder, surprise, fear, or pity

'Ele'ele - black; name of Elder Pele's (female) family/house

Hā - Breath, life

Hānai - Foster, adopt, raise, feed

Hale - Home, building

Haumāna - student

Hilahila - shame, embarrassment

Hina - gray/white; Elder Hina (female) of the Ke'oke'o (definition: white)

Honua - Earth, World

Ho'oponopono - To correct

Hopohopo - Anxiety, uncertainty, doubt. A non-derogatory label for Manaful beings who fear, doubt, and have anxiety about their innate magical powers. They rejected the learning and usage of

Mana except in health or safety purposes. They have telepathic abilities. Some use them, but most do not. Their vulnerabilities are far and wide due to this rejection. Powerful mental forces of others can control Hopohopo.

I'a - Fish or marine animal including big and small creatures like crabs and whales

Ikaika - Main Protagonist. Means strong, powerful. Grandson and heir of Elder Puna one of the highest ranking Manaful 'Ohana leaders in their world.

'Iliahi - Sandalwood

Ipu - Water gourd or dancing drum

Kāko'o - uphold, support, assist

Kāholo - Hula steps: repeated side steps

Kalakoa - Showing varied, calico patterns of colors all at once

Kalo - Uphold, support; taro plant; mythological and theological significance in Hawaii

Kauhale - Group of houses comprising an ancient Hawaiian estate or community: women's eating house, family church, family gathering house, canoe house, etc.

Keiki - Child

Kolohe - Mischievous, rascal, naughty

Kōkua - Help

Kumu - Tree, foundation, teacher

Kukui - Candlenut tree used for light, incense or indigestion

Kūpuna - Grandparents, ancestors, older relatives or close friends

Kuleana - Responsibility

Laulau - Wrapped ti leaf packages of steamed or broiled meat or other foods

Lima - hand

Lua - Hole, grave, toilet

Maka - Main Protagonist and Elder of ʻŌmaʻomaʻo ʻOhana, a teenager and one of the youngest Elder leaders; definition: eyes

Māku'e - brown; name of Elder (male) of the same name

Makana - gift

Makani - wind

Melemele - yellow; name of an Elder family

Manakō - mango

Manu - bird

Maui - one of the main Hawaiian islands; with a kahakō over the "ā" as in Māui the word refers to the legendary demi-god

Menehune - legendary race of small, dwarf people in who built bridges, temples and more secretly at night, hidden from Human sight though heard sometimes in the wind; not capitalized "menehune" is a verb meaning to work or gather together to complete a task

Moa - chicken

Momi - pearl; name of house/family of highest Elder Alaka'i and his daughter Charmaine

'Ohana - family

'Ōlelo - language

'Ōma'oma'o - green; name of third highest Elder family in Manaful

'Ono - delicious (food or other things)

Pahu - box, drum

Papakōlea - An actual Hawaiian homestead community near Punchbowl Cemetery in Honolulu, Hawai'i

Piko - metaphorical center of being; literally umbilical cord, navel, genitals

Polū - blue ref to clothes and things; referencing the sky or ocean use uli; Manaful Elder (male)

Poni - purple; Manaful Elder Laka's (female) house/family name

Pule - pray

Pulelehua - butterfly

Puna - Main Protagonist. A Manaful grandparent and Second Highest Elder; definition: spring of water

Tita - (slang) sister

Tūtū - *grandparent*

U'ala -- sweet potato

'Ula'Ula - (color shade) red, house name of second highest Elder family in Manaful

Uli - Main Antagonist (after Lapu), visited in flashbacks, deceased former Elder of ʻŌmaʻomaʻo family, grandfather of Elder Maka, who killed him in a battle at the end of Book 1.

Uli - (color/shade) deep, dark color including the sea, sky, clouds, body bruises, etc. Mythological connotations of evilness, magic for malevolence.

SECOND EDITION

DORIMALIA WAIAU

AND EASA MOHAMED

The Secret Club and the Manafuls, Second Edition

Library of Congress Number: TX 9-399-740

Front cover image and book design by miblar.com
Back cover author image by Monica H. Waiau
Be Manaful Logo ™ 2024s
Printed by Dorimalia LLC., in the United States of America
Second printing edition 2024
Dorimalia LLC website: dorimaliawaiau.com

For the TSCEI and TSCM, Ed 2
D2D et al Hard Copy ISBN: 978-1-965985-02-1
D2D et al Print Copy ISBN: 978-1-965985-01-4
D2D et al EBook Copy ISBN: 978-1-965985-03-8
KDP excl. Hard Copy ISBN: 978-1-965985-00-7
KDP excl. Print Copy ISBN: 979-8-9877972-9-7
KDP excl. EBook Copy ISBN: 978-1-965985-04-5

Still and always for the Māhoe

PROLOGUE

Storyteller in Papakōlea, Hawai'i
January 13, 2022

"You enjoy reading about magical beings, yes?" Aunt Ellie asked her niece, Ari. "Your imagination flows when you do?"

"Oh, yes, I love it," Ari said, smiling. "Tell me about the Manafuls you mentioned yesterday."

The middle-aged Hawaiian woman and her eleven-year-old niece sat together outside her mountain home on a warm, sunny morning. The cool Honolulu breeze wafted the scent of breadfruit and gardenia trees towards them as they reclined on the front lanai couch.

"Manafuls are brown dwarves with magical powers," Aunt Ellie began. "They live in a world unlike ours."

"Where?" Ari asked.

"In a parallel dimension."

Ari stared at her aunt. "What's that?"

"It's a place that exists at the same time as Earth, except beyond a time portal."

Ari bounced. "Like in a fantasy novel?"

Aunt Ellie nodded.

"Exactly. Although once humans enter Manaful, Earth time stops for them—"

"The clock stops behind the portal?" Ari scratched her chin, working through this puzzle out loud. "When they come back home, the clock starts again? It's as if they hadn't left?"

"That's right," Aunt Ellie said as she high-fived her niece. "Guess how the Manaful communicate?"

Ari hummed. "Like space aliens? Telepathically?"

"Right again, smart girl. All Manafuls can project their thoughts and receive others' thoughts, and they can also talk like you and me."

"What languages do they speak?" Ari asked.

"Any language in the universe," Aunt Ellie said. "With their magic, all things are possible."

"What! Wow, I want those powers, Aunty! That and telepathy too. Don't you?"

"The magic, definitely," Aunt Ellie said, then frowned. "But maybe not the telepathy. I wouldn't want to read people's minds. Some people have ugly thoughts."

"Oh, yeah, like those bullies at my school. I know what's in their head," Ari said.

"Bullies?" Aunt Ellie's voice raised slightly. "Has something happened to you at school?"

Ari sighed. "Not to me, but it happens at school."

"What do you do?" Aunt Ellie hid her worry.

Her niece wiggled. "If the bullies knew that I snitched, they'd hurt me too. So, it's our secret, okay?"

Aunt Ellie looked grim.

"If that happened to me," Ari whispered, turning away, "I'd tell my counselor and give them the bullies' names."

Aunt Ellie gently turned Ari by the shoulders to face her again, looking into her niece's eyes. "You'd be doing the right thing, Ari. The counselors know what to do. There are rules to protect people who help. I'm glad you don't physically or verbally intervene. I wouldn't want you to get hurt."

They hugged, then Aunt Ellie shook out her hands to ease the tension.

"Are there good and bad Manafuls?" Ari asked.

"They aren't inherently good or bad," Aunt Ellie said. "Some make negative or catastrophic choices."

Ari understood. "Oh, they're like us. We may have grown up learning bad things, right?"

"The Manafuls do that too," Aunt Ellie said. "Some Manafuls even refuse their magic. Those ones are called the Hopohopo. They have to purchase the use of magic to run things, just like we purchase electricity and gas for our homes and cars."

"Why would they need to purchase magic if they could make things run themselves with their own magic?" Ari wrinkled her nose in confusion.

"Their rejection of Mana prevents them from learning how to use its force and power," Aunt Ellie said.

"That's just sad, Aunty. I don't understand the Hopohopo. Like an angel cutting off its wings and powers, refusing to fly and heal humans. Do they communicate telepathically too?"

"They can, but only a few do."

As Ari shook her head in disbelief at the waste of such gifts, Aunt Ellie smiled at her inquisitive niece. Manaful Word was just what Ari needed.

"Well, Ari, maybe we could get to the story now, hmmm?"

"Hey. Don't let me hold you back!" She bobbled her head and laughed, then checked the other side of her aunt for a bag. "Who wrote this Manaful story?"

"I did. It's mine. I'm making it up as we go. Are you going to give me a chance to tell it?"

Ari smiled and clapped. "Of course. I love your stories. Let me have it!"

Aunt Ellie raised her brows. "You promise not to interrupt?"

Ari sighed. "Don't you like my questions? You said to always ask questions. 'Don't be afraid to ask!'"

"True. You're right again."

"Ready?" Aunt Ellie folded her hands before her.

"Yes." The little girl mimed zipping her mouth, but a giggle still came out. "Hee hee."

Aunt Ellie hugged her niece. They lay back together on the couch. The story began.

Chapter 1

Manaful World
January 13, 2022
Koa Forest

"*Some humans don't understand love,*" Elder Puna, a Manaful elder, telepathically projected to his grandson, Ikaika. The dwarvish duo wore only clothing of their family color—red. The pair stood out under hundred-foot koa trees, falling leaves caressing their cocoa faces on their descent to the forest floor. The branches brushed Ikaika's shoulder and his grandfather's glowing robe like "Hellos" soothing a beloved. Soft voices in the wind reached out to the grandfather and grandson, "*Hey, we're here too, we understand love!*"

Elder Puna turned from Ikaika, telepathically answering his verdant family, "*Aloha, dear ones, I know you do.*"

Koa, the tree leader of the forest, stepped forward, bowing. He answered, "*We will help you welcome this new group of young humans to our home.*"

Koa's towering presence carried the weight of wisdom and peace. He swayed his body from crown to roots. The reverberating sounds echoed around the dwarves as all the other trees matched Koa's rhythmic dance.

Bump...bump...swish. A heartbeat flowing energetic power through each limb and vein of the trees. Koa invited the elder to dance, "*Join me.*"

Elder Puna floated up into the air, grabbing a bough. Koa's stepping roots pattered a pattern on the forest floor. The other koa trees formed pairs, intertwining their branchy limbs in dancing pairs.

Ikaika laughed as Elder Puna's robe formed hands of luminous textile, grabbing the youngster to tow behind his grandfather. Koa, Elder Puna, and Ikaika now formed a whimsical conga-line, swerving around other koa trunks. Ikaika was radiant in the glow of his grandpa's robe, enthralled by Koa's energy.

After a while, Koa and the forest fell back into place as Elder Puna bowed in gratitude. "*Your musical gifts captivate my soul, Koa. Mahalo as always for that dance. Yes, please join us in our welcoming chant to the human children.*"

Koa and his trees answered together, "*We would be honored, Elder Puna. We are forever in your service.*"

Elder Puna shook his head, "*We are as one in service to the Source. Embrace the Mana.*"

The Koa forest rustled, echoing him, "*Embrace the Mana.*"

Koa stretched to his full length, "*Here, create your screen against me, so you may observe your preteens.*"

Elder Puna acknowledged Koa's offer, "*Mahalo.*"

He raised his hand and conjured a magical Shimmery Wall against the forest guardian's body. It was like a twenty foot pool of water but vertical. The Wall served as a viewing and time traveling portal between Earth and their world, Manaful.

They observed the objects of their interest. Three Wright Middle schoolers. The grandfather and grandson were telepathically connected as they watched the three humans, the senior teaching the junior amidst a halo of sparkling mist.

Ikaika wondered how he'd explain the full depth of Manaful ways of life to their preteen guests. There were so many layers to every facet of their world.

A pink butterfly landed on Ikaika's shoulder, reading his thoughts. When he was with his grandfather, he sometimes let his mind screen fall. That wasn't wise for many reasons. The butterfly fluttered its delicate wings to get Ikaika's attention.

"An open book!"

He turned his nose to her. *"Hello there, Pinky."* He stuck his finger to his shoulder. She hopped on so he could bring her before him. He liked speaking eye to eye with Manaful beings.

Pinky, the butterfly, projected into Ikaika's mind, *"You must protect yourself."*

Ikaika blew a gentle breath on his friend, *"I know. When Grandpa's around, I take for granted that he'll screen us both. We got distracted when we danced with Koa."*

Pinky giggled as a breath of wind lifted her wings, *"Perhaps, Elder Puna wants you to learn how to protect yourself, as I do for my own mind."*

Ikaika bowed to Pinky in his cupped hands. She jumped on his palm to wave her wings up and down, tickling Ikaika's palms. Her tinkling laughter filled his heart. She cocked her head at him before swooping away on the breeze.

"Guard your mind and emotions, Ikaika. Put up your mind screen at all times. Don't rely on others to do it for you," she projected over her thorax.

"Mahalo always. Be safe!" Ikaika waved to his lovely friend until she became a speck in the sun's rays shining through the koa canopy.

"Pinky's right, Ikaika," Elder Puna tapped Ikaika's elbow, guiding his attention back to the Wall. *"Never lose track of your mind."*

"It's confusing, Grandpa. How much must I open my core? Am I supposed to live in shut-in fear?"

Elder Puna passed his hand over Ikaika's head. His grandson's tension disappeared. Ikaika let out a sigh of relief, shoulders relaxing. An invisible rubber band twanged around his forehead.

"I love when you do that!" He appreciated the peace that came with Source's Mana. He nudged his grandpa's foot with his own in thanks. The impish Cloth of his grandfather's robe reached out again to Ikaika, tickling his toes. Ikaika slipped away from the robe's spry "fingers". *"Ha, ha! Stop that, Cloth!"*

His grandfather's floor-length elder's robe represented the Manaful ʻOhana leader status. The waist-cinched loose garment was made of bioluminescent silkworm fibers. Every hue of the red spectrum rippled through it with his motions as if the colors were afire. It also had a living personality. Sometimes, like now, Cloth would reach out to others for fun. Ikaika's earliest memories were being held by his grandpa and Cloth. It massaged as well as tickled forming fingers with the threads.

Ikaika kept a fair distance from his grandfather and the mischievous Cloth. Elder Puna chuckled at Ikaika's wary expression.

"Your core will know who to trust," Elder Puna brought them back to their conversation on mind-screening. He motioned and Ikaika's head, heart and midriff lit up like festival LED's, making him giggle.

"I must always keep the screens up, just in case?"

"Correct."

"Even around you?" Ikaika raised a brow.

"There are great forces out there preying on the minds and bodies of Manafuls," Elder Puna regarded his grandson. *"Times are ever in flux."*

Ikaika pursed his lips to review the lesson at hand. *"As far back as I can remember, Grandpa, you'd say, 'Put up your screen! Talk to your mind, heart, and body – don't let your attention stray from them! When you are not aware of them at all times, your screen is down. Anyone or anything can manipulate you, control you."*

Elder Puna nodded, lifting his hand to his heart. *"Good work, Grandson, that's the key. Remember that."*

Ikaika beamed at his grandfather's praise. He did a little happy dance, the pebbles on the forest floor celebrating with him. They rose up on their pointest edges to wiggle by his feet. The rounder pebbles jumped on their pokier pals' shoulders to join in on the happy moment. The clicking of their bumpy surfaces added to the symphony of rustling of leaves around Ikaika and Elder Puna's toes. Creating a wave effect, the flowers bobbed, opening and closing their petals in time. The pollen-laden bees bounced too (though a little off-beat, Bzz, bZZ, Bzz!).

Elder Puna shook his head at his grandson's ability to rouse everything around him. He couldn't hold back a chuckle. The child's energetic glee had always been contagious. The elder raised his hand and stillness came over the forest again. The pebbles did one last click together, the flowers sank down contentedly, and the bees buzzed off at the opportunity to get back to work. Even the ants, who'd stopped their flurrying to watch the magical party, bowed out and proceeded with their duties.

Elder Puna raised his brows pointedly at Ikaika, redirecting him to the Wall.

Ikaika winked at his grandfather. It took a lot of Mana to 'wake' the forest like this, so he was content to let his core rest for a bit. "*What did you mean earlier: some humans don't know love?*"

"*Many humans do not understand each other. Love is a product of mutual understanding.*"

"*Why not just mind-meld?*"

"*Aye, how's an old fellow supposed to explain love?*" Elder Puna threw his hands up frustratedly. For a dwarf of three and half millennia in age, he had impressive biceps. Ikaika levitated to squeeze his grandfather's muscles.

"*Wow, you've been lifting weights?*" Ikaika poked.

"*I mālama myself; that's what.*"

"*They look like us, Elder Puna,*" Ikaika observed, pointing at the Shimmery Wall.

"*Time is not the same in their world, Ikaika.*"

"*Seems the same.*"

"*The Manaful to human age ratio is different,*" Elder Puna projected.

"*Do they use telepathy like us, Grandpa?*"

"Some humans on Earth do. There are some powerful people there."

"You never talk about that bit."

"With the preteens, we'll be able to project into their minds," Elder Puna went on.

"Won't that scare them?" Ikaika projected worriedly.

"They'll adjust."

Ikaika frowned at his grandfather. *"Are they dangerous? Why are we inviting humans into our world if they may be loveless?"*

Tired of peering through the Shimmery Wall portal, Ikaika released his levitation and sank back down to play on Koa's roots, balancing on the foot holdings. Koa loved to play with the young dwarf, moving his roots left and right.

The Manaful stretched his arms and legs in a surfer's stance for balance. Koa tipped him over as an ocean wave would, tumbling him like a downed surfer. His out of breath laughter enlivened Koa and his arboreal kin. They clapped their branches together for Ikaika's surfing performance. The pounding of wood created more wave patterns catching Ikaika by surprise. He fell on his saronged butt on the wet mossy ground. This lifted the trees' cheerful vibe even further. The trees shook with mirth, foliage falling around the dwarf like snowflakes in a winter wonderland. Thousands of birds burst from their branches in a symphony of surprised squawking. The Heir entertained the forest endlessly.

Ikaika learned his lesson not to mess with Koa's wily roots. He brushed the damp earth from his bottom, moving to stand behind his grandpa. Koa never messed with the elder. Before returning to his portal lesson, Ikaika stuck his tongue out at Koa, *"Ha! Can't trip me from here!"* The Shimmery Wall against

Koa's trunk shook a little. Elder Puna raised his brow at them. Koa immediately stood up straighter as did Ikaika. His grandpa, used to his grandson teasing everything and everyone around him, winked at Koa.

Refocusing on his portal class, Ikaika projected, *"What are they wearing? Looks uncomfortable."* He looked down at his simple yet dirty sarong. He conjured a new one. A cleaner version immediately replaced the soiled one, wrapping itself expertly around him. His attire was cut from the same Cloth, albeit not as glittery as his grandpa's.

"We have been watching them your entire life. You tell me why they wear varied clothing," Elder Puna projected, testing his grandson.

"Well, Gramps, human societies have changed over time. Some humans are still nude, depending on their culture."

"We're talking about clothes, sonny."

"Others have thinner or thicker clothing due to their geography," Ikaika projected mental imagery for good measure. Elder Puna nodded and waved for Ikaika to share more of his learning.

"Errrr. Clothing types depend on their time period and subculture, too," Ikaika puffed with pride as he remembered. *"Like fashion and novelty wear, leis and ti-leaf skirts, turbans and scarfs."*

Images in the Wall flitted to mirror the young Manafuls speech, showing the tale of a thousand human cultures through the lens of attire.

"You know a lot, Ikaika. You need to trust what's up here and in here," Elder Puna projected, pointing to his head and heart. He was smiling at the beauty coruscating within the portal, pulled straight from the mind of his Heir.

Ikaika shared a smile with a passing Jackson chameleon who projected a quick, "*You, go Buddy!*" before crawling into a koa tree crevasse.

"*Is this Manaful's first encounter with humans? Why are we inviting this particular three?*" Ikaika wanted to know. The Wall shimmered, going back to the human kids.

"*No, these are not the first humans. Nor the last. As for why, this is related to cosmic alignment. You will learn with them,*" Elder Puna projected.

"*Don't you mean becoming Manaful? How can they embrace Mana if they're humans?*" Ikaika projected, squishing his eyebrows together. "*They don't really seem to know Source either.*"

"*They do,*" Elder Puna projected as he raised his arms to the Shimmery Wall portal to Earth. The edges fizzled as the image within became holographic, gaining depth. Ikaika perked up. He closed his eyes to sense his grandfather's Mana, or power.

The elder's core rang out bell-like, seeking the accompaniment of the forest. Shivering awake, the trees around the pair lifted their roots from the ground in a stomping motion. Rhythmic thumps echoed under the canopy as the koas marched in place, nodding their crowns in time to the beat. The wind added its part, a whistling harmony hearkening a windfall of change. The birds joined in with their notes. Frogs croaked their percussion along moss-edged streams. Every forest being was part of the orchestra.

Elder Puna chanted their welcoming song to the special trio of youths. Ikaika sang with him.

Elder Puna and Ikaika's Welcoming Chant:

"We welcome you, dear children.
There is a place for you outside of time.
A place to rise above the storms outside and within.
A place of presence power in the now.
A place to heal somehow.
A place to be.
The purpose of being is to be in harmony. "

Elder Puna and Ikaika's song flitted through the Shimmery Wall between Earth and Manaful. Voices carry.

CHAPTER 2

Earth
Honolulu, Hawaiʻi
January 12, 2022
4 p.m.

The Manu home in Papakōlea, Honolulu, was its usual quiet place. Petite Malie Manu lay on the couch, reading. Books were the shy eleven-year-old's only friends. A latchkey only child, she had an ear out for her widowed mother's return from her nursing dayshift. On cue, the sound of a car engine coughed up their driveway.

"I'm home!" Pili Manu said from the front porch. She took off her PPE, dumping them into the lanai trash can outside.

"Hi, Mom!" Malie said, sitting up on her cushions. "How was the hospital?"

"Omicron's kicking our butt!" Pili's shoulders slumped, fearful of bringing germs into their home.

She made her way toward the kitchen of their four-bed, two-bath home. An only child as well, Pili inherited the house from her deceased parents. Mortgage free. Hallelujah. "How was your school day?" Pili said over her shoulder to her daughter..

"My life is Groundhog Day, Ma," Malie sighed. She returned to her book. "Same drill, different day."

Pili frowned at the paperback hiding her daughter's face. "New book?"

The book bobbed, Malie's voice answering from behind its spine. "Librarian Heluhelu loves me. I picked up this new release."

Malie picked up a second book and waved it. "Plus one extra."

Having missed her daughter's elfin features all day, Pili pushed the book down. She wanted an eyeful of that face. Large, round, faux-tortoise-shell glasses dominated Malie's hazel, owl-like eyes, wispy pale brown brows raised in question.

"Let's have your Math worksheets," Pili said.

"It's on the table by the mail," Malie said, lifting her book back up to continue reading.

Math checks took most of Pili's focus upon coming home. Pili had long ago given up on mother-daughter movie nights. For the eleven-year-old bookworm, books were supreme and the TV was boring.

"Why watch someone else's interpretation of the words, when I can imagine my own moving images?" Malie would say.

"It's about family bonding, not the show!" Pili would reply at the book in front of Malie's face.

Wild chicken clucked in their yard. The neighborhood street cats meowed at each other, scrambling for free kibble. The nightly evening news sang its intro montage from their neighbor's window. Malie had put pot pies in the oven. Cheesy broccoli called Pili's name, the cheddary scent beckoning her.

"Thanks for putting the pies in!" Pili said from the kitchen.

"You're welcome!" Malie answered from the beige loveseats she'd moved to. The cozy, oversized seating were perpendicular to each other. Malie's wavy, light-brown hair suddenly swished across her shoulders as she popped up on her knees to face Pili.

"Aren't you going to jump into the shower? Omicron grosses me out! Bah, yuck!" Malie made a throw-up

face and laughed.

"Agreed. Bah, yuck!" Pili responded. Making her own matching gross sounds brought on resounding laughter. The tired nurse made her way to her bedroom. She waved, loving her daughter's lingering giggles.

Malie said, "Wash off that grossness, Ma! Blah! Ha ha!"

"I'm going."

"I'm rhyming!"

Pili missed her deceased husband, Kimo. She reached her master ensuite and knelt on the edge of her sunken tub.

"Oh! If only you could meet your daughter, Kimo," Pili said to herself. She poured the fragrant lavender bubble bath into the tub as it filled with water. The steam fogged the room with a garden-like aroma. Bubbles thickened over Pili's rippling reflection in the water. She closed her eyes and hummed a song to her late husband.

Kimo's Song:

"Wherever you are my dear.
I am wishing you were near.
I know you keep us in your sight.
Your memory is locked up tight.
Holding you close with all my might.

Be with us through the stars up in the sky.
Be with us through our breaths and each sigh.
Be with us!
I hope our daughter knows.
She won't have to worry, I suppose.
Knowing you're here, in some sense, brings comfort.
It just makes my heart twist and contort.
Thinking too much and living without family support.
Be with us through the stars up in the sky.
Be with us through our breaths and each sigh.
Life's a result of the decisions we make.
Who could've predicted so much heartache?
With this virus here, I am out of sync.
It's like going in circles in an ice rink.
Help me, my Kimo, bring strength to your daughter.
Lifting our girl up is all that really matters.
Be with us. Be with us."

CHAPTER 3

Earth
Honolulu, Hawai'i
Across town
January 12, 2022
4 p.m.

"Hut. Hut," the DMW League football coach shouted to his athletes in their sweaty jerseys and pads. Cleats splashed mud everywhere, but the boys lived for it.

"Oohhh," the lithe Pierre Martin groaned in pain. One too many sacks. Where's the O-line? Oh, right, COVID vaccine requirements stole his protectors.

The preteen, Martin, is a French, Hawaiian, and Chinese-American transplant from California. He and his parents literally sought refuge at his Hawaiian maternal grandmother's Mānoa home in the Spring of 2020. They fled the astronomical COVID numbers in Los Angeles, arriving in Honolulu before the scientists made the vaccines.

Though only eleven years old, Pierre had the promise of a lifelong athlete. A broken nose from kickboxing saved his exotic interracial features from being too pretty.

Gabe Martin, Pierre's French actor father, taught kickboxing before COVID shut those close-contact courses down. Gabe's youngest pupil, a first-grader named Kenji, broke Pierre's nose out of the blue.

It had been like any other Saturday class. The students had lined up and marched forward, counting and kicking as one.

"One-two-three kick!"

Six-year-old Kenji and then eight-year-old Pierre had been facing forward, moving synchronously. They'd struck the air and kicked on the count of three.

"One-two-three kick!" They shouted and progressed.

"One-two-three kick!" They continued, but Kenji suddenly jump-kicked sideways into Pierre's nose. Blood had splattered everywhere, creating tie-dyed-like art on their white Gi.

Pierre had never known why Kenji turned. Three years later, Kenji never let the older Pierre forget the beating. '#Nosejob' is what Kenji's tagged Pierre ever since. God save us from tech-savvy fourth graders!

Wow, that was pre-COVID California. It seems like a lifetime ago. The DMW League star quarterback pulled his helmet off. He shook sweat around himself like a dog after a bath. Practice rosters weren't as full, with Omicron depleting the team's enrollment. The athlete vaccination mandate restricted dozens of boys from participating. Ultimately, it was the family's choice to vaccinate. Everyone had an opinion about vaccinations—to do it or not. It's a political quagmire Pierre didn't want to fall into. Even school turned into a battleground between the vaccinated and anti-vaxers.

Wright Middle handled COVID all right. The kids had the option of wearing masks or not on campus. Pierre just wished he could wear a paper bag over his head. Who'd have thought being attractive was a shame? The girls kept getting too close. If only they knew he didn't swing that way. Hmmm. Maybe then Pierre would get some space from their fawning. It's flattering, yet heartbreaking.

If only he could just say it: *I like boys.*

God forbid. If he came out, he could forget being in the DMW Football League. The team would fall apart. The sacred mantrust would be gone. Pierre reached the benches, swallowed a liter of water, and poured another liter over his sweaty head.

"Great practice, son!" Coach Jackson, a fit middle-aged Asian-American, called all his players "son."

Coach Jackson nudged Pierre's shoulder and smiled. "All-star arm, young man, you've got it!"

Pierre smiled back. "Thanks."

Gabe Martin approached his son amid the other parents and exchanged fist bumps with Coach Jackson. Gabe was between acting gigs. His TV series in Honolulu was on hiatus due to COVID. Pierre inherited Gabe's height and Parisian features, minus the broken nose a la Kenji. Yet, Pierre had Shelly 'Uhane Martin's Chinese features too. A Eurasian modeling agency appealed to Shelly and Gabe Martin scouting Pierre. They'd imagined him doing commercials and print work for Asian product lines overseas. Gabe had puffed up when that happened. "Chip off the old block!"

Pierre's mom shut down the modeling idea swiftly. Shelly refused to let her son grow up as a starving artist as they had.

She never ceased to remind Gabe of their early married years in poverty. They'd raised baby Pierre in run-down LA walk-ups. They used food stamps and relied on State social services. The younger Gabe's roles were barely legit. Their bread and butter came from Gabe's "French Boy with Flowers" acting extra roles. "Hey, those roles paid the bills!" Gabe always reminded Shelly. Of course, they could have accepted money from her parents, but they'd been proud nineteen year olds.

Shelly 'Uhane was studying Accounting at USC on a full academic scholarship when she fell in love with the French actor. She'd been a pregnant full-time student and Gabe took those acting roles. God bless his parents for sticking things out, albeit stubbornly and independently.

Pierre and Gabe bumped shoulders as they left the field for Gabe's car.

Pierre said, "How's Ma?"

"She says you're spending way more time at school than necessary," Gabe said, as they got into their Lexus.

Pierre laughed hysterically. "Guess that means extra hugs."

Gabe Martin's current co-starring role as a European Vice Officer paid the bills now and then some. His French accent lifted the show's ratings, not to mention his handsome face. This role made that decade of living hand-to-mouth worthwhile. He was grateful for the pandemic hiatus on many levels. Though Omicron ran rampant in Hawaii, Gabe loved this time off to watch his boy play football. When his TV show was rolling, the pandemic on-set restrictions drove some mad. Not Gabe, though. He rolled with the punches. The local cast teased him, but Gabe loved them and the crew.

"If you can't laugh at yourself, you're taking yourself too seriously!" Gabe would say. Filming beach scenes across Oahu were his favorite days at work. Gabe was filled with gratitude for this life. He didn't miss the LA traffic jams or smog. Hawaii was "Da best!", as the locals would say. Gabe agreed.

Hands on the wheel, Gabe glanced at Pierre. He had a hunch that his son was having a crisis in puberty. Gabe wished Pierre would come out of the closet. He and Shelly had always known.

When Gabe took his family on a film set, he would notice his son mooning over teenage male co-stars. Once, Gabe's teenage co-star eyed Pierre right back. Kane Roberts was very flirty, fiery, and all of fifteen.

"Hey, Pierre," Kane smiled, giving Pierre the elevator look.

"Would you come to my trailer and help me with my lines?" Kane had said, winking suggestively. Gabe gave Kane's manager-parents a talking-to after that invite. At a traffic stop, Gabe peered at his son's profile. As a protective father, he wished Pierre didn't possess his mother's lovely features.

Sexuality clues were something parents instinctively felt.

Some families oppressed, punished, or ignored those signs. Thankfully for Pierre, Gabe and his wife were nothing like that. They loved Pierre unconditionally. They supported him wholeheartedly. Gabe especially appreciated the advice of Trevor Mālama, a close family friend.

"Let him be! I never came out until we were in our late teens!" Trevor would say. "I'm his godfather. When it's time, who better to come out to than me?"

Gabe worried about Pierre's professional football dreams. Will the real Pierre ever be safe? They'd reached his in-laws' property deep in the wet, green valley of Mānoa.

Gabe released a sigh of appreciation. He was infinitely grateful to be in Hawaii. Tūtū's garden spanned a half acre of lovingly doted-on property. Tūtū, his mother-in-law, is a gregarious Hawaiian woman in her late fifties. She took over her husband's garden after he died. The land had been passed down from Grandpa's Chinese plantation working family. Tūtū is of Hawaiian heritage and fell in love with Grandpa's connection to his land.

Upon arriving, Gabe knew Pierre wanted to check on Tūtū. He told Pierre to grab his football gear and school bag later. Pierre gave him a one-armed hug and immediately ran to roll up the long garden hose for Tūtū.

She was still hardy and fit, but her scoliosis acted up sometimes. She kissed his cheek, greeting him, "Aloha, my love!" He was her only grandchild. She gracefully glided up the pathway on his arm, a hula dancer since she could walk.

Pierre breathed in his grandma's garden, filling his lungs with the jasmine and rosemary-scented air. The sun's retreating rays barely reached the treetops. The gloam of evening begged him to sit and to just be. Still grimy from practice, Pierre resisted the temptation. Tūtū went off down an eggplant path, leaving Pierre in a secluded copse in a pool of sunlight. Something in his midriff vibrated, flushing his body with an inexplicable joy. It compelled him to share his heart. He sang, but softly.

Pierre's Garden Song:

"Trees get to be with trees.
Leaves mingle in flight with their friendly peers.
Bumblebees dancing in the bushes fearlessly.
Why can't I be as free?
Free to be me
Buzz into the sky like a happy-go-lucky bee
What will happen, when I'm free to be me?
Flowers titter in their pretty garden parties.
The caterpillar curls up into its chrysalis on a tree.
When is my turn?
When's my butterfly moment?
When will I be free to be me?
Tell me garden, what will it take?
When will I make fewer mistakes?
Could it be just in my head?
All of this frustration and horrible dread?
Help me, garden.
Help me, trees.
When can I be me?"

CHAPTER 4

EARTH
Wright Middle School Gymnasium
January 12, 2022

Nicole Moku burst into the gymnasium bathroom after basketball workouts, disappointed in herself. Her jersey and shorts were damp with sweat. She headed to the wash section to freshen up before mom rolled in to take her home.

She was supposed to be a military brat. With her faceless African-American father from Texas and beautiful Native Hawaiian mother, she possessed a deep skin tone, luscious screen-worthy lips, and tightly curled hair. Yet, her bloodline is all that was left of her Navy-enlisted father.

He must have been tall. Not the reedy type, but big boned. Swole. Nicole often got a shock herself seeing how big she was in mirrors. Then her eyelids would come down, ashamed, not wanting to see reminders of the dad who wasn't there.

Nicole was the result of a one-night stand; her father never knew about his baby girl. Knowing about her existence was neither here nor there. Her maternal grandfather had known. In fact, he'd disowned his pregnant daughter, having never met baby Nicole either. Mr. Moku kicked the newly turned eighteen-year-old Kaleo out upon discovering the pregnancy.

"Nobody gave the slightest damn," Nicole muttered, slamming her bag on the sink counter. She bent to wash her face. Thinking of her mother overwhelmed her most times.

Pregnant and homeless, Kaleo was rescued by her best friend Nick Fine and his two dads. Nick and Kaleo were soul siblings. The pair became close buddies in elementary school. By the twelfth grade, they'd been bonded for more than a decade. Nick's dads—psychologist Drs. John and Court Fine—had all but adopted young Kaleo since grammar school.

Reruns of Nicole's chosen-family history were frequent, as the Fines believed in talking your heart out for mental healing. She loved them to bits.

They were the nurturing father figures Kaleo never had. A widower, Kaleo's dad struggled to raise his daughter. The Drs. were loving and understood Kaleo's hardships. They'd predicted that she'd eventually leave her father's loveless home. This was simply sooner than expected.

Proud and strong, Kaleo refused to take handouts; she wouldn't be a burden to Nick's family.

Nicole's mother became their live-in housekeeper throughout her community college, undergrad, and grad school studies. She eventually became their tax attorney. The Fine husbands proudly cheered their "kids," Kaleo and Nick, as they marched across the stage to accept their respective Juris Doctorates from William S. Richardson School of Law.

Leaving the bathroom, Nicole investigated a ping from her backpack, retrieving her first ever phone (Thanks, Uncle Nick). Of course it was her mother: *I'm here! Parked out front, Luv!*

After a few years, Kaleo left corporate law to hang a virtual shingle for patrons with tax issues worldwide. God bless the World Wide Web. Who'd have thought the pandemic would benefit online law practices? A baby and a career made the past twelve years worthwhile, according to Kaleo..

Sadly, there were only four other Black or part-Black students at Wright Middle. Nicole was an outsider in her own homeland. She didn't fit in with the local Hawaiian girls, nor with the handful of Black students. She always knew she should've been a military brat. At least they have a clique in whatever school they landed in. It hurt being caught between two worlds.

There wasn't a time when Nicole didn't grumble about her hair, cursing the curly, puffy hassle it was. She wore her kinky hair in a soft, fluffy mahogany cloud around her face. Detangling with coconut oil was her morning routine.

Fussing it, Nicole sang to herself in the gym's locker room.

Nicole's Duckling Song:

"Ugly duckling,
You float in the wrong crowds.
Your identity just might be flawed.
Make my isolation less bleak.
Can comfort come from your beak?
Do your feathers offer hugs?
With this hair, I am a bug

Let's dive deep into the water.
Just you and me, pal.
The water cleanses us
Nothing else shall.
Help me discover my truth
Is it like a romantic carnival booth?
Appreciation through and through?
Is self love true blue?
Let's dive deep into the water.
Just us, my feathered pal.
My story has a catch, Ugly Duckling.
Unlike you, I'm neither duck nor swan.
Where's my magic wand?
Did I forfeit my fairy tale?
My tears fill up many pails.
Let's dive deep into the water.
Let me be purified deep in the water."

CHAPTER 5

Storyteller in Papakōlea, Hawaiʻi
January 13, 2022

Aunt Ellie sat up from lounging on the couch, stretching her arms. She laughed at Ari's messy hair.

"These children are really cool, Aunty Ellie!" Ari laughed. "Time sure flew. Why does the story begin today?"

"Ari, I want you to imagine it all happening now, practically the present day. These kids could be you," Aunt Ellie said. "Let's take a break and grab a snack. Are your legs asleep? It's been an hour."

Ari bounced up like a sprite.

"Let me help you up, Aunty!" Ari giggled and stretched her hands out to assist her aunt.

"I still want to know more of the story. Tell me about Wright Middle." Ari said.

"I thought we were taking a break?" Aunt Ellie laughed, nudging her niece with her hip.

"Can't you multitask, Aunty? Come on."

Aunt Ellie shook her head at her tanned, half-Caucasian and Hawaiian niece. Ari's parents (her sister and brother-in-law) were very busy. She appreciated every minute with her niece. They grabbed some bananas and iced tea to sit on the back porch. They had an unobstructed view of Punchbowl and the Pacific Ocean beyond it. Homemade macaroni and cheese baked in the oven behind them. Its delicious aroma made Ari excited for dinner.

"Aunty Ellie, is their school a big one?"

"Hmmm. Wright Middle has three hundred students. It's located in Honolulu, on the lower mountains below the Papakōlea Hawaiian homestead community."

Ari was happy that her aunt was writing about their neighborhood. "Oh, Wright Middle is near the Makiki area then?"

Aunt Ellie nodded.

"I like your description, but you sound like a travel site," Ari said.

"You want to return to the story?" Aunt Ellie laughed.

"I don't mean to insult you!" Ari was hard to resist.

"Thank you. Tell me where we left off."

"Malie's lonely, Pierre's conflicted, and Nicole's mad about her kinky hair," Ari said, sighing. "She's not ugly."

"I agree."

"But that was the day before their adventure began," Ari said, leaning forward.

Aunt Ellie drank some tea and continued the story. "Their lives changed forever the very next day. Picture this—"

Chapter 6

Earth
Wright Middle School
January 13, 2022
2:45 p.m.

The school bell rings at the end of lunch, pushing students to their last period. A trio of children bump into each other outside of their gym class. Strangely, they'd never spoken to each other. It's this timely meeting that transports them out of time.

Nicole, Malie, and Pierre came together onto that hallowed path from different directions. The trio was just out of reach of Ms. Marco's class. Her call of welcome was a warm hug.

"Glad you're here! Dress out and roll call in five!" Ms. Marco pumped everyone up. Except this time, voices from afar pulled at them, an enchanting song just for their ears only. They were drawn to a symphony of faraway instruments. Another world called the children with rhythmic pounding and reverberating harmonies. Tribal, almost. The three converged around various bends to meet dumbstruck, staring at one another.

"Am I being Punk'd?" Nicole broke the silence.

She looked behind Malie, sure she'd find hidden cameras. Malie hugged her paperback book to her slim chest, intimidated by the outspoken girl.

"Sshhhhh, there's chanting!" Pierre cocked his head at the girls. "You're getting it too? Not just me?"

Malie nodded her head vigorously. Accustomed to speaking only to her imaginary book people, Malie blushed as the young man smiled at her in gratitude.

He winked at her. "Goodness, you saved my sanity. Thought I was falling off my rocker!" he said. He was charming. "Pierre." He pointed to his chest.

"Malie." She pointed at herself smiling at the silliness of introducing herself to her gym classmate.

"Ding-dongs, we're in the same class," Nicole said as Pierre waved at her.

He laughed at Nicole's manner.

Malie ignored the two of them and approached the lichened back wall of the gymnasium.

The chanting was coming from the moss.

"Hey, Malie. What are you doing? Careful." Nicole sensed an off putting heaviness in the air. "Ms. Marco's taking attendance by now, girl. Let's head to class," Nicole urged her petite and usually shy classmate. She was about to tap Malie's backpack. Pierre must've felt the same Mother Hen-like instinct as he reached for Malie too. The symphonies blasted louder, and the air tingled.

Swooosh!

Next thing they knew, there was a twenty-foot-tall by twenty-foot-wide glittery, water-like Shimmery Wall where the gym wall had been. Malie stuck her hand into what looked like "water." Her palm came out dry. Thankfully, she was still in one piece. The wet-less waterfall wall reminded Malie of a portal.

"We could time travel! Wow!" she bounced. They looked at each other silently asking: *"Should we?"* They turned towards Ms. Marco's voice, cringing at the thought of gym class. The Shimmery Wall invited them. With the recklessness of youth, they nodded in mutual agreement to go in. They reached for each other's hands and approached the portal. They leaped together on Nicole's count.

"One, two, three!"

Their bodies broke down into molecules that separated and reconfigured in another dimension. Via this Molecular Travel (MT), the kids' particles remained conscious, their atoms singing.

The Trio's Molecule Song:

"Parts afloat and buzzing around.
Moving faster, round and about.
Strangers meeting on hallowed grounds.
What is happening to us?
It's like being hit by a bus.
Bursting our forms into smithereens.
Are we going down a fun-slide of dreams?
Where are our bodies? I don't weigh a pound.
This is freaky and no joke.
What if we turn into artichokes?

Please, tell us we're alive.
Let's survive! Let's survive! Let's survive!"

CHAPTER 7

Manaful World
January 13, 2022
2:45 p.m.

Pierre was the first of the trio to enter the world of Manaful that day. Their weird little song rang in his head.

"What happened? How's my body?" He checked his hair to ensure his stylishly gelled black 'do was still in place. He also checked his important body parts.

Nicole popped in after him, catching him in the act. "Are those parts your priority?" she teased.

"Yes!" Pierre laughed at himself.

Malie appeared seconds after them. "I thought we jumped together." She was looking for her book and backpack. She'd had it on. Her belongings were gone.

Nicole felt in her bra for her cell phone. "Hey, where's our stuff?" Nicole asked anyone in this magical world.

Elder Puna and Ikaika popped in via Molecular Travel (MT) in front of them out of nowhere. They stood up straight in their 'Ohana's attire. Ikaika wore just his sarong and Elder Puna wore his bioluminescent robe. The elder's presence was filled with the Mana Mist, the powerful ether element manifested around him as opalescent droplets.

Malie was in awe of the dwarves. This was overwhelming, her heart beat sped up. She wasn't sure where to start. Was she shocked by their teleporting? Was she shocked that little brown dwarves joined them? Was it safe here? Can she breathe here? Will her skin melt off? Hey, why are the older dwarf's clothes moving? Was she hyperventilating? She tried to breathe. Pierre turned to her worriedly. Nicole was too mad to pay attention.

Elder Puna lifted his hand toward Malie. She suddenly felt calmer. As she took a big breath, flowery scents filled her lungs. A breeze picked up around her, cooling her overheated skin. She looked at the dwarves. Were they doing something to her? She shook her head; it didn't matter. Her anxiety was whisked away.

Nicole, ever the blunt one, said, "What are you? Why are you so short?" Pierre laughed in discomfort and surprise at Nicole's frank greeting. Malie waved.

Elder Puna telepathically group projected, *"You are in Manaful. I am Elder Puna, an elder leader. This is my grandson, Ikaika."*

"What the heck?" Nicole said. "Did you get that in your head?"

Malie nodded.

Pierre said, "Yes, he said he's Elder Puna, and the younger one's Ikaika, his grandson."

"I got that too," Nicole nodded.

"How did he send his thought-speech into all our heads at the same time?" Malie asked.

"It's TGP," Ikaika projected.

"How do you know how to speak English?" Pierre asked.

"We speak whatever language is in your head." Ikaika projected.

"Woah, back up a little," Nicole said.

Ikaika and Elder Puna stayed put. The trio of human children backed up on their own. They walked through the grass out of earshot.

"First things first, where are we and how did we get here?" Nicole asked.

Elder Puna projected from a distance, *"This is Manaful. You wanted to be here, and our world wanted you."*

Malie and Pierre nodded in sync.

"Are you hypnotizing them?" Nicole demanded, hands on her hips.

"No. We are just harmonizing them."

She herded the other two away from the dwarves.

"What would you like to happen here?" Elder Puna's presence loomed large in the trio's head whenever he "spoke", like a mental pulse.

Malie and Pierre said, "Magic!"

Nicole stared at her peers and snapped her fingers in front of their faces. "Wake up, people! This is fishy!"

The middle-aged brown dwarf transported the short distance to them with the younger. The corner of their eyes crinkled at Malie and Pierre.

"Where is Manaful?" Nicole asked, frustratedly waving her hands in front of Malie and Pierre.

Ikaika informed the trio, *"We are a parallel dimension accessible from Earth."*

Nicole squeaked, "What?"

Malie and Pierre snapped out of their trance and looked at the younger dwarf.

"Did we molecularly transport here through the Shimmery Wall by your magic?" Malie asked.

Ikaika nodded, pointed to Elder Puna, and TGP, *"My grandfather opened the portal for you. We chanted a welcome song."*

"It was transfixing," Pierre said.

Elder Puna smiled, and Ikaika lifted a high-five to Pierre, who immediately high-fived him back.

Pierre mimed the high-five motion. "How'd you know to do that?"

Ikaika projected, *"I've studied Earth beings all my life through the portal."*

Nicole said, "That's creepy! Interdimensional stalking!"

Malie elbowed Nicole. "Hey, I'm sure he didn't mean it in a pervy way, right?"

"You seek guidance." Elder Puna stated.

Nicole laughed, "Sure, from a counselor, not some alien dwarf people on another planet!"

Pierre and Malie looked at Nicole at the same time. They grabbed her hand and dragged her away from the dwarves for a huddle.

"What are we doing?" Nicole said.

"Pep-talk. Like a football team," Pierre whispered, putting his arm around their shoulders.

"I think they're onto us," Malie whispered back and returned the gesture, hugging their waists.

"We're not a football team!" Nicole shook her head, but kept her voice low and put her arms around them too.

"We're more like a trio or a club," Pierre said.

"Yes! A secret club like in my favorite detective books!" Malie said.

"Why do we need a secret club?" Nicole asked.

"We can't tell anyone back home that we were here meeting these 'people' or whatever they are," Pierre answered.

"No way," Malie agreed. "Back home, they'll think we've lost our marbles!"

"So, what are we going to do here?" Nicole asked.

"I vote to learn and absorb as much as we can. Stay safe and support each other," Pierre said.

"I second his vote!" Malie said.

"What is this? We're not doing parliamentary procedure in a football huddle on some alien planet!" Nicole's voice rose.

"Ssshh!" Malie and Pierre said.

"Just go with the flow, Nicole." Pierre said.

"We're all good, Nicole," Malie said.

"Okay, let's face them together, Secret Clubbers!" Nicole humored them with a fake cheerleader voice, "Go, team! Go!" She stood up straight with one fist on her hip and one in the air.

Her sarcasm was lost on sweet Malie. "Clubbers?"

"Gee, we're too young to be night-clubbers!" Pierre said.

"Give me a break, you two." Nicole rolled her eyes, breaking her pep-squad stance. They turned around and saw Elder Puna and Ikaika watching them. Nicole had a hunch they'd picked up every word with their telepathic powers. Not to mention, they were loud.

The newly formed Secret Club re-approached the Manaful pair, who stood beneath a humongous koa tree. The aura of the atmosphere reminded Pierre of Tutu's garden. Pierre felt a wave of peace come over him. He closed his eyes and took a deep breath. Nicole was the first to find her voice after their huddle.

"This isn't right. My Uncle Nick's a prosecutor. This is kidnapping! Let us out now, or else," Nicole said. Those were brave words, yet she couldn't control her anxiety as she fisted her hands.

Elder Puna, the Manaful elder, stepped closer with open arms. A wise, deeply sonorous voice TGP into the Secret Club's heads: *"You are free to come and go at will."*

The elder lifted his chin towards the tree behind them, and seconds later, it became the Shimmery Wall again. The trees on the human side were at a standstill. A mynah bird's wings were caught in mid-flight. A dried pinkish-brown plumeria freeze framed a foot off the ground. Earth time had stopped.

"Manaful is a parallel world. We are not aliens," He TGP to the children, watching them process his thoughts.

"I got this, Gramps. They're my age. Let me show them around!" Ikaika puffed up his chest. He stepped closer to the preteen humans. His wavy light-brown hair fell in messy locks around his ears, bangs grazing his friendly eyes. He waved at them again.

"Once again, call me Ikaika. You are Pierre," Ikaika pointed at Pierre and fist-bumped him. Pierre bumped in awe.

"You read my mind?" he said, staring at the dwarf, whose lips never moved except to smile.

Ikaika nodded and made his way to Malie as she hid behind Pierre. *"Hey, Malie. Sorry about your books, bag, and cell phone,"* Ikaika TGP.

She fist-bumped him back. For once in her life, Malie felt large. She was giddy. Maybe it was from inhaling all the sparkly mist in the air.

Nicole's lanky frame towered over Ikaika. He raised a double fist bump to her like Rocky Balboa standing triumphantly at the top of his steps. "*Yo, Nicole, double fist-bump for you,*" he projected in a low voice mimicking the fictional boxer. Nicole laughed, raising both of her arms for him. His energy and telepathic powers befuddled her.

It was strange enough to be frightening, for a worrier like Nicole.

Chapter 8

Storyteller in Papakōlea, Hawaiʻi
January 13, 2022

Sitting on the back porch with Aunt Ellie, Ari drank her tea and put her chin on her fists.

"Why did you stop, Aunty? I want to know what they're doing in Manaful. Nicole's scared? Nervous?" Ari said. "Don't they want to know what the Manafuls are?"

Aunt Ellie stood and patted Ari's shoulder, "They are trying to get over their fear of molecular travel."

Ari sighed. "MT would be really cool. I'd love to go through that molecular change, wouldn't you?"

"I think you watch too many Sci Fi movies."

Ari groaned. "Do I have to do my chores? Is that why you stopped?"

Aunt Ellie nudged her, "Yes, the dryer just sang its finishing song."

Ari stomped her feet toward their washer and dryer combo. "Why does the dryer jingle? It's not like I enjoy washing more with a pretty tune than a buzz."

Aunt Ellie laughed. "Get to it!"

Ari was a good negotiator. "Okay, but after I fold and put away the clothes, you'll continue the story?"

"Deal."

Twenty minutes later, the pair met again in the living room on rainbow gymnastic mats. They stretched, while Aunt Ellie shared more. "You're enjoying the story, aren't you?" They both felt the flex in their legs.

"Yes, I like their name. What happens next for the Secret Club?"

Aunt Ellie was quiet. Ari tapped her arm. She smiled then began.

Chapter 9

Manaful World
January 13, 2022

"*Ikaika will be your guide.*" Elder Puna telepathically projected into The Secret Club's minds. "*You will be safe. You have my word.*"

The elder dwarf glowed with energy and power. He didn't intimidate the children, but was awe-inspiring. The swarthy sage had a welcoming presence. He held his hands over his heart.

Pierre and Malie wore twin expressions of reverence. Pierre instantly thought of Tūtū. She made that "I'm so touched" facial expression too, holding her hands to her chest like Elder Puna was doing. It happened especially when Pierre completed gardening chores without being asked.

Malie's heart tugged as she looked at Elder Puna. She wished she'd met her mom's parents before they'd died. She never knew her dad's parents. They'd disowned their son after he'd married her mom. Pili's financial situation was "beneath them." Having a sweet grandpa would be amazing.

Nicole stared at the elder dwarf. Her Club mates may be transfixed by these magical beings. She had yet to get the allure. Her Granddads, Drs. Fine, instilled the stranger-danger concept since she could walk. She grabbed Malie's and Pierre's shirt sleeves.

"Can Elder Puna manipulate my mind? He reads it and projects his thoughts to us. Manipulating minds isn't far off." Her peers frowned in unison. They thought alike, both agreeing she was paranoid.

"No!" Malie and Pierre said. They smiled and said, "Jinx," then fist-bumped.

"Okay, okay. One of us has got to be the devil's advocate here!" Nicole said.

"Free will is of utmost importance to Manafuls, just like with humans." Ikaika projected.

Malie agreed with the Manaful. "Yes, one hundred percent agree about free will. How could we live without it?" She was raised by a single mother. Female empowerment and free will were part of her makeup. "By the way, can you show me how to access telepathic powers?" Malie asked.

Pierre studied the Shimmery Wall. Using the Wall must be like streaming online with limitless service providers. "I think they observe us twenty-four seven, three-six-five," Pierre said.

"Pierre's right," Ikaika projected, smiling.

"Creepy. Did you watch me shower?" Nicole said.

Pierre and Malie gave her a twin look of dismay. "Melodramatic much?" Pierre said.

Malie looked ashamed of Nicole and tried to apologize for her. "Ikaika, we don't think your people are peeping toms."

Ikaika's patient facial expression reminded Malie of her mother's kind features. Ikaika's face appeared to be that of a teenager, but the light in his eyes was mature. Malie had a hunch that human years didn't equate to Manaful ones.

"That's neat how you do that with our brains, Ikaika." Malie said.

"I'm guessing you're not eleven years old like us," Pierre said.

"I'm seven hundred and seventy Manaful years and eleven human years old."

"Oh, just like the dog-to-human ratio times ten," Nicole said.

Pierre and Malie twinned gasps of shock. "Nicole, did you lose your manners coming through the Shimmery Wall?" Pierre said. "You're slipping up."

Malie hiccupped, elbowing Pierre, "Hey, maybe we should go with the Nicole flow. She's right about the Club needing a devil's advocate."

Pierre frowned.

Nicole offered a fist bump to the pair.

The Club shared a look of agreement and made another team huddle.

"Strategy meet! Should we stay or go?" Nicole said, squeezing Pierre's and Malie's shoulders.

Malie stood up for herself, "I vote for staying!"

Pierre patted her shoulder and nodded. He lightly head-butted Nicole, who stood closer to him in height than Malie. "Nicole, we've got to try."

Nicole closed her eyes and groaned. "Will you two always overrule me?" She took a deep breath. She squeezed their shoulders again. "Alright. Let's do this!"

Malie laughed at Nicole's battle-ready attitude. She and Pierre shared a twin look of gratitude. Pierre wanted to do a team shout. He held his hand out flat, facing down, motioning the girls to put their hands on top of his. They stood in a circle. He shouted, "Yeah! Say, 'Secret Club' on three: one, two, three!"

They shouted in unison, "Secret Club!"

CHAPTER 10

Manaful World
January 13, 2022

Elder Puna looked upon the Secret Club, amused by the quick camaraderie. The trio had only known each other in passing, yet stepping into Manaful unified them. He contemplated his purpose for bringing them there. Ikaika smiled and hopped around on Koa's roots, awaiting his Manaful tour-guide role.

Nicole was the first of the Club to re-approach the dwarf family again. With her ever-present bluntness, she said, "If you aren't aliens, then what are you?"

Ikaika looked to Elder Puna, who nodded.

"This is our parallel dimension, Manaful World. Your Earth time stops when you are here. We are Manafuls. We've been here for thousands of human years." Ikaika said.

The Secret Club nodded their appreciation at the new learning. They were in a daze as they strolled down the grassy hillsides. The trio kept bumping shoulders.

Malie enjoyed her surroundings. She took in the damp forest atmosphere, birds chirping all around them.

She smiled, realizing how similar Manaful was to the backwoods of her home, Tantalus Drive in Honolulu. The bushes and trees were thickly laden with fragrant vines. It appeared to be maile vines. The maile lei was thick, hunter green, and a lovely adornment worn like long, decorative stoles. People wore them around their necks for Hawaiian celebrations back home, such as a wedding or a graduation ceremony. On the other hand, Tantalus Drive didn't have Manafuls with telepathic powers.

"Elder Puna and the other elders here do not invite humans that often." Ikaika projected.

Nicole noticed Ikaika's grandpa mostly stood still, observing them. He'd MT closer if they went too far. "Why doesn't Elder Puna talk more?" Nicole pointed at the solemn yet resplendent dwarf elder. She'd never get over his robe. It reminded Nicole of her favorite lipstick counter displays. Every imaginable shade of rouge danced within the cloth.

"You will have a safe and fascinating visit. You are free to come and go as you wish," Elder Puna projected, levitating cross-legged.

Malie and Pierre shared twin looks of awe at his floating. Nicole was over it, focusing on their freedom.

"We can leave? Just like that?" Nicole snapped her fingers. "Through the Shimmery Wall in the blink of an eye?"

"You are not prisoners. You are rare guests, Nicole." Ikaika projected.

Pierre was dazed, needing something to lean on. He found a waist-high limestone rock boulder. About six feet in diameter and four feet tall, the stone glistened despite its coral texture. It must be pokey. The path behind the boulder led to what sounded like a flowing river. Dampness hung in the air. The water trickled through a beaver's bridge with a plucking sound like the Japanese koto.

"Can we transport to different places in your world?" Pierre asked.

"Oh, yes. Not on your own. You don't have our Mana or magical powers. With Mana, you could molecularly transport wherever you wish," Ikaika projected.

"Hey, could you get out of my head?" Nicole grumbled. "Don't you have vocal chords?"

"We do. I apologize," Ikaika laughed and answered aloud. He had a fun-loving, warm tone.

"That's better. Thanks." Nicole said, shaking her head back and forth as if to make sure he's out of there.

"You normally use telepathy, don't you?" Malie observed, leaning on Pierre's legs as he sat on the huge limestone boulder. The glistening green stone texture looks bumpy. She initially thought it might be a misplaced reef. However, as she jumped on it, the small patterns were smooth rather than rough, like porcelain. She elbowed Pierre, pointed down, and nodded. He winked, acknowledging her.

"Nice texture, yeah?" Pierre said. Ikaika's melodic tenor captured their attention again. Talking aloud was preferable for the preteens. Telepathy still blew their minds, especially Nicole. He answered Malie's question about his natural telepathic inclination.

"You're right. Almost everyone is telepathic here," Ikaika said. He nodded and appreciated Malie's observation.

Pierre twitched his lips like a rabbit. He then ran his fingers through his hair, further messing it up. He'd gelled his straight dark hair this morning. Stylish hair was important.

Malie said, "You speak English fluently. Can you understand all human languages? Do you just pluck them from their heads and understand it?"

Only half interested in the linguistic conversation, Pierre leaned back on his limestone boulder; it was comfortable and wide. He smiled up at Malie, proud of his bright buddy.

"Yes, we have linguistic programming in our brains created by Source," Ikaika said.

"That's very mystical. I want Mana. That's what your magic's called, right?" She said.

Ikaika nodded, "Mana is the magic and life power from our Source Creator."

Nicole laughed at Malie's questions. "Get a clue, sister! This whole place is Mana-land! How do you think we got here?" Nicole said.

"Hey, don't be jelly of the poor guy's inherent qualities!" Pierre said.

"You are in good hands, children. Ikaika will guide you. Align with Source," Elder Puna said sagely. He then bowed and disappeared. His voice had been soothing and low, fading away in a swirl of momentary mist.

"Uh, goodbye for now?" Malie said to the empty air. "Where did he go?"

"Hasta la vista?" Pierre said to the empty space too. They don't know where Elder Puna went.

The Secret Club stared at the empty air before them. Nicole converged with the others. They sat squished together on Pierre's boulder, unaware that they were now holding each other's hands.

"Ummm," Malie said.

"Bababawa," said Pierre.

Then, the no-longer tongue-tied Nicole said, "What the heck just happened?"

Nicole continued, demanding, "Tell me, does Elder Puna always disappear like that? Poof? Now he's here. Blink-blink. Now he's not?" Nicole looked down at Pierre and Malie holding hands. Nicole raised her brow as if to say, "Why are you two holding hands?"

Pierre released Malie's fingers, shaking his head. He was surprised to be holding onto her.

Ikaika smiled.

Malie grinned at Pierre and said, "No big deal."

Ikaika had the patience of a wise old man. He nodded at Nicole, answering with the kind tone of a preschool teacher. "Elder Puna's a busy Manaful leader. He trusts me to show you what's what."

Malie raised her hand like she was in class.

Ikaika smiled up at her and pointed at her like a teacher would. "Yes, you had a question, Malie?"

Nicole swatted Malie's leg. "Give me a break, girl. We aren't in school."

Malie ignored Nicole and said, "Please explain Mana more. What is it?"

"Good question, Malie." Pierre winked at her.

Ikaika fell silent and led them deeper into the woods. They stared at the tree canopy ten stories above their heads. The dwarf appeared to be meditating. Pierre and Malie were confused. Nicole crossed her arms over her chest and stopped walking. She tapped her right foot on the rainbow of pebbles on the forest floor.

Nicole motioned for her phone. "Ikaika, could we have our devices?"

Ikaika shook his head. "We're off the grid here. Try to center your being and stop relying on your device."

Nicole's eyes widened. "That's hardcore. I cannot imagine life without my cell. It's my lifeline," the tall girl said.

Pierre laughed. "Sad life, Nicole. Dreary."

Malie giggled and nudged Nicole. "That's how I felt about my paperbacks. Being here is freeing."

Pierre explored the lovely rolling fields beyond the koa treeline. Ikaika walked backward beside Pierre, signaling the girls to catch up. The kaleidoscope of plant life and flowers expanded like a never-ending walkway, ferns unfurling. The farther they walked, the more land opened before them.

Manafuls flitted in the forest, never approaching. They seemed curious, not afraid. Perhaps other humans had visited before. Some Manafuls waved, then disappeared without disturbing a branch or a bush. Some hovered from place to place instead of walking. Some disappeared into thin air, like Elder Puna had. Most of them wore red attire, but plenty of other colors were in the mix. None of them were elders, since their clothing lacked an elder's bioluminescent robe.

Malie wished to see a pink elder's cloth. That would be beautiful.

Ikaika nudged Malie, agreeing, "Yes, Elder Ākala's robe is breathtaking with the fuchsias, flamingos, and violet shades in motion."

Malie tripped over her own feet. Right, Ikaika reads minds. She keeps forgetting. She checked on Nicole, who was watching a Jackson chameleon chasing moths. Pierre was a little ahead examining minuscule burrowing owls on the forest floor. Malie breathed easier and shushed Ikaika.

"Don't tell those two you can read our minds. Pierre would be cool, but Nicole would flip."

Ikaika nodded but made no promises.

Despite Ikaika's mind-reading revelation, she was enjoying their interlude in this magical world. Malie hummed to herself. The serenity here inspired her to sing.

Malie's Koa Forest Song:

"Safe havens are in my mind.
I hate it on Earth when they stare from behind.
All those people's eyes on me.
Sometimes I wish I didn't act so meekly.
Stop being like an old fut.
Stand up tall no matter what.
That's what my mom tells me to do.
I try, but end up stepping in poo.
Our Secret Club will help me.
Together, we've survived these pandemic days

Our Secret Club will help me.
School life is like being in a haze.
Our Secret Club will help me.
Mahalo to my pals and the Manafuls too
Together, we'll figure out what to do.
Pierre and Nicole will know what to do.
So a safe haven's really found in people?
Like being blessed with water under a steeple?
Is it the love found in friendly faces?
It's moving past one's weaker traces.
Getting over the lockdown's madness.
Our Secret Club helps us all."

Ikaika smiled at Malie with pride for her lyrics. He projected, "*You got it!*" to her mind alone. They fist-bumped and laughed. She didn't mind his mental conversation.

Ikaika moved a few yards ahead to Pierre. The football player was admiring some wild trout lilies that were bobbing in a cloud of rainbow mist. The sepia petals brought on nostalgia. Flowers, thanks to Grandpa and Tūtū, were one of Pierre's first loves. His teammates would fall over themselves laughing, if they knew. When he was younger, his now-deceased Grandpa, regularly sent special flower arrangements to Pierre in LA. Fresh from their Mānoa garden, the flowers were artfully arranged by Grandpa himself. Tears prickled Pierre's eyes as he remembered those precious deliveries. He'd made a herbarium of Grandpa's flowers pressed in parchment, a loving memorial and keepsake. Ikaika placed his hands over Pierre's, sympathizing with Pierre's loss. Strength flowed between them

The girls were calling up to a flock of rainbow parrots that came down to entertain them. The birds pecked at each other's bright wings, squawking as if in a busy meeting.

Nicole admitted to herself that this was a neat place.

Ikaika and Pierre had moved on together farther down the path between hedges of burgundy bougainvillea. Pierre stuck his fingers on the sparkling petals and delicate white pistils. The thorns poked him a little, but still captivated him. He was mesmerized by the mist inundating beneath the sepals.

"The girls are back there," Pierre whispered to Ikaika. "Look at all those Manafuls peeking around the corners. How different is this world? Do you accept everyone? Wait...do you know everything about us?"

Ikaika nodded.

"Are there gay Manafuls?" Pierre continued, flushing.

Ikaika patted Pierre on his arm, calming the nervous young man. He knew sharing one's deep fears is easier with strangers, even otherworld ones. There's less fear of exposure and no danger of losing a relationship.

"We love all beings." Ikaika said. Ikaika had observed Pierre's inner struggles with his orientation via the Shimmery Wall. He had a hunch it was one of the reasons Elder Puna invited Pierre there—to heal.

Pierre stared out at the flowers waving in the breeze. There were lemongrass sprinkled across the meadow pathway. It was leading them deeper into the forest. Ikaika's easy acceptance of diversity surprised him. He needed to sit. Suddenly, the same limestone boulder appeared on his left.

"Hey, Ikaika, where did that limestone boulder come from? That wasn't there a second ago. Is that my same boulder from back there?"

Distracted from the topic at hand, he circled the limestone. He recognized a foothold on the back of the boulder. Even the corallike patterns that Malie had rubbed were there. Ikaika looked smug. He'd done something.

"Did you use Mana to bring my boulder here?" Pierre queried. Wrapping his head around how magic worked was not easy. Not to mention he was getting self-aware of an internal conflict through what he could only call his *core*.

Ikaika nodded again, grinning.

Their minds melded for a second like two caressing feathers dancing in a zephyr.

That's right. Core.

Pierre took a deep breath, and, with closed eyes, found a semblance of peace. He was okay with all this transparency. They were a whole bunch of peas in one pod. It was comforting having someone preempt his needs—taking care of him without ever having to say a word or go to the stores for grocery. Pierre laughed, imagining Nicole's reaction. She'd go a little crazy.

He hopped on his boulder and leaned back back on his palms. The squirrels squabbled as their little legs and claws disturbed carpets of dry leaves. The fresh water stream flowed nearby as fish leaped, splashed. This world helped him forget about trying to live up to others expectations.

Now, if he could get an orange, life would be perfect. Seconds after thinking of it, three delicious oranges fell into his lap.

Pierre hugged the oranges to his chest to prevent them from rolling off. He'd caught them with his quarterback reflexes.

"What the?" Pierre held the orange out to the dwarf before him. "Did you? Again? Like my boulder?"

Ikaika nodded and wondered if Pierre realized he kept referring to the limestone boulder as "mine." Nature did that to some humans— helped them anchor themselves. He offered Pierre tangerines too.

Pierre laughed, "Gosh, no! That's enough. You've outdone yourself."

Ikaika bowed and brushed away the compliment. "Those were parlor tricks."

"Remember Malie asked about Mana?" Ikaika said. "The elders of every family have unbelievable Mana. Life changing powers."

Pierre tucked two oranges into his pockets and hugged the remaining one. Malie's lilting voice neared behind a growth of bushes. He scooted over on his boulder, making room for them. Pierre anticipated their expressions when they saw his orange. Heehee. This is going to be good. He thought. Nicole is going to flip out when she realizes Ikaika and Elder Puna read all of our thoughts! She's got a temper. Pierre noticed Ikaika nodding.

Ikaika winked, sharing a smile with the blushing Pierre.

"Hey, it's another boulder," Malie said as they made the turn onto the guys' path. "This big limestone sure seems out of place here by the bougainvillea. Hmmm." She poked her chin with her pointer finger.

Accepting Pierre's hand to sit beside him, she thanked him for sharing his boulder. Malie patted a spot beside her for Nicole to hop on. Nicole shook her head, patting her hair down. Its mahogany puffiness had a life of its own. The breezy, fresh air lifted the kinks, giving her an ethereal halo of hair.

Ikaika revealed, *"I molecularly transported Pierre's boulder from the other side of the koa forest. Manafuls read minds all the time, always. I've been reading yours since you got here."* He figured he'd rip off the bandaid. They all stared at Nicole, knowing this would shock her.

Nicole snapped, "Hey! I asked you to get out of my head! Vocalize, dwarf! What do you mean? All this time, you heard our thoughts? Even when we were farther away in our huddles?" Nicole raised her fists as if she were in a boxing ring.

"Here we go!" Pierre said, sharing a look with Malie. The petite girl nodded at Pierre, pointing to her head and everyone else's. Pierre's jaw dropped in surprise. She already knew about Ikaika's mind-reading?

"Yes, Malie figured out that I read your minds. Minutes before you did," Ikaika projected.

Nicole whipped quickly to her two pals. They were in on this too?

Pierre and Malie wiggled and said, "Oops!"

Nicole noticed the dwarf's peaceful expression. Then she saw Malie and Pierre's twin expressions of dread. They expected her to blow her top. She took a deep breath, opened her eyes wide, and stretched her arms to the sky. She found peace in singing, so that's what she did.

Nicole's Song for Peace

"Peace be to the tall girl in the trees.

Lift me up, forest; give me harmony.
Dispel the angst that follows me
What is happening to me?
Why am I always off-key?
Why get so bent out of shape?
It's like eating sour grapes.
What makes my chest hurt all the time?
With anxiety, there's no rhythm or rhyme.
Peace be with the tall girl in the trees
Explain this stress that's always overflowing.
The Post-COVID effect brings such hurting
Looking up at the bright blue
Helps me make sense of all the whys
Granddads would hold my hand
Trying to understand
I must be a calm person inside
Processing and setting stress aside
Peace be with the tall girl in the trees.
Peace be with me."

Malie and Pierre approached Nicole as her song died down. They held their arms outstretched for a group hug. She frowned, whimpered, then enveloped them both. Ikaika smiled at the preteens comforting each other.

A little while later, the kids made their way through a sunny meadow where flowers bobbed and pranced. After her song, Nicole didn't have any commentary. She was too leery of wild animals. Would they creep up from behind them? They were slinking through the bushes and sniffing under the logs. How many animals were out there?

"Are there wolves, snakes, pigs, or bears ready to eat us alive? How safe is this adventure?" Nicole said.

Ikaika shook his head. "They are out there watching us, but I told them you are under Elder Puna's protection. He has Mana over them. This is his Territory."

On cue, a herd of deer sprung past, stopping to share respectful bows with Ikaika, which the Manaful returned. The Secret Club stopped to stare at Ikaika. Their eyes were popping out like cartoon characters.

"Your telepathy extends into animal minds too? No way!" Malie said.

"Waaaaay," Pierre replied for Ikaika, recalling his oranges. Mana was cool to have.

Nicole just noticed the fruits bulging out of his back pockets. She pointed at Ikaika, "Where'd he get those oranges?"

Malie patted Nicole's shoulder. "You said it, Nicole. This is Mana-land. Remember Pierre's limestone boulder that Ikaika moved?"

Ikaika nodded approvingly at Malie. She's on target. They continued walking. Nicole was still making sense of everything.

She frowned. "Okay, Ikaika. Let me get this straight. You move people and things, even help people jump interdimensionally via molecular travel. Plus, you read minds and telepathically project your thoughts? Now, you talk to animals?" She was getting red. Was she going to lose it?

Pierre stopped to look at Nicole. Malie caught up from behind. They sandwiched Nicole between them. Nicole looked left and right, taking in their concern.

"You two should have a stand-up comedy show. This twin thing is hilarious!" She *was* losing it.

Malie and Pierre shook their heads at the same time, both frowning at their friend.

Nicole sighed. "Spit it out, you two."

Malie and Pierre shared another worried look. Malie shook her head at him. Pierre nodded in silent assent. He'd do it.

"Hey, Nicole, your song mentioned anxiety." He leaned in to check her pupils. "We're here to help you. When that pain fills your chest, grab our hands. Don't say anything. We got you." He said.

Malie nodded and grabbed Nicole's hand, squeezing the taller girl's long fingers in her own smaller grasp. Nicole smiled at her petite pal, squeezing back. Pierre opened his hand for her; she grabbed it and squeezed Pierre's hand. He offered his free hand to Malie. She accepted. They stood in a circle of understanding and unity.

Ikaika absorbed their happiness.

Pierre let go first, nodded, and walked towards the river. He admired the mini yellow butterflies. Ikaika beckoned the girls to go ahead of him.

He said, "Manafuls are similar to humans." He made a prayer pose. The girls respectfully remained quiet. After a few minutes, Ikaika's voice came back, "We are our own predators."

Malie groaned, "I didn't want to know that. It was nice thinking we were in our own safe haven."

Ikaika comforted her and said, "All places, here and in your world, are safe havens. It depends on your state of mind."

Nicole rolled her eyes. "You sound as philosophical as my granddads. They're psychologists. 'Everything is in your mind,' they'd say." She mimicked their voices for the last part.

Ikaika motioned them closer and called Pierre back to them. "Let us hover together!"

The Manaful had them line up side by side. He stood directly in front of them like a drill sergeant. He turned around with a quick pivot, snapping his fingers. Suddenly, they floated together over the duff.

"We're levitating." Nicole screamed.

"Hovering, Nicole, like he said," Pierre said, as if he did it every day. His posture had adjusted for liftoff.

"This is better than any book I've ever read!" Malie clapped her hands. They ascended together as though they stood on a rising invisible floatie.

"We're leaving the river? I loved it." Malie said.

"Don't worry, there are rivers everywhere," Ikaika said as they sped forward, rising all the time.

"The rabbits were really cute in their hovel, all fluffy and cozy," Malie remembered.

"Of course you would notice the wildlife while I'm getting a grip on my fears!" Nicole said.

"They were playing in a log," Malie sighed. "A mossy log."

"Malie observes and studies everything," Pierre said.

"As if we actually know each other," Nicole said.

He shook his head. "Every gym class, I watch people," Pierre said. "She's an observer too."

Malie made a heart with her hands for him. "Thank you, Pierre."

Nicole tutted.

Ikaika wanted to dig. "Why didn't you talk to each other in school?"

"Don't you know that already? You've been watching us all your life!" Nicole said.

Ikaika wondered how to best explain. Nicole stressed herself out. "I don't watch you specifically. More so humans in general."

That actually piqued her. "Are you a human sociologist?" Nicole asked.

"No, no, nothing so professional as that! I only watch out of concern. Elder Puna and I are peaceful observers," Ikaika said.

Malie clapped her hands, cheering, "Yes! Yes! I knew it! They want to help us," she shouted. "Maybe they invited middle graders because there's more hope for young people?"

Ikaika was impressed. "You are very intuitive and astute, Malie." He turned his back to them, "We're here!" Ikaika waved them to follow, as if they were disembarking a ferry. He gently deposited them on a hilltop. Their feet made a squishy sound landing on the damp grass.

They'd hovered quickly from the koa forest's floor to that hilltop, which rose at least 300 feet. That didn't help ease Nicole's fear of magic. She actually knelt down on the ground, afterward.

"Nicole, what are you doing? Get up!" Pierre said, embarrassed.

She stood up straight, wiping dirt off her palms, "I'm happy to be standing on solid ground."

Malie giggled. Nicole was entertaining.

CHAPTER 11

Manaful World
January 13, 2022

They were on a plateau with an ocean visible in the distance. There were thousands of trees around them. Pierre filled his lungs with the cool mountainous air. "Hey, there's the river!" He noticed how it drained into estuaries, which fed the ocean. "Wow, even swampy mangroves look fantastic from up here. The leaves are like green cell phones waving at us in a concert as if we were the performers."

Nicole laughed at his imagination. "When's the last time you've been to a concert?" she asked.

"A while. COVID canceled so many events. Things are coming back," Pierre acknowledged.

"I like your imaginary concert crowd," Malie said, pushing her glasses up her button nose.

"Both of you are strange," Nicole said. "It's just trees, albeit fragrant ones. The cedar and pine scents take my breath away, Ikaika."

"Don't you notice all of them dancing," Malie insisted.

"I notice the wind," Nicole sniffed, hugging herself.

Two blankets popped out of nowhere. She squeaked and grabbed onto them. She pulled them around her broad shoulders, raising her brow at Ikaika. He winked. She spread one out on the ground to sit on.

Pierre's heart burst with joy. The wind had picked up at this elevation, blowing the scent of wildflowers around them. He watched Malie, who was running her hands through the baby's breath thick around their blanket. Millions of white petals drifted in the wind. Some of them lingered on her fingertips and arms. Pierre relaxed next to them on the blanket. He thought of his limestone boulder. In a blink, it appeared.

Pierre shouted, "Yes!" He leapt up from his boulder's cool surface. Was he part kangaroo? He just hopped from a prone position.

Nicole's jaw dropped, then she grinned. "What else have you got, Ikaika? Ice cream cones?"

"Nicole!" Malie and Pierre chastised her.

"Jinx!" they chorused.

Malie climbed up on the boulder next to Pierre. She had less agility, of course. However, her legs were lean and she had spunk.

Ikaika whisked the blanket away when he and Nicole joined them. It was a boulder party minus food. Wait! Nicole's ice cream request? Sure enough, a second later, they had chocolate sugar cones in their hands.

"Better eat them before they drip on your fingers," Ikaika said. "Sorry if you don't like chocolate," he nudged Nicole's foot with his. "Chocolate's my favorite. Oh, you like raspberry ice cream instead? Done." Her cone switched flavors in a snap.

"Hey, get out of my head, Manaful!" She grumbled. Ikaika apologized but noticed she chowed down on her desired flavor.

"So, explain again about the ice cream, the boulder, and our hover-traveling," Nicole said.

"It's Mana," Ikaika said with a sudden serious tone. He grimly continued, "We are born with the capacity to harness Mana, yet many families reject its power. They fear a loss of control."

Malie and Pierre twin-nodded, which made Nicole's lips twitch. Those two were meant to "meet" today.

Malie asked, "How did you come into your Mana training, if many generations have neglected gifting their children with Mana development?"

Ikaika perked up at her question. This little one was very sharp. He nodded at her and said, "Every Manaful 'Ohana has an Elder who embodies varied types of Mana. By the way, did you notice the different cloth colors? Elder Puna's dancing robe? The light in the threads?"

Nicole made a 'mindblown' expression: "Boom!"

She said, "Did I notice? That's why I freaked out and had the huddle/vote to get out of here. The power coming off Elder Puna gives me goosebumps!"

Ikaika appreciated Nicole's enthusiasm. Pierre urged Ikaika to finish explaining about parenting and Mana training. "You were raised by Elder Puna?"

Ikaika nodded and made a prayer pose again. The Secret Club shared a frown. Attempting to lighten the mood, Pierre lifted his foot to his mouth. He was pretending that he'd put his foot in it. Malie giggled in amazement at Pierre's continual displays of agility. Still hungry, Pierre dug out the oranges from his pockets, handing them to the others. Ikaika declined; instead, he snapped his fingers three times. The peels of an orange disappeared at each snap. Pierre and Malie clapped and laughed. Nicole rolled her eyes at Ikaika showing off.

Ikaika bowed, then his face became solemn.

He said, "Lapu killed them."

The Secret Club asked in unison, "Lapu? Bad dude?"

They amused Ikaika. These three were the Three Stooges. "Lapu is not a person," Ikaika said.

The triad were on a roll, saying together, "Huh?" Like dominoes, Nicole elbowed Pierre, who elbowed Malie. They argued with their eyes.

Nicole blew out a big breath, "Okay, I'll ask. If Lapu isn't a person, how did it kill your parents? Is Lapu a hurricane name? On Earth, we have these seemingly random names that meteorologists give storms and hurricanes, like Ivan and Sandy."

Ikaika studied each human slowly. The kids raised their hands, changing their minds. It was too soon to ask. Ikaika's parents were dead. Sticky subject.

After a minute of silence, Nicole said, "Hey, let's pause in the Lapu conversation." They all took a big breath, agreeing not to speak of Lapu murdering Ikaika's parents.

"Hey, Ikaika, instead of an orange or ice cream, could I get a pair of Nikes?" In the blink of an eye, the new Nikes appeared on Malie's feet. She noticed it formed after the strange mist manifested around her ankles.

"Wowza!" Malie hopped to the ground and did a happy dance in the baby's breaths. The little flowers covered her pink shoelaces.

Malie unstuck her sticky fingers, raising her brow at Ikaika. The Manaful winked at her. Pristine, warm, wet washcloths popped into their hands. They were the same as those distributed on tongs after dinner at five-star restaurants. The cloth even had an emblem: a fiery rose. She smiled and thanked Ikaika. Nicole reluctantly thanked him, too. Pierre bowed his head. As soon as they'd wiped up, the washcloths disappeared in a snap like Pierre's orange peels had. Manafuls don't litter.

"I vote we go on a hike, buddies! Let's explore this world!" Malie said.

Nicole shook her head at the petite bundle of energy.

"Sugar rush?" Pierre said. He worried about them being bigger than the Manafuls.

Ikaika bumped Pierre's hip with his shoulder. "It'll be fun. Perhaps you three will be jungle gyms for the toddlers."

Pierre laughed at that, answering, "I don't mind you in my head. I appreciate all the encouragement I can get."

Malie nudged his other hip, adding her two cents, "I'm sorry we never talked before on campus. I never thought a popular guy like you needed encouragement."

Pierre grinned left, then right. They sandwiched him with Aloha. Not wanting to be left out, Nicole nudged Malie's other hip.

"Yo, Ikaika, let's go exploring! Malie, you can break in your new shoes," Nicole said.

Malie jumped up and down. She said, "Ohhhh, maybe we could molecularly travel? That really changes our bodies in interesting ways. Then, it puts us back together. I wish I could learn how that works. I would become a Nobel Prize Winner!"

Nicole rolled her eyes, hard.

Pierre patted Malie's shoulder and said, "That's an admirable aspiration. Do you enjoy watching sciency things on YouTube?"

Nicole laughed, "Sciency? Is that a word?"

Malie said, "Oh, yes. Mom and I used to watch 'How It's Made' and 'Mythbusters.' Anything with 'How' in its title floats my boat."

"How about we don't molecularly transport?" Nicole complained, "We've got to do that to go home. That's enough for me. Before that, no thank you!"

Pierre raised his arm up, saying, "I vote that we actually exercise our leg muscles and hoof it!"

Malie jumped up to tap his hand in midair. Pierre smiled at her.

She said, "I second the walking vote! I'd better use my new shoes before they disappear."

Ikaika nodded in apology. She can't take them to Earth.

Nicole was curious about magic. "Do you learn in school or train with a master wizard?"

"I do homeschooling with my own master of Mana, Elder Puna," Ikaika puffed up.

"How much magic does a Manaful know when they are born?" Pierre asked.

"Very little," Ikaika replied. "It grows stronger only through knowledge gained over time."

"You guys have it all set," Nicole whistled.

"Remember, many generations of Manafuls refuse to believe in their Mana. They are the Hopohopo."

"Hopohopo," Malie repeated.

"They doubt their powers and magical capabilities. Our Mana is latent at birth. It takes awareness and training to harness the Mana for the good and not for the bad. Hopohopo dwarves deny their babies this gift." Ikaika frowned and put his hands together to do a quick prayer for the Hopohopo babies.

Malie and Pierre shared a look. They bowed their heads, too, for the babies.

"For the bad?" Nicole repeated after him. Of that entire speech, all her brain hooked onto was that. Maybe they shouldn't visit here? "There's good and bad Mana?" she said with fervor, eyes wide.

Ikaika watched her. Was her blood pressure increasing? Maybe they should pray for Nicole. He projected just that to Pierre and Malie. The three of them agreed, bending their heads again. Nicole watched them. She took a deep breath, closed her eyes, and bowed her head too. She didn't know what they were praying for. She prayed for herself. She'd never know that they'd prayed for her too, or maybe she'd felt it? Hmmm...

Ikaika raised his head and saw Nicole's head bow in prayer. Malie and Pierre noticed too. The three of them shared a grateful smile. Nicole was taking care of herself.

When Nicole raised her head, she picked up on their concern. "What?"

Pierre and Malie shared a twin thought, *"What do we say?"*

Ikaika stepped in, "Yes, Nicole. Mana can be used for good and bad. Power comes with polarities. It's just like Earth."

"How bad are the Manafuls you're talking about?" Pierre asked.

Ikaika's face fell. Malie pinched Pierre. He mouthed, "Sorry!" to her.

Malie changed the subject. "Manafuls don't have formal schooling? Are all minors homeschooled like you?"

Ikaika shook his head and decided to get them moving. It's a tour, after all. He waved for The Secret Club to follow him down the other side of the hill. They were entering the sandalwood forest. Pierre smiled at the changing woodlands, marveling at Manaful's environmental differences.

Ikaika read Pierre's thoughts, "The tree species change from hill to hill. The Manaful families that control each area have their own preferences from way back."

Pierre enjoyed the scent of sandalwood with its soothing aroma. The essential oil from these trees make for heavenly massages.

Ikaika winked, "Best oil for soothing you after a stressful day." Then, Ikaika laughed as Pierre jumped a little. Had he forgotten Ikaika was always in his head?

He fist-bumped Ikaika in thanks for reading his mind and explaining. Nicole frowned at Ikaika while Malie smiled approvingly. The girls had their own Ikaika-reading-my-mind opinions.

Ikaika nodded at Pierre and said, "Let's add a wiggle and 'woosh'!" He bumped Pierre's fist, adding wiggly fingers to the fist-bump gesture and the "Woosh!" sound.

Pierre laughed. "Yah! Let's do that again!" They fist-bumped, opened their hands to wiggle their fingers, and both said, "Woosh!" Laughing, Pierre turned to Malie for her to try it.

They did it: fistbump, wiggle, woosh! Malie happily turned to Ikaika. They fistbumped, wiggled, and wooshed too.

Malie then excitedly turned to Nicole with her fist bump ready. Nicole crossed her arms over her chest.

She tucked her hands under her armpits. "No. Just no."

Malie sighed, and they all continued down the hill.

The scent of the woods waved a welcome to them along a path lined with wildflowers of every color. A gardener's dreamscape. The Manaful World's climate allowed for extraordinary combinations of blossoms and fragrances. Malie hummed at the deep purplish-pink orchids dancing in the breeze beside the long stemmed sunflowers. The latter out-sized Ikaika.

Pierre shook his head, making sure it wasn't all a dream.

Nicole refused to get caught up in the scenery, riveted on the topic of homeschooling. "Do the Manaful children get stir crazy at home with one teacher for twelve years?"

Ikaika shook his head at her. "Manaful Elders of each family possess specialized Mana. This is similar to your vocational, medical, technological, and other educational fields."

Nicole raised a brow. "Medical Mana? Like healing powers?"

Malie stopped on her path to stare at Nicole. "That would be wonderful. COVID has killed so many. It's been a heartbreaking two plus years."

Pierre didn't want to think of COVID deaths. He swung his arms around, itching to run and use his muscles. Ikaika laughed at Pierre's neural overload. He was amazed at how much Pierre loved action. It's likely the reason he did well in sports.

"Go for it. Try it. Fifty yards from here to there. How fast did you say you were?" Ikaika dared him. He pointed to the fifty yards between them and the sandalwoods. It would be good for Pierre to stretch his legs. Pierre nodded and was gone. He got to the forest entrance in a handful of seconds: *Professional Combine, here I come!* He thought and laughed as he bent over to catch his breath.

The girls and Ikaika wooted and cheered for his sprint. "Woohoo!"

Pierre lifted one arm in thanks; he was otherwise occupied with catching his breath.

Ikaika turned back to the girls, pausing to recall what they'd been talking about. Oh, yes, about Manaful education. He answered, "Yes, we have hospitals here filled with medical professionals. Training begins at the age of five. There are fields like Manaful physiology, psychology, and pharmacology."

Malie's eyes widened as she said, "Wow, Manafuls know that young what they want to be?"

Nicole's brows furrowed, commenting, "Were those babies forced to learn healing?"

Ikaika shook his head at Nicole. They watched Pierre leapfrogging over little limestone boulders in the area. The football player had an affinity for that stone family. Malie smiled at Pierre's happy vibe and energy. Nicole was focused on Ikaika, awaiting his response.

Ikaika turned back to them with the utmost patience, "Each elder has a specialty. If they are in the medical or marine science field, babies in their families begin in that field."

Nicole puckered her lips again. "Families choose to take on the Mana voluntarily, right?"

Malie lost track of their conversation. They got nearer to Pierre's make-shift workout area near the forest. The birds' calls crescendoed as they approached the treeline.

Nicole was determined to learn more about their social system. "What do babies or children who don't have Mana learn?"

"Each village has a special role in the larger society, like fishermen, carpenters, and entertainers," Ikaika explained. "Legally speaking, if their parents reject Manaful vocations, they can learn it upon reaching their majority without parental agreement. That would mean leaving their family."

Nicole hadn't picked up on Ikaika's mood. She instead perked up and did a little shoulder jig. "Oh, legal speak," she smiled. "That's like my second language growing up with Uncle Nick and Mom practicing law."

Ikaika already read that in her head and nodded. Malie said, "Ooooohhh, coolio! My mom watches Law and Order."

Nicole laughed, "TV lawyers aren't like real ones! Though they look and sound like it."

Malie grinned, "I know. My mom watches for the handsome actors."

Ikaika smiled as the girls shared. He didn't pick up the Manaful home-schooling conversation. He preferred to let the Secret Club set the pace of their learning here. The vibe was smoother and mellower that way.

They reached Pierre, who'd found his giant limestone boulder again. Ikaika winked at Malie when she pointed at the stone and then at him.

Ikaika was sweet to bring the boulder along for Pierre. She understood Pierre's Aloha for it. Some people don't believe rocks have elemental power or calmness in them. She and Pierre were of one mind.

Since "meeting" his giant limestone boulder in the other valley, he'd formed a bond with its sturdy presence.

Pierre's Limestone Song:

"What was it like before I knew about being still?
Why'd I turn little things into molehills?
Will I still have this inner strength outside of here?
Will the ways of my world still bring me to tears?
Limestone, power me up with your glistening shine.
Help me be true to this heart of mine.
Limestone, lift me up with your strong presence.
Help me accept my own essence.
Limestone, help build up my beliefs.
Remind me to be cool even in grief.
Limestone, help me rock it!
Help me rock it!
Football, classes, friends, and family.
Help me rock it!
I rock!
Is there a safe space for boys like me on Earth?
Do people accept different love well-sought?
Can I conquer football and still be free?
What would the locker room be like for guys like me?
Limestone, help me rock it!
Help me rock it!
Football, classes, friends, and family.

Help me rock it!
We rock!"

At the end of Pierre's song, the girls and Ikaika clapped. He bowed and exchanged a fist-bump wiggle-woosh with everyone except Nicole. She wasn't buying its silliness yet, though she was tempted after that song.

Pierre smiled. He knew Nicole would join in one day. They made their way onto a small path into the sandalwood forest. They continued their earlier conversation about babies with Mana.

Ikaika read the confusion in the girls' minds.

Ikaika said, "Well, families who believe in Mana teach babies to wield it safely from the early toddler stage. That's as far back as I remember. They don't want us to harm ourselves, other Manaful, or other beings."

Malie agreed. "Oh! Yes, of course, no harming others. Are Manafuls vegans?"

Ikaika shook his head. "Epicurean choices are respected here. We have elders who telepathically 'talk' to animals here, like my Gramps. The animals that are going to be consumed give themselves like sacrifices. It's a glorious reciprocity. Those who eat the animals give thanks for their gift of life."

Nicole wondered if Elder Puna and Ikaika were vegetarians.

Ikaika nodded at her in assent, reading her mind.

Nicole raised her brow and frowned at him for being in her head.

Ikaika mouthed, "Oops!"

She shook her head, and fought off a smile. His enthusiasm for life was contagious; he had a big personality. Having Mana doesn't hurt, either.

"My Tūtū believes in not harming other beings, but she's not vegetarian," Pierre said.

"By other beings, what do you mean?" Nicole asked Ikaika.

"Everything around us is alive, even if they seem inanimate," Ikaika said.

Nicole chortled, "Ridiculous!"

Pierre and Malie grimaced, pointed at her, and shook their heads. Ikaika grinned at their twinness, unbothered by Nicole.

"Nicole! Rude." Pierre said.

"Well, it's impossible not to harm things or people. We're always hurting someone or something. That's life!" she said.

That disturbed Malie. "What do you mean?"

Nicole pointed at herself. "I'm not vegetarian. Are you two?"

The other children declined to answer.

Nicole puffed up and raised her voice. "All of the protein we consume comes from living beings. As for non-eating circumstances, pain is inevitable. We step on ants, we swat flies, we tease people, we wear leather and pearls, we shoo away stray chickens and cats all day, we neglect homeless people, and more!" Nicole was on a roll. Her cheeks were flushed. She moved her head back and forth like a bobble toy.

Malie reached for Nicole's hand and squeezed. Nicole closed her eyes. She went quiet and took a deep breath. Pierre checked her eyes. "You okay, friend?"

She nodded. He met Malie's eyes. Malie nodded, too.

Pierre walked away to get some space. Nicole's mercurial moods saddened him. He let the forest soothe him. He liked the different textures of the trees and bushes. Some of the tree barks were golden brown with dripping resin, while others were of darker tones. Maybe they were mahogany or eucalyptus trees. What were they doing amid the sandalwood? Strange mixture. He thought of Tūtū again. She'd appreciate these flowers and roots.

Nicole wanted to get moving and was grateful to have her gym shoes on. "I'm itching to discover some mountain trails. Let's go foraging!"

"Forage for what?" Malie asked, poking a giant fern to watch it sway with a tinkling sound.

"There's nothing like a breathtaking hike through the forest," Nicole said.

"You're on. Let's go. We're in sync." Ikaika said.

Nicole whooped.

"I appreciate my new hiking shoes, Ikaika!" Malie said, staring at her pink Nikes. "These are cute. I'm glad my gym shoes are in my backpack." She jumped in place, appreciating the bounce of her shoes. "These fit perfectly and are my favorite color."

"You read her mind too, didn't you? Style, size, and color of the shoes?" Nicole raised her brow at Ikaika.

"Hey, 'gotta do what you gotta do?'" Ikaika mimicked Nicole's accent and stance. His hands were on his hips, and his head bobbled on his neck from side to side like hers does.

Pierre, who'd returned to the group, shouted, "You sound like Nicole!"

Malie high-fived Ikaika, "That expression was all her!"

Nicole pointed at Ikaika, "Ha, ha, ha! You are all comedians," Nicole nudged them all. "I'm onto you, Ikaika! Watch your back, dude!" she said.

He waved her towards him. "Bring it, girl!" He mimicked her accent and tone.

That brought the other two to tears, hugging their bellies with laughter.

Nicole's lips twitched. The dwarf was getting to her. Seconds later, she was laughing too. She was the first to head out, "Let's go, everyone!"

Geckos rushed across their path as they made their way through young mulberry bushes almost as tall as Ikaika.

A large white owl manifested out of a rainbow burst of Mana Mist, droplets of light dancing on its feathers. The glowing owl perched on a thick sandalwood branch over Pierre's head. The glorious old one made "woo-woo" sounds, projecting to Ikaika: *"New guests, Heir? Give them my welcome. Friends of Elder Puna are friends of mine and my own."*

The wise old owl's telepathic projection humbled Ikaika. He stopped in his tracks. The Secret Club bumped into him like successive waves on a beach.

"You okay, Ikaika?" Malie was struck by Ikaika's meditative expression. He stood still and stared peacefully at the bird. She sensed that they were having a telepathic conversation. She shushed her peers, nodding towards the giant avian above them. Nicole got goosebumps. Pierre and Malie bowed to the bird in unison.

Ikaika turned to the Secret Club to introduce them. "People, this is Maluhia. He welcomes you, and his family will always keep an eye on you."

The kids waved at Maluhia. The owl didn't twitch or blink. It "woo-wooed" again, then disappeared. Beneath the shady tree canopy, the luminescent colors of his departure made the children gasp in awe.

The suddenness of the owl's appearance and disappearance gave them the shivers. This Mana Mist was very powerful yet beautiful to behold. They'd never been up close with a big owl like that, much less one that magically pops in and out from misty rainbow lights. The whole forest was powerful to be in. They looked up, appreciating the rustling of the trees and the cool mountain winds. The peaceful aura of Manaful nature embraced them lovingly.

CHAPTER 12

Manaful World
January 13, 2022

They continued to trek through and appreciate the sandalwood forest. Reaching for a puakenikeni tree, Nicole drank in its beauty. Its delicate, pale yellow blossom exuded perfume sweeter than a Parisian perfume.

Nicole asked, "Hey, Ikaika, about Mana again. What's the catch?"

Pierre didn't follow. "What do you mean by catch?"

"Oh, well, if there's magic, does that mean there's no work or money?" Nicole wondered.

"Who needs money with magic?" Malie said.

"I can't imagine a world without money," Pierre said.

"We have silvers and golds, which are used like you use money," Ikaika said. "The coins are part of an economic system for those who reject Mana. The Elders' Council invented the coin-wealth system for them."

Nicole frowned, "That makes the Hopohopo seem like second class citizens!" Being raised by lawyers and shrinks, Nicole was always fascinated by legal and sociological conversations. Being part AfricanAmerican in a post-George Floyd era, Nicole was cognizant of inequalities.

"If magic's available at birth to everyone, why is money still needed?" Nicole said.

Pierre and Malie were speechless.

Ikaika said, "For survival."

Nicole harrumphed.

They continued through the forest. The leaves and smaller branches scrunched under their feet. Nicole moved aside taller vines in Malie's way. Malie smiled at her, nodding her thanks.

Ikaika noticed the branches hitting Malie. Like a conductor he waved his arms once from left to right. With a wise expression beyond his years, he communicated to the trees as he did with Maluhia, the owl. The path widened in seconds. The trees and plants had squirmed aside. They moved backward on both sides like soldiers on command. Ikaika bowed to them in gratitude. Deep, resounding tree voices projected: *Travel safely. Ikaika, be aware.*

"Holy moly! Shut the front door!" Nicole shouted, turning to Malie and Pierre. She pointed at Ikaika, "What did you just do? Did you just order the trees back, and did they just TALK BACK?" She screamed that last part.

Ikaika smiled up at her. "Yes, to both."

"I saw that too!" Pierre squeaked.

"Did you just squeak?" Nicole laughed like a crazy person. "That was loud and high, Pierre!"

"Hey, you could be a falsetto, brother," Malie elbowed him.

"Hey, you have to admit it was astounding! You screamed too, Nicole." Pierre said.

"Hey, hey, no shame in screaming!" Malie hugged his arm. "I agree telepathy and mobile trees are freaky. Mind-blown!" She motioned "poof!" face, holding her hands over her head.

Pierre patted her arm and waved at trees.

Nicole and the group walked along the forest path. She stared at the thirty-foot canopy of greenery, mouth agape. She mumbled to herself, "This can't possibly be happening!"

She took a deep breath, closed her eyes, and felt a small dwarf hand squeeze hers. A calmness enveloped her, and her heartbeat slowed to its regular pace.

They walked together, a girl and a Manaful. They were an odd pair. Nicole felt a rare peacefulness. Was Ikaika sending calming energy through their hands? Was it the trees' Mana? Maybe it's both. She went with the flow.

Pierre smiled at Nicole's acceptance of the dwarf.

At this slightest hint of being seen while vulnerable, Nicole dropped Ikaika's hand.

"Hey, Ikaika, tell us more about the money and Hopohopo," Pierre was curious why a being would reject Mana.

"Mana comes in different forms and purposes, like money," Ikaika said. "Mana comes from Source, refined through a family line into more nuanced skills."

"Family line? Like ancestors?" Malie wished she knew her family tree.

"Yes. The magic flows through the bloodline for thousands of years." Ikaika took the lead down the palapalai, lace fern, path. Its fragrance captivated them, as well as the feathery fronds. Hula dancers on Earth loved the plant, linking it to their Hawaiian goddess, Laka.

"Manafuls have lived for thousands of years? How is that possible?" Nicole asked.

"Gramps appears 'middle-aged' to you." Ikaika sprung over a fallen tree branch, which grew new shoots that reached for the sky.

"He's about the age of my granddads." Nicole said.

"Elder Puna is three thousand and five hundred Manaful years or fifty human ones." Ikaika laughed at their flabbergasted faces.

"No way, he can't be that old. He has great skin!" Pierre balked.

"What's the ratio, again?" Malie asked.

"We already asked that question," Pierre nudged her, "Seventy years to our one human year."

Nicole hit her knee and bent over laughing at something in her head. "It's dog-years times ten!" Nicole joked.

"Thanks, Nicole. Yes, we're like dogs." Ikaika said.

"Or petri-dish bacteria," Nicole went on.

"She didn't mean that," Malie frowned at Nicole.

"Nicole's working on her filter," Pierre said.

"Gee, just joking, people!" Nicole sniffed. Some people have no sense of humor!

Ikaika focused on Nicole's forehead for a second, and she did the same with an exaggerated stare of her own.

"Are you reading my mind again?" She made 'crazy eyes' like the albatross in Rescuers Down Under. She'd watched it with mom last week. Kaleo flashed in her mind's eye and Nicole abruptly ran out of sass.

Ikaika winked.

“Nicole’s kind hearted,” Malie said.

“We just met today, but in class, you’re always cheering on the underdog,” Pierre added.

“You all don’t have to get sappy on me!” Nicole blushed.

“Let’s get back to Manaful ages and their Mana,” she reined in the conversation.

They passed a spongy log that looked like a good resting spot with its lush maile vines perfect for seating. Pierre wished for his limestone boulder. In a flash, it appeared, matching the forestry. He smiled at Ikaika, before lounging on his green comfort stone. He patted the space beside him. They all jumped on. Malie needed a little lift. They sat that way under the teal light of the sun reflecting off the leaves and flowers. The hoots of sleepy monkeys amused them.

CHAPTER 13

Manaful World
January 13, 2022

"Elder Puna is one of the original Manafuls. While not immortal, my grandpa possesses some of the greatest powers in our world," Ikaika said with humility.

Pierre and Malie frowned, contemplating the implications of such power.

"Does that make him the president of your people?" Pierre asked.

"They're not regular people!" Nicole said, correcting him.

"You know what I mean." Pierre kept his eyes on Ikaika.

"More like vice-prez, Pierre," Ikaika said. "He and Elder Alakaʻi are the two oldest and most powerful Manafuls."

"Wow!" Malie mimed being mind blown again. "Boom Shaka!"

Nicole was concerned about Ikaika's parentage. How long has he lived with his grandpa?

"What happened to your parents?" she said.

Pierre nudged Nicole, frowning. Since "meeting" her, she's had a thing for getting too personal.

"They were killed in a power grab." Ikaika bent his head.

He put his hands together before him in prayer motion again. Their boulder meeting had gotten somber.

They gave him a moment of silence. Malie and Pierre, who sat on either side of him, put their arms around the dwarf's shoulders.

"I'm sorry, Ikaika," they said as if they were of one mind. They didn't say "jinx," remaining solemn.

Even Nicole gave Ikaika his moment of peace.

"It was a while ago, and I'm blessed to have Gramps." Ikaika wiped his cheeks.

Malie and Pierre worried and shared a thought. "*What should we do?*"

Nicole broke the ice.

"Hey, Ikaika, how about we go back to that stream in the koa forest? We could molecularly travel there."

Her willingness to transport surprised Malie.

This got Ikaika's attention too. He nodded and levitated, waving for them to follow.

"Thank you, Nicole." Ikaika saw only good intentions in her mind. He directed them before transporting. "Let's take each others' hands in a circle. Now, close your eyes. Good. On the count of three: One! Two! Three!"

They disappeared, and seconds later, their bodies were transported to a rocky embankment.

"I'll never get used to that!" Pierre exhaled, reaching for his hair and his boy parts.

"You're funny, Pierre. We're all good. It's a reconfiguration of our molecules!" Malie said.

Pierre shook his head at her, wiggling his arms and shaking his legs out. Malie laughed, mimicking Pierre's dance. She shook her head and body.

Nicole looked at them. "What are you two doing?"

"Nothing!" Pierre and Malia said. "Jinx!" This simply irritated Nicole more than before. Their twinness never ends.

She stomped after Ikaika, who was "talking" to the stream. He wasn't voicing, but she knew there was more going on. He was having some telepathic conversation again with the beings around them. Everything was listening to him. The wind stopped, the river froze in time, and a beaver's arm was stuck mid-wave. Nicole closed her eyes to relax in the silence. Then there wasn't.

As sudden as everything stopped in time, they all woke up. Maybe she'd imagined it all? Probably not. Ikaika turned to her, waiting for her question. Then his brain penetrated hers and he nodded.

She said, "Hey! Get out of my head!"

He said, "You're not imagining any of this."

She nodded. "Okay. Thanks for confirming, but stay out of my head!"

He saluted her. "Aye! Aye!"

She laughed and pointed at him with a fake-serious "I'm-on-to you!" glare.

The Secret Club and Ikaika had molecularly transported near a slow-moving stream in the sandalwood forest. It had been closer than going back to the koa forest brooke. The water was at least three feet deep. Malie clapped at the jumping rainbow fish. They may be koi fish. She looked at Ikaika for confirmation.

He nodded, "Yes, koi."

Malie crouched on a rock, watching the smaller kelp nipping at the baby barnacles on the submerged base. Then she sat and took her sandals off.

Nicole said, "Hey, I wouldn't put my foot in there!"

Malie answered, "Why? Afraid of those parasites that hijack animal brains? Will we become worm-controlled pod people?"

Nicole laughed, "Nature documentaries?"

Malie nodded. "Pods-are-us wouldn't happen. I'm sure Ikaika already telepathically told all the worms to leave us in peace."

Nicole hid her wince at the truth in Malie's words. Shoot, she'd just witnessed Ikaika doing that. She masked the gravity of the Mana between Ikaika and the creatures behind casual laughter.

"Wow, Malie, was that sass and snark from you?"

Malie nodded. "Wayyyy. I'm irritated with humans. I wish we could live at peace like this with other beings."

Nicole sighed, "You're telling me about peace? A half-Black person? Peace between people, much less other beings, is a pipe dream."

Malie offered her fist to Nicole for bumping, nodding her head in encouragement. Silently she said, "Come on, Sister. Give me a fistbump-wiggle-woosh!"

Nicole grudgingly fist-bumped-wiggle-wooshed! Malie.

The petite girl leaped up and cheered! "Yes! Yes!"

They both laughed at the silliness of the shared hand gesture, yet they appreciated each other's presence.

Ikaika joined them at the stream, conjuring a large fluffy beach towel for them to sit on together. Nicole smiled at his

Mana/manifesting of things out of thin air. He shrugged his brown dwarf shoulders as if to say, "What can I say?"

"Why am I not thirsty here?" Nicole asked him. The girls and Ikaika sat cross-legged in a circle, facing each other.

"We are in a parallel dimension, Nicole," he said. "Just a moment in time has passed for your body."

Nicole's nose scrunched up in confusion. "So, time stopped at home? My body thinks it's at home?" Nicole asked.

"Exactly," Ikaika said.

"What's the purpose of bringing us here?" she said.

"For you to form your Secret Club," Ikaika said without hesitation.

Nicole hummed and realized the three of them may have never connected on the other side, left to their own devices. Nicole closed her eyes, raising her face to the warm sky. She pondered Ikaika's surprising revelations. Opening her eyes, she sang for release.

Nicole's Questioning Song:

How now? How can there be just The Now?
Will I ever live just in the Now?
Wrinkles, old bones, and hearing loss.
Time shows its power like a coin toss.
Diplomas, careers, kids, and marriage vows.
What do they all mean: Live only in The Now?
Does he mean I must value each moment?
Is that life's biggest component?
How now? How can there be just The Now?

Will I ever live just in The Now?
Less figuring out why I'm always mad.
Less wondering the truth about my dad.
More loving friendships filled with support.
More sassy comebacks and silly retorts.
Yes to possibilities and dreams.
Yes to living well and happy memes.
How now? How can there be just The Now?
Will I ever live just in The Now?"

After singing, Nicole felt lighter inside, a tension release. Malie patted her hand and Ikaika nodded at her. She walked away from her friends and moved closer to Pierre's flower meadow. She wasn't surprised to discover him resting on his limestone boulder. She laughed as a butterfly landed on Pierre's crooked nose. He wiggled his head while asleep, and the monarch flew away.

She continued towards the sandalwood treeline, letting him have a moment too. Without Ikaika doing his Mana thing nature was at rest. Almost normal. She hummed as she circled back towards Malie and Ikaika's spot at the stream. She sat next to them quietly.

The baby koi kept jumping and splashing droplets on Malie's eyeglass frames. They were young and likely new to the environment. The petite girl's toes dragged in the water in hopes of a baby fish pedi. It was a good time-out for all of them. Malie smiled at Nicole through the water droplets on her lenses and sang a song of her own.

Malie's Stream Song:

"Hello, little fish. Nibble, nibble at my toes.
My brain leaps for joy; it just goes
At home I'd sit for hours to write
It's hard to think, trying with all my might
As I pull my hair, making up a story.
Bad guys losing, heroes get the glory.
Now I find some peace in a stream,
Words flow out as if from a dream.
Little fish, nibble, nibble at my feet.
That's how stories become complete.
Writers have something to express
Sometimes it can be such a mess
Book friends can bring people home
Nothing beats a great tome.
Mahalo, little fish nibbling, for now I know.
Mahalo for helping me realize I get what I sow"

Nicole and Ikaika bowed at Malie in appreciation. They understood her need for quietness. She silently thanked them for listening to her song with a nod.

Unaware of the girls' musical inner journeys by the stream, Pierre remained on his boulder. He was on a limestone island in the middle of a rainbow dandelion sea. The wind blew the wispy mini umbrellas up to his legs and arms. He smiled at the heavens, singing to himself.

Pierre's Meadow Song:

"Shiny, floaty flowers glowing around me.
Reds, blues, and greens that fly up then flee.
How I love what you represent.
All of you are my favorite presents.
Lifting yourselves up into the air.
Celebrating life, ignoring all the stares.
Shiny, floaty flowers glowing around me.
Your rainbow seeds bless those who wish to repent.
Giving them acceptance no matter how they're bent.
Boys, girls, or none of the above.
No one judges you for who you love.
Rainbow colors, Oh, I love what you represent."

Chapter 14

Manaful World
January 13, 2022

Ikaika smiled at their singing. It's The Secret Club. It was time for them to return to their world for now. He gathered the children together. That was when his childhood friend, Maka, molecularly transported into their presence.

Ikaika's face lit up and he hugged the newcomer's muscled arm. Unlike Ikaika's expressiveness, Maka's silent assessment of Ikaika's human guests was stoic. Ikaika did a happy hover-dance that his favorite Manaful was here to send off the humans.

Maka projected only to Ikaika, "*Who are they?*"

Ikaika responded, "*This is The Secret Club. You'll love them!*"

Maka grunted. "*What's special about them?*"

Ikaika squeezed Maka's arm, "*I'll show you in the Wall.*"

Maka raised his brow at Ikaika, but he squeezed Ikaika's arm in turn. His sarong was green.

"Hey, Ikaika! Don't be rude! What are you two projecting? Who's your friend?" Nicole insisted, always the one to break the ice.

In a lower tone voice than Ikaika, the broader Manaful introduced, "I'm Maka. We will get to know each other next time."

Pierre's eyes widened at Maka's low sonorous pitch. Wow, Pierre was thrown back by the dwarf. He appeared to be Ikaika's age, yet his voice was a beautiful bass. Pierre rubbed his throat, curious about the changes in his own 'reedy' voice. He hoped it lowered into a low tone like Maka's.

He shook off the thought and implored, "There'll be a next time, Ikaika?"

Malie high-fived Pierre and moved towards Maka for a high-five. Ikaika's friend separated himself from Ikaika and crossed his arms.

Malie frowned, but was undeterred. She smiled and waved, "Hi, Maka! I'm sorry we're leaving just as you've arrived! It'll be great to bond with you next time."

Nicole's eyes narrowed at Maka, cautious about this one's quiet, gruff demeanor.

Pierre smiled at Maka and offered a fistbump.

When Maka shook his head still frowning, Nicole laughed. Ikaika saved the fistbump instead.

Malie stepped closer to Pierre, nudging him with her hip.

She took his hand, "I was thinking about returning too, Pierre! Mahalo for asking."

Nicole shook her head at their twinness.

"Why am I not surprised that you think alike?" Nicole said.

Ikaika jumped for joy. "You may return when you wish. Simply come together as The Secret Club to sing a Song of Request. Elder Puna will create a Shimmery Wall for you."

They all thanked him.

"What's a Song of Request?" Nicole said.

"It's a chant of love and humility. You all sing, putting your hearts into the words and sharing how you're doing." Ikaika said.

Nicole wasn't connecting the dots. "What does that have to do with visiting here?"

Malie patted her shoulder and said, "Elder Puna and Ikaika care about our well-being, Nicole."

Pierre said, "It's important that we gather often and keep singing. It's good for the soul!"

"Yes, let's keep our bond on Earth," Malie said. She squeezed Pierre's arm.

"What's with you two? You've become siblings in one afternoon," Nicole said.

"We love you too," Malie said, reaching to give the other girl a much-needed hug.

"Hey, hey, give me some space!" Nicole said with her hands up. "Don't go all sappy on me, too."

Despite her denials, she couldn't help liking these two bozos.

Nicole hip-bumped Pierre, "Hey, when we get back, let's exchange digits. Keep this on the down low, got it?"

Malie stared wide-eyed. Pierre laughed.

"Digits? Down low? Really? Are you a hip-hop artist?" Pierre said.

Ikaika raised his hand, and the Shimmery Wall appeared.

"Wow! That's amazing. You never explained that family Mana stuff and the degrees of power." Nicole reminded Ikaika.

"I will, promise. Come back soon." Ikaika bowed.

"None of that formal stuff!" Pierre said. He hugged the dwarf they'd come to treasure in one afternoon. Malie came in for a group hug. Pierre opened one of his arms, raising his brows at Nicole.

"Bring it in, girl!" he said.

Nicole groaned and made a pretend angry face. Then she laughed and joined their group hug. Then they lined up and held hands, prepared to leap back home.

"Here we go. Molecules, stay together, please!" Pierre said.

"Have faith!" Malie said, squeezing his hand tighter.

Taking the lead, Nicole shouted, "On three. One! Two! Three!"

They jumped through.

Pierre was the first to molecularly reconfigure. They'd returned to Earth time before gym class. He wasted no time, checking over his boy parts and hair.

"Hooh. I'm all here!" He said.

Nicole and Malie reconfigured after him. He was still checking his limbs and arms.

"Pierre!" Nicole groaned.

Their bags popped into their hands suddenly. Malie checked her backpack for librarian Heluhelu's book, bringing it out to hug. She noticed her Manaful hiking shoes were replaced with her original sandals.

Malie shifted her weight, squishing her lips like fish. Who was she? The Manaful World Malie or the shy Malie of Earth?

"We're going to be late for gym class! Vamos, people!" Nicole nudged Malie's backpack and nodded to Pierre. The Secret Club headed to class together. But not before appreciating their cell phones' reappearance and exchanging digits.

CHAPTER 15

Earth
January 13, 2022,
Secret Club's three homes
8 p.m.

The Secret Club's Nightly Mobile Meeting

Malie: I call to order The Secret Club
Pierre: Nice. Yes, leader!
Malie: I'm blushing.
Nicole: I'm rolling my eyes.
Malie: I'm here.
Pierre: Here.
Nicole: Really, sister. Procedure again? Want to vote next?
Pierre: Voting now? For what?
Malie: She's ribbing me.
Nicole: Come on, people. Freaking out about today yet?
Pierre: Today was real. Really scary, exciting, and amazing.
Malie: I wanted to tell my mom.
Pierre and Nicole: Stop!

Malie: I didn't. Really? She's a nurse practitioner. Three words for how she'd respond: meds and shrink.

Pierre: My two words: vaccination reaction.

Nicole: I nominate that we keep Manaful World a secret.

Pierre: Isn't that the name of our Club? Secret Club? Redundant much?

Malie: Yes, yes. I second.

Pierre: Nicole, now you like procedures?

Nicole: Touché!

Nicole: Confirmed. Resolved. Manaful World = secret. Tell no one else.

Malie: Drawback.

Pierre: What?

Malie: Mom reads texts, emails, and history.

Nicole: Let's Google about Manafuls.

Malie: What if others have been there or posted about it?

Pierre: Too risky for Google or social media.

Nicole: We voted, people! It's a secret.

Malie: Let's get this straight, Pierre.

Nicole: Straight?

Pierre: I would if I was!

Nicole: ...

Malie: ...

Pierre: Girls?

Nicole: I called it! Called it!

Malie: When?

Pierre: All my life.

Nicole: Gym class. Boy, if being gay was a secret, I'd stop checking out our male classmates doing pull-ups!

Pierre: Oops! You figured me out.

Nicole: Plus, Uncle Nick is gay. Granddads John and Court are gay. Married before I was born. I just know, and still, I heart you!

Malie: Ditto! Proud of you, Pierre.

Nicole: Football?????

Malie: Secret Club is here for you. Anytime. Day or night.

Nicole: There you go! Ditto.

Pierre: Who says, "Ditto?"

Nicole: We do now. Anyway, watch the movie *Ghost*. Stream it. Classic.

Malie: RIP Patrick Swayze.

Pierre: Awwww.

Malie: Oops. Mom's home. Late workshift. Want to check on her. I officially call this Secret Club meeting closed.

Nicole: My mom's tired a lot too. It's good to check on them.

Pierre: I second.

Nicole: Resolved.

Pierre: Night, Malie. Tomorrow.

Nicole: Pierre, hang up quickly. I'm calling you.

Pierre: Yes, ma'am!

He leaned back on his bed. With one foot on his knee, he tucked the mobile between his ear and shoulder. Next time they should FaceTime. He used both hands to toss a football above his head. He tried not to regret what he'd revealed to the Secret Club.

"Nicole, what did you mean about gym class? Am I that obvious?" Pierre asked once he got her on the phone again. He was awestruck. He hadn't known he spent class watching boys in that manner. What if he acted like that at football practices unknowingly? What would his teammates do to him? Coach?

"Stop worrying. It's my gay intuition," Nicole said. "You're the bravest person ever!"

Pierre sat up on his bed, switching to his Pods because his shoulder was sore from holding the phone. He groaned and exchanged the pigskin for his pillow. He squished the purple feather pillow, hugging it.

He said, "Not that brave, really. Does telling two girls and an otherworld dwarf count?" A strange realization came over him.

"Hey, Nicole, how would you describe Manaful to anyone?"

There was a large stump and bump from Nicole.

"You okay there?" He checked.

"Are you kidding me?" Nicole had fallen off her bed.

She rearranged her pajamas. "We just voted never to describe it to anyone else!"

The pitch of her voice was hysterical. Pierre winced, pulling his Pods away. He made a raspberry with his lips. The sputtering sound made her laugh. Oops. She jumped from her bed to pace her room.

"No. No, not sharing with anyone!" She said, "Secret. Two hundred and ten percent secret."

"Mum's the word!" Pierre backpedaled, reassuring her. She calmed down and slowed her breathing. Holding her chest to keep her heart in there. The line went quiet for a while.

Ooookay, divert her attention, Pierre thought. "Nicole, do you talk to yourself?"

She perked up. "Yes." Psychoanalysis was like breathing in Granddad's home growing up.

"Yes, everyone does, at least in their head. It's when we talk badly to ourselves that causes anxiety—like in my case," Nicole added.

Pierre said. "You've got to stop doing that in the future. Talk to someone when those bad self-thoughts seem to take over."

He recalled Coach Jackson's pep talks about mindset and positive affirmations. "On a positive note, I know what I'm talking about. Before a game, I pump myself up with positive thoughts," he said.

Nicole smiled, imagining Pierre jumping in place, geared up in his helmet and jersey.

"Pump yourself up. Then, when you're anxious, talk yourself down," Pierre said. "Text me whenever you need to. I've got your back!" he said.

"You too, Pierre. I have my own cheerleaders in you and Malie. Today was a life-changing day. We were there for the Club. We were strong for all of us." Nicole was happy.

Encouraging him helped her forget about her own worries. The Secret Club and the Manafuls. Nicole was still getting over that new development in her life.

Like, woah.

"Thanks," he said after her speech. "You've got it backward. You're our fearless leader, Nicole."

"Ha ha," she said, "Night. Until tomorrow."

"Ditto!" Pierre replied with a smile. He hung up with her laughter in his ear. Pierre lay back on his bed. He imagined a future life like Nicole's granddads. He'd be happily married to his ideal man. He started to hum, then stood up with gusto to sing to the mirror.

Pierre's Ideal Guy Song:

Give me. Give me. Give me. Give me.
Curly hair that's ginger, brown, blond, or black.
Straight hair or no hair. I like them all; it's like that.
Top hats or ball caps, either would suffice.
When finding the right guy, it's all really nice.
Give a guy a choice, then it'll be alright.
Let's all rejoice and call it a night.
When we come into our own,
When our true colors are shown,
Good things start to happen.
Our lives start to reshape and—
Give me. Give me. Give me. Give me. Give me. Give me.
The guy of my dreams!"

CHAPTER 16

Manaful World
January 13, 2022

Elder Puna and Ikaika watched the Secret Club close out that day. Through the Shimmery Wall, the Elder and his grandson swiped through the images like surfing the internet. They laughed at Pierre and Nicole's hilarious yet profound post-Secret Club meeting conversation.

Ikaika projected, "*Will they be back, Grandpa?*"

Elder Puna grinned at Ikaika, projecting, "*Want to place a bet?*"

Ikaika sputtered. "*What?*"

Elder Puna laughed, "*Always wanted to say that: 'Want to place a bet?'*"

"*You're mad.*"

"*Human idioms are quite entertaining.*"

Ikaika shook his head. "*Don't do that to me, Gramps.*"

Elder Puna laughed. Who'd have thought this new batch would affect him this much? He waved his hands. The Shimmery Wall disappeared with a swoosh and a fizz.

CHAPTER 17

Storyteller in Papakōlea, Hawaiʻi
January 13, 2022

Aunt Ellie and Ari were in the living room before bedtime. "It's been a long day for you, Ari," Aunt Ellie said.

Ari cheerfully wondered what it would be like to meet the characters in real life.

"School was fine, Aunty," she said, "but I loved learning more about the Secret Club and the Manafuls. I'm not tired of them and never will be"

"The Secret Club had their first big journey together." Aunt Ellie said.

"Well, did you put away the dishes?" Aunt Ellie's brows went up.

"I wish we had a dishwasher," Ari complained. "Wiping dishes is irritating."

"Don't complain about simple chores like that, my dear," Aunt Ellie said, "Tsk, tsk tsk."

Ari winced. A lecture on the impoverished was forthcoming. One, two, and—

"There are children who have no food. They don't even have dishes to eat off. They don't have clean water to drink, to wash dishes, or to shower," Aunt Ellie said.

Ari turned her head sideways, hiding a big eye roll like Nicole's.

"I understand, Aunty." Ari said. "I am blessed. My bad."

It was Aunt Ellie's turn to roll her eyes at sayings like 'my bad.'

"When I was young, 'bad' was slang for 'good.'"

Ari frowned. "Huh?"

The older woman just shook her head.

"They should tell their parents," Ari said.

"I'm proud of you. I pondered that option too." Aunt Ellie said.

Ari was glad. "Well? What was your author's decision?"

"You have to wait." Aunt Ellie said.

"Oh! I will be restless tonight!" Ari said.

"You will rest well," Aunt Ellie said, messing up Ari's hair.

"Thank you for a good day, Aunty," Ari reached up to kiss her Aunt's cheek. "Good night!"

It had been a good day for everyone, real and unreal.

Chapter 18

Storyteller in Papakōlea, Hawaiʻi
January 15, 2022

Aunt Ellie and Ari walked through their garden, enjoying the scents in the air. The rosemary herbs grow thick and tall, and the papaya tree's juicy fruit were yellow-orange. The breeze lifted Ari's hair as she set out a metal bowl of kibble for the stray cats. She refilled and cleaned out a metal water pan daily. Ari kept it under their porch ramp to remain cool.

"What is the Secret Club up to today, Aunty Ellie?" Ari asked.

She brushed dirt off a bench. Wild hens clucked next door, while their chicks peeped.

"First, how was your school day, Ari."

"Well, I'm adjusting to a new school. Middle school is a huge transition."

"That's exactly what the Secret Club is doing, dear," Aunt Ellie said.

"They're like me. Yay" Ari danced.

Aunt Ellie winked. "Tell me, Ari, what would you like to happen next?"

Ari said, "Our club should communicate with each other in school too."

"Hmmm. Good suggestion," Aunt Ellie said. "Alrighty, January fifteenth, from the top!"

Chapter 19

Earth
Wright Middle School Cafeteria, Breakfast
January 15, 2022

Nicole walked through the cafeteria breakfast line to pick up her plate. She likes chocolate milk and cereal. The fruit looked yummy—half sliced oranges and apples with apple sauce served in small cardboard containers and cinnamon sprinkled on top.

The basement cafeteria, with its white linoleum floors and cement columns, was like basic training camps in military feature films. Yet, the students were not nearly as orderly as new recruits. Cafeteria workers tidied up after the middle schoolers.

"Hey, Nicole!" Pierre shouted out from his table of football boys and adoring groupies. She rolled her eyes at the gawking girls sitting at Pierre's elbows. Don't they know we're still supposed to be socially distancing? The girls' skirts were way too short, breaking the school dress code.

Nicole waved at Pierre. She was about to walk past him. The Secret Club was a secret, after all. That meant their friendship was too, right? Pre-COVID, she'd been socially awkward. Post-COVID, she was rude.

Pierre felt a twinge of sadness. She was avoiding him or the hassle of friends. For some, it was easier not to try. Why bother if you'll just be dumped for "better friends?"

"Hey, Nicole! Want to take a walk before class?" Pierre called after her. Maybe he hadn't gotten the idea of secrecy. He was smiling at her as he got up from the table. He was at her side with his empty plate in a jiffy. Must be those quarterback quick steps. Wow, he was one of the considerate ones. He'd actually picked up his plate and taken it to the trash bin. She was impressed. Really.

Pierre sanitized his hands and offered his fist for a fist-bump-wiggle-woosh!

She stared at his fist, then held his gaze for a second.

He raised a brow, daring her to be silly.

Her lips twitched, and she let out a big breath, finally relaxing her shoulders. She hadn't known until that second that the tension was building in her trapezoids.

He continued to wait for a fist-bump wiggle-woosh!

She did it! Their laughter rang out in the cafeteria, bringing curious glances from tables nearby. They made their way up the stairs out of the cafe and towards an adjoining building.

"What class do you have first?" Pierre asked Nicole.

"English," she said, now more relaxed around him. Despite her seeming aloofness, she was glad to have Pierre as a friend. She'd find Malie at the library later.

Nicole stepped out of the immediate pathway. They stood by a water fountain. It was not on the main thoroughfare in and out of the cafe stairway. There were fewer kids coming and going there. No one drank from the old-school water fountains anymore. Post-COVID, even the filtered fountains were avoided.

"I'm good, we're good," she said. "I'm just surprised. You've never spoken to me outside of gym class."

"Well, yesterday was a life-changing day for me," he said.

She agreed, laughing.

"I'm going to need to adjust to having two buddies on campus," she said.

"That's right, you do. My name is Buddy!" he said, laughing and pointing at his chest. His white t-shirt had flowers reading "May Day is Lei Day Momi Elementary."

She studied the pre-COVID date on it wistfully. He looked down at his shirt, too. "Oh, I know. Those were good ole days."

She nodded. "My life used to be delineated and marked by pre- and post-COVID life. Now, it'll forever be pre- and post-SC life with you and Malie," Nicole said.

"Right?" Pierre said. "SC! I like it." He was smiling. If this were a Manga book, sunbeams would be shining from his eyes, kawaii.

She blocked her eyes. "You're too bright. I need sunscreen just standing next to you!"

Pierre said. "Oops! Shushhh, Nic!"

"Wow, dial down the shine! How are you so radiant?" Nicole said.

She tried not to laugh again. Pierre's personality was uplifting— a small smile tickled her lips.

"Has anyone ever told you that you have great lips?" Pierre appraised her.

Coming back to school without a mask was amazing. N-95 masks were preferred in small, closed spaces, but the mandate was gone.

"Hey, are you flirting with me?" she said.

"Just appreciating you. We need to do that for each other!" Pierre said.

"Oh my god! You sound like my granddads! That's all they tell me: 'Nicole, appreciate yourself and others always!' Her voice mimicked Granddad John's low voice.

"They're right!" Pierre said.

"Pierre, I web-searched our Manaful World date, January thirteenth. It freaked me out."

"What? Why?" Pierre scratched his chin.

"Don't you remember four years ago there was a false missile alert?" She was bouncing on her feet now. "The same day we 'Clubbed'!"

"Holy smokes! That's right. I was in LA. We were scared as heck, especially for Grandpa and Tūtū. My mom kept their farewell voice message. We kept playing phone tag with them after the false alert."

"Mom was blubbering till she got to me," Nicole recalled her own experience, at ease with Pierre's recounting.

"It was frustrating trying to catch each other, so my grandparents left a VM."

"After she got me, dead silence."

"Sort of a shock. My mom was like that too. Grandma and I did all the talking."

"I think I felt ice in my stomach."

"Still makes me cry, remembering what we all thought would be their last message. Tūtū was frantic and crying. Grandpa was very calm, almost Zen-like." Pierre said.

"Wow."

"Thanks for bringing this up."

"Really?"

"Not being a sassybutt."

"Just glad it turned out to be a false alarm,"

"I'm going to go home and hug Tūtū. I'm going to tell her how I'd appreciated her and Grandpa's VM. It had been a lifeline having their voices, thinking it was the last time connecting with them. God!"

He blinked the tears from his eyes and waved his hands in front of his face. "Grandpa died that year, too. 2018 was just the crappiest year ever. That is, 'til COVID came. Thousands of kids lost their Grandpas when COVID hit. Oh, my heart!"

Nicole held his hand. "Hey, do you want to visit your counselor? I'm sorry about your Grandpa and for bringing up the alert. I didn't think about an out-of-State family's point of view. Geewiz!" She slapped her forehead, sparking a teary-eyed laugh from Pierre.

"How crazy that SC was formed on the false missile alert day?" Pierre shook his head.

"I know! I'll never forget January thirteenth, 2018!" She sighed and took a deep breath.

Pierre patted her shoulder. "Me too, girl. Me too! Breathe. Breathe." He was really good with that.

The first period bell rang, and he motioned 'text me' with his fingers. They hugged and he ran to class. She stared after him, still agog that she had two buddies here.

It was a lonely time at middle school last year—a lonely everything. Virtual learning was a fudged-up time for everyone. Kids didn't turn on their cameras. Many were locked in their homes depressed. Distance learning took on a whole new meaning during the pandemic. She'd been distanced from school, teachers, peers, and her sanity. That's why the Granddads intervened with their weekly "check-on Nicole" visits.

She shook the sad memories away. Thinking of the Secret Club instead, a small smile formed on her lips again. Wow, she was grinning. Even her eyes smiled. This was ra

CHAPTER 20

Earth
Wright Middle School
January 15, 2022

Nicole sat in her English class a few minutes later. As her teacher took roll call, she flashed back to that fateful morning of the false missile alert in Honolulu.

It was Saturday morning, and her heart felt like it had stopped. Her mom had been home. Thank God. Nicole had slept in that day. She'd wished she'd slept through the whole dramatic mess. The governmental retraction that it wasn't a real alarm but an employee's "wrong button" error took too long.

Now, how about that employee? That's a different can of worms. She felt sorry for that person. He got fired. She hoped he was alright now. Nicole wouldn't wish the "wrong button" pusher's fate on anyone.

Anyway, that morning, she'd been resting in her room listening to music streaming on her laptop through her earphones. She'd been out of the loop, having missed the false ballistic missile alert.

"Nicky! Nicky!" Mom had pounded on the door.

Her frantic voice had scared Nicole so much she'd jumped. Her earphones hung from her ears, pulled out from the laptop.

Once Nicole had unlocked her door—yes, privacy was important even for seven year olds—her mom stumbled in. Kaleo had been in her yoga clothes, ready to stretch in the parlor.

She had grabbed Nicole and held her tight. She'd begun crying and mumbling through broken breaths about a warning. "I love you! I love you!" she had said as she squeezed Nicole. Her tears had dripped onto Nicole's back. Kaleo's broad, swimmer's shoulders enveloped Nicole's.

"Missile attack!" Nicole had finally understood Kaleo's teary mumbling. Kaleo had held her phone in her tight fist—Yes, her mom still had a flip phone back then. I know. She'd shown Nicole the "BALLISTIC MISSILE THREAT INBOUND TO HAWAII. SEEK SHELTER." A cold sweat had broken out over Nicole's body, and she'd stumbled backward onto her bed.

She recalls being frozen for she didn't know how long. "What do we do?" Nicole had asked her mom.

"I don't know," Mom had whispered.

Nicole hadn't been sure why her mom's voice in that instant changed. Now serene. Kaleo had been frantically screaming her name and pounding on her door minutes ago. Yet, at that moment, her mom looked calm. She peered into her daughter's eyes and nodded. It was as if Kaleo had come to accept death, appreciating Nicole's presence.

Her mom held her as they lay on the bed. It was the warmest Nicole had ever felt. If the world were to end, it was alright because they'd be together.

Queensrÿche's "Silent Lucidity" played on repeat from Nicole's still-running streaming service. The singer's haunting, deep voice prophetically sang about their very situation. Blame Uncle Nick for the deep, retro music preference. The words were serendipitous. The magnitude of the song had never been more poignant than at that moment.

Thirty minutes later, Kaleo got a text that it was a false alarm. They had still laid there, crying, even after they knew it had been a mistake. They'd been relieved and grateful for each other.

"Beep!"

"Beep!"

The yellow rubbish truck lifted the fragrant dumpster bins outside of Ms. Taniguichi's window. The English class was one of the fortunate ones to be situated by the dumpsters. Not. The truck logo read "Call Us. Let's talk trash!"

Hee hee. That's funny. Nicole laughed as tears welled in her eyes, remembering her seven-year-old self.

"Nicole?"

"Nicole?"

Ms. Taniguchi was calling her. She pointed at something for Nicole to read on the smart TV in front of the class. The bell rang. Ms. Taniguchi sighed, dismissing them. Nicole was saved by the bell.

Chapter 21

Earth
Wright Middle School Library
January 15, 2022

After school that day, Malie waited outside of the library. "Bye, Ms. Heluhelu!" she said to the librarian. She did a jig, patting the new books in her bag.

Buzz. Buzz.

Text from Pierre: Where are u?

Malie: Outside the library. U?

Pierre: Just finished tutoring. Headed your way. B right there.

Malie: K.

Pierre: C u soon.

Malie laughed at the chatter of green parrots on the Spanish tiles of the rooftops. The sun's afternoon rays reflected off the white stucco, blinding her.

"Hey, Malie!" Pierre greeted her.

He wore faded jeans, old tennis shoes, and a white Momi Elementary t-shirt. He brushed his styled, dark hair back. They stared at each other for a second, unsure how to act. He broke out into a big grin, opening his arms. She giggled and they hugged.

"Glad I caught you!" he said, releasing her and exhaling a big "Whoo".

He'd ran from his study hall. She stepped back and pointed downstairs where her mom would be picking her up.

"Gee, take a breather," Malie said "What building did you come from?"

"I was on the upper campus," he said. "It's downhill from there, but I didn't want to miss you."

"I wouldn't have ditched."

Pierre didn't reply. A lot of people didn't show up. He wouldn't take her for granted. They walked leisurely down to the driveway. Parents idled in their cars.

"Today was a long day—Fridays." He said.

"I know. Whenever you want the weekend to start, the day drags on."

"Well, no paperback," Pierre pointed to her hands.

"I have two new ones," she patted her backpack, "but I'm trying not to stick my nose in a book. I will think of the SC instead. Books shouldn't be a crutch!"

"The SC, huh?" Pierre laughed. "Nicole said that too."

"What can I say? Great minds think alike."

"It's okay to carry around your book still." Pierre said.

"Yes, but talking to you is better. What time's your ride home?" Malie said.

"Oh, I'm not headed home for a few hours. Got football practice soon. We're in the DMW Football Champs tomorrow!"

"That's right. Congrats!" Malie said. They fist-bump-wiggle-wooshed.

"We're going to win! It's all in the mindset," he said.

"I believe in you, Pierre. I'm glad we're friends," Malie said.

"Agreed. Nicole mentioned not having buddies here before SC," Pierre said.

Malie nodded. Well, her books were her buddies, but those don't count.

"SC nightly meeting tonight?" Pierre asked.

"Yes! You might be tired after practice. We don't have to talk for long." Malie said.

"No worries," Pierre said.

Buzz. Buzz.

"That's Mom. She's around the corner." Malie looked at the notification. "Gotta run!"

Pierre saluted her and signaled "text me" on his phone.

"Okay!" she said as she left.

When the car pulled up, Pierre waved to the Hawaiian-Caucasian woman in the driver's seat. It was a white Chevy convertible. Malie waved again as they left and he smiled back.

CHAPTER 22

Earth
The Secret Club's respective homes
January 15, 2022
7:30 p.m.

"I like FaceTime more than texting and phone calling," Pierre said.

"This is a phone call," Nicole said.

"Phone with video," Malie said.

"You know what I mean, girls!" Pierre said.

"I call The Secret Club's second meeting to order!" Malie said. A rubber ducky squeaked three times.

"Wow." Nicole said.

"Malie's building her repertoire," Pierre said.

"Hee hee, that's right, Pierre," Malie said.

"First topic up for discussion is telling our moms about Manaful World and our Secret Club," Pierre said.

"No way," Nicole said.

"Dissention strikes!" Malie mock-gasped.

"I'm not seconding that!" Nicole said.

"I do!" Malie said. "I don't like keeping secrets from my mom."

"Then why the heck are we called The Secret Club!" Nicole said.

"Just our moms, no one else, Nicole, please." Pierre said. "Puh-lease!"

"Not grandparents, dads, or classmates," Malie said, "Just SC mom's."

"SC moms," Pierre said.

"Ugggghhhh!" Nicole said.

"How about a compromise?" Malie said.

"Huh? What kind?" Nicole said.

Telling the truth didn't bother her. Her mom might call the granddads and double the weekly check-ins. She loved her granddads but hated their therapeutic interventions.

"There's no way to avoid therapy in your family," Malie shared her wisdom.

"Yes, I know, and it's been necessary for not just me," Nicole said. She frowned, contemplating COVID's effect on teens worldwide.

"Here it is. We tell our moms we've created a fantasy storytelling club. All that happens in Manaful is open to share with them." Malie said.

"That's a good idea," Pierre piped up. "The Mana blows my mind still. Our moms wouldn't believe it's real anyway."

"So, they know we're buddies?" Nicole pursed her lips.

"Yes." Malie said. "Mom asked about Pierre this afternoon."

"They'll be happy about us." Nicole said. "I've been a little anti-people since March 2020."

Pierre teased Nicole, "Just a little antisocial?"

"Me too," Malie said.

"Books don't count as people," Nicole said.

"I know!" Malie said, blushing.

"Football has kept me together mentally. Yet, I wouldn't trade our SC for anything!" Pierre smiled at them. He put his phone on his lap and made a heart with his hands.

"Awwwww!" Nicole and Malie said.

"Jinx!" The girls laughed.

"Back to the 'Mom Moments' tonight," Malie said, clapping her hands.

"Gee, look at you, all commanding and reining us in," Nicole said.

"Mom Moment?" Pierre said.

"Yes, we vote and resolve now to have Mom Moments tonight. We reveal our friendship and fantasy storytelling club," Malie said. Her voice was confident and clear.

Pierre winked at her.

Nicole put her phone on her lap and wiggled her hands above her head in the sign language clapping sign.

"Motion up for vote!" Pierre said.

"I vote, yes, to both. The Drs. Fines' double intervention will be forthcoming, but what the heck!" Nicole said.

"Second!" Pierre and Malie said.

"Would the granddads meet with me?" Pierre said. Maybe he could talk things out with them, after getting his parents' permission? As gay grandparents and psychologists, they were in a unique place. From Nicole's talking about her granddads, Pierre already liked them.

"Yes! Let's set that up. Better they focus on you than me. Ha ha!" Nicole said.

"That's beautiful, Pierre. Now, back on track. We're decided? Pinky promise?" Malie said.

"Pinky promise." Pierre said.

He smiled, remembering doing that with his best friends in California. Initially, it was difficult leaving them. Things happen for a reason. He had the girls now.

"Who does a pinky promise anymore? We're eleven, not seven." Nicole said.

"I say we text, 'It's done.' when we've finished telling our moms," Pierre said.

"It's done... sounds so dramatic, like a spy mission." Nicole laughed.

"It's done, Sir!" Nicole says again in a serious low secret agent voice. She fell back onto her bed with laughter.

"Yes! Like that, minus the 'Sir' part." Malie laughed too.

"High-five, gals. We're set. I motion to end this meeting. I've got my Mom Moment and a game tomorrow," Pierre said.

"Hey, that's my line," Malie said. "Well, not the game part."

"Don't step on the gal's toes, Pierre!" Nicole said. "Best wishes on your football champs, too."

"Sorry, Malie. Mahalo about the game. I'm excited. Going to tell Mom now." Pierre waved at them.

They waved back.

Click. Click. Click.

CHAPTER 23

Storyteller in Papakōlea, Hawaiʻi
January 15, 2022

"Aunty Ellie, I hate cliffhangers!" Ari said.

"Are your lunch bag and clothes ready for tomorrow?" Aunt Ellie asked. "Your parents have another business event. Sleepover, again!"

"I know. Miss them. More storytelling would help. I'll prepare my lunch and clothes later," Ari said.

Aunt Ellie said, "No, but nice try." She pointed to the kitchen.

"Oh!" Ari got up and did the hokey-pokey. They'd been at it since this afternoon. Aunt Ellie was in stitches watching her. Ari got a fruit cup from the fridge and prepped a PB and J sandwich. Homelunch was something her aunt insisted Ari make to save time for study hall during lunch. She played video games during that period instead. Her secret. After packing lunch, Ari laid out a polka-dotted A-line dress with earrings and matching socks for tomorrow.

"Okay, I'm done! Back to the SC-reveal to the moms?" Ari plopped back onto the recliner.

"Hey, sit nicely. You'll break that poor old chair," Aunt Ellie said.

"Oops. About the SC?" Ari said.

"How would you like things to go?" Her aunt asked.

"Huh? How would I know? You're the storyteller." Ari put her hands on her hips.

"Stretch your brain. Make predictions," Aunt Ellie said.

"Okay. All of the mothers think the kids are crazy and forbid their friendship," Ari said.

"That would be the end of the story," Aunt tsked.

"You said to predict."

"Thank you. Interesting effort, young lady." Aunt Ellie said. "Half your sentence hit the mark. The Moms. They think about a lot of things."

CHAPTER 24

Earth
January 15, 2022 between 6-8:45 p.m.
Secret Club Moms

Nicole's Mom

Kaleo Moku was in her home office alone. She stared at her daughter's happy face in a group *ussie*, standing between her two granddads, Court and John. The image was her favorite desktop wallpaper.

"What's happening in your life, my child?" she spoke to Nicole's image.

"How can I help you adjust to these preteen years?" Kaleo wasn't sure she was parenting Nicole correctly.

Kaleo sighed. "Should I buy you video games? Should I sign you up for ballet or swimming classes?"

Many programs were closed due to the COVID crisis. Some athletic clubs were open for those who have been vaccinated. Nicole took all her shots and boosters.

"Need more time with the Granddads?"

During the lockdown, she'd worried about Nicole's mental health. She was still worried.

Maybe we should get a dog. The responsibility of a pet is a great one for children.

At breakfast time that day, Kaleo had mentioned a courthouse internship. "Uncle Nick is very busy as a prosecutor. Yet, he suggested you do an unofficial internship there. It would be good for you." Nicole's big "No way!" wasn't a surprise.

Timing is everything. She'd try again soon.

Kaleo laughed at herself. It was better than weeping. The COVID lockdown had put a strain on their bond.

"There is such a thing as too much togetherness," Kaleo said. Kaleo's mild OCD clashed with Nicole's "I'll clean it later" mantra.

Working at home is a boon and a drain. A boon financially, as many people sought legal services online now. A hardship because who wants their mom always underfoot?

When school returned, first part-time, then full-time, Nicole had been ecstatic. "Let me out of here!" her eyes said. Kaleo didn't take offense.

* * *

Pierre's Mom

At football practice that evening, Shelly Martin watched her son Pierre. He dug himself out of the pile of muddy jerseys. Champs were tomorrow.

"Congrats!" one of the other parents said.

"Yes, thank you," Shelly replied.

"Your boy is going places!" another parent said.

"He's sooo cute. Could you help us get his autograph?" Three preteen DMW League cheerleaders ran up to Shelly.

"Sure, let him settle down and hydrate," Shelly said.

"Hey, Shelly! Do you, Gabe, and Pierre want to come over for dinner tomorrow after Champs?" One of the other football mothers smiled at Shelly.

It would've been a good idea, especially since Chloe was a great chef.

Pierre made his way to his parents. Gabe ran towards his wet, muddy son.

"Raincheck, Chloe? My mom's planned something special for our boy. Thanks, though. I love your cooking, girl! I'll text you later." Shelly smiled at her friend with gratitude. She then turned as her husband grabbed their son.

"My boy! That's my boy!" Gabe shouted and lifted Pierre up over his shoulders. His son wasn't a little guy anymore. Still, Gabe used his kickboxing-master muscles, carrying his son around like he weighed less than a sack of potatoes.

Shelly laughed. "Put him down, Gabe! I want to hug him too! Don't hurt yourself. Save your congrats for tomorrow."

Pierre laughed, too, and shook his head at his parents' demonstrative love. It's no wonder he was a hugger too. Gabe put him down. Shelly opened her arms with a 'give me some' gesture.

"No, Mom, I don't want to get your outfit dirty," he said, peering down at her yellow sunflower-printed romper. Mom was a very girly girl when she wasn't in her banker business suit.

"Oh, get over here!" She'd kept her arms open and they embraced.

"I saw Sawyer's mom, Aunt Chloe, speaking with you just now. Are we going to their house for dinner tomorrow after Champs?"

"Oh, Buddy, about dinner at Sawyer's. I don't think so," Gabe said. He was a wise husband. He'd read his wife's frown and negative shaking of her head about dinner at Sawyer's. No husband wants to be in the dog house.

"Mom, please?" Pierre wiggled.

"Tūtū made a special dinner for you, using her garden veggies. Plus, she handcrafted Grandpa's dumplings you love," Shelly said.

Tūtū went overboard sometimes for her only grandchild. Who could blame her? Generosity and Aloha were part of her ʻohana's way of life.

Her parent's organic garden fed their entire lane in Mānoa Valley. Tūtū had donated to those in need during the COVID lockdown and has continued to do so. Admittedly, during the pandemic, many people were jobless, appreciating free fresh veggies.

"Oh, I forgot," he said with chagrin, "She was sewing my lei yesterday and creating a little feast earlier this morning."

Pierre loved his Tūtū above all others. Whenever she asked how he was doing inside, he guessed that she knew about his homosexuality. She told him stories of her māhū cousins growing up. In their Hawaiian culture, which he loved—agender individuals had been valued since Pre-Christianity old Hawaiian times.

Coach Jackson approached the Martin family. "Yes! Yes! He had a great scrimmage! Tomorrow we'll smash those Tantalus Tarantulas!" Pierre hid his wince at Coach's imagery.

"This boy is going all the way, Shelly!" Coach said, "Get ready for those private school recruiters!"

Shelly sighed with resignation. They'd already started to hound the family. This list included private high school recruiters, collegiate scouts, and pro flag football league managers. Was she getting ahead of herself with her worries for Pierre? What to do about her talented son? She sighed again.

Soon they'll have another child to raise. She rubbed her secret baby bump again and said, "Heaven help us!"

* * *

Malie's Mom

That night, Pili Manu came off the hospital floor exhausted and Personally Protected to the hilt. The cool antiseptic hospital corridors gave her chills daily. The morgue had been filled to the brim at the peak of the COVID lockdown. They'd rented freezer trucks as a make-shift crematorium for deceased patients due to the overflow of death. Morbid. Pili shuttered at the memories of those days between 2020 and 2021.

She came back to the present with the ping of the elevator and shuffled into the empty box. It was eight p.m. She arrived at the employees' parking lot. Beep! She shut her car alarm down and, upon turning on the engine, asked Siri to call Malie.

"Hey, Mom!" Malie answered on the second ring. There was a nervous energy in her voice.

"Coming home now, Sweetie. Are you alright?"

"Oh, I was on the phone with some friends earlier," Malie chirped.

"The one I saw today when I picked you up during my break?" Pili asked as she waited at a stop light.

"Yes," Malie answered but didn't elaborate.

The light changed. "What are they like? Boys, girls, or non-binary?" Pili inquired. She was an open-minded mother. She encourages Malie to accept and welcome all kinds of people into her life with love.

"I've made friends with a boy and a girl in my grade," Malie said. Beep. Beep. Beep.

Pili slowed down, switching lanes to make room for an eighteen wheeler reversing out of a grocery store. The big hauler entered the road with the aplomb of an experienced commercial driver's license holder.

"Tell me about your new pals when I get home, okay? Love you," Pili said.

"Love you," Malie said before they disconnected.

Pili felt the streetlights and headlights reflecting across her skin. There were white and red beams propelling her home. The stars shone overhead, accompanied by a full moon.

"Siri, turn on soothing piano elevator music." The rhythmic sounds came through the speakers, adding a mellowness to her cool drive home.

Pili's patient load at Stanton Hospital was still heavy as the Omicron numbers increased. What was the best part of her shift? The end. Her work used to be joyous, as she'd helped pregnant mothers and their babies. She'd comfort them when their newborns were delivered prematurely. Now, each pandemic day of ventilating and praying took its toll.

Pili looked at the dashboard time: 8:45 p.m. "I hope my girl had a good day," Pili said under her breath. ETA, five minutes. It was Tako Friday. Note: it's tako not taco. Her girl loves homemade octopus soup. Cooking together was a more successful mother-daughter adventure than watching TV. Putting a smile on Malie's face made the whole day 'all good'.

* * *

The three mothers, while alone, sing to themselves about life.

The Moms' Song:
Pili:

"Give me one day with all my checklists completed.
Help me, Kimo, my dearly departed!
IRS, PMS, or EMS, they're my life in a looping cycle of stress.
Three-letter acronyms, though tiny, cause so much distress.
Yet, being a mommy is something to treasure.
Finding joy in simple pleasures.
I crave a smile, a hug, a 'How was your day?'
After those, there's no room for dismay.
I'm simply taking it as it goes, as it goes, as it goes."

Shelly:

"Settled in for the night,
My guys are settled in for the night.
Pre-game playoff run-downs at dinner.
Win or Loss tomorrow; he's always a winner.
If only they knew what was happening within me.
Thank God for this cathartic melody.
Heating pads, swollen cankles, and sensitive breasts.
Is it safe to birth a child during pandemic unrest?
I'm just taking it as it goes, as it goes, as it goes."

Kaleo:

"The bandwidth isn't strong enough.
Working from home requires that I be tough.
I'm sick of my videos buffering.
Building a business online can be suffering.
My brother Nick says, "We could use you at the D.A.'s."
I've been there, done that—I don't miss those court days.
Working from home can be priceless.
I enjoyed Nicole's presence.
I just take it as it goes, as it goes, as it goes."

Chapter 25

Earth
Jan. 15, 2022
9-10 p.m.
Mom Moments at each of the Secret Club members' homes

Nicole's Mom Moment:

Nicole knocked on her mom's open office doorway. "I put away the clothes, Mom. Did you eat the baked potatoes and salmon I left in the heater drawer?"

Kaleo swiveled her chair around, resting her pen on her chin, and glanced up from her legal pad.

"Oh, no. No dinner yet. Skipped it again. Will you switch the heater off and let the meal cool, please? Later, put it away. Alright?"

"Mom, you demand that I take care of myself and eat three squares a day. You must do the same! 'Positive role modeling is good parenting,' remember like Granddads say?" Nicole motioned quotes, mimicking Granddad John's serious voice.

"Gosh!" Kaleo pushed air out of her mouth. Worrying came naturally to Nicole via her mother. The apple doesn't fall far and all that. Kaleo had tax season around the corner and needed to clear out her current dockets.

"Mom, ready for our nightly talk? It's nine p.m." Nicole moved onto the loveseat in the corner of Kaleo's office—a sweet little window nook. Outside, the Honolulu City lights shone from their twenty-third-floor condo. Nicole missed Granddad's two-story with the fun backyard and huge in-laws' suite over their garage. It was cozier and larger than their condo. Plus, she missed their warm daily presence. She complained about the weekly "check-ins," but she missed being near them whenever she wanted.

"Wow, nine o'clock already? I'm beat. How was your day?" Kaleo swiveled her chair to face her daughter. She rolled closer and rested her feet on her daughter's lap when Nicole patted her thighs. Kaleo appreciated their nightly massage/bonding time.

"Ahhhhhhh! That's good!" Kaleo relaxed as Nicole pushed her thumbs into her soles, hitting those acupuncture points.

"Mom, I have a story to tell you. You can't interrupt until I'm done. Got it?" Nicole kept her tone mellow. She breathed in and stayed calm, imagining her two pals sharing the same moment right then.

Kaleo perked up, her lawyer intuition kicking in. What's this about? Is Nic in trouble? She tried not to imagine the worst. She took a deep breath as well and forced those thoughts out of the way.

Nicole steadied herself like an Olympic diver, ready to leap off the platform.

Her daughter was focused and in a zone; this was a new, self-collected Nicole. Kaleo raised her brows and pulled her feet off from Nicole's lap.

Nicole moved her hands face-up onto her upper thighs and closed her eyes for a few seconds. She opened her eyes and looked her mom straight in the eye.

Wow, who was this child?

"Mom, yesterday before gym class, I made two new friends," Nicole said.

"That's good for you; it's been a while," Kaleo said.

It had been. COVID locked down the world and many preteen friendships.

"I know, Mom. It's been hard these past years," Nicole sighed, determined not to lose her nerve.

"Tell me about your new friends," Kaleo refocused Nicole, not wanting her daughter to take a downturn. Stealing back one's faith in oneself and others after these past two COVID years is a goal for everyone.

"We created a fantasy storytelling secret club," Nicole smiled.

"Oh? That sounds fun," Kaleo said. Was it like Dungeons and Dragons? Oh, that's cool.

"Yes, Mom, it's fabulous! I love it. In our story world, we leaped through the Shimmery Wall portal and left this Earth. We entered another world of brown, magical dwarves who speak telepathically and molecularly travel with magic from place to palace!"

Nicole's speech picked up. She knew she was blabbering and speaking too fast. She couldn't help the tumbling of thoughts.

Like throwing up when you're got a stomach bug—your body can't stop the actions. It's involuntary.

Kaleo reached for Nicole's hand, sensing her daughter needed to calm down again. Nicole's pulse had picked up. Kaleo rubbed her thumb over it.

"Nicole, you're excited. That's great, but there's no rush to tell me about that world. Relax. We're not going anywhere. Take your time," Kaleo soothed.

Nicole took a deep breath. Okay, she could do this. She closed her eyes again and returned to the zone.

"We explored their Manaful world—that's what it's called. In our storytelling, I mean, we explored Manaful," Nicole corrected herself. "I made really good friends: Pierre and Malie, from my school."

Kaleo smiled and squeezed Nicole's hand. She liked the light in her daughter's eyes. She hoped these children were positive associations. A mother could never be too sure.

"We're called the Secret Club because we promised to keep our Manaful World story a secret," Nicole continued.

Kaleo gave Nicole a high five with her other hand. "Thank you for breaking your secret pact and telling me."

Nicole continued, "You're welcome. We'd voted to make an exception for our mothers. It's not healthy to keep things from one's mother." Kaleo brought her hand to her heart. Awwwww, that's sweet. "Yes, we voted on that tonight," she said.

"Voted?" Kaleo raised her brow. This was new. Kids these days come up with all kinds of role-playing.

"Yes, we have fun meetings via our mobiles. We make motions, vote, and call things to order and closure," Nicole laughed. "Well, Malie leads us."

"Really? There are just three people in your Secret Club?"

"Yep. Pierre's warm and generous; Malie clever and sweet." Nicole smiled.

Kaleo contemplated how else to respond to her daughter's revelations. She enjoyed Nicole's new enthusiasm. She wanted those other kids to be kind and loving presences in her daughter's life. It was heartwarming. It was an answer to her prayers. She'd talk to the Granddads later about how to handle the fantasy group. They may have some ideas about it. For now, she'd be gracious and easygoing. It was a blessing to have psychologists in one's family.

"Thank you for sharing that, Nicole." Kaleo kept a nonjudgmental and sympathetic voice.

Being a lawyer helped when one needed to assuage and soothe another. She couldn't fool her daughter. Did she even think she could?

"Mom, don't use your 'calming my client' voice!" Nicole laughed.

"Can't get much by you, huh?" Kaleo laughed too. "Alright, I'll tell you straight: I'm not sure how to take the world-leaping stories. Yet, I'm pleased that you've made good pals. I hope you continue to have positive, strong bonds."

Nicole smiled. She'd take that. Mission accomplished.

"Woooosh!" Nicole felt great. She wanted to break out her phone, but her mom didn't like phones during their bonding time.

"I wasn't sure if you'd think I'm crazy, Mom." Nicole made a funny face.

"Well, you have a great imagination," Kaleo said. There's nothing wrong with that.

"Mom, you're not going to make me tell the Granddads, are you?" Nicole grumbled.

Kaleo hedged, "Well, it is a new avenue for you." Mom and daughter had an eye duel. Brows up and down. Eyes squinching and widening. Nicole lost and blew a raspberry.

"I knew it! I told the SC you'd make me do more therapy!" Frowning, she pointed at her mother.

"Everything's confidential between therapists and clients," Kaleo said.

"They're not my therapists, Mom!" Sitting between the granddads as they listened and held her hands was intense. It was a psychological triage.

"It's just like normal weekly check-ins, Nicole." Kaleo's voice took on the 'The Law' tone.

Nicole stood up and was about to stomp out.

Kaleo grabbed her daughter's hand, pulling her back. "Hey, where's my post-bonding hug? Never close the day on bad terms." Kaleo raised her brows. Hugs were good therapy too.

"Okaaaaayyy!" Nicole said, forgetting her ire and sinking into her mom's arms.

"Good night, Mom." Nicole nuzzled her mom's hair bun. The gray streaks blended with the dark brown tendrils falling about her face. Her mom was a cloud of fragrances, jasmine, baby powder, and peppermint.

"Good night, my little one!" Kaleo kissed her daughter's kinky hair.

"I'm not a little one anymore!" Nicole mumbled as she dashed off to her room. She was eager to send off her 'mission accomplished' text. She wanted to be the first one that had finished the job. Alone in her room, she texted the Club.

"It's done."

Once it was sent, she hoped the others' Mom Moments went as well as hers did.

* * *

Malie's Mom Moment

Pili Manu stood over her tako soup pot beside her daughter, Malie. They put their noses side by side over the pot. The steam filled their kitchen with oceanic aromas. The Audubon bird clock peeped the pretty sounds of the red-winged blackbird. It's nine o'clock at night.

"Aahhhhh! Yummmmm!" they moaned together as their stomachs rumbled.

"Tell me about your day," Pili said. She was curious about Malie's new friends. She didn't want to push the subject. How can she be subtle, though, when Malie's been alone for years? Books are good, but they aren't your friend. Malie would disagree with that.

"I had a wonderful day, Ma, and that's outside of my books," Malie said.

Pili put her hands on her hips. "Really?" What would her daughter do without sweet librarian Heluhelu? Wright Middle

School scored when they hired that lovely teacher a few years ago. When her daughter entered middle school, Pili was worried about Malie's transition to a new library. Since she could walk, libraries were her daughter's safe zone or home away from home. Every child needed to have that. Having that safe place on campus was cause for celebration.

"Malie, stir that pot so the meat doesn't sit on the bottom to burn," she said. Scrubbing burnt meat from a pot was not fun.

"Is it time to mix in the seaweed?" Malie asked. The seasonings and greens were the yummiest once they'd soaked and gotten soft in the salty soup base. It was like marinating your barbeque vegetable skewers before throwing them on the grill. The tako needed to soak up that juicy marinade.

"Sure, put the seaweed in. I'll check on the rice." Pili moved to the back porch table where the ceramic rice pot cooked the brown and white grain mix.

"The stories on TV and the web have nothing on my new secret club, Mom." Malie tried to build context. Malie was often in her dreamy book worlds; she brought up subjects out of the blue and out of context. Pili was used to it, but she appreciated Malie trying to think about other people.

"Secret Club, huh?" Pili said. "Tell me the whole story instead of the middle part first."

"Oh, yes, from the top, right?" Malie laughed.

"From the top," Pili said.

"I made two new friends yesterday," Malie frowned. "They were in my class all along. Yesterday was my first time hanging out with them."

"Oh? Two friends from which class?" Pili asked. She was proud that her daughter had looked a peer in the eyes or even had a conversation. Pre-COVID, Malie was so quiet that her teachers often emailed home: "Malie is not fully participating in her collaborative groups." She would give monosyllabic responses in class, but she'd do her part of her team's labors. She wasn't the weakest link, per se, just the quietest one.

That she "hung out" with peers tickled Pili.

Malie tried to elucidate her thoughts, always tougher with adults. "My new friends are a boy and a girl from the sixth grade like me."

"You've never spoken to them before, but they've been in your class since August?" Pili asked.

"Just gym; Ms. Marco."

Wow, maybe the class was really large? Maybe the gym teacher allowed Malie to read her book during class on a side bench? No, she doubted the latter was the case. Gym is about kinesthetics and putting the rec book away. It was rec body time, not rec reading time.

"I don't talk in classes," Malie admitted.

Why was Pili not surprised?

"The other day, before gym class, we bumped into each other and started talking," Malie continued.

"Oh? About what?" Pili asked, grabbing dishes to set the table. Malie relaxed more when her mom moved about doing her thing.

"We sat together and began storytelling." Malie's heart sped up. Maybe this half-truth thing wasn't the right way to go. Would Mom believe her if she told her they leapt through a Shimmery Wall that appeared out of nowhere into another dimension? A whole new world? She straightened up and took a deep breath. She can do this! She hadn't opened her phone, but she'd felt it vibrate in her butt pocket. She knew it was the SC. One of them had accomplished their mission. Now it was her turn. She moved to the dining room table, taking the forks from her mom's hands.

"We'll be fine, mom."

"You love stories; your classmates have read the same ones as you?" Pili smiled as Malie finished setting up the table.

"Oh, no, Mom, we made one up. We created a secret fantasy world and a club to protect our stories for just us," Malie spilled out.

Pili blinked. That was a lot to take in. She noticed her daughter clattered the ceramic coffee mugs together as she held them.

Pili grabbed the mugs from Malie, placing them down. Malie laughed and thanked her.

"Why are you nervous? Was it upsetting? Did they offend you?" Pili said.

"I'm not upset. It's exciting, Mom. We time traveled. We met dwarves. They had magical powers!" Malie laughed as it all tumbled out. Oh, no. Time to dial it back.

"You made up fantasy stories with each other?" Pili's voice went up in surprise.

Oh, she didn't believe her daughter. This was good. Malie could run with that.

"Yes, exactly, Mom. We're a fantasy storytelling club. They're my new besties!"

Pili raised her brows when she'd said the "besties" part.

Oh, maybe Malie went overboard on that part.

It was true, as Malie's been in non-friends mode her entire life. With that big weight having been lifted off her shoulders, Malie smiled to herself. She watched her mom return to the kitchen to ladle soup into their bowls.

Malie did a little happy dance in place. Then, she pulled her phone from her butt pocket to check her messages. Yup! It was the SC. Nicole's "It's done." Two Mom Moments down. One to go.

She breathed in the amazing wafts of tako soup. Yummy. Before her mom could lay down the "No Mobiles at the Dinner Table" law, Malie wiggled her cell at Pili.

"We've video called twice and texted, too," She shook her phone, then put it away again when her mother frowned at it.

Pili was happy about the enthusiasm in her daughter's voice, though dinner time meant no cell phones. She smiled when Malie put her device away.

"I'm happy for your Secret Club, my dear," Pili said. "Be careful what you text, and don't forget to do your homework before spending all hours video calling!" She added in a serious tone. Pili didn't know that they'd already had their SC Nightly Meeting.

"Yeesssss, Mom," Malie sighed. She did another little dance. She got it done. That was easy. Okay, maybe not.

Pili watched her daughter dance and smile to herself. What was happening here? Should she be pleased about Malie's new pals? Is a fantasy writing club a good thing?

It's been a difficult past two years with this pandemic. Witnessing the heartbreak daily in her hospital shifts makes her appreciate little things. She was grateful for this small gift: Malie made friends. She was smiling and dancing. Here's hoping this club stays strong.

Malie excused herself to the restroom.

She texted "It's done" as soon as the door closed. Sitting on the closed toilet seat, she covered her mouth to hide her relieved giggle. Her mom had been really cool about everything. The SC had been right: Manaful World was too unbelievable for a parent to conceive. The storytelling club idea had worked. She hoped Pierre's Mom Moment was going well.

* * *

Pierre's Mom Moment

Shelly sat on her porch swing overlooking her parent's garden. The birds called to each other in the night, saying their piece. They made her smile. Mānoa Valley at nearly ten pm was a cool, breezy, and peaceful time.

After the swashbuckling adventures attending football games and practices, her banking career, and her non-profit accounting work for Grandpa and Tutu's garden, Shelly rested. She loved the fragrant night air.

She made it a habit to share the beauty of nature with her baby bump. The darkness was lit only by the stars above and the solar lanterns farther down the garden path. She left the porch light off to avoid the hovering termites.

Shelly leaned back on a pillow sideways on the swing with her legs stretched across the bench. Her feet left some space for someone to join her. The back porch door squeaked and then banged against the porch railing. The old door screws needed WD-40 oil.

Excited footsteps sped up towards the swing, then slowed down as if pulling the brakes. It was her son. He mostly ran around the house with uncontained jubilance, facing the day/night/whenever. Tonight was the night before Champs. Perhaps he was eager to share his thoughts on tomorrow's game. After helping Gabe with the dinner dishes and taking out the trash, Pierre ran to his room without a word.

"Mom?" Pierre appeared before her. He pointed to the swing, hoping to join her. He was always courteous, knowing that sometimes she didn't want company. Her 'outside at night time' was not to be interrupted. She was getting space and harmonizing with nature.

Something must be going on for him to break that unwritten Mom rule. She smiled up at him, grasped his hand to pull him closer. She pointed to the space left by her feet on the swing. He squeezed her fingers before letting go to sit there.

He harrumphed.

"Can I tell you something?"

"Sure, Babe. I have something to share with you, too. Good news, in fact." She patted her baby bump. His eyes widened. With his mouth agape, he started blubbering, "Ba ba ba wa ba ba baby?"

She laughed at him, placing his hand on the two-month-old raspberry-sized baby inside her womb.

"That's my surprise. What's yours?" She teased and nudged her still-shocked son. He took a deep breath, as if preparing for something big.

"Wow." He took his hand back and clenched the bench beneath him. "My surprise isn't as big as yours! How did this happen? Wait. Wait. I know how it happens," he laughed at himself. "Um, I mean, when did you know?"

Shelly smiled. The family had talked about having more kids pre pandemic. Things changed when everything locked down. She was surprised it took this long to conceive.

She hoped Pierre would go with the flow as he usually does. He loved people.

"Mom! Is it a boy or a girl? What month is it coming? Will I have to change doo-doo diapers?" The questions tumbled out of him, one after the other.

She laughed and nodded.

"Mom, you're a great mom, and this little one will be lucky to be in our family."

She teared up a little. It's the hormones. "That's sweet. Now, tell me what your good news is." She was eager to know what had shaken him up earlier.

"Oh, it's nothing like this. You've outdone me. It's insignificant compared to this." He nodded and stared at her belly more. He ran his hands through his hair, making it spike up due to the sweat on his forehead. He'd been nervous coming out here. Now, his sharing felt anticlimactic to him.

"Whatever you have to share isn't insignificant, Pierre. Your life is always a big deal to me."

"Thanks, Mom." He smiled. What would he do without his mom? His little sibling was indeed fortunate to be born into his family.

"Well, I made new friends." He smiled at the momentousness of it all. Wow. What an adventure they'd had. There would be more. Guaranteed.

Shelly noticed his change in mood. His happiness was contagious. Oh, this was going to be good. Did he meet a special boy? A mom knows all.

"Football guys and gals?" she said. She didn't want to push the gay topic. He'd come out of the closet in his own time. Shelly and Gabe had lifetime LGBTQIA+ family and friends.

"Oh, no, two girls from my gym class. I hadn't spoken to them before." He felt confident sharing about his new buddies. The SC came along at a good time.

"Well, that's great. You're expanding your contacts! You're never too young to network." She smiled.

"Yes, expanding." He liked that. "We're expanding our minds by creating stories, Mom."

"Oh, stories? You're in a book club?" She tried to hide the surprise in her voice. Her son was more on the street-smart side than book-smart. This was wonderful for him. A child should never stop growing.

Pierre hadn't noticed the surprised lilt to his mom's voice. He stood up and began to pace, unable to contain himself.

Shelly smiled. This was her son. He always leaned toward the kinesthetic learning side. Hands-on teaching was what she told every teacher, every year. That's what her son needed to be successful in their classes. She couldn't imagine him sitting in a book circle group. Maybe it was an interactive story group or drama club?

He turned to her, wiggling his hands and legs. Even at ten p.m., he couldn't contain his energy.

"Oh, no library is needed for us, Mom. These gals have a great imagination. We made up a time traveling fantasy world." His chest puffed up.

She found this interesting, both his description and his glee. "Really? You sat with them and made up your own adventures?" She pulled more of the story out of him. This was a new interest for her son.

A storytelling club could be fun. Since her father's death to cancer in 2018, Shelly has cherished every day with her family. She didn't waste a moment on misaligned expectations between Pierre and herself. If this club made him happy, she'd support him all the way. She'd happily meet his new friends. She'd express her appreciation for the joy they give her son. She shook her head and refocused on him. How did she run away with those thoughts? Could she blame it on the hormones? Pierre waved at her.

"Are you still with me, Mom?" He laughed and pointed at her. "You were in la-la land for a moment!"

"Yes, sorry." She laughed at herself. "You were saying something about stories?"

"Yes, there are magical dwarves who communicate telepathically," he added.

"Oh, that's very creative." She marveled at the characters he talked about. Shelly wasn't sure where her son was going with his news. She was glad he was branching out with new friends.

Different people brought varied life experiences. They helped her son grow. She was pleased he was broadening his perspectives. Not video gaming but fiction writing with friends?

"Wow, son, tell me about your new friends." Shelly kept it light, letting him take the lead on the girlfriend topic. He wasn't dating them. Eleven was too young to date, right? She didn't think he preferred girls, anyway. Hmmm. She dropped that thought. Too intense.

"Malie and Nicole are as different as two people could be in looks and personality." He laughed.

"But it's 'good' different, right?" She didn't want to insult his friends.

"Oh, yes. They make me laugh!" His eyes shone.

"I'm glad, Pierre. You deserve to have positive people who are honest with you." She didn't want to say "gay you."

"Yes, Mom, I can be the real me with them."

His immediate and obvious affection for the girls was fascinating. A little nudge wasn't out of order.

"What is the real you, Pierre? Or who is Pierre?"

"I'm not sure, Mom," he said. "Will you give me time to figure things out?"

Wow, he was trying to understand himself. She began to cry. She pushed him back a little to look at his face, started shaking her head with laughter, and then she pulled him back in. She held him tight.

"Hormones! This baby is bringing on hormones. I'm crying at the drop of a hat these days!"

"Mom, you're squeezing me. Are you okay?" He patted her back.

He was soothing her.

She pulled away and returned his gaze.

"Oh, my son, take all the time you need." She reached up, gripping his shoulders.

"I love you!" She was crying again. Oh, boy!

"It was the storytelling, Mom. I'm learning about myself when I'm in there," he said, looking off into the garden.

"In there?" Shelly asked, making him flinch and catch himself.

"In the story, I meant. It's a secret, our story. We're The Secret Club, okay, Mom?" he said.

She nodded, perhaps humoring him about the club's need for secrecy. He was grateful for her.

"Just one secret tonight, son?"

"Yes, please." He nodded.

"Are you ready for tomorrow's DMW State Champs?" She let him go and sat again, pressing her hands to her back. Oh, standing and sitting quickly hurts. Maybe she ought to return to yoga class? She used to love her yoga, but then COVID happened. She had a fave YouTuber, but in-person yoga class was fun. The energy of the class and teacher lifted her spirits. Now that in-person classes had opened up, she'd make the time. Namaste.

Pierre walked down the stairs, breathing in the plants and flowers. The darkness of the night brought a serenity he loved. He stopped his thoughts, sucking in a huge gulp of mints and the woodiness of the shrubs nearby.

She watched him, knowing the thought of football sometimes frustrated him. Shelly knew it was tied to his homosexuality.

Pierre turned around and came back to the swing. "I don't know about the game, Mom. I should be peppy and proud that we've made it this far. Winning games is good. It's just my head. I must return to my visualizations of winning, as Coach says."

With a confused sigh and an expression of uncertainty, Pierre sat on the lowest porch step. He pulled at the crabgrass trying to take over the footpath. His mom gave him silence. Let him be. That was the best part about sitting outside at Tūtū's house. Being here was easier. Just being.

"Focus on resting tonight; then, let things be." She read his mind. Mom was Zen like that.

He smiled and fist-bumped her. "Thanks, Mom. Congrats on the baby." He pointed to her stomach.

"Congrats to us all! We're blessed in more ways than one!" She laughed.

"Yeah, Mom. We are."

He stood up and lent her a hand up from the swinging apparatus.

"Hey, maybe you shouldn't sit on that." He pointed to the swinging bench. She could fall out, couldn't she? Is it safe?

"I'm good. Don't fuss. Your dad does enough for all of us. He said I shouldn't be driving. The nerve, huh?" She laughed at the ludicrous idea.

"Yeah, nuts. Can't hold you back!" He nodded, knowing his mom's determined nature.

She went inside after kissing him on the cheek. He plopped back down and swung back quickly on the chair.

"Hmmmm."

He noticed the girls had texted their "done" messages.

He typed in his own response.

"It's done. I'm last."

Beep Beep Beep

Nicole: I was first.

Malie: Second.

Pierre: Better late than never.

Nicole: True. I have to tell the Granddads about our storytelling club. Called it!

Malie: That's good. They'll keep it confidential. They love you. You're blessed.

Pierre: I'm not ready to tell her about being gay.

Malie: There's no rush. We've got you! Heart to you!

Nicole: I'm with Malie; take your time. Hey, want to come over and talk to the Granddads? You can't get better gay role models than them!

Pierre: Def. It's on my future agenda.

Malie: She's right about her granddads. I want to talk to them too.

Nicole: Thank you, yes, they are. They raised me. My family.

Pierre: Awwww, that's sweet. Strong gay men like that are beautiful. That's me one day.

Malie: Buzzzz! Wrong. That's you now. You're stronger than you give yourself credit for, Pierre.

Nicole: I second that.

Pierre: Appreciate it, gals. I'm going to hit the sack. Big game tomorrow.

Malie: Yes, DMW State Champs. Best wishes for you. Be safe and injury free.

Nicole: Yes, injury free, man! Remember Will Smith's movie *Concussion?*

Pierre: Yes, I'm aware. My coaches and parents take it seriously. Concussion protocols are no joke. I'm good.

Malie: You're always in my thoughts now. Both of you.

Nicole: That's really sweet, Malie. We just met, and you're all sappy.

Malie: It's quality over quantity of time that matters.

Pierre: True. Night, gals!

Nicole: Night.

Malie: Night.

They all disconnected. Yet, they remained connected in their hearts.

CHAPTER 26

Storyteller in Papakōlea, Hawaiʻi
January 16, 2022

It was another lazy Saturday morning at Aunt Ellie's home, where she and her niece were strolling along the yard's garden pathways. Ari checked on her cat's water. Maui had killed a bird the other night and left it near the bowl. The sight made her stomach turn; a stark reminder that Maui isn't domesticated. Feeding a stray cat for a year didn't make it non-feral. She sighed, grossed out remembering the strewn feathers and bloody carcass. She'd almost thrown up raking it up. She'd sterilized the rake and pan afterward.

Following her Aunt into the home and to the laundry room, the preteen busied herself with the washer. Ari was good at helping her aunt with daily chores. When she was younger, she'd mix the whites with color loads. That got her in trouble. Mom likes her cream blouses to remain so, not pinkish cream. Aunt was always at her aunt's home. They mostly cleaned, enjoying each other's company. Her mom and dad were busy with their jobs and volunteer work. Aunt Ellie was her "babysitter," but Ari didn't like that term. She wasn't a baby anymore!

Ari and her aunt sipped Mamaki tea on their front porch stairs, next to the aloe plants and gardenia bush. Aloe was pokey but provided quick antiseptic remedies. It wasn't as pretty nor fragrant as the gardenia, yet its utility was priceless.

The ramp up to the roadside began just a few feet away. When she was a toddler, she'd tire herself out running up and down it. All of that energy expended made it easier for Aunt Ellie to put her to sleep.

The mid-morning's glaring sun would be out soon. The lovely cool lull between eight and ten was that sweet spot in time.

"Aunty Ellie, why didn't Pierre tell his mom he's gay?" Ari asked.

"Ari, the question is not 'Why?' but 'Why not?'" Her aunt said.

"Oh! What do you mean?" Aunt Ellie had lost her. Ari squished her lips in confusion.

"Any time a child or person comes out of the closet, it is an amazing and life strengthening time." Aunt Ellie pinched Ari's cheeks. "Stop making that face."

"Life strengthening?" Ari shook her head. "It's scary not strengthening."

"Yes, it is. The person is stronger in his/her/their lives once they tell loved ones," Her aunt said. "They've held something hidden for so long. That's painful for many. Like they're hiding from life or ashamed of their life."

Aunt Ellie took a deep breath, closing her eyes.

Ari patted her aunt's shoulder. "Are you okay, Aunty?" Ari worried for her. Now, after her aunt's passionate words, she was more curious than before.

"What if their loved ones aren't accepting of them? That's not strengthening," Ari insisted.

"It's still strengthening whether people love and accept others for who they are." Aunt Ellie turned on the porch with her arms outstretched. "Hug time!"

Ari giggled, loving hug-time. Aunt Ellie had instituted it since Ari's birth.

Her aunt would hold newborn Ari in her arms and say, "Hug time!" to baby Ari. She hasn't stopped since. Ari ate it up! Aunt Ellie rested her head on Ari's soft hair, breathing in the citrusy shampoo.

"I wish all families would accept their kids no matter what," Ari said.

"Me too, Ari. Me too."

They separated, and Ari's brows furrowed as she noticed Aunt Ellie wiping a teardrop from the corner of her eye.

"So, why didn't Pierre tell his mom?" Ari couldn't drop the subject.

"Are we back to that?" Aunt Ellie raised her brows.

"Yes, you're the writer, Aunty," Ari pushed.

"True, I am. There are magical things happening in their lives, Ari," Aunt Ellie said.

"Magical things? Oh, you mean the Manafuls? Are they visiting the Hawaiian dwarves again?"

"Who said they're Hawaiian?" Aunt Ellie said.

"Their names are Hawaiian. Even their land looks like beautiful Hawai'i." Ari said.

"Let's keep an open mind, Ari. I couldn't pretend to know all things Hawaiian, nor appropriate a culture like that." Aunt Ellie's voice was very serious.

"Appropriate?" Ari perked up. She loved new words.

"Yes, appropriate, Ari." Aunt Ellie continued, "The Manafuls are pretend beings, not the true Menehune. I cannot revamp the traditions of Hawaiian families for generations like the Menehune. That would be disrespectful."

Ari's eyes brightened, and she bounced to her feet with an "Aha!" moment.

"You're doing the right thing, Aunty. I get it. Mom talks about culture stealing, too. Though I'm a little confused, because we're Hawaiian. Heck, we live on Homestead land. You couldn't get more Hawaiian than that!" Ari puffed up with cultural pride.

Aunt Ellie nodded. She stayed silent for a moment.

"I concede. The Manafuls can be Hawaiian. Let's call them a new generation of fictionally inspired Hawaiian beings rather than historically accurate Hawaiian beings?"

Ari squished her lips again, frowning. "You lost me again, Aunty."

Aunt Ellie laughed at her niece's expressive face.

"Aunty, I think we should change the subject for now. You've got to watch your blood pressure, you know?" She patted her aunt's knee. Her mom did that when her dad went off about politics. Her mom would say, "Uh-huh. Yes, dear." It is always better not to engage. Just be cool. Let the person wear themselves out.

Aunt Ellie laughed at Ari's mature yet humorous actions.

"So what's happening next for the Manafuls?"

"What would you like to happen?" Aunt Ellie asked.

"You always ask me that! I'm not the writer!" Ari laughed.

"You're excited now, aren't you? This story has stirred you inside?" Aunt Ellie asked.

"Oh my goodness, which story? How do you balance the two worlds in your head, Aunty?"

Aunt Ellie didn't respond, picking up where she left off instead. There was a lot to unpack before the real story started..

Chapter 27

Manaful World
Sandalwood Forest,
Elder Uli's Manson,
June 16, 2022
10 a.m.

"*COVID is a blessing in disguise,*" projected Elder Uli to his grandson and only living relative Maka.

Elder Uli, a Manaful family leader like Puna, watched the Secret Club on his Shimmery Walls.

He'd set up a theater room in his mansion with three portal viewers. Their sandalwood tree house mansion was chic and techy like that. The forest generated essential Mana Mist which fueled all things around them. The Mana Mist is strong in the mansion as the trees are perpetually connected to all the elements of nature in which Mana Mist exists. Ether surrounds them. Elders coexist with this powerful energy as they align with Mana.

Being magical didn't hurt when 'building' one's home. Elder Uli and Maka lived in the sandalwood treetops perhaps thirty feet above the forest floor. It was an intimidating ten thousand-square-foot abode.

Elder Uli was third in line for seat inheritance in the Elders' Council, and he craved first place.

In Manaful, wealth and power came from Mana, not money. Elder Uli was younger and less trained than Elders Puna and Alaka'i, his two nemeses in line above him. He'd come upon his Mana the "smart" way—murder.

He'd killed all of his relatives (multiple generations) and inherited their magic. Simple. Not.

When they died, Manafuls transferred their Mana to their closest living kin. At the time of death, the Mana goes through transmutation. This is when the magic in their bodies mutates into energy and ether, all things that make Mana Mist. That magical energy travels from the ground up into the eldest living relative. It was a heavily spiritual, divine process.

Not every Manaful could survive it, especially if the entire family dies or is killed. That's a lot of transmutations and power surges going into one body. Not all the magic transfers. Sometimes the transferring process kills the living kin.

After each death in his family, Elder Uli had gained most of his relatives' Mana. He'd outlived his parents, his uncles and aunts, his siblings, and his only child and daughter-in-law. The latter two were Maka's parents.

How he committed all that murder without soiling his hands was the biggest secret in their world. Every Manaful suspected he'd murdered his 'Ohana for their Mana. No one could prove it. All of Manaful either hated, feared, or wanted to be Elder Uli. Only one Manaful even remotely loved him. That was his grandson, Maka.

Now, back to the theater room where three Shimmery Walls displayed a Secret Club member in freeze frame. It's as if Elder Uli had pressed pause on three streaming videos. The Elder was studying The Secret Club. He hated Elder Puna. What will Elder Uli do to the human children?

Maka, Ikaika's soul-brother, frowned at Elder Uli's menacing tone. It was fascinating that he could never call Uli Grandpa, Grandfather, nor Gramps. It was a very formal household. Maka felt the sinister Mana of the Spirit named Lapu at work here. Maka wouldn't be part of his grandfather's plans. This choice may cost him his life.

Growing up under his grandfather's wing had been a life-time challenge. The Elder drank too much and mistreated everyone, including Maka. Yet, the Elder was all the family he had left. His grandfather hadn't always been the menacing being he was today. Maka knew that Manafuls across the land gossiped about his grandfather. They said he'd kill Maka too one day. Maka shut those rumors out. He both loved and feared his grandfather.

Is it still love if one is afraid for their life? Was it a victim's codependency? Maka tried not to go all therapist-speak about it. He spent a lot of time with Elder Puna, talking it out. Fortunately for Maka, his grandfather was too selfish to care where Maka went nowadays. Uli neglected Maka's schooling in Mana. He neglected Maka, period.

Elder Puna tried to get Maka to talk about his anxieties and fears. Elder Puna and Ikaika were the only loving dwarves in his life. He'd known them his entire life. Both of their families were nobility, so to speak. Both Maka and Ikaika were heirs, who were supposedly trained from birth in Mana.

The preteen boys would become future Elders or 'Ohana leaders. It was both an onus and honor for Maka and Ikaika.

Thankfully, Maka wasn't imprisoned at his sandalwood mansion anymore. He was free to come and go via MT, hovering, or good old hoofing it. Maka wanted to transport to Ikaika's presence now.

Elder Uli blasted a projection into Maka's head. A mental scream, loud and clear. Maka winced.

"Pay attention, Boy!"

Maka used the mental screen Puna had trained him to create. By using Source's Mana, he could shield his grandfather's penetrating and evil projections out of his head and heart. Emotions and mind needed screening. Maka was a turbulent, sensitive person.

"Puna can't win! He never will! I am the lord of our World," his grandfather projected when he felt Maka's mental screening. It had traces of Puna's Mana all over it. This raised his ire even more. Puna was secretly stealing Maka away from him .

"You were saying COVID's the best thing?" Maka projected. *"We don't have COVID here, Elder Uli."*

"It doesn't matter what reality is or isn't," Elder Uli cackled, eyes wild. He was out of control. Maka shook his head behind his grandfather's back.

Oh, no! Maka worried that Elder Uli was scheming again. What did an Earthly pandemic have to do with Manafuls?

Elder Uli bragged about his plans. *"What matters is the illusion you feed into gullible minds!"* Elder Uli added with terrifying glee. "*The Hopohopo are just begging to be enslaved. They chose this . Dumb fools.*"

"*There is no disease that can't be cured in the Manaful world,*" Maka insisted. "*COVID was devastating to witness on Earth. Let's not make light of it.*" Maka cringed, recalling the human death toll since 2020. He knew he shouldn't engage with his grandfather. Instead, he put his mental screen back up and observed.

"*I'm grateful for the healing in Mana,*" Maka projected. Elder Uli ignored him.

"*The Hopohopo will believe my 'Humans brought a fatal virus' propaganda. They believe what I tell them. What I put into their minds,*" Elder Uli projected.

"*What do you mean?*" Maka was scared as he was getting the picture. Uli was right. The truth would hold no sway under total mind-control.

His grandfather was going to brainwash and infiltrate the brains and emotions of the Hopohopo. They'd believe The Secret Club brought COVID here. It was like political gaslighting, minus the advertising. Who needed ads when Uli and his Protectors could mentally break through Hopohopo's bodily systems? Maka had to get through to him. "*They're just Earth children! They'll be vulnerable if Manafuls think they're dangerous!*" Maka could pinch himself. If Ikaika were here, he'd tell him to guard his concerns for the SC.

Fortunately, Elder Uli wasn't paying attention, perhaps uncaring about the children.

"*Being Manaful is a power struggle every day, Maka,*" Elder Uli lectured. "*When you don't have money or Mana, you eagerly do whatever it takes to get it.*" His projections were sinister.

"Umm, Elder Uli? What's happening to you?" Maka started to back up. A suctioning force came from his grandfather. Was he doing his Lapu seances again?

After Maka's parents were killed, the dark Spirit Lapu came into their home and into his grandfather. Maka knew it could happen again. He suspected it had happened often in the past. Lapu sought out powerful Manafuls, particularly elders. Elders were charged up with Mana from Source. That elemental energy fueled the dark Spirit, Lapu, as well.

"I am disappointed in you, Maka. You could've been as great as me!" Uli projected.

"I'm not done growing up, Elder Uli! I can be as great as I want to be!" Maka stamped his foot like a child having a tantrum. *"I'm seven hundred and seventy years old! I have a lot of time!"*

Maka was suddenly afraid Elder Uli would make Manafuls sick with Corona. What if he simulated a pandemic? *"That virus, any virus, doesn't exist in our pure dimension."* Maka needed to get through to his grandfather.

This was playing with fire—Manaful genocide.

Maka pointed to the Secret Club, still frozen on the Shimmery Walls.

"Ikaika introduced them to me and it's been a pleasure," Maka smiled.

Elder Uli's eyebrows bunched up, contemplating disowning his do-gooder grandson. His robe was bioluminescent, like Puna's shades of red. Elder Uli's robe covered every imaginable shade of green on the continuum, from deep moss to mint shades.

Puna's Secret Club was Uli's prime focus. Maka's grandfather unpaused the three Shimmery Walls , scanning the scenes of each Clubber's life in real time.

The Elder watched the DMW Football League quarterback doing drills, the petite and bookish brunette baking muffins, and the hardy, kinky-haired girl laughing with her mom as they did calisthenics.

These children will be Puna's downfall and Elder Uli's celebration. Ignoring his grandson, Elder Uli transported their home. No 'Goodbye.' No 'Love you.'

Maka watched the Secret Club in the Walls. His grandfather's machinations gave him the chills. This was spying with bad intentions; it was discomfiting. He passed a hand at the walls, turning them off.

He wished Lapu wouldn't possess his grandfather. He wished they had a loving bond Ikaika and Elder Puna had. Maka was grateful for Elder Puna and Ikaika taking care of him after his parents' deaths.

He loved the 'Ula'ula House.

He projected his thoughts to Ikaika across the Manaful World: *Hey, Buddy, want to hang out?*

Ikaika quickly responded: *Sure, you okay? Problems with Pops again?*

Maka laughed at Ikaika's disrespectful reference to his grandfather. Ikaika never dared to call Elder Uli that in person, of course. That would've been catastrophic. Elder Uli had no sense of humor. Nada.

Maka transported to the hills below Ikaika's house.

Ikaika had a mansion in the sky, too. Except, his home was higher and invisible. It was grand in size and magic, yet beautiful in different ways. It was Cloaked, an invisibility spell requiring great ʻŌhana Mana.

The two highest Elders, Alakaʻi and Puna, had created it together combining their Mana. That dual-Mana swept Maka off his feet. Elder Alakaʻi was Ikaika's spirit-father like a godparent. Lucky Ikaika.

The four walls, ceiling, and floor of Ikaika's invisible floating mansion were made of magical, impenetrable glass. Ikaika lived in a gym-sized glass box high in the sky. It was a skyscraper penthouse without the other one hundred floors beneath it.

The birds never flew into them, as embedded magnetic forces warned their keen natural senses to avoid the gigantic invisible object. The Mana of the mansion kept Ikaika and Elder Puna safe.

Maka never asked, though he could guess that the uber security was to protect Ikaika from Elder Uli. It was ironic that Maka came and went there daily. Ikaika's home was one of the few off-limits places in Manaful to Elder Uli.

"Ikaika!" Maka projected, waiting on the grassy hills next to the koa forest. The winds swept his hair up, filling him with peace.

Maka was relieved to be away from the sandalwood forest. He was paranoid that one of Uli's men would harass him. Truly, more daunting goons Manaful has never known. They might eavesdrop on his telepathic projections, if that's even possible. One never knew with magic; there were so many ways to use it. Maka's Mana was still growing, yet he was no match for his grandfather's power.

Elder Uli's Mana could be shared with his goons. He'd witnessed their violence when his parents died. That's why all those deaths in his family were never pinned on Elder Uli himself. The goons were the assassins.

Elder Puna's Mana was the second-highest and strongest in Manaful. Being near Ikaika and Elder Puna's home was a comfort in security. Elder Alakaʻi was the most Manaful dwarf alive. Ikaika had two grandpas.

Maka imagined Ikaika's home somewhere above him.

"Ikaika! I know you're up there!" Maka searched the sky for his buddy.

"I'm right here." Ikaika's voice projected invisibly in front of Maka.

"Ah! Shoot, don't do that! Where'd you come from?

Maka clutched his chest. He glared at the laughing Ikaika, who was now visible within a sphere of dispersing mist.

"You are just too easy to trick!" Ikaika reached out his fist for a bump. Maka frowned.

"Come on, relax." Ikaika nudged Maka's limp arm with his fist.

Maka sighed. He couldn't stay mad at Ikaika for long. He grasped Ikaika's fist, pulling him in for a tight hug.

Ikaika squeezed him back, comforting him. Maka often needed hugs after going at it with Uli. *"Hey, buddy. You okay?"* Ikaika patted Maka's back.

Maka shook his head, gave one last squeeze, and let go.

Ikaika wished Elder Puna could hānai, or adopt, Maka. That would protect his friend from Uli's unpredictable rages. Maka would receive more Mana lessons, too.

"Don't you know the invisibility spell?" Ikaika raised his brow at Maka.

Maka shook his head. *"No, I missed that lesson. Grandpa doesn't teach me anything."*

Ikaika swore under his breath. Didn't Uli want to strengthen his family? The Ōma'oma'o House, its knowledge, was important to their world.

Maka smiled about invisibility. *"Wow! I hope Elder Puna teaches me that soon. I appreciate all the Mana learning I can get, even though I'm always catching up to you in Mana lessons."*

"I could teach you anything you've missed, Maka, but getting the Mana lesson from an Elder is wisest." Ikaika said. *"Remember the telephone game the kids play on Earth?"*

Maka laughed. *"Yes, the original telephone message became messed up by the time the message hit the third or fourth caller."*

The kids would sit in a circle for the game. They'd laugh at how different the last telephone message was from the original.

Maka sighed, understanding the parallels between learning lessons from Ikaika versus an Elder.

Ikaika read his mind. *"You got it, Maka. Source imbues my old man with tremendous power."*

Maka smiled. *"If you teach me the same Mana lesson, it wouldn't be as profound or powerful."*

"You got it! Let's catch up with Gramps now. Maybe it won't be the invisibility spell, but there's always something to learn from the old man." Ikaika winked.

Maka shook his head at the misnomers Ikaika gave to such a powerful Elder: "Gramps?" and "old man?"

Only Ikaika would call Elder Puna that. He does it to his grandpa's face too! The nerve, huh? Unlike Elder Uli, Elder Puna laughs right back at his grandson's joking name calling.

"Sure, I'm in. Let's find Elder Puna." Maka bounced with excitement. Once Elder Puna had transported them to him while he was healing a herd of sick deer.

Ikaika nodded, agreeing with Maka's thoughts. Being near his grandfather brought humility and appreciation for nature.

The dwarf preteens had both lost their parents in a power grab. Their common loss bonded them.

Ikaika nudged his buddy's shoulder. Maka didn't budge, being half an inch taller and fifty pounds bulkier. Though they were both tanned brown and had brown hair, their similarities ended there.

Maka was built like a football linesman. Pierre had taught Maka some tackling strategies. It was humorous watching the lean human wrestling with the thickly muscled dwarf.

Nicole would shake her head at them. Malie loved it. She'd clap her hands and cheer for whoever could pin the other first.

Though Pierre's limbs were long, Maka's core was taught. He always won, even without Mana. Ikaika was the ref, assuring Pierre that Maka wasn't allowed to use Mana in their matches. Fair's fair. Ikaika's body was more like Malie's, slender yet strong.

Before transporting to Elder Puna, they asked for permission to join him. It's like knocking on a door prior to entering another's room. Maka stopped Ikaika before he projected to Elder Puna.

"Hey, Ikaika. My grandfather was spying on the Secret Club."

Ikaika's eyes widened. *"No!"*

"Yes."

"Often?"

"Maybe. There was a familiarity to the way he talked about them."

Ikaika blew out a big breath. *"We better tell Elder Puna as soon as possible."*

Maka nodded.

"Where are you, Grandpa? Can Maka and I visit you? Would we be disrupting?" Ikaika telepathically projected across the Manaful World.

In a blink, Elder Puna transported them to his side. To remotely transport people demanded great Mana. The young dwarves hadn't gotten to that lesson yet.

As their bodies reconfigured beside Elder Puna on a huge pier, Maka's *"Wow!"* resounded over the rough waves.

"I love when you do that!" Maka smiled at Ikaika's grandfather. The elder's aura was immense and loving. This gave Maka warm fuzzies every day. He was blessed to have Elder Puna in his life.

Ikaika waved at his grandpa. He laughed at Maka. Really? He's tagged along with him and his grandpa for eleven years. He's still in awe of the Elder?

Maka stared out at the ocean below. Its waves stretched forward over the horizon. He smiled and sang.

Maka's Elders Song:

"How did I get cursed and blessed, huh?
Is it possible to live a life that's so messed up?

Hell at home but heaven with friends?
Both sides make me confused to the end.
Elders come in all shapes and sizes
Some are filled with life, others with surprises.
Elders out there, bring peace to our World.
Make it safe for all Manafuls.
Let us have a life that's fruitful.
Elders out there, bring harmony, please.
Don't let my grandfather bring that cursed disease.
How did I get cursed and blessed, huh?
Give me the choice to release from Uli's Mana.
Strengthen me as I face my fears,
Lift me up from a life filled with tears.
Let me be strong when the going gets tough.
Elders support me! Enough is enough!"

The words filled his soul with courage. Maka shivered under the cold, wet spray from the waves swamping the pier.

Elder Puna projected an acknowledging, "*We will help you,*" to Maka.

Ikaika fist-bumped his pal. Elder Uli would turn against Maka someday. The showdown was coming. Ikaika prayed his buddy would be ready to face his grandpa's ugliness.

"Elder Puna," Maka began, "Elder Uli is planning to use The Secret Club as scapegoats in a fear mongering campaign."

Elder Puna nodded. Maka guessed he'd plucked out the idea from Maka's thoughts.

Elder Puna's voice had a Gregorian chanter's vibe: "*Monopolizing fear is a common Lapu tactic. Uli could be just another victim of a greater scheme.*"

The boys moved to each side of Elder Puna, reaching for his hand. The elder squeezed their hands and put a calming spell into them. The pressure of their grasps lessened, and they closed their eyes.

The three dwarves moved to sit together on a fiber mat. Their legs were crossed, their hands loose on their knees. The sea breeze lifted their hair, seagulls calling to each other in their dives for fish. The Manafuls' thoughts drifted to a peaceful place.

After twenty minutes, the boys noticed Elder Puna talking to a large sea turtle.

The turtle projected, "*The hurt is seeping into my stomach. I'm old, but still enjoy coasting the waters. Will you heal me so that I may swim for a while longer?*"

Elder Puna lifted his right hand, a shimmering mist coming to life around his fingers.. The turtle's carapace had patchwork-like patterns whose full beauty was revealed when it hovered out of the water. The 200-pound loggerhead was neither bothered nor surprised by the levitation of its body as it leveled with the pier.

Elder Puna telepathically shared his observations of the reptile's body. Cancerous tumors grew in its cells and cysts clung like cauliflower clumps on its body. Ikaika wanted to cry, and Maka gasped in horror. Maybe it was nicer to euthanize the old fellow?

Elder Puna nodded to the turtle. The elderly reptile nodded its big head in return. Elder Puna projected: "*Align to Mana.*" The honu closed its eyes and returned the blessing.

Before their eyes, the tumorous growth disappeared. The turtle's shell gleamed as if having completed a luxury car detailing job. It sparkled with glistening water.

Its flippers flapped with readiness to stretch newly refurbished muscles.

Elder Puna laughed: *"Alright, alright, you're welcome."*

He placed the turtle into the water once more as the boys stared, mouths agape.

They'd witnessed Elder Puna's Mana-healing before, yet each time was astounding to see. The positive energy and love between Elder Puna and the loggerhead were palpable. That was the key to the elders' Mana—love.

Elder Puna's red robe glowed against the blue skyline. It reminded Maka of his grandfather's robes, also radiant despite its owner's nastiness.

Maka avoided eye contact with his grandfather much less watching him while in his presence. The dark, negative energy was hurtful.

Prior to Lapu's presence in his grandfather's life, Maka remembered a warmer side of Elder Uli. His parents had been alive. Maybe it was wishful thinking. Elder Uli changed after the murders of Maka's family members. They all fell like domino blocks, one after the other.

Ikaika shook Maka's shoulder. *"Hey, pal, don't go there again. Stop looping memories of him."*

Maka nodded. *"Thank you."*

Maka gave Ikaika a one-armed hug. Ikaika laughed, loving the affection. All their lives, that was his kuleana or responsibility—cheering up Maka. It comforted Ikaika to do that. Death after death, Maka had needed his friendship with Ikaika and Elder Puna more and more.

A pod of whales approached the solitary mid-ocean pier. A mama blue whale corralled her baby whales bumping and playing with each other. Kind of cute, as long as they didn't whack down the pier.

The Mama blue whale approached so rapidly Maka was rattled. .

"*Woooah, slow down, Mama,*" Maka projected.

Ikaika laughed, "*No worries, she's a friend. Her babies are sweet, yeah?*"

Maka nodded, "*Uh, huh. Whatever you say. Sure, only you could call 5,000-pound calves 'sweet.'*"

Ikaika laughed again. Maka wasn't used to the big ones. Elder Puna Mana-healed them all: from itsy-bitsy spiders to hauntingly seductive twelve-foot-long king cobras. Those snakes were easily four times the height of a Manaful.

"*What's he doing?*" Maka projected to Ikaika. The blue whale Mama and her calves were now half a football field away from his grandfather.

The boys had backed away. Far away from the Elder. They were now at opposite ends of the fifty-yard pier. Ikaika closed his eyes. "*Grandpa, what's happened to the whales? Do they need healing?*"

Ikaika opened his eyes and shared with Maka. "*Grandpa says the calves lost their birth mother,*" Ikaika's face fell. "*The Mama whale there is their adopted Mama.*"

Maka frowned, too. "*Ohhhh, that's horrible.*" He asked Ikaika, "*How could they have gotten separated?*"

"They weren't separated," Ikaika projected softly as a tear flowed down his cheeks. *"She was killed by hunters."*

Maka stomped his foot. *"I thought that was an Earth thing."* He was stricken and surprised, *"Why would a Manaful need to hunt whale meat when they could simply conjure meat?"*

"Right?" Ikaika said, *"We don't need to hunt anymore. However, the Hopohopo do."*

Maka thought of his grandfather. Elder Uli had mentioned them. Those were the ones he'd brainwash about The Secret Club.

Ikaika nodded, *"Hopohopo are prone to manipulation by powerful Manafuls."*

Maka conjured a cozy bench for them to wait on. Ikaika thanked him. They sat and stared at the whales.

Ikaika nudged him. *"I know, buddy. It's hard with your grandpa. Sing some more. Let the music in your core heal you. Just softly, okay?"* Maka smiled, agreeing.

Maka's Song for Strength (sung softly):

"Creeping vines pull me apart.
Thorny fingers splitting my heart
Into pieces with sinister notions.
Grandpa, you turned to Lapu for His evil potions.
My loyalty's been truly tested.
A tree of life that's totally infested.
Creeping vines won't stand a chance,
Pruner in hand, I advance!
Give me strength all above and around.
Manaful World is filled with sight and sound.

Every dwarf brings energy, either light or dark.
Finding allies is no walk in the park.
Give me strength all above and around.
Grandpa, will our bond ever return?
Why has our family ended up in urns?
Our ancestral line was so strong and full.
You came forth and attacked like a bull.
Give me strength all above and around.
Give me strength."

Ikaika clapped and cheered for Maka. The latter's eyes were closed, tears dampening his eyelashes and streaking his cheeks.

Ikaika hugged his friend's arm, hoping Elder Puna was done healing the whale calves. They'd come for Mana-healing of the psychological and spiritual kind. Animals and humans alike needed that.

His grandfather was a busy dwarf. Busy elder. He projected, *"Grandpa, you done over there? Maka needs healing over here!"*

Elder Puna projected to them both, *"He's fine. You're a good soother, my boy! Proud of you."*

Ikaika perked up, looking across the pier as his grandpa turned from the whales at that moment to make eye contact with him.

Elder Puna's eyes sparkled with white fire; Source's fire. Elder Puna smiled, and then he returned to the whales.

Ikaika blushed with pride. Maka laughed, having caught their exchange in full. Maka punched Ikaika's arm. *"Chip off the old block, huh?"*

Ikaika projected, *"If you'd like to speak with Gramps after he counsels the whales, we can wait."*

Maka nodded. *"Sure, I like it here. I've got nowhere else I'd rather be. Let's keep watching Elder Puna work."*

Ikaika appreciated his friend's patience. They were a good pair.

CHAPTER 28

Earth
Wright Middle School Gym
July 5, 2022
8 a.m.

Reluctant students dragged their feet across the Wright Middle School campus. Everyone was recovering from the Fourth of July holiday.

The Secret Club had voted to visit Manaful World every Thursday, rain or shine. Barring family emergencies or appointments, they continued their visits with the dwarfs. Being in Manaful was the Secret Club's time-out from the stressors in life. They could spend as long as they liked exploring the magical world every visit.

Neither of them attended Summer School that year. The gym wall was their favorite spot to cross over. Pierre Martin did stretches against their wall, often first to get there after practice. Football, for him, was never off season.

Buzz. Buzz.

He continued his stretching, but answered his cell phone.

"Hi, Tūtū," he said, "No, I didn't forget the shopping list."

Tūtū shouted, "Add my favorite International Delight Italian creamer!"

Pierre winced, tutting at her volume. His grandma had recently begun to lose some of her hearing. "Tūtu, you forgot your hearing aids." Shopping for her was something he and his mom did twice a week. "You could call my mom too or text your add-ons," Pierre urged for the hundredth time.

"The aids give me headaches with the ringing and buzzing," Tutu complained. "Your mom puts me in voice mail. I don't like talking to machines. Then, that texting thing..."

Pierre rolled his eyes as she went on one of her rants. He looked up as a mongoose skittered beneath a pinkish-orange plumeria tree. The brush of curled-up green-brown leaves revealing their path. There were burrows of mongoose families on the hilly middle school campus. He breathed in, relaxing a little.

He tuned back into Tutu's cell phone complaints with more calmness.

Tūtū was saying, "I tried the emojis, but some are inappropriate. A brown pile of poop? Why would someone want that in their message?"

Pierre laughed at that.

"Oh, my Korean drama's starting. Bye." Abrupt silence. She'd hung up. Just like that.

Pierre was accustomed to her calls and long winded manner. He shouldn't ignore her. She was lonely. Everyone needs a sounding board. He talked to himself about being compassionate like Elder Puna.

"Hey, Pierre," Malie Manu called out from the stairway leading to a parking lot. The breeze rustled up the dirty, broken branches. Her dress was floral. Pierre appreciated the blue bonnet pattern.

They fist-bump-wiggle-wooshed and hugged as if they hadn't texted daily for seven months straight.

"Was that Tūtū?" She pointed to his cell phone.

He laughed, "How'd you guess?"

She smiled, mimicking his shoulders. "Your posture changes when you listen to her," Malie replied, arms at her sides like a soldier at attention.

She returned to her usual slouch, "Aren't you aware of your body tightening?"

Pierre scrunched his face. "I started stretching..." he paused. "Then she'd called, and my impatience took over. Then, I talked myself down from any impatience."

Malie nodded. "Another monologue? Oh, that last part. Good on you!" She winked at him.

He smiled and nudged her shoulder.

Malie had bonded with Tūtū over the past months. She didn't know them as "The Secret Club," but rather, "the girls."

"How are her pink orchids?" Malie adored Tūtū's garden, especially all the flowers. She bounced in her matching blue and white flowered tennis shoes. Her ponytail jumped in harmony with her movements, too-large tortoise-shell glasses sliding down her nose.

"Hi, people! I'm here!" Nicole Moku, that vibrant wonder of a girl, spread her arms out wide as she came around the corner. She added a Broadway boogie, laughing.

Nicole's good moods were apparent. She wasn't as over-the-top cheerful as Malie and Pierre were, but she was learning.

Everyone heals at their own pace.

"What an entrance," Malie teased. "No jingle for us?" They all did a group fist-bump-wiggle-woosh!

Nicole's eyes sparked as she said, "Sorry I'm late. Mom gave me chores before letting me out. Blah, she's a cleaning freak. I'm a 'let it lie there 'til later' gal."

"Me too," said Pierre.

The deserted spot at the back of the gymnasium helped. Most of the teachers were on summer break. If anyone saw them jump through the portal, there'd be some explaining to do.

"Let's get this show on the road!" Nicole said. "On the count of three..."

The Secret Club broke into song, an otherworldly harmony ringing beneath their voices. The portal opened and they were off.

The Summer Re-Entry Song:

Together:
"Moving places and crossing spaces."

Pierre:
"Does it ever get less funky?
Could I reshape into something hokey?"

Nicole:
"That's hilarious. You'd have to be hokey first."

Malie:
"Do you ever wonder why we never thirst?

No drinking or eating. Except for that first time.
We ate oranges and cones. Let's ask for pie, maybe key lime?"

Together:
"Moving places, crossing spaces."

Nicole:
"Do you ever wonder about the Manaful races?"

Malie:
"What? Just check out their Hawaiian faces."

Pierre:
"It's not like Ancient Hawaiian Kings and Queens.
It's more like Atlantis, if you know what I mean.
Except for the falling into the ocean part, gee!
No way, don't think of anything so freaky."

Nicole:
"Hey, people, focus your minds and molecules.
In order to get there, we must follow the rules."

Together:
"Moving spaces, crossing places. Moving..."

Their molecules sang as they crossed through the Shimmery Wall. They reshaped in Manaful World.

Chapter 29

Manaful World
Koa Forest Elders' Council Chambers
July 5, 2022
8 a.m.

Manaful Elder Uli was tall for dwarf standards at three and three quarter feet. His dark complexion complimented with his green bioluminescent robe. At 3000 years old, he was one of the younger elders. He was at least a thousand years younger than some of his fellow 'Ohana leaders. Rumor has it that Uli had killed his family.

Today, an entire rainbow of 'Ohana cloths were present. It was a rare occasion for them to gather. Annual council meetings were held, of course, but this was an emergency assembly.

Meeting more than annually was avoided for mental health reasons. Elders often came away from them with migraines due to the great amount of verbal communication required. They were telepathic beings, hence the long argumentative meetings were a chore.

All the Elders were top-notch magical healers. They represented the most powerful Manaful beings of their world. Thus, their meetings should not be a problem.

However, it was reminiscent of a family reunion. One is forced to be pleasant with relatives they'd rather avoid. That condescending aunt. That pervy uncle who has no filter. He'd say things like, "Eh, did you get fat?" or "You're still single?"

It took a year to get over the Annual Assemblies.

The Elders sat around a large circular koa table in hierarchical order. It was reminiscent of King Arthur's Round Table.

The Prime 'Ohana leader, Council Seat, wore pristine opalescent robes. He was the oldest and had the most Mana. While Mana was transferred generationally via transmutation upon death, that hadn't happened to Elder Alaka'i yet. He's the original Manaful created by Source. He was at least 4200 years old in Manaful years. That's sixty human years. Manaful was a young world in the grand scheme of the universe.

Alaka'i and Puna went way back, having known each other most of their lives. Aligned with Source's Mana, Alaka'i founded the Elders' Council. Puna was the second elder to join, then Uli's uncle was the third. When their buddy, the original Uli, was killed, Puna and Alaka'i mourned.

The current Uli was the third most powerful Council member. He'd gained most of his family's powers but not their loving hearts and wisdom.

Elder Alaka'i spoke first. "Elder Puna has requested this emergency council for the protection of his human guests—The Secret Club."

Grumbling voices and rebuttals came from various Elders at the table. Elder Alaka'i raised his palm for quiet. The room immediately settled down.

He continued, "Interestingly, Elder Uli hasn't offered his family's security company Protection Force Bodyguards to watch over The Secret Club. He instead promised said company will not harass the children in our world and theirs."

Puna pondered Uli's magnanimous promise. Uli always had an ulterior motive. Uli's security company was superfluous. It fed on the fears of the coin-wealthy Hopohopo Manafuls.

The Hopohopo were afraid of those who used Mana. Coinwealthy Hopohopo controlled the lives of impoverished Hopohopo under a Governor's system. Uli's bodyguards were assassins, yet it couldn't be proven.

Puna wanted to help the homeless and suffering Hopohopo. They refused Mana. Refused to change their belief systems, preferring poverty. They lived in fear.

Uli used and manipulated those Hopohopo. Uli invested all of his time training his Protective Force guards in Mana, but not alignment.

Some Manafuls feared the Spirit Lapu possessed those bodyguards. That could bring annihilation.

The elders around the table squabbled

Some yelled, "On what grounds is Uli's denial of protection?"

Others shouted, "This is bigotry!"

Another elder's voice complained, "This is unworthy of an Elder! Uli should be reprimanded! Where's his Aloha?"

Puna observed and waited for his pal Alaka'i to call the council to order. He raised his brow at the latter, projecting to him: "*How about some order, buddy.*"

Alaka'i smiled at Puna. Then he shouted, "Order! Order!" He pounded his mother-of-pearl gavel, motioning for peace. He pointed to Uli. "Elder Uli, explain yourself. Why aren't your forces available to guard The Secret Club?"

Uli puffed his chest out. He looked at the other elders. They sat around him beneath floating kukui nuts lit like candles, creating halo-like spheres around their heads. The intoxicating mixture of oils and resin in the air complimented the beauty of the elders' robes, a contrast to the tension in the chamber.

Uli scoffed at Alaka'i, causing a flurry. He was so disrespectful. His voice boomed, "One word: COVID. Puna's Secret Club is the first wave. They'll bring COVID, kill off our people, and transport more waves of humans here. They'll steal our home."

Puna stayed calm. He knew Uli would go there. He understood his fellow elder's megalomania and narcissism. Puna interjected, "We have no viruses in our dimension. Never have, since the beginning of our world!"

The gavel pounded. "Puna, wait your turn!" Alaka'i shouted. He was angry as heck about Uli's accusation, but he had to let Uli talk.

Uli went on,"Unexpected things always happen. Isn't it better to be safe than sorry?" Uli's extraordinary blue eyes shone with glee. The fear of the unknown was key. He planted a seed of fear into the council.

Puna's face reddened as he clenched his teeth. "Elder Alaka'i, is it my turn yet?"

Alaka'i looked at Uli. "Well? Anything else to add?"

Uli had one last point, hammering the final nail in Elder Puna's coffin. Uli smirked at Elder Puna. "Some of my 'Ohana have shown flu symptoms since The Secret Club began their weekly visits seven months ago. Cancer growths are becoming common in nature and the cities. Severe depression is rampant."

Silence. Not a pin drop. No swish of robes. Then, there was yelling.

Elders standing and shouting their heads off in fear. The whole council became an uproar. All except Puna. He sat still and serene.

Puna and Uli held each other's gaze all the while. A silent war. Each elder knew the other's intent. One for peace. One for strife.

"This is the beginning of the end!" some Elders claimed. "Uli's right! Humans are going to kill us off!" other Elders conceded.

The pro-Puna group became calmer as Puna projected soothing thoughts into them. He was unable to breach the phobia within the pro-Uli camp. They tended to be the younger generation of elders.

Puna's supporters said, "Let's be calm, elders. Maybe Uli is exaggerating. There's got to be a spell to heal them."

Puna projected to Alaka'i: "Got control? Rein your leaders in, brother." Alaka'i agreed but was irritated with Puna always telling him what to do. Who was the leader here, anyway? Before Alaka'i could take control, Uli's supporters began to chant:

The pro-Uli Crew's Song:

"The end is coming over the bend.

How can ripped seams ever mend?
Generations stretching back for millennia lost.
Three hasty children banished is a small cost.
Close the Shimmery Wall.
Safety first, most of all.
Sweethearts or not, we must protect our own.
Imagine your great grandbabies' sickened moans.
The end is coming."

As their words died down, Uli and Elder Puna still stood in a high noon staredown. If looks could kill, Puna would have dropped dead.

CHAPTER 30

Manaful World
Koa Forest
July 5, 2022
8 a.m.

Pierre was the first to pop through the Shimmery Wall. He checked his body and hair. Some people never change. Nicole came through next with Malie right after. Their phones and bags had disappeared as usual.

Nicole looked around at the flower meadow they'd landed in. Pierre left their side to run through the field, loving it.

Malie plopped on a patch of grass, wondering where Ikaika and Elder Puna were.

Pop. Pop.

Ikaika and Maka arrived as if Malie had called them here.

Maka nudged Ikaika, projecting, "*You never taught me that invisibility spell!*"

Ikaika said aloud, "Maka, stop projecting. It's rude."

Maka mimicked Ikaika, albeit aloud, "It's rude."

Malie stared at the tanned dwarves, one donning his green sarong while the other wore his red one. They never wore shirts or shoes. She wondered if they ever got foot calluses or if they could get pedicures in Manaful.

Maka laughed at her thoughts. "Pedicure? We don't need foot beauty care, Malie. We use Mana-care. Get it? Like your 'Medicare' on Earth—Mana-care?" Maka slapped his knee, laughing at his own joke.

Nicole stared at the brawny dwarf. She often did that, never quite getting his jokes. They were droll, but she liked that Maka made her friends smile.

Maka once joked that she had a stick up her butt and she should loosen up. She didn't like that and let him have it. She'd surprised him by wrestling him to the ground, tickling him until he called, "Peace! Peace! I give. No more tickling, please!"

Ikaika and Elder Puna forbade Maka from using Mana on The Secret Club. He'd been at her mercy, in stitches with laughter. He'd forgotten how ticklish he was. Ikaika and he used to tickle each other as toddlers. They'd matured and stopped doing that. Too bad. It was fun.

Pierre ran up to them, high-fiving the dwarves. "Hey, guys! I'm happy you're here."

Ikaika nodded and patted Pierre's arm. "Sorry. My bad, Elder Puna was checking out a crime scene."

Malie giggled at his "My bad." She pointed at him. "You sound like us."

Nicole grinned. "Yes, it's cool. We'll teach you more."

Pierre was struck by his words "crime scene" instead of his use of slang. A crime scene in peaceful Manaful?

"Can we transport to the crime scene to observe Elder Puna?" How does Puna handle those cases?

Ikaika shook his head. "No. He's in an Elders' council meeting right now. Non-elders aren't allowed to attend those."

Maka nodded. That's where his grandfather MT today. They'd been arguing when Maka opened his mouth about The Secret Club visiting. He could punch himself.

Ikaika projected, *"Stop that. You can't tell your heart to stop loving. Inside, you'll always want to trust him. No matter how hard he hits you or insults you."* Maka stared at his friend.

Nicole watched their silent exchange. She put her fists on her hips. "Stop doing that around us!" She shook her pointer finger at them.

Malie laughed at Nicole's tone, nodding in agreement. "Share guys, we'd all like to know what's in your hearts and minds."

Pierre fist-bump-wiggle-wooshed Maka, sensing something was up.

Maka took a big breath. Huhhhhhh. Sighed and stared at the kids. They truly cared.

"Long story short?" He asked.

They nodded. "My grandfather hates Elder Puna. He's using you to disrupt the world. Says you plan to kill us all."

Nicole was the first to react with a succinct F-word that rhymes with duck.

Malie began reaching up to cover her mouth. Pierre did it for her.

Nicole whipped Pierre's hand away.

"Language, Nicole!" Malie said. She gave the dwarves an apologetic look on Nicole's behalf.

Maka laughed, "No, I agree."

Ikaika nodded too.

CHAPTER 31

Manaful World
Koa Forest
July 5, 2022
8:30 a.m.

The Secret Club remained in Manaful World, offended by Elder Uli's plans.

Pierre needed his limestone boulder. Ikaika transported it to them ASAP.

Malie lay back on the limestone boulder's smooth surface beside Pierre. She was glad her pal wasn't ashamed to ask for his boulder. The whistling wind through the nearby trees soothed them.

Nicole had huffed and preferred a spot by a nearby stream to the limestone boulder. She hovered with Ikaika there. Molecular transporting still freaked her out.

Maka sat on the grass beside Pierre's limestone boulder. He weaved them lauhala branch hats, insisting they were great protective headgear.

Malie reached for a branch to try weaving too, wishing he would conjure them hats.

Maka smiled, "I could do that," he was in her head, "but I like making things."

Malie didn't mind him in her head.

Nicole still lost her temper about their mind-reading. That blew her fuse. Both Malie and Maka laughed. Yes, Nicole's temper was something. She was happier in some ways, but not all.

Malie asked, "What was your grandpa like, when you were younger?"

Maka said, "It was hell, Malie. Still is."

She made a heart with her hands. Maka returned the gesture.

Pierre perked up from his restful pose. "Ssshhh. Someone is coming."

Maka nodded, acknowledging the presence of Uli's Protective Forces. Two females in their thirties approached them. They wore Maka's 'Ohana cloth of forest green designed in the style of a sarong. Their simple attire was a trick, as the pair possessed dangerous Mana.

His grandfather had trained them. They were neither Hopohopo nor Manaful, but caught in the middle of Uli's mechanisms..

The Protective Forces stopped twenty yards from the children. They hollered to the youth: "You don't belong here. Elder Uli ordered us to watch you. Don't spread COVID."

Pierre and Malie hid behind Pierre's boulder. The tall stone couldn't have protected them from Uli's Mana. Ignorance is bliss.

Pierre said, "We are Elder Puna's guests. We come in peace."

Uli's Protective Force guards stared at him and then at each other. Though the guards stood less than three feet tall, the humans knew looks were deceiving.

Choosing a soft approach, Maka said, "What's going on, Aunties?" The guards were his relatives.

The taller of the pair projected: "*We mean no harm. Yet, you must take them away. Your grandfather won't be as kind.*" That made Maka's blood boil.

Malie gasped, reaching for Pierre's hand.

Maka positioned himself in front of the children. The Protective Forces were doing his grandfather's dirty work. Still, he was tired of playing nice.

He rooted his body into the soil and called the forces of Source. Mana Mist flowed into his feet and through his blood. Sparkling light energy lifted from beneath them. A forcefield flashed to life as it enveloped them in a bubble of safety, stirring the dirt around them into floating particles.

Chin down, Maka projected: "*I call on Source for Mana to keep my friends safe. I stand by Elder Puna's decree to keep them protected from all dangers. Leave now.*"

The second Protective Force guard stepped back and shook her head. She pulled her partner back. "*We mean no harm. Yet, you must take them away.*" Then, the two ladies transported out from there.

Malie asked, "Your grandpa sent people to stalk us?"

Maka nodded.

Pierre waved at Maka. "You were glowing. There was an energy field around us!"

Maka sighed, "It's from Source. Aligning tires me out."

Pierre and Malie stared at each other and then nodded.

Maka looked at their foreheads, and he nodded too. They must find Elder Puna.

Down by the stream with Nicole, Ikaika stopped communing with nature. He listened to Maka's projection: *"Come back. We need you to take us to Puna. The Protective Force was just here, warning us off. The kids are spooked."*

Ikaika and Nicole molecularly traveled there mere seconds after Maka's projection. The hair on Nicole's arms bristled but she kept mum. Maka frowned and hugged Ikaika.

"Need Elder Puna's help." Maka said. He was crashing. Adrenaline rush. Calling on Source's Mana exhausted him. He did what he loved the most. He sang.

Maka's Plea for Help Song

"Taking sides hurts my insides.
Isn't home where the heart resides?
The Family Head has lost control.
Falling deep into a dark hole.
Innocent children have been framed.
This can't go on; they can't be maimed.
Help me, Ancestors!
Grandpa's wrongdoings are crippling.
He's lost it; he's surely slipping.
Our family's falling apart.
I don't know where to start.
It's up to me to put him down.
Oh, my gosh! Get out of town!

Euthanizing the mentally ill is the hardest task.
First, I must remove his mask.
Make it known the harm he's transgressed.
Only then, will we be blessed.
Help me, Ancestors!
Help me!"

After his song's final words, the whole group surrounded him in a hug. The children gave their support in solidarity a

CHAPTER 32

Manaful World
Koa Forest
Elder Puna's mansion
July 5, 2022
9 a.m.

It was the first time The Secret Club had visited Elder Puna and Ikaika's home.

The kids couldn't get over the magnificence of the huge, invisible, floating gymnasium-sized glass cube in the sky.

Malie ran from one side of the mansion to another, each lap taking twenty seconds. The open floor plan reminded her of home. A grander version.

She stopped at the glass walls, looking way down. "How far are we up from the koa forest?"

Maka laughed at her reaction. He'd been here hundreds of times and was still in awe.

Ikaika's home was both a sacred and loving space. Something, Elder Uli's mansions lacked.

"We're a hundred feet above the forest floor," Ikaika stood beside her. They enjoyed the koa vista together.

The ceiling was transparent too. Malie waved at the birds and clouds passing above. The floors were made of flowing pearlescent gray marble that seemed alive. It moved like an elder's bioluminescent robe.

The cool, lavender-scented air relaxed Nicole. She looked for a diffuser like her mom keeps in her office.

The children were about to ask about furniture and rooms. No kitchen, restroom, or bedroom. Nicole squirmed, needing the bathroom urgently.

Maka smiled, relieved at the distraction their reactions provided.

Ikaika projected to Puna. "*Grandpa, I need you. The Protective Forces approached Maka and The Secret Club. Maka's shaken up, but he's hiding it well.*"

Puna projected back: "*The Forces? They weren't supposed to harass the kids. Trust Uli to lie to the council. The council's in turmoil. I'll be there soon. Align with Mana.*"

Maka laughed at Nicole's wiggling need for a toilet. "Imagine a bathroom," he told her. She gave him a "you're nuts!" look, but she did it.

Out of thin air, a hallway appeared with an ornate koa door to presumably a private bathroom. Her shock made everyone laugh.

Malie clapped her hands. "I want to manifest things too! Wow!"

Nicole, still amazed, went into the bathroom.

With an equal amount of astonishment, Pierre shook his head. "That probably doesn't work for money or a puppy, huh?" He pointedly looked at Ikaika, who smiled back.

"No, this is my sanctuary. I use restraint with Mana." Ikaika said.

Malie created colorful landscapes for the glass walls.

Ikaika allowed her artistic pleasure.

She progressed to a red velvet loveseat. It floated a few inches off the dolphin gray floor. She relaxed on the cushy chair, happily conjuring a paperback by her favorite author.

Pierre laughed. "Figures!"

Pierre then elbowed Ikaika, "How do you have this magical crib?"

Malie perked up, interested too.

Ikaika sat beside her. "Elders Alaka'i and Puna made this house for me mainly because Gramps travels a lot. He surveys and heals many beings at all hours of the day."

Maka conjured a sandalwood armchair across from them. He added. "Sometimes Ikaika and I would MT to Elder Puna's location. We'd watch him heal or counsel creatures. He teaches us a lot about different beings and Mana."

Ikaika nodded. "It's beautiful how Grandpa does that. That's part of my and Maka's training."

He continued. "To learn Mana takes a lifetime of training. Most times, my training involves visiting Manafuls or animals all over the world. That's why I needed a solid abode, a comforting landing pad."

Pierre laughed at Ikaika's humble descriptions of a "solid abode" and "pad" for this gorgeous 'Create Your Own' mansion.

Malie said, "Your Manaful training is to listen and heal beings every day?"

Pierre said, "Cool schooling." He had a hunch Mana schooling was deeper than that. There were many more layers to this training.

Maka stared at Pierre's forehead. "You got that right, my friend."

Nicole returned from Ikaika's five-star hotel-like bathroom. She could soak in that huge clawfoot tub for hours. She caught the guys' exchange, shaking her head at Pierre. She didn't understand how Maka reading his thoughts didn't bother him.

She said, "What is it like being an heir, Ikaika?"

Ikaika cringed. "I don't like to imagine Puna's death and my inheritance. Yet, that's how it works."

Maka said, "Elder Puna is the second most magical Manaful alive. He is most loved as well. It would be a Manaful World loss like no other, when he dies." He bowed his head.

Ikaika and The Secret Club bowed their heads as well. The four of them broke into a song together.

Gratitude Song (Everyone singing except Maka):

Together:
"Precious guardians are precious presents.
They have a precious presence.
Power flowing from above and below.
Don't let life take its toll.
Let your love for them show."

Malie:
"She comes home late.

Yet offers help—won't hesitate.
Spoils me with girly things.
Her hugs and hearts mingling."

Nicole:
"She's tough as nails,
Won't let me go off the rails.
She wants me to stand up to bullies.
There's no space in life for wussies!"

Pierre:
"She's very pregnant and moody.
He's ambitious and pushy.
They want the best for me.
Believing in my destiny."

Ikaika:
"A Puna-less world would be heartbreaking.
His love for all things is striking.
Birds would stop singing.
Whales would spout water simultaneously.
Ants would trip in their marching.
Wolves, coyotes, and dogs would howl hopelessly."

Together:
"Don't let life take its toll.
Let your love for them show."

They ended their song, filled with love for their families. All eyes stared at Maka's downtrodden features. He hadn't sung with them, nor expressed gratitude for his family. No one could blame him.

Chapter 33

Manaful World
Sandalwood Forest
Elder Uli's mansion
July 5, 2022
10:30 a.m.

Elder Uli scowled at his two Protectors, awaiting their explanations. They'd projected their frustrations about Maka and the humans.

Protectors Kōkua and Malka'i awaited their deaths. Elder Uli underestimated their goodness. They were sweet ladies. Elder Uli's Mana couldn't break down their loving natures.

Kōkua wanted to help the children. She served the elder for money as many did. Most of his employees did: for money or for fear. Elder Uli was an opportunist and murderer. She shunned that thought while in his presence, he'd read her mind.

He had no true core. Lapu filled that vacancy.

Uli took in the Protectors' report. Maka tapped Source's Mana. Uli was too conceited to believe his stupid, incapable, softy grandson could do that. If he did, it must have taxed the little sod. These two Protectors were pathetic.

He lifted his hand to their faces, stretching the skin taut on their bones. Open-mouthed, the guards tried to breathe, fingers scrabbling out to him in vain. A harsh wind came into the mansion, picking them up. Squeezed them, twisted their bodies. Watching their skin turn blue, he laughed and dropped his hand.

The wind dissipated. The guards fell on the hardwood floor like a ton of bricks. They struggled to breathe and felt their skin rebound painfully back into place.

He projected, *"Do the job right next time!"* He spat on them and walked to the kitchen for a drink.

Maika'i crawled to a chair to support her legs as she stood. She wiped her face with disgust.

From the kitchen, a soda can fizzed. A wine bottle uncorked. Ice chips clinked.

The ladies held each other, wobbling down the hallway past the mounted portraits of Uli relatives.

Maika'i and Kōkua stopped briefly to look at Moemoe Uli's portrait. He was Maka's father and Elder Uli's only child. He'd been a kind-hearted and promising heir.

In the mansion's employee changing room, the ladies centered themselves. Maika'i's head hurt from the stretching and sudden drop to the floor. Her forehead was bruised and her ears were ringing.

Kōkua's arms hurt from bracing her landing. Other guards died from the stretching, suffocating in midair. Today she'd been lucky.

Maikaʻi was a stout two feet tall brunette. She washed her face again repeatedly. Kōkua put her hand over Maikaʻi's shoulder to settle her down.

"It's going to be alright. We'll report Uli to the Elders' Council." Kōkua said

Kōkua's long blond hair was a filthy mess. The whirlwind had swept twigs and dirt into their hair and on their sarongs. Kōkua shook her lithe frame. She was alive, walking out of here, and bringing this tyrant down.

They changed out of their tattered sarongs and into their cleaner, personalized ones. Though it was shapeless over her curvy figure, Maika'i liked the little decorations added to it. Her mother's embroidery and ruffles on her hem brought her spirits up. She felt stylish, swinging her material left, then right.

The ladies exited the changing room and stopped at Elder Uli's shout from a staircase, "Stop!"

He said aloud, "Those humans don't belong here. Puna's going to lose! I'm the winner!"

Kōkua and Maikaʻi jumped to attention. Drunk or not, he was still powerful in Mana.

He continued his stink-breathed ranting, "You two will continue to report their whereabouts to me!"

Kōkua and Maikaʻi said, "Yes, Elder Uli!"

He nodded and disappeared.

Relieved that he'd left, they were about to transport home. Their faces became serious as Kōkua stopped Maikaʻi.

"Heart monitors," she whispered.

"What?" Maika'i squinted one eye.

Kōkua leaned towards the wall opposite the changing room. "You of all people! Listen!"

Maika'i's had a whole former life as a Mana-care physician. She was immediately on her toes. There was a corridor down the hall. It was an isolated, not often used, area of the mansion.

Kōkua vaulted forward, waving Maika'i over to a paneled wall further down the hallway. She signaled for Maika'i to be quiet: Use your doctor ears; it's ventilators!

Maika'i nodded. They pressed against the wood. Maika'i's senses were jumping around, her heart saying, Get in there quickly!

The two Protectors tapped along the wall, picking up on the hollow ring. Maika'i felt along the panels and pressed a loose one. The wall split open like double doors. The pair burst through at once.

The room resembled a hospital room with pristine beds, sheets, monitors, and other medical gadgets necessary to preserve life.

Different fragrances warred for attention. A clean citrus scent rose from glistening hardwood floors. The soft 1000-thread-count bedsheets were doused in eucalyptus oils. This room was beautiful and hotel-like despite its Spartan simplicity, and concealment.

Kōkua, ever on guard, held her hands up in case there were authorities or medical practitioners ready to kick them out. Or worse, goons. When she saw no one but the five sleeping dwarves in the corner, she stood at ease. Kōkua took a deep breath.

Approaching the beds, she recognized one of the patients as her missing cousin, Kai. "Oh, Gosh! No! No!" she whispered as her heart raced, "Cuz!" She ran to his bedside.

Maika'i reached Kōkua's cousin first and stopped her friend. "Kōkua, let me check his vitals and sense his body first. Please."

Maika'i rubbed her arm. "We'll help him, Kōkua. We'll MT with them all to the Elders' Medical Center, if necessary."

Kai blinked awake as Maika'i examined his breathing and unhooked his IV.

"Where am I?" Kai wasn't coherent, but Kōkua was happy he'd remembered his home.

She squeezed her cousin's shoulder. "Your tomatoes can wait. Let's figure out why you're here, Cuz. Does Ala know where you are?"

Kai tried to sit up, but that wore him out. He shook his head, looking distraught. "I want to get out of here." His heart monitor started beeping.

"Hey, Kai, calm down. Your blood pressure and oxygen levels are dangerous!" Kai nodded, trusting that whoever was with his cousin was one of the good guys.

Reading his thoughts, Maika'i apologized and introduced herself, "I'm sorry, Kai, my name is Maika'i. I used to practice medicine to heal Hopohopo, before I joined the Protectors." She smiled, "Yes, I'm a 'good gal'.

Maika'i missed being a healer; sadly, being a Protector paid more. She'd had her kids to consider. She'd been raised by Hopohopo and had more to learn about her Mana. She at least had her healing Mana powers. For that, she was grateful.

Kai started to cry. Maika'i gave Kōkua a speaking look, projecting: *Venting is good, but ask your cousin to breathe deep and relax. He's not looking well.*

Kōkua nodded, hugged Kai, and hummed a familiar tune from their childhood. Maika'i smiled, remembering the sweet tune about ladybugs.

Kai leaned into Kōkua's arms, enjoying her gentleness. After a few moments, he shared how he got here.

"I was in my garden pulling weeds. Out of nowhere, a dark figure with a syringe attacked me. Then there was darkness." Kai started to shake. He was panicking again. "Let me out of here!"

His eyes pleaded for immediate departure. Kōkua projected to Kōkua, "I will take him to the Medical Center. They can quarantine him if necessary. I'll need to be checked out too, if Uli gave him something contagious." Kōkua picked up her weakened cousin.

Maika'i agreed, "Embrace the Mana, my friend."

Kōkua nodded, "You too."

Maika'i wondered if the others had been kidnapped as well. She wasn't sure what to do. She didn't know who to trust. Uli is one of the most powerful Manafuls in the world.

She'd never called upon the highest elder, yet she guessed this presumption would be forgiven. Hopefully, Elder Alaka'i wouldn't ignore her projections for help. He must filter thousands of projections and pleas. With his Mana, separating official from nonofficial class was a simple thing like swatting a mosquito.

"Elder Alaka'i, please help me. I'm a Protector in Elder Uli's mansion. He's drunk and asleep. I've found sick Manafuls. I don't know what he did to them. I align with Mana."

She added the last part as a pledge that she was true to Manaful and not the knots of Lapu.

A voice rang in her head, and she shivered. It was him, Elder Alakaʻi. Star-struck, she almost dropped the medical papers in her hands. Like meeting a king, it was breathtaking.

"Source aligns us. Thank you for contacting me. I sense five Manaful patients in that room of varying energy patterns. Some are very weak. Investigate further. MT with them to the Medical Center once you've ascertained their condition."

Maikaʻi thanked Elder Alakaʻi, returned his *"Embrace the Mana,"* and grimly set upon her triage of the patients.

Empowered by Elder Alakaʻi's vote of confidence and fueled with the familiarity of healing, Maika'i examined each patient.

She lifted her hands above the four patient's sleeping forms, eyes fluttering, using her healer senses. She felt their weakened energy as Elder Alakaʻi had said. How does he scry all across Manaful World?

Eyes closed, she sensed the journey each patient had made to this destination. Images flashed across her mind's eye like stolen dreams. They'd been tranquilized like Kōkua's cousin, Kai, had shared.

Maikaʻi didn't pick up viruses, injuries, or any other health complications. Were they kidnapped here, sedated, then placed in a holding pattern? For what? What had Uli planned for them? She no longer hesitated to wake them up. She didn't condone kidnapping.

The Manaful teenage girl closest to Maikaʻi woke up next. The youth's voice was high pitched and scared. She said, "Where the hell am I? Who are you?"

The girl flinched away from them. Maika'i explained the situation, adding, "I am a healer. What the other guards did to you was wrong. Why were healthy Manafuls sedated and brought to this mansion?"

The teenager voiced, "Name's Rhoda Honua. I think this has to do with COVID. Last I recall, the City was in a panic."

Maika'i wasn't surprised the girl couldn't project her thoughts. Rhoda was from the City, having not yet attained full Manaful status, exactly like she and Kōkua. People like them were in-betweeners, often called Aspiring Hopohopo.

The young girl couldn't have been much older than her children. Maybe 1000 years old or about fourteen human years? Maika'i felt sorry for the youngster's predicament.

Rhoda stared up at the healer. She dug deep to project her thoughts. She aspired to be Manaful. "I sensed you in my mind while I slept."

Maika'i nodded, glad Rhoda was open to tapping Mana. "Yes, I was a healer at one time. That's why I know you don't have COVID. The virus, any virus cannot exist in Manaful World. Our elders of each element would stomp out such a pithy thing compared to their Mana."

Okay, maybe Maika'i went overboard. She was a bona fide elder fangirl.

Rhoda rolled her eyes, then laughed. Older Manafuls were all about the elders of each element. Her parents lectured her daily about their Mana.

The magical elements were B-O-R-I-N-G.

As a teenager, she never spared a second on metaphysics and Mana. She rebelled from her family's Mana training, casting the magic aside. Rhoda scrunched her face, remembering the guards' whispered conversation.

Uli's guards had snatched her from the streets. She'd been hanging out with some Hopohopo teens. They'd bundled her up in a rug after knocking her out with chloroform. She was lucky to be alive and unmolested.

They'd piled up the other unconscious patients in the bed of their truck. She had been the last pickup. They needed Manafuls to be "pretend COVID" patients. The red-head's subconscious had picked up and retained a lot of information even when knocked out.

Strong brain, Kōkua thought, looking at the fiery one.

Maikaʻi swore and started pacing. She had had enough with Elder Uli. He had gone too far. Maikaʻi declared to Rhoda, "This has to end. I will wake the others and MT us all to the Medical center. The elders' security agents will likely question you all once you're deemed fully healthy."

Rhoda perked up, smiled, and took Maikaʻi's hand.

"You've got this, sis," Kōkua said.

Maika'i lifted her hands over their forms, making the urgent determination to transport with them.

NOW.

The air electrified around the little group in Uli's hidden room, and everyone gasped.

She did it—rescued them.

Upon arriving with the patients, Maikaʻi felt validated for taking them out of Elder Uli's mansion. Center staff tended to them till Elder Prime arrived. Alakaʻi was grim as he examined them himself. Maikaʻi had to abstain from fangirling. His eminence and aura blew her mind. His healing powers were unreal and incomparable across their world.

As the ʻOhana Elder Prime, Alakaʻi felt responsible for every Manaful's well-being. His chest ached from Uli's betrayal. Alakaʻi felt like a failure for not predicting Uli's plans. Uli was no longer aligned with Source. This was an alliance with Lapu.

Alakaʻi stood with Maikaʻi on the healer's observation deck. He needed guidance. Only one other Manaful in their world could help.

Alakaʻi projected to Puna, *"I have endangered my people by falling for Uli's lies and fear mongering about COVID. Please come to the Medical Center."*

Elder Puna MT to Elder Alakaʻi in an instant. He brought the forlorn Maka with him. He did this for Maka's safety.

The Elders mind-melded for a few seconds, mentally sharing each other's goings-on. Elder Puna was not surprised by Elder Uli's schemes. He said a prayer for the healing patients Maikaʻi and Kōkua had rescued.

Before leaving the medical center, Elder Alaka'i thanked Kōkua and Maika'i. He accepted their formal resignations on behalf of Elder Uli. He put them under his protection, offering them positions at the Medical Center or with Prime Elder's security.

Both were honorable positions. The Manaful ladies bowed and accepted the honor of Elder Alakaʻi's job offers with pride.

Maka recognized the former guards, apologizing for any miscommunication they'd had earlier in Koa Forest. The ladies shook their heads and hugged Maka. All was forgiven.

He was Moemoe's son. Maka's father would be proud of his son. He hadn't followed his grandfather's questionable path.

Maikaʻi and Kōkua sang at the entrance of the medical center. They smiled at the sky and felt a great weight lifted off their shoulders.

Maika'i and Kōkua's Mana song:

"What happened to Moemoe?
His life was flung about like a toy.
We know his death was a cover-up.
Uli made sure we all shut up.
Moemoe, your son will avenge you.
Fight this cancer from within.
Afraid for our lives we were of him.
Like turning corners on your rims.
Opening your mouth was a risk,
As a guard, we'd search and frisk.
Moemoe, your son will avenge you.
The Uli family will win.
Fight this cancer from within.
Anyone who dared ask the wrong questions.
Their disappearance was under contention.
Sunken to the bottom of a river?
Stones tied to their legs, one quivers
Serving the darkness of Uli, we've come aground.
No longer, we're free and turning around.
Moemoe, your son will avenge you.
The Uli Family will win.

Fight this cancer from within."

Maika'i and Kōkua bowed and thanked their makeshift audience outside the center. Many appreciated the passion in the ladies' voices. Their song helped Maka, and he praised their creativity and musical talent. They preened, glad to cheer up Maka a little. He needed it.

Chapter 34

Manaful World
Elder Puna's Mansion
Koa Forest
July 5, 2022
11:30 a.m.

"Hey, Nicole, we met two of Maka's aunties in the koa forest," Pierre piped up. The Secret Club were relaxing in Ikaika's extremely cool home. Puna had come and gone with Maka. There'd been an urgent matter with those same aunties and his grandfather.

"The aunties had served as Elder Uli's guards, but they uncovered a grave plan," Ikaika informed them from his faux-leather lounge. Maka had projected an update to Ikaika.

Malie remained on her loveseat while Pierre and Nicole were antsy. They'd manifested a weight equipment center and video gaming room. Hands-down, Ikaika's house was the bomb.

"How do you get any Mana training done with all of these toys?" Nicole asked. This place was lit. He didn't need to buy anything in a human or Hopohopo sense. Using coins, that is.

"Nope!" Ikaika answered her thoughts.

"Hey, get out of my head, Manaful!" Nicole joked. Truly, she was lightening up a little. How could she not? There was so much to do. She could conjure an indoor swimming pool in this floating mansion.

"Yup, I could! Wanna take a dip?" Ikaika smiled up at her.

His mind-reading was sharp. He answered her in real time. No delay, live all the time. He nodded to that thought too. She laughed. What a life!

Malie watched Elders Puna and Alakaʻi in the adjoining "room". They were shut out from their convo by the floor to ceiling soundproof glass partition. Meeting Elder Alakaʻi flipped The Secret Club. They all felt like dropping to their knees in a Wayne's World "I'm not worthy" moment. He was the first Manaful, a biblical Adam. The Elder greeted them graciously.

"So, Puna, this is your Secret Club?" Elder Alakaʻi bowed and winked at Elder Puna. Ikaika said they'd been buddies, like brothers, almost their entire lives. He was Ikaika's spirit-father.

Not wasting time, the two elders and Maka popped out of the room. They'd been in that inner cube of a conference room for forever, Maka between them. Nicole worried that they'd never get the scoop.

Ikaika sat beside Nicole on the couch . He nudged her shoulder. "Hey, it'll be fine. Maka's grandpa hired those protectors who approached our friends. There was a grand plan to blame you three for spreading COVID here."

Malie jumped up from her loveseat, and Pierre came to kneel near Ikaika and Nicole's legs.

Ikaika conjured two armless chairs for them to sit on. "Be comfortable!"

Nicole blinked. She'd never get used to his split-second magic. Her two buddies scrambled onto the chairs.

Ikaika continued the story Maka had projected to him before the elders corralled him into the conference room.

"Maka's grandpa got caught by the aunties, Kōkua and Maika'i. They became rescuers, saving victims of Elder Uli's fake-COVID plan." Malie said a quick prayer for the victims.

"Hope they're all right! " Nicole said.

Ikaika turned his chin, pointing to the conference room. Maka's in there sharing his fears about his grandpa. The elders are planning with him their next steps.

Pierre started to pace. He wanted to do something. Their powerlessness was frustrating.

Ikaika bent his head in prayer. He tapped all the healing power within him, calling on Source. Help us be calm. Help us be patient.

Nicole understood his need for solemnity, bowing her head too. Malie and Pierre followed. A wave of soothing peace came over them.

They closed their eyes and breathed. Just breathed.

CHAPTER 35

Manaful World
Koa Forest Elders' Council Chambers
Secret Meeting without Elder Uli
July 5, 2022
12 p.m.

Elder Prime Alaka'i frowned from his Council Seat at his paranoid peers. He pounded his gavel, calling the second meeting that day to order. He cringed before speaking, hating the vocal part of these meetings. "Telepathy rocks," as The Secret Club says. He agreed with them. However, navigating a tangle of thoughts was harder than a tangle of words (easy as it may seem to little girls and boys).

"All here, honorable Elders, we've uncovered a distasteful scheme run by one of our own. The one who is in absentia."

Uli's empty member seat was scrutinized by many eyes.

Pro-Uli Elders grumbled under their breaths, waiting for the full story. Elder Alaka'i explained further, "The Protectors and Maka Uli, Uli's heir, were hoodwinked and gaslit to the extreme. Vile mental manipulations have been crafted. Tainted Mana has been casted.

"We are the supporters of every element that creates this world. Tainted Mana may be involved in our current predicament, but let me remind you it is just one cog in the bigger wheels of the cosmos. The spirit force can be balanced in Manaful. There could never be a virus that can defeat our Mana. Uli tried to make some of us doubt our alignment with Source."

"I don't doubt," roared Elder Polu, Left Hand of Seat.

"Nor I," said the prim Elder Laka.

"*Some* were tricked into thinking something as meager as a virus could decimate our world," Alaka'i pushed ahead. "We let the waked one, Lapu, haunt our cores as he has possessed Uli's. Lapu creates that Fear. Fear took hold of some of you today. "

"Don't you mean It," a halo of gold interrupted. Elder Melemele. Lipstick and bling on.

"It has no identity," Elder Alani of the venusta hues agreed, ever the highlighter.

"Nevertheless," Puna, Right Hand of Seat, restored order with a core pulse.

The Seat inclined his head and droned on. "You, as elders, represent every element. Combined, you are all the universal forces. You have forgotten your worth by falling victim to fear. Some of you spit on Source today. Shame on you!"

It was a fire and brimstone speech.

It was the Hands' turn. Polu went first. His navy blue robe, threaded with turquoise, was agitated like choppy seas.

"I've never liked sitting here on land when I could be out there riding my porpoises," he began in his crashing voice.

"And me my tunnels," rasped Elder Mākau'e.

"But I come because our Mana melding is important for the world."

"Just get to the point," Elder Pele erupted, smoldering in her secluded corner.

Elder Polu turned his nose up. "I've notified the Council on several occasions over the past hundred years of a vile mana sneaking around my coral gardens. They rise from the bedrock like geysers. My ecosystems are decimated, animals infected."

"I have dealt with the leaks," Elder Mākue's closed eyes turned to Polu.

"My animals remain infected," Polu said. "Tainted Mana rises within their cores, making their cells cancerous. I don't know how it's still spreading if you've fixed your leaky little vents. It makes me sick!"

There was an uncomfortable stir at the last word.

Puna whispered a verse from an almost forgotten song: "*Once upon Source there was a great Hā.*"

Even the robes sat very still, as if expecting more of the tune. The air rang with the dragging notes, the kukui nuts crackling. But when the last syllable echoed out Puna launched into a regular monologue in soothing tones.

"I am investigating this," Puna began. "Elders Polu, Lilinoe and Hina are ever willing to lend their Mana to resolve cases of this cryptic cancer. Only by collecting knowledge and learning can we find the best solutions to reach our full potential. So we have learned."

"Tell them what we learned!" Polu slapped his own thighs, impatient in his cocoon of swirling water.

Puna hammered in the nail. "Lapu has begun manifesting using tainted Mana Mist."

"Dead Mana?" Elder 'Ākala leaned forward.

"It happened slowly over the past hundred years. And it's still happening. Something is supercharging Lapu's core. This is not about Earthly microbes at all. This is bigger than Lapu. It's about the grand scheme of things, the cosmic cycles When spirits come to life. When eras change. Listen close, Elders."

By the end of his momentous revelations, pro-Uli Elders began to cry with guilt. They ripped off their masks. They hugged their pro-Puna neighbors and begged Elder Alaka'i for forgiveness.

Elder Prime continued, "I must apologize to you all, too. I was a poor role model. I gave Uli the benefit of the doubt. Let me show you my truth."

As always, there was a Shimmery Wall viewer mounted on a platform in the Council Chambers. The imagery within shifted to show them Uli's actions from Alaka'i's point of view. Most of it was Screened, hazy and ambiguous, but the Seat filled in the blanks.

Every elder now realized how Uli, an opportunistic Manaful young enough to be their child, became third most powerful. It's Lapu's doing.

When the elders settled down from their outpouring of guilt and forgiveness, they resumed their seats at the koa round table. Elder Hina, in her light gray, almost white, bioluminescent robe, asked to speak.

She represented the moon and had skill over the tide. She'd torn off her transparent mask, appearing ready to beat her now ex-pal Uli to a pulp. How could he have led their crew of younger elders astray? The prior Uli had been their mentor.

"I was one of the tricked elders."

Hina's hair swayed with her impassioned speech; it was a gorgeous platinum river flowing to her hips. The natural shade contrasted with her tan skin and hazel eyes. She was enchanting.

Elder Lilinoe held Hina's hand. They were siblings in spirit. Lilinoe wore a deeper gray robe representing stormy rains and mist.

"I motion that all elders converge on the sandalwood forest to punish that lying scoundrel!" Hina's words resonated with everyone.

Elder Lilinoe raised her hand.

Elder Alaka'i nodded at her empathetically.

Lilinoe admitted, "I was scared of a fearsome pandemic, too. I second my sister's motion to converge on Uli's private home. He won't get away with this!"

The other elders cheered in support, eager to broadcast their decision to the rest of the world via the Elder Link, a telepathic "public channel" so to speak. Elder Alaka'i pounded his gavel.

"Order! Order! Lilinoe, did you have more to share?"

She wiped a tear from her eye, nodding. "We must use our 'Ōhana Mana to return peace to our world! No Manaful should live in constant fear!"

Elder Puna started. Ikaika had said those exact same words not too long ago. Constant fear.

Lapu had indeed managed to reach more souls than ever before. Yet, panic won't do. Puna cleared his throat.

"Fear not. Lapu is still weak," he reassured the tense chamber. "We will figure out what the spirit is devising behind Its newfound Blocking power. If His essence comes from tainted mana, then that is to our advantage also. We have our own master of it."

Puna inclined his head toward the earthen mound on which sat Elder Māku'e's basalt throne. This elder never opened his eyes at council meetings. He stroked his beard with a hand that was made of living grit, but remained silent, granular robe shifting with his movements with a skittering rustle. The kukui nuts around him were flameless; he did not like light.

"We will persevere; love will conquer all," Puna concluded.

Lilinoe and Hina bowed in unison to the red Elder. Lilinoe humbly shared, "My sincerest apologies for speaking ill of you and The Secret Club!"

"Mercy aligns with Source," Elders Alaka'i and Puna chorused. "We are ever open to forgiveness."

The koa chamber became loud with sorries and praises for the brave Uli whistleblowers, Maika'i and Kōkua. Their images flashed on the Shimmery Wall platform.

Elder Alaka'i pounded his gravel again. "Order! Order!"

Puna raised his hand for a song. The leader laughed at his childhood friend, sure he could add his two cents better in rhyme. Why not?

Everyone settled down. Alaka'i silently marveled at his friend's gravitas. Puna raised one brow at Alaka'i's compliment.

Puna puffed up his chest with pretend pompous air, projecting, "*Hey, when you got it. You got it.*"

Alaka'i laughed at Puna's attempt at levity.

Just as quickly, Puna became serious again. He solemnly looked at each elder. One by one, they met his gaze, projecting their apologies directly. Aligning with the enormous presence of Source, he rallied his compatriots around his majestic core.

Elder Rally Song:

"Bring out your elements. Use your Mana.
Embrace the 'ōhana skills you represent.
Take on all challenges by being present.
Lift our world from this slump.
Don't let Uli kick you in the rump.
Fear takes away all love and hope.
Can't let that happen. Nope. Nope. Nope.

Heave out your elements. Use your Mana.
Believe in our big Manaful family.
Work together to spread harmony.
He tried to weaken us.
Infected our minds like a pus.
I've had it up to here.
The time to be righteous is near.
Bring out our elements. Use your Mana."

At the end of Puna's song, the elders were up and cheering. They all shouted, "Align with Source!" They MT without further ado to the sandalwood forest.

Elder Alaka'i pounded his gavel, trying to get a hold of the situation as everyone disappeared one after the other. Mana mist swirled in the chamber in their wake. All over the world, hundreds of Manafuls headed to the sandalwood forest to support their Elders. The sound of zinging mass telepathy was deafening in Alaka'i's venerable head.

"I didn't ask for a stampede!"

Puna stayed back, patting his friend's shoulder. "You try too hard, buddy." Alaka'i shook his head and slumped in defeat.

It was a lost cause. The elders were out to get Uli. Puna looked at his friend and shrugged. "What will you do, Alaka'i?"

"Great rousing chant."

"You flatter me."

"Got them out there."

"Mahalo."

"I couldn't have done better," Alaka'i offered Puna the compliment with a fist bump. Puna fist-bumped him, laughing, and Elder Puna laughed with him, elbowing his pal.

A bell-peal rang in their heads with immense weight. It was Elder Prime's heir. Charmaine Momi

"Daddy! I'm going to Maka's!"

"Stay put in the villa, young lady!"

"Daddy!"

"No!"

"Ugh!

"Absolutely not!"

"You can't stop me from helping him!"

Her projection winked off with a note of victory. The sudden loss of her incredible presence humbled them both. She was a unique being in their world. With her around...

“Want to bet on Uli’s chances?” Puna had a thing for jolly bets now. The Secret Club’s idioms were rubbing off on him. Alaka‘i shook his head. They MT to the battle scene, hoping they hadn’t missed the show.

CHAPTER 36

Manaful World
Elder Puna's Mansion
Koa Forest
July 5, 2022
1 p.m.

The Secret Club watched the set-up for a battle scene in real-time from Ikaika's Shimmery Wall. Malie begrudgingly "let" Ikaika erase her landscape murals and move her red loveseat to another room. The Secret Club and Ikaika huddled together on a newly conjured velvet sectional.

They loved the huge movie-sized Shimmery Wall before them. Apparently it was set to viewing mode. The trio and Ikaika saw all the Manaful elders converge into Uli's sandalwood forest to avenge Maka and Manaful World.

Uli had long since lost the honorific "Elder" title in their eyes. Truth be told, Nicole wanted to refer to Uli as a poophead. Ikaika had laughingly plucked that thought out of her head. He shook his head at her, "No, Nicole. Don't lower yourself to insults. Uli's not worth it."

Strangely, Nicole almost felt sorry for Uli. "This is like watching a wipeout football game, where there's no chance for the underdog."

Pierre high-fived her for the football imagery. "Nice, Nicole!" Pierre scratched his chin and bounced on the cushions. "I wonder what it's like down there in the heat of things?"

Malie shook her head at him. "No, thank you. I like watching from here with you. Safe and sound." Ikaika nodded, agreeing with Malie.

He worried for Maka. Elders Alakaʻi and Puna had picked Maka up from the mansion just minutes ago. They'd had to twist his arm to join them at the front line. He'd been scared.

"This could be dangerous, elders!" Maka had paced Puna's mansion. They'd met here just an hour ago; that had been prior to their second Elders' Council meeting.

The Elders had left him there to mull over the council meeting's likely outcome. The Secret Club and Ikaika had waved at him once the elders left. Maka had given them a thumbs-up through the glass. "I'm good. Just need some space."

The Secret Club had nodded, resuming whatever they'd been up to. Ikaika had lingered on the other side of the glass, lifting his hand to the pane. Maka had gotten up and put his hand to his friend's through the glass. *"I'm here. When you're ready. Be strong, Maka."*

Maka had heard Ikaika's projection and felt his Mana warming the glass beneath their hands. He nodded his thanks and returned to the cushy, ergonomic chairs he was partial to. He sat comfortably, but he'd been stressed out.

Ikaika's heartbeat quickened, watching in real-time on portal viewers as Elders Alaka'i and Puna arrived with Maka at Uli's front yard. Ikaika sang a brief, silent prayer-song for Maka.

Ikaika's Prayer-song:

"Don't be afraid, my friend.
Stand tall fighting him to the end.
Let Manaful elements empower you.
All that's good in Manaful praises you.

Here we are rooting for you.
We're your cheering squad
I know it all seems odd
Believe in the Mana of Source
Let the past go without remorse.
Amen. Amen. Amen."

The Secret Club clapped for Ikaika, repeating after him together: "Amen. Amen. Amen."

Chapter 37

Manaful World
Sandalwood Forest
July 5, 2022
1:05 p.m.

In Uli's front yard, there were no Protective Forces anymore. They'd been disbanded, and some of them apprehended by Elders' Security. Most of them spilled the beans after the incident that morning at the Medical Center. Some of them escaped with Lapu's help.

There was no one looking out for Elder Uli now, except Lapu. That was, unless even the Spirit ditched Elder Uli, throwing him under the bus. Lapu was like that, unloyal to His followers. When an acolyte was no longer useful, Lapu disposed of them.

Every elder except Uli was present. Together, they formed their rainbow of bioluminescent clothing, resplendent against the sandalwood forest's sun-scattered backdrop.

Maka stood between elders Alaka'i and Puna. They nudged him, pointing upward to Uli's treehouse. It sat in a tangle of bare boughs that looked like a claw.

"Go face him," Elder Alaka'i said as if telling Maka to eat his porridge. Elder Puna nodded encouragingly. A face-off was coming. Maka shook with fear and anxiety. He wasn't ready for this. He turned to the elders around him.

They stood for the earth, air, water, fire, and all other fundamental and living beings. They represented the many complex forces of nature Manafuls take for granted. His eyes pleaded with them for help.

They all sent their energies out to him. The forest became an amalgamation of power. Their combined Mana surrounded Maka from all sides, levitating him in a transparent bubble above the ground. Through their empowering beams of Mana, Ikaika's prayer song uplifted Maka from afar. All of their support rejuvenated him. He sensed it all in his core.

Did he believe in himself enough to accept this surge? Through Source, there would be no Mana inaccessible to him. Though containing all that power may get him killed.

He opened his core, and flinched with the burn of sheer energy that welled in. Surge Alert. Already he was trembling.

Elder Uli's laughter broke through Maka's protective sheath. Lashing out his Mana, the senior threw out a net of electrified force that burst the bubble. Maka dropped to the forest floor, head ringing with the rush of magic.

"Haaaa-haaaa-haaaa! Isn't this the sweetest moment," Uli said, forming a heart with his hands. His robes were green fire. Ferns curled up into dead black crisps under his feet as he hovered across the clearing.

"You have succumbed to despair," Maka grunted, balking at his pulsing core as he aligned with Source. Or tried to.

Heir and Elder locked their minds in a mental battle, bracing themselves against the magnetic pulse of their presences crashing into each other in unseen space. Uli's pulse grew steadily bigger, pushing Maka's feet back through the dirt. Both Manafuls began to spark and fizzle with energy as their cores powered up.

Uli suddenly struck, lifting Maka to stretch him to death. Maka rose several feet above the ground, being pulled in four directions like an execution by quartering.

Maka drew on his core to tap the spectrum of elements saturating it. Source's Mana welled up deep inside him, flooding every fiber of his being. He dropped to the ground, free.

The teenager felt elder Mana radiating through his pores. They circled the two fighters, grandfather and grandson. They gave them a thirty-foot diameter ring of space.

It was a lot of room, yet for Elders Alaka'i and Puna, it was too much space. They wanted to interfere and pulverize Uli.

Back at Ikaika's mansion, he and The Secret Club were of one mind with Ikaka's grandfather and spirit-father. They wanted to interfere.

"Why isn't your grandpa stopping Uli?" Nicole screamed at the Wall. They watched at the end of their seats. Eager to jump into the fray, Pierre jumped up to pace behind the viewers' couch.

"What's happening to the other elders? Why are they glowing in different shades?"

Ikaika off-handedly answered, "Those are their 'Ohana colors. They're passing their core-powers into Maka. It'll help him defeat his grandfather."

Malie clapped, "Yes! I love this unified support for our guy!"

Nicole was still confused. This wasn't a fair fight. "Why did they force Maka to fight alone in the ring against Uli?"

Malie said, "I get it. It's for the ʻOhana leadership. One must earn it. Like Maka's proving that he's worthy of holding the title."

Ikaika applauded Malie's intuition, giving her a one-armed hug. They all still faced the screen.

Back in the ring, Maka had a rainbow aura around him. He began to shake, trying to balance the overwhelming Mana. He was just a preteen. It was all hard to handle.

Uli tried to push Maka's shoulder to the ground, "Kneel! I subjugate you, fool!"

He backed up at the heat rising from Maka's body. Uli boomed, "What are you doing? You're not worthy of their Mana! You owe me!"

"Owe you what, exactly?"

"I raised you!"

"You're not my Creator"

"I am your Lord!"

Maka leaned forward with his hands out, accepting the elemental powers of each elder. "Source is my Lord! You can't gaslight me with your rubbish!"

Maka saw plasma sparkling between his curling fingers. He could kill his grandfather with this great infusion. He felt like a bubble about to explode.

Suddenly, Maka didn't want to do it. Doubts crept in.

Uli sensed Maka's hesitation, jumping at this weakness of doubt. Maka's fears were Uli's fuel. It energized Uli. He seized the sandalwood trees all around them with his Mana, sliced them into needles in the sky above, and directed them to rain as arrows upon him.

"Aah!" Maka went down, looking like a hedgehog. Sandalwood reeds stuck out of his back. He bled on deadened turf.

The other elders shouted and tried to leap forward. They wanted to squish Uli like the bug he was. But this was not a schoolyard fight. Mana Mist manifested around them thickly.

Elder Alaka'i projected, "This is Maka's fight. He must believe in himself."

He put up an invisible force field separating the fighters' ring from the audience of elders. "If Maka dies, I will let you take care of Uli!"

The impatient elders grumbled, some cursing Elder Alaka'i under their breaths. Some elders reinforced their energies into Maka again— no force field could stop the flow of Mana.

Uli snorted, and lifted up into the air in a storm of sand and twigs. A sphere of rot exploded from him, withering the grass and shrubs in a ring as it expanded. Maka raised his hand as if to block a punch. Already weak, his defense proved futile. Maka was blasted backward, his skin seeming to crisp like parchment on fire. Even his blood curdled, flesh paining like he'd never felt before..

Back in Ikaika's home, The Secret Club screamed! "Ouch! Ahh! No!"

Nicole let her swear words fly, not giving a rip about manners. Malie lifted her brow at Nicole's language.

Nicole answered, "If I can't curse now, when else? Maka's over there, covered in spikes, for Christ's sake!"

Pierre understood. The spikes injuring Maka were gruesome. It reminded him of the infamous arrow scene in Akiro Kurasawa's classic samurai movie Throne of Blood. Pierre and his Grandpa had enjoyed black and white samurai films together. The contrast between his beloved grandfather and Uli couldn't be more stark than now. Pierre was pissed at Uli's murderous intent.

Malie worried about Ikaika.

The dwarf was losing it. When the spikes rained down on Maka, Ikaika started crying and yelling at the Wall. Malie's expression changed as he glanced sideways at Malie. No one has a bigger heart than her.

Malie was rubbing the dwarf's back. Ikaika patted her knee, repeating like a mantra, "He has to defeat him. He has to defeat him!"

Meanwhile, in the fighter's ring, Maka was seriously getting whooped. The SC cringed as their friend was lifted and slammed to the ground repeatedly, driving the wooden needles deeper and deeper into his wounds.

Uli stood over his grandson. Strips of wood ripped from the trees all around orbited the rotten elder. They twisted, coiling like ropes into a whip that seemed alive. He caught it.

"So damn weak!"

Swaaaaat! Uli now flailed a Sandalwood cat-o'-nine-tails, relentlessly flogging Maka's arms, legs, and back. The rope splintered the thorns sticking out of him. Some thorns got pushed deeper in.

"Aahhhh!" Maka shouted in agony. The thorns pierced his organs, weakening him as blood dripped down his face, chest, arms, and legs.

Uli was on a roll, "What good are these elements if you refuse to Manaful up?"

Swaaaaat! Uli was an expert at mind games. He knew that defeating Maka was ninety percent mental and ten percent physical.

Uli was winning. A hopelessness swirled in the air, an unseen nemesis. Maka's mind was turning against himself: *I'm too young. He's defeated our whole family. How am I different?*

Uli laughed, "Haaaa-haaaa-haaaa! I'm winning! You dummy!"

Swaaaaat! Uli's whipping broke Maka down as he cried, "Please, stop!"

Uli struck again and again. "Never! I must teach a lesson to all of them, too." He meant the screaming elders on the other side of the force field. The whip decayed into dust as Uli blasted out surges of rot again, chipping away at Maka's flesh.

Then, out of nowhere, Source's presence expanded to contain ground zero...

Maka was falling in and out of consciousness. He was having an out-of-body experience. His spirit drifted out of his broken body.

Uli freeze-framed. The spectator noise was muffled, replaced by ephemeral voices that whispered like waves on a beach.

"Am I dead? " Maka asked Source.

Voices rose from the ocean of whispers, getting clearer.

"We love you!" It was the elders, Ikaika, and even The Secret Club. Voices from all over the world.

"We love you!" Someone suddenly grasped his left hand, icy. Someone else held his right. His eyes widened in recognition of his parents, Moemoe and Nina. They floated beside him in non-corporeal form. The three of them looked down at his bloody figure and his grandfather's frozen arm in mid-strike.

"We are with you, always, son." His father said, "We love you."

His mother said, "You are ready to ascend."

Floating Maka hugged them both. "I love you so much. Miss you."

She patted his back. "We're always with you. Believe in Source, the preserver. Believe in yourself, your core."

He nodded. "Okay, I can. I mean, I will. I do." They smiled and disappeared like an unspooling thread.

Woooooosh!

Maka's spirit wooshed back into his body. Time restarted in a snap. He looked up through the blood in his eyes and hair. He took back that ninety-percent-mental game. He stood on shaky legs and willed the thorns out. They shot out of his flesh straight at Uli.

Ducking the projectiles, Uli's eyes widened. He sensed a change in Maka's strength.

The crowd of elders sensed it too. They cheered. For a while there, they thought Maka was down for the count.

"Yah!" Came their shouts and hollers of support. They'd turned into a crazed crowd at a prizefight. A possible KO round makes a turn for the better. The downed fighter has found his feet for another go.

Uli wasn't having it. He hadn't given up on the mental game: "Get back down, loser!"

Maka was no longer the same dwarf. He was no longer a means to an end. Maka smiled wryly at Uli.

He was all in now—one hundred percent body, mind, spirit, and soul.

Maka took a deep breath and called on Source. He believed. He believed Source had his back. A heavy, reverberating bell-strike rang in his head, deep, heavy.

Winds rustled around Maka and Uli. They became encircled by manifesting Mana Mist, a vortex that sparkled in the overcast light of day. Thunder rumbled over the forest canopy.

Buzz! The force field vibrated loudly as it began to rain.

Torrents drenched Maka and Uli, cleansing Maka's wounds. The water purified him, just as the magical mist was healing him. A cloud of nature's Mana Mist enveloped Maka. Nature's magic was waking. He finally accepted the rainbow of elements from the elders and his Piko—core—exploded into life.

All of them are parts of the Source. All the colors now flowed through Maka, balanced. Waves of voices encompassed him. The whistles of whales. The squalls of the ocean filled him with strength as flocks of seagulls flapped their wings. Pele's swooshing fires and lava bursts burned hot as his core. Every creature one could imagine linked to him at once. He finally felt it all. Such might! His fear vanished.

Uli watched the flow of elemental spirits within his grandson. He felt it happen in his own core, rotten as it may be. The rain froze around them like diamonds lost in space, all noise muffled.

A cosmic force held them all in a fist.

The grandfather was now afraid for his life.

He tried projecting Lapu. Only silence came. He tried transporting out of the ring. That didn't work, either; the mists held him prisoner. This was it for Uli.

Maka aimed his hands toward Uli.

His grandfather faced his death with dignity. His hands were relaxed and empty to his side. He closed his eyes and lifted his chin. The mist attacked his living form. It broke his atomic bonds, unraveled his form and core. He literally melted back into the forest. His skin turned into greenish-brown tar, which dried to cracked dirt, and then his core winked out of existence with a small shockwave, leaving behind only the robe. It's light dimmed. The textile became ghostly, limp in midair.

A deafening bell rang out in all minds of Manaful except the humans. Otherworldly, large, as terrible as it was awesome. A statement from Source.

Uli was annihilated.

Maka fell to the ground and cried in relief, utterly exhausted. His wounds were painful. His nerves were on fire.

There was grief too. Sadness for the "What ifs."

What if I had a good grampa?

He prayed in gratitude for his life and for the support of the elders around him. He thanked his parents, who had visited him in non-corporeal form. He had no idea what had happened, but it had given him such strength.

Elder Puna was the first one to float into the space Uli had rotted, cutting through the frozen raindrops. He knelt next to Elder Maka, soothing his new peer. At only 770 years old, Elder Maka would be the youngest in Council history. Maka hugged Puna.

"We did it, dear Elder!"

Puna started. He shook his head. "It's just Puna now. You got it wrong. It was all you out there! Proud of you!"

Maka bawled.

"There, there."

"I didn't want to kill him! He loved me, deep down."

"Ehem."

"I know it!"

Puna nodded, understanding Maka's piety.

Still, Maka needed to understand the bigger picture.

"Uli hasn't been himself for a long time," Puna said carefully. "The self-abuse and temptations of Lapu stole your grandfather long ago. Toxicity like that steals the love from a Manaful's heart."

Puna hugged Maka and felt Maka nod against his shoulder, but well after the rain burst back into a real-time drizzle. The pitter-patter of water drops grumbled on the humus.

"You must lead your 'Ohana now. The Elders' Council will perform the final transmutation of your family's Mana," Puna said, emanating strength like Uli had rot, potent waves of it.

Chief Elder Alaka'i approached, radiant. He gathered all the Elders in a circle around Maka. They held hands, surrounding him in a smaller ring this time. The elders sang for Maka as Source gifted him with his 'Ohana's Mana. You could see it happen, the mists dancing and ringing like music in motion.

The Elders' Song of Transmutation

"Generations of Mana transmuted to a new
'Ōma'oma'o Elder.
He'll manage the vital crops like no other.
He will bless and serve his family with love.
He brings the peace of a dove.

Envelope him with all of your goodwill.
Transmute through Source, with our Mana and powers.
Keep his body, mind, spirit, and core within your bowers.
Safe transmutation!
Safe transmutation!
Safe transmutation!"

An emerald light embraced Maka as he sensed the energies of every tree and growing plant-life. They "spoke" to him, and he greeted them in return.

His grandpa's robe bobbed over like a dying oarfish. It seemed reluctant to let the Mana Mist take it to its inheritor. Maka poked an arm into a sleeve and the other slapped him. He looked round at Puna, holding his cheek in shock.

"Just grab it and put it on," Elder Alaka'i suggested, bobbing impatiently.

Maka reached out but the robes twitched away. It tried to flee but he grabbed it with a deft M'T. He and Cloth had a little tussle in the wet air as the Elder Council watched patiently, and finally got the upper hand. He put on his 'Ohana robes and the fibers came back to life, lighting up the rain. Its color returned in blending greens.

Alaka'i smiled at Maka, whose only injury now was a receding black eye. "Welcome to the Council, Elder Maka Uli."

Maka winced. "Maka, please."

Puna nodded and elbowed Alaka'i. The latter frowned. Alaka'i loved to stick to formalities. "Ah, yes, I understand," he said to Maka and Puna.

Everyone congratulated Elder Maka. Then they gradually MT away to their own homes. They were all eager to share their experiences. They'd had front-row seats to unprecedented action.

Elders Maka and Puna teleported to Ikaika's floating mansion. When the greatly tired elders popped into the room, three emotional humans and a very relieved dwarf rushed them. They all formed a group hug.

Finally, the arms broke apart except for Ikaika and Maka. They were crying, swaying, and hugging. Ikaika felt Elder Maka's back for arrow puncture wounds. He stepped back with a raised brow.

Elder Maka projected, "*The transmutation ceremony healed me, and now I receive the constant yammering of all woodlands, crops, gardens, and more.*"

Ikaika beamed, "*You'll get accustomed to it sooner or later. Gramps and Elder Alaka'i have.*"

That didn't surprise Elder Maka. "*That's not news. Those two are practically as old as Manaful World itself.*"

The Secret Club listened in via their connected minds. Projections were still strange after all these months. They preferred voice and using their vocal cords. Yet, the kids understood how tired Elder Maka must be. Telepathy was his first language.

Elder Maka was utterly tired and probably ready to hit the sack. They would be.

He pointed at Ikaika's huge Shimmery Wall. Ikaika frowned and almost broke into tears again.

He projected to Maka, "*Yes. You went down, and he kept whipping you. I projected a prayer song to you. I pushed all my strength into it, hoping you'd receive it and fight back. You were so very still on the ground after a bit. We thought it was the end. Thought. Thought. Thought you were dead."*

Ikaika was blubbering now. The kids and Elder Maka were now group-hugging him.

Elder Maka continued to hold Ikaika close, and the others did too. The new elder was tearing up again. He projected for everyone, "*I love you all.*"

Elder Puna silently observed the group. He'd stepped back to give all the young ones space. He turned to the Secret Club, saying aloud this time, "Are you three ready to cross over to your neck in the woods?"

Elder Maka held his hands up, laughing as he switched to voice. "No more forest metaphors for today. Still sensitive here."

Pierre laughed and hugged Elder Maka again by himself. The girls sandwiched-hugged him from each side.

They fist-bumped-wiggle-wooshed Ikaika, who pulled them in for more group hugs.

They all laughed and took a deep breath together. They'd witnessed an ordeal together—the entire day had been like a journey. Nonetheless, when they jumped into the Shimmery Wall, no Earth time would have transpired. That's what interdimensional travel was like—a trip, in all meanings of the term.

The Secret Club bowed to Elder Puna. Ikaika's grandpa guided them to the same Shimmery Wall they'd just seen life change within.

Pierre said, "Wow, we can enter Earth from up here in the clouds?"

Elder Puna waggled his brows sassily. "Not always."

The Shimmery Wall switched to traveling mode, so to speak, and Elder Puna held his arm for them to enter it. The Secret Club turned one more time to the room and waved. The three Manafuls waved back. The kids held hands and leapt through the Shimmery Wall.

Chapter 38

Earth
Wright Middle School Gymnasium
July 5, 2022
8:00 a.m.

Pierre felt for all of his body parts. Nicole jumped up and down. Malie wiggled. They all felt like a lifetime had transpired. Before leaving for their respective homes, they sang a song for the Manafuls in their safe space behind the gymnasium.

The Secret Club's Family Song:

Together:

"You can take it with you.
With you. With you.
You can take it with you.
With you. With you."

Pierre:
"Loss of family breaks your heart.
Many things can pull you apart."

Nicole:
"Virus or not
Be honest. Don't let love rot."

Malie:
"Manaful or human, it doesn't matter.
Holding pain inside makes glass shatter."

Together:
"You can take it with you.
With you. With you."

Pierre:
"Friends lift you up when you need them.
Having them there during the mayhem."

Nicole:
"It's essential to say, thank you.
They appreciate you too."

Malie:
"Mama says, 'Pay attention to where you are!'
But don't forget to also pay attention to what you are."

Together:
"You can take it with you.
With you. With you. "

Pierre:
"You're a beautiful person, no matter what.
Never listen to those who don't give a fut."

Nicole:
"Take it from me, making friends changed my life.
They lift me up and save me from strife."

Malie:
"So never forget the love they gave you.
They'll be there. Just give them a cue."

Together:
"You can take it with you.
With you. With you.
You can take it with you.
With you. With you."

They hugged, promising to FaceTime that night. Their nightly meeting was going to be exciting. Recaps always were.

Chapter 39

Manaful World
Ikaika and Elder Puna's mansion
August 4, 2022
7 a.m.

Elder Puna and Ikaika watched the Secret Club grab their lunch bags and don their jackets at their homes. They were all headed to school. Today was a big day for them: the first day of seventh grade at Wright Middle.

Ikaika chewed on a mint leaf. Its cool, tingly flavor was refreshing and good for his indigestion. Being able to conjure anything to eat can upset one's stomach. That morning's mushroom pizza and taco weren't jiving well in his belly.

A swoosh of air swept behind him. He found Elder Maka there. He'd come to watch the Secret Club through their Wall. Technically, as an elder, Maka could conjure Shimmery Walls wherever he stood. His Mana was that bad butt.

That term made Ikaika smile. The Secret Club girls argued about swearing on the reg. Nicole would say, "bad a**" while Malie would say "bad butt." Ikaika didn't care either way, but when his gramps was around, he kept his language clean.

Elder Puna nodded at his new elder peer and winked at Ikaika. "*Yes, please, avoid swearing in my presence,*" his grandpa projected.

Elder Maka's new Elder's cloth suited him. In the post-fight and transmutation exhaustion, Ikaika hadn't noticed his pal's robe.

Had he been blind? Maybe he was, then. Not now, though. Elder Maka's robe was more beautiful than Uli's had been. Elder Maka's bioluminescent cloth shone like the fresh Maori paua or abalone shells. Glittery pearlescent greens, blues, teals, and browns lived in Elder Maka's robe. Wow.

His grandfather's red bioluminescent robe had amazing fiery colors that were dramatic. Elder Maka's robe had a subduing, almost trancelike vibe.

Ikaika was a little jelly (another human term he loved). However, he wouldn't trade the Elder's kuleana for any gorgeous robe. No way! Ikaika liked being young in mind and body.

Elder Maka pointed at the Shimmery Wall. The split screen showed the kids singing in their cars and talking with their respective parents. Elder Maka turned sideways to his friend to inquire, "How have they been, Ikaika?"

Ikaika smirked, answering sassily, "Hey, you're a powerful elder now. You could simply mind-meld and read my history of knowledge."

His friend shook his head vigorously at that. "Ikaika, I'm shocked you'd suggest that. That's not ethical. Mind-melding is a mutual, consenting bond."

Ikaika playfully punched his friend's arm. "I know. I'm pulling your leg. Grandpa would have my hide."

Elder Maka laughed at that and didn't mind the playful manner in which Ikaika still treated him.

"You've been really busy, huh? It's been a month. Are you good?" Ikaika was serious now.

Elder Maka appreciated his concern and was amused by Ikaika's adoption of human idioms. He gave it back. "No worries, dude. I'm all G."

That made both Ikaika and Elder Puna laugh. Ikaika held his stomach and tried to catch his breath. He was practically 'Rolling On the Floor Laughing', as The Secret Club would say in their nightly mobile meetings.

Elder Maka rolled his eyes hard, which was another Nicole thing.

Ikaika saw that and literally dropped to the floor this time.

Elder Puna watched his grandson on the floor as he grappled with his self-control, bemused.

Ikaika finally settled down, though he stayed down there flat on his back. Arms out, he huffed and puffed.

His prone position was an invitation for the three new puppies Elder Maka had recently gifted Ikaika.

Cookie, Brownie, and Cupcake—named after all of Ikaika's favorite foods—tumbled all over themselves to get to their master. Cookie looked like his chocolate chip namesake with beige fur and black smudges. Brownie was all brown. Duh. Cupcake had a white frosting-colored head and a black body.

The baby labradors were five weeks old and transitioned to the bottle. Elder Maka had been given Mele, the labradors' mama, and her pups soon after Uli died. His aunt, Maika'i, the former protector guard, moved her family to a no-pets condo closer to the medical center.

She'd returned to her former career as a healer. Elder Maka was grateful for Mele and the pups. He knew Maika'i's family missed the labrador family. Maika'i and her family transported to his mansion to visit Mele and her pups when they could.

Yet, Ikaika knew his pal needed the healing bond of his dog. Besides, the young elder's big new mansion needed Mele.

Elders Alaka'i and Puna had melded their Mana to break down and rebuild Uli's mansion. The former gigantic treehouse abode was now a copycat house but with more natural light.

Elder Maka asked for a replica of Ikaika's glass house. The elders laughed and granted their new peer's wish. The huge, pearlescent cube of home looked odd in the canopy thirty feet above the forest floor. It's not invisible, just transparent.

Its clear glass walls were double-reinforced and darkly tinted. Elder Maka was adamant about his privacy. The thick foliage up there was like a private hedge-fence.

Ikaika hugged his pups and accepted the levitation the elders offered. It was strange standing between them.

Ikaika absentmindedly offered the elders on either side a mint leaf from his sarong pocket. Both accepted, humming in appreciation.

Elder Maka bowed and projected, "*Thank you, mint.*"

Ikaika raised his eyebrow. "*Did you thank me or the plant?*"

Both Elders laughed, answering at the same time, "*Both. Both you and the plant.*"

Ikaika laughed again. "*You two could be a comedy act!*"

His grandfather patted his shoulder. His friend grinned and patted Ikaika's other shoulder.

Ikaika turned back to the Wall. Life was funny.

CHAPTER 40

Earth
Wright Middle School
Gymnasium Locker Room
Lunch Recess
August 4, 2022

As far as the first days of school went, Nicole's didn't go so well. Three tall boys in her team sports class bullied her. They sneakily waited until everyone left the locker rooms. Should she have changed faster? Who knows?

It began in class when the three tall boys picked Nicole for their basketball team. They'd made two assumptions. You know that saying about the word "assume?" After making an a** of themselves, the boys regretted choosing her.

First assumption, at five foot two, Nicole was one of the tallest people in the seventh grade. Naturally, she must be a great B-ball player, right? Buzz! Wrong.

Second assumption, Nicole's part African-American. B-ball is in her blood, right? Buzz! Wrong, again.

Like the game show buzzer, the basketball buzzer rang loudly against their team.

Nicole missed a shot. Buzz!

Nicole traveled, again. Buzz!

Nicole allowed a legal turnover. Buzz!

Got the picture? That last one was unfair. The school prohibits skins versus shirts. Therefore, how was she to remember who her teammates were?

It's the first day of school. Give a girl a break. After changing her clothes, she stepped out of the girls' locker room. The three tall boys from her team cornered Nicole outside the door. They stood head to head with her, though broader and meaner. They made rude animal squawks at her. The largest of them began to abuse her in time with his crude sounds.

Wack! He pushed her shoulder against the wall.

Wack! He kicked her shin.

Nicole twisted her body, blocking his next attempt and their arms and legs entangled. They almost fell to the floor.

He disengaged himself, but stepped back.

Another one didn't approach her, but he shouted, "Yo, Ken, it's the phony baloney, Nicoley!"

Nicole's ears perked up at the name. That's right!

The large one's name was Ken. She didn't know the others, though they were on her 'team.' At that moment, she regretted signing up for team sports class as well as Regular Gym class. Why'd she voluntarily surround herself with this much testosterone? He pulled her gym bag from her, throwing it on the floor.

The third one grabbed her backpack, opened it, and pulled her deodorant out. He smiled wickedly at the label, Pure and Soft. He shouted, 'Lookie here, she's Lovely and Soft. Not! More like Wack at B-ball and Soft!" He threw the deodorant at her head. She ducked and it landed at her feet. The top popped off, smudging the linoleum tile with the fragrant, creamy substance.

Nicole had had enough, she was about to reach down for her things and make a run for it. Ken, the large one who was pushing her, blocked her path. His chest almost touched hers. The proximity made her cringe.

He pressed closer. Ken's breath was disgusting. She wished everyone was still masked-up. At least they wouldn't breathe on her, much less spread their germs.

He raised his hands toward her boobs, adding in his crass voice, "We should get a basketball ball. Dodgeball, anyone? First, look at these girls here. Wow."

Nicole was about to knee him in his boys, when a shout came from behind the bullies. "ARRRRGGGGHH!"

From behind the three bullies, a short, dwarf-like skinny boy waved his arms above his head and screamed. A book and backpack lay at his feet. "STOP! Ken! Stop that! I'm telling Mommy!"

The small boy was about four feet tall. He reminded Nicole of a skinner, pale-skinned version of Ikaika. He stopped hopping around and shouting his warnings. He'd distracted Ken enough that she was able to shimmy away from the boys. She backed up a few feet from Ken's vile closeness. The cute little savior held Nicole's attention from running away.

Ken narrowed his face at his brother, shouting at him, "Shut up, Kona, or I'll shut you up next!"

Kona puffed up his face and bravely raised his fist. "Oh, yeah? Remember three strikes and you're out? You've got priors! One more, and it's Juvie for you! Ha! Eat that!"

Ken's buddies nudged Ken, nodding and acknowledging Kona's words. The two bullies backed away from Nicole, letting Ken bury his own grave.

Wow, Nicole was impressed. Kona was right. Uncle Nick was a prosecutor.

Nicole almost wanted to hug little Kona. Ken's buddies had already lit out. Ken followed them as if someone lit a fire under his butt.

Kona watched the guys fleeing. He was small for sixth grade, having skipped a grade level. His thickly framed glasses kept slipping down his nose. He held a paperback against his chest like a shield.

Nicole smiled at him. He reminded her of old Malie. That's before they were the SC.

She nodded to Kona. "Thanks."

He nodded back.

She took a deep breath, closed her eyes, and wished she could MT home. Oh, to be Manaful would be cool! She left the gym to find a bench to eat lunch.

How ironic that this place of bullying was also her place of peace. That's life. Walking around the back of the gym, Nicole sang to herself about the bullies.

Nicole's Song for Bullies:

Put away your mean words.
You're being absurd.
Bullying others makes you a turd.
It's only pain that you bring.

Stop it now. Learn to sing!
Sing out your pain. It's okay to be off-key.
Trust me on this, just listen to me.
Put away your mean words.
Don't touch me or breathe on me.
Go walk in nature, hug a tree.
Hitting people is a crime.
You'll end up serving time.
Get some help. Get therapy.
Seek out a newfound family.
Put away your mean words."

Nicole found a bench to eat her home lunch. She wasn't that hungry; instead, she texted The Secret Club.

CHAPTER 41

Earth
Wright Middle School Cafeteria
Lunch Recess
August 4, 2022

Pierre sat at his regular lunch table with his football pals. He'd adjusted well in Hawaii since moving from California before COVID. Rodney, an offensive line, was also in Pierre's algebra class.

"Pierre, did you understand Mr. Nakamura?" Rodney's confusion about class was normal these days. Many students were still adjusting to in-person learning post-pandemic.

In class, Mr. Nakamura still wears his mask. His instruction sounds muffled at best. Only a few teachers have the energy or wherewithal to post their lesson notes online.

Pierre smiled. "I'll share my math notes with you later. Text me, and I'll share the doc." Rodney's tense shoulders dropped in relief, and his brows straightened out.

He mumbled, "You're cool," with his mouth full of spaghetti. Tomato sauce stuck at the corner of his lip.

Pierre laughed. Eating in the cafe was a risk, as the students weren't socially distancing anymore. It was a risk many took these COVID days.

Pierre looked at each of his classmates and wondered where Nicole and Malie were. He missed them and looked forward to meeting them at the gym after school.

Thursdays were their special days. Manaful days. Too bad they only visited once a week. They needed to rethink that—he'd make a meeting motion tonight.

Beep. Beep. Beep.

Pierre's SC group text notified him. Nicole.

Nicole: Where are u 2?

Malie: Library. Come up. U both. Heluhelu loves u.

Pierre: Haha. Not. She likes quiet.

Nicole: Not sure

Malie: U ok, girl?

Pierre: U good, Nicole?

Malie: Really. Come up. Put ur phones on vibrate pls.

He got up, excusing himself. He changed his settings to vibrate. He sang about the library.

Pierre's SC Library Song:

"The SC's meeting at the library
It's like taking a ride on a ferry.
Nothing else is this merry
Makes me wonder about being lonely and alone?
They both almost have the same tone.
Both mean there's no one else there.

You're solo, single, and not a pair.
Lucky for me, I didn't qualify.
I'm none of those things. Testify!
The SC's meeting at the library
It's like taking a ride on a ferry.
Is there anything else merrier?
Best friends make good company.
The Secret Club and the Manafuls
Being with them is funny.
Funny how I forget my worries.
Funny how they give me the glory.
Lifting me up, accepting me as I am.
That victory was flush after dodging spam.
The SC's meeting at the library."

Pierre finished his song upon arriving at the school library a minute later. He felt good singing and letting go of his emotions.

Nicole had beat him there. She sat quietly beside Malie, texting something. He bet it was hard for her to stay still and not talk.

Malie felt Pierre's presence. She tapped Nicole's hand and pointed at him. Nicole's shoulders visibly relaxed. Pierre's brows furrowed. He wondered if she was okay. She looked sad.

He waved, putting his finger over his lips. His lips formed a soundless 'Ssshhh'. He pointed to librarian Heluhelu, who eagle-eyed him.

Having reached their table, he lifted the chair and placed it softly on the cool tiles. Not making a squeak. He gingerly sat, belying his size. He'd bulked up some over the past month as he anticipated another championship DMW football season.

Malie smiled, mimicking his silent 'Shhh.' Bless her funny face. Nicole looked him right in the eye. She pointed to their phones.

Both Pierre's and Malie's phones vibrated. Nicole had texted them just now.

Nicole: Bully run-in again after team sports class.

Pierre's chair dragged loudly against the tiles as he suddenly rose. He didn't bother texting. "Who? Where?"

Malie was upset, too. She hadn't bothered shushing him; she'd stood too. "Nicole?" Malie asked too loudly.

The librarian made her way to the trio. "Excuse me. Please take your conversations outside." Her narrowed gaze focused on Malie, seeming disappointed in her favorite patron.

Malie snapped out of it, remembering her manners. "Oh, we apologize Ms. Heluhelu. Yes, we will be leaving now."

She swiped up her book bag and pulled on Pierre's sleeve. Pierre motioned his head at Nicole. Chinning in the direction of the door, he encouraged her to follow.

Nicole was the last to close the Library door behind them. Malie spoke up first, her hands waving around excitedly, "Tell us again. From the top!"

Pierre folded his muscled biceps across his chest. He nodded in agreement at Malie's order.

Nicole rolled her eyes hard. God, these people never quit. Well, that's why she opened her mouth just now. Oh, she'd texted, technically, but that's beside the point.

"In team sports, I made some bad basketball moves. My teammates were pissed that we lost. They stalked me outside of the locker room. It got a little hairy with three tall guys to one me. The lead guy, no names, was checking me out and hinting he'd beat me up."

When she'd said "no names," both of her friends swore and spoke over her.

Well, not exactly. Malie used "Shoot, no! Tell us! Those dumb farts are going down!"

Pierre didn't hesitate, "Forget that. Let me at 'em!"

Nicole put her hands up. "This isn't the way to handle it. During my last class, I'm going to the Veeps. I didn't tell you to start a vendetta!"

Malie did her breathing practices that Ikaika taught her. "1… Whooo. 2… Whoooo. 3… Whoooo. 4… Whooo."

This distracted Nicole unintentionally. Malie looked really funny with her eyes all big and her chest moving exaggeratedly. She was an owl, even sounding like one. Nicole imitated her, minus the numbers: "Whooooo. Whoooo. Whoooo. Whoooo."

This cracked up Pierre, too. Wow, what an icebreaker, huh? With tears in their eyes, they took each other's hands in a circle. Bowing their heads together, they did a silent prayer for a few minutes.

CHAPTER 42

Earth
Wright Middle School Counselor Kealoha's Office
August 4, 2022
1 p.m.

During Nicole's last class, her teacher wrote her a pass to visit her counselor. Counselor Tawny Kealoha is a sweet lady. She'd immediately taken control of the situation once Nicole had explained what had happened with the bullies. She named everyone except Kona.

All would be well, the school Administrator, Vice Principal Cynthia Kalani, assured Nicole. She would open up the CCTV recordings and conduct a formal investigation.

Counselor Kealoha called Nicole's mother to come to campus. Kaleo Moku, Esq., was a force to be reckoned with. She'd gotten there in fifteen minutes; being her own boss had its perks.

Nicole breathed easier after conferencing with her mom, Counselor Kealoha, and VP Cynthia Kalani. The bullying investigation was on its way. In the initial stages, she wouldn't have to meet with the boys alone or at all.

Her mother had called Uncle Nick immediately. He'd advised her to keep her cool. Let Wright Middle School Administrators do their job. He'd step in and call his pals in the Juvenile Crime Unit, if necessary. Uncle Nick, who could always cheer Nicole up, asked to speak with her.

Uncle Nick's voice brought tears to her eyes. She breathed deeply, smiling a little as she recalled Malie's owl-breathing technique.

"You're all right, my girl? Need anything?" He had a kindness in him she'd always, always cherished.

Why he was in criminal law rather than family or child advocacy, she'd never know. "Unc...Uncle," her voice trembled a little. "Um, there were these boys." Big breath. Whooooo. "I was scared." Big breath. Whoooo. "I thought of you and had my phone ready." Big breath. Whooo.

Hey, it was working. Oxygen is amazing. Duh. Uncle Nick praised her for breathing deep and self-managing her anxiety.

"That's good, my girl. That's good. Breathe deep. Keep breathing." She felt her mom's hand rubbing her back. Keeping her eyes closed, she kept breathing and holding the phone tight. Tears simmered beneath her eyelids. She didn't care that her mom and Counselor Kealoha were sitting right there next to her.

VP Kalani had headed out after her walkie chirped. She was needed for some other urgent matter.

"Nic, come over to Granddad's tonight with your mom. Hot chocolate, Hurricane popcorn, and hugs?" Nicole laughed. How could she resist her favorite things?

"Yes, we'll be there!" Nicole hadn't bothered to check with her mom. Oops! She opened her eyes and looked at her mom apologetically for changing her plans for the night.

Kaleo didn't hesitate. She leaned closer, speaking into the cell, "We'll be there, brother! Letting you go. Love you!"

Then he added, before hanging up, "Nic, stay strong. I'll be with you tonight. Love you!"

Nicole teared up again. He was the ultimate uncle! She stared down at the mobile after disconnecting. How'd she get such a great family?

CHAPTER 43

Earth
Wright Middle School Gymnasium
August 4, 2022
2:45 p.m.

Nicole was the first one to arrive at their gym wall. She sat on the cement steps leading up to a teachers' parking lot. She pulled at the tall weeds at her feet.

Pierre found her there, staring at her scuffed black booties. She liked the no-heel boots. Comfort mattered. Her team sports shoes were in her backpack beside her.

"Hey, Nicole, you took care of the matter?" Pierre sat next to her on the step. It was squishy, but she didn't care. They rubbed shoulders—he was getting broader.

They didn't have their phones out. That was something they did less—screen time. Hmmm. It was likely a result of the Manafuls. In their world, they'd go hours and hours without devices.

She was quiet, which was unusual for Nicole. She was biting her nails—a habit she only did at home. She disliked appearing as a weakling.

Pierre was flattered that he was one of those "homes" for her. He was sad and mad on her behalf. If he knew those bullies, he'd make them sorry.

He hadn't realized his fists were shaking until Nicole covered them with her hands. She continued to hold him, looking into his eyes. She breathed deeply. "Whoooooo." Breathed deeply. "Whoooooo."

This made him laugh and loosen up immediately. His shoulders were now shaking in mirth. He squeezed her hands before letting go of Nicole's fingers.

"That's Malie's owl-breathing! Gosh, she's going to do a happy dance!" Nicole nodded her head, grinning now. Yet, she kept doing it. Deep breath. "Whoooo." Deep breath. "Whoooooo." She waved at him to try it.

He shook his head, then made a face. "Why not?" He exclaimed happily, joining in. Synchronously, they breathed deeply. "Whoooo."

Breathed deeply. "Whooooo."

Malie turned the corner and came upon them doing her owl breathing. She ran the rest of the way to them, dropped her book bag, and put an arm around each of them.

"Oh! You two are owl-breathing!" She loved it. She turned around to sit on the second lowest step on their shoes. She wiggled her little butt on Pierre's Converses and Nicole's booties and leaned back on their knees. They all laughed at her antics.

After relaxing for a bit, they stood up and prepared for their Portal Song.

Before grabbing Nicole's and Malie's hands to sing and leap, Pierre checked on Nicole one more time. "Hey, Nicole, do you want to share?"

Malie peeked around Pierre, "Yes, you okay? You talked to the admin.?"

Nicole nodded to both of them. "Yes, to all of your questions, buddies. I'm good. I'll explain on the other side with the elders and Ikaika present, okay?"

Her friends nodded. They understood her need to wait. There's no sense in repeating her story once they crossed over. They held hands and sang.

The Secret Club's Portal Song:

"Moving places, crossing spaces.
Moving places, crossing spaces.
The Secret Club and the Manafuls
How many hits will it take?
How many words will they make?
To bring me down.
To break my crown?
Dear Manafuls, with their open arms,
Supports us, never lifted in harm.
Moving places, crossing spaces.
Moving places, crossing spaces.
Stop him! Stop her! Stop them!
A swat on the face, a ripped hem.
A push against the wall. An accidental fall.
How much will it take?

Being with them's a mistake.
Moving places, crossing spaces."

Their molecules floated through the Shimmery Wall. Whether they arrived safely or not was a good question.

CHAPTER 44

Storyteller in Papakōlea, Hawaiʻi
August 4, 2022

"No, Aunty, continue please! What do you mean by 'If they arrived unsafely?'"

"I didn't say that at all."

"Whether—they are safe is a good question?"

"Close."

"We'll, you know what I mean!" Ari was adamant.

Aunt Ellie sighed and stood up from their living room couch. She smiled down at her slender niece. Ari's light brown tendrils had spilled out of her ponytail.

"There will be other days and adventures, dear," she laughed at Ari's forlorn look.

"What about the Manafuls? What happened to Ikaika and Elder Maka? Aunty!" Ari bounced on the couch, pleadingly peering up at her aunt.

Aunt Ellie gave in, "Okay."

Ari hugged her aunt's legs. "Oh, I love you, Aunty!" Her aunt laughed, "Love you, too."

EPILOGUE

Manaful World
August 4, 2022
3 p.m.

Near Elder Maka's mansion, at the scene of the battle In the sandalwood forest, Ikaika and Elder Maka were perched on Pierre's limestone boulder. The boulder was a heartwarming reminder of The Secret Club.

Ikaika lay back with his head in his palms. His buddy sat ramrod straight next to him.

Elder Maka's bioluminescent green robe put off an aura glummer than its owner. The textile was chameleon-like. Right now, Elder Maka's robe matched the shade of the limestone.

Ikaika smiled up at his buddy's tense shoulders. The weight of the world seemed to rest on those shoulders. Ikaika harrumphed, staring up at the sky sharing his Mana with the growing saplings of the sandalwood forest Uli had burnt.

He recalled the battle here one month ago.

They were a football field away from his friend's new mansion. His gramps and spirit-father, Elders Alaka'i and Puna revitalized the forest soil but Maka had declined their help from there. Grass had already grown, but the trees were still young.

Ikaika missed the thick, thirty-foot rows of majestic wildlife. Elder Maka worked hard everyday to rebuild this portion of his forest with his Mana.

Bark! Bark! Ikaika's labrador puppy triplets tumbled over to the boulder. They loved being here. Their mama, Mele, barked at them to behave and stay on the grass next to Ikaika and Elder Maka. She was on guard and alert, a great mama.

Ikaika marveled as some sandalwood trees to the left grew in rapid timelapse. The trees grew speedily from seedlings to baby shoots to thrice the Manaful height. Maka had become so strong. Wowza.

Ikaika loved watching his friend flex those new Elder muscles. The lovely woodsy scent of new life blessed them.

The Secret Club will be here soon.

Their Thursday visits were a treat. Ikaika avoided watching their first day of seventh grade on the Shimmery Wall. He didn't want them to feel his eye on them all the time. It would freak them out. Besides, Nicole ribbed him, literally and figuratively, whenever he said he'd watched her. "Stalking much?" She'd sass, then tickle him.

Watching Elder Maka speed-grow the trees, Ikaika felt like he did with Elder Puna. Peaceful. His friend's newly supercharged core was palpable like a strong magnetic field. He had a calmer, old-man vibe now. It was a little strange, as they were only 770 years old—preteens.

Elder Maka still laughed and smiled. It's not like his wits died. Yet, his presence was different because elders were aligned with Source every second of every day.

Ikaika couldn't imagine that kind of existence yet.

Really.

Literally being aware of Source's presence looming over you, vast and all-encompassing, all the time. Elders harmonize their whole lives to this cosmic presence. That was the alignment Ikaika was being trained to achieve himself, one day.

Suddenly, Elder Maka jumped off the limestone. Mele picked up Brownie with her mouth and held down Cookie and Cupcake with her forearms, practically sitting on them, stricken. Bark! Bark! Bark! She was loud. In a snap, Elder Maka sent all four labs to his treehouse via molecular transport.

Ikaika projected Elders Alaka'i and Puna: *Help us! Something's here. Think it's Lapu!*

In seconds, the elders popped in. They stood like a fence between Ikaika, who clung fearfully to the limestone, and the approaching trouble.

Elder Maka bowed to his mentors and peers. They nodded back. They stood strong together.

The stomping of hooves, the buzzing of wasps, and the caws-caws of bird calls surrounded them. The animals were stampeding, scared. The senior elders hummed, perhaps talking to the animals telepathically? Maka hadn't gotten that down pat yet. The animal noises stopped as abruptly as they'd started. The air thickened with a dark mist, saplings swaying furiously. Ikaika wiggled his extremities and loosened his body. It wasn't as if he could help. Still, he felt good letting go of his fear.

"Do you want to go home?" His grandfather's projection came in.

"No way, Gramps," he answered. Elder Puna nodded.

The darkening sky and whirling wind gave Ikaika goosebumps. Lapu was here. The Spirit's drizzling essence was sticky, dense with fear unlike Mana Mist. He stirred the trees and frightened the forest creatures.

The Lapu essence whipped around like a sentient pillar of smoke. Leaves began to wither, carpets of grass and shrubs decayed, monkeys and parrots started to scream. Black fire exploded around all save the Manafuls, who were safe within the forcefield Alaka'i conjured without moving a muscle.

In one fell swoop, Elder Maka's new forest turned to smoking ruins. Ikaika groaned, feeling for his friend. He'd worked for a month to nuture these young growths.

"Give me your faith, not pity!," Maka's mind whispered in his friend's ear.

Ikaika winced and projected. *"I'm sorry. You've all got this! With backup like this, Lapu doesn't stand a chance!"*

Both Elders Alaka'i and Puna grinned. Well, at least he could break the ice. Expecting Lapu's next step was nerve wracking.

As if Lapu had caught on to their impatience, menacing laughter whipped around them. A formless core was riding the currents, a Spirit who woke up a thousand years ago. First of its kind in this world, but not the last.

Elder Maka was the least patient of the three Elders. His core rang bell-like as he blasted a projection, the force of it making him levitate

"Come on! Do something or scram! Be gone!" He was so upset that veins bulged on his neck, throat wanting to scream.

The other Elders turned sideways simultaneously like twin soldiers. They lifted their hands onto Elder Maka's shoulders, sending soothing energy into him. A force field of Mana Mist kept their minds and bodies safe.

Lapu's toxicity tried to get to them, His dark mist circling Alaka'i's forcefield like a ghost shark.

Maka's core burned hot, his emotions getting ruffled by the Spirit's presence even from a distance. All the little things that sucked in life suddenly became more important than all the things that are perfect. It kindled a chaos that fuelled roiling fear and anger.

"Do not give in to the turmoil. Don't feed It." Elder Puna projected.

"*Who're you calling eeet?*" hissed a voice like rusty nails dragging on tin, but bubbly underneath like gloopy tar, coming from the cloud of dark mist. Trying way too hard to sound dangerous.

"Are you nothing, then," Alaka'i projected, raising a flowing brow. Despite the prickling suffocation the venerable elder looked quite good humored. His opalescent robes rippled sedately.

"*I will become just like youuu.*" Lapu skittered around them on the rising and falling gusts that caught up detritus like a hesitant, very self-aware tornado in a weaker stage of life. "*A he, a she, perraps a zey; defo nyet yen eeet.*"

Ikaika's eyes went round. "*Huh?*"

"*It's just another petty tactic of his,*" Puna projected a private aside. "*Sowing chaos. Just keep your core steady.*"

"*Tee hee hee!*" Lapu buffeted wildly. "*Haven't you noticed I can be seen now?*"

"Nothing new, just smoke," Maka said snidely, aloud.

"It's my very own mana," hissed Lapu, also aloud as if showing off. Now the voice was the susurration of a trillion grains frictioning in a sandstorm.

"Using Mana Mist in this way harms only you, Lapu," Alaka'i projected, keeping their forcefield strong. Beyond it trees continued to decay, and the ground was again barren.

"*Wrong*," Lapu taunted. "*It harms everyone.*"

A replay of the time Uli withered life, but much more devastating. Maka and Ikaika connected their cores to warn all animals in the danger zone away. The trees were not fast enough to escape the expanding waves of rot.

"Stop your destruction across the lands," Alaka'i continued. *"You have a rightful place in our world. Go there."*

"*I always go there, you old buzzard.*"

"*Well, next time you do, stay there.*" With that, Alaka'i brought his halo to life. A burst of mana mist manifested in the air to attack the darker mist. They met with sparks, ionizing, crackling.

"Eeek!" screamed Lapu in his gravelly voice, wafting around to escape the rainbow droplets trying to consume him.

They watched the fighting clouds of magical essence, one pure from nature, the other tainted by a vagabond Spirit. Nature was strong here with the elders and Ikaika supporting it. Lapu fled beyond the charred clearing into the thick of the forest, a serpentine rainbow mist giving chase.

The clearing was dead.

Maka groaned. *"Took me a month to plan out a canopy design!"*

"You have to start over," Ikaika agreed.

"They were almost adult trees," Maka shook his head, twisting his robe sleeves restlessly. He hovered about in circles, lifting up tendrils from the ground to inspect. It was dead dust.

Puna tutted. *"Just let us help regrow this faster."*

Maka looked at Alaka'i and Puna, nodding. He mustn't allow his pride to dictate his choices. A whole month of trying to regrow this patch only proved that he had a lot to learn, that he still needed help. *"Thank you. I'm exhausted."*

Elders Puna and Alaka'i put their hands on their midriffs, activating their cores to their full potential. The very sunlight bent around the two. They channeled the Mana welling up within their cores, and mists of the air reacted to it, flurried to stitch the broken patch of forest back together. The wind came in again, bringing seeds and minerals from other corners of the forest.

Alaka'i condensed water vapor to dampen the frothing soil. Grass began to grow. Newly arrived seeds burrowed into the humus into their beds. Points of green speckled the moist earthen circle around the Manafuls.

Ikaika was grateful for all three elders. Lapu would probably have eaten him for dinner. The Spirit was gone now. They all relaxed, no longer sensing his presence.

"You can come back now," Ikaika mass projected to his team of forest guardians, including Maluhia. It was the signal for the animals to return with gifts to their ʻāina, or land.

The chipmunks came with stuffed cheek pouches, the butterflies frisked pollen off each other, and varicolored birds busily scattered seed pods over the barren hills. In the Manaful World, everyone except spirits loved their ʻāina with every fiber of their being.

Together, they healed.

GLOSSARY 3

Alignment - process of self improvement through mental ascension to reach and harmonize with the Higher Dimensions.

Annihilation - getting wiped out of existence. It is a Council banned spell, even Elders only allowed to use it as a last resort. It is risky because the spell will backfire on the caster if Source invalidates the annihilator's self-justification for casting it. It is one of the most dangerous spells in existence. In Manaful, Source is often the direct decider of natural annihilations.. Death is a lesser annihilation.

Clothing Colors - Manafuls are a family-based society with nobility. The monarchy is replaced by an Elders' Council (see Elders' Council). Each Family has a primary leader or chief called the elder. Each family only wears the spectrums of color that run in their family. The closest comparison would be the family tartan patterns in Scotland.

Core - Referred to the harmonized center of your balance, made up of your body, mind, heart and spirit. The core exists in both worlds, physical in one's bodily dimensions and in the spirit realm as Piko.

Elder (s) - Manaful World is led by elders or the royalty of each family or ʻohana (Hawaiian word for family). Each ʻohana wears spectrums of one color. Elders wear a magical, bioluminescent version of their family's color. They don a bathroom-like robe with a belt over their undergarments and clothing. Only elders have the power to wear these magical robes. An elder can be male, female, or agender. They range in ages from birth to 4200 years old. The elders hold the greatest magical power in their ʻohana.

Elders' Council and Elder Prime - Manaful World is a special society led by royal elders. All elders have a seat in the Council, a governing body. It is the ruling body of the Manaful World. Some elders are more magical and powerful than others. Upon their death, an elder's magic is passed down to the next eldest (male, female, or agender) living relative. They are the heirs. The heir takes their seat in the Council. The nobility of elders is represented in the Council. The Prime or leader of the Council is Elder Alakaʻi. He is the first documented living Manaful. He is the most powerful, magical Manaful in their World. His vice-Prime, second in the hierarchy, is Elder Puna. He and Alakaʻi grew up together. Puna is the second most powerful in magic on Manaful. Every other Manaful after them follows in their rank: 3rd, 4th, 5th, etc. The rank is according to their family's age and magical power. The older the family, the more magic it possesses.

Elder Link: Telepathic multisensory real-time broadcasting on a private or public mental communications line between Elders across Manaful World.

Hānai - Hawaiian word that literally means adopt, foster, care, and feed a child or adult, recognized at the discretion of the Hawaii State Family Court System.

Source: Hawaii Revised statutes. 2021. Hawaii Revised Statutes Chapter 587A-4.
https://www.capitol.hawaii.gov/hrscurrent/Vol12_Ch0501o588/HRS0587A/HRS_0587A-0004.htm

Hopohopo - Hawaiian word that literally means having anxiety, doubt, and fear. Non-derogatory label for Manaful beings who fear, doubt, and have anxiety about their innate magical powers. They rejected the learning and usage of Mana except in health or safety purposes. They have telepathic abilities. Some use them, but most do not. Their vulnerabilities are far and wide due to this rejection. Powerful mental forces of others can control Hopohopo.

Source: KAI LOA Inc. and Ke Kula ʻo Samuel M. Kamakau, Laboratory Public Charter School. "Hopohopo." Manomano, 2017, https://manomano.io/definition/9235, 25 December 2022.

Lapu - in Hawaiian it means spirit, apparition or ghost. More specifically, it is a night monster that haunts people. For Manaful World, Lapu is a being or haunting spirit, male in gender. He tempts Manafuls to hurt others and murder for power. Once the Manaful is no longer useful, Lapu kills them or leads them to self-destruct. He then finds new Manafuls to manipulate.

Source: KAI LOA Inc. and Ke Kula ʻo Samuel M. Kamakau, Laboratory Public Charter School. "Lapu." Manomano, 2017, https://manomano.io/definition/21171, 27 December 2022.

Māhū - In Hawaiian culture, māhū are accepted and highly regarded third-gender homosexuals who are of great spiritual and religious significance.

Source: KAI LOA Inc. and Ke Kula ʻo Samuel M. Kamakau, Laboratory Public Charter School. "Māhū." Manomano, 2017, https://manomano.io/definition/23212, 28 December 2022.

Mana - Magical powers from Manaful's Source or God-being that created their World 4500 Manaful years ago. The Source grants Mana or powers to all animate and inanimate things and beings. Manafuls have the most Mana and control over non-humanoid creatures: elements, weather, trees, animals, rocks, tables, money, etc. The most powerful, magic wielding beings are the elders (see Elders). Not all Manafuls accept, learn, or use their Mana (see Hopohopo).

Mana Mist - It is an airy substance akin to ether, misty, and entirely present everywhere, coming from oxygen and water. It is visible when light catches upon thicker clusters of the organic substance. Being one of the five elements of life and from the Manaful Source/God, Mana Mist is a most potent magical resource and energetic force to be reckoned with. Its ubiquitous presence makes the mist an ever desirable utility for Elders, good and bad alike. Natural beings like trees collect the most Mana Mist or ether, as it is rooted in the soil, absorbing the mist from outside and within continuously.

Manafuls - Magical dwarf (four feet is the tallest) beings of humanoid biology from a separate dimensional world from Earth. They are advanced in technology and magic, speaking telepathically or orally in all human languages. They may travel by foot, but it's more natural to them to travel by transporting themselves molecularly (see Molecular Travel or MT). They wear only one clothing color, their family color.

Manaful World - Fictional magical and technologically advanced world reached only by invitation via a time portal. It is an Earth replica, with the same biosphere and oxygen/carbon dioxide symbiosis. Same gravity. Same forestry, animals, clothing, etc. Imagine an Earth doppelganger minus global warming. Humans can breathe safely there. It's in a separate time dimension from Earth. Upon entry, Earth time stops. When returning to Earth, the time you left restarts like a parallel dimension. It is a young World only 4500 Manaful years or 64 human years old.

Mental Manipulations - these are dozens of Manaful ways to telepathically manage or control other "cores" (mind, body, spirit)

Mental Screen(ing) - Elders teach Manafuls from a very young age to mentally, emotionally, and spiritually screen themselves in all ways from telepathic, mental control by others. When their mental screens are down, Manafuls are prey to mind-control, manipulation, and evil intentions of others to brainwash them. Hopohopo who have telepathic abilities can learn to mentally screen themselves, yet they more times than not refuse to do so. It's this rejection that leaves Hopohopo very vulnerable to darker Manaful forces like Uli and especially Lapu.

Mind-meld - to mentally connect and remain connected with another Manaful. Only done Manaful to Manaful. While mentally connected, Manafuls can share past and present thoughts and memories. Only very powerful Elders can use mind-melding to combine their powers to build things or to heal others.

Molecular Travel (MT) - Magically changing your body into molecules to travel through time; and, to and from places. Your body breaks down into molecules and reconfigures itself in the new place or time. Time traveling is done molecularly. This form of transportation is done via magic or Mana. Only Manafuls who use/accept Mana can do it. Manafuls can MT themselves and humans anywhere in Manaful.

Piko - Physical and spiritual center (literally umbilical cord)

Projection - In Manaful World, a projection is a mental calling out of your thoughts via telepathy. This is like a mental telephone call across their world in split seconds. In the novel, projections are in italics and quotes.

Spirits - the life force that fuels the cores of living beings. Pure energy. AKA "The Fires of the Cosmos".

Shimmery Wall - A magical 20 x 20 foot wet-less shiny waterfall time portal. The Shimmer Wall is used to leap interdimensionally (from Earth to Manaful World and back) and intra worldly (within Manaful World). Also called "Wall," it can be used as a live-stream or real-time television portal into Earth or anywhere in Manaful World. Could serve as a spy cam that doesn't need installing. The beings or people being viewed have no way of knowing they are being observed. Only elders or elders' heirs have enough magical power to use or conjure the Shimmery Walls. There could be an infinite amount of them, but will sap the core energy of the conjurer. SW's could pop out of nowhere as the elders and their heirs could conjure them at any time or at any place.

Source or Source Creator - God figure for the Manafuls. It (no gender) exists in all things, living and not living. It created Manaful World, Manafuls, and all spiritual beings like Lapu. It's alive, living, and present in all things and beings. Source creates all of the five elements and most importantly the Mana Mist. Source imbues the core of Elders with 'Ohana Mana within as well. Elders harmonize with Source to gain extra powers via the Mana Mist. Elders encourage all Manafuls to access this alignment, too. It's not forbidden, rather it's encouraged. Elders say, “Align with Mana” to mean linking to the Creator (Source has many names) . Mana or magical powers come from Source. By embracing Mana, a Manaful taps Source’s love, protection, magic, powers for the positive purposes.

Telepathically Group Projection (-ed, -ing) - Abbreviated TGP, it is to telepathically group send, like group texting, thoughts to only specific and select individuals from your brain to their brains.

Telepathic Projection - To telepathically send out or mentally project your thoughts privately to one person only.

Transmutation - Slightly borrowed from scientific and historical definitions, transmutation means the transformation of something. In Manaful World, it refers to the changing, transferring, and moving of magic, energy, and spiritual powers from one Manaful to another. The powers come from their God or Source who transmits the five elements of life into all the world: soil, water, fire, air, and ether or Mana Mist. It can be lent to another Manaful in spurts or large amounts. It can be passed down almost entirely (all an elder’s powers) from one Manaful to their heir upon death.

Source: Google’s English Dictionary. “Transmutation” OxfordLanguages, 2022,
https://www.google.com/search?q=transmutation, 27 December 2022.

ACKNOWLEDGMENTS

Praise and all thanks to God/Allah.

Love you to our families in Hawai'i, Maldives, and across the planet.

Mahalo to HitRECord; Roosevelt HS 'Ohana; Heather Sangster of Strong Finish; Jon Kirk, Anthony Harvison, and their team at Palamedes PR and The Double Agents Talent Agency; and, Tania, Julia, and their teams at Miblart.

Much appreciation for friends, supporters, and associates worldwide.

ABOUT THE AUTHORS

DORIMALIA WAIAU & EASA MOHAMED

Dorimalia Waiau, a born and raised Papakōlea lady, is a storyteller and musician to the depths of her soul. As a high school English Language Arts teacher of two decades, she has always loved children and words. The purpose of this novel and the seven more from The Secret Club and Manafuls series is to spread love and joy for all beings around the world. She would love to collaborate with her readers at:
https://hitrecord.org/users/DorimaliaWaiau/records.
Visit her website: www.dorimaliawaiau.com .

Easa Mohamed hails from the Maldives and started as a journalist, going on to work in communications and marketing. He has a lifelong interest in creativity and explores it through literature and sketching.

www.ingramcontent.com/pod-product-compliance
Lightning Source LLC
Chambersburg PA
CBHW030341310726
48979CB00001B/140

* 9 7 8 1 9 6 5 9 8 5 0 0 7 *